Corcitura

A Novel

Melika Dannese Lux

Corcitura

Books In My Belfry and colophon are trademarks of Books In My
Belfry, LLC

Front cover photo © iStockphoto.com/Carina Lochner

Cover Design © 2012 Melika Dannese Lux

ISBN: 0615722091
ISBN-13: 978-0615722092

To my 7, for always believing.

Contents

BOOK THE FIRST: THE NARRATIVE OF ERIC BRADBURRY PART I: 1888

BEGGARS AT THE GATE	1
TWO ENGLISHMEN IN PARIS	12
OPÉRA PHANTASMIQUE	29
HELLO, GOOD-BYE…HELLO	51
A CHANGE OF PLANS	65
THE HAUNTER OF DARKNESS	90
OUT OF THE FRYING PAN, INTO THE FIRE	116
A TAVERN IN VENICE	166
THE HUNTED	192
THE RATLIFF HORROR	237

BOOK THE FIRST: THE NARRATIVE OF ERIC BRADBURRY PART II: 1894

THE PERSONAL REPRESENTATIVE OF MRS. ROBERTA B. IVES	266
NEW YORK, AUNT ROBBIE, AND THE MILLIONAIRES' BALL	292
FIRST LOVE	329

BOOK THE FIRST: THE NARRATIVE OF ERIC BRADBURRY PART III: MARKED — 1894-1895

THE LETTER	390
THE TIGHTENING OF THE NOOSE	421

BOOK THE SECOND: THE NARRATIVE OF MADELAINE BRADBURRY 1895: ALONE

BELODODIA'S BELFRY	474

BOOK THE THIRD: THE NARRATIVE OF ZIGMUND FERTIG 1895: THE FOUNDLING

SPECTERS OF THE PAST	536
FULL CIRCLE	608

EPILOGUE

Melika Dannese Lux

Cologne, Germany: 13 February 1895   667

POSTSCRIPT

Legacy   695

Book the First: The Narrative of Eric Bradburry Part I: 1888

Beggars at the Gate

"*C*all me Penniless!"

Oh, yes, Eric, that's lovely. And what are you going to say next? Which way to the Pequod?

I flung *Moby Dick* aside. Obviously, there was nothing between the covers of *that* book that I could lift and modify to suit my purposes. Maybe if I'd read more than the first five pages, I'd feel differently, but that kind of logic was neither here nor there.

Time for round two. I grabbed one of the other novels I'd strewn across my bed. I hoped I'd have better luck with this one.

"A grand tour won't be a grand tour unless we've got gobs of money to spend." Hmm...a bit patronizing, that. *Thanks for nothing, Louisa*, I thought, tossing *Little Women* across the room. This filching of famous first lines had seemed like a fabulous idea when I'd thought of it two hours ago, but I could see that it was getting me nowhere fast.

Deflated, I reached for the last novel, my final hope for inspiration. Ah, yes, here we were. Jane wouldn't let me down. I could never go wrong with her. "*Ahem*...It is a truth youthfully acknowledged that a young lad in possession of little to no fortune should want infinitely more than the lot he's got. I know I've never given either of you any particular reason to trust me with even *five* quid, but let's put that unfortunate past history behind us, shall we? After all, you must spend a little to reap great rewards, right? Well, that being said, Mother, Roddy...how about you extend to me those three hundred pounds?"

Botheration! Not even plagiarizing Jane Austen was going to get me what I was after. That tack was all wrong. Roddy was like clay; he needed to be pummeled till I got him into the right shape—the *giving* shape, which would take some work, since he'd always treated me more like a poor relation to be tolerated than a stepson.

I swung the mirror back up and straightened my necktie, then thought better of it and mussed the cloth till it hung at a suitably dissolute angle. There was no need to look modish when I was about to go begging. I was deluding myself if I thought this was going to be easy. Even after practicing for months, the approach was still lacking, and I'd run out of ideas. I had no idea how we were going to convince our parents to give us the money, yet we had already gone too far to quit now.

Seven months ago, Stefan Ratliff, my closest friend since childhood, had hit upon the scheme of using a grand tour as a cover for our own exploits. Educational pursuits were fine for the average man, but we two saw this as an opportunity to indulge in as many extravagances as possible as we tramped from one capital of Europe to the next. It would be a final lark before we said farewell to youth and became men of the world that fall, at which time Stefan and I would both become inmates at Oxford.

Only now did I realize that Stefan had somehow passed the baton to me without my knowing it, putting the onus on me to prove the soundness of this venture to our parents. *I* was the one who had to do the coaxing. *I* was the one who would be offered up as the proverbial sacrificial lamb. Imagine having to tell Roddy that this grand tour was the best idea since the Reform Act of 1867. No wonder Stefan balked. Still, it was a rum trick if there ever was one. I'd make sure to get back at Stefan soon, once we were underway and far from home, of course. There'd be no sense in murdering him outright, not with all the scandal it would cause in the papers. I'd wait till we reached Paris, then do away with him in the Tuileries Gardens and blame the murder on the ghost of Robespierre.

So cheered, I sat down on the edge of the bed and mulled over my misfortune. I wasn't as preoccupied with getting my parents' consent to travel abroad as I was with convincing them to lend me capital. Money had always been my chief problem.

My association with Roderick Caldwell had begun ten years ago when my mother, Laura, took it into her head to marry the man. What possessed her to make such a hash of our lives, I will never know, but there was no denying that Old Roddy was well loved and loved just as ardently in return, where Mother was concerned at least. The picture of connubial bliss would have summed them up nicely. Roddy was a fine catch and Mother was the belle of her set, although a widow, but he was willing to overlook this trifling detail. If you were to poll the citizenry, the results would show that Sir Roderick Caldwell was an upstanding citizen, a model husband, and adored by all.

Quite a lot of rot, that, but it wasn't for the "fly in the ointment," namely *me*, to say at the time. I was only eight years old and my job was to be neither seen nor heard, except when I was trotted out on special occasions to do my stepfather credit.

There were times throughout the last decade when I had often wondered if Charles Dickens had used Roddy as the model for Ebenezer Scrooge, but I suppose, if I were pressed to admit it, that I was being too hard on the old man. He was generous to a fault with his own causes, but when it came to me, he suffered from what one might call extreme tightfistedness. Yet Roddy was by no means suffering from want. There was the house in Mayfair I shared with Mother and him, for instance, that was certainly not a hovel, and then there was his little villa in the South of France, not to mention the pension in Corfu, though he claimed that really was more of a business investment. Ha ha, it is to laugh.

Still, none of this mattered when The Stepson reared his head. I remember once asking Roddy for tuppence to buy some Turkish Delight and receiving instead a lecture on the wastefulness of the English youth in today's modern world. Not quite what the average school-age boy wants to hear when he asks Papa for some lolly to buy a sweetie.

Things hadn't changed much over the last few years. Though Roddy grew a shred fonder of me, he kept my allowance to a rather bare minimum, based on his opinion that I was a wastrel and would most assuredly spend his "hard earned" wealth on drink and depravity. I suppose he was still sore about the tuppence incident. His was an entirely baseless surmise, mind you, but, since he was Mother's and my only means of survival, I was forced to bite my lip and keep trudging through life on two bob a week.

Try as we might, though, the prospect of embarking on a grand tour was something Stefan and I were unwilling to give up without exhausting every option. Today was already the twelfth of June, and the time was ripe for us to seize our chance, carpe diem and all that palaver. We could no longer afford to keep putting the scheme off. I knew that if we were to have any hope at all of setting out before month's end, we would have to act this very night, which was why we were planning to wine and dine The Older Set (on Stefan's allowance, of course) that evening at the Café Royal.

After the second course, I would rise from my seat, raise my glass in toast, and spout forth a torrent of arguments so convincing that by the time I had ceased and earned a round of thunderous applause, Roddy would fall to his knees and beg me to take the money off his hands. Maybe I was putting a little too much faith in my oratorical skills, but one must be optimistic. Besides, if I ever hoped to make it to those hallowed halls of Parliament one day, I could hope for no better person to practice on than the one-man Inquisition that was Roderick Caldwell. Compared to my stepfather, Torquemada was a cream puff.

The clock on the landing read a quarter to eleven by the time I made my way downstairs. I was mentally re-rehearsing my arguments for the thousandth time and was so absorbed in my thoughts that I didn't realize Stefan and our parents had already gathered until I was nearly halfway into the drawing room.

I glanced at Stefan. He looked like a lit Roman Candle, his shock of red hair swept up into a Brutus style that had died out of fashion more than sixty years ago. I had a mad urge to grab the fireplace poker and jab him in the ribs. Anything to get him to show some emotion. His face was unreadable, so that I wasn't sure if we were winning or had already been soundly defeated. The fact that he was avoiding my eyes didn't do anything to calm my nerves, either.

All four of our parents were silent. Mr. Ratliff was leaning over his tented fingers. Mrs. Ratliff idly stirred her tea. Mother sat up much too straight in her chair, and Roddy, well, Roddy was worst of all. He was standing with his back to the hearth. His eyebrows were raised, his eyes fixed on a water stain on the ceiling. I knew that look. And I knew what would happen if I didn't do something to keep him from travelling down that moral highroad he was so fond of traversing.

So I did the only natural thing. I started blubbering like an imbecile. "I, for one, think it would be a grave error in judgment to deny us this opportunity. Lord knows we are mature enough!" I piped up, my voice sounding like the squeal of a baby who has just been tipped out of its pram. "Think of the good this journey would do myself and Stefan. Why, we would come back practically self-sufficient men of the world, ready to take London by storm!"

All their faces still wore that vacant expression, although Mrs. Ratliff's showed the most signs of life. She'd always liked me, I thought, so I ran to her first, divested her of her teacup, and shoved my hands into hers. "After all, we are the future of England, and let it never be said that the British were not magnanimous when it came to expanding the cultural and educational horizons of their youth."

Nothing had gone according to plan, but I was certain I had presented my points well...or as well as could be expected, given the circumstances. To my horror, Mrs. Ratliff began to laugh. It started out as a little melodious chuckle, one I had grown accustomed to hearing over the years, then burgeoned into something very near a guffaw. I looked around the room and saw that not only did Mr. Ratliff and my mother share in her mirth, but wonder of wonders, Roddy was laughing, too! This was indeed a day for firsts.

"Mrs. Ratliff, I..."

"Eric, you fool, *please.* Less is more." The relief in Stefan's voice made me suddenly hopeful. My brow furrowed in confusion as I looked at him, for he began to laugh, too. Why the devil was he laughing if all our plans had crumbled around our ears? I knew then that we had won, but our victory had been attained through no efforts of my own. Rather, it had been secured before I had even entered the room. And I had been a complete and utter fool to worry.

"Oh, Eric, dear," Mrs. Ratliff said, patting my hand. "I think this idea of a grand tour is marvelous. And I am so pleased that you and Stefan will be expanding your tour to include Romania, my homeland."

"Don't forget Austria-Hungary, Mother," Stefan chimed in, giving me a wink. This little extension of his was news to me. I began to wonder what else Stefan had promised our parents in order to get his way.

"Of course, my love. Eric," she said, rising.

"Ye...Yes, Mrs. Ratliff?" I responded, rather groggily. I was still stunned by the sudden turn of events.

"Your parents and Mr. Ratliff and I have been conferring, and we all believe that you and Stefan would benefit greatly from this grand tour. We will make all the necessary preparations for the two of you to set out on the twenty-first of this month."

I stared at the woman, and it would not be a falsehood to say that I gaped, for this news was beyond wonderful. How long I stood in this manner I cannot say, but when my mother brought me back to consciousness, it seemed as though I had been gone for at least half the day.

"Close your mouth, you fool," she whispered in my ear. I did as told and presently found that she had placed a small blue envelope in my hands. "This is from Roderick," she said, looking intently at the little parcel, "please try to spend it responsibly. Lord knows it's probably the most you'll ever get out of the old skinflint."

She motioned for me to put the envelope away in my waistcoat pocket, then returned to her seat. But I couldn't resist the urge to see just how generous Papa Caldwell had been. I slid my fingers beneath the lip and pulled out a stack of bills, which, after a quick, discreet count, I realized totaled four hundred pounds! It was an exorbitant sum. Obviously, that blasted pension must have been a much more profitable investment than I had given Roddy credit for.

I fingered the bills, counting them again to be sure. My heart pounded faster as I ticked them off one by one, but I had not been mistaken.

This generosity was beyond anything I had ever dared to hope for. I was not even expecting a hundred quid from the old blister and had resigned myself to being the "poor relation" of our duo, living off Stefan's wealth for the duration of the tour, but old Roddy had come through in the end in a way I never thought possible. Gone was my resentment over the Turkish Delight. Nothing could mar my opinion of him in that beatific moment, not even the thought that he might be giving me such a large sum of money in the hopes that I would be suspected of robbing the Bank of England and end up getting locked away in some foreign jail. No, I would not countenance such evil notions. Roddy had changed—he was human after all.

I stuffed the bills back into the envelope and looked upon Roddy in open adoration. Such unaccustomed attention from his stepson must have made the old coot uncomfortable, for he began to fidget and look behind him as if he thought my adoring gaze was meant for the clock above the mantelpiece.

"My dear, *dear* father," I said, clasping my hands about his. What was the world coming to? Not twenty minutes before I had been lamenting ever crossing paths with this gentleman of sterling character. *Eric Bradburry, you've been a fool.* I continued to shake Roddy heartily, all the while chuntering on about his generosity in a stream of words that I'm certain made absolutely no sense to his ears, much less my own.

"All right, all right," he said, extricating himself from my hold. "That's enough of that. It is my sincere hope that you will use this money *wisely* and not waste it on frivolity."

"You need have no fear of that, Roderick," I replied, in what I hoped was a sincere, man-of-the-world tone of voice.

A chuckle from Stefan's corner brought me to my senses. I cocked an eyebrow at my coconspirator. And that's when I heard Roddy clear his throat.

Oh, Lord. I knew that sound did not bode well for us. He must have uncovered a flaw, a chink in the armor. One word from him and our entire scheme would be shot to Hades.

Ever since his brilliant success that morning, I had come to think of Stefan as a second Wellington at Waterloo, so it was unfathomable to me to even entertain the notion that he had not taken into consideration every objection my stepfather could possibly make. I was puzzling over just what these objections might be, when Roddy began to speak.

"There is one thing that gives me pause, though. The absence of guides. Now, I could arrange..."

"Oh, of course we will have guides, Mr. Caldwell!"

Guides?! Since when had Stefan arranged for us to have guides?! Another shock like this and I would have to be taken to hospital. He knew full well we intended to take up with whatever local cicerone we could find, and *that* only when necessary. After all, going it alone was half the adventure, until the language barrier made guides a must. In truth, though, I doubted we would need the guides. My smattering of languages, not to mention my trusty Baedeker travel guide, would see us through France and Italy just fine, and Stefan's native knowledge of Romanian would allow us to journey through the Eastern European countries as easily as if we had been locals. I was about to protest this plan, until I caught the warning glance Stefan shot my way.

"Yes," he continued, turning his attention to Roddy. "I took it upon myself to contact Father's associates in each country, and they assured me that we will have guides waiting at our beck and call the minute we set foot on foreign soil. There is no need to worry about *anything*."

The speech was a little too confident and a trifle cloying, but it served its purpose.

"Well, then," Roddy said. He looked at my mother in bewilderment, then seemed to realize the futility of objecting any further. His shoulders sagged a bit, but he recovered himself before anyone else had a chance to notice this momentary display of defeat. "I suppose all that is left to say is Godspeed."

"Godspeed!" Stefan and I answered simultaneously. If our smiles could have been any broader at that moment, I believe our faces would have split in two. I slapped Stefan on the back, still unable to believe we had won.

"How in the world did you pull it off?" I asked. "And since when did we decide to go to Eastern Europe?"

He nodded toward the doorway and motioned for me to be silent until our parents had left the room.

"That, my dear boy," he replied, his eyes gleaming in triumph, "was the key. You know money was never a problem, my parents being millionaires and all. The real trouble was convincing them it was a sound venture. And that's where good old Eastern Europe came in. I knew my mother would be absolutely giddy if she knew we were going to visit the country where she and I were both born. So I just happened to mention that we were thinking about stopping over in Romania for a day or two. And there you have it. Simple, really, don't you think?"

It must have been my day to gape like an idiot, for that was what I was reduced to once more. I stared at Stefan, his face triumphant, then burst out laughing.

"Bravo, lad, bravo! A stroke of genius! Now, if I may make a suggestion? Let's stop standing here congratulating ourselves and start packing for this grand tour!" And with that, I shoved him into the hallway and left him to his own devices. I still had a lot to work out before I could relax. I'd never been as cavalier as Stefan about life changing events. My head was still spinning from everything that had happened. It was so impossible to believe we had succeeded. But as I began taking the clothes out of my wardrobe, the truth finally sunk in.

In nine more days, Stefan and I would set out on the grandest adventure of our lives.

‡

On the twenty-first of June, Stefan and I stood on the deck of the *Erinyes*, the ship that would guide us away from Dover and across the Channel. Our parents were somewhere down on the quay amongst the throng who had gathered to see us off. I peered down into the crowd, searching for their familiar faces, but all I could distinguish were dozens of arms waving handkerchiefs and flags.

Stefan was about ready to burst from anticipation. He had given up looking for our parents long ago and was instead gazing across the opposite side of the ship toward where the coast of France was waiting to meet us. I smiled as I looked at him. I knew what he was feeling. It was a giddy sensation, setting out on your own for the first time. Here we were, Eric Bradburry and Stefan Ratliff, two intrepid young Englishmen ready for whatever life had in store.

"Finally free. And about time, too."

"Sorry?" I asked.

"I thought we'd *never* get away from them."

"That's not like you," I said. He'd looked nothing like his usual, jovial self when he'd said that.

"Maybe it is and you just never knew it."

"What an odd thing to say," I ended up saying to his back, since he'd turned and seemed to have forgotten I was there. Bother Stefan; he was being enigmatic again. He'd been acting like this a lot lately. I didn't know why, but it unnerved me. Still, there was nothing I could do about it, and frankly, I didn't want to. I was too excited to care about his changeable moods at that moment.

A thundering blare erupted from the smokestack above us. I leaned over the rail and saw the gangplank being drawn up. My heart thudded against my chest. Now it was *my* turn to feel as though I would burst.

"This is it!" I shouted above the din to no one in particular. "Paris awaits!"

~10~

Corcitura

Two Englishmen in Paris

*T*he crowd on the platform at Gare Du Nord was quite possibly the largest mob I had seen in my life. Ever since we left Calais three days before, I had kept my nose buried in my Baedeker, reading up on the culture of today's modern Parisian and familiarizing myself with the history of the sights I would see in the city. From what Baedeker and Co. had to say, I had felt assured that all mobish tendencies died out after the Revolution, so why did I feel like Sydney Carton going to his doom the moment I clapped eyes on the throng? If I had told Stefan my feelings, he would have looked askance at me and said I was experiencing fear of the unknown and just a bit of foreign prejudice, not to mention that I was being ridiculous—and he would have been right on all accounts. It also didn't help that the only book on Paris I had read apart from my Baedeker was Dickens' *A Tale of Two Cities*. Not quite the introduction you would want, but it was too late to remedy my mistake.

I latched onto Stefan's arm, dragging him along behind me, and somehow the two of us managed to push our way through the press of bodies and get as close to the exit doors as possible. This part of the train was nearly bursting with tourists. I clutched my valise to my chest and turned to Stefan. "When that door opens," I said, "you'd better run."

Corcitura

He wasn't paying any attention to me whatsoever, I could
tell, but some of my words must have registered for he
nodded, waved his hand dismissively, and muttered an
abstracted "Yes, yes, of course," before refocusing his gaze on
the commotion taking place outside. He had been acting this
way since we left Calais; I suppose the cause of his aloofness
had been my fascination with the Baedeker. Honestly, I was
surprised he hadn't thrown the book out the window by now.
Although I was beginning to feel like an overbearing
governess, I didn't trust Stefan's plan for guides, so someone
had to take the cultural aspects of the trip in hand. After all,
I would have to report to Roddy when we returned—a task I
was dreading—and I couldn't afford to come up wanting in
either eloquence or substance. Lord knows he would be
looking for holes in my story so he could trip me up.

The door of the compartment was opening. I could feel
the anticipation hovering in the air. I could also feel an
overexcited tourist stepping on my foot, but a quick flick of
the shoe put him in his place.

A wave of humidity struck me in the face as the door
opened. Before I had the chance to steel myself against the
outflow of passengers, I was swept off the train by the tide of
humanity.

I held my valise above my head as I was dragged forward.
Someone knocked into me so hard that I nearly dropped my
valise, while another equally hospitable Frenchman ran over
me in his haste. I had a strong desire to throttle that one, for
after he crashed into me, he laughed as though the sight of
my sprawled body was the most amusing thing he had seen
in his life.

I'd made up my mind to go after the blackguard, but a
sudden break in the crowd made me forget all about him. I'd
nearly squeezed through the opening, when I was pushed
back to the ground.

My suspicion that the mob had been concealing
pitchforks underneath their overcoats did not seem as
farfetched to me now as I sat huddled on the platform,
rubbing my injured foot. I had a feeling the offender was
probably the same man from the train, but then a torrent of

French invectives hit me and I looked up in shock to see that my assailant was a bent old crone! She flung her hands in my face and shot me a venomous glance as if to say she couldn't believe I had had the gall to get in her way.

"What is the world coming to?" I asked aloud as I watched her totter off, but no one was there to help me answer the question. This little incident had done nothing to lift my spirits, and, to top it off, I had lost Stefan.

To my relief, the crowd began to recede. I heaved myself off the pavement, balancing on my good foot, and looked around for my erstwhile friend. A glance at the train showed me Stefan was nowhere in sight. So he'd got off the train. That was something. But where the devil was he now? The stationmaster would know.

I was halfway to the stationmaster's office when I heard a familiar laugh that stopped me in my tracks. Off to the side, separated from the crowd, I saw Stefan chatting with...no! It couldn't be! As I studied the man—the same long, lean form; the tousled black hair; the sardonic twist to the mouth; the look in his eyes that told the world the man's high opinion of himself—I began to feel sick. It was him...the selfsame Parisian who had bowled me over not ten minutes before.

I hobbled toward them, my unease growing as I saw that they seemed to be getting along famously. In fact, they appeared to be thick as thieves, laughing and carrying on in *English*, no less. That one fact alone made the man's purpose almost certain, though I couldn't bring myself to admit it.

Please don't let it be our guide. Please don't let it be our guide.

"Ah, Eric, there you are," Stefan said as I came upon him and his new friend. "May I present Luc, who will be our 'fearless leader' while we are in Paris."

It's our guide...blast.

Oh, well, I thought to myself, *I might as well make the best of it, seeing as how I have no choice.*

"Charmed, monsieur," I said in French. That would leave him speechless.

"No need to strain yourself," he returned in English. "I speak your language like a native."

Corcitura

Well, that point was debatable, but I wasn't willing to go to war over it. I could see this pompous cove and I were going to have a prickly association. We stood there—he with his arms crossed, I struggling to balance on my good foot as nonchalantly as possible—sizing one another up as though we were two gladiators getting ready to tear each other's heads off.

A cough from Stefan brought me out of my gloom. I had learned over the years that this gesture was his way of urging me to forgo conflict and take what he called the *superior path.* Oftentimes, this meant I had to be the bigger man and give in, even when the quarrel had not been my fault. Usually I did, but this time I had to make a concerted effort. This Luc fellow was a little too cocky, and I was tempted to mutiny just to see if Stefan would really pop a vein. But the more mature part of me won out in the end. Roddy would have been proud. Besides, the bursting of an artery was a decidedly messy business and we weren't going to be in Paris long enough to make a side trip to hospital.

I cleared my throat, pretending to take no notice of Luc's barb, and flashed him a smile. "Shall you be dropping us at our hotel first, or are we to traipse all over the city carrying our trunks?" I ignored Stefan's pointed look and kept my eyes fixed on Luc. I might have been taking the superior path, but that didn't mean I had to be a saint.

"And just how many trunks would that be?" he asked, that sardonic grin still plastered on his face.

"Two."

"Ah, très bien! If you will follow me?"

I let him take the lead and motioned for Stefan to keep pace with me a few steps behind.

"Where did you find this man?" I whispered.

"*I* didn't find him. *He* found *me.* Materialized the minute I set foot off the train. I can't explain it."

"Well, that's not the least bit alarming," I countered. "And yet you've agreed to let him be our guide."

"He offered, I accepted. It's as simple as that."

"As simple as that. As simple as you losing your senses the minute we crossed the Channel?"

"Steady on, Eric. Spread your wings. Live a little."

I stewed over his laissez-faire attitude, unsure of what I could say to make him see reason. "Luc. Surely there's a last name to go with that?"

"How should I know what it is?"

"Stefan!" I shrieked, causing Luc and several other people to stare at me.

"Oh, I thought I saw a rat, ha ha," I said, laughing nervously. Luc gave me an odd look, and several other people began inching away from what I'm sure they thought was an unhinged foreigner. "Railroad rats, very large, very dangerous," I continued babbling, trying to justify my outburst, but they had all lost interest in me by then, thank heaven.

"Get a hold of yourself, Eric. You're acting like a buffoon."

"I'd rather be a live buffoon than a dead one. You don't know that man's last name. And do you know why, Mr. Man of the World? It's probably because he doesn't even have one. Luc, *ha*! That could be an alias for all we know. He's probably going to shanghai us for our passports. And then what do you think will happen? We'll end up dead somewhere in a gutter. He'll have one of his troupe do the job, and the fellow will probably turn out to be a descendent of Charlotte Corday. A knife in the heart, I can see it now. Ta-ta Eric and Stefan. End of story. What a lovely grand tour this was."

"You are becoming overwrought."

By the time I'd thought up a particularly biting retort, we had already passed out of the station and were standing on the curb in the sunlight of the Parisian afternoon. My animosity lessened somewhat, until I saw Luc waiting near the street, leaning on our two trunks, which had somehow magically appeared. I faltered a step at the sight of him, for I found it impossible to believe that he had secured our trunks so quickly when he had been with us the whole time. So, he wasn't only a potential murderer—now he was a necromancer! The man worked in mysterious ways.

I walked up to him, fixing on him what I hoped was a penetrating stare. "So, Luc,"—and it was all I could do not to say, "if that's your real name"—"what are you planning to do with us and our trunks, hmm?"

Instead of answering, he smiled one of his irritating smiles, placed two fingers in his mouth, and whistled.

I half expected a hook-handed man to pop out from behind a corner at the summons, but was surprised by what I saw. A stallion was drawing a barouche, its sides decorated with streamers in the colors of the French flag, straight up the drive. Luc reached out a hand and stroked the steed's flank as it drew up next to us on the sidewalk.

"Gentlemen!" Luc said with all the flourish of a ringmaster introducing a tight-rope-walking bear. "Your chariot awaits!"

Stefan hopped into the barouche and settled himself in. I, however, was still intent on being obstinate and was getting annoyed with myself for not being able to think up further obstacles to this pleasure trip. Something was not right about all this, but I couldn't say what.

I watched Luc in silence as he heaved our two trunks into the barouche, then I pulled out my Baedeker and leafed through it, searching for the page I had marked.

I heard a sound that was too slight to be considered a gasp. For some odd reason, Luc was staring at me in horror. No, that was not correct, he wasn't staring at *me*. He was staring at the Baedeker.

Ha! So, Monsieur Sans-Surname had a bête noire! I had a momentary desire to wave the book in his face and see if he would cower before it like a vampire recoiling from the sight of a crucifix, but I restrained myself.

"So, my good man," I said, hardly able to conceal my smugness. "Where shall you be taking us first?"

If it was possible to blanch even more, Luc did so that moment. His Adam's apple bobbed erratically as he tried to swallow.

"Why don't you take a seat in the barouche, Monsieur?"

"Very well."

I settled in beside Stefan, while Luc pulled himself up onto the driver's seat and took the reins in his hands.

I drummed my fingers against the Baedeker and chuckled to myself, which made Luc wince. The man looked positively beaten, but I had a feeling he wouldn't admit defeat so easily.

"What are you so happy about?" Stefan asked.

"Oh, nothing. I just think this is going to be a lovely day after all."

‡

"Good God, what is that thing?!"

"That, my young friend, is La Tour Eiffel, or soon will be."

I couldn't understand why Stefan had taken such a dislike to the half-built edifice. It didn't look that terrible for a monument under construction, but then I caught snatches of the conversation of the Parisians that had gathered near us, and I had a feeling Stefan was adopting this foreign sentiment to ingratiate himself with the entire populace of Paris.

The debate amongst the little group grew heated. The men gesticulated wildly and the women, disgust puckering their rouged lips, made several biting comments and smirked haughtily at what one of them called the "inverted spider." Strange analogists, these French...

Luc sauntered over to me. He had somehow regained his savoir faire between here and the Champs-Élysées, curse him. "Monsieur Eiffel's Eyesore is what *we* locals call it."

The emphasis on the "we" was for my benefit, of course, but I ignored the barb and his pointed stare. I wasn't going to let the blighter ruffle me. I had a secret weapon, one which I had already used to devastating effect when we had stopped at the Arc de Triomphe an hour ago. He knew better than to push me now or the little red book of death would be brought out again. On the way back, I had indulged in a vision of Luc falling to his knees, screaming, "No! Not Le petit Livre Rouge de Mort! Anything but that!" and had chuckled darkly, causing Stefan and our guide to look at me warily. They were both probably wondering if the strain of the journey had caused my mind to snap. If they wanted to speculate, I would

~18~

do nothing to relieve their worries—I was enjoying this game far too much.

"No, I see no merit in it whatsoever," Stefan said, resigned. "It's a monstrosity. I pity the poor souls having to look at it every day. If only they had made it more appealing. It mars the beauty of Paris. I could understand if it were grand and regal like the Arc de Triomphe, but this? *This*?!" He threw up his hands in exasperation.

"It caused quite a riot among the literati, let me tell you," Luc said, throwing me a look that let me know he was relishing the fact that this info was not to be found in my book. "Zola nearly had a fit, as did de Maupassant and others, what with their petition to halt its construction, but they couldn't stop it. They even went so far as to call it the 'Tower of Babel,' and I must admit, I agree with them."

"Typical French," I murmured, for I had taken to the thing immediately and felt I had to defend it.

"What was that?"

"Nothing." He wasn't going to corner me that easily. This was only a minor skirmish. We still had to see the Obélisque de Luxor in the Place de la Concorde before retiring to the hotel. I was content to await my moment and choose my battles wisely.

"They say it will be completed next year, but I don't believe it," our guide rambled on. "It's up for the Exposition, but after that, they'll probably realize what a disastrous mistake it was and tear it down, regardless of the twenty-year lease." He looked pleased with himself for imparting that bit of local gossip.

I wanted to retch.

The two of them stood there lost in conversation, neither of them showing any sign of wanting to leave. What were they doing, waiting for the Tower to tell them its side of the story? It was nearly four o'clock, tea time would be missed, and, though I had grown fond of the Tower, I had no intention of loitering about all day contemplating its shortcomings or fate.

"Well, shall we be moving along?"

That seemed to spark life in them, for they both finally tore themselves away and followed me back to the carriage.

Luc carefully guided the barouche past the countless Mesdames running to and fro down the boulevard. I swear I did not see a single woman who did not have at least two bandboxes tucked underneath her arms. They loved shopping in Paris, that was for certain. Mother would have been in heaven. Roddy would have had an aneurysm.

During the whole journey, Stefan kept muttering to himself about the Tower's flaws, while Luc whistled a jaunty tune, obviously happy I hadn't broken out the Baedeker.

Excitement overcame me as I saw the Obélisque coming into view. The Place de la Concorde had been the one landmark I had the greatest desire to see, what with my fascination with the Revolution and all. I couldn't wait for Luc, lollygagger that he was, to traverse the few more feet to the spot, so I jumped out of the barouche and raced past the gilded fountain with its merfolk statues, and made straight for the Obélisque.

"Come on, come on," I called to my bewildered companions, "quickly!" I didn't even have to crack open my Baedeker. I had already memorized the passage about the Place's history. "This was the exact spot where Marie Antoinette and King Louis XVI were beheaded in 1793." I looked up at the Obélisque, studying the hieroglyphs carved into its sides, and marveled at this ancient gift that had been given to the French by the viceroy of Egypt more than fifty years ago. The setting sun caught my eyes, and I turned around to see its rays glinting off the dome of the Hôtel des Invalides—or Napoleon's tomb, as it had come to be known—on the other side of the Place. I was going to impart a tidbit about this building when Luc inserted himself between Stefan and me and pointed to the ground at the foot of the Obélisque.

"And they say," he said in an exaggerated whisper, "if you look closely, you can still see the stains from the blood that dripped from Marie Antoinette's severed head when the executioner held it aloft to the crowd." He stopped suddenly, looked over his shoulder as if he were afraid of being watched, then motioned for us to draw closer. "Some say that while he was displaying her head to the mob, he slapped her cheek and she blinked..."

This really was too much. "Of all the ghastly things to say! Nowhere is that mentioned in Baedeker!" I said hotly.

"Well, Baedeker doesn't know everything, does he?!"

In spite of my resolve to fight him every chance I could, I recoiled slightly at this vehemence. It was the first real sign of annoyance he had shown me all day. His nostrils flared and his hands were clenched at his sides. The pair of us were on the verge of coming to blows. Well, if this was what he wanted, I was not going to back down from a fight. I had already rolled back my cuffs, when Stefan stepped between us and put his hands on either of our shoulders.

"Lads," he said. I did not like the gleam in his eye as he said this. It was far too conciliatory for my purposes. "I hardly think this is a proper place for fisticuffs. It wouldn't do anything to further good relations between our two countries, let me tell you." And here he laughed a little too loudly and drew Luc and me closer. I knew what was coming, and I felt like pushing Stefan into the fountain behind us. The cheek of my friend amazed me sometimes.

"Now, be civilized men and shake hands."

I would have rather spit in Luc's eye, but it seemed Stefan expected me to take that blasted superior path yet again. Reluctantly, I stuck out my hand, and about two minutes later, Luc shook it—barely.

"Now, then, shall we make for the hotel?"

"Yes, but first I want to show you the view from the Pont Neuf. Nous allons. Follow me."

My spirits lifted at the idea of taking in the view from Paris' oldest bridge, so I decided to hold my tongue and go along. I could tell Stefan was very pleased with himself for diffusing our little war, for he kept a smug smile on his face throughout the duration of the trip. Luc, on the other hand, had undergone a complete transformation. This new attitude of his was making me a trifle uncomfortable. He persisted in whistling some French ditty that was catchy the first few bars, but after hearing it repeated twenty times in the space of five minutes, it started to grate on my nerves. I was sure he had something devious planned to put me in my place, but what that could be, I hadn't the slightest idea.

The lamps dotting the Pont Neuf were being lit as we turned onto the bridge. Luc brought the carriage to a halt beside an old woman selling flowers. While he busied himself with catching up on local gossip with this grande dame, Stefan and I leaned over the railing of the bridge and studied the hundreds of grotesque faces decorating its side. I laughed as I came nearly face-to-face with a particularly ugly specimen who reminded me of Luc. "Stefan, you need to see this..."

"Oh, forget your war and look at this." Stefan seized me by the arm and dragged me to the opposite side of the bridge. "Notre Dame, Eric," he said with a reverence for the sacred which he had never shown until this moment. "What a sight!"

I had to agree. Not even Baedeker had prepared me for the vision of the cathedral in all its Gothic magnificence. The lamplight cast its twin bell towers in an ethereal glow. The fading twilight pierced the stained glass of the rose window and splayed a rainbow of refracted light upon the Parisians strolling below.

We were close enough to make out the row of saints on the cathedral's facade, but too far away to see their features. I remembered skimming through this section in Baedeker and not truly paying any attention to the list of saints, so I pulled the book out of my pocket and leafed through it until I reached the page that dealt with Notre Dame. I skimmed the page and had nearly reached the spot I was looking for, when I felt my skin prickle and realized that Luc was standing beside me.

"May I see that please, Monsieur?" he said, extending his hand.

Something about his tone of voice made me hesitate. Warily, I held the book out to him and watched his eyes for some sign that would betray his true intentions, but there was none. He reached for the book and I relinquished it, albeit reluctantly.

"Hmm..." he said as he flipped through it. I turned to Stefan and raised my eyebrows. In that moment, I saw a flash of movement from Luc's direction and turned back in horror to see the crazed Frenchman flinging my Baedeker into the Seine!

I shrieked and leaned over the rail, flailing my arms in the air in a futile attempt to grab the book before it plunged into the water. Thankfully, the book had not fallen into the Seine, but rather onto the deck of one of the petite bateaux that was steaming along underneath the bridge. An old man on deck picked the book up and turned it over curiously before looking up and seeing my stricken face. His eyebrows rose when he saw me, and he held the book aloft.

"That's right," I said, motioning for him to throw it to me. "Toss it here, toss it to me! Toss it back! Come on, man, do it!"

The man was about to throw it up to me, when Luc, blast him, shouted something in a dialect of French I did not understand. Whatever it was, it doomed my hopes, for the man laughed and threw my precious book into the Seine.

"What on earth have you done?!" I growled, rounding on Luc with every intention of tossing *him* into the river.

"Good form, old boy, good form!" cackled Stefan, who was doubled over with laughter.

Et tu, Stefan? So this was how Caesar must have felt. Well, Stefan wouldn't be laughing so heartily in a few moments. If I had my way, he would be taking a swim next.

Luc smirked and flicked something off his cuff. "Who are you going to trust? A stupid book or me?"

"I suppose I don't have any choice, now, but to trust you!"

"That is right. It certainly took you long enough to learn it."

I couldn't decide who I was angrier with—Luc for his suave command of a situation I thought I was in control of, or Stefan for throwing in his lot with this foreign devil. Either way, I had been defeated, and it was a feeling I didn't like.

"Come on, lad, don't give me that pitiful look," said Stefan as he put his arm around my shoulder.

"I, for one, don't see what's so funny!"

"Eric, you have no idea how annoying you've been."

"What?!"

"I've been wanting to do that since we left Calais!"

I felt as though I did not know Stefan. Yes, I might have been a little overzealous with the Baedeker, but did my best friend have to take such obvious delight in my humiliation? It was as if setting foot on foreign soil had altered Stefan past distinction, and I was not so certain I liked this new Mr. Ratliff.

"It's time to go. I have plans for the evening," I said, walking back toward the barouche. Of course, this was a lie, but Stefan didn't need to know that.

"Oh, really?"

"Yes, really, and if you have any sense at all, you will join me, instead of hanging about with *him*."

"I'm not so sure about that."

I let the comment and our conversation die. I had no desire to talk with either of them until we reached the hotel. Mercifully, Le Grand Hôtel Intercontinental came into view shortly thereafter. I couldn't help marveling at its almost palatial exterior. At five stories tall, it took up a swath of city blocks and sat in all its glory directly opposite the Opéra Garnier. It was grander than any hotel I had seen in London, and I was willing to bet it even outshone Roddy's precious pension in Corfu. If the outside was this impressive, I wondered what majesty would be found within.

I'd jumped out of the carriage and strode to the gilded, etched-glass doors before Luc had even stopped the barouche.

I halted on the threshold of the grand foyer and turned back to see Luc entrusting our trunks to the porter and then handing Stefan two strips of paper. Luc pointed at the papers then jerked his thumb in my direction. He and Stefan seemed to be settling on an arrangement of some sort, for the two of them smiled and shook hands, then Luc disappeared around the side of the hotel and Stefan walked toward me.

"What are you two plotting?" I asked as we passed through the hotel's doors.

"Oh, so you've decided to talk to me again?"

"Look, Stefan, it's just that this man...he doesn't seem trustworthy." Stefan pulled up and drew me aside into an alcove. "Come now, Eric," he sighed. "You're doing it again."

"What?"

"Being small-minded. Trust me. We're practically brothers. Would I let you down?"

Before I could answer, he produced the papers and waved them in my face. "Now, look what I have here."

"How can I look when you keep waving them about like an idiot?" I said, laughing. I took the papers from his hand and read over the script written on them. "Stefan!" I shrieked, barely able to contain my excitement as I realized what the papers were. "These are tickets to tonight's performance at the Opéra Garnier! How on earth did you get them on such short notice?"

"You can thank Luc for that, though I know you won't. The fool went and got two tickets, but I'm not wasting my only night in Paris on some ridiculous opera."

"*Arabella, the Romany Child,*" I said, reading the title of the opera aloud. "Sounds intriguing."

"Sounds dead *boring*, if you ask me."

"Well, what are you planning to do?"

A wicked gleam lit Stefan's eyes. "Just you wait and see," he said, patting me on the arm as if I were a child. "Now, take this," he said, handing me the key to our room, "and make yourself presentable. Meet me down here when you're done and you'll find out."

And before I could protest further, he turned on his heel and walked off toward the concierge's desk. I was mystified by this sudden turn of events and would have stood there goggling like a buffoon if the tolling of a clock had not brought me back to the present. Six bells. I only had an hour and a half before the curtain rose.

I raced up the marble staircase and the four ensuing stairwells—nearly crashing into several people in my haste—before finally reaching our room. When I opened the door, I was stunned by the grandeur in front of me.

Louis XIV chairs cushioned in rich red and gold velvet filled the large anteroom. Several Carrara marble tables were placed about to form a sitting area. On the white paneled walls, there hung copies of some of the world's most famous works of art. The paintings were of such magnificent artistry that I wondered if anyone but the most seasoned critic would be able to tell they were copies. Fragonard's *The Love Letter* was perched above the marble fireplace, and Boucher's *The Toilet of Venus* kept watch over two divans clustered around a glass table in a far corner of the room.

As I looked down, I noticed that the floors were made of oak so polished one could see one's reflection in the surface. I had seen paintings of Versailles, but even the opulence of that palace seemed to pale in comparison with our suite.

Off of the sitting room were our sleeping quarters, which were no less grand. I would see to it that this first room would be mine, for it opened onto a magnificent view of the Opéra Garnier. The building was so close I could have almost reached out and touched the golden statues adorning the opera house's roof. Stefan's room, or what I had already decided would be his, was reached by an adjoining door. I was about to appraise his quarters, when I noticed something lying on the chair next to my bed. A top hat, cape, pair of gloves, and an evening suit had been laid out, along with a small white envelope sealed with red wax that bore the emblem of the hotel. I tore open the envelope and extracted the note.

Compliments of your guide, or as you would have him called, Luc Sans-Surname...don't let my generosity go to your head, Anglais.

I was dumbfounded and more than a little disturbed. How had he known I had called him that? I had never spoken it aloud...or had I? The man unsettled me and made me doubt myself, but I seemed to be the only one who felt this way. He and Stefan had been matey ever since they met. Maybe I was letting my imagination run away with me again. I *had* voiced my suspicions rather incautiously at Gare du Nord. Maybe Luc had overheard my little rant to Stefan. That must have been it.

The mantle clock in the sitting room began to chime. My time was nearly up. I was determined not to let my doubts about Luc ruin my evening.

I quickly donned the suit, grabbed my hat and gloves, and made my way downstairs. Stefan was a grown man, so let him sort things out himself. If he wanted to cavort with this supposed mind-reader, that was fine with me. I was certain there was a logical explanation for the man's omniscience.

I passed underneath the massive gas-lit chandelier hanging from the foyer ceiling and stepped out into the crisp night air. How long I would have to wait for Stefan, I did not know, but I hoped he wouldn't tarry. I had just pulled out my watch when I saw Stefan and Luc—dressed in top hats and tails, each of them carrying a walking stick and looking for all the world like two dignitaries—sauntering down the boulevard toward me.

"What ho, old boy?" Stefan chimed as he came to a stop before me. "Ready to spend an evening with your precious Arabella?"

"Don't you both look très beau monde. And just where are the two of you headed?"

Stefan and Luc smiled rakishly. "Well, we think it would be a terrible miscarriage of justice if we did not partake in some of the local color, so to speak."

"And what would that be?"

"Girls, girls, girls!"

"Doesn't that sound like fun?" shot in Luc.

"Um hm, a dancehall, I take it?" I ventured, knowing full well this was exactly what they both had in mind.

"The boy is perceptive!" Stefan taunted good-naturedly. "Now, the only question is, which one do we choose?"

"There are two that come to mind. La Perle de Paris and The Folies Bergère," said Luc.

"Which one is more respectable?"

"Oh, La Perle, no doubt."

"Good! Then it's settled. To the Folies we go!"

"But that's not the more reputable one," I couldn't help adding, trying hard not to laugh at Stefan's sudden transformation into a Bohemian.

"What do I care for reputability?" he said, shrugging his shoulders in a very Gallic gesture he had no doubt learned from Luc. "Roderick's not *my* father. Come, Luc, dissolution and degradation await!"

"And what of your ticket?"

"Give it to one of those poor fools hanging about outside. Or save it as a souvenir. I've no use for it tonight. Oh, Eric, stop being a prude. Let's have some fun. Come with us."

"No, thank you," I said, looking down at the tickets in my hand. "You don't have the wrath of Roderick to scare you into submission. Are you sure you won't change your mind?"

"There's no possibility of that," he said, patting my arm condescendingly. "I have no desire to relive my own Romany childhood, much less witness that of the unfortunate Arabella. I wish you luck, old man, and now we must be off."

"Promise you won't do anything you'll regret?"

"Yes, *maman*," he said, smiling rakishly again. "Besides, I hardly think it's possible to commit every deadly sin in a single night, but I'm game to try."

I laughed at this bravado. "Just don't expect me to show up with the gendarmerie to save your neck."

"Wouldn't dream of it."

And with that, we wished each other *bonne nuit*, and the two of them strode off arm in arm, singing *La Marseillaise* at the top of their lungs. I laughed again as I thought of Roddy. Their little jaunt was definitely not what my stepfather would consider a "cultural experience."

A commotion across the way drew my attention to the crowds filing into the opera house. I consulted my watch again. Ten minutes to spare. I straightened my top hat and walked off toward Garnier's palace, where my box seats and Arabella were waiting.

Opéra Phantasmique

I thought I had reached my quota of astonishment for the evening, but as I crossed the threshold of the opera house, that notion was shattered. Spreading out before me like the wings of a giant eagle was the Grand Escalier. The main flight of shining marble steps led up to a landing before branching off into two more grand staircases, one leading off to the left, the other to the right. As if that were not enough, two bronze nymphs bearing a trio of candelabras adorned the marble newel-posts at the base of the Escalier and beckoned to the milling patrons, welcoming them into the opulence of Garnier's palace.

Up above, angels and figures from mythology flitted across the frescoed panels of the ceiling. Apollo in his chariot raced across the pale sky, while in another panel, a woman bearing a shield was being crowned by an angel. At her feet rested a man clasping a triton in his hand. I was certain these two were meant to represent Athena and Poseidon. Set into the ceiling above the frescoes was a skylight, now darkened by the shadows of night. The lobby must have been even more magnificent in the daytime, with sunlight streaming through this opening and glinting off the gilded statuary and marble floors of the Escalier.

As with the Eiffel Tower, I didn't understand the people's aversion to this place. It had been called gaudy, garish, and overdone when it was unveiled in 1875, but now the people adored this grand palace. The lobby was full to bursting with men and women dressed in their finest, and the small balconies protruding from the gallery around the second landing were filled with more resplendent patrons gazing down upon the dignitaries gathered around me.

I had been informed by the attendant that Box Five was on the second level. After passing through the sea of gowns and tailcoats and journeying down a hall carpeted in red velvet, I finally reached a door bearing a small wooden plaque with the words *6 Places 5* painted onto its surface. Stepping across the threshold, I collided with a mass of crushed red velvet, and as I drew this curtain aside, I was nearly blinded by gaslight. A blur of red and gold swayed before me. I shielded my eyes until they could adjust to the brilliant light being cast by the chandelier.

As I walked toward the edge of the box, my eyes still downcast, I noticed that several plush chairs were scattered about. I had wondered if I would be the only one in the box that night, but this was a ridiculous notion given that the opera house was growing more and more crowded as the evening wore on.

By this time, my eyes had regained their focus, and I was now free to take in the spectacle of the chandelier. Strands of crystals were strung between the bronze tiers, while several more diamond-like facets were encrusted into the chandelier itself. Dozens of gas-lit candles and orb-like spheres were interspersed throughout and made the entire chandelier glow ethereally.

I was so absorbed in studying the chandelier that I nearly toppled over the balcony rail when I heard a woman's voice cry out behind me.

"Oh! Hello!"

I turned to see a woman wearing a high necked black gown decorated with enough jet crystals to rival the chandelier. Her hair—I couldn't tell if it was brown or aubergine—had been swept up atop her head in a style that would have made Madame de Pompadour jealous, and her face was one of those enigmas that make it impossible to determine age. She could have been anywhere from forty-five to sixty.

I stared at her, unsure of what to say, then finally managed to find my voice. "Bon soir, Madame...wait, you're *English*?"

"Yes, of course, you silly toff! You gave me a dreadful fright! I wasn't expecting anyone else to be in my box. You see, Lady Windermere abandoned me the moment she found out it was another one of Vladec's productions. Pleaded a dreadful headache, although we all know she can't stomach these Romanian operas. And then of course my husband chose to be indisposed. In fact, he's usually indisposed whenever one of Vladec's operas opens, now that I think of it, although no force on earth can keep him from this place when one of those tacky French farces is staged. I suppose his would be termed a 'selective indisposition.'"

Here she pulled out a pair of opera glasses from her reticule and chuckled giddily to herself. My head was reeling from all this information, which had been delivered without pause for a breath. I was going to suggest we take our seats, when her eyes grew even wider then they had been during her entire recitation, and she started up again.

"Of course, I'll return home to find him wrapped up in furs on the settee, feigning an attack of rheumatism, quite badly feigning, I might add, and looking for all the world as though he is at death's door. Poor, *dear* Horace. Acting was never his forte. He's probably at the club with Lord Windermere as we speak."

She beamed at me, then must have noticed my bewildered expression, for her hand flew to her mouth and she shook her head swiftly from side to side. "Oh, for goodness' sake, listen to me rambling on! I'm Guildy."

"Guildy?"

"Well, if you want the full title, I'm Lady Elspeth Guildford," she chimed, extending her hand for a kiss, which I dutifully bestowed. "All my friends call me Guildy," she said, taking her seat, "and I've decided that you and I are going to get along splendidly, *Mr...*"

"Bradburry, Eric Bradburry."

She was in the act of raising the opera glasses to her eyes, but halted abruptly after hearing my name. "Not Eric Bradburry of Mayfair? Sir Roderick Caldwell's boy?"

Of all the people I could have crossed paths with on this trip, I had to meet one who knew Roddy. "Guilty as charged," I said ruefully.

"So, you're the wastrel son!"

I laughed a mirthless laugh. "It seems my reputation precedes me."

"He told me of the Turkish Delight," Guildy said apologetically.

Was there no end to the humiliation?! "But that was ten years ago!" I half shrieked.

"You know how Roddy is. He never forgets anything."

"Yes, unfortunately."

"Stuff and nonsense, lad, stuff and nonsense," she said, patting my knee. "Never mind. Now, what brings you to gay *Paree*, hmm?"

I was beginning to think I could learn a few lessons from this woman, for I had noticed that Guildy never let anything dampen her spirits for more than a second. Might not be a bad attitude to adopt. "My friend and I are on a grand tour..."

"How lovely! I remember...oh! Lionel! Penelope!"

I didn't remember a Lionel or a Penelope, but then I realized that an elderly couple had entered our box and Guildy had completely lost interest in what I was saying. Small mercies still existed.

I rested my chin on my fist and looked down at the seats below. A tug on my sleeve made me turn, and the next thing I knew, Guildy shoved her opera glasses into my hands.

"Just some old friends who came to see me before the opera begins," she said in her breathless manner. "Take those and have a look about before things start up. Half the fun of coming to the Opéra Garnier is watching the people. I shan't be a moment." And she disappeared with Lionel and Penelope behind the curtain.

I put the glasses to my eyes and looked over the crowd. A few people were still loitering in the main aisle, but nearly everyone else had been seated. A portly man was chatting loudly in French with another reveler whose look of boredom spoke volumes to all but the man he was conversing with. Suddenly, the portly man stopped talking and his bored companion's face no longer looked so devoid of life. The pair of them gamboled up the aisle, their arms whirling about excitedly. When I saw what had caught their attention, I nearly dropped the opera glasses.

A young couple, both of them probably no older than twenty-five, had appeared in the entryway. As they walked to their seats, those who were still gathered in the aisle spread apart almost deferentially so that the pair would have an unhindered path down which to travel.

The man's jaw-length blond hair was slicked back against his head, which allowed his high cheekbones and steel-colored eyes to appear to their full advantage. He was dressed in an evening suit nearly identical to mine, although he appeared to be a full head taller than me and was of a stronger physique. Strangely enough, I thought of Stefan at that moment. The man reminded me of him, though Stefan's hair was red and his eyes were emerald green. Besides, this man looked far more Slavic than my friend.

If the man was striking, then the woman on his arm was quite possibly the most beautiful creature I had ever seen, and I could tell my opinion was shared by the many male admirers who were also gawking at her. She wore a white gown and opera gloves of the same color sheathed her bare arms up to the elbows. The dress looked like a second skin, for her flesh was as white as porcelain. Any other woman would have looked sickly in such an ensemble, but the dress's lack of color only enhanced the woman's striking beauty and drew one's eyes away from the immaterial.

Her silken black hair hung loose and was so long it reached past the crimson sash tied around her waist. Her eyes were large and as black as her hair, and her lips were full and red. Around her neck she wore a pearl choker from which dangled a large golden *L*. It reminded me of a necklace I had once seen that had belonged to Anne Boleyn. I had always thought the style gaudy and cumbersome, but on this woman, it suited her swanlike neck perfectly and made her look even more elegant.

As I continued watching them, something inside my mind snapped me to attention. I had been so bewitched by their appearance that I hadn't noticed anything wrong before, but it struck me now that even though they were both beautiful, their manners differed sharply and made them seem somehow incompatible. The man was relishing the attention of his admirers, but the woman seemed to be recoiling from the stares as if she were afraid of being struck. She kept her eyes downcast and let the man lead her along, which he seemed perfectly happy to do.

They finally came upon the portly Frenchman and his companion, who both appeared to be great friends with the Slavic man. The Frenchman clapped the Slavic man on the back and kissed the lady's hand. "Monsieur Salei et Mademoiselle Bianchetti!" the Frenchman boomed.

So, they were not married. For some unexplainable reason this fact made my heart leap.

The woman inclined her head and drew her hand out of the Frenchman's grasp. If there had been a discreet way of doing it, I had no doubt Mademoiselle Bianchetti would have torn off that glove and ripped it to shreds—so appalled and disgusted did she look. Although I had thought him haughty and self-absorbed from the start, I had apparently not given her companion his due, for he seemed to sense her discomfort. He took her hand, but instead of kissing the spot where the Frenchman had placed his lips, he turned her hand over and kissed the palm, then linked her arm through his and patted her hand reassuringly. She seemed to soften at this gesture and raised her eyes to his, but instead of the love I was expecting to see, she turned on him a look of bewilderment that bordered on fear.

Maybe I had been staring at her so long that she began to sense she was being watched, or maybe it was something completely coincidental, but in that moment, her eyes left the face of the Slavic man and stared directly into my own.

I felt as though my soul had been laid bare. I was exposed and wished I had something to hide behind. The voice in my head kept telling me to look away, but I was transfixed by those mesmerizing black eyes and couldn't move.

Her eyebrows contorted into a v as she continued to stare at me, her head tilting slightly to the side as if she were confused. A flash of gold obscured my view and I blinked to clear my vision, only to be confronted by the raging eyes of the Slavic man when I regained my focus.

Only then did I realize I was still starting at them through the opera glasses.

The glasses fell into my lap. I felt constricted around my throat and I couldn't say why. The man's look had been threatening, but he was too far away to harm me. Why, then, did I feel as though he'd stolen something from me? Why should I feel as though I was somehow less?

A moment later, I hazarded a look. Whatever feelings of wrath the Slavic man might have felt toward me had seemingly vanished. He and his lady had taken their seats, and their attention was now fixed on the stage.

I still felt uneasy. It was foolish of me to stare so blatantly at perfect strangers, but I knew if given the opportunity, I would be as blatant again. I couldn't rid myself of the fascination that woman had engendered in me.

A rustle behind me let me know Guildy had returned. I turned to her, but my questions would have to wait until the intermission. The roll of the timpani filled the auditorium and the curtain began to rise.

In the middle of a woodland clearing, a girl sat among her sheep. She seemed to be lost in a reverie, until the blast of a trumpet shook the stage and she came to life. I wish I could say that was a good thing, but alas, Arabella was far more appealing when she kept her mouth shut. Not that her voice was shrill, but it had a sweetness that was unnatural and made one want to stop up their ears. And as if that weren't enough, the entire opera was being sung in Romanian.

From what I could gather, Arabella was a Cinderella-type figure, complete with a wicked stepmother—whose witch-like appearance reminded me of something out of the Brothers Grimm—and two hideous stepsisters who took great delight in trying to overpower their sibling's mawkish voice, but failed miserably.

After about fifteen minutes of watching Arabella flitting around through meadows, I began to wish I *had* gone to the Folies with Stefan and Luc. It would have been even better had I been able to convince Stefan to abandon the whole idea and come to the opera with me. At least then he would have been able to translate. But no, that was selfish. I wouldn't want to subject my worst enemy to this kind of torture, much less my best friend. I was managing pretty well on my own anyway, and I had a feeling she was singing "woe is me" in as many different styles and ranges as she could, for there was much swooning and histrionics involved, not to mention the forlorn expression she kept plastered on her face throughout.

I glanced at Guildy and saw that her left eyebrow was arched and her lips were pulled back in a grimace. I was glad to see I wasn't the only one who didn't find the Romany child charming. This whole production was reminiscent of the type of Gothic melodrama penned by Ann Radcliffe and mocked by Jane Austen, and I wondered how the person who wrote this so-called opera hadn't been jeered into oblivion ages ago.

As bored as I was, it was only natural for my thoughts to wander, and that's exactly what they did—right back to the Bianchetti woman and her companion. I hadn't been able to get the pair out of my mind, especially when I knew they were seated so close. My eyes roved over the seats below, trying to make out their shadowed forms, but the gaslights had been dimmed and it was impossible to see anything beyond the footlights of the stage. This was probably done intentionally by the opera's creator, for the thing was so frightfully dull, audience distraction was a given.

Mercifully, the mournful tones of a bassoon heralded the end of the first half. The final scene found Arabella lying prostrate in yet another meadow, wailing and stretching out her arms in supplication as her prince was hauled away by a rival band of Gypsies.

The curtain fell to a smattering of applause and more than a few exhales of relief that half of the travesty was over.

"*Whew!* I'm glad that's done with," said Guildy, rising to stretch her limbs. "I'm starting to think Lady Windermere and my husband were right to give this one a miss."

"I don't understand the appeal. It's awful."

"It may be awful now, but they usually make it somewhat worthwhile during the second half. You should have been here for last year's production. *Captain Codrescu's Bride.* Appalling."

"Was it as bad as this?"

"Let's just say it was a rather uncensored version of *Bluebeard*, complete with the chamber of horrors. And there's *always* a cloaked figure, just you wait. They must have an obsession with the bally Ghost of Christmas Future to keep sticking shrouded phantoms in these things."

"The people don't seem too enthused," I said, glancing at the less-than-thrilled patrons.

"Oh, ho ho! Don't let their stoic faces fool you. They're too stuffy to admit they like to indulge in a good bloodbath every now and then. They're still pining for the excitement of the Terror. Give them La Guillotine and the Morgue and they'll come running. Vultures the lot of them. And as long as he funds these fiascos, Vladec can stage whatever productions he fancies."

"Vladec?" My heart skipped a beat at the name. I had a suspicion I knew whom it belonged to.

"Vladec Salei, that's him down there," she said, pointing to the Slavic man. "The tall, blond gentleman. And the lady you couldn't take your eyes off of is Leonora Bianchetti, the fair maid of Milan."

I felt my face grow hot and tried to hide my embarrassment. I hadn't known Guildy was watching before. I would have to keep an eye on her from now on.

"Leonora is his *traveling companion*," she continued, raising her eyebrows at me so I would understand the implication. "Scandalized half of Europe, that relationship, but for a man like Vladec...well, he can get away with anything and still be the toast of society. It's a wonder every man didn't follow his example and start trekking across the world with a Milanese mistress after he showed up with her.

There's a rumor they met and fell in love and became engaged in Greece years ago when they were both there on holiday, but honestly, I don't believe it. She's barely twenty herself, and Vladec, well, he *does* look younger than he actually is, so it might have been possible, now that I think about it. It's still a rather pat excuse if you ask me, and if it's true, it's the longest and most unconventional engagement I've ever heard of. We've been waiting for years for him to make an honest woman of the poor girl."

"How old *is* he?!" I asked, horrified, discounting everything Guildy had rattled off after this one bit of information. I had a vision of Vladec, wearing a black cape and bandit's mask, storming into the twelve-year-old Leonora's bedroom and whisking her off into the night. I shook my head and banished the thought. Arabella was starting to have an unhealthy influence on my mind.

"Oh, at least *thirty!*" Guildy's eyes twinkled. She was enjoying jesting with me, naïf that I was. "You have a lot to learn about the world of *high society*, dear lad. And speaking of high society, here come the impresarios now."

I was astonished to see yet another striking pair heading down the aisle toward Vladec and Leonora. This time, I was careful to keep my gaze a little elevated, so that if they caught sight of me, they would think I was looking at something across the way.

The woman's gown was a deep shade of crimson that nearly blended into the red velvet seats surrounding her. The color suited her, but what was attracting the attention of the male contingent was not the shade of the gown, but the dress's plunging neckline and also the woman's bare arms. Several matrons gasped and pointed, but the woman did not appear to be shamed by their reproaches. She seemed to be enjoying the attention her scandalous attire was receiving, for she smirked and continued to saunter on undeterred, even going so far as to stare some of the offended grande dames directly in the eyes as she passed them by.

Unlike Leonora, this woman had an olive complexion and lighter eyes, although I was having difficulty determining the color. They seemed to change hue depending on how the gaslight illuminated them—looking alternately green then blue.

Her hair was quite extraordinary and was also worn loose about her shoulders. Although it was not as long as Leonora's, it had a sheen of an entirely different nature, the color being somewhere between deep red and black.

There was something earthy about her sinuous movements, yet something also garish and brazen. Everything about her seemed overdone, much like this entire opera and Arabella's sickeningly sweet voice. The woman was too much to take in at once, too overtly sensual, too false. I couldn't help comparing her to Leonora. Whereas Leonora intoxicated you with her beauty, the beauty of this one was suffocating.

I stifled a laugh as I turned my attention to the man. He was no less brazen than his companion, whom I knew at once had to be his sister. Their hair was almost the same hue, although the man's was sootier and curled. He was a born rake, I could tell, what with the way he was leering suggestively, his eyes roving over everything wearing a dress. The same scandalized grande dames pushed their daughters behind their backs so that the man wouldn't be able to ogle them, but that only served to delight him further and make him leer all the more. He played the bohemian role to perfection, with his bowtie askew and a certain devil-may-care attitude that I could tell the younger ladies found irresistible.

"Who are they?" I asked Guildy.

"The Golden Ones. The Boroi siblings: Augustin and Sorina."

I looked back at the pair, who were now chatting with Salei and Mademoiselle Bianchetti.

"The toast of Paris, those four, although they only pop round for the summer season. Who knows where they flit off to in winter. Maybe they go off to *Greece*," she said, winking, and jabbed me in the ribs. "They're the reason people come to these things. An opera by the Boroi siblings is très beau monde. It would be an egregious faux pas to even consider missing it."

She reclaimed the glasses from my lap and brought them to her eyes, not even trying to hide the fact that she was staring blatantly at the Golden Ones. I admired her pluck. "That one there," she said, pointing to Sorina, "has been hailed as the second coming of Marguerite de Navarre. She rules at her brother's side and is his artistic expert. He's the musical genius, if you can call *this* music. The tortured soul, the brooding artist...you know the bit."

I stared at the man a moment longer and realized I had seen him somewhere before. Without the cape and plumed hat, I hadn't recognized him, but now that I got a better look, I knew who the rake was—Arabella's prince!

"Ah, you've noticed!" said Guildy the perspicacious wonder. "They always put themselves in their performances. Rather nepotistic and self-aggrandizing if you ask me. I'm quite surprised she hasn't shown up in this one yet, but there's still a whole half to go."

And with that depressing thought, the lights grew dim and the familiar roll of the timpani, which I had come to think of as the knell of doom, heralded the beginning of half number two.

I had expected much of the same, but was surprised when the curtain rose to reveal a scene starkly different from everything that had come before. Somehow, since the last act, Arabella had been transported halfway around the world. Olive trees sprouted from craggy hillsides and gravel had replaced the grass of the Romany countryside. Arabella stood in the middle of a circle of revelers who looked like they'd just spilled out of the Doge's palace in Venice. She was surrounded by a sea of leering, sneaking, devil's faces— carnival masks concealing the true identities of the festival goers, for a festival was what this bacchanal undoubtedly was.

At the edge of the circle stood a man. He was perched behind a carnival booth of some sort, his chin resting on his hands. He glared at Arabella hungrily. Even from where I sat, I could see the sardonic expression on his face. Suddenly, the man snapped his fingers and the crowd closed in around Arabella.

Corcitura

The cellos struck and drew out a cord so low, it not only made the stage rumble, but I felt the vibration all the way up in our box. Arabella looked as wary as the rest of us. I knew she wasn't acting.

From behind the booth, the man withdrew a top hat and cape. *Overly theatrical*, I thought. As soon as he'd donned these garments, the man turned toward the orchestra pit. Once again, he snapped his fingers, and as he twirled back around, fixing his attention on the hapless girl, the orchestra struck up a mad, frenzied csárdás. The revelers swayed in time with the music, twirling and dancing faster and faster. Arabella was pulled and pushed and spun so that I didn't know how she kept her balance. Even I was growing dizzy. She stumbled into one masked partygoer, who laughingly tossed her to the next, and all the while the man in the top hat and cape, the leader of this danse macabre, cackled and spun about the stage like a possessed top.

A break in the crowd revealed a figure I hadn't noticed before. I scanned the faces of the audience, but no one seemed to notice this new entrant. Their eyes remained riveted on Arabella.

The revelers continued to whirl like dervishes, oblivious to the dark shape circling on the periphery—the dark shape that was so maddeningly ill-defined, I began to wonder if it was actually there.

The crowd surged round Arabella, bandying her between them like a rubber ball. The girl had been jostled so much, I wasn't sure if it was fear or nausea that made her grimace.

The ringmaster—for that was how I'd come to think of him—cavorted through the crush of bodies, shrieking in a language I did not understand. The music whipped up into a frenzy, roiling and growing, making me want to tear off my skin—anything to stop that ululating, pulsating beat from burrowing deeper into me. I looked over the rail, crazily thinking it wouldn't be such a bad idea to jump. Had that been the intention? Absurd. But I only had a moment to think on these unpleasant things, for the ringmaster shouted something that sounded like "Avanti," and everything changed.

Sparks exploded near Arabella's feet. Just as quickly as it had started, the mad farce jolted to a halt. I thought the man had hurled dynamite at the girl, but the sound that erupted as the sparks hit the floor was made by the clash of five pairs of cymbals and the striking of the timpani—a noise so jarring, it sounded as though the earth were breaking apart.

The audience gasped as smoke billowed over the stalls.

"They're trying to suffocate us so we won't survive to write letters to the opera's management," I heard Guildy choke out behind me.

Arabella was doubled over, hacking on the smoke she and all the rest of us had inhaled. The smoke smelled strangely like incense. It whipped round my head, stinging my eyes and making me sneeze. I batted it away, finally succeeding in clearing a patch.

Smoke still swirled around the center of the stage, obscuring the ringmaster and half the revelers, but the other half and Arabella were plainly visible. The revelers pushed the masks over their faces, revealing eyes as lifeless as those of a corpse. There was no feeling toward the whimpering girl, there was no compassion. She was as good as dead to them.

Slowly, they backed toward the wings, receding into the darkness. The last of them halted a moment, but this seemed to be only part of the ruse—a last bit of cruel theatricality. The figure quickly passed on without a word, leaving the girl even more destitute than before.

I'd seen the lividity of their faces, the absolute lack of color in their eyes. They'd abandoned Arabella without even flinching.

Enough, Eric. I was feeding into the fantasy. I had to remind myself that this was all part of the opera. Yet I couldn't help remembering that Arabella wasn't Arabella at all, and if she were acting, then she was the greatest actress I'd ever seen, even better than Bernhardt.

A shriek from the stalls pulled me back to reality. The smoke had finally cleared. A new actor had taken center stage.

Guildy had been right about the Borois' obsession, but even Dickens' specter couldn't compare to this figure rising up from its crouching position. Instinctively, I leaned back as the figure, swathed in a black, hooded cloak, rose to its full height.

I tried to swallow, but my throat had gone dry. The music, which had been nonexistent since the crash, undulated menacingly as the figure lifted its head. I caught a glimpse of deathly pale skin before the creature pulled its cowl down, shielding its face from view.

Arabella hadn't seen it. I had the absurd notion of shouting to warn her, but the thing hissed and made its presence known before I could.

Arabella stumbled, falling to her hands, scrambling back toward the edge of the stage. Her face had gone as white as chalk. She should have fainted from terror by now. Any normal person would have. *I* would have.

Was there no one to help her? The ringmaster! He was still on stage, leaning against the wall near the left wing exit. His arms were crossed, his demeanor casual. How could he be so relaxed?

Because this is only an opera, Eric. He's acting. Of course, surely. How ridiculous of me to think otherwise.

Arabella stretched out her hand toward him, but he shook his head and backed away, holding out his arms as if to say, "What can I do?" But his expression belied his desire to help. As he vanished into the recesses of the stage, the auditorium filled with his laughter.

Arabella and I were a mirror image of each other—both our mouths hung open in astonishment. A rapping in the orchestra pit caught her attention and mine as well. The conductor, not looking the least bit unnerved, raised his baton, and Arabella, to my amazement, began to sing.

All this time, the figure had remained rooted to the middle of the stage. I could sense it waiting, feel its tension, almost hear it breathing as it slinked upstage, beckoning the girl to follow it.

Arabella walked toward the figure as though in a trance. Her voice had completely transformed and no longer bore any traces of its former sentimentality. The closer she drew to the creature, the more plaintive her voice became. My heart began to race as I watched helplessly. She would be within the thing's reach in a matter of moments.

The creature suddenly halted. A dead white hand emerged from the folds of the cloak. That broke Arabella's trance.

She recoiled and let out a pitch so high that I clapped my hands over my ears to block out the piercing shriek. She turned to run, but the creature latched onto her arm and dragged her into the shadows.

And as the creature was stealing her away, all the lights in the theater went out.

"Oh, now they really have gone too far!" I heard Guildy exclaim behind me. "What cheek! Vladec will hear from me about this. The Borois are letting their morbid Transylvanian souls get the best of them."

Panicked voices murmured below. It would only be a few moments before pandemonium reigned. Guildy grabbed me by the arm and had started to drag me from the box, when the lights suddenly flared on again. They must have rehearsed this several times or had some grand master valve I had never heard of before. It seemed impossible to me that so many gaslights could be extinguished and relit so quickly, for not only had the lights of the chandelier been put out, but all the footlights as well.

The brilliance lasted long enough to calm the patrons, then the lights dimmed once more, and the opera resumed.

The creature appeared as before, but the girl standing resplendent in the center of the stage was *not* Arabella. They had placed a light behind her so that she radiated an almost angelic glow. Gone were her tattered frock and loose, virginal tresses. This new girl was dressed in a gown of shimmering gold. A coronet sat atop her flowing hair—red hair so dark it was nearly black.

Sorina.

The voice that rose from her throat was low and husky. As she advanced on the creature, I realized the roles had reversed. The false Arabella was the one who now held the power.

The creature shielded its face from her radiance and shuffled back, trying to escape into the safety of the shadows, but Sorina pressed on and showed no signs of abandoning her purpose, whatever it might be. The creature had backed up as far as it could. I was expecting her to strike it, but instead she bent down and pressed a kiss onto its head.

The creature crumpled into a heap. I grasped the box's rail, certain the specter's collapse would bring about another trick with the lights, but instead the floor underneath the thing's cloak began to glow.

The creature writhed beneath the black folds of its garment. Nervous whispering rippled through the crowd. Even Guildy's breathing had grown heavier, but everything fell silent as the creature threw off the cloak. It, or rather *he*, had been transformed as dramatically as Arabella. The light reflecting off his jewel-encrusted doublet was blinding, and as I narrowed my eyes to diminish the glare, I saw that the man now standing in all his glory, clasping Sorina's hand, was Augustin Boroi. The Prince and been set free.

False Arabella and her Romany Prince embraced, then linked arms and walked off into the night, the scene panels parting as the couple passed through. The music became melodious for the first time, yet there was still a touch of menace that hinted all might not go well for Arabella and her Prince in the future. With a final blare from the trumpets, the curtain fell, and I breathed a sigh of relief.

For such a spectacle, the applause that ensued was enthusiastic, but then again, my fellow patrons could have been as relieved as I was that the farce had finally ended.

I suppose Sorina and Augustin had meant for the opera to be an allegory of the transformative power of true love, but all their macabre antics had drowned whatever symbolism there was, and as the lights turned up and I looked at Guildy, I could tell she felt the same.

"What a lot of rot," she huffed, grabbing my hand. "You come with me and we'll get to the bottom of this."

"Where are we going?"

"Why, to find Vladec and give him a piece of our minds, that's where!"

I recoiled at the thought of facing the man, but then my heart began to beat faster at the prospect of seeing Leonora again. I let Guildy drag me out of the box and down the Grand Escalier.

Someone sailed into me when we reached the landing. I lost hold of Guildy's hand and was thrown upon something so cold that I felt as though I had been thrust against a block of ice. My first thought was of the marble banisters, but when I looked up I found myself staring into the cool grey eyes of Vladec Salei.

I had no doubt he recognized me. His eyes had narrowed to slits that barely left any of the irises visible. I was about to retreat, when I felt someone grasp my arm and turned to see Guildy standing beside me.

"There you are! Vladec, I really must have a word with you about this entire production and those Borois you insist on supporting."

"Theatrics, Madame. Nothing more. The people love it and it garners our actors fame. Everyone wins."

His English was highly cultivated and held just the hint of an accent. I was again reminded of Stefan, for he too had a slight foreign tinge to his speech that only surfaced when he was extremely excited or on the verge of losing his temper. From the look on Salei's face, I hazarded a guess he was of the same constitution as my friend.

I stepped back and left Guildy exposed to his wrath. Yes, it was not very chivalrous, but Salei didn't seem like the type to be crossed.

"I beg to differ," Guildy continued, undaunted. "You scared half that congregation out of their wits. What are you going to try next? A live beheading?"

A shadow crossed over Salei's face at Guildy's last words. "Did it frighten you, Madame?" he said, his voice strained. "You must work to strengthen your constitution."

I thought Guildy would sputter a rebuke for that bit of insolence, but instead she laughed and patted Salei's arm. "You know me better than to think I'd be scared by your theatrics. It was just a word of warning, that's all. By the way," she said, looking behind Salei. "Where are the Borois and Mademoiselle Bianchetti?"

"I am here, Madame." The voice was so quiet it startled me, as did the presence of its owner, whom I had not noticed until this moment. Leonora emerged from behind Salei and linked her arm with his.

"Splendid! Allow me to present my young friend, who is a great admirer of yours."

My face grew hot again. I had to struggle mightily to suppress the urge to throttle Guildy. Leonora didn't seem to notice, although Salei threw me a look that conveyed his desire to impale me to the floor.

"Your servant, Mademoiselle. Eric Bradburry." I tried to meet her gaze as I placed the kiss on her hand, but she kept her eyes averted. She didn't look well at all, now that I could see her up close. There was a marked pallor to her skin. I wondered if she were an anemic, or had some other such wasting disease. Of course, this realization only made me warm to her more. I'd spent too much of my youth reading tales of knights errant rescuing maidens from dragons, I remembered, eyeing Vladec Salei.

"Well, now that we're all acquainted," Guildy chimed.

"If you'll forgive us, Lady Guildford," Vladec said, inching toward the steps, "we really must be going."

Panic seized me. They couldn't just leave, not like this. I had to see Leonora again, though I didn't know what I hoped to accomplish. I just knew I *had* to see her at least once more before Stefan and I left Paris.

"Your accent...Romanian?" It wasn't the most tactful start to a conversation, but I was desperate.

Salei stopped on the last step of the Grand Escalier and turned on me a look so disdainful I shrank back.

"And why would you think that?" he nearly spat.

I wanted to say, "Maybe because you only fund Romanian operas and seem to enjoy keeping company with the Romany people, so how the devil should I know," but I bit my tongue. For Leonora's sake, I would be diplomatic.

"Well, my friend and I are making a sort of grand tour. He's originally from Romania, and I was thinking the two of you would have lots to talk about."

"How *fascinating*," he said, his voice dripping with sarcasm.

Without saying another word, he headed for the exit.

I had made a fool of myself, and for what? I trudged down the last steps, ready to bid good night to Guildy, when I noticed Salei loitering before the doors.

"It's Russian," he said, not turning round to address me to my face.

"Beg pardon?"

"My accent. It's Russian. From Novorossiysk. What did you say his name was?"

"My friend's? I didn't."

Salei's eyebrows rose.

"Oh, sorry, well, yes, all right, then. His name's Stefan. Stefan Ratliff."

"*Stefan...*"

"Ratliff."

Salei didn't answer.

"Yes, well..." I coaxed.

"It is settled. Be at the Louvre tomorrow at noon. And be sure to bring this little friend of yours with you."

I almost collapsed at this news, but more so because Leonora lifted her head and smiled at me over her shoulder as Salei guided her through the doors.

"Good show, lad!" Guildy said. I could barely keep my balance, so drunk was I with my success. "Now, here's my card."

I looked down to see that she had placed a small, filigreed card in my hand.

"How long are you staying?"

"We leave for Marseilles tomorrow evening, but we'll be stopping over for a few days on the way home to London."

"Capital! Call upon me when you return. I'd love for you to meet Lord Guildford. Hopefully, by then, he will have recovered from his indisposition."

I caught her sly wink and laughed. Guildy was a treasure. I was glad we had met, and not only because she had been the one to throw Leonora and me together.

I tried to take Guildy's hand, but I should have known she wasn't one for formality. She hugged me so tight I could scarcely breathe, then made me promise to see her when we passed through Paris again. "And remember," she said, holding me at arm's length, "if you are ever in need of anything, you know where to come. I sense more than a bit of fire in you, Eric Bradburry, so if you find yourself in a nasty scrape, just call on me and I'll find a way to rescue you from the gallows." She winked at me again and chucked me under the chin—a joker till the last. I somehow knew I had made a friend for life.

I walked back to the hotel lost in my own musings. A burst of fireworks jolted me from my reverie and brought Stefan to mind. *Stefan!* I hoped he had returned. I was eager to talk with him about my evening and our plans for tomorrow, and he was no doubt bursting to tell me of his night at the Folies. I was certain he and Salei would have stimulating conversation, but as for me, my mind was fixed on Leonora.

When I reached our suite, I found it empty. I was momentarily disappointed that he hadn't yet returned, but then I caught sight of the éclair and café au lait that had been set upon the table by my bed. Luc's handiwork no doubt. In all the excitement, I hadn't bothered to eat since we had stopped for crêpes on our tour that afternoon.

I had just changed into my nightclothes and settled down with my feast, when the door to our suite was flung open and Stefan danced in.

"You certainly look happy," I said through a mouthful of éclair.

He shuffled his feet, then twirled about like a mad thing. "I danced with Fifi La Femme and I dipped Le Rondouillard!"

"Who in the world are they?"

"I have no idea, but they seemed quite popular. Ah, Eric. I am in love!"

"Oh, so Mademoiselle La Femme captured your heart? Or was it the butterball?"

"No, *genius*," he said, tapping me on the head with his walking stick. "I'm in love with PARIS!"

"Well, get over it quickly because we're leaving tomorrow. This is not your grandfather's grand tour, after all, and unlike you, my hideously wealthy friend, my money won't last forever."

"Pshaw! You have hundreds of pounds!"

"Hundreds of pounds can go just like that," I said, snapping my fingers, "especially when you're around. Oh! And I have some news of my own to share with you."

I related to him the events of the evening, omitting several details that would have made me appear in an unflattering light, and ended by telling him of our plans for the Louvre.

"So, what do you think?"

I had to endure a good five minutes of hearing Stefan fighting with the duvet in the other room before he finally answered. "Leonora sounds lovely," he said on a sigh. "But I'm not so sure about this Salei character. What do I want with a Russian anyway?"

"Oh, come now, Stefan," I protested, fearful he wouldn't go through with the plan, "it would do you good to befriend more of your Slavic brethren. Besides, Russian culture isn't that different from Romanian."

"Ha!"

"What do you mean by 'ha'?"

"You'll find out tomorrow."

And so saying, he pulled the duvet over his head and turned to the wall. That was my signal to do the same.

I lay back against the pillows and looked out at the fireworks still exploding in the sky. Tomorrow I would see her again. What would happen between us, I hadn't the slightest idea, but as I closed my eyes, I saw her face and knew it would be a day to remember.

Hello, Good-bye...Hello

"**W**ake up, Rip van Winkle!"

Pinpricks of light wavered before my eyes. For some reason, the floor was getting closer— much closer, until I finally understood that someone had lifted my mattress and I was about to become intimately acquainted with the hardwood beneath my bed.

"Stefan, bloody hell! What time is it?"

"A quarter past seven."

"A quarter past sev...why the devil are you already dressed?" I said, taking in this fact for the first time.

"Why am I already dressed?" he asked, shocked, as if my question were absurd. How silly of me! Of course, it was perfectly normal for him to be up and about at this ridiculous hour after a full night of reveling. "Because half the day has been wasted waiting for you to get up! I promised Luc I'd meet some friends of his before we have that rendezvous with your lady love and her paramour at noon."

At the mention of our guide, my headache grew worse. It was bad enough Stefan's antics had given me a bump on the forehead, now he had to rub salt into the wound by talking about Luc. Well, he hadn't said anything about *me* accompanying him on his little jaunt, and for that I was thankful. And it was a testament to my muddle-headed state that I hadn't registered his insult to Leonora until this moment. Paramour indeed...I'd see about that.

"All right, then," I said, anxious to get him out of the room before the idea of conscripting me into the outing struck him, "you flit off and I'll meet you at the Louvre."

"I'll be sure to tell Luc you wished him well."

I groaned, but Stefan's bubbling laughter drowned my protest. I raised myself up off the floor, closed the door to our adjoining room, and prepared to face the world, but more importantly, Leonora. Their relationship did not bother me one whit, since Salei had no greater claim on her than a prolonged association, which I was certain had been trying and possibly even violent, judging from that fearful look I had seen on her face the night before. What I hoped to gain by the meeting, I had not the faintest idea, but I wanted to make a good impression on the off chance she would fall in love with me at third sight.

By the time I had washed and dressed, Stefan was gone, yet apparently not far away, for the sound I heard outside my balcony was Stefan's laugh. I opened the door and looked down. Sure enough, there was Stefan...and Luc, and two other people I did not know standing in the street underneath the window.

These were Luc's friends, no doubt. A decidedly striking pair, but I had other concerns and couldn't waste time on these new arrivals.

I had half-turned back into the room, when something about the woman's appearance triggered a memory. Spying had done me a world of harm last evening, but spying was what I would do again now. I didn't feel safe gawping at her in the open, so I slipped behind the curtain, shielding myself from view.

She was swathed in a gown of scarlet much like the one she had worn the evening before, although this time there was nothing scandalous about her ensemble. A veil of black lace covered the entire bottom half of her face, leaving only her changeable eyes visible, and was affixed to a smart looking scarlet hat she wore perched atop her red-black curls. In her gloved hands, she grasped the handle of a matching scarlet parasol, holding it low above her head to keep out the sun. The sun...it was blistering already, yet she appeared as calm and comfortable as if it were a mild midwinter day.

The man now shaking Stefan's hand was dressed just as heavily as his sister. Although it was fashionable for a lady to wear gloves during the daytime, the thick, leather ones covering the man's hands seemed excessive, especially given the heat. Even more so, he, too, had a sunshade, although it was black and austere compared to his sister's.

I had thought I had seen the last of Augustin and Sorina Boroi, but I was mistaken. Apparently, Luc knew everyone in Paris. What business they had with my best friend, I couldn't even begin to guess, but the sight of them with Stefan made me uneasy. I should have been happy, overjoyed even, that the three of them had somehow been brought together, for if Stefan would have anything in common with anyone, it would be the Borois. Yet for some reason, if I could have, I would have wished him to the ends of the earth to get him away from that cat-eyed woman and her rakehell brother.

Luc be hanged, I had to get Stefan away from those Borois. I stepped out onto the balcony with every intention of yelling to Stefan to wait for me. The word *stop* was in my throat, but all that managed to come forth was a strangled gasp, for at that moment, Sorina turned her eyes on me.

I froze. I could not move, but not because I was afraid...I didn't have the power. And as this horror dawned in my mind, a suspicion that something was not right about that woman arose.

She was the one who had robbed me of mobility.

They had paused to look at Opéra Garnier. At least, Stefan and Augustin had. Although her arm was linked through Stefan's, Sorina's eyes were still fixed on me. She stared, unblinking, drawing me deeper into her gaze, until a smile lifted one corner of her mouth into a smirk, and she turned back toward her brother, who was gesturing excitedly at the opera house. I caught the word *Arabella* and knew he was relating to Stefan his *triumph* of the night before.

For the first time since she looked at me, I had feeling in my fingertips. I began to hope that I had been freed of her hold, but somehow, in my exuberance, I must have given myself away. She turned her head once more, her chin tilting ever so slightly over her shoulder, and kept her eyes demurely downcast. It was a sidelong glance, yet it held all the power of a full glare, as if she had been staring me dead in the eyes.

If someone had passed her on the street, they would have thought her conduct irreproachable. She appeared to be just an exceptionally beautiful lady of quality out for a stroll with her brother and beau.

I envied their ignorance.

Her left eyebrow arched in a challenge, yet still she did not look at me. My heart hammered against my chest. I heard her laugh, but the laughter was inside *my* head. She was speaking something in Stefan's ear, yet that maniacal, taunting laughter continued to ring through my brain.

I wanted to strike my head against the balcony rail—anything to stop the shrieking of this fey creature—but still I could not move. I felt as though someone were striking a giant gong inside my head. I couldn't even clamp my eyes shut to at least alleviate some of the din. The noise was too great. Too great...I had to find a way to move...one step over the rail and my pain would end...

Maybe it was never her intent to drive me to suicide, or maybe the novelty of our secret joke was wearing thin. I know not the reason, but Sorina finally turned her head away and released me from her hold.

My legs gave out beneath me. I crumpled to the hard marble floor of the balcony. I felt boneless, as though my limbs were made of gelatin, and I shuddered despite the heat. With what little strength I had, I turned my head and looked out at Stefan, arm in arm with Sorina and Augustin, through the spindles of the balcony. A flash of black caught my eyes, and I noticed Luc trailing at a distance. I had forgotten he was there at all.

This new Luc was so unlike his former self that for a moment I doubted my eyes. He seemed positively skittish. All traces of his previous self-assurance had evaporated in the presence of those two. What's more, he seemed quite content to be ignored by his companions and kept nervously twisting his hat in his hands. Every few seconds or so, he would cast a look over his shoulder then shuffle on dutifully behind his three charges. There was something about his manner that suggested fear, but of what, I could not be certain. It couldn't have been the Borois, for the outing was Luc's idea...or was it?

I shook my head to clear my mind of these thoughts. That in itself was progress, for I had not been able to move much since I collapsed. I might have stayed prostrate all day had not the sound of their fading laughter spurred me into action.

Shakily, but with growing strength, I stretched out my arms and managed to push myself up off the floor. How I reached the lobby without falling down fifty times along the way was beyond me. I must have been urged on by the feeling of dread certainty I felt in the pit of my stomach—the feeling that Stefan would let slip our plans for the Louvre and those blasted Borois would have no trouble ingratiating themselves into our meeting with Salei. And, I thought selfishly, would find a way to keep Leonora and me apart. If she could, I was certain she would, for I was convinced Sorina thought she had staked a claim on me that morning with her little incident at the balcony. Well, if luck were on my side, I would never have to see her again. But even if she were there, I vowed I would not let her, nor her brother, nor Luc, nor Salei, nor even my closest friend, destroy my plans.

‡

"The Winged Victory of Samothrace, or Nike, as she is known, came to the Louvre in 1884."

We were standing at the Daru staircase underneath the giant headless, armless stone statue of the winged maiden of the Aegean. I had latched onto an English-speaking tour and seen all the great spectacles of the Louvre in the interim, but now the time was ripe for me to escape in search of Stefan. It was a quarter past noon already, and still he had not shown himself.

I hung back as the tour moved on. Once they were out of sight, I hastened away and made for the Melpomene Gallery, taking a cursory glance at the giant statue of the hall's namesake on my right as I passed by. I had thought Nike was gigantic, but this muse made her seem almost Lilliputian in size. Apparently, all Louvre statues were enormous. It must have been a prerequisite.

I walked down this gallery and came out into the Salle des Caryatides. As I moved into the hall, I caught sight of my erstwhile companion, thankfully Boroi-less, staring at a large canvas that had been propped up in the center of the salle. I thought it odd that a painting would be on display in a hall filled with statues, but I didn't let the incongruity of the situation trouble me for more than a second.

"There you are! I've been looking everywhere for you. Where have you been?"

I was expecting to receive a response and would have been happy with one of his sarcastic remarks, but he acted as though I did not exist. *Very well, then.* I decided to give it another go. "Been walking the same halls as the Kings of France and that great poisoner herself, Catherine de Medici, have you?" I was beginning to sound like Luc.

Still nothing. He just stood there, head tilted to one side, his hand on his chin, absorbed by the painting before him. It had taken me forever to finally locate Stefan, and this was all the response I received? Not even so much as a flicker of an eyelid. Now we would have to rush out to the entrance to meet Vladec Salei, whom I hoped by some miracle was still waiting for us. My plans were crumbling before my eyes. And did he care? Absolutely not. He was as still and lifeless as the statues surrounding him. "Honestly, Stefan," I said hotly, "what's so bloody fascin..."

I stopped dead when my eyes finally flashed toward the painting. I hadn't bothered to look at it until then, but now as I took in the nightmarish spectacle painted on that canvas, a shudder passed through my body and chilled me to the marrow.

A woman, shrouded in white, was draped over a divan in a dead swoon, her arms hanging limply over her head. In the background, a horse, nostrils flaring, eyes aglow, stuck its head through the crimson drapery. The horse looked crazed. Its lips were drawn back in a grimace that made it look as though it were sneering. But the most horrifying aspect of the painting was not the half-mad horse, nor the seemingly dead woman.

It was the demon.

A grotesque, dwarfish creature crouched atop the woman's chest. They weren't very visible in the foreground, but I could just make out the shadows of the thing's horns reflected off the curtain. The creature's entire visage was hellish, yet there was something taunting about its colorless eyes, pug nose, and grim, frowning mouth. I felt as if the thing were challenging me to push it off its perch. I doubted I would have possessed the courage to do so had this tableau been real.

I laughed nervously and immediately felt ridiculous for chuckling aloud. The incident this morning with Sorina had turned me morbid. Try as I might, I could not shake the feeling of unease the painting had instilled in me. Nor could I make myself turn away. It was demonic, yet fascinating, and it had captured Stefan's imagination, too, for his eyes were still fixated on the painting.

"Amazing," he whispered. "What do you think it is?" he said, addressing me without taking his eyes off the canvas. "A demon?"

"A vampire."

The voice must have come from the painting, it had to have—there was no one else around. I looked about warily, trying to avoid the now self-proclaimed vampire's eyes, but could not discover any other source from whence the voice could have come. But there *was* someone there, as it turned out. A slight cough signaled his arrival. I still couldn't figure out where he'd materialized from, but here he now was, standing at Stefan's side.

Strangely, my first reaction was not relief at the sight of Vladec Salei but rather confusion as to why he was fully cloaked indoors. I thought it odd that he had not bothered to remove his overcoat and gloves. Maybe he had stumbled upon us through mere chance as he was making for the exit.

I sent a silent *thank you* heavenward, but I doubt it ever reached the Pearly Gates. My heart sank as the confusion of the moment dispersed, and I saw that Salei was alone.

"An incubus, to be exact," he continued.

"It looks as though it crushed the life out of her." Stefan was still staring at the painting. I wondered momentarily if he had even realized the person he was conversing with was not me. Nothing seemed to be getting through to his brain this afternoon.

I, for one, had had quite enough of Mr. Fuseli's *Nightmare*, as I now knew the painting to be named. A small placard bearing a short history of the artist and painting had been set up beneath the canvas. I failed to see what the Swiss artist's work had to do with the Roman statues surrounding it, but some genius must have made a connection that was lost on me, so I let the matter drop.

"Nightmare," I said, musing over the title. "How appropriate." I turned my attention to Salei, who was staring rather amusedly at Stefan. "Oh, pay no attention to him," I said lightly, unsure of what to make of the look in Salei's eyes. "That's his morbid Transylvanian soul talking." I knew Guildy's phrase of the night before would suit nicely someday. "He has an inherent fascination with death."

Apparently, it was my day to be ignored. "You are quite right, my young friend," he said to Stefan. "Although it is the Vrykolakas that crushes its victim to death."

"Vrykolakas?" Stefan asked.

"Yes. A vicious Greek vampire, though some believe it to also be a werewolf."

"That's tidy," I shot in. "How nice of the Vryko-what's-its-name to be so accommodating. A vampire and a werewolf," I concluded, chuckling. Did he take us for complete imbeciles? I'd never heard such nonsense in all my life.

Salei skewered me with a look of contempt that made me shrink back despite my resolve to not let him rattle me.

He angled himself closer to Stefan. "The incubus there, well, it has more *carnal* motives, if you take my meaning."

For the first time, Stefan tore his gaze away from the painting and looked at Salei with an expression so wide-eyed it was almost comical. "Oh..." he said, then, "Oh! Yes, well, of course, I mean, *rather*," and laughed awkwardly.

I am by no means a prude, but Salei's last bit of information made me feel decidedly uncomfortable. And it didn't help that he seemed to be warming to the subject.

"You see, it subsists on the life force of its chosen *incubator*, in this case the woman, which explains why she looks nearly drained of life. So in essence, it is in fact a vampire, or could at the very least be considered one. I, for one, am more inclined to believe that than the demon myth."

I half expected him to finish this little lecture with a flourish by saying *voilà*. "You seem to know a great deal about it," I said icily. I did not see the point of this morbid conversation, for I was certain I would never need to make use of this knowledge. And, furthermore, Salei's interest in the subject disturbed me. I was beginning to think the Borois had learned everything they knew about the macabre from their patron. Maybe this visit wasn't such a good idea after all. He could have been a second Gilles de Rais or Marquis de Sade for all we knew. And since my prospects with Leonora had now vanished, I didn't see a reason for us to keep company with Vladec Salei a moment longer.

I wanted to bolt from the room with Stefan in tow, but then I noticed that Stefan was rapt. Utterly, completely in thrall to Vladec Salei. From whence this fascination stemmed, I had no idea, but it was there, plastered all over his face.

"It is a hobby of mine," Salei explained. "Obscure folklore fascinates me. Your friend and I met at the Opéra Garnier last evening. So *you* must be Stefan. Allow me to finally introduce myself. My name is Vladec Salei."

It must have been that Slavic bond. Apparently, becoming matey at once with a complete stranger was what Stefan had meant by "Ha!" I should have been gloating over my success. After all, it was I who had been certain they would have so much to talk over. But all I could feel was a childish discontent that bordered on jealously—anger that my best friend no longer needed me. Not that Stefan ever had, but still. We hadn't even been gone a week, and although we certainly had not come to hate each other, I felt as though something between us had changed the moment we entered France.

For the next hour and a half, I idled, mentally cursing Fuseli for not keeping his fantasies to himself, the museum's curators for their complete loss of sanity in displaying a copy of the blasted painting in a hall of statues, and Vladec Salei for being a walking encyclopedia of esoteric knowledge. Once or twice, they had asked me to comment on some triviality, but for the most part, I was ignored. Obviously, there was no place in their conversation for my non-morbid English soul.

I knew when I was not wanted, but I also knew the day was waning and we had a train to catch.

"Well, it's been wonderful, truly, Mr. Salei," I said, leading Stefan away, "but we really must be off."

"And where are you two headed?"

"Rome."

If I had struck him a blow, it wouldn't have produced anywhere near the jarring effect the name of the city did. His face contorted so severely, I doubted he would be able to return it to its normal expression of hauteur when this little outburst of his subsided. "Rome!" he nearly shrieked with a vehemence I could not fathom. But all the venom of his tone was consigned to that single word, for after he had shouted it, he seemed to regain his composure. "Detestable city," he said calmly and with his former high-class disdain restored. "Filthy, not a single thing worth viewing there. Filled with nothing but shrines to false prophets and run by men so old and obsolete they should have been bricked up in those supposedly sacred vaults ages ago. Men as archaic as the basilicas themselves."

Well, he had established that he wasn't a churchgoer. And I did not intend to stay around and have him infect Stefan, who had seemingly become as impressionable as clay while in Salei's presence, with his noxious ideas.

"Why don't you come with Leonora and me to Greece?"
He said it so innocently, yet there was a persuasive
undertone to his words, like a man trying to bribe a child
with a sweetmeat. He knew my weakness, the cheeky devil.
And, fool that I was, I actually entertained the notion of
giving in.

"What a splendid idea! Eric told me all about...ahh!"

"*Ahh?*"

"What he means is," I said, shooting Stefan a glance that
warned him to keep mum or he would get another jab in the
ribs, "we really would love to, but we can't get to Greece for
another few weeks. So sorry."

"I see. We'll be in touch, then?"

"Of course, good-bye!"

And without waiting for him to say more, I bustled Stefan
down the hallway and didn't stop until we had exited the
museum.

I was halfway into the cab when Stefan grabbed my arm
and pulled me back out. "Wait one moment. This whole
blasted Louvre scheme was your idea. Why are you in such a
hurry to escape?"

"No, *he* suggested it. I merely agreed, which was a
mistake, I now see."

"And just exactly how?" The stubborn gleam had come
into his eyes. There was no reasoning with him when he was
in one of these moods. Years of experience had taught me
that he was capable of any sort of mischief in this state, and I
wouldn't have been surprised if he rushed back to Salei and
agreed to the Grecian scheme just to spite me.

I motioned to the driver to wait, then cast a glance back
toward the Louvre to make certain Salei hadn't followed us.
"Something's not right with him. I don't know what it is, but I
wouldn't trust him from here to that lamppost. So get it out
of your head because we are *definitely* not meeting up with
him when we get to Greece."

"You're doing it again!" he said, exasperated. "What
happened to all that twaddle about fostering relations with
my Slavic brethren, eh? And I don't see any reason why we

shouldn't take his advice. Who wants to go to Rome anyway...stuffy, detestable city that it is."

Parroting someone else's words was the first sign of intractability. In many ways, Stefan had never grown up. He was still that sulky little orphan David and Marishka Ratliff had stumbled upon in Romania.

But on this matter, I wasn't about to budge. "Look," I said, pulling out my watch. "The train to Marseilles leaves in two hours. And unless you want to journey there on foot, we have to go now. So forget all about Vladec Salei and let's try to get on with this blasted grand tour of yours, all right?"

"Fine," he said, and huffed into the carriage.

I settled into the seat across from him and shouted to the driver to take us back to the hotel. Stefan, arms crossed, face clouded over, wouldn't look at me. I knew he would hold his defeat against me. He had always had a vindictive streak I could never understand, but I had overlooked that and many other things over the years.

I leaned my head back against the cushion and studied his averted face until I felt sleep tugging at my eyes. A short rest before reaching the hotel was just what I needed. My eyes had begun to close, but then I had the unmistakable feeling that I was being watched. I looked across the way to see Stefan staring at me. He was smiling, but something about the smile made me uneasy. It was secretive, threatening, and somehow knowing all at once.

"Why are you smiling?" I asked, not truly wishing to know the answer.

"Oh, nothing," he said quietly. "I was just thinking of your friend Sorina Boroi."

The mention of that name startled me. I had purposely not said anything about the Borois to Stefan. My shock, coupled with my failure to press him for further details about this woman, made my guilt apparent, which I knew was just what he had intended to do.

The smile was now self-satisfied. He looked down at the floor, snorted softly, then leaned his head back and closed his eyes. I no longer had any doubt that he knew what she had done to me that morning. And, horribly, I felt he was glad of it.

What had she shown him during their outing? His face was like a mask, unreadable, Sphinx-like. Whatever secrets she had imparted to him, I knew he would keep hidden, for he seemed to have taken her side against me, though he had known her scarcely more than a few hours. If I spoke now, I would only make the situation worse. I needed time to think, to plan my strategy...to reevaluate my relationship with the friend I had called *brother* for the last thirteen years.

I shoved myself into a corner of the cab and focused my attention on the passersby, trying to distract my mind from the gnawing anxiety in my chest.

This grand tour had seemed like the adventure of a lifetime. But now, in light of my fears, I was beginning to regret ever agreeing to Stefan's blasted scheme.

☦

"If that is all, Monsieur..."

Not even the prospect of leaving Luc forever could cheer me. *He* had facilitated the meeting between the Borois and Stefan. I didn't care how small a part he had played. I was willing to shoot the messenger, no matter how blameless he might be.

I took the valise from Luc's hands and heaved it onto the rack above my seat. "Yes, that is all," I said curtly, stuffing a few Francs into his waiting hands. "Good-bye, Luc."

"We never say good-bye. It is always au revoir. Will it not be the same with us?"

"Good-*bye*." I turned my back on him and looked out the window. The sound of the door sliding into place told me he had left, and I let out a sigh of relief. I heard him and Stefan prattling on in the hallway, then the door slid open once more and my friend joined me in our cabin.

"Said your au revoirs, have you?"

"Yes."

This was the attitude he had adopted ever since we left the Louvre and Vladec Salei behind. Monosyllabic answers, no more. I heard him settling into the seat across from mine, but still I did not turn to face him. "What, no tears?"

A laugh—that was progress. The sound startled me. I turned away from the window.

"No," he said, "I will see him again on the way home."

"Well, *you* will, but *I* certainly won't. I'm meeting Guildy when we come through again. You can tell him that I...."

I nearly choked on the words. My eyes blinked frantically in a desperate attempt to dispel the vision standing on the platform outside. Luc had his arm around her. He whispered something in her ear that made her laugh brazenly, her red-black curls shaking free of her hat. The laugh was echoed by her brother, who strolled up with a valise in each of his gloved hands. He handed one of the valises to his sister, then reached into his pocket and pulled out an envelope. He gave the envelope to Luc, and the guide walked off.

Luc had nearly vanished into the crowd, but for some reason he turned back to look over his shoulder, turned back to look at *me*...and smiled.

The voice was so quiet I scarcely heard it. "I promised her."

I rounded on Stefan, terror battling with my fury. "What did you promise her?!"

"He wants to see it as bad as she does, so I had to promise her."

I planted my arms on either side of him, trapping him in his seat. "*What did you promise her?!!*" I shouted into his face.

"They're coming with us to Rome."

A Change of Plans

hen I opened my eyes, I found that the train had come to a halt. I stretched and reached for my watch, which I had placed on the arm of my chair the night before. It was already past mid-day. I hadn't realized I had slept so long. It didn't really matter much now anyway.

A loud blast shook the last vestiges of sleep from me. I looked out the window and saw Stefan and Sorina Boroi standing on the platform. Beyond them, a cloud of smoke rose from the funnel of the small steamer that would take us to Rome.

We still had nearly three hours to spare until we departed. I settled back into the seat, not wishing to face our new companions just yet. I had hardly talked with Stefan the entire journey. He, likewise, had been avoiding me and had only returned to our cabin when sleep was necessary. Even then, he had only come back maybe twice. I had my doubts he was sleeping at all, especially when I noticed the purple hollows beneath his eyes. He was too busy keeping company in the dining car with Augustin and Sorina Boroi.

A tap on my window drew my attention. My eyes were not quite focused yet, but I could see well enough to know it was her. I nearly tumbled to the floor when I realized that the face smiling down on me was Leonora's. Her laugh was muffled by the pane of glass separating us, but her joy at seeing me was undeniable. She nodded toward the harbor, motioning for me to join her outside.

I grabbed my watch, stuffed it into my waistcoat pocket, and reached for my shoes. The fact that we had traveled on the same train without meeting seemed unfathomable, as did the reason for her being here, but I wasn't going to spend my time puzzling over a mystery I had no hope of solving. I held up my index finger to signal that I would only be a moment, to which Leonora nodded vigorously and smiled again. *God, that smile could blind a man.*

My heart was hammering so hard I was surprised she couldn't hear its frantic beating through the glass. She looked radiant, more alive than I had ever seen her, and I had the delicious thought that maybe her happiness was due to me.

My hand was on the latch of the sliding door when a shadow fell across the window. Of course. How could I have been so naïve? Wherever Leonora went, he was never far behind.

I turned toward the glass, knowing who I would see. Standing beside her, his arm wrapped possessively around her shoulder, was Vladec Salei.

The look in his eyes told me everything. He was not blind; he knew how I felt. Yet I suspected he would not do anything to compromise his gentlemanly veneer. He was one of those aristocrats who expect people to submit to their will without thinking otherwise. Well, I didn't give a fig for his will, or his hoity-toity rank, for that matter.

I met his gaze without blinking. As one man to another, he was warning me silently with his eyes to stay away from his prized possession. But from the look of her face, I knew Leonora wasn't impartial to me. Salei be hanged. I was going to take my chances.

I felt reckless in my new resolve, so much so that I raised my hand and waved to Salei. The look of shock he turned on me was nearly too much to bear, and I had to face away momentarily to keep from laughing at his bulging eyes and gaping mouth. He turned on Leonora, who was struggling to look suitably horrified, and mouthed something I didn't catch. That would teach him. He had underestimated his opponent. I was determined to make him never discount me as an adversary again.

I slipped through the door and walked down the hallway until I came to the passageway leading to the exit. As I stepped off the train, I nearly crashed into Augustin Boroi.

"Ah, Bradburry!" he said in heavily accented English. So Stefan had given him the particulars. I didn't know whether to be thankful for that or not, so I just mumbled a greeting and made my exit before the male half of the Boroi duo had time to detain me further.

"It's so good to see you again, Mr. Bradburry."

"Eric," I insisted, taking Leonora's hand. She was a vision in white muslin, with a lace parasol and gloves to match. I feasted my eyes upon her face—noting with satisfaction that she didn't appear as pale as before—until Salei butted in and cast a pall over our reunion.

"Bradburry...a pleasure."

"Salei, likewise."

It nearly killed both of us to be civil, but Salei, ever the aristocrat, played the part well. I was hoping to somehow be rid of him so Leonora and I could stroll to the harbor alone, but there didn't seem to be a way to divest ourselves of him without arousing suspicion. I was almost ready to include him in the party—anything to be with Leonora—when intervention came from a source, not divine, but astonishing all the same.

"*Dearest* Vladec...and Mr. Bradburry. My word, it is a surprise to see you."

A born actress, this Sorina Boroi. I couldn't decide if she were lying on purpose or had truly begun to believe her own version of reality. She had seen me on the train, and seen me to disadvantage, for I had once accidentally walked halfway into the dining car before realizing she was there and had rather conspicuously about-faced and sped off down the hallway.

"Madam," I said sternly. I stared her in the eyes, knowing she would not flinch. Sorina did not disappoint.

"It will be so lovely to be in your company again, Eric," she cooed, letting her fingers brush across my arm.

"What do you mean by again, Sorina?" Leonora's voice was quiet, but the vehemence of her tone could not be denied.

"Well, dear, while you were locked away in your little hotel, supposedly ill, Eric and I had the good fortune of becoming acquainted. Do you not remember?"

Her cat-like eyes roved over every inch of me. A more modest woman would never have been so brazen. But then again, this was Sorina Boroi I was dealing with.

That blasted knowing smirk was playing about the corners of her mouth again. She pulled off one of her black lace gloves and extended her hand for a kiss. But if Sorina Boroi expected me to be as weak as her other conquests, she was mistaken. I looked down at her hand in disgust and met her gaze with one as equally steady as hers—a gaze so hard and unflinching that she started back slightly at the look in my eyes.

I left her hand hanging in the air and offered my arm to Leonora. "Let's walk, shall we?"

"Yes, let's."

There was some sort of rivalry between the two women. I had a feeling the object of the spat was Vladec Salei, whom it seemed Sorina had designs on. This afternoon, Leonora seemed inclined to let her adversary win a small victory, though undoubtedly she would make Sorina pay for her insolence later on. Leonora was demure, but underneath that placid facade, I sensed she could be as unflinching as Sorina when something vital was at stake.

I looked over my shoulder to see Sorina pulling on her glove with such force, I was certain she would be in need of a new pair very shortly. She was not used to being denied her every whim; it amused me to see her huffing about and railing at Salei in Romanian. He said something to her, which seemed to make her soften, then took her hand in his and walked off toward the harbor in the direction opposite the one we were traveling.

He was a clever one, Vladec Salei. He would grant us our time together, but by taking a diverging path that terminated at the same point, we would be forced to meet him eventually. I had won a small battle, but he was still victorious when it came to the war.

Two more figures were waiting for Salei and Sorina at the end of the platform. I squinted to make out their identities— Stefan and Augustin Boroi. Where Stefan had vanished to the minute I walked off the train, I hadn't the slightest notion. All I knew was that when I looked through the window, he was there, but when I came onto the platform, he was gone. Maybe Sorina had sent him on an errand, or, more likely, maybe he was sick of the sight of me and had taken himself off voluntarily. Truth be told, I wasn't too kindly disposed toward him at the moment anyway, so it was all for the best. Whatever their little quartet had planned for the next few hours did not interest me. I was glad they were gone. Now, I had Leonora all to myself.

‡

"So, what's your story?"

I handed her the lemonade I had just procured, and the two of us settled down onto a bench overlooking the harbor.

"I'm afraid it's not very interesting."

"Oh, I doubt that very much."

She looked up at me, her eyes dancing with mirth, then turned away to gaze upon the vessels sailing out of port. "I was born in Milan but spent most of my early life living in Germany or Greece. My father was an archeologist and professor of antiquities. He was fascinated by the ruins of the Aegean. I suppose I was born with some of that fervor and madness for ancient things, too. I was the one who accompanied him on all his digs. My mother never could understand his fascination, not that she ever tried to, but she wasn't alive long enough to know him like I did.

"The world thought a boy would have been better suited to being his assistant. It was a great disappointment to his colleagues at the university when Signora Bianchetti presented the Professor with a useless girl, but my father never once held my sex against me. I wish more men could be as open-minded as he was."

She studied her glass of lemonade. I knew at once whom she was referring to, and I was thankful he was halfway across the harbor with Stefan and the Borois.

I expected her face to be tear-stained, but it was clear and untroubled when she turned her eyes to the harbor once more.

"Then, during the summer when I was sixteen, I met Mattias Fertig. How I loved him, Eric. Mattias was a student at the university in Cologne where my father had been teaching. The way they took to each other was uncanny. Mattias was like no one I had ever met before. He was as mad as my father and I about people and artifacts that had been moldering beneath the earth for centuries. We were married in Greece not long after we met. You look surprised!" she said, turning those dancing eyes on me once again. "Am I that repulsive?"

"No, no," I sputtered. "It's just that I thought Vladec..."

"No," she said firmly, staring down into her glass again. "Vladec was not the first."

I didn't know how to continue. The two of us sat in silence for a time, but I was not content to let the story end there. I felt she was holding something back, yet I knew she was willing me to ask her the question that had come into my mind. "And what happened to Mattias?"

"He died."

It was what I had expected, but hearing it said aloud made it seem much worse, much more final.

"We were on a dig in Greece when it happened. My memory of that time is not very clear. I try not to remember, to be honest. It is too painful."

"You were left alone, then?"

"No, my son..."

Son? "Did he..."

"I don't want to talk about that part of my past, Eric. I can't."

"I'm sorry, Leonora. It must have been awful." The words were feeble, but I couldn't think of anything else to say. Nothing I said would have comforted her anyway.

Silence reigned once more. I was afraid to continue after such a revelation, but Leonora was the one who picked up the strands of the story again. "A month after their deaths, Vladec found me. Vladec *saved* me. I'd lost my father in an accident during that month, too. If Vladec hadn't taken me in, I don't know what I would have done. I was quite mad by that point."

My beautiful Leonora...mad? I couldn't imagine it. Yet would I be any different? Could I hold on to sanity if those I'd loved most in this world had been taken from me?

"I'm sorry," I said again.

"Yes. So am I."

Something did not make sense to me. "If all those terrible things happened to you in Greece, why do you go there so often?"

The veins in her temple throbbed. "It's complicated." Was that the only answer I'd get? Her hands strayed to her skirt. She grabbed onto a fold of the garment, clenching her fist around it so tightly that her nails tore through the fabric. All this time, her eyes were fixed on the steamer we'd be boarding soon.

"Leonora..." I reached for her hand, but she pulled away from me as though she were afraid of my touch.

"Look what I've done," she said. I heard the hysteria in her voice. Her nerves seemed as frayed as the fabric she'd just torn—torn without realizing what she was doing. "Greece holds many painful memories for me, but I had a life there, Eric. A happy life, till my world was destroyed. I cannot hate that place, though I've tried.

"And there you have it," she said, handing me her empty glass. "I suppose it's not as interesting as the stories they circulate in Paris. But then again, the truth is never quite as enticing as a good bit of scandal."

I blushed to my ears. I had believed those vile rumors and now felt ashamed that I had thought ill of her, if even for a moment.

There was so much I still wanted to ask, so much I still needed to wrap my mind around, yet one aspect was so clear it did not need further reflection. In all her talk about Vladec Salei, she had never mentioned love. The love she had for Mattias was evident. Any fool could have seen she still adored him, but when the story turned to Salei, her voice had become taut, strained, and cold, even though she'd admitted he'd saved her. Saved her *how*?

"I know what you're thinking, Eric," she said. "Why hasn't he married me? Vladec is not the marrying kind, which is good for me in a way because I could never be married to anyone other than Mattias."

It was strange logic, yet I understood. She had also said it with an unmistakable finality, which I knew meant the conversation had come to an end as far as she was concerned.

She smiled at me one last time before turning to walk along the dock. Against the failing light, she looked ghostly in her colorless garments. The thought hadn't occurred to me before, but now that I watched her, I found it curious that Leonora always wore white. From the parasol she carried, down to the Mechlin gloves she wore on her hands, her ensemble was always colorless. White...the color of purity. She was beyond that now, it pained me to admit, but if her body was no longer pure, at least her heart was, for I was certain she only loved one man and that man was not Vladec Salei.

The thought of Mattias triggered a memory long since buried. When I was at Eton, I had learned that Mary, Queen of France, had been forced to wear her widow's weeds after her aged husband died, but instead of the traditional black we English were used to, the custom in France was to wear white, the color of mourning. I smiled wistfully at the remembrance and wondered if Leonora had chosen to always wear this color to honor the memory of Mattias Fertig.

A blast from the steamer jolted me from my reverie.

"That's our signal to head out," said Leonora. Her transformation from cowed, quivering creature when in Salei's presence into this mysterious, untamable beauty when he was away was astonishing. I wished there was some way I could free her of him forever. From what she had told me, I reasoned she was about twenty-four years of age. Six years older than myself. That wasn't such a large difference. It would be a marriage of convenience. I knew she could never love me, though I was already neck-deep in love with her. Yet ours would be a happy union, I was sure. If there were a way I could convince her to accept the notion, I vowed I would make her my wife as soon as we were safely in Rome.

I took her arm and led her farther down the dock, where Salei and his three charges were waiting. All our trunks and valises from the train had been placed in a little pile beside the gangplank and were in the process of being loaded onto the ship.

Stefan was talking animatedly with Augustin Boroi, while Sorina—wearing the new pair of gloves, scarlet this time, I knew she would be in need of after her tantrum—was leaning into Vladec Salei, muttering something to herself. The moment she caught sight of us, she jerked away from him and sauntered forth, challenge in her eyes.

"Ah, there you two are! Finally! We've been waiting forever. I trust you found a nice, secluded spot for your idyll? Have a pleasant tryst?"

If it weren't against my nature, I would have struck that woman in the face. I hated the way she took delight in taunting Leonora, and I hated the way she baited me every time we had the misfortune of being thrown together.

"We had a lovely, illuminating chat, thank you," I replied. "And did you enjoy your time with Salei? You seem to love keeping company with him."

"Yes, I do," she said saucily. I hadn't expected her to blush, but I also hadn't expected her to agree so readily that she was after Salei for her own. I looked at Leonora, expecting to see some sign of anger, but her face was emotionless.

"I think we understand each other perfectly, Eric, *dear*," Sorina cooed, slipping her arm through mine and leading me up the gangplank.

"Oh, yes, I understand your type all too well."

"My type? And what might that be?"

"I couldn't say in public, Madam, without causing a scandal."

That had the effect I was hoping for. She yanked her arm away and glared at me, her breast heaving in anger, before flouncing back down the gangplank toward Salei. I didn't envy him having to bear the brunt of that harpy's rage.

"Thank you for that," Leonora whispered to me. My heart leapt at her gratitude. The next few days would be crucial to my plans. I wasn't about to let Sorina Boroi distract me for an instant.

‡

As it turned out, Sorina Boroi distracted me for quite a few instants. I don't know whether it was her idea, or whether Salei wanted to be rid of her, but everywhere I went on the steamer, she was at my side.

It started the first day when we were pulling out of port. I had gone topside to catch a glimpse of the infamous Château d'If off the stern. Apparently, my jab on the gangplank hadn't been as long-lasting as I would have hoped, for when I turned round, whom did I find at my elbow but Sorina Boroi?

"I've been inside," she whispered. "And have known many men who languished in there. Some claim I was the one who drove them mad and not the prison itself." Her eyes were glistening. I couldn't decide whether her words were bravado or madness, since the fortress had been shut up for years. Her half-truths—I guessed there was some slim thread of veracity mixed into her lies—disconcerted me, but I had a feeling she was just trying to goad me into bantering with her again this time.

I turned away in disgust, watching the Château receding in the distance. The horror of being confined with this creature for the next few days seemed worse than the tortures Edmond Dantès had experienced behind the prison's walls. I had hoped to have at least a few moments of free gazing to myself, but the incident with Sorina Boroi had sapped my interest in the Château d'If. I left my perch on deck, not having any desire to contemplate further the cruel fate Dumas made his Count of Monte Cristo endure for all those years.

Sorina followed in my wake. A mad desire to run seized me, but then I remembered that my only hope of escape was to hurl myself overboard. After a few more days of her shadowing, I would be willing to take my chances with the sharks.

Whenever I sought a moment's peace, I would hear the hated rustle of silk and would find her standing beside me, that blasted smirk twisting her lips. I had even tried to intentionally mislead her, telling her I would be in one part of the ship when in reality I would be as far away from the designated spot as I could, but still she would find me. She had the uncanny ability of knowing exactly where I would be at all times.

And then there was the trouble with Leonora. Ever since the first night aboard ship, Leonora had stayed in her cabin. I didn't know whether she was truly unwell or had chosen seclusion to avoid Sorina, but I had a suspicion it was the latter. Stefan was no help, either. He, Augustin, and Salei kept company with each other in the steamer's small smoking room for hours on end, talking over God knows what.

Desperate to get away from the blight known as Sorina Boroi, I sought out the company of the few other passengers on the ship. Yet whenever I tried to start a conversation, a strange sort of panic would come over my fellow travelers. They'd start blubbering like idiots and back away from me as if they were afraid I would pounce on them. I could not even begin to fathom why they had reacted in such a hysterical manner, but then I saw that Sorina had materialized at my side again, and I suspected she was somehow responsible for poisoning their minds against me.

"Such a pity," she said, laying her gloved hand on my arm. "I can only wonder what their fevered minds are conjecturing now that they know the reason the young Bianchetti woman is staying in her cabin is to avoid the most unwelcome attentions of Mr. Bradburry. And then they've seen you lurking about, looking half mad, for the last few days. Poor dears. They would have never known had I not told them. And now they are all privy to the story of your father and the madness that runs in your family. And they've witnessed it—yes they have, on that first day you boarded. The way your eyes glazed over whenever you looked at Leonora. What a shame."

I was too horrified to move. In one fell swoop, she had destroyed my reputation and cut me off from every means of aid should I need it, and I certainly felt I did at that moment. At first, the scheme didn't make any sense at all, but as I looked over the past few days, I realized that it had all been plotted and executed to perfection. All her tricks, all my attempts to avoid her, had all been working to the same end—discrediting me, distracting me and making me seem crazed, and I had played right into her hands. I suspected Salei was behind this, yet Sorina was so spiteful and followed her own rules that I couldn't be sure this was not all part of her own sick little game.

Although the vessel was small, and the passengers few, I had learned that they were all quite prominent in their circles. The Italian was a magistrate in Rome and the Greek an aide to the government in Athens. The Frenchman worked for the Sûreté, which was enough for me to avoid him at all costs, given what I had experienced in Paris at the hands of this minx. It would be their word against mine, and who would take the ravings of a supposed madman seriously when these masters of the law condemned him as a lunatic? Oh yes, Sorina, you had left no room for error, you witch.

My position was precarious at best, yet I no longer felt fearful. Fear had turned to anger, which in turn had evolved into hatred. I felt the need to fight, to somehow show her I would not bow down so easily.

"I know what you are."

For a moment she did not answer, and I got the distinct impression she was trembling. Fear? I doubted it. I hadn't the slightest idea what she was and she knew it, but the statement had caught her off guard.

"No, dear, you have no idea," she said. "And who would believe you now that they know your true nature?"

"You'd be surprised." I could be just as enigmatic as she could.

"Would I?"

"Yes."

She smiled, but it wasn't her usual confident smirk. The smile was forced and she struggled to keep her lips from twitching—she was nervous.

"What exactly do you want?"

"*You.*"

The way she said it turned my blood to ice. She did not say it with desire, nor in the caressing tones of a lover, but there was a hunger in her voice I could not identify. She was looking at me as though she wanted to devour me.

"But what about Salei?" I said, my voice a desperate squeak. She had backed me against the railing. One false move and I would be meeting those sharks sooner than I liked.

"Oh, I want him, too," she said, leaning against my chest, "and I'll have him eventually, but now he's too busy turning your friend into his protégé. I am content to wait for my prize. But you...*you* would prove to be a nice little distraction. And I know Leonora is fond of you, so it would be doubly sweet."

"Would it, Sorina?"

Hers was the last voice I expected to hear. I looked behind Sorina and exhaled in relief as I saw Leonora walking toward us, magnificent as an avenging angel.

Sorina's hand hung suspended in front of my chest. She had unbuttoned my shirt at the collar, but had recoiled and frozen like a thief caught in the act when Leonora's voice had sounded through the darkness. "I see you have recovered," Sorina said sourly.

"Yes, and just in time, apparently."

I slipped away from Sorina and offered my arm to Leonora. "Thank you," I mouthed. I had feared Leonora would think I wasn't averse to Sorina's seduction, but when she smiled up at me, the warmth of her eyes eased my mind. She knew I was innocent.

"It's time to go in for dinner. And do take a moment to compose yourself, Sorina. Vladec is very fond of the ice sculpture on our table. We wouldn't want you melting it in your overheated state."

Sorina's eyes flashed in the darkness. She opened her mouth as if to retort, but there was nothing she could say. I suppressed a chuckle as we passed her by. Poor little Sorina Boroi. She was so used to being pampered and getting whatever she desired. But not tonight.

We had walked on a few steps when a ragged breath escaped from Leonora. I pulled her to a halt, but she shook her head and motioned me to move on. "Stay away from her, Eric," she said, her voice wavering, "she's dangerous."

"I think I've learned that first hand tonight. But hold a minute before we go in." We were standing outside the dining room. I could see Salei, Stefan, and Augustin Boroi through the windows. They were already sitting at the large circular table we had shared the night before. Stefan and Augustin were carrying on loudly in Romanian, while Salei looked on like a benevolent uncle and smiled at his young charges' mirth every now and then. The only other occupants of the dining room were the Greek government aide and his wife, who were sitting at a small table on the far side of the room. They didn't look as though they were enjoying themselves, and I had a feeling it was because of my friend's carousal with his countryman. The situation did not improve when Sorina huffed in through the room's double doors and started spouting off to Salei, no doubt recounting our little incident. A pained look crossed Salei's face. I wondered if he was beginning to realize what sort of monster he had created. Poor devil. Short of killing her, he would never be able to get rid of her, especially now that she had him in mind for her next conquest.

I turned my attention back to Leonora. "It's worse than that, though, I'm afraid." I then told her of the rumors Sorina had bruited about aboard ship.

"Strega," Leonora spat. "The witch. Whatever can she be about? You just stay near me until we dock tomorrow and then you'll be safe, all right?"

If she only knew I had been praying for this since we left Marseilles. Now, I would certainly have time to tell her of my plans before we reached Rome.

I squeezed her hand and smiled in answer as we walked through the door to the dining room.

"Ah, there you two are!" Stefan shot up from his seat and held out a chair for Leonora. He was glaring at me wolfishly, but I gave him a look that soundly disabused him of whatever insinuations had been dancing through his mind. He was in an exceedingly good mood, too, which was surprising, given his coldness of the last few days. Whatever the reason for his present mirth, I was happy to see him returning to his old self.

The only seat available was next to Salei. I took it because I had no choice. He didn't seem to be the kind to move down a chair to accommodate anyone. And besides, I knew he didn't want me sitting next to Leonora.

As I took my seat, I glanced up to see Sorina Boroi staring me dead in the face. The result of this unenviable position was that I had been placed directly across from her. So, with Salei on my right, Augustin Boroi—who was already drunk—on my left, and Sorina Boroi watching over us all, I was certain this wouldn't be a pleasant evening. My one consolation was that Leonora was only a chair away, so at least I had an ally relatively close at hand if need be.

"Drink your sherry, boys," Sorina cooed.

I hadn't looked at the glasses yet, but now that she'd drawn attention to them, I noticed that Stefan and I were the only ones not drinking red wine. Odd, that, but I didn't really mind. Stefan, on the other hand, seemed extraordinarily put out.

"Why can I not have what you're drinking?" Was it really his intention to sound so petulant? He looked like a sulking child. I half expected him to stick his thumb in his mouth and tug on his ear until she gave him what he wanted.

"In time, *precious*. You'll have to wait until you are truly ready," she said, smiling viciously. I'd never noticed how white her teeth were until then—how white and gleaming and sharp they looked in the candlelight.

"Now, then, enough prattling. Come, come," she chirruped, clapping her hands for the waiter. "Bring out our feast." She had apparently assigned herself Queen O' the May for the evening.

I didn't think we had arrived late, but when I looked down at our plates, I saw that our salads had begun to wilt. They had been doused with oil and there were strange looking crumbles of white cheese mixed in between the lettuce. I glanced at Stefan, who mouthed *Feta* back to me. Greek cheese...odd. The night before, we had feasted on pasta and Italian dishes in preparation for our arrival in Rome. Why the sudden change in cuisine?

Moments later, two waiters bustled in, each bearing a pair of covered trays. They set them down, amidst Sorina's squeals of delight, and removed the covers with a flourish, revealing pieces of meat and sliced vegetables on skewers. On another tray were tentacles that looked so lifelike, I wondered if the rest of the octopus had secreted itself underneath the tray's cover.

"Lamb kebabs and grilled octopus! How delightful!" Sorina said. "Now, everyone, enjoy!"

I didn't think I would enjoy eating the tentacles, and the kebabs didn't look any more appealing to me, so I just picked at my salad instead. Stefan caught my look and passed me his glass. "Here," he said, "you can have my sherry. I've gone off it completely."

I nodded in thanks. My mind was in a whirl. I couldn't reconcile myself to this strange turn of events, not to mention this odd feast and Sorina's new attitude. Her laughter was so false it would have been comical if it weren't for the fact that I suspected there was a sinister motive behind her assumed mirth. I didn't like the way her eyes kept darting toward Leonora. It was almost as if she were hoping to somehow strike her dead with a glance.

I took another sip of the sherry to fortify myself, then decided to have a go at conversation. "So..."

"That's such a beautiful necklace, Leonora," Sorina shot in.

Leonora touched the *L* at her throat. "Thank you," she said, bewildered.

"At first I thought the *L* stood for lover, but then Vladec told me what it meant. Where did you say you got the idea? Anne Boleyn? Clever woman."

"Yes, she was," Salei said tightly. I could see his jaw clenching in anger. I didn't blame him. I was furious with Sorina myself.

"Such a shame about the beheading," she rattled on. "But I suppose that was the only way Henry could be certain he had truly rid himself of her forever. There's something so *final* about a beheading," she said, stroking her neck with her long, red-tipped fingers.

"Yes, w-well," Stefan broke in, stuttering as his eyes drifted to Leonora and took in her mortified expression, "this is all stimulating, but I fail..."

"Tell me, Eric," Sorina said, rounding on me, her eyes blazing. "What letter do you think suits me? Would you buy me a golden *S*?"

Every pair of eyes in the room was trained on me. Not a single person at our table was breathing. In a matter of seconds, the tension had grown as taut as a bowstring.

The look I turned on her was so full of hate, not even one as brazen as Sorina Boroi could help flinching. "No, madam," I said quietly. "I'd buy you a scarlet *A*."

Affronts to her reputation pierced her to the heart, though I couldn't understand why, since she had very little character left to defend. She picked up her knife and fork and savagely bit down on a piece of lamb, biting her lips so hard in the process that blood spattered onto the tablecloth.

So Sorina Boroi had a weakness. I smiled to myself as I looked toward Leonora. She had recovered, thank goodness. I was rewarded with a nod and smile of thanks.

I had thought I had put an end to Sorina's bravado for the evening, but apparently a bite of the lamb and a drink from her brother's glass of red wine were all the stimulants she needed to lash out again.

"Greece can be so dangerous this time of year, what with all those banditti around, don't you agree, Vladec *dear*?"

"Greece?" Suddenly, I knew why the menu had been changed.

"Oh! Did Stefan not tell you?" she said, looking the picture of innocence. "There's been a change of plans. I gave orders to the chef to grant us this feast in honor of our destination. We dock tomorrow afternoon in Athens."

I shot a death-glare at Stefan, but he avoided my eyes. "No, he failed to mention that little fact," I said through clenched teeth. "Especially when he knew we had planned to go to Rome. I suppose you diverted the steamer, too, Sorina?"

"Silly boy," she said, laughing. "Of course not. Vladec had this ship bound for Greece all along."

"Is that so?" I looked at Salei, who met my glare with equal intensity. There would be no cowing him.

"Well, given this new state of affairs," I said, rising from my seat, "I think it best to retire. Stefan?"

"Oh, you can't leave yet," Sorina protested, saving Stefan from my wrath for the time being. "We still haven't had dessert. And, Leonora, I have a special dessert just for *you*."

"Really?" Her voice quaked at the announcement. I could see she was as fearful of what Sorina had in store as I was.

Sorina clapped her hands again; once more a waiter appeared, bearing a small tray, which he set before Leonora. He uncovered it to reveal a small pastry dotted with fruit and drowning in white syrup.

"Voilà!" Sorina said. "Baklava with strawberries and cream. Doesn't it look delightful?"

If it had been a severed head on that plate, Leonora could not have looked more horrified. The knife she had been holding clattered to the table and struck the plate on which the dessert was resting, chipping off a piece of porcelain before falling to the floor. Her movements were so horribly slow as to be almost dreamlike. Her hands shook as she brought her napkin to her gaping mouth. I had no doubt she had done this to suppress the scream rising in her throat. Her breath was ragged and sounded like a death rattle, and her eyes—those black eyes that had been smiling at me a moment before—were dilated in horror.

"Oh, how silly of me," Sorina said quietly. Her eyes were aglow in triumph. "That was Mattias's favorite, wasn't it? And the two of you shared this dessert the day he died, didn't you... *Dearest*, I had forgotten you told me. How careless I have been."

Leonora lifted her eyes to her assailant's face. I felt a stabbing pain pierce my heart when I saw the look of profound sadness Leonora turned on Sorina. "Vladec," she whispered, placing a trembling hand to her forehead, "I feel one of my headaches coming. Help me, please."

Salei had her in his arms in an instant. I watched in silence, growing more jealous by the moment, as he lead her through the double doors and out of the dining room.

"Poor weak creature," Sorina said, turning her attention to her food. "She suffers from terrible migraines and chronic anemia. They've been treating her for years. Vladec has the best doctors, but they have tried everything and failed. The best they can do is feed her foods with lots of iron. And then there are those tablets she insists on taking. Well, I suppose the weak constitution is a family deficiency. It's the reason her brat died, after all."

I had risen when Leonora left the table. I was still too appalled to retake my seat. Steel glimmered up from the floor. I leaned over to pick up Leonora's knife. I gripped the handle, wondering what it would feel like to plunge the blade into Sorina's heart.

Stefan must have sensed my intentions, for he snatched the knife from my hand. "Eric, go to bed," he whispered nervously.

"You and I will talk later. Come see me once you've had your fill of Lady Dark Heart's company."

And with that, I left him alone with the witch and her drunken brother.

‡

Sea spray struck me in the face the minute I walked out on deck. The skies had been clear not ten minutes before, but now the ocean had begun to roil and the ship was starting to pitch violently. I stuck out my hands and gripped the railing to steady myself as I walked up the deck.

A streak of lightning split the night sky and was followed by a boom of thunder so loud it was a miracle I wasn't deafened after hearing it. Seconds later, the air crackled and another bolt of lightning forked across the darkness. In that flash of illumination, I saw Leonora standing at the bow of the ship. Vladec Salei was nowhere to be seen. I didn't like the way she was leaning out over the railing. There was no reason for her to be out there alone, especially in this weather. Then I saw her take a step up the rail and my heart leaped into my throat.

I charged up the deck, slipping on the now soaked boards, and flung myself at Leonora. The instant I caught her in my arms, a wave washed over the bow of the ship. I had no time to grip anything. In a minute, we would be dragged overboard. I clung to Leonora as we were swept along on the tide, but instead of feeling the waves drowning us as we hit the water, I felt a sharp jab against my back—the railing surrounding the bow had prevented us from plummeting into the depths below.

The impact sent the seawater spewing from my lungs and knocked Leonora from my arms. I collapsed against the deck, coughing and spluttering, my throat feeling raw. Another crack of thunder exploded over our heads. If we stayed topside any longer, we'd be washed overboard when the next wave hit.

I wrapped my arms around Leonora and guided her into the lounge. Thankfully, no one was there but a steward who came to our aid directly with a tankard of brandy and a pair of wraps. I draped one of the robes around Leonora, then took off my soaked jacket and shirt and threw the other robe about my shoulders before the two of us settled into a divan near the fireplace.

"Why were you trying to kill yourself?" I croaked, gagging as the brandy fought against the seawater still in my throat.

"K-kill myself?" she said, her teeth chattering. "Is that what you th-think I was t-trying to do?"

"You were leaning over the railing. You looked as though you were going to jump."

"One of my gloves had f-fallen on a lower r-rung and I was trying to reach for it. Then you c-came along and nearly knocked me overboard."

"Sorry for that," I said sheepishly, though I knew she wasn't angry. If I hadn't been there, Leonora would have been washed away.

"Besides, it wouldn't do any good. I can't kill myself."

"I'm glad you feel that way because I've never thought suicide solved anything."

"That's not what I meant."

I stared at her, willing her to look at me, to explain that odd statement, but she'd focused her attention on the fire dancing in the grate.

I would have loved more time—to prepare, to calm myself, to think of the best way to convince her my wild scheme would work—but this was the only chance I had to be alone with Leonora before we reached Greece, and however inopportune this moment was, I would have to make it work.

"Leonora," I said, taking her hand in mine. "I can take you away from all this."

"All of what? What are you saying?"

"Marry me, Leonora. I love you."

My heart leapt when I saw tears welling in her eyes. I was convinced they were tears of joy.

"Eric, please," she said wearily, rising and turning her back on me. "You're not thinking clearly. Go to bed."

"Give me a reason why you won't."

"I can give you a thousand reasons and you would never believe any of them."

"You don't love Salei, do you?"

She rounded on me. I expected her eyes to be filled with rage, but the sadness I saw reflected in them made my heart ache for her. "Our relationship is none of your concern."

"Answer my question, Leonora. If you love him, look me in the eyes and say so."

She cupped her face in her hand and sighed in exasperation, shaking her head slightly as if she could not understand why I was persecuting her with questions she could not answer. She smiled ruefully and turned away again, but I wasn't going to let her leave until I knew the truth. I pulled her toward me so she had no choice but to look at me.

"Answer me."

"Oh, Eric," she cried, her resolve finally breaking. She rested her forehead against my chest, and I soon felt my wrap growing damp from her tears. "If only I could tell you everything."

"Then tell me," I coaxed.

"It's not that simple."

She brushed away her tears, then patted the wrap where her head had lain. Her brow furrowed at the sight of the water stains. "I'm sorry," she said. I didn't know if she were apologizing for the wrap being wet or because she couldn't give me the answer I wanted to hear. "When we get to Greece," she said, breaking away from me, "you and Stefan will continue with your tour, and Vladec and I will go on our way. I want you to forget we ever met."

"I could never forget you, Leonora."

"I wish I could believe that."

"You can."

"Yes...I know...that's the problem."

She laid her hand against my cheek. I didn't want to let her go, but the moment was over before I could think of a reason to keep her near me. I watched her walk through the lounge's doors and make for the corridor to her cabin. *Her* cabin... It was the first time I'd realized she was not sharing a cabin with Vladec Salei. The separation gave me hope—hope that his hold on Leonora was weakening and hope that she would find it in her heart to accept my proposal in the morning. A fool's hope, maybe, but it was something to hold on to after this day on which nothing had gone according to plan.

‡

It was already well past midnight when I finally settled into my cabin. And, surprise of surprises, Stefan's bunk was empty when I walked through the door. Ah, well, I suppose he was still getting drunk in the dining room with Augustin and Sorina Boroi. Devil take the lot of them.

I briefly contemplated hitting myself over the head with one of my shoes, but that blow would not have been strong enough to induce sleep. Besides, I was still nursing the bruise Stefan's antics had inflicted on my forehead, and I felt strongly disinclined to add another lump to my skull.

I pulled out my watch. A quarter to two—and still Stefan had not returned. The prospect of sleeping at all this night didn't seem likely. If I didn't get to sleep in the next five minutes, I would light the lamp and compose a letter to Mother and Roddy. She would be worried, for I had not had time to write while in Paris, and he would be expecting a full report of all I had seen and done since I left Dover. My account to him would be a nice, dull travelogue—exactly the sort of thing he'd love. I would be sure to leave out a few details here and there, especially the bits about Sorina Boroi.

I had laid a sheet of paper out on the desk between our beds and was uncorking my inkwell, when I heard voices in the cabin next to mine. I could not make out what they were saying from where I was sitting, so I abandoned the letter and walked toward the wall separating our cabins.

"The English brat is the one you need to watch, not the other." The voice belonged to Vladec Salei. And I knew he was talking about me.

"But, Vladec...can I not at least have Stefan for a while? He is so amusing." I shuddered at her words. Did Sorina Boroi's lust have no bounds?

"No. Stay with him always."

"Stefan?" She really was dense, but I hoped she was right this time. I held my breath, willing him to say yes, that it was Stefan she was meant to shadow.

"No. It must seem like an attack. You've done very well on this ship. Now, you must finish your part in Greece. I will be waiting with the authorities to catch him in the act. Whatever you do, make it convincing. I have no intention of letting Eric Bradburry leave that country alive."

I reeled back from the wall as if I had been scalded. A thousand and one scenarios raced through my mind, each more horrible than the last. The blood pounded so loudly in my ears, I thought my head was going to explode.

They planned to frame me. But to what end? He wanted something with Stefan. Sorina had even said Salei was making Stefan his protégée, but that certainly didn't necessitate offing me. The only thing I could think of was that he somehow needed Stefan's money. But a man like Vladec Salei, who had half of Europe in his pocket, had no need of money, so what other reason for this mad scheme could there be? Granted, Salei had hated me on sight, and the feeling was mutual, but I had certainly done nothing to merit this drastic reaction.

It didn't make sense. Whatever solution I worked out was punctured by a million and one improbabilities seconds later. The one thing I knew for certain was that I had to stay away from Sorina Boroi at all costs. If she weren't near me, she couldn't frame me, for apparently she was to be the victim of one of my supposed mad rages.

I came out of my fog long enough to totter over to the door and shoot the bolt. I leaned against the frame for a moment, my mind still spinning, then I stumbled back toward my bunk and rolled onto the mattress. I was too shocked to move, let alone care that I had locked Stefan out and left him at the mercy of Sorina Boroi. I hoped he would be safe, but I was taking no chances. Whether he had a protector or destroyer in Vladec Salei, I did not care. All I knew was that he had been chosen to live, while I, for some reason, was going to be sacrificed.

Their net was closing in. I would appeal to Leonora tomorrow as soon as we docked, although I didn't know what good that would do, nor even if they would let me near her, now that their plan had been set in motion.

My mind grew more fevered by the moment. If I weren't careful, I would make myself go mad before morning. Wouldn't Vladec and Sorina love that?

Corcitura

No. I had to keep my wits about me. I would not get any sleep on this night. I couldn't afford to let down my guard. For all I knew, they were lurking in the corridor now, trying to find a way to break down my door and do away with me while I slept. They were crafty, yes, but then a thought struck me, and I smiled in spite of my fear.

They did not know I had overheard...

Somehow, in the solitude of my cabin, that thought seemed to me the most comforting thing in the world.

The Haunter of Darkness

"**S**o, here we are: two weeks early and at the mercy of someone who wants me dead."

Stefan shook his head and handed me my valise. He was still having trouble believing my story. I suppose my feverishness of the early morning hours did not help matters. He maintained that it was the knocking about the wave had given me—swallowing seawater was enough to set any man's fancy raging. Well, if Stefan wanted to keep denying the truth, he could do it alone. I was determined to sever all ties with the Borois and Vladec Salei the moment my feet touched Greek soil.

As I had expected, Leonora was nowhere in sight. I reckoned he was keeping her hidden until I was safely off the ship and no longer a threat.

Salei and the Boroi contingent had gathered around the gangplank, ostensibly waiting for Stefan so they could all continue on their little Greek holiday together—without me.

The streets below were teeming with travelers. My throat tightened at the sight of them. Now that Greece was practically overrun with tourists, we would be hard-pressed to find a room on such short notice. Then again, Stefan had his small fortune, and I my money from Roddy, so we might just find a way to buy ourselves in.

Stefan was already arm in arm with Sorina Boroi by the time I turned around. So the hunt had begun... Wouldn't Salei be pleased. But when I looked for him, I was shocked to see him advancing in my direction.

"Gentlemen," he said, beckoning to Stefan, who sauntered over with the blight still affixed to his arm. "I feel terrible for inconveniencing you." For someone who was supposedly stricken with remorse, he certainly was beaming rather triumphantly. "The porter has just informed me that a room has become available at my hotel. Sadly," he said, turning his cold eyes on me, "there is only room for one of you."

"I'm not going without Eric."

"What?" Salei and I said simultaneously. I nearly toppled over the railing. Could it be? Had Stefan awoken from his temporary madness? I knew he would come to his senses. Apparently, he *hadn't* forgotten the time I had saved him from drowning in a foot of water in the Serpentine when we were lads. Stefan was back!

"I...I am afraid that's impossible," Salei stuttered. What a joy it was to see the unflappable Vladec Salei at a loss for words.

"No, Vladec, it's not. We will make do, isn't that right, old boy?"

"Of course you will, and I intend to see you do." I was already shocked by this turn of events, but hearing the voice of Sorina Boroi nearly put me over the edge. Having her suddenly become our advocate was unexpected, not to mention highly suspicious, and I wondered if she had spoken poison into Stefan's ears and convinced him to refuse Salei's hospitality.

Salei's eyes blazed into hers. I took a step back, not wishing to get caught in the crossfire when he finally decided to strike her dead, for that's what he appeared to be on the verge of doing. "Sorina, we already settled this."

"Yes, but I changed my mind. You know I'm not very good at following orders. Untamable, you once said." Her mouth twitched up at the corner. Ever the coquette—flirting even in defiance to a man who wanted to strangle her and would have if she hadn't grabbed Stefan and me by the arms and led us down the gangplank before Salei could wrap his hands around her throat.

We had already traveled more than halfway down, Salei trailing behind us helplessly, when a man rushed up the gangplank and nearly knocked the three of us overboard. I caught the words "frantic" and "Constantinos" and saw Salei blanch. He was pale to begin with, but now he looked as white as a corpse. He seized the man by the collar, then released his grip when he saw me staring at him. It was a momentary lapse, but I had seen his fear, although I hadn't the faintest idea why those words should make him so terrified.

"Sorina," he said, his voice once more smooth and cultivated. "A word."

Sorina released our arms and sauntered over to Salei. The moment she was within reach, he grasped her arm and twisted her around so that his lips were inches from her ear. Whatever he said, we could not hear. He kept his tone controlled, but I could tell he was furious. I could see his jaw clenching and unclenching as he fired the words into her ear. Anyone else would have given in after such a savage display of force, but not Sorina Boroi. She met his eyes with a gaze as equally fierce as his own. I half expected her to spit in his face.

"Why should I be afraid?" she hissed. "It was not *I* who stole his mistress!" And with that, she wrenched free and flounced off toward us, grabbing our arms so roughly and cantering off so quickly we had to run just to keep pace with her.

As we rounded the corner, I looked back and saw Salei railing at Leonora as she came out on deck. Whatever those cryptic words meant, they had obviously upset his precious plans. And whatever the reason for Sorina's defection, I was thankful for it. It might have just saved my life.

‡

"Charming, isn't it?"

We were standing in the cramped, dirt-floored room for which we had just paid a small fortune to inhabit over the next two weeks.

"That's not the word I was thinking of," I said sourly, gathering a palm-full of dirt and sifting it through my fingers.

"Well, we're here now, so it can't be helped."

I wanted to berate Stefan, but after the incident on the ship, I thought better of it. He had remembered I was his best friend, after all, so telling him we would never have been in this situation if he hadn't got all matey with a complete stranger wouldn't have helped the brotherly mood I was striving to maintain.

"Why don't we go explore?" I said amicably.

"I have a better idea."

"Which is?"

"Why don't *you* go explore and tell me about it when you get back?"

I folded my arms, my eyes narrowing at his sly face. "I'm beginning to think you used me as a means to your own ends," I said without rancor.

"Perhaps."

Deuced honest, he was becoming. "I don't think that's such a good idea. I wouldn't want to leave you at Lady Dark Heart's mercy."

"Oh!" he said, feigning surprise. "Jealous because Leonora isn't free to do as she chooses?"

"Look, Stefan," I said seriously. This was no longer a game. "Sorina's not free to do as she likes, either. She just puts on a brave act and flouts her supposed freedom in Salei's face every chance she gets. I don't trust her, and you would be wise to follow my example."

"May I remind you that I'm a full two months older than you?"

"Technicalities," I said dismissively. "You may be older in years, but as for smarts, you're no wiser than a lad of ten."

"Oh, really?" The right side of his lip had begun to twitch. The gesture took me aback, for I had never seen Stefan display that sign of anger before. But I *had* seen that same reaction on the face of someone else, and that someone else was Vladec Salei.

"Yes, really," I said hurriedly, masking my apprehension behind a firm tone. "Now, make a sensible decision for once in your life and let's be off, all right?"

"No."

"*Stefan...*"

"Bah! You and your ridiculous worries. You're worse than my mother. Come, now, out you go. I'll see you tonight."

Before I could protest further, he had bunged me through the door and bolted the lock behind me.

Short of breaking down the door and dragging him out, there was no way Stefan would willingly go along with my idea. I consulted my watch; it was already half past six. *Fine.* Let him have a few hours to himself. There'd be time enough later for me to knock some sense into him.

The thought of him alone did not trouble my mind, but the thought of him keeping company with Sorina Boroi was quite another matter. She had been leaning against the side of the hovel, ostensibly studying her fingernails, but I was not blind to her triumphant smile as I came up beside her. She couldn't mask how happy she was that Stefan had thrown me out.

That she had designs on Stefan was obvious, especially after hearing her pleas to Vladec Salei the night before. And as for Stefan, well, he wasn't exactly a paragon of sound judgment. Regardless, I knew I was not wanted here, and no matter what I tried to say, nothing would convince him when he got into one of his intractable moods. Yet I knew I could not let them be without saying something—threat, warning, directive, I didn't know what to call it—to her, however baseless it might sound.

"If you do anything to him, I'll..."

"You'll *what?*" she snorted.

She had me there. I couldn't think of a single thing I could do, but she didn't have to know that.

"You just wait."

"Oh, I *will.* With baited breath."

She was practically oozing self-satisfaction. *Fine, then, Lady Dark Heart. Believe you've won for now.* I'd let her have her fun.

I felt a certain satisfaction as I walked away, knowing I would expose her when I returned that evening. I didn't know what I was going to say or how I was going to make him believe me, but I would somehow find a way to discredit her, to tarnish her reputation, or whatever was left of it, as soundly as she had destroyed mine. Nothing would stop me, not even Stefan...or whatever was left of *him*...

Good Lord, why should I think such a dreadful thing?! I shook my head and continued walking, not wishing to indulge in such morbid thinking for even a second more. She wasn't a cannibal, after all. Yet the feeling of unease still gnawed at my heart.

I had nearly reached the village, but something made me look back toward the hovel. Sorina was still standing there, looking secretive. She reached out her hand and raked her nails across the door. Seconds later, the door opened inward and Stefan, now wearing an evening suit, peered out. He looked about, no doubt to make certain I had finally gone, then linked arms with Sorina and walked off in the direction of the Acropolis.

Atop the hill, light flickered off the pillars of the Parthenon—flames from a bonfire, most probably. I heard the sound of voices as I leaned closer. I could just make out some cries, though faint, but they didn't sound like cries of alarm. Rather, it sounded as though some revelry was taking place high up on that hill toward which my friend and Sorina Boroi were now heading.

Maybe the Greeks celebrated a version of Walpurgis Night, for all I knew...or cared. If he wanted to debauch himself with that night crow, so be it. I was tired of spending every waking moment worrying about Sorina Boroi. There would be time enough to deal with her later.

‡

"Drink, drink!"

I took the glass from the man and downed the drink in a gulp. Fire scorched my throat and I yelped, my eyes beginning to water.

"More, more!" he said, handing me another glass.

"No! That's quite enough," I managed to croak. I was already on fire. One more shot of that liquid heat and I would flame up like a torch.

I bid the man good evening and walked on through the village. There was some sort of festival going on. Children ran through the streets chasing each other, while their fathers and brothers entertained everyone by playing the stringed instruments I had learned were called tambouras.

Someone pushed me from behind, and I was thrust into the midst of the parade. *Well, when in Greece...* I followed along, dancing in turn—and probably looking like a fool—for what must have been a mile as the parade continued to wend through the streets.

As we passed a tavern, one of the children stopped and handed me a kebab and a hunk of that peculiar white cheese I had eaten on the boat.

"Efharisto," I said, "Thank you."

The parade showed no signs of stopping, but my legs were wearing out, so I excused myself and settled down at one of the wooden tables in the small courtyard outside the tavern. How long I stayed there eating my little feast and watching the stream of locals dance on by, I don't know, but when I pulled out my watch, it read a quarter to midnight. I had been gallivanting for over five hours.

It would take me at least twenty minutes to trek back to our hovel. I wasn't expecting Stefan to have returned, but on the unlikely chance he was there, I didn't care if he was sleeping or not. I would fill his ears with what I thought of him and Sorina Boroi.

I took one last look at the parade, then set out for home.

The flames near the Acropolis had died. I cocked an ear, but didn't have to strain this time, for there were no longer any revelers at the top of that hill. Stefan must surely be back by now, unless Sorina Boroi had spirited him off to yet another den of iniquity.

I retrieved my key from my pocket and slid it into the lock. When I tried to push against the door, it held fast. "Stefan," I called out. "Stefan, are you there?" I asked a minute later. Still, there was no answer.

I shouldered my weight against the door again. Nothing. It had been jammed.

I was ready to try the hole that served for a window at the back of the hovel, when I heard a sound coming from within—a low sibilant sound, like the hiss of a snake...a very *large* snake.

Stefan was in there with that snake. A boa constrictor, an anaconda—whatever other foul kind of snake that was indigenous to Greece could have been in there strangling the life out of him.

I jangled the lock, making a terrific noise that surely must have caught its attention—drawn it away from Stefan and turned it toward me. But nothing happened.

Then I heard the sound again. This time it was different, more defined, almost human—a low, rasping voice, sounding as though it were struggling to speak, as though its vocal chords had been damaged and it couldn't talk above a whisper.

I tried to swallow. My mouth felt as though it was full of sand. I pressed my ear against the door and heard the voice hiss a name...*Zigmund.*

A gurgling sound snaked through the wood beneath my fingers. My hands clenched, causing splinters to embed in my skin. I could care less about the pain. My only thought was that this couldn't be happening.

Snakes could not laugh.

Stefan was in there with that horror, that gurgling horror, whatever it was.

I threw my weight against the door and it gave way. The blackness disoriented me; the room was so dark, I couldn't see a foot in front of my face. Not even the moonlight pierced through the window on the other side of the room.

I took a step forward. My foot knocked against something on the floor—something that gave off a low moan. Startled, I sprang back, colliding with the overturned crate that served as a night table. The din that erupted was enough to wake the entire village. I slid to the floor, trying to conceal myself behind the crate, but the creature either did not hear the noise or was too busy to care.

I reached up my trembling hand until my fingers closed around the neck of the oil lamp resting on the crate beside the bed. Slowly, carefully, I settled the lamp next to me, then reached up once more in search of the matches.

There were none.

Lovely. They had been there that afternoon. Where the devil had they gone? I was ready to give up, but then I realized they might have been knocked to the floor. When I stretched out my hand, one of the matches snapped beneath the weight of my probing fingers.

The snuffling above me ceased at once. My arm remained stretched out. If I tried to move, the rustling of my clothes would give me away. This was an entirely new problem. The thing seemed not to care about loud sounds, but make the tiniest of noises and it would go berserk.

I could hear it moving...coming closer...leaning down from its perch on Stefan's bed. Stefan's bed! He couldn't still be in it? The thing on the floor...no, that was definitely *not* Stefan.

A gust of hot air was expelled against my arm. I had to bite my lip to keep from choking. The stench of the thing's breath was unbearable—like the dead earth of centuries-old graves.

There was no wind that night, but something was ruffling my hair. *Oh, yes, that's wonderful,* I thought. The thing was sniffing inches above my head, but the room was too dark for me to discern anything. Why hadn't it attacked me yet? Was it blind? The thought gave me courage, for if it was, I had an advantage, though the thing sounded as big as a bear.

I slouched lower and drew my knees to my chest, trying to tighten myself into a ball. The match was between my fingers. I drew my arm in as slowly as I could. For some reason, the thing jerked away at that moment and went back to its incessant hissing, cooing over whatever it had trapped beneath itself in the bed.

I didn't know what I hoped to accomplish by lighting the lamp. I suppose I was counting on the thing being scared of light. Whatever happened, I had to know what was there, no matter what, yet to strike the match and light the lamp before being seen was surely impossible. I had no weapon, save the lamp, which I already planned to hurl at the thing if the situation turned desperate. But what good would that do? Stun it for an instant, during which I would have to run like mad to escape before the thing realized it should be giving chase? Ridiculous.

As if it had read my thoughts, the thing began to laugh low in its throat.

That decided me. This mocking devil would be unmasked now. No more waiting, no more fear.

I struck the match, threw it inside the lamp, then wrenched the turner up as far as it would go and leaped to my feet.

The light blazed forth so strongly I was blinded for a moment. I lowered the lamp to lessen the glare, and that's when I saw what I was up against for the first time.

It had started to screech—a terrible, high-pitched yowl—yet I was too petrified to run and could do nothing but stare at it in horror. It must have been a man at one time, but now it was plague-ravaged beyond distinction. Although it was still screeching, its tongue seemed to have a life of its own. The barbs encircling the tongue lashed against the thing's face with each jerky movement—puncturing holes in its cheeks from which blood dripped forth. I swallowed hard to keep the bile from rising in my throat, but still I could not turn away.

Sores split the death white skin of its face. There was a bulge underneath the cloak where its stomach should have been, a bulge that was much too large. This was not fat. The thing was engorged and had most probably just fed—on whom, I did not even want to venture a guess.

Red-rimmed eyes stared out from that pale mask that looked more like a skull than a face. The cowl of its cloak had fallen back to reveal a baldpate with more of the same oozing gouges. They weren't as fresh as the ones on its face; something must have stabbed it in defense during an attack some weeks ago. But from the way the tongue lashed and whipped about, I suspected that the creature, in a moment of desperation, must have been driven mad by its own bloodlust and inflicted the wounds on itself.

I swung the lamp toward the creature's face; it screeched and reeled backward, tumbling off the bed.

And that's when I heard Stefan groan. He had been on the bed...being crushed to death underneath the monster's weight.

Madness and terror took hold. I threw the lamp at the thing's head. There was a burst of flames and a horrid scream as the lamp shattered against the creature's face. Shards of glass imbedded in its head, its flesh hanging in strands. A huge piece of the glass protruded from its cheek, which was bubbling underneath the flames like melting wax. Nothing could have survived those injuries. The thing would surely collapse in a dead heap, but all my assumptions were wrong tonight. The beast yanked the shard from its cheek, and its skin began to change.

The flames flickered then disappeared, seemingly sucked into the creature's face. A ripple broke out underneath the ravaged surface...and then the skin stretched until it had grown taut over the wound. I blinked in disbelief, for the cheek had been restored—becoming as smooth as if there had never been an injury. The horror of this transformation was too great for me to fathom. Why should the self-inflicted gouges remain, yet the cheek I had nearly burnt off heal at will?

I now had nothing left with which to defend myself. If the thing wanted me, it would get me. But I wasn't going to let it attack Stefan again. If it wanted *him*, it would have to take us both. I balled up my fists and advanced.

I don't know if it was because it had used up all its strength to heal itself, or because it actually was as terrified of me as I was of it, but all the fight seemed to go out of the creature the moment I took that first step toward it.

The barbed tongue shot out of its open maw. Was this a prelude to attack or one last show of bravado? The creature's eyes darted to the right. Salvation was only a few feet away. I couldn't cut it off from the opening in the wall, and the creature knew it. In one wild leap, the beast yanked the cowl down over its head and thrust itself through the window.

I heard it screeching long after it had loped off. I had already wasted enough time worrying over something that I'd never, *hopefully*, encounter again. My concern was all for Stefan now.

I leaned over him and tore open what was left of his shirt. Large, purple blotches bruised his torso. A thin red gash ran down the middle of his chest. On closer inspection, I saw that it was thankfully only a surface scratch. *But still...*

I reached for his wrist, feeling for a pulse, but there was none. He couldn't be gone. I refused to believe it.

I looked around for something with which to revive him—water, sal volatile, spirits, anything—but there was nothing in this blasted hovel.

"Stefan, Stefan!" I shouted, shaking him by the shoulders. "Wake up! You are not dead, do you hear me?! You are *not* dead!" I slapped him. Nothing I did produced any signs of life in him. Hot tears burned my eyes, but I refused to give in. Not yet. Not now, even though I knew the battle had been lost and my best friend was gone.

I pounded his chest, trying to revive his heart, but that didn't work either. My hands shook uncontrollably as I tried to lift his body. What was I hoping to do, raise Lazarus from the dead?

I'd come too late.

I released my grasp and let him slump down upon the pillow.

He couldn't be gone. He wasn't supposed to die, not like this at any rate. How could he go now before we had even had a chance to really live? I shuddered, for wasn't that what had caused all our trouble? Our desire to live? To forsake all caution and strike out on our own? I choked on the sob in my throat. Now my brother was dead...what good was freedom if it got you killed?

I felt nauseous. My reason was slipping away. I couldn't lose control now, yet what need had I to keep up the pretense any longer?

I was alone.

I turned away from the lifeless body of my best friend and buried my face in my hands.

Tears had been blurring my vision and streaming through my fingers for what seemed like an hour before I heard the sound. I thought the creature had come back, but then I heard him gasp and felt his hand latch onto my arm.

"Eric..."

Stefan was alive! I was so relieved, I didn't consider how drained of energy he was and crushed him in an embrace that would have snuffed out the rest of his life had I not realized what I was doing and released him before more damage was done.

"What happened? What the devil was that thing?"

"I have no idea," he said, barely above a whisper. "We had come back from the revel at the hill and had just entered when there was a knock at the door. Of course, we didn't know who it could be, so we did not answer. Then there was another knock and a voice...a *voice*..." he faltered and broke off.

"Go on," I coaxed.

"A voice, Eric, too horrible to describe...a voice that hissed 'Zigmund' over and over again. 'Zigmund,' '*Zigmund,*' always that dreadful name. Sorina wanted to fetch Vladec, but there was no time. We bolted the door...it was already too late. It knew we were inside. The window...we forgot the window...I tried to fend it off, but it knocked me unconscious, and Sorina...Sorina...*God*, Eric, where is she?!"

He bolted upright in bed, but immediately collapsed for lack of strength. It was at this time that I noticed a trickle of blood near my foot. A rivulet, streaming down a hill. The hovel was on an incline. Why had I not noticed this before?

I struck a match and lit the lamp on the opposite side of Stefan's bed. Light flashed into the gloom. My eyes followed the stream of blood, the light in my hand revealing all.

I nearly retched when I saw what the shadows had kept hidden.

"C-Constantinos..."

Her death gurgle rang in my ears as I drew closer. There, lying on the floor, her throat ripped open, was Sorina Boroi—drowning in a pool of her own blood.

"E-Eric..."

"Sorina, don't speak," I said, averting my eyes from her exposed windpipe. "It won't do any good."

"No!" The vehemence astounded me. Any other person should have been dead by now.

"Sorina," I whispered, the words feeling like ashes on my tongue. "What's keeping you alive?"

"I wish I could say s-sheer force of will." I placed my hand underneath her neck to raise her up. Suddenly, my hand felt warm...and wet...and I looked down to see it covered with her blood.

"Let me alone," she choked. I lowered her to the floor. Raising her was only making it harder for her to speak.

"Listen to me. I haven't much t-time. I discovered a disturbing little s-sec-ret. It seems V-Vladec deceived us all. He wanted me to l-leave, he was just p-pretending, putting on a l-little s-show this morning on the g-g-gangplank. It wasn't t-terror you saw in his f-face. It was e-excitement. C-Constantinos..." she said, and raised her hand to where the creature had been crouching.

"What, that thing has a name?" My guess about it having once been a man seemed to have been correct.

"Shh," she hushed. A look of horror came into her eyes and a cough racked her body so violently, I feared she would expire on the spot. But she rallied and seemed to gain strength from the episode. She was still holding on, for whatever purpose, with a dogged determination I could not understand. "L-let me finish," she said. "C-Constantinos is a loose c-cannon. Vladec has never been able to d-depend on him...until n-now. He used me as b-bait. Vladec knew that if we s-s-somehow stumbled on C-Constantinos, he would kill me, just as he has all other w-women he has come across who were not *her*. And S-Stefan would have s-survived..."

"Stefan is alive, Sorina. He was only hurt a little."

"Thank the devil..." Her eyelids fluttered. I thought she was gone.

"Sorina," I said, shaking her. "Sorina, please, what else?"

Her eyes shot open. She fixed on me a look of surprise, as though she had never seen me before in her life. She blinked rapidly and seemed to regain her focus. "Vladec knew C-Constantinos would not k-kill Stefan, but the b-beast lost his head. P-poor Stefan. I s-suppose you could say he was attacked by m-m-mistake."

"He is fine, really."

"Oh, E-Eric, how little you know."

"Sorina, please...what...*oh, God*," I groaned, for at that moment, blood spurted through her throat and dribbled down her lips. She didn't have long.

A racking sound shook through Sorina's body again. I thought it was another cough, but then I realized it was Sorina attempting to laugh.

"Sorina?"

"I used to f-fancy the taste of blood, but this is ridiculous."

I didn't understand what she was trying to convey, yet I couldn't suppress the feeling piercing my heart. My chest ached. No matter how horrifying her words were, or what they meant, I felt something akin to pity for the creature dying in my arms.

"Don't pity me, Eric. I would do it all the same if given another chance."

She was fading fast, yet she no longer stuttered. Sheer force of will indeed...

"I'm not asking for your forgiveness. I have done no wrong according to my kind. I never meant to turn you. I just wanted to have a little fun with you before they took you away. They will be coming soon. Vladec made sure they wouldn't believe you, didn't he, and I was his tool, what with those stories I told aboard ship. So he has destroyed us both, hasn't he? Your reputation and my life... It was not the way he planned it, but he still got everything he desired in the end. Now you will be locked away forever, and I will go quietly into the night, no longer a threat. Oh...I hear them now. That will be the police. Vladec has told them where to find us."

"I hear nothing."

"You will in a moment." And just then, I heard faint cries in the distance, as of a mob running through the streets.

"Eric, wait." She stretched out one deathly pale hand and drew me down toward her lips. "Tell Vladec," she whispered, "I'll see him in *hell*."

As I looked at her in shock, her head fell back and her eyes, once so bewitching in their changeability, glazed over and saw no more.

I had hated her, yet what had been her life? As I removed my blood-soaked hand from underneath her neck, I realized I didn't want to know. I tottered back over to Stefan, who was staring in horror at the body of his almost-lover.

"She...she..."

"Stefan, get a hold of yourself. She's dead."

"She kicked and bit him, Eric, and then...and then...I saw...she showed me things. Things no living person was ever meant to see. Oh, God, Eric, oh, *God!*"

"*Stefan!*" I slapped him harder than was necessary, for his words filled me with a nameless fear. Who were these people, if they could even be called people?

A crash sounded against the door.

They were here.

I turned back to Stefan and was shaken by how terror-stricken his eyes had become.

"*She's not dead, Eric.*"

The way he whispered those words set every nerve in my body on edge. "How can she not be dead when her head was nearly taken off?!" I snapped. "She just died in my arms!"

"That's just it. I saw her...saw her like I'd never seen her before. And then him...Eric, oh, *no!!!!*"

He recoiled against the headboard, dithering and tearing at what was left of his shirt.

As he ripped away the fabric, I saw the slash on his neck.

It was no more than a few inches in length, yet the blood had congealed on it like a second skin. I leaned in closer, trying to examine it better, but I couldn't give it more than a cursory glance, for the mob was closing in.

I grabbed Stefan and dragged him over to the hole in the wall, boosting him up and forcing him through the window.

The moment our feet touched the ground outside, I heard the door give way. A chorus of enraged voices flooded the house. Then a collective gasp went up.

They had discovered Sorina.

Something crashed inside the hovel—the other lamp. The fire would be their problem now.

Stefan had gone limp. It was all I could do to keep him from falling in a heap on the dirt. I draped his arm over my shoulder and supported his weight as I slowly inched around the wall to the back of the hovel. No police had come this way, thankfully. I cast one last glance around just to be certain, then hobbled off toward a cluster of rocks a few feet away. The bracken would give us some cover until Stefan recovered enough to make a run for it.

"We'll be safe here," I said when we reached the rocks. "Don't worry, the worst is over. We're safe now." Stefan's head lolled against my shoulder. I doubted if he was even still conscious. I kept a firm grasp on his arm and was about to move off, when I heard a sound that stopped my heart. I flattened myself against the rock and tried not to move.

Something above us, snuffling, growling... *hunting...*

The creature.

It had returned to finish what it started, and from the look of Stefan, whose bruised skin was turning an alarming shade of blue, that wouldn't take much effort.

I slumped down lower as the creature scrabbled about frantically on the rock. It was searching for a hold. I hoped its claws would find something to grasp soon, for if the creature lost its footing, it would fall right on top of us.

The moonlight became obscured as a hand with impossibly long nails jutted out above my head. So this was how it would end... Slashed open just like Sorina.

Corcitura

I felt light streaming back into my face not two seconds later. When I opened my eyes, the claw was gone. What's more, the snuffling and growling had been replaced by new sounds—gunshots and dozens of voices screaming in terror.

I eased Stefan to the ground and peeked out over the rock. Half of the police force was in pursuit of a figure loping over the rocks in the distance, while the other half was charging in the opposite direction, away from the hovel that was now engulfed in flames.

I couldn't believe what I was seeing. One oil lamp could not have caused such a blaze. Then I remembered the gunshots. I had a terrible feeling that this conflagration was no accident.

Not all the police had fled. Two officers emerged from behind the hovel. One motioned to the other and they both crossed themselves, then turned toward the house and spat—the action the Greeks took to ward off the devil.

The taller of the two mouthed something to his comrade that I was too far away to hear, then looked around nervously before throwing...no, it could not be. But it was. Firewood to feed the blaze, the blaze that had been set on purpose.

I was still so close I could feel the heat from the great bonfire, smell the burning tinder...and something else—something too horrible to put a name to.

My throat was closing. I was on the verge of gagging when I suddenly thought of my grandfather. Years ago, he had told me a story he had never imparted to me before, a story about his combat in the First Afghan War, but not one of the thrilling tales he had fired my imagination with so many times before. This one was different, and much darker. He spoke of the horrors of the battlefield, the casualties of war, and the smell he and all soldiers swore they could never forget, no matter how hard they tried.

The scent of burning flesh.

And as the vision of my grandfather faded, I heard a sound I knew would haunt my dreams till the end of my days.

Sorina...screaming.

"I told you she wasn't dead." Stefan shuddered in the darkness. He had known, for he had seen her as she truly was in the moments before the attack. As I looked down at him, I knew he would never tell me the truth. He would take the secret of her true nature with him to the grave.

I wanted to plug up my ears, to hurl myself into the Aegean or hide under a rock—anything to stop that agonizing death-cry from clanging about in my head.

"Brace up, Stefan," I said, shouldering him once more. "We're leaving." My mind was made up. I had to press on, regardless of the horror. I wasn't going to spend another waking moment in this hellish place.

All our clothes and belongings had gone up in the blaze. Now, we only had the money in my waistcoat and whatever Stefan had had the presence of mind to stuff in his pockets for his evening out, which I doubted amounted to any considerable sum. I had no plans beyond this night. My one aim was to leave this godforsaken land before something else tried to kill us.

We had traveled a distance of some feet and had just crested a hill when I saw the creature.

"Damn its dogged insistence!" It must have set the police on the wrong scent. The beast crouched down on all fours, and I got the uncanny feeling it was trying to blend in with the rocks surrounding it. But then I saw something snakelike whip out of its mouth and knew it was not trying to hide. The hunter was about to give chase.

"Stefan, run...*run!*" The urgency of my voice must have jolted him awake. His head snapped up and he let out a shriek at the sight of the thing, then grabbed me by the arm and shot off toward the woods.

The trees hampered its pursuit but nearly killed *us*. I dodged round the trunks, narrowly missing being decapitated by the low hanging branches. I lost hold of Stefan twice and tripped once, which nearly cost me my head, for the creature was right behind me. My pants were torn, my knees bleeding, but I didn't give my injuries a second thought as we broke through the other side of the forest ahead of our pursuer.

Corcitura

The vista we had burst upon brought tears to my eyes. We had stumbled upon a train station. Smoke rose through the air, the smoke of a departing train.

"Can we make it?" Stefan asked, looking at me anxiously. The same idea had struck into his mind.

"We'll have to run for it, but there's no doubt we..."

The trees behind us splintered apart as the creature smashed through our last line of defense.

"Now?" said Stefan, getting ready to bolt.

"*Now!*"

We would have to make a mad dash and leap to bridge the distance between ourselves and the back of the train.

I thrust out my hand, but Stefan was not there. Panic gripped me. The creature had taken him! But when I looked back, I saw that Stefan was only a pace or two behind me. His legs were giving out. If I didn't do something quick, the thing would be upon him, for it had given me up and was making for the easy bait.

"Make for the train! I'll take care of it."

"Eric, no!"

"*Just do it!*" I pulled up and barreled into the creature with all the force I could muster. The blow stunned the beast, knocking it to the ground—and taking me along with it. Its black cloak twined around my head, suffocating me. My limbs tangled with the clammy arms of that undead thing as we rolled over the gravel, the beast clawing at my head. A rock hit the creature in the skull and it loosened its hold enough for me to break free and savagely kick its engorged stomach. The beast shrieked in my ear, but deafness was something I was willing to live with.

I was free.

I bolted for the train. Stefan was scrambling up the back step. An unearthly howl shook the ground, but I didn't turn around. I knew what was coming for me. I could almost feel its fetid breath bearing down on my neck.

"Come on, Eric, *reach!*"

I lunged for Stefan, grabbing his outstretched hand, but I had misjudged the distance.

I hung limply in the air, my legs dragging along in the wake of the train. Stefan clutched my sleeve, but his grip was loosening. He was too weak to hold on to me much longer.

I reached for the iron railing, but the train was jolting too violently and the bar was too far away. The step bucked beneath me, knocking me about, the metal banging into my chin. Blood pooled in my mouth. The taste of it was vile, nauseating. I spat out a great glob of it, which landed on Stefan's hand. That was the worst thing that could have happened, for it seemed to singe him. He skittered away from me, clutching his hand, his face torn between confusion and an emotion I couldn't believe I was seeing—*longing.*

I fell against the metal with a great crash, more from surprise at Stefan's reaction than from the erratic motions of the train. Frantically, I reached out and laced my fingers through the iron grating of the boarding step just as something tugged at my leg.

I looked back to see the creature's claws wrapped around my ankle.

This was the end. Stefan didn't have the strength or the will to pull me up. He was too mesmerized by the blood—*my* blood. The creature was clawing at me so forcibly now, I couldn't hope to hold it off much longer.

I lifted my other leg and was trying to kick the beast in the face, when I heard the door to the back of the train open, and watched my salvation coming toward me in the form of the last person in the world I wanted to be indebted to, or thought I would ever see again.

Vladec Salei emerged onto the platform. He reached into his overcoat and pulled out a revolver.

One shot and I was released.

Salei reached down a hand and yanked me up as though I weighed no more than an infant.

"Stand aside," he said.

A protest was on my lips, but then I saw the creature, very much alive, charging headlong toward us.

"It won't do any good," I said, convinced nothing could kill the thing.

"So you say."

"Trust me. I've had experience with him."

"So have I."

Another shot did nothing to discourage the beast. What's more, Salei was out and had to reload. The thing had latched onto the iron railing and was pulling itself up so that it was nearly eye-to-eye with us, but Salei didn't seem to be flustered in the least.

"Shoot, shoot! Fire the bloody gun before we all die!" I screamed. For one agonizing moment, I stared the creature dead in the eyes. Its barbed tongue whipped out. The last thing I would feel before I died was the sensation of hundreds of tiny daggers ripping into my throat.

I entreated Salei again, but all I got in return was a sour twist of his lips, and the next thing I knew, he lifted the gun and fired a shot straight into the creature's gaping mouth.

The beast rocketed backward so quickly, I didn't even have time to notice if its head was still attached to its body. When the dust cleared, I saw the creature sprawled on the track a good twenty feet behind us—looking quite lifeless, I was relieved to note.

"My dear gentlemen, you have been to hell and back it seems," said Salei, ushering us into the cabin. "I somehow feel responsible for all this."

No matter that he had just saved our lives. He had an uncanny way of showing up when we most needed him, yet he was also the cause of all our ills, and regardless of what had just occurred, I would stay quiet no longer. "It bloody well is your fault!"

"Eric, please..." Stefan had been given a blanket and a cup of steaming chocolate and was now huddled in the corner of his seat. If he wanted to be conciliatory, he could do it alone.

"Stop defending him. He knows what that thing is, and I don't intend to beat about the bush any longer! Tell us what you know."

"My guess is as good as yours," he said. Damn his calmness! He crossed his legs and folded his arms and was staring at me as a doctor would look at a raving lunatic he is about to recommend for commitment. "Have a seat, won't you?"

"No, I won't. Where's Leonora?" A horrible dread overcame me, and I panicked at the thought that he had sacrificed my beautiful Leonora to that creature, too.

"Though I don't see how it is any of your concern," he said tightly, "I sent her and Augustin on to Romania. Greece is too dangerous for her now that that thing has returned."

"I would love to have a word with you about that. What exactly *is* that thing and how much of this was your doing?"

"I am innocent."

"Ha! Tell that to Sorina Boroi."

"What do you mean..." It wasn't a question. I knew he was well acquainted with the answer. It wasn't even a statement. It was just the obligatory thing to say.

"She's dead."

He looked over at Stefan and sighed as though it was news he wasn't surprised to hear. "I knew she would come to grief sooner or later. It's what one expects from such a woman. I tried to warn her, but she wouldn't listen to me."

"She said you used her as bait, that your outburst was just an act."

"That's jealousy speaking. Sorina couldn't accept that I would never leave Leonora."

"Leonora has never been any man's mistress." I spat the words out before I could stop myself. Now he knew that I had been told her history. Somehow, I had a feeling he was already aware of my knowledge. I expected him to leap upon me in fury, to smite me to the floor with a single strike of his fist. That I would have accepted, but not this dead calmness he presented. To me, this was worse than a blow.

"How true."

The words stung like ice, as did his glare. We stared at one another for a moment longer, then he leaned over to Stefan and patted him on the knee. "You'll be all right in a few hours," he said, all smiles. "As for me," he continued, rising from his seat, "I must go consult with the conductor. I think it best we put as much distance between ourselves and that beast as quickly as possible. Don't you agree, Bradburry?"

I couldn't speak, but managed a nod. In return, Salei's lips twisted into what I was learning was his way of smiling. He turned and exited the cabin.

Now was my chance. I thought I had had my fill of running, but after this incident with Salei, to run was exactly what I intended to do. The creature was dead, or nearly dead, as the case might be. It wouldn't be coming back for us. But *this* one, this suave, disarming man was much more of a threat to me, much more dangerous because I didn't know what to make of him. I wasn't sure what to think, or what *he* was thinking, and that to me was far more terrifying than the blatant horror that was Constantinos.

Constantinos. It was the first time I had thought of that horror by name.

I pushed aside that thought and focused my attention on our surroundings. We were alone in the main cabin. It seemed we were the only ones on this train. I had not seen anyone else—save the steward who brought Stefan his blanket and chocolate—nor heard any noises whatsoever from the other compartments. Salei had us at his mercy yet again.

That he wanted my best friend for some nefarious purpose was becoming blatantly obvious. He had been after Stefan since he first clapped eyes on him. It wasn't carnal lust, I knew, but it wasn't a natural inclination either. Salei, like Sorina Boroi, always got what he wanted and what he wanted now was Stefan. As long as I was alive, I wouldn't let him succeed. And if I hoped to stay alive for even an hour longer, I would have to take matters into my own hands.

I pulled Stefan to his feet and guided him to the back of the train.

"Once we reach Bulgaria, we'll write home, or even to Guildy, and they'll send help, you'll see."

"What are you saying?"

"We're leaving."

"I'd rather stay here where it's safe."

Poor misguided naïf. Even after all he'd witnessed, he was still unwilling to think ill of Vladec Salei.

"It's not safe, Stefan," I said gently. "Think about it. Our lives have been turned upside down ever since Salei came into them. And that is partly my fault, I'm sorry to admit. But we don't have to be beholden to him forever."

"He saved your life…"

"Only so he could take it from me later on. We will never be safe or have a moment's peace if we stay…and that's why we're jumping off this train."

"*What?!*"

I hadn't expected him to like the idea, but we had no alternative.

"We'll jump on three, all right?"

"I haven't given my consent!"

"You have no choice."

"But what about that *thing*?"

Constantinos…again I was thinking of it as a man. "That *thing* is dead." For all I knew, the bullet could have killed it, though I had my doubts. But Stefan didn't need to know this. "Salei blew it to bits. What have we to fear?"

He grumbled, but took my hand. Victory, however short-lived, would be mine. We would make for Thessaloniki, then catch a train to Sofia. With any luck, we would reach Bulgaria without incident. Along the way, I would send my letters and hope that Mother, Roddy, or Guildy, who was the closest, would send someone to guide us home.

"On my signal. One…two…*jump!*"

A rock struck me in the back as we landed. The pain wasn't searing, just uncomfortable, but even if it had been excruciating, I don't think I would have cared. Stefan had somehow hit the dirt without a scratch and was in high good humor. He had good reason to be, too. We had cheated death many times this night.

As I watched the train hurtling into the distance, my mouth twitched into a smile that would have rivaled one of Vladec Salei's smug grins. There he was, oblivious, chatting with the conductor and thinking he had us right where he

wanted us. And here we were, safely out of his clutches—
finally.

We would be halfway to Thessaloniki before he even knew
we were gone.

If only I could see his face when he returned to find that
we had vanished. A part of me was slightly disappointed that
I would be unable to witness this final moment of triumph.

Oh, what a pity.

Out of the Frying Pan, Into the Fire

A decision made during a moment of weakness can ruin your life.

To date, I had made three.

Going on this blasted grand tour, which had seemed like a lark at the time—the time, I had to keep reminding myself, that was barely a month ago—was one. Spurred by my mad desire to see Leonora at all costs and therefore agreeing to meet Vladec Salei at the Louvre was another. And the last and probably most grievous of all: jumping off that train in Athens.

Even though staying aboard would have meant putting ourselves at the mercy of Vladec Salei, after what we had been through since, I regretted my hasty decision profoundly. In hindsight, it would have been better to keep the devil in my sights than have him sneak up on me in the dead of night, which I feared he would find a way to do.

For the past three weeks, we had been traveling alternately on foot and by train, trying to blend in with the local population as thoroughly as possible, for I knew we were being followed. We had spent these twenty-one days looking over our shoulders at every turn, jumping at the slightest sounds. I still found it hard to believe we had survived as long as we had.

Corcitura

As I had correctly guessed, what Stefan had stuffed into his pockets amounted to quite an insubstantial sum—namely, nothing. I cursed myself daily for not shoving all my allowance into my pockets. Nearly all my money had been burned up in that fire in Greece. Between our lodgings, which were pitiful, the clothes we had needed to buy, and the fare for whatever trains we were lucky enough to stumble upon, my remaining share of our budget had been depleted to little more than seventy-five pounds, and on that sum we would have to find a way to last until reaching London.

Our plans had been nebulous at best, but once we crossed into Bulgaria, we had reconnoitered and decided our surest course would be to make for Romania directly. To stretch our funds, we had been forced to sometimes go without food. This was a good strategy, strangely enough, for our stomachs grew so numb and accustomed to being empty that after a while we were immune to the pangs of hunger.

I kept my resolve to write to Mother, Roddy, and Guildy, hoping my letters home would not go astray or be intercepted by some unknown force. I doubted the letters would do any good, but at least our family and friends would know we were on our way, even if they couldn't reach us in time. Hoping for some miracle of the post, I had put the address of our hotel in Romania—the one we were originally supposed to stay at—on my last letter to Guildy. It was a foolish thing to do, but I was desperate at that point and could no longer afford to hesitate because of my fear that Constantinos or someone else would intercept our letters and lie in wait for us at our next destination. It was a risk I had to take.

Perhaps the greatest gamble we had been forced to take was staying overlong in Sofia. I suppose it couldn't be helped. We were both weak in mind, body, and spirit, and needed a respite before we were forced to become fugitives once again. We had stayed to ourselves, not venturing out too often during the day or night, and would have most probably stayed longer if it had not been for the incident with the wolf.

We had taken lodgings in a place similar to the one we had been forced to inhabit in Greece. One night, not long after our arrival, I heard a snuffling outside our door, a sound that was much too similar to that which Constantinos had made when he'd been sitting on Stefan's chest. Stefan heard it, too. From his reaction, I knew if I didn't do something, the little strength he had regained would be sapped, and he would relapse into a semi-invalid state—making escape impossible.

I had no other weapons but my hands and was dreading the encounter, but when I looked out the window, I saw that my fear had been unwarranted. It was only a wolf scrounging for its next meal. The glow of the moonlight revealed its size, which was nothing above average, and something else...

Red-rimmed eyes.

I must have cried out, for Stefan had pushed me aside and taken my place at the window by the time I came to my senses. When I looked out again, I saw that my eyes had been deceived by a trick of the moonlight. The wolf's eyes were normal. It was just a wolf...just a harmless wolf.

The incident might have been a complete coincidence, yet we were both too unnerved to stay in Sofia any longer and left the next morning.

Bucharest had been no better, but the two days we spent there were relatively peaceful. We had already decided that our main target in Romania would be Brasov. Stefan had conveniently forgotten to mention to me that he had shared his birthplace with Salei when we were onboard the ship to Greece. Of course, if he had shared this little pearl with *me* a few countries ago, I would have struck out on a course in the opposite direction. But it was too late for that now. We had both made mistakes, it was just that mine were accidental...I wasn't so sure about Stefan's.

That he had shared more than he should have with Vladec Salei, I was certain. Although I didn't have a clear notion of just how detailed he had been, from comments made here and there throughout our journey, I had a vague idea that it had to do with Stefan's six older sisters who had scattered after his father was murdered and left Stefan to fend for himself until David and Marishka Ratliff had stumbled upon him wandering the streets of Brasov half dead.

Corcitura

Onward to Brasov we trudged, the looming Carpathians shadowing our every step. If I had any hope of finding an ally, it would be in Brasov. I was sure Salei had sent Leonora to this city in anticipation of our arrival. How to find her without encountering Vladec Salei was another matter, but I would deal with that when the moment arose...if it arose at all. I even entertained the notion that Augustin Boroi might side with me once I told him of Sorina's death and Vladec's betrayal, which I was sure Salei had failed to mention. Even so, I didn't harbor any great hope for that scheme, knowing as I did the control Salei possessed over the surviving half of the Boroi contingent.

We crested a knoll and caught sight of a massive medieval fortress set high on a hill, far back amongst the trees. The castle seemed familiar. I vaguely remembered learning something about it a few months back in a book on Romanian history that Stefan had forced me to read. I should have known he wasn't feeling a sudden surge of national pride, but rather was foisting the responsibility of being the knowledgeable one on me again, even though I had no idea he was planning on including his homeland in our tour at the time I read the book.

I focused my attention on the castle, trying to recall what I had read about it. It was said that some fifteenth century tyrant, I forget who it was, had passed through there and spent a few nights before setting out on the warpath again. I could not deny that the fortress was beautiful, though it filled me with a sense of foreboding. There was something about those high stone walls, the tiny windows, and even the fluted spire on one of the turrets that made me shudder and conjure visions of dread and dark deeds taking place within the bowels of the keep.

I was becoming more and more disquieted and wanted to push off, but Stefan seemed entranced.

"Castle Bran," he said on a sigh, his eyes alight with memory. "My sisters and I used to come here as children. We played at the base of the hill, sometimes daring to venture near enough to call out to the spirits of those dead Wallachian soldiers trapped within. My sister, Dacia, once swore she saw one wave to her from atop the battlements. But she was always rather fanciful, so we never really believed her, though I wanted to. I was very morbid in those days."

"Yes, and you still are, so can we make for town, now, please?"

I didn't like what the place had done to him. It was almost as if some sort of change had occurred in him the instant we crossed the hill. What's more, he seemed inclined to stand there all day, gazing wistfully at his Castle Bran, when he knew full well that every moment was precious to us.

Suddenly, he came to life and clapped me on the back as if nothing untoward had passed between us over the last month.

"Turning over a new leaf?" I said as we walked on.

"There was never a need." Typical Stefan, never saw what he did wrong. "Besides, I'm home, Eric. After thirteen years, I'm finally *home*."

In the past, if we had ever been able to trade lives for even a moment, I would have, so to hear him bemoan the life David and Marishka Ratliff had lavished upon him smacked to me of ingratitude. That he missed his sisters was a given, yet he would never have had the opportunities, nor the wealth, nor the *love*, I might add, that his adoptive parents had given him if he had stayed in Brasov, which had been his home for barely five years.

Something had indeed changed, but I was hard-pressed to identify what it could be. He had been a different person since we left for the tour, so I was fairly sure that the change had nothing to do with the attack in Greece. I had been stealing furtive glances at the slash on his neck when Stefan was asleep. As far as I could tell, it was healing nicely, although it had turned a frightful shade of purple and the blood had not yet crusted off. I was no doctor, but it didn't seem life-threatening to me, so I hadn't bothered him about it anymore, since the mere mention of it recalled that dreadful night and cast him into a gloom so deep it took hours to restore his spirits.

Corcitura

Maybe the idea of returning to Brasov had been more overwhelming than I had first suspected. Or, more probably, perhaps the thought that his six sisters were somewhere alive and well between here and Cluj was working on his psyche more powerfully than he was letting on. And then I had a notion that rocked me to the core. What if he had used me only as a means to get to Brasov and be reunited with his sisters? Or, more horribly, what if he intended to desert me and disappear with them into the wilds of Romania?

Ridiculous. I was letting my imagination run away with me. He was my best friend, my constant companion for the last thirteen years. Surely he wouldn't be so duplicitous? Besides, if he were this master planner I was envisioning him to be, he wouldn't have been so foolhardy as to throw in his lot with a specimen like Vladec Salei. But then my fevered brain set off on another track...what if it had been Stefan's idea, not Salei's, to be rid of me? Did I really know the man walking by my side, or had that been another error in judgment? There were rumors that he had somehow been responsible for his father's death all those years ago. I had never credited them, for Stefan had been but a child of five, and what could a lad that young possibly do to cause someone's death?

As we walked on, drawing ever closer to the place of his birth, I realized that I was at a loss to explain anything that had befallen us this past month, and the thought that Stefan might have been the genius behind all our troubles, save for the hitch with Constantinos, filled me with dread.

We walked on for another hour or so before reaching the city. The atmosphere about the place was bucolic and would have been charming had the town exhibited some signs of life. Everything was seemingly deserted. It had also grown noticeably colder as we walked on and was now positively frigid for a summer evening, what with the unseasonably cool breeze that whipped round our heads.

Stefan's face had clouded over. Disappointment that there were not more people around to witness his second murder, perhaps? Enough! My mind was becoming feverish again. Vladec Salei was the cause of all our ills, not Stefan, and to suspect my friend of anything more than poor judgment in the choice of his companions would have been wrong of me.

I held open the door of the hotel as Stefan passed through. Exposed beams, with bunches of wheat and husks of corn hanging from them, crisscrossed the low ceiling. Toward the center of the room, a large oaken counter had been set up to receive guests. Crouching behind the counter was a short, balding man with a hangdog look affixed to his ruddy face. That he was trying to avoid us was evident, for he had shrieked on catching sight of us and tried to dive behind the counter.

"This is your territory, lad," I said, pushing Stefan forward.

"Why didn't you pay more attention in school?" he retorted.

"I don't recall them offering a class in the Romany language at Eton."

"That's true. All right, enough with the delays. Let's get this over with, shall we? He doesn't seem so ferocious on closer inspection."

That was how it had been all our lives. The banter, the brotherly camaraderie. It had flashed in and out over the last month, but every time it came to the forefront again, I was willing to forget all the harsh words and misunderstandings that had passed between us. If he could still revert to our old ways, what was to say he had changed at all? Maybe he had just been swept along by the glamour of the Continental Elite and was now beginning to regret pushing aside years of friendship for some flash in the pan association with a man we didn't even know. I could only hope this was the case.

The man flinched as Stefan drew near, but did not try to hide again. I remembered my letters and told Stefan to ask the man if we had received any. Stefan fired off a string of Romanian to which the man said something in the tone of a question. I distinguished the words *Bradburry* and *Ratliff*, then, when that produced no effect, Stefan for some reason said *Belododia* and the man nearly fainted dead away. He tottered back and caught the countertop just before stumbling to the floor. Stefan remained unmoved by the spectacle. Why he had mentioned his true surname was beyond me, but then I pieced the puzzle together and realized he was trying to elicit a response to the name in order to discover something about his sisters.

"Stefan, now's not the time," I said, trying to draw him away.

"Now's the perfect time, Eric. I may never have another chance like this," he said vehemently, snatching his arm from my grasp.

"Why do you want to dredge up the past when all that's there is pain? Hasn't your life been good enough?"

"It's not that. The money, the riches, all the wealth, the parties, *you*...nothing can fill the void they left in my heart. Sometimes I wish David and Marishka would have just left me alone."

"Stefan, you can't mean that," I said, horrified.

"Why else do you think I wanted to come to Romania? I have to know they are still alive."

So I had been right. He had used this tour as a means to see his sisters again. I suppose it was only natural, yet I felt used and wanted nothing more than to knock some sense into him...*literally*.

"Thank God your parents aren't here to witness this betrayal," I said bitterly.

"My parents are dead, Eric, and if I had my way, David and Marishka would have followed them to the grave years ago..."

I gaped at him in astonishment, and Stefan returned my gaze with equal shock. To wish death on the two most loving parents any child could have asked for was beyond vile and he knew it. A second later, he shook himself and seemed to regain his wits. It was as if he hadn't been himself at all.

"Eric, I, you...I didn't mean it..."

"Come, we're leaving. Something's not right."

"Nothing's right about any of this..." he said faintly.

"Now you're talking reason. Let's get away before..."

"Buna ziua, *Bradburry*."

Stefan gripped my arm so tightly, I heard my bones contract. I stopped dead at the sound of that voice...that smooth, cultivated voice, the owner of which I had so doggedly tried to escape.

Looming in the doorway, his broad form blocking out the morning sun and casting us in shadow, was Vladec Salei. Augustin Boroi, his eyes wild, was standing right behind him. The Romanian looked feral and half-mad—and he was staring straight at *me*. Surely he couldn't think I had killed Sorina? I knew Salei was capable of spewing any malice against me, but this was low even for him. Of course, having to contend with a crazed brother whose lust for vengeance knew no bounds would prove the perfect deterrent to my protecting Stefan.

Boroi was twisting something between his fingers. *No, there was no possible way...* It couldn't be, but as I narrowed my eyes, I saw that it was indeed a lock of red-black hair— *Sorina's.*

How the blazes had that come into his possession when he and Leonora had been sent off to Romania hours before Sorina was killed? But that inventive story had been nothing more than another of Salei's lies—a lie to throw us off the scent, a lie devised to trap us. Which set my mind wondering on yet another track...where was Leonora?

Salei walked toward us, his hands spread in a gesture that was meant to convey camaraderie but reeked of falseness. "I thought that since you beat such a hasty retreat in Athens, you suspected you were being pursued," he said. "I am here to offer my protection."

Ha! Protection? From his double-dealing? He couldn't be serious. We didn't need to be protected from Constantinos; we needed protection from Vladec Salei. I would have taken my chances with that thing that attacked us in Greece. At least I could see Constantinos for what he was.

"Let's walk, shall we?" he said, sliding his arm around Stefan's shoulders and leading him through the door. "Such a lovely day, it would be a shame to stay cooped up."

Corcitura

He was by no means our Virgil, but I had a feeling he was leading us into hell nonetheless. If anyone could have found us, it would have been him. Why had I even bothered to flee?

I shot a pleading glance toward the man behind the counter, hoping for reassurance or some sign of solidarity, but he had already returned to his tasks and was ignoring us as though we were invisible.

I was on my own again. We walked into the square, Salei and Stefan in front, and I and Augustin Boroi bringing up the rear. The sun had slid behind the clouds, casting the town into a shadow so dark it seemed like dusk at midday. I tried to keep pace with Stefan and Salei, wanting to hear whatever poison he was feeding my best friend, but they were always a step ahead.

Salei was leading us out of town, back up the hill toward Castle Bran—the perfect isolated spot. He could do anything to us up there, and no one would know otherwise, save for those dead Wallachian soldiers Stefan had mentioned before.

I was faced with a conundrum. I couldn't desert Stefan, but getting both of ourselves killed wouldn't solve anything. What could I do but go along with the plan and pray Salei's intentions were honorable? The fact that he seemed matey and innocent did nothing to ease my worries. He was a master of dissembling, with moods as changeable as the wind.

The nagging suspicion that Vladec Salei wasn't all he seemed continued to eat away at me. I had to draw his history from him no matter what. Who knew? It might very well prove to be the last bit of knowledge I learned before he sent me to my death.

We had nearly passed beyond the center of town when I looked back and caught sight of a girl loitering in the middle of the square. From what I could see, she was beautiful and looked to be about my age or a few years older. I discerned a pair of large, emerald green eyes set deep within her face. A scarf had been tied around her hair, but the unruly mass of auburn curls would not be contained and several strands had come loose. The girl was striking, and I couldn't shake the feeling I had seen her before. There was something about the way her nose turned up at the tip that reminded me of someone...and also the quizzical way she tilted her head to one side as she noticed I was looking at her.

A mad urge to make her acquaintance seized me then. I had no idea how I would press my suit, or why I should even have a suit. I suppose I was desperate for an ally, even though I had not the slightest notion what help this girl could give me against the likes of Vladec Salei and Augustin Boroi.

I had settled on the idea, but Salei must have noticed I was gawking, for he shouted to me to keep pace and herded us on. Not that I really should have even considered dawdling. Augustin Boroi had been casting death-glances at me all morning. I didn't know what he'd do if Stefan and Salei left me alone with him.

Just then, the Boroi excrescence hovered into my sightline. I thought the girl was going to die of fright. The change on her face was awful. I knew at once this was not the first time she had clapped eyes on him.

He was leering at her, taunting her, daring her to run away. And he succeeded. The shock of seeing him again, looking at her in that suggestive manner, must have been too great, and she darted off as though the devil himself were at her heels.

For his part, I knew his intention had been to make his presence felt, both as a warning to me and as some sadistic show of power to the girl. I wanted to wipe that self-satisfied smirk off his face, but could think of nothing wilting to say. This certainly wasn't the behavior of a man who had just lost his sister. Then again, Augustin Boroi was as much a paradox as Sorina had been. I gave up trying to understand his ways and walked on.

After a few paces, curiosity got the better of me and I looked back, hoping to see some glimpse of the girl. A movement at the doorway of one of the stores betrayed her presence. She looked around before attempting to set foot outside the door, presumably to make certain her tormentor was out of sight, then bravely stepped out into the square again. Poor thing. I would have to remember to mention her to Stefan.

Inexplicably, Augustin Boroi chose that moment to head back toward the town. He hadn't seen the girl, but I had the unsettling feeling he sensed she had returned. What he would do if he saw her, I didn't even want to imagine. And so I did the unthinkable. I reached out and pushed him ahead of me, saying in response to his furious protestations that the morning was waning and if we had any hope of reaching Castle Bran in time to enjoy the view, we'd have to hurry.

I was getting my fill of danger because of women. It had been this way ever since we reached Paris. First Leonora, then Sorina, now this girl whose name I didn't even know. And if Augustin hadn't hated me before, he certainly did now, for I had interfered with whatever he'd been planning to do to that girl.

He looked as though he was about to boil over and inflict some sort of wrath on me. I had no intention of being at his mercy for the remainder of the journey, so I jogged a few paces and was finally able to catch up with Salei and Stefan. We walked on in silence for a time, the two of them continuing to chat in their matey, effortless way, while my mind ranged over why in the world we should be going to visit Castle Bran, an hour away from civilization.

"So, Vladec," I said as nonchalantly as I could, "what do you think that thing that attacked us in Greece was?"

"A madman, no doubt."

"A madman, is that all?"

"Of course, what else could it be?"

I could think of a hundred and one other things it could be, and all of them were irrational. Nevertheless, I pressed on, determined to trap Mr. Unflappable into revealing himself. "And what do you make of that name it kept repeating over and over...*Zigmund.*"

At the mention of the name, Salei's lips twitched slightly. Though it was only a small sign, I could tell my questions, and the repeating of that mysterious name, irked him.

"Undoubtedly the name of some poor unfortunate it killed," he said dismissively.

"Or *you* killed," I muttered.

"What did you say?"

Melika Dannese Lux

"It's getting a bit chilled," I said quickly, wrapping my arms around myself for good measure.

"*Yes...*" He eyed me suspiciously, then turned back to Stefan and walked on.

As we crested the hill, Castle Bran came into view once more. Its forbidding visage disturbed me. I couldn't put a name to my fear, but something about the place made me want to run for my life in the opposite direction.

"This castle holds many memories for me," Salei said, gazing almost longingly at the fortress. "And does it hold the same for you, my young friend?"

"Indeed it does," said Stefan, becoming more animated than I had seen him in weeks. "My six sisters and I used to play at the base of the castle for hours on end when we were children. I was telling Eric how we used to call out to the spirits within, daring them to take us away."

"I'm sure they loved that," Salei said wistfully. I wasn't sure if he meant the dead soldiers or Stefan's sisters. "Tell me about these sisters of yours."

"There's not much to tell. I was only five when we parted. But I remember they were lovely."

Lovely my eye. If they were so lovely, they wouldn't have deserted him when his father was murdered.

"Ruxandra was the ringleader, the most beautiful of them all," Stefan continued, "but Magdalena declared herself our queen and used to lord it over us. Dacia and Irina were so close in age they were practically twins—and acted like it. They shared some sort of secret bond and kept to themselves. They were always off somewhere in the woods, larking about like sprites. Olga was the grounded one, the *sensible* one. She didn't approve of our games. Said we were enticing the occult and would pay for our unhealthy curiosity one day. And as for Nadia..." Here Stefan broke off and pretended to shield his eyes from the sun. It was another of his gestures that I'd grown accustomed to over the course of our lives. He would have rather died than let anyone, especially Salei, witness such sentimentality.

The only thing I knew about Nadia was that there was some great tragedy surrounding their parting. It was Nadia who had been at Stefan's side when their father was murdered.

"Nadia is dead to me, her story is no longer important," he said quietly. And that was the end of it, or so I thought.

"It must have been awful to be dragged away from her," Salei continued doggedly.

That simple statement lit a spark in Stefan's eyes, and they shone with a malignancy that was frightful to behold. If anything could have been a deterrent to this conversation, that look was it, but Vladec Salei didn't seem to notice.

When Stefan did not answer, Salei let forth a booming laugh and said something to him in Romanian, which seemed to lighten my friend's mood. Salei continued laughing and Stefan joined in, while I sat in silence, disgusted by their falseness and changeability, and Augustin Boroi stood off at a distance, muttering to himself and still savaging the lock of his dead sister's hair.

"Come, it grows late," he said, guiding Stefan back toward town. "We will talk further at the hotel. Perhaps one night we can come back here and see it in the light of the full moon. I promise you, there is nothing more glorious."

"That would be wonderful."

"Someday, then...soon."

Someday soon, I mimicked to myself. I would see to it that that never happened.

I rose to my feet, mystified beyond belief. I could not see a point to this entire escapade, save for Salei to wax nostalgic. He could have very well talked of all this at the hotel.

And then it hit me. He had wanted to draw the information out of Stefan and had used Castle Bran to trigger memories of things Stefan had no wish to remember. I had hated Salei before for reasons I did not understand, but now I loathed him all the more definitely for the vile, silver-tongued deceiver he had revealed himself to be.

This plan of his, whatever it entailed, could have but one outcome and that was the total disintegration of my hold, however tenuous, on Stefan's mind. If he could isolate Stefan from me more than he already had, then Salei's way would be cleared for whatever destruction he was plotting.

I struggled to wrap my mind around this mad, nebulous scheme. The thing that I kept coming back to was that Salei had asked to be told more, yet had not been surprised by the answers he had received. It was as though he needed Stefan's affirmation to a story he was already well acquainted with. There was something in Salei's manner that betrayed his prior knowledge, and this omniscience frightened me more than I cared to admit.

The need to reveal Stefan's sisters made no sense, unless Salei had designs on them, too, or worse, had already worked some mischief against them. The look Augustin Boroi had shot that girl in the square told me he at least was familiar in these parts. I had a feeling if the Boroi blight was known, surely his patron had a reputation here as well, and I could guarantee it wasn't a good one.

A grumble from Augustin Boroi caught my attention. I could tell he was on the verge of trying to goad me into an argument, but I was in no mood to truck with the hot-headed Romanian at my side. I set my jaw and shot him a look so dark even he couldn't help but flinch. Let him mutter to himself all he wanted. He would get no rise out of me.

Before I knew it, the walk of an hour had passed, and we were once again at our hotel. I wanted nothing more than to have a few moments alone with Stefan to clear his head, but my plans were once again ruined, for Salei ushered us all into the dining hall and made us sit at a large table by the hearth.

I was settling myself in for what would be a long, uncomfortable evening, when a shadow fell across my chair. I looked up to see the man from behind the counter. Apparently, he also served as the maître d'hôtel for this *fine* establishment.

Salei had on a "hail-fellow-well-met" expression that was sickening, for me at least, to witness, given what I had learned of his true nature.

Corcitura

True nature... The words reminded me of Sorina Boroi. I shook my head to clear it of the image of her bloody corpse lying in my arms.

Salei spoke rapidly in Romanian, laughed, and cocked an eyebrow at the man, apparently expecting him to chuckle at whatever the joke had been. The man looked confused and more than a little nervous, then must have realized Salei was waiting for some show of mirth, and responded with a dutiful snort.

This seemed to please Salei. The challenging look left his eyes. He fired off an order so rapidly, I was only able to catch three words: pogaca, which I had learned was a type of bread, and *Brasov's Best*, which I assumed was the name of the local vintage. The recitation had been said in a combination of English, Russian, and Romanian. I didn't know if Salei had somehow managed to get drunk before drinking any wine, or just wanted to show off his wealth of linguistic knowledge, but I had a feeling it was the latter.

The man bustled off. As I followed him with my eyes, I nearly jolted out of my chair, for the person waiting for him at the end of the corridor was the selfsame girl I had seen in the square that afternoon.

The minute he reached her, he railed at her with a savagery I couldn't understand, stretching up on his tiptoes and flailing his hands in her face. She, for her part, faced him unflinchingly, and it was only when he shouted at her the loudest and pointed toward our table that she showed any signs of wilting. What he told her she obviously dreaded, for she backed through the doors to the kitchen, never taking her eyes off us, or, more accurately, from Vladec Salei.

"Tell me more about this Nadia of yours," Salei said, staring at the doors as if he wished to see through them to the frightened girl within. I pitied the creature. I did not like the hungry look in Salei's eyes. He'd probably marked her as his next conquest. Poor Leonora to be subject to the whims of such a man.

"There's not much to tell," Stefan said placidly.

"I'm sure you can think of something you haven't shared with us, *dear* Stefan," he said insistently. The man was relentless. He obviously took great delight in tormenting people, but what made me even more furious was that Stefan obliged Salei in all things and seemed not to bear him any resentment.

"Nadia, well, Nadia was special. We were the only ones who witnessed the incident, you know."

The "incident" I knew at once meant Stefan's father's murder.

"I remember hearing of this case some years back when I was passing through Romania to gather some rare ancient texts and artifacts for some clients of mine."

"The folklore again?" I said, unable to keep the sarcasm out of my voice. In anyone else, this penchant for the esoteric would have been considered a morbid obsession. With him, it was a scholarly pursuit.

"Yes, quite right, young Bradburry," he said smoothly. I doubted it was a business venture. More likely some hunt for strange and unhallowed things he had undertaken for his own pursuits. Honestly, did he take us for fools? Stefan's father had been killed thirteen years ago. If Salei was now indeed thirty, what business could he, then a seventeen-year-old, possibly have had with *clients*? It would have been laughable if I had known him well enough to discount its truth. But the look on his face drained all my smugness. I had to remind myself once again that we didn't know much about Vladec Salei, apart from the scant bit he had let slip...the things he wanted us to hear.

"So, this Nadia," he persisted, "why should she be the one you were closest to? What's so special about her?"

"Nadia was the one I killed my father for."

"*WHAT?!*" I shrieked, and so did Augustin Boroi, who had apparently not been informed of this fact either. Stefan looked as calm as though he had just made some comment about the weather instead of admitting to murder. I had asked him if he was the one responsible for the death of his father years ago, but instead of the placid, direct response Salei had received, I had been given a firm tongue-lashing, had been told I had a vile mind to think such awful things of one's best friend, and then had been forced to endure a week of Stefan's silence as punishment for my transgression. Yet here was this stranger, this confounded man who could elicit any truth from my friend at will as easily as if he had snapped his fingers.

"He was forcing her to become the servant of a farmer we all knew would have done terrible things to her. It was the night before he was to take her away. Father was drunk, as usual. He had beaten Nadia so that she was nearly dead. That was his going away present, he said afterwards. I hated him for killing my mother..."

"*Murder?*" Salei asked eagerly.

"No," Stefan answered, his eyes as glassy and unseeing as if he were in a trance. "Exhaustion. Seven children born in twelve years, not to mention the four miscarriages. She never was the same after I was born. I suppose that's why Father blamed me for her death, why he treated me worst of all. I couldn't understand why he should hate me, though, since he never loved my mother anyway.

"Nadia took care of me after Mother died. She was my protector, my world, my everything. I couldn't bear to think of her being prey to that farmers' lusts. So, that night, after Father went to bed, I took the knife and did the deed. One swift swipe across his throat. It's as simple as that."

"As simple as that," I heard a hollow voice say, then realized the voice belonged to me.

In a matter of minutes, the man I had called my brother for the last thirteen years had completely dissolved before my eyes. My mind raced over everything we had been through together, trying to read into it, to see if there was any mark of the sinister I had somehow overlooked out of friendship. If he had hidden this from me, he could hide anything. And as the truth sunk deeper and deeper into my mind, I realized I did not know Stefan at all.

"And then they came for you, didn't they?" Salei said.

"All my other sisters fled, but Nadia remained. Until they came and took me away from her. I kicked and screamed and begged them to leave me alone, but they wouldn't listen. Nadia tried to save me, but one of their party threw her against the table where I had left out the knife. The last thing

I saw as they dragged me away was Nadia cradling her arm where the blade had sliced it open. I don't even know if she survived. They tore us apart, and for that *I will always hate them*."

He spat his last words out with such malice, such unadulterated venom, that for a second I thought I had misheard. Surely he would never speak of his parents—the only *real* parents he had ever known—in such a hateful way? After all they had done for him, he couldn't possibly be that ungrateful. He was acting as though taking him in when the world had turned him out was the worst offense they could have committed against him. But then again, blood was thicker than water, and it seemed Stefan had held to this maxim for years without anyone knowing.

"Of all the thankless..." I couldn't help saying, but my words were cut off by a strangled gasp and the sound of glass shattering against the floor.

I had been so stunned by the revelation, I had forgotten all about the girl and the drinks, but she was now standing at my elbow, the broken bottle of *Brasov's Best* lying shattered at her feet. I started as I saw the hem of her dress, for the wine had already soaked it through. The vintage was so thick and dark it looked as though her dress was drenched in blood. She had hidden her hand in the folds of her apron, but not before I saw a long scar snaking up her arm. *Impossible...* As I looked away, I received another shock on this day of revelations.

Stefan and the girl had locked eyes and were staring at each other in horror. No, not horror—recognition.

She must have heard his revelation, heard it and remembered—she was the reason he had committed murder. I now knew what it was about her that I had found familiar— her eyes. They were the same emerald green orbs staring out from Stefan's face.

They stared at each other, both too shocked to move, until a great commotion erupted and the man emerged from the kitchen and started railing at his clumsy servant once again. His display was nearly comical, what with all his gesticulating and choked exclamations, but the girl showed no signs of listening, and that's when the man reached up and yanked her savagely by the hair. She yelped in pain. Before any of us could react, the man was sprawled on the floor, clutching his bleeding nose.

"Touch her again and I'll break more than your nose!" Stefan loomed over the man. If I didn't intervene, Stefan would have another soul's blood on his hands.

I reached out to stay his hand, but Salei got there first. "Come, come, Stefan," he said soothingly, "this is not necessary. The girl should be getting back to her work anyway. Sit. There."

All the rage seemed to go out of Stefan's body at the sound of Salei's voice, and he slumped, deflated, into his chair. He glanced a final time at the girl as she backed away from our table. I saw a look pass between them—a knowing look, which I suspected was a silent confirmation of a meeting at a later hour.

"Pretty girl, yet all thumbs, I'm afraid," Salei said, chuckling. I wanted to strike him. He knew the girl was Nadia, yet he still continued to play his game. "This story of yours troubles me, Stefan."

"Why should you take an interest?" I asked, not bothering to conceal my contempt.

"Dearest Stefan," he continued, ignoring me, "I see in you the very image of myself when I was your age. Lost, in need of guidance...and salvation. I can give you all those things."

My skin prickled at his words. Who did he think he was? God?

"*Yes...*" Stefan answered listlessly.

"I cannot reconcile myself to the actions of your stepparents. Such brutality, such falseness. And lest you forget, your entire real family could very well be alive."

Save for your father, I wanted to add.

"And I know you miss your sisters *terribly*. As you miss Romania. I see it, Stefan. I know the longings of the heart all too well. Think of all you have lost since you have lived in exile in England. Isn't it time to make things right?"

Stefan sat in silence, staring at his hands resting atop the table. He seemed to be struggling within himself. I dreaded what he would say. I had a feeling he wouldn't be averse to whatever it was Salei was offering him. If I said something now...but what? It didn't matter, just so long as I distracted him. Silence on my part would only increase the chances that Stefan would agree to anything.

"Your parents weren't responsible for what happened to Nadia," I said. "You must see that, Stefan. Surely..."

"Silence, *boy!*"

Salei's voice was so piercing, I raised my hands instinctively to cover my ears. That booming voice seemed to wake Stefan from his trance, but only for a moment. Stefan's lids drooped as Salei continued talking in that low, persuasive voice of his.

"What were you going to say, dear lad? Come, tell us. You are among friends."

Stefan looked around uncertainly, avoiding my eyes, then seemed to be seized with a fury. "Yes, by God, *yes!*" he shouted, bringing his fist down against the tabletop.

I felt like I was in some feverish den of anarchists. The way they were slapping each other on the back—Stefan without even knowing what Salei was planning—made me sick.

"Stefan, it's late and you've had a nasty shock."

"What are you talking about?"

"You know what I mean," I said, and gave him a look, the import of which he gathered instantly. "We have much to plan for tomorrow, since we will be heading on in a few days' time...*alone.*"

I had intended to give Salei a jolt, but he remained as calm and collected as ever. "Go along, Stefan," he said confidently, "I'll catch up with you tomorrow. Stefan and I also have much to talk of, Bradburry, and you can be sure we *will.*"

We'd see about that. I wasn't going to argue with him a second further because I knew whatever I said wouldn't matter. I would not win the fight with him in this gloating state.

We left the pair of them alone. I didn't say anything—no wishes for a good evening, nothing. I couldn't have thought up a decent thing to say if my life depended on it. Not that I wanted to be matey with either of them anyway. Roddy would have been shocked by my lack of manners. Well, that was a ludicrous thing to think. Who was I fooling? Roddy would have been shocked by *everything* that had happened since I last saw him, my lack of propriety being the lowest rung on the ladder of offenses.

I guided Stefan toward the stairwell, which was lit only by a few candles guttering feebly along the walls.

"Um, it's a tad…"

"What?" I said, exasperated. "You wouldn't think twice about going into hell with Vladec Salei, but you can't handle this little darkness? Get up the stairs," I said, giving him a shove.

I had been expecting a small room, rather quaint, and probably without the comforts of a modern hotel, but the room we set foot into a few moments later made the one in Greece seem almost grand.

Firstly, there were no proper beds. Two small and decidedly lumpy cots had been set up on either side of the room. There were no furnishings, save for a tiny washstand stuck into a corner. And the walls were the worst. They were covered in sickly yellow paint and smudges of brown marred nearly every surface of the walls. The stains could have been dried blood or dirt or something else I didn't want to think about, not that the stench gave me any great hope it wasn't this last. And probably the most disconcerting fact of all was that there were no windows.

"Lovely," I said, "the room's a firetrap."

"We've no need to make a mad dash in the night," Stefan said pedantically, "so I don't understand why you're so upset."

"*Really?* In case you haven't noticed, things haven't exactly gone according to plan. Given our recent history, I wouldn't discount escape as an option. But I'll be damned if I'm going to jump off another train because of Vladec Salei."

"That makes two of us."

"At least we finally agree on something."

I left Stefan sitting on his cot and went over to grab the washstand and lean it against the door. It wouldn't prove much of a deterrent, but at least it would momentarily halt intruders and gain us some time to gather our wits and formulate some sort of defense.

I stepped back and surveyed my handiwork, all my enthusiasm vanishing as I noticed for the first time that the door had no bolt. *Wonderful.* Something was not right about this room, nor this place, for the look of the dining hall and exterior of the hotel had done nothing to suggest the squalor we found here. I had a nagging feeling Vladec Salei had had a hand in suggesting this room be given to us.

"I'm rather glad Leonora is not here."

I gaped at Stefan, but he returned my gaze unflinchingly. I had been so busy hating Salei and trying to make sense of him that I had completely forgotten all about Leonora, who, as Stefan pointed out, was nowhere to be found.

"What has that devil done with her?" I asked, rounding on Stefan with a fury I could not contain. "If you know something, Stefan, so help me God, you'd better tell me."

"All right, all right," he said with an unflappability that was maddeningly akin to Salei's. "There's no reason to get so cross. She's in Paris."

"What?! Why?"

"He sent her on ahead."

"*Alone?*" The thought of her traveling unaccompanied through this wild land and the ensuing countries was appalling. I couldn't believe that even Salei would have condoned such a scheme.

"Apparently."

"When did you learn all this?"

"He told me when you were stewing on the way back from Bran. Why do you hate him so?"

"Why do I hate him so? Would you like the condensed version or the full report?"

"Don't take that tone with me, Eric. You're just jealous."

"Jealous?!" I shouted in disbelief. "Why should I be jealous that a madman has taken a fancy to you?"

"Vladec is not a madman," he said petulantly.

"No, I'm beginning to think he's something much worse."

"Worse than my supposed parents?"

"Stop that right now," I said, resisting the urge to strike him across the face. "You know very well all that babble you spewed downstairs was untrue."

"Was it? They might not have witnessed the brutality their man inflicted on my sister, but they did nothing to rectify the situation. To me, they are just as guilty, and I will never forgive them."

"The problem with you, Stefan, is that you have too high an opinion of yourself and can't admit when you're wrong. And you were *dead* wrong to impugn David and Marishka to the likes of Vladec Salei, and you know it."

"You'll never understand."

"You're right, I won't. How could I hate the two people in the world who saved me from a fate worse than death and gave me a second chance?"

"They could have given Nadia a second chance, too."

"Well, she seems to still be in one piece after all these years."

"Then you know?"

"I'm not blind, Stefan."

"I must see her."

"Tomorrow."

"Vladec can arrange it, I'm sure."

"*No*, Stefan," I said with more terror in my voice than I wanted him to hear. "She knows of you and you of her. Why drag Salei into it?"

"This coming from the one who initiated our relationship in the first place," he said with ill-concealed contempt.

"Fine, yes, I take the blame. Mea culpa, mea culpa, mea *maxima* culpa, Stefan, but you compounded the problem by throwing in your lot with Sorina Boroi."

"And now she's dead," he said quietly.

"Yes, thanks to that thing—that *thing* that's probably still got a taste for your blood."

"Don't say that, Eric. You don't know how horrible that was."

"I know," I said, softening at the obvious distress the remembrance caused him, "but it won't do any good killing each other over who is to blame. The important thing is to stay united. Salei is not honorable, I can tell you. I don't want you near him."

For the first time since Vladec Salei had found us that morning, Stefan seemed to become clam and regain his normal demeanor. "I felt like I didn't know myself," he said in a mystified voice. "I couldn't think clearly. *God*, Eric, what's he doing to me?"

"He's using some sort of mind control on you. Sorina Boroi tried that with me, and she had me for a few alarming minutes, but I somehow managed to break free. Now, the thing is..."

"Hush, did you hear that?"

I listened intently. Indeed, there was a sound coming from within the corridor outside our door—the unprotected door, whose washstand bastion now seemed ridiculous. The sound, which I now knew to be footsteps, halted outside our door. The silence was broken by labored breathing, as if the stranger's vocal chords had been damaged. And then we heard a sound all too familiar—a laugh low in its throat...

Constantinos.

Stefan rose from the cot, despite my whispered protests, and slinked over to the door. Carefully, so as not to make a sound, he looked through the peephole, then spun about violently and slumped back against the door with a crash, muttering incoherently to himself.

Tension shot up my arms. I looked down to see my hands clamped around the bedclothes. I hadn't even realized I had clenched my fists.

"It's him," he mouthed.

If the creature hadn't heard Stefan, then somehow between here and Greece, it must have gone deaf. But then I remembered it was sensitive to small sounds, yet loud noises, like the thumping Stefan had just inflicted on the door, didn't seem to bother it. I pushed Stefan aside and squinted through the peephole. The lights were nearly out. I couldn't make out much, but I was able to discern a black-robed figure making off down the corridor. Something about its gait was wrong. The loping, almost animal strides of our attacker were missing. This being was too human. Then I heard a cackle and knew at once that this was not Constantinos but someone else entirely.

"Augustin Boroi giving in to his theatrical impulses," I said, turning round to face Stefan.

"It can't be…"

"It was."

"Why would he do such a thing?"

"Undoubtedly, he did it at Salei's bidding. Don't you see? They're trying to scare you out of your wits and force you to agree to whatever mad scheme he has in mind."

He was silent for a moment, letting my words sink in. "I have to see Nadia," he said. The firmness of his tone gave me hope.

"Tomorrow we'll find her. I promise you. Now get some sleep. I'll keep watch."

He seemed to take comfort in this and turned over on the cot. It was some minutes before I heard his breathing regulate and knew he had finally fallen asleep.

The lights in the hallway had been fully extinguished. The room was now plunged into an even deeper gloom than before. Thankfully, I didn't have to force my eyes to stay open. I couldn't have slept had I wanted to. After what I had witnessed, I was wound as tight as a coil. I probably wouldn't be much use the next day when my lack of rest caught up with me, but I was not about to sleep, knowing Salei or his minion could come back and set upon us at any time they chose.

I looked once more at Stefan, then leaned back against the wall, my legs dangling over the side of the cot. I don't know what caused the feeling, for the room was stuffy and oppressive, but a cold sensation shot through my body at that moment. Carefully, I drew my legs up onto the bed. The wood floor looked solid enough. I saw no sign of trapdoors. Although my fears might have been absurd, I felt much better now that my legs were safely tucked beneath me.

There was no shame in being cautious.

‡

I must have dozed off despite my resolve to keep watchful. When I woke up, I saw a sliver of light filtering in underneath our doorway. It had to be midday already. Someone was shaking my shoulder. I glanced up to see Stefan leaning over me, saying something in a hurried voice.

"So get up now. We have to hurry."

"Hurry for what?" I said, unsuccessfully trying to stifle a yawn.

"To meet Nadia."

"Where?"

"In the town square. She wouldn't tell me anything else."

I thought that was smart, given Stefan's hopeless naïveté when it came to Vladec Salei. I wouldn't have been surprised if he had let him in on the whole scheme.

As I rose from the cot, I noticed that Stefan had moved the washstand back to its corner and filled it with water so I could have a quick wash before we set out. I also noticed that the valises I had bought in Bucharest and left in the lobby downstairs had been brought up to the room. I wondered just what else Stefan had been doing while I was asleep. I hoped he had avoided Vladec Salei as I told him to, but the fact that he was evasive when I asked him this very question made me wary of this outing with his sister. It seemed she and I were the only two of this group who understood just how dangerous Vladec Salei was. Vigilance would be the order of the day.

As soon as we came into the square, I saw her. She had wrapped a shawl around her head and was holding the end of it before her face like a veil, no doubt so she wouldn't be recognized by anyone who wasn't part of our expedition. Stefan saw her immediately and motioned for her to lead the way. She gave a slight nod to convey she had understood our signal then walked a few paces ahead of us. In a matter of minutes, we were standing in front of a large Gothic church.

"Biserica Neagra, the Black Church," she said rapidly in English. I was surprised to hear her speak the language and even more surprised that her voice was not tinged with a heavy accent. Perhaps she had condescended to speak our language because she had supposed Stefan had forgotten Romanian. "Follow me, they cannot harm us here."

Stefan had told me once that the church got its name after it was nearly burned during a war in the seventeenth century. Part of it had been charred nearly past distinction, but since then the church had been rebuilt and was now fully functional and quite beautiful.

We stepped through the gate and crossed the threshold into the magnificent nave, where soaring Gothic and baroque arches and flying buttresses greeted my eyes as I gazed up at the ceiling. Music floated down. I looked behind me and saw a massive organ at which the choirmaster and his pupils were practicing an aria from one of Handel's compositions.

As we walked down the nave, I noticed several magnificent carpets hanging from the walls of the church. They looked Turkish with their weaves of gold, red, purple, and every royal color imaginable. As I looked closer, I remembered that they were indeed Turkish, for they were the Anatolian carpets that had been donated over the years by merchants returning from trips abroad.

Stefan and Nadia settled into a pew away from the organ at the far side of the church. I followed at a discreet distance. I had already decided to stand nearby in case they needed me, but not so close that they felt hindered in their talk. I sat at the end of the pew and pretended to be listening to the choir, when I was actually listening to Stefan and Nadia.

"How is your arm?" Stefan asked gently.

"It's fine. The years have been good to you, brother."

"And you as well. *Help me*, Nadia, I can't do this anymore."

"Help you how?" I was surprised she could keep her voice so calm in the face of Stefan's anguish. I didn't know if she was cold by nature, or if she was just as overwrought as her brother but knew how to control her feelings better.

"Vladec has promised me salvation if I give in." Give in to what?

"No, Stefan," she said. For the first time I sensed fear in her voice. "Whatever he promises you is a lie. You cannot trust him. He is evil, I know."

"How do you know?" he asked. I shuddered as I heard him. There was no terror in his voice, only fascination.

"I've seen what he can do. That's why I tried to flee when I saw you in the square. Augustin Boroi is no better, but he is nowhere near as dangerous as his master. Vladec has no power over me so long as I stay strong, but if I even show the slightest weakness, he can take me just as easily as he took our sisters."

"No..."

"Yes, Stefan. Ruxandra, Magdalena, Dacia, and Irina. They've all been turned."

Turned. This was the second time I had heard that word, and I *still* couldn't fathom its meaning.

"That's only four. What of Olga?" Stefan asked

"I lost track of her years ago. She escaped his grasp, but the others are lost, Stefan. He preys upon the weak. Don't let your mind succumb to his power."

Stefan was already much farther gone than Nadia suspected. And as I sat there, listening to the chords of Handel flooding through the nave, I realized I didn't know how to turn Stefan off this path he had already committed to taking.

"One day you're going to look upon a face you have no desire to see, and that face will be yours, Stefan, if you let him change you."

"What choice do I have?" he asked helplessly.

"Fight it!"

"I can't! I've already begun to change."

I heard a sound that was too strangled to be a gasp and turned to see Nadia's eyes filled with sorrow, yet no tears spilled forth. "Constantinos," she said. It wasn't in the tone of a question. She knew.

"Yes, I've noticed little things, strange desires...abnormal *cravings.*"

"Then you are lost."

"But Vladec can save me," he continued feverishly. "He said if he put his plan in place, my blood would be tainted and Constantinos would lose the scent."

I was shocked to hear Nadia laughing. "What a set of options," she said, half to herself. "So, what's worse? Having that thing come after you, or becoming another Vladec Salei? Complete with all his lusts and unnatural hungers. You'll give in to get rid of one devil, only to gain an even greater evil than the last. You don't know him, Stefan. No, listen to me. You think you do, but you don't know him at all."

"I know that I can't go on living like this. I know I can't survive much longer on normal fare. And I know if you don't help me, Vladec will, and whether I'll be lost will no longer matter. I fear I already am."

A long, tense silence followed. I was sure Nadia was as shocked as I was by what Stefan had just revealed. "Why did you come here, Stefan?" she finally said in a voice so quiet I had to lean in closer to hear. "Why did you risk all this?"

"For you. I had to know you were alive. I never thought *I* might not be by the end of this journey."

"But what of the others?"

"They were only memories before and are dead to me now, but you remained and always will."

"Because of Dragos?" she asked.

"Because of Dragos," he affirmed. In my heart, I knew they were talking of their father, even though that was the first time I had heard his name.

"Will you help me, Nadia?"

Once again, she paused, and when I heard the rustling of cloth, I looked over to see she had drawn her arm from the folds of her dress and had taken Stefan's hand in hers. "I don't know what I can do, but I can research some things and try to find someone who can help. There is no shortage of hunters and scholars in our country. How much time do we have?"

"Not long."

"Then we will have to hurry. If I can, I swear to you, Stefan, I will save you from this."

"I know."

"But you must promise me. Don't see him ever again. Don't even go within a hundred yards of him. It would be your death."

Stefan seemed to be vacillating, but finally he gave his promise, although it sounded halfhearted to me. His back was turned toward me, so I could not see his face. I wondered if he looked her in the eyes as he made his vow.

The choir had stopped singing and the organ was now predominant, the organist playing some minor-toned affair that made the hair on the back of my neck prickle. I placed my hand against my forehead. When I drew my hand away, sweat coated my fingers. I began to tremble, yet my body felt as though it were on fire.

I looked around the church, half expecting to see a candle rack like the one back home at the Church of the Immaculate Heart of Mary, but there was no rack to be found. In fact, there were no lit candles in this church, so why should I feel heat as though a thousand flames had ignited behind my back?

"*Eric...*"

The heat was still there, but at the sound of Stefan's voice, something inexplicable happened—I felt both chilled and blazing hot at the same time. He and Nadia were both staring at the door we had passed through. It had been thrown open. Beyond the threshold stood a cloaked, bent figure with a death's head for a face.

"Don't be ridiculous, Stefan," I said, my voice breaking. "It's just Augustin Boroi again."

"I don't think so..."

As the creature stepped closer to the doorway, I knew Stefan was right. Although Augustin Boroi was a master of the theatrical, even he would have never been able to maneuver that lashing tongue as naturally as Constantinos could.

We were as good as dead once he got into the church. I slid over to Nadia and Stefan, intending to shove them out some back door—assuming such an escape existed—but Nadia held up her hand and pointed to the entrance.

Constantinos advanced then stumbled back as though he had been repelled. Undaunted, he gave it another go, but met with the same results.

"I told you we would be safe here," Nadia said calmly, as though the sight of that spawn of hell trying to enter the church was the most normal thing in the world to her. "He'll go on that way until he tires himself out, which shouldn't take much longer."

I doubted her certainty, but since I couldn't think of any other plan of action, I decided it was best to stay quiet and watch.

He flung himself against the open doorway again and again, banging himself more fiercely against the invisible shield blocking his path every time, until I was certain the exertion would kill him. Suddenly, he stopped and began stalking back and forth on all fours before the entrance, glaring at us, his unattainable prey, safely ensconced within the walls of the church. His eyes were so full of venom. I didn't even want to think what our fates would have been had this unseen protection not been granted to us.

He was panting like a dog, his tongue lolling out of his mouth. His desire to get at us would kill him. One more mad flail and he'd be finished. This thought hadn't even gone out of my head when he stopped in mid-stride and stared straight into my eyes, fixing on me a look so cagey, I suspected he had somehow read my thoughts.

He reared up and threw himself against the doorway more frenziedly than he ever had before. His bloodshot eyes protruded so dramatically, I wondered what force was keeping them from falling out of his head. His tongue, over which he had never had much control, lashed about so maniacally, it had already torn off several chunks of his own flesh in the minutes since his latest attempt at gaining entrance into our sanctuary had begun.

I was growing sicker by the minute. We had to get out of here, if only to preserve our sanity. I moved to the left, and so did he. I took a step to the right, and he advanced.

I watched him, rapt, like a mouse before an owl. He crouched down on all fours, his hackles rising. *Hackles*?

Fangs more suited to a wolf extended from his mouth, and I knew what he was about to do.

"Go, now! *Go!*"

I hustled Stefan and Nadia down the pew, but it was too late. The church shook from the roar that ripped from the throat of the beast.

The chaos that erupted drowned the echoes of his howl and the screams of those within the church. I raced back toward the doorway, my arms above my head, shielding myself from the falling bits of masonry. Frantic, wild thoughts darted through my mind. If he destroyed the church, if he even shook the church a bit, maybe the protection would evaporate.

When I reached the doorway, I expected him to be there waiting for me. But there was nothing—no sign that he had ever been there, save for a set of very large foot and hand prints in the dirt. He was gone.

Bells clanged in my head, reverberations of his roar. I tried to pop my ears, but nothing worked. I still felt like I had a head full of cotton wool. What had been his intention?

His...

The simple word sent a chill through my now restored body. I had become anthropomorphic, for I had thought of Constantinos as *he* during that entire display, though he had been more animalistic than ever.

"See?" Nadia said nonchalantly. "I knew it was only a matter of time."

"You've met with him before, I take it?" I asked rather gruffly. Her familiarity with the ways of these creatures unsettled me.

"With him, yes, just once. Several years ago." She turned away. I sensed she did not want to be questioned further on the subject. "Now we must hurry," she said, addressing Stefan. "He cannot harm us at my home, either. Follow me."

She drew the scarf across her face again and led us through a door in the side of the church. A large crowd had gathered to inspect the destruction, which was remarkably not as bad as I had thought. A few stones lay strewn about in the courtyard, but that seemed to be the extent of it. The real damage had been done to the choristers' nerves. I wondered if they even had the slightest clue as to what had caused the destruction.

Thunder clapped overhead. That was too convenient. Maybe Salei was actually Zeus in disguise. Nothing about him would have surprised me now. Most of the crowd was pointing to the sky, gesticulating with their hands. It seemed the storm would be blamed after all.

I passed by a girl who I had seen near the organ. Her eyes met mine. No, the others might have blamed the weather, but this one...this one had seen *him*. This one knew.

I passed on without a word, not wanting to draw attention to myself. I was expecting Nadia to make straight for the house on the opposite side of the square, the one I had seen her take shelter in the day before. Instead, she led us on a roundabout path, through alleys and behind houses, so that we arrived some fifteen minutes later at the back of the house we could have reached in moments by simply crossing the square.

The doorway was stooped. As I leaned down to avoid striking my head against the lintel, I caught Nadia's eye.

"It's best Salei does not know my movements in this city," she said, removing the scarf from around her head and placing it in one of the drawers of a small wooden sideboard. "If he did, I'd have no end of trouble from him. It's best to keep the wolf off the scent for as long as you can, don't you agree?"

"Of course," I said, once again mystified by the calm with which she faced the uncanny.

She walked past me toward the door, which she closed firmly. I was astonished to see how many bolts she had on the door, but she, like me the night before, obviously felt no shame in being cautious either. With the door now secured, the room grew very dark. I noticed that all her windows were shuttered and bolted, too.

"Do take a seat," she said as she lit an oil lamp. Stefan complied. As I was passing the sideboard, I saw that she had not closed the drawer where she had stored the scarf. Pushed to the side beyond the scarf, I saw a large, intricately carved

Gothic cross. Scrollwork laced down the sides and the edges were sharply cut. The long silver chain it hung on, for it was obviously a necklace of some sort, was piled up in a little heap next to it. Set into the center of the cross was a red cabochon. From this distance, I couldn't decide if the stone was a ruby or not. I stretched out my fingers toward the cross but yanked them back immediately, for Nadia slammed the drawer shut so quickly that if I hadn't recoiled, my fingers would've been severed.

Her hands were still on the drawer as she turned her eyes on me. "*Sit*, Eric," she said tightly.

I rubbed my fingers, nursing the injury that never occurred, and did as she ordered. Only when I was settled at the table did she step away from the drawer and the precious object inside. I wasn't sure of Nadia, but I had been feeling favorable toward her ever since I met her. Now, I didn't know what to think. Either she was hiding something or she thought I was a thief. I expected it was the former. She had shut that drawer a little too quickly for the cross to be just a meaningless trinket. And she was a little too obvious in her desire for me to let her secrets lie undisturbed.

"Eat," she ordered, placing wine, bread, and cheese on the table. She took a seat across from me. "Tomorrow, I will make the necessary inquiries and we can start planning what our next course of action will be."

"And if we leave, will you not come with us, Nadia?" *If* we leave? I started at the words and nearly upset my wine goblet. Of course we were going to leave, weren't we? Eventually we would have to, and the sooner the better, as far as I was concerned. The day's events had simply been too much for Stefan's mind to handle. I couldn't imagine staying in Brasov forever...or was that what he had meant? I turned back to my bread, catching sight of Nadia's strained look as I did so.

"I have a life here. I have my duties," she said wearily. "Just know that I am alive and that I love you. Maybe one day we can be together again, under different circumstances."

"Nadia, *please*."

"No. Stefan, you have to trust me. I can get you away, but I cannot leave. It would be disastrous…" She trailed off and let the words die, leaving us to speculate over what she had left unspoken. I searched her face for some explanation, but that shuttered look had come into her eyes once more.

She sighed and rose, coming to a halt before Stefan's chair. "Sleep well, my dearest brother," she said, leaning down to kiss Stefan's head. Her eyes shimmered in the lamplight. I saw her lips twitch in the effort to hold back her unshed tears. I suspected she never wanted to let her brother see her cry. She was his guiding force, his salvation, and the idea of showing weakness must have terrified her, especially when she knew Stefan was only a single step away from succumbing to a darkness neither he nor I understood.

The face I saw when she stepped away showed no signs of its former anguish. The moment had passed, the tears were now gone, and she smiled at me faintly before turning to walk toward her chamber.

She had passed into the shadows beyond the circle of lamplight when something made her pause, and she looked over her shoulder at her brother. "Stefan," she said, her voice low and grave, "do not go anywhere near that hotel. Salei will be hunting. There is no reason for you to leave the house at all. I will bring you all you need." Here she paused and looked off into the space beyond our line of sight. "If you keep your wits about you and do not let your mind puzzle over things you should have no knowledge of, you have nothing to fear."

And with that, she left us in the near darkness, *my* mind at least wandering despite her warning.

We sat in silence for several minutes before one of us finally ventured to speak.

"It's impossible to know what time it is by the sky," said Stefan, affecting a light tone as he looked at the shuttered windows, through which not a single crack of light shone. "What does your watch say?"

I reached into my pocket and pulled out the watch. "Good gracious, it's half past eight!"

"Then I think we best retire, too."

I took the lamp from the table, and we traveled down the corridor to the only other room in the house. Although it was smaller, the room we set foot into in Nadia's home was far superior to the one at that wretched hotel. There were two small beds on the far end of the wall, with a table between them. I set down the lamp on this table and looked about the room. Two more of Nadia's shuttered, bolted windows were set into each of the walls and a few rugs had been placed here and there on the stone floor. It was quite cozy and would have been a nice retreat, save for the circumstances.

I sat on the bed I had claimed for my own and tried not to let the bolted window behind my back unsettle my mind any more than it already was. As I let my eyes travel round the room, I realized we were once again possession-less, having left our valises back at the hotel. Well, no matter. Nadia had taken us in hand and would see to our needs. Thank goodness I had all our remaining money safely tucked away in my waistcoat pocket.

"No need to keep watch this night, not that you were any good last evening," Stefan said, settling into the bed opposite mine. He wasn't angry, nor should he have been, but I had found it hard to read him these past weeks, so it was a relief to hear the laugh in his voice.

"Very droll," I said, enjoying our banter, "but you're right. She's got so many bolts in this place, you'd have to be superhuman to break in." I instantly regretted my words, for they made me think of Constantinos, who, if not human, was incredibly strong. But Nadia had said he could not touch us here. I didn't know if she was putting too much faith in the protection of the bolts or if some unknown power was at work here, too, as it had been at the church. She might have been concealing something from us, but she was no liar, and I would have to be content to trust her judgment for the time being.

"I have a feeling our luck is about to change."

"Well, it can't get much worse," I said as I settled into bed.

"You'll see. Things always look less frightening in the morning." Either he was becoming loopy through lack of sleep, or his sister's influence had calmed him more than I had guessed. "Let's try to get some sleep, shall we?"

"After what I saw in that church today, I doubt I'll ever be able to sleep again." As soon as I said the words, a violent wind howled outside and rattled the bolted windows. I shivered and sank down deeper into the bed. Though I hadn't mentioned him by name, I felt that Constantinos was near— *waiting.*

I rolled over onto my stomach and winced as a sharp pain bit into my chest.

The watch.

I reached into my pocket and pulled out the watch, settling it onto the table between our beds. I was near enough to the table to hear the ticking as loudly as if the watch had been resting on the pillow beside my ear. Yet instead of setting my nerves on edge, the incessant tick-tick-tick was strangely calming. I felt my eyes beginning to close.

I was spiraling into twilight, not yet asleep, yet still awake enough to be vaguely aware of movement in the room. Stefan must have risen to bolt the door. Yes, that was it. *Heart, why do you pound? There is no need to fear. A scream? Where? I hear it not. I only hear the voice...the voice...and the darkness. The darkness is coming...yes, sweet darkness come and claim me, I am so tired of fighting, but tell that voice to be silent. That voice, so faint and low...that voice I've heard before...*

"Pleasant dreams, *Bradburry.*"

‡

I woke up and did not know where I was. My eyes were wide open, yet blackness was all I could see. For a terrifying moment, I thought I had gone blind.

I tried to move my hands, but they were bound behind my back. My feet were just as useless, for they had been bound, too. I was sitting on damp stones and the air was frigid. It was still nighttime. But where the devil was I?

"Wondering where the devil you are?"

Augustin Boroi.

"What have you done with Stefan?!" I screamed, lashing about and doing harm to no one but myself.

"Your friend is in the best of hands. You will be seeing him shortly. Would you care to join in the hunt?"

"Hunt, what do you mean?" I asked. He was toying with me. His calmness sent a chill through my heart.

"Allow me to shed some light on your situation."

I felt his hand atop my head. With a swift yank, my vision was restored, and I looked up to see Augustin Boroi holding a burlap sack in his hands, his form silhouetted against the moonlight. I blinked to focus my vision and looked around, trying to discover where they had brought me. I was in a courtyard, in the center of which was a covered well. The walls were nondescript and told me nothing, and it wasn't until I looked up and saw the fluted turret that I knew where I was.

Castle Bran.

"Up with you." I had seen no knife, nor had I felt him cutting my bonds, but at the command, I found I could move freely. The moment I got to my feet, I bolted from him as fast as I could. I leaped over a low wall beyond the well and sped off down a corridor, expecting Augustin to be hard on my heels, but all I heard was wild laughter ringing through the night air. Cackling, chortling, gasping laughter, horrible to hear. I paused a moment to listen and then bolted off again, for the laughter was not Augustin Boroi's, nor was it male. The laughing was being done by women, several of them, if the voices were to be believed.

I clapped my hands over my ears and raced on. When I came to the end of the path, I found myself back in the courtyard. Augustin Boroi was still standing near the wall...and he was not alone.

"Stefan, thank God!" I said, racing over to him. I no longer cared about the laughing wraiths, whoever they were, nor did I think it strange that Augustin was not interfering and trying to keep me from leading Stefan away.

I had dragged him past the well to a moonlit alcove, when I suddenly felt him grab me by the arm and pry my fingers from around his wrist.

"Eric, no," he said. The sadness in his eyes confirmed my worst fears. We had been unhindered because Stefan had no intention of leaving. "I've made my choice."

"What...what choice?" I croaked, the words lodging in my throat. "Surely you can't..."

"Constantinos will no longer be a threat. Vladec has the answer."

"Yes, and the answer is death," I said desperately. I wrapped my hand around his wrist again, hoping to somehow sway him from this path, though I was terrified Stefan was already beyond my reach.

"For some, yes, but not for me." He wouldn't look at me. For the second time he wrenched my hand away. I nearly stumbled from the contact, the coldness of his touch cutting like a knife through my flesh. I didn't understand why I hadn't felt it before, until I saw the glove Stefan was clutching in his now exposed hand.

"We have to stop running into each other this way, Bradburry."

His low, rumbling laugh rang through the night. Standing by the well, surrounded by several women whose beauty was terrible in its otherworldliness, was Vladec Salei.

"So nice of you to join our midnight party," he said, advancing toward me, his lips contorted into that maddening smirk I had come to hate.

"Join you?" I cried. I glanced from him to Stefan, who had come to stand by his side. He was looking grave and avoided my eyes, as if he were ashamed of what he was about to do, whatever that might be. To me, this hesitance betrayed his fearfulness. I was fired with a new hope that all was not yet lost. I advanced toward him, only to be yanked back the minute I took my first step.

"Oh dear, oh dear," Salei said, tut-tutting. "I fear it will be necessary to restrain you. We cannot have you interfering with our plans. Augustin," he said, snapping his fingers, "tighten your hold."

"Stefan, no!" I shouted before the brute constricted his arms around my neck and crushed the breath out of me. I clawed at his arms, trying to dig my fingers into his flesh, but

I was succeeding only in exhausting myself, while his hold grew tighter. My distress must have greatly amused the women. They all began to cackle and jeer at me as I struggled to break free. One of them, the tallest of the group, thrust out a long, slender arm and motioned to her cohorts to follow her lead. They moved as one as they advanced from the shadows. I was able to see them much clearer now.

What struck me first was their similarity—they all looked alike—yet as they drew closer, I realized this was because they were all wearing the same type of gown. White, diaphanous fabric encased their bodies, covering everything but their arms and legs. The skirts of their gowns had thigh-high slits on each side, and as they moved closer—their gowns billowing in a breeze that had whipped itself into being the minute they came toward me—I noticed for the first time how pale their skin was. It was so translucent I could see the blue veins throbbing beneath the surface.

The tall blonde one reached me first. I tried to pull away, but Augustin Boroi held firm. The woman stretched out her hand, placing a long finger underneath my chin and tilting my head upward. In that instant, I thought I was lost. I could not tear my eyes away from the two green orbs set into her face.

No human being could have possessed eyes like hers.

I quailed at the thought and forced my eyes shut, for the vision of her ripping those eyes from a cat's head was enough to nearly shatter the remaining vestiges of my sanity.

A scream unclouded my mind. I looked beyond the woman to see one of her cohorts pulling a girl from another shadowed alcove and dragging her into the center of the courtyard. The tall one still had my chin clamped between her thumb and forefinger, but turned her face toward the screaming girl, so that I saw the horror the creature's hair had been hiding from my eyes.

Two holes had been burned into her neck, directly atop a vein that was throbbing wildly. From the size of the holes, it looked as though someone had thrust the tips of a drafting compass into her neck. The flesh was not burned in the usual sense, for the scarred skin would have eventually healed over the holes. Instead, the holes were open and black, with a circle the color of ash surrounding each one. Whatever had come into contact with her flesh had corroded the holes into a state of perpetual openness, yet they looked old, as though they had been inflicted years ago. But why had they still not closed?

My jaw shook as a shout rang through her body, but still she kept her attention riveted on the writhing girl. I heard a chinking sound and tore my eyes away from the holes. Resting in the hollow of her throat was a large, golden pendant sculpted into the head of a dragon or wyvern. The thing was ghastly, its red eyes bulging, its fangs exposed.

Suddenly, a cry went up. The remaining women had joined hands and formed a circle around the body of the cowering girl. Moonlight fell directly on their forms a few paces away—they were all wearing the dragon pendant, too.

Wild theories gamboled through my mind. I recalled stories about secret cults and ancient rites designed to appease elder gods and demons. The girl was a sacrifice, just like in the medieval tales of old where the kingdom offered up a virgin to slake the dragon's lust.

This was madness, insanity, but it was undeniably real, and I nearly lost my wits when the circle opened and I saw that the girl cowering in the middle of it was Arabella.

At the sight of her, I jolted back so violently that the woman's nail drew blood from my chin. I winced as I felt the blood trickling down onto her hand.

"Why thank you, *dearest*. How did you know I was hungry?"

It took every ounce of my strength not to retch as she licked the blood off her fingers.

I was breathing as heavily as a horse after a race. I felt as though my heart would burst through my chest if I had to witness any more of this. I wanted nothing more than to close my eyes and drift off into a dreamless sleep, but no matter how hard I tried, I couldn't force my eyes to obey me. This, too, was some trick of Vladec Salei's to keep me awake to witness the destruction of the innocent girl.

Melika Dannese Lux

"Augustin?" Salei said. I wilted at the barely concealed joy in his voice.

"Yes, Vlad?"

"I have a surprise for you. Leave the boy to Ruxandra and come join me here."

I thought the moment Boroi released me, I would be free, but instead I was rendered immobile. The only thing I could move was my head, which I turned toward the scene unfolding in front of my eyes.

Boroi stood before me, obscuring my vision. I shouted to him, hoping to distract him from his errand, but my scream was strangled in my throat, for the woman I now knew as Ruxandra had come behind me and slid her arms around my neck, holding me in a death grip fiercer than Augustin Boroi's.

Her sickly sweet breath tickled my ear as she whispered words in a language that wasn't of this earth. Ruxandra. I hoped it was a common name, but the likelihood of her being someone else was impossible. This creature was one of Stefan's sisters whom Vladec Salei had turned.

The circle parted. Arabella looked up at her destroyer in horror.

"Hello, darling," Augustin Boroi cooed.

The girl screamed and shrank away from his outstretched hand, but the women formed an impenetrable wall that she could not break through. The circle closed around Augustin Boroi and his victim as a shadow fell across the moon and shrouded the courtyard in darkness.

There was a shriek and then I heard a sickening crunch as Arabella's cries died to a whimper. Something thumped against the ground as Augustin Boroi stepped back and drew his arm across his mouth.

The sleeve of his shirt had doubled as a napkin. It was no longer white when he pulled it away.

He mumbled something to the women. Snarling, they crouched down and set upon what I could only guess was Arabella's lifeless body. Biting, sucking, crunching, gulping—all these abominable sounds permeated the night. I planted my feet more firmly against the flagstones. My stomach was so knotted that if I didn't get a stronger foothold, I would collapse.

The clouds had passed. The courtyard was once again bathed in moonlight. As the women stood up, I noticed something different about their faces. Their lips had been just as pale as their skin before they crouched, but now they were rouged. With a shock, I understood that it was not anything cosmetic that had given the tinge to their lips—it was blood.

Arabella's blood.

Her body lay shriveled in the center of the circle, completely sucked dry.

I shook uncontrollably at the sight, convulsing against the witch still holding me in her grasp.

"Shhh," she said, her voice whispery and seductive, "they needed to feed. The next one will be less gruesome."

"*Next?*"

"Watch."

Vladec Salei emerged from the shadows and gazed down at his minions with a smile, like an indulgent mother hawk watching her fledglings tearing off the heads of field mice. At his side was Stefan, who had remained in the shadows with his mentor.

"Stefan, are you ready?"

"Yes, Vladec," he said, trancelike, yet there was no denying he was the master of his own senses. He wanted to do this. He wanted to kill...*again.*

"Brother, we have brought you a present," said the raven-haired one. So they were all indeed his sisters. I doubted the term had been used simply as a mark of solidarity. Augustin Boroi disappeared behind the well and returned seconds later, dragging a stunningly beautiful girl by the hair.

Not again...

She was dressed in a gown like the other women, only she did not have the same raw sensual look about her body or face, nor were her eyes shining with an inhuman light. She wasn't wearing the wyvern pendant either.

She clawed at her captor's hands, scratching Augustin Boroi enough to draw blood, but he tightened his grasp on her white-blonde hair, savagely yanking her into the middle of the circle.

"She's yours, Stefan," he said, finally releasing his hold.

The girl rose to bolt, but as Stefan emerged and loomed before her, she fell back onto her hands, her mouth forming a horrified *O*.

"Stefan, I do not wish it!" she cried, tears streaming from her eyes. "Spare me, brother, please! I am your sister! You loved me once!"

"And I still do," he said calmly, falling to one knee before her, "which is why you must join us or be lost forever."

"Sisters, help me!" she shrieked, darting her head from one passive face to another. But her cries fell on deaf ears. Her sisters remained unmoved. "You are damned, all of you!" she cried desperately.

"We do not think so."

"Because all of you are in thrall to that father of lies!" she screamed, flinging her hand out toward Vladec Salei.

"Speak not of what you know nothing about," Stefan growled. The girl grew silent. I thought it was fear that made her cease, but her eyes were cunning. She had a plan. I feared it was a desperate one, for I didn't see how she, or any of us, would get out of this situation alive.

I turned my attention to the sisters, standing as still as stone, and something inside me snapped. What had happened to Nadia? She should have been taken away, too, but she was nowhere in sight.

Nadia gave us away.

She must have. She had sacrificed Stefan to Salei's lusts, and the family was going to be made whole once more—a family of dark creatures I couldn't yet put a name to. She had betrayed us, but then I remembered the way she had looked at Stefan last night, and the entire notion of her treachery seemed ridiculous. Nadia, wherever she was, was not to blame. Whatever devilry had brought us here, it was solely the work of Vladec Salei.

Stefan moved closer. That's when I decided I had to act. Some force within me gave me strength, and I could only believe it was God granting me a last chance to save my best friend. I willed myself to shout despite the harpy's grip on my neck.

"Stefan, Stefan, listen to me! He is a liar! He is a demon, a monster, and you will become just like him if you do this. A killer, a murderer, a lost soul! Think of what Nadia said, Stefan, please! Think of Sorina! You have to listen to me!"

"Constantinos killed Sorina," he said quietly, "and he will come for me."

Why had I mentioned her?! It was too late for hindsight. The name had been spoken. "Yes, but if it hadn't been for Salei, she would still be alive! He betrayed her, as he will betray you all!"

"*Liar!*"

I had caught his attention at last. In one stride, Vladec Salei stood before me, his face inches from my own. A flash of animalistic fury crossed his face. For one terrifying second, I saw him not as a man, but as a creature of nightmare, with serrated fangs and eyes the color of blood. The look was one I would have expected to see on the face of Constantinos, not Vladec Salei.

"*What are you?*" I managed to say, despite my terror.

"What am I?" he cried in disbelief, his face restored to normal. "*What am I?* I thought you much sharper than this, Bradburry. Can you not figure it out? Have I not given you enough clues? I admit the day walking must have thrown you off a bit, but we are not all condemned to be night crawlers. If you knew how many different kinds of us there are, you would sleep with one eye open for the rest of your life. It is our world, Bradburry. You're just living in it...for now."

I didn't have time to be shaken by his words. The girl began chanting in Romanian. All eyes turned toward her. I thought her plan would be a desperate one, and I had been right. Somehow, she had concealed a dagger in her gown, for she now had the tip pointed at her heart.

"Olga, don't!" Stefan cried. For the first time that entire night, he was himself. He reached for her—too late.

With a cry in which I sensed her elation at escaping a fate worse than death, Olga plunged the dagger into her heart. Her breathing was ragged and gasping, then grew shallower until it stopped completely.

"What a horrible thing is death," Vladec Salei said grimly. For once, shockingly, he sounded sincere. He walked over to Stefan and knelt beside him, draping his arm around Stefan's shoulders. "Magdalena, see that she is properly disposed of."

The dark-haired one gave Salei a look that made my skin crawl. With strength that she had no business possessing, she dragged the body of Stefan's dead sister off into the shadows.

"She could have joined us. She could have lived," Salei continued, undaunted. "You don't want to end up like that, do you?"

"No..." Stefan said between sobs.

"Yet that is exactly what Constantinos will do to you if he finds you. He wants you dead, Stefan, but I want you to live...*forever*."

"Yes...yes, so do I."

"Eternal life and eternal youth. An incorruptible body that will last for ages. Isn't that what you want? Isn't that what you've *always* wanted?"

"Yes..."

"It is time for you to embrace your destiny. Step onto your chosen path, the path that your family set for you. Surrender to me and I will give you this gift."

"*No!*" I tore at the woman's arms, frantic to break free. He was talking madness, and Stefan was giving in. I would not lose him, I *could not* lose him. I'd die before letting Salei turn Stefan into another bloodsucking corpse.

"Silence!" Salei was in front of me before I could master my emotions.

"You cannot do this! You are not God! You cannot create life on your terms!"

"*God*?!" he shrieked. "What does God have to do with me? Did he interfere to save me? No, I do not need God to create life, nor to destroy it. I'm doing just fine on my own."

"The natural order of life will rebel," I pressed on. It was suicidal to keep defying him, yet I couldn't stop myself.

"Your...creations will turn against you. They will destroy you in the end!"

"There is no order but my order. Learn to live with it."

So smug, so self-assured...so unstoppable. *Damn him.*

"Now you will be a witness to that which you have dreaded."

"Why are you doing this to me?" I begged as he stuffed a dirty rag into my mouth. Tears streamed down my face and soaked the rag, causing its filth to wash down my throat. The taste was sickening. I felt bile rising, but I swallowed hard to press it down. I was not about to drown on my own vomit.

"Bradburry, Bradburry," he said with mock sympathy. "Why? Because I want you to suffer. I want these images to be burned into your mind forever. I want you to abandon all hope and give in to a despair so dark you will never recover. I want you to understand that there is no one but me who will intercede for you, no one but me who will order your life. There is no God, there is no heaven, there is no hell. There is just *me.* You will be mine without my ever having to turn you. It's remarkable really. You can try to evade me, but I will come for you in the end. Have your life, enjoy it, prosper, but always know that all you do is for nothing.

"And knowing all this, I want you to remember that you will *never* be one of us. When you are dead and rotting in your grave, know that Stefan will live on forever. I brought him salvation. And you brought him to me, Bradburry, on a silver platter. You are responsible for all this, only you...I want you to live with that guilt for however much longer you have, knowing you failed your best friend...your *brother.*"

It's a lie, it's a lie! I wanted to shout, but all that came forth were stifled screams.

Stefan was kneeling in the middle of the circle. Ruxandra had joined the group...which meant Augustin Boroi had taken his place behind me once more. I was so dazed I hadn't even noticed the change.

I was choking, I couldn't breathe. I wanted nothing more than to die and wished they would end my life before I could witness Stefan's destruction.

With one last smirk, Salei walked away from me and entered the circle. He tilted Stefan's head to the side and ran his fingers over Stefan's exposed neck.

"I will show mercy, Eric." I didn't know who had spoken. The voice had been a woman's, yet all the women were in the circle. Augustin Boroi was my captor, but no, that was not true, for Augustin Boroi was standing by the well.

The grip around my neck loosened. As I turned to look into the face of my oppressor, I felt my heart leap into my throat.

The eyes that stared back into mine were Nadia's.

"Pay no attention to what he said. You'll thank me for this one day."

How could you? my eyes pleaded.

"I had to do it, Eric. I have to preserve myself. I'm the only one left. I *won't* end up like them."

I reached for her hand, then felt something hard strike my head. I fell to the ground and looked toward the circle, my eyes beginning to close as unconsciousness overtook me. Stefan was hunched over, his hand pressed against his neck. Standing above him, his arms outstretched, was Vladec Salei, his lips spattered with blood...*Stefan's blood.*

God, save me from this darkness...

‡

I woke up in a bed more comfortable than the one I had fallen asleep in. No, that was fancy. I was still in the little room at Nadia's house. Thank God it had all been a dream—a nightmare.

I rolled over and grabbed my watch off the table by my bed. It was a quarter past four on the morning of the twenty-ninth of July...two days later than when I had gone to sleep.

Two days! I leaped out of bed and staggered back as moonlight shone into my eyes. Impossible, unless Nadia had unbolted the windows, which I doubted.

I shut my eyes and stuck out my hands, using them as guides as I tottered toward the window, which was no window at all.

Corcitura

My hands closed over an iron railing. I peered out into the night, sleep no longer blurring my vision. The sky was lit with stars. I could smell the sea salt in the air and hear a lilting voice below. The voice belonged to a man, who was serenading a young couple as they drifted in a gondola along the canal below.

Canal?

Another look proved that it was true. And with the realization came a feeling of panic that threatened to drive me over the edge.

In two days' time, Vladec Salei had brought us from Brasov to Venice.

A Tavern in Venice

*T*he sun's rays shone on the canal, making the surface of the water shimmer in the morning light. For the past five hours, I had sat as one dead, watching the moon set and the sun rise over a city I shouldn't be in yet. Six times in the last half hour, my hand had flown to my neck, checking to see if I had been granted the marks of the elect, but each time I drew my hand away, I breathed a sigh of relief. My fingers had encountered no holes.

The fact that I was unharmed gave me hope. I even allowed myself to believe that the entire ordeal had never happened—that it had been nothing more than a fevered nightmare. Yet no sooner had I convinced myself than I looked at my surroundings and knew what I had witnessed had been no dream. And as I raised myself off the floor and finally mustered the courage to look at myself in the mirror, the black and purple blotches marring my throat gave me all the proof I needed.

I tossed the watch onto the bed and stumbled toward the water closet. As I passed the door to the suite, I saw the handle turn. Instinctively, I drew back, looking for a place to hide, but I need not have feared. It was only Stefan, looking more vivacious than I had seen him in weeks. In fact, there was a healthy glow about him. His thin lips seemed fuller somehow...and ruddier.

"Eric, thank goodness," he said, shutting the door behind him. "I feared you were lost."

"Lost?" I asked in disbelief. If anyone were to be lost, it would have been him. I was as healthy as a horse. "What do you mean? I'm perfectly all right, despite the fact that we somehow managed to make a journey of thousands of miles in two days. And did I mention I don't remember making the journey at all? Why are you looking at me like that?"

He was staring at me as if I were an idiot. "Eric," he said slowly, "we left Brasov three weeks ago."

"No, that's impossible!" I shrieked. I could feel reason slipping away from me. It was another one of his lies. It had to be. I had just checked the watch not five minutes before. "Today is the twenty-ninth of July. Look at my watch!"

He nodded as one would to placate a lunatic, then gathered the watch off the bed. I saw his eyebrows rise and felt a rush of triumph surge through my body. Ha! There could be no denying the date, now that he had seen it so plainly on the face of the watch. "Don't tell me my business, Stefan..." But my triumph was short-lived. The look he turned on me froze my heart.

"Read the date, Eric," he said quietly, handing me the watch.

"Read the date," I mocked, trying to hide my fear. "I don't need to read the date. I just told it to you. But to appease you, I'll look. See? It says it right here..." The watch fell from my hands as I staggered back against the wall.

Not again. It was happening all over again. The illogic of it all would drive me mad. "No, no," I dithered, trying to back farther away from Stefan, but there was no place to go.

"It's there for you to see," he said, his calmness maddening. "Today is the twenty-third of August, your birthday."

"No, no, it's a trick, a trick the two of you devised! You're trying to drive me mad, and you're succeeding." Hysterical laughter rang through the room. I did not know where it was coming from, but once I shut my mouth it ceased.

The laughter had been my own.

"Dear me," he said, sighing. "I was hoping the fever had passed, but it seems you have still not recovered. Perhaps a walk in the sun will do you good?"

"Don't you dare touch me!" I shouted, cowering behind the side of the bed. He stood expectantly on the opposite side, but if he were thinking of using some mind control on me, he could abandon the notion because I'd die before crossing this barrier I had set up between us.

"Eric, please," he said, thankfully staying on his side. "I'd never harm you."

"Ha!"

"Don't you remember? You fell into the Danube in Budapest. Plummeted right off the bridge. If Vlad hadn't been there…"

"*Vlad?!*" I cried. *Vlad?* So all formality had indeed been dropped between them. I should not have been surprised, given that they were now blood brothers…*literally.*

"You expect me to believe that Vladec Salei, who would have let me drown if given the chance, dove in to save my life? Come, Stefan, you'll have to do better than that."

"I expected you to say as much, especially after hearing what you said about him in your delirium."

"My delirium?!" What was he talking about? Did he expect me to believe this…this…fabrication of theirs?

"Yes, I'm afraid that was a side effect of your near drowning. You were in a fever for a week, raving about secret cults and creatures that drink blood. Of all the ridiculous notions. Vlad would be appalled."

Wouldn't he just, I thought bitterly. Yet could it be true? Could I believe them, or, more importantly, Vladec Salei? For one brief moment, I entertained the notion, then banished it as quickly as it had come as the image of Arabella's shriveled body flashed into my mind. A dream? Not bloody likely.

Of course I couldn't believe Stefan, nor would I *ever* believe Vladec Salei. What had Olga called him before she died? The father of lies. Yes. An apt title.

I peeked over the side of the bed to where Stefan was sitting. Strangely, he was wearing a high-necked coat, despite the heat. The perfect cover, for those who didn't have any reason to be suspicious. But I wasn't one of those people, especially not after what I had witnessed in the courtyard of Castle Bran.

"Let me see your neck," I said innocently, finally rising to my feet to face him head on.

"Whatever for?" he said, a little too defensively. He pulled at the collar and fastened the top button, making it impossible for me to see what the collar concealed.

Yet still I persisted, not so much because I wanted to see the marks I knew were there, but rather because I wanted to gauge Stefan's reaction. I wanted to know how far I could push him before he would reveal his new nature. "I want to see if that wound Constantinos inflicted on you has finally healed, that's all."

"It has, now let's get some fresh air," he said, rising so quickly he upset the stool at the foot of the bed. Nervous? Yes, he was, which gave me courage, and even a faint sense of hope that all was not yet lost.

"Very well, then. Fresh air is just what I need," I lied. "Just give me a moment to change, and I'll meet you on the street."

He nodded, still clutching protectively at his collar, and left the suite. The minute I heard him close the door, I crumbled to the floor, the charade no longer necessary. I feared for my life, yet I feared for his, as well. By agreeing to the walk, I might have very well put my life in even greater danger than it already was in. Yet I could not abandon him without knowing if Vladec Salei's hold was complete. It might have been a fool's hope, but I was not yet willing to accept that Stefan was lost.

I felt exhaustion stealing over me. I couldn't let myself tire out before my task had even begun. I'd be forced to make a decision soon, and I was dreading what that would entail. If Stefan and Vladec Salei had made some pact with each other, I wouldn't be able to stop them. And so I would have to abandon Stefan and pray that one day he would somehow find redemption.

Maybe I could contact Nadia when I returned home. No, not Nadia. She would be the last person I'd go to for help.

She'd told me something before I lost consciousness, something that I could not remember. But it wasn't something heartening. Although she had saved my life, she had done nothing for her brother. I still didn't understand what part she had played in this affair, but that she was involved was a certainty. Try as I might, I could not rid myself of the feeling that she had betrayed us, indirectly or outright. Somehow, she had given us away to save her own skin, to offer her brother as some sort of blood sacrifice to Vladec Salei so he would be content to leave her in peace.

The sacrifice to the dragon.

Yet that made no sense, either, for if she wanted to rid herself of Stefan, she wouldn't have gone through the trouble of protecting us from Constantinos. Wild speculation, that's all it was. I was making myself dizzy just thinking about it. What did I know? All these notions could have been true, but they seemed more inconceivable the longer I reasoned over them. I was just looking for a scapegoat, and Nadia was the obvious target. I suspected her because I didn't know her and now I never would.

Then there was the problem of what to say to Stefan's parents when I showed up on their doorstep without their son. The hatred Stefan had spoken against them made me worry for their safety. Under Vladec Salei's influence, there was nothing Stefan would not do, however unwilling he might be. In some ways, I thought it would be better if he never went near his parents again—better for them, as well as Stefan. There was no telling what could happen in one of his fits of passion.

I could try telling them of Nadia, although I doubted they would remember her. I wondered if they even knew of her existence. How much had they been told when Stefan had been brought to them? Very little, I guessed, especially not the part about Stefan slitting his father's throat.

Well, when the time came, I'd have to tell them *something*. The safest story would be that Stefan had found his sisters again, which was true in a sense, and had decided to stay in Romania. It was ridiculous, laughable, outlandish, but it was the best I could come up with now.

The next few days would be crucial. Within this time, I would have to find a way to work some sort of miracle. I didn't want to lie to Stefan's parents, yet in order for this not to occur, I would have to succeed in somehow saving Stefan and then find a way to restore him—if that were still possible—so that they wouldn't suspect anything had ever been amiss. I had always been an optimist, but this line of reasoning was stretching credulity even for me.

I reached into my pocket and pulled out the money. The stack was noticeably thinner. I laughed bitterly after I had counted the bills, for my funds had been depleted to little more than thirty pounds.

Thank you, Salei. Leave it to him to make it look as though I had spent the money between Brasov and here when I had been unconscious the entire time. *Wonderful attention to detail.*

I stuffed the bills into my pocket and rose, stopping to look out the window before I headed off to join Stefan. I caught sight of him loitering underneath the window, looking around nervously, his hand still clutching the side of his collar. The day was sweltering. I wondered how much longer he would submit himself to that torture just to hide the markings we both knew were upon his neck.

What a day this would be. He was growing impatient, I could tell. I had a sudden fear that if I didn't hurry, someone else I had no desire to see would come and claim him.

That decided me. It wouldn't do to keep Stefan waiting any longer.

‡

Ten hours later, I was back in my room. Stefan and I had agreed to meet in an hour's time, when he and I would have an evening "on the town" to celebrate my nineteenth birthday. I prayed that when I entered the lobby he would be alone. I could not stomach an evening in the company of both him *and* Vladec Salei.

As I readied myself, I was struck by the silence in the room. It was the first time in all our travels we hadn't shared a suite, or at least had adjoining rooms, and I took that as a sign that Salei's influence was growing. Stefan was somewhere on another floor, doing God knows what. I suspected he had used changing into evening clothes as an excuse to be rid of me, since he was already dressed for dinner and had been since that morning.

For all my hopes, the day had revealed nothing. The only thing that had occurred to peak my interest was when Stefan mentioned Leonora. Somehow, as we were passing through St. Mark's Square, we got to talking of her, which sparked Stefan's admission that he thought it would be a good idea to take a mistress, preferably an Italian one, since we were, in fact, in Italy. "Carpe Feminae," he had said, "seize the women."

It would have been hilarious had he not been serious...and had I not noticed the wicked look in his eyes. When I discouraged the idea, he had said I had a very narrow conception of morality, to which I had countered, striving to maintain a light tone, by saying he was a libertine.

"So right!" he had said merrily. "If I had been alive during The Merry Monarch's time, that's exactly what they would have called me."

I had expected him to be offended, but he wasn't in the least. In fact, he seemed to be enjoying the banter. I had begun to chide myself for thinking ill of his game, but stopped dead when I saw the way he was ogling every woman we passed by. The way he was leering made me nervous. I had seen that same hungry look in the eyes of Augustin Boroi.

I had watched him tramp through the square and had felt sick, for the transformation had already started to take root. While Stefan exclaimed over the Doge's Palace and the statuary within the square, I could do nothing but walk on as though in a trance, realizing more and more that everything I had witnessed in that courtyard had been real...*very* real.

I knew it was unwise to travel out with him again, especially at night, but I had learned nothing. I was beginning to believe this night would be my last chance to discover how great was the hold Vladec Salei possessed over my best friend's mind.

Best friend. He was no longer that to me...he was no longer *anything* to me. He had been cold and distant and even cruel several times that day already, as if he were deliberately trying to make me hate him. Yet every time I had caught his eyes, I saw in them a pained, hunted look, as though he were warring with two sides of his nature: the one that loved me for the brother I was, and the one being controlled by Vladec Salei, the side that told him I was a danger and needed to be eliminated.

I was expecting to find Stefan looking like his new, devil-may-care self, but when I saw him in the lobby, he looked worse than ever. His cheeks were sunken and his hands shook despite his efforts to control them. He reminded me of a painting I had once seen entitled *Death Walking*, and it wasn't comforting to think that given my newfound knowledge, this might have been a truer assessment than I would have liked.

"Stefan, are you all right?" I asked as I came to a halt before him. His eyelids flickered, but that was the only sign of life my question elicited. I stared at him for what felt like an eternity. After about five minutes, I realized there would be no response. He was as still as the marble statue of Francesco Foscari we had seen adorning the Doge's Palace that morning. To Stefan at that moment, I did not exist. His eyes were focused on something at the far end of the lobby. As I turned my attention to the point where he was gazing, I saw a flash of gold.

"My ill luck be damned," I swore under my breath. I would be forced to spend an evening in the company of that silver-tongued devil after all. What a night this would be. But as I looked again, relief washed over me. I had been mistaken. My fears, and Stefan's seeming trance, had exaggerated the entire situation. The man idling in the opposite corner of the lobby resembled Salei only slightly. We were safe, for now. Vladec Salei was close, I could feel him, but he was not here—not yet. If we hurried, we might be able to throw him off the scent, for this night at least.

I spoke to Stefan again. This time, a flicker of recognition registered in his eyes, and he seemed to come out of his coma.

"Oh, Eric. I didn't see you standing there."

The tone of voice in which he said this sounded drained of all life. It was all I could do to restrain myself from checking for a pulse to ensure that he was still living. "Stefan, you look...*horrible*," I stammered, giving up the charade.

"Well, I would, wouldn't I, seeing as how I haven't had a good rest in days."

I felt a pang of alarm at the admission. What had happened to him within the last hour to make him look so haggard? Days, he had said, but I knew it had only been two, impossible though it seemed, since Nadia had knocked me unconscious in the courtyard of Castle Bran.

I would have given the world to be back in London at that moment, but if there was one thing Roderick had burned into my mind, it was to never flee from a situation because of fear. And what had I to fear anyway? Just the fact that a strange man and his coterie had attached themselves to us in Paris, and we had since been subjected to terrors I had not even experienced in my worst nightmares? Nonsense! Well, that was what my step-father would have liked me to believe, but I was of a different mind.

I took Stefan by the arm. "Come, I'm getting you out of here at once."

For all his seeming lack of strength, the grip Stefan clasped my arm in was crushing. "What?" he said. I winced at the hatred in his voice. "Leave before I give you your surprise? No, no, Eric. It is your nineteenth birthday today, and, by God, we are going to celebrate in Continental style!"

He released my arm and sauntered toward the door as if he possessed all the energy in the world. He was losing the battle with his better nature, and this realization plunged me into a despair that nearly drove me to tears, for once the other half won out, he would not only be lost to me, but to anyone who could have helped him before he fully succumbed.

Corcitura

I watched dumbly as the porter opened the door for him. I was mildly surprised to hear Stefan wish the man "good evening" in perfect, unaccented Venetian. When had he mastered Italian, let alone the Venetian dialect? Stefan, whose first language was Romanian and who only learned to speak English out of, as he said, a highly inconvenient necessity? This ability must have been just another facet of Vladec Salei's "gift."

I stood there growing angrier by the second, only noticing after a good three minutes that Stefan was waiting for me to join him on the pier.

For what must have been the thousandth time that night, I second-guessed my course of action. I vaguely sensed that he was taking me somewhere dangerous, yet I couldn't let him loose in a strange city when he was obviously struggling to control something he had not yet learned how to master. The sane thing to do would have been to run as far away from him as I could while I had the chance, but the situation was not as desperate as that...yet. There was nothing for it but to join him.

Stefan was already getting into the gondola by the time I arrived at the pier. I expected the gondolier to be garrulous or start singing as soon as I took my seat, but the man seemed bent and cowed and had a strange abstracted look in his eyes, as if he were an automaton carrying out a duty he had no interest in.

The gondola drifted slowly down the canal as I took in my surroundings. The night was brilliant, with millions of stars dotting the sky. A full, blue-tinted moon peeked out from behind a few stray clouds and illuminated the water, which glowed faintly green in the moonlight.

I tried to think up something to say to Stefan, but was unsuccessful in my attempts. He, in turn, showed no inclination to talk during our journey, but instead draped his arm over the side of the gondola and let his fingers trail along the water's surface, his eyes remaining transfixed on the moon. The one thing I had to stop myself from asking him was how he had enjoyed his hour with Vladec Salei. By the time I thought up a banal comment on the beauty of the night, something that could not possibly be construed as intrusive, we had arrived at our destination.

"Here we are!" Stefan boomed, coming suddenly to life and nearly upsetting the gondola. "A splendid taverna, don't you think?"

I had to laugh in spite of myself because the so-called "taverna" looked more like a palazzo. Dozens of flaming chandeliers were affixed to the building's exterior. Everywhere you looked, from the balcony on the fourth floor to the pier at the entrance, people were milling about with goblets grasped in their hands. "Rather a misnomer, don't you think?" I said.

"This is no laughing matter, my good son," Stefan said. For that one instant, it was as if the old Stefan had returned, so jovial and natural was his tone. But when he looked back at the taverna, all his joviality vanished and a vacant look entered his eyes.

"La Dimora di Notte," he said, almost reverentially. He closed his eyes and stood there as though he had been transported by some unknown bliss. I was already wary of this nocturnal escapade, but upon hearing the name of the place, a chill went through my body. I involuntarily looked over my shoulder, certain my eyes would light upon a face I was not prepared to see.

"The Dwelling of Night?" I asked uneasily.

Stefan's eyes flickered open, and he seemed to regain his composure. His moods were so erratic that it was almost impossible to determine how he would react in any given situation. A mere word, question, or glance, however harmless it might have seemed, could have sent him into a rage or the deepest melancholy. He was becoming as changeable as Vladec Salei.

"Roughly translated, yes," he said, shaking his head as if to clear his mind. "Catchy, isn't it?"

"A rather strange name for a tavern, don't you think?"

"Not at all!" he said, smiling. His better nature was at the forefront. How long this would last, I could not say. "It is night, people dwell here. It's all very fitting. The top floor is where we are headed. Come, step lively. We've already tarried long enough."

Stefan punched me in the arm and we headed down the pier toward the brass double doors, which swung open ceremoniously before we reached them. I thought they had opened of their own volition and was momentarily startled until I saw that a porter was standing on the inside. Stefan said something to the man in an undertone I couldn't catch and jerked his thumb back at me. The man laughed suddenly and Stefan joined in his mirth, sharing in the private joke that had no doubt been made at my expense.

I smiled despite my annoyance and followed Stefan up the first flight of stairs. At the first landing, I noticed that there was a passageway that led off to a private room. The door was closed to public eyes, but the sounds that pierced through the brass told of some great revelry taking place within. I could hear glasses clanking and voices raised in jubilation. Someone let out a screech that sent chills down my neck, but I was apparently being oversensitive because a great burst of laughter followed what I had thought was a cry of pain.

The stairwell did not match the undoubted opulence of this secret room, however. The walls were whitewashed and peeling in several places. There was no light at this stage. Had it not been for the brilliant golden beam that was visible underneath the doorway of the private room, this entire landing would have been cloaked in almost total darkness.

"Isn't it divine?" Stefan gushed, obviously feeling right at home.

"That wasn't exactly the word I was thinking of," I answered.

"Oh, stop being a prude, Bradburry."

My head snapped up at the sudden use of my surname. He had never called me Bradburry before, even in jest, and the fact that this had occurred in such a disreputable place as I was discovering this "taverna" to be, filled me with a sense of foreboding I could not repress. Only one other person had ever called me that—Vladec Salei.

We walked up to the second landing in silence and were making our way to the third, when I was nearly knocked off my feet. The man sagged against me and didn't seem to be conscious, until I collared him and he came to life with a vengeance. He rushed me like a thing possessed, his arms flailing about, his fists punching madly at the air, but I countered with a blow to the jaw that sent the man reeling. He staggered back against the wall, clutching his face and moaning pitifully, and I was astonished to see that the man who had attacked me was our gondolier.

"Well, look who we have here!" said Stefan in that same perfect Venetian he had used before, shocking me by going over to my assailant and placing his arm around the man's shoulder as if they were the best of friends.

I'd heard of being kind to one's enemies and turning the other cheek, but this was ridiculous.

"What an unfortunate incident," he said soothingly. I half expected him to pat the man's hand as if he were merely a child who had fallen and scraped his knee. "Now, do the sensible thing and get upstairs and refresh yourself, my good man. Off with you, now!"

The man looked as bewildered as I was, but upon hearing that he was not going to be detained, relief registered on his face and he scurried up the stairs.

"You must be kind to these poor wretches," Stefan said magnanimously, straightening his jacket, although this action wasn't necessary, since he had taken no part in the scrum. "He is in obvious need of stimulants. Besides, he is our ride home"

"I think stimulants are the last things he needs. The man is obviously drunk beyond reason. Who knows how many more of his friends are waiting to ambush us upstairs. And how did he even *get* upstairs before us, for that matter? And if you *think* for one moment that I am going to get into the same gondola as that raving madman, well, you don't know me at all. I think it's time we left."

"Absolutely not!"

His voice reverberated through the vacant stairwell like a clap of thunder. His face clouded over so dramatically and his eyes grew so dark that only the huge black pupils were left visible. I stared in horror at what I could have sworn was no longer Stefan, but a demon released from the bowels of hell.

Just as quickly as the fury had come, it vanished, and Stefan was once again himself, or as near to himself as the other side of his nature would allow him to be.

"We've come this far already," he said in a soothing tone I had never heard him use before. "Are you, the 'Man of the Hour,' going to let one drunken reveler spoil the entire evening?"

I looked at him warily, knowing it was just another trick, this cajoling of his, to get me to go on. I had no desire to spend another minute in this wretched place and was on the verge of making my feelings known, when I suddenly felt the urge to discover what it was that Stefan and the other patrons found so enticing about this mysterious fourth floor. Against all my better judgment, I gave in. The pull of this place, coupled with my inordinate curiosity, was becoming too strong to resist.

"Very well," I agreed.

"Splendid! Come, the hour is growing late."

I watched him dart up a few more steps before I began to trudge along behind.

As we passed the third landing, I noticed for the first time that Stefan was carrying a cane of some sort. Why he hadn't used this to stop my attacker was beyond me, and the thought that he had had a weapon handy and had done nothing with it made anger well up inside me all over again.

I hurried after him, trying to catch a better glimpse, since the light was growing a trifle brighter at this stage. But when I finally saw it, I wished I hadn't. My heart somersaulted in my chest. The top of the cane was made of gold and had been carved into the shape of a beast's head.

A wyvern's—exactly the same as the pendants Stefan's sisters had worn.

The only difference was that the gems that were set into the eye sockets were emeralds instead of rubies, yet they still sparkled with an unearthly intensity. I had never seen him with that cane before, but the sinking feeling in my stomach told me it had been a gift from his newest and dearest friend, for it had been personalized just for Stefan. The eyes were green like his, not red like Salei's had been when he had revealed himself to me, if only for an instant. This wyvern was fiercer and more striking than the others. I wondered if it had been designed to symbolize Stefan's transformation into a monster more powerful than even Vladec Salei.

"So it has begun..." I said, but the words faded away.

We had finally reached the fourth floor.

I thought I was standing on the threshold of a seraglio. Silk hangings of red and gold, crimson and brilliant ochre, met my eyes everywhere I looked. The room was nearly full to capacity, with people lounging about on overstuffed cushions or sitting at one of the few tables scattered around the chamber. As I looked up, I saw several gold chandeliers dangling from the frescoed ceiling. Each chandelier contained a single candle that guttered in a red Venetian blown-glass holder. The effect was striking yet eerie, since the lights cast a reddish pall over the room, making everyone appear to be bathed in blood.

I looked over at Stefan to see if he shared my concern, but he was smiling so broadly I thought his face would split.

"What did I tell you?" he said, taking my arm and guiding me over to an empty table at the farthest end of the room. "A birthday to remember!"

Stefan signaled to a waiter and ordered the man to bring us two glasses of the taverna's finest wine. The man gave me a sidelong glance that made me feel decidedly unwelcome, then bustled off to the elaborate, mirrored bar at the other end of the room. There must have been over a hundred bottles of wine encased in the intricately wrought Venetian glass holders resting on the bars' shelves. I had no desire to join Stefan in fraternizing with our neighbors at the next table—whom he seemed to be getting along famously with— so I decided to make a count of the bottles to keep my mind occupied until the drinks arrived.

I had counted twenty bottles before I noticed the gondolier sitting at the bar, glowering at me over the rim of his wine glass. My mood did not improve when I saw that *he* was advancing to our table, our drinks set atop a golden platter he was carrying.

He placed Stefan's glass down first. After Stefan gave him a pointed look, he set the other glass before me.

"Grazie," said Stefan, but the gondolier was already walking back to his post at the bar.

"I'm not drinking that," I said, pushing the glass into the center of the table. "Why in the world would he be giving us our drinks?"

"A member of the brethren."

"Beg pardon?"

"It's a guild they have here," he said, waving his hand dismissively. "I remember reading about it before we arrived. Quite powerful, I've heard. Its members are not limited to a single profession."

He was mocking me. I could see his mouth beginning to lift in a maddening smirk, a smile that was half sardonic and half secretive, as if the fate of the world depended on the answer to a riddle only he knew and would never share.

I looked away from him in disgust, my eyes lighting upon the goblet I had refused. In all the tumult, I had not paid attention to the contents of the glass. Now that I studied it, I realized that it was the most viscous looking drink I had ever seen in my life. It did not look anything like wine, but rather resembled a thick, red-black custard. I felt sick just staring at it. Stefan shouldn't drink that. Who knew where it came from and what it even was. I reached for the glass, but stopped myself before my fingers could close around the stem. Something distracted me, something I hadn't noticed until that moment.

Everyone else in the taverna was downing the same drink.

"At last," Stefan said, eying the glass hungrily. "It has to be drunk in one fell swoop, so the locals say. Well, when in Rome, eh, old friend?" And before I could answer, he set the glass against his lips, tilted back his head, and the liquid was gone. After a minute, he let out a satisfied sigh and opened his eyes. "Not bad," he said. "Not bad at all."

The entire spectacle filled me with a dread I could not explain. And the most alarming aspect was not that he had drunk the liquid so easily, but that when he spoke, his voice was not his own. Something had changed. There was a marked difference in tone, but that still wasn't it.

The accent!

He hadn't spoken with such a heavy Romanian accent since he was a child. The fact that it had resurfaced the moment after he drank from the cup seemed too uncanny to discount as a mere coincidence.

Stefan signaled to the gondolier again. "Another two glasses of Sangue di Vita for me and my friend here," he said in Venetian. By the time the gondolier turned away, Stefan had claimed my glass and drunk the wine in that goblet, too.

"Tell me, Eric," he said, licking a droplet from the corner of his mouth. "Have you ever tasted blood?"

My mouth was so dry I could barely find the voice to answer him. "What an odd question..."

"But a valid one. Well, have you?"

"I've cut my lip before, so yes, I suppose I have tasted blood, but..."

"Not your own, you foolish boy." He let out a short, derisive laugh and leaned in so that he was only a few inches from my face. "I mean the blood of another."

"Good God, Stefan, of course not!"

"Pity..."

I jerked away from him in horror. There was such genuine disappointment in his voice when he said this that I believed he had finally gone insane.

"Stefan, this is madness," I said, my voice cracking in spite of my resolve to remain calm, "listen to yourself. What are you saying?"

"I'm saying that there are things in this world you cannot understand. Things you don't even want to imagine."

"And why should I be concerned about any of this?"

The gondolier returned with two more glasses of the wine. Stefan inclined his head in thanks, took the goblet between his fingers, and looked me dead in the eyes. "Because, my dear Eric, I have tasted the secret knowledge. I know how much to say and when to pull back. I know what to see and not see. And now that I have become whole again, I can never go back. All these things he has given me. Better than my supposed mother and father ever could. For that, I owe him my life and allegiance."

"Stefan, this is nonsense!" I cried. My voice echoed off the walls of the suddenly silent room. Apparently, my outburst had made our table the center of attention. Dozens of bloodshot eyes were now leering at us. And all of those eyes looked...unnatural. It was something about them, the way they were illumined in the darkness, as if they possessed a light all their own. Of course, it could have been the sheen that occurs when one has had too much to drink, but I doubted that was the reason. I had seen the same glassy look in the eyes of the gondolier when he had attacked me...and in the eyes of Stefan's sisters just before they tore into Arabella.

I felt the room closing in on me. My first thought was to run, but that would have aroused even more suspicion. Given the fact that I didn't know what kind of men, if they were men indeed, I was dealing with, staying calm just might save my life.

"He has poisoned your mind against your parents, Stefan. He has poisoned your mind against *me*. Have you learned nothing from what we have gone through?"

"He told me you'd say that," he said smugly, his eyes lit with a cunning gleam I had never seen in them before this night. "He knew it would be too much for you to handle, but I insisted. I wanted to give you this one last chance."

I didn't know what he was saying, nor did I want to. He wasn't making any sense at all. One last chance for what?

"Join us, brother."

"What are you talking about, Stefan? Join you in what? And who is this 'us'? Vladec Salei? Become a part of his cult, is that what you're saying? I'd rather be damned."

"You see, Eric," he said sadly, "that's the problem. You already are. This can be your only way out."

"What has he told you?" I shrieked. "You can't be serious, Stefan? Think of the consequences."

"It is too late," he said simply.

"No, it is not too late! Listen to me," I said, pleading with him in a whisper I hoped only he and I could hear. "If not for me, think of your parents. Think what this would do to them. How can you forsake a lifetime..."

"It's not a lifetime!" he exploded, slamming his fist down upon the tabletop so hard that the other glass of Sangue di Vita, the glass meant for me, went careening through the air and shattered upon the stone floor.

Something hissed behind me. When I looked back, I saw one of the few women in the room preparing to pounce upon the spilled liquid. The gondolier, who was still standing at Stefan's elbow, shouted something at the woman in a language I did not understand. The woman reeled back with a screech, cowering against the wall, raking her fingers across the exposed stone. I prayed she wouldn't draw blood. There was no telling how the others would react if she did.

She looked so feral that I thought she was on the verge of doing herself harm. But all she did was sit there, whimpering pitifully, her other arm raised in front of her face as though to shield her eyes from the sight of her oppressor.

"What is this place?" I wondered aloud.

Stefan's eyes had clouded over once again. He had suddenly become very quiet...too quiet.

"How does one start over?"

"Stefan?" I asked, for I thought he was addressing me.

"How does one go on after doing such unspeakable things?"

His eyes were focused on the glass still clasped within his hands. He was not talking to me.

"It's all rather simple, really," he continued, speaking in someone else's voice. "Say to yourself, 'What things?' And it becomes clear...you are blameless. They brought it on themselves. What have they ever done for you except control your life? They tore you away from your sister; they ripped you from your home. Did you ask to be saved? No! They forced their supposed love upon you when you had no need of it. And then they brought you down, made you feel inferior, lavished their wealth in your face. *Damn them!* Forget them and start over...with us, your true family, my Corcitura, my *own*."

"Yes, I see it now," he said, coming out of his trance. "I know what I must do."

And as this bizarre internal conversation came to an end, it was as if Stefan had been reborn. Gone was the insecurity, the changeability, the uncertainty—the fear. One of the natures had finally taken over, and it was *not* the one I had been hoping would win out. I shuddered at the thought that had fixed itself in my mind, but I could not deny its truth.

Staring at me now, he looked *exactly* like Vladec Salei.

"A toast to you, my brother," he said, lifting his glass. "May your eyes be opened on this night, and may you see as you have never seen before. Knowledge is a very powerful thing. Drink and be free."

Red light shot through the glass, red light reflected from the candle guttering in its holder above my head. My eyes darted up toward the ceiling. First impressions are tricky things, and mine had been wrong—horribly wrong. There were no angels in these panels. What had I been thinking before? Demons cavorted in a pit of rocks and shattered skulls. Fire licked their hellish bodies as they danced through one torture scene after another. In the center panel, a huge, black-winged beast devoured something that was still kicking as it was being forced down the devil's gullet.

How could it still be kicking? Or, more importantly, how could I *see* it kicking?

The figures in the panel were moving.

Their movements were slow, tortured, dreamlike, but real—undeniably real. I watched, entranced, unable to turn away, as one poor soul after another was raked across hot coals or had its ashen flesh stripped by one of the devil's overseers.

I put my hand to my mouth, but still my eyes remained riveted to the ceiling. The other panels did nothing to cure my nausea. Eleven horned beasts—looking like crosses between satyrs and devils—formed a circle around a giant creature, half dragon, half man, that held a severed head aloft in its clawed hands. Blood dripped from the stump, falling into the waiting mouths of some of the beasts, as the others caught the liquid in black chalices.

The fresco was blatantly hellish, but its living replica was even worse.

I had lied to myself from the very beginning, deceived myself into believing that I was being fanciful and overly imaginative. Surely such monstrosities only existed in nightmares? Yet I had lived through a nightmare these past months, and that was no dream at all.

I was still fighting against the awful truth, not wanting to give in, searching my mind for a logical explanation—but there was none. And the most horrible realization of all was that I *had* known, somewhere deep inside, ever since the day I first set eyes on Vladec Salei.

Plague carrier.

Living death.

Drainer of life.

The phrasing did not matter. No euphemism could strike fear into the hearts of men the way that single word could.

Vampire.

And for me, the uninitiated, that single word meant death.

Sweat trickled down the back of my neck. I could feel every pair of eyes in that wretched den trained upon me, waiting for my next move. Here I was exposed, my true nature on full display for all of them to see—the outsider, the one who did not belong...*yet.* And that was when I made my choice.

Run or die.

A jump from a fourth floor window would surely break my legs. Of course, there was always the possibility I'd be killed as soon as my body hit the stone. But I had to chance it. There was no way I would survive a mad dash to the doorway. Stefan was in league with the forces at work in this place. I knew better than to expect any help from him. The rest of them would be upon me before I could take one step. To tear me limb from limb would be the work of an instant for them.

Corcitura

There was nothing for it. However short-lived my chances might be, I had to risk it, but then a thought struck into my mind. I remembered that the front side of the taverna sat directly on the canal. From the fourth floor it would be a sheer drop of some twenty-five feet straight into the water. It was perfect. I almost smiled at the thought, until I looked down and saw the gondolier reaching for my neck. I lunged behind Stefan's chair and grabbed the wyvern-headed cane. The gondolier turned so swiftly that the blow I dealt him was more of a reflex than an actual strike. Even so, he staggered back, stunned by the impact of the cane to the side of his head.

A deafening, inhuman scream rattled the room. I thought it had been the gondolier, but the unearthly howl had come from Stefan. I turned to see him overturning the table and tearing his way toward me, his eyes fixed on the cane still in my hands. I was already halfway to the window by then.

I glanced down at the cane. What I saw was definitely not a trick of the light.

The wyvern's eyes were glowing.

"So," I thought aloud, "there is more to this cane than he would like me to know."

"Yes, and it belongs to me, now give it back!" Stefan had covered the distance between us in less than a second and now stood shoulder to shoulder with me by the window. It was either fight or jump. From the look of him, it would be a battle I could not win.

I looked behind him. The crowd was inching their way forward. Distraction was my mistake, for in that second when my attention was averted, Stefan seized his opportunity. He latched onto the cane and flung me against the window.

I had planned to use the cane to shatter the pane, but there was no need for that now. My body would do it for me. I braced myself, expecting to be pierced by a thousand shards of broken glass, but all I heard was a splintering of wood. Instead of pain, the only thing I felt was a humid breeze against my face as I dangled in the air, twenty-five feet above the canal. It had been so dark in this corner, I hadn't realized the window was paneless and divided by only a thin strip of wood, a fact I was thankful Stefan and I had both been unaware of.

But my joy at still being alive was fleeting. Stefan had not lessened his hold on the cane. I clung to the wyvern's head with all my might, as Stefan, with strength I had never known him to possess, began to slowly pull up the cane—and me along with it.

The distance between us was lessening at an alarming rate. I had to act fast. I didn't relish the thought of him sinking his newly sprouted fangs into my neck. Raising both my legs, I got a foothold on the side of the building and yanked down on the wyvern's head with every drop of strength I had left within me.

A strange look spasmed across Stefan's face. At first, I thought someone had struck him from behind, but then I realized that the stricken gaze was not a look of pain but of horror.

Something was happening to the cane.

What I thought was the cane's natural outer coating was actually a scabbard—and it had started to come loose. A gleam of steel flashed in the moonlight, followed by a sound as of something being unsheathed. The next thing I knew, the cane and I went hurtling through the air to the canal below.

The last thing I heard before the water closed over my head was Stefan's agonized shriek of defeat.

The coldness of the water stunned me, nearly causing me to drop the cane, which I now saw was a sword. I still had air in my lungs. Surfacing now would be certain death. I swam off toward the canal wall and floated along it until I was sure I wouldn't be spotted. Better to let Stefan think I had drowned.

My lungs were beginning to burn. I had been underwater nearly three minutes. The time had come to surface, vampires or not.

As I broke through the water, I could still see the taverna from my vantage point beneath the pier. Stefan was still leaning halfway out the window. He was frozen in the same position I had left him in, clutching the empty sheath. A few of his ilk had joined him and were scanning the canals for any sight of my body.

A terrible thought darted across my mind and set my heart racing. If I could see them, who was to say they couldn't see *me*? After all, I had no idea how potent their heightened senses could be.

All right, Eric. You've been in the water long enough. It's time to go.

I treaded back so that I was flush against the canal wall. With the sword still clutched in my right hand, I pulled myself up over the wall, cast a quick look in the direction of the taverna to make sure I had not been spotted, and slinked off in the opposite direction.

I didn't go back to our hotel, for that would have been too obvious. Instead, I ran as far away from it as I could until I came to a pension on the outskirts of the city. The place was far enough from Stefan, yet still afforded me quick access to the boat that would take me to the mainland the next morning.

The room I secured on the second floor of the pension was small and possessed only one window, for which I was thankful. The minute I stepped across the threshold, I set to work. The biggest piece of furniture in the room, the wardrobe, I pushed up against the door, which I made sure to bolt upon entry. A divan turned on its end made a good barricade against the window. Everything else—the bed, a night table, a chair, and a small sideboard—served to reinforce the wardrobe in front of the main door.

Satisfied with my makeshift defenses, I slumped down against the divan and buried my face in my hands.

How does one start over?

I couldn't get Stefan's words, or the horrible images I had seen on that ceiling, out of my mind.

How does one go on after doing such unspeakable things?

I racked my brain in an effort to remember anything from the little I had read on the subject. But how can one prepare for this? The shock of finding out your best friend, your *brother*, has become a creature you had always consigned to the shadows of legend, was too great.

These thoughts would get me nowhere now. Facts were what I needed, yet facts were something I had precious little knowledge of.

Silver was one way, but where would I find any now? It was hopeless. Wait! That was not true. I looked down at the staff still clutched in my hand. The blade glinted, showing off the scrollwork etched into the silver. I had a strong desire to break the blade in two, but until I learned the full truth behind this staff he cared so much for, I had to keep it safe.

As soon as I resolved to protect the staff, the full import of what I had done hit me in the pit of my stomach.

My life would never be the same.

Stefan would not let me go so easily. I could have been rid of him, could have severed our lifelong relationship that very night, had I only let go of the staff.

And now it was too late. The hunt had begun.

He would never let me rest until he had reclaimed his property. He would dog my every step until we reached London...and I would be there, waiting for him.

If there were any chance to kill him, I would have to take it. No amount of sentiment could prevent me now. No scruples could stay my hand. But given what I had witnessed in Greece, I had my doubts that a mere shard of silver would end the life of the monster Stefan Ratliff had become.

I glanced at the clock on the mantel. It was only ten minutes to ten.

We had been gone just one hour.

It had seemed like a lifetime. Some otherworldly devilry of Vladec Salei's must have been responsible for the delay of time, but I was too exhausted to exert any more energy puzzling over what still made no sense to my overwrought mind.

"God, see me through to the morning, I beg of you," I prayed. Nine more hours until the boat left. And then another day until I could be on the train bound for Nice. Until then, I still had to endure a night of watching—and waiting.

I tightened my grip around the wyvern's head and settled back against the divan.

Corcitura

Stefan had been right. No matter how hard I tried, this was one birthday I would *never* forget.

The Hunted

*O*ne week later, I arrived in Paris, after having nearly been caught at least six times throughout the journey. They had been dogging my every step since the morning I fled. It was only by sheer luck, or Divine Providence, more likely, that I didn't barrel directly into Vladec Salei as I got off the boat at Nice.

I hadn't slept in the last forty-eight hours, not so much because I was afraid of being caught, but because I could no longer afford lodgings at any of the hotels, even the most inexpensive. Even if I had had the money, I only really had one choice. I couldn't stay and rest up, no matter how brash I tried to be, for they would undoubtedly take advantage of my weakness and find me. My only course was to forget I was exhausted and buy train passage at every stage I could. I had to reach Guildy as quickly as possible. The fear that they would catch me and do God knows what before I could reach her was enough of an incentive to drive me on.

The only things I had to my name were fifteen pounds, the card with Guildy's address—which had been nearly obliterated when I plummeted into the canal in Venice—and the blasted silver sword. It was because of that silver sword that my funds were now even more depleted. I had been fleeced in Lyon by a merchant who assured me it was quite common to pay thirty pounds for a "genuine" leather sheath.

But what could I have done? Salei, Stefan, and that pustule, Augustin Boroi, were hard on my heels. I didn't have time to be choosy. I had been lucky to have traveled that far without being stopped—having devised a way to conceal the sword in newspapers and such—but now that I was in Paris, I couldn't very well walk the streets brandishing the thing like some homicidal maniac.

I pulled the card from my pocket and studied the writing that was hardly legible. The number of the house was almost smudged beyond comprehension, but I was able to discern what I thought to be a five and an eight, followed by the words *Boulevard Montmartre*. That was a start. I hoped the fifty-eight was correct. I didn't have time to hang about and knock on doors until I found her. My pursuers weren't far behind, yet something had changed when I stepped off the train. I could feel them drawing close, but it was almost as if they were giving me a wide berth...or, looked at from another angle, enough rope to hang myself with.

My pursuers...one of whom was Stefan...who was dead to me.

I ignored this train of thought and walked on. This was no time to dwell on the past. I knew I would see him again, and I was dreading the encounter.

I walked past a few houses until I reached the forties, then stopped to study the card again to make sure. Something in the air made me look up, but the attack came before I even had the chance to realize I was in danger.

My knees buckled underneath me. I flailed the staff, but gained no purchase and choked in panic when I found that I couldn't cry out. An arm encircled my throat, crushing the air out of me as thoroughly as Augustin Boroi had done once before. It was the night of the ritual in Castle Bran all over again, and I was just as powerless to stop this attack.

Whoever my assailant was, he was incredibly strong, and dragged me backward as though I weighed next to nothing. I couldn't turn my head to see who he was or where he was taking me. When I tried to raise his arm to my teeth, he just tightened his grip.

My vision began to blur. I only had seconds left before I lost consciousness. What he wanted with me, I didn't know, but that he was more than a pickpocket was certain. He was probably some hired hand of Salei's, for the arm didn't belong to any of my three pursuers.

I blinked frantically to steady my gaze and was able to see that he had dragged me into an alley. So this was how it would end... Done away with in some back corner of Paris. All my struggles, all the running—all for naught.

"I'm sorry I had to do this to you, Eric, but it was the only way."

Hope surged through me as I recognized the voice. I never thought I would hear it again. In fact, I had vowed I never wanted to. But compared to my three other options, the voice that spoke to me now was a godsend.

"Luc, what the devil did you do that for?" I said, rubbing my neck. He had released me and slinked toward the end of the alley, motioning me to follow. I stumbled forward, looking my assailant in the face for the first time. Strangely, I wasn't angry, nor was I fearful. The look on his face told me I had no reason to be afraid.

"Are you hurt?"

"Not any more than I already was."

"They're after you, you know."

"Yes, I'm aware of that." It suddenly struck me that he was being very calm about the entire situation and knew a great deal more than he should have.

"How do you know so much?" I asked suspiciously, backing away and unsheathing the sword.

"Eric, you have nothing to fear from me. Put that thing away!"

He recoiled at the sight of the silver. I nearly dropped the blade in shock. I knew there was something wrong with him, but I never expected it to be this. "So you're a vampire, too?"

"No. The fangs were withdrawn before the transformation could take effect. But my blood had already been tainted."

"That's the most absurd thing I've ever heard."

"I have the marks to prove it."

I wasn't ready to witness a repeat of the scene in Castle Bran, but Luc had already raised his hair, and I'd no choice but to look at the scars on the side of his neck. Thank God they were nowhere near as grisly as Stefan's sister's had been. The scars were miniscule, practically invisible, save for the smooth, slightly raised pink skin. The marks were barely noticeable unless you were on top of him, or knew they were there in the first place.

"I'm a wraith, Eric," he said in a voice completely devoid of the arrogance he usually affected.

"A what? What do you mean you're a wraith? Wraiths are ghosts."

"Not when vampires make them."

I stared at him blankly, which must have amused him. His mouth twitched up at the corners, but the smile was no longer sardonic.

"All of the symptoms but none of the perks," he said grimly.

I regained my bearings. "Meaning?"

"I tread the line between both worlds. I can never belong to theirs, but neither can I return to my own. I am an outcast in both."

Despite my resolve to hate him for what he'd done, I pitied him then—pitied him, yet feared what he was, for wasn't this exactly what Vladec Salei could do to me? He didn't want to turn me. He'd told me so himself. But this option... The desire to run was fiercer in me at that moment than it had been all of last week, when I'd been fleeing for my life.

"I suppose I'm a little bit vampiric."

"That's like saying you're a little bit pregnant. Or a little bit dead. You either *are* a vampire or you aren't. Which is it?" Enough shilly-shallying.

"It's not that simple, Eric."

"In my book it is."

"But not in mine. You can sheath that blade now. I'm not here to harm you. I'm here to warn you."

I eyed him warily. How could I be sure of this man who lived in a shadow world of near vampirism? He had thrust

Stefan and the Borois together. Yet now that I knew he was a wraith....Heaven help me, this was ridiculous. A wraith? A ghost? A specter? Did such things even exist? Of course they did. I'd seen them. I'd witnessed their blood rituals, and it had almost killed me. No, Luc was a servant, a puppet. Whatever part he had played in Stefan's destruction, he had done it at the bidding of Vladec Salei.

"Tell me what you know," I said, sheathing the sword.

"They were delayed on the way. You have at least a day's time. Enough to get help and head for London. Listen to me, Eric. There's more I wanted you to know. I couldn't let you go on without knowing the truth. It was meant to be you."

His words made no sense. *Me*? "Surely you can't mean..."

"You had no connections. You weren't nearly as rich as Stefan. You were the logical choice, but after the night at the opera when Vladec saw you for what you were, saw the danger you posed to his hold on Leonora, he changed his mind. I doubt anything would have come of it if he hadn't discovered Stefan was a Belododia."

That night swam before my eyes. I saw myself in Box Five, catching Leonora's eye and earning Salei's hate. If I hadn't been so eager, if I hadn't been so besotted, none of this would have ever happened.

"No, it can't be," I said, choking on my words. "He...he," but the words would not come. *I* was the guilty one. *I* deserved to die. I had killed my brother as thoroughly as if I had stabbed him in the heart with a knife. How could I go on after this?

Forget them and start over...with us, your true family, my Corcitura, my own.

Those words—Salei's words spoken through Stefan. Hidden in them was something I hadn't understood until now, something that made everything Luc said a lie.

"Don't feed me that pack of lies. It was never meant to be me. You know it, I know it, Vladec Salei knows it. Otherwise, why should it matter that Stefan was a Belododia? Why should that *one fact* make Salei choose Stefan over any other? I saw how Salei reacted when I told him Stefan's last name. He knew there was something off with it being Ratliff.

Don't tell me it was coincidence. It was *always* meant to be Stefan."

"Fine, yes," he said. He wasn't agitated. Oddly, he seemed relieved. "That was Salei's game. He knew Stefan was somewhere in Western Europe, but Vladec has a terrible sense of direction."

"I don't believe that."

"Regardless, there was a familiar odor about you that night. Don't look so disgusted. Their terminology and ideas don't seem so absurd when you've lived with them for as long as I have."

"Exactly how old *are* you?" He didn't look a day over forty.

"When they...changed me, I was thirty-six."

I knew better than to ask him just how long he'd *been* thirty-six.

"The odor was the smell of Stefan—the smell of murder. Once you've taken a life, a vampire can smell that life on you no matter how long ago you committed the crime. Stefan was marked to begin with, but after setting himself apart by killing his father, it was only a matter of time before his past caught up with him. Of course, Vladec might have been mistaken, or so he thought. He'd been disappointed before. It could have been something else, some other familiar scent that threw him off, but when you said his name was Stefan *Ratliff*...Ratliff and Stefan do not go together, especially for a son of Romanian blood. Vladec knew he had found his man."

His man. Exactly what kind of claim did he have on Stefan?

"It is not your fault," Luc continued. "Vladec would have found him sooner or later. They are cursed, that family. It's a miracle Stefan lasted this long. David and Marishka Ratliff simply delayed the inevitable when they snatched him from Romania."

I didn't even bother to ask how he knew this. What was the point? He seemed to know everything. "Then he must have known about Constantinos, too," I said, half to myself.

"Constantinos?" Shock registered in Luc's eyes. So there *was* something this all knowing, all seeing, not-quite-a-vampire didn't know. "He's still alive?"

"Yes, I'm afraid."

"Then Vladec is still trying to succeed where he failed in the past, nearly five hundred years ago."

"You can't be serious."

"Well preserved, no?" he said bitterly. "His history is tied up with the Belododias and Istratescus more thoroughly than you could ever imagine. Blood for blood. Turned and killed, turned and killed, turned and killed, down through the ages. If Stefan hadn't killed Dragos when he did, Vladec would have done it himself sooner or later.

"The name Belododia is as good as a curse in Romania. Dragos was a devil. He sold out all his children to Vladec Salei to save his own skin. The only Istratescu who was never turned or killed was Florin. He knew Vladec when Salei was young, and I don't mean artificially young. He knew him when he was turned at the age of seventeen in 1395."

"But that's impossible," I said, my voice hollow. My head was reeling from these revelations. They were ridiculous, horrifying, and undeniably true.

"I wish it were. The ones who died were lucky. The ones who killed themselves I'd like to think of as blessed. Surely God would have mercy on their souls, knowing the kind of life they would have been forced to lead had they lived. Florin was one who died by his own hand, but not before he siphoned off some of his blood and that of Vladec Salei's. Florin knew it would only be a matter of time before Vladec succeeded in his mad scheme to create the Corcitura, the half-breed, mongrel vampire no one could kill. Another Upyr wouldn't have produced the hybrid effect. The specimen has to be bitten by *two* different species of vampire, otherwise he'd just retain the characteristics of whichever vampire was the first to get to him. There were only Upyrs in Russia. That's why Vladec decided to travel, and it was in Greece where he met his match."

"Constantinos."

"Yes. I still to this day don't believe Salei knew what he was getting himself into with that one. Not all vampires are created equal, you know."

In truth, I didn't know, but he was so involved in his storytelling that I didn't want to squabble. I had a lot to learn about the internecine world of vampiric politics, but Luc wasn't the one I would ask.

"Constantinos is as savage as they come, but once found, Vladec was unwilling to let such an opportunity pass him by. So they struck an alliance. Vladec's plan couldn't fail...in theory. Constantinos was always a difficult partner. He didn't exactly appreciate being told what to do or who not to kill. I could fill the sewers of Paris with their failed experiments."

"It must have been a grisly business," I managed to say, swallowing hard.

"You have no idea. It didn't help that Constantinos rebelled against Vladec's stricture that he not attack women. *I* could have told him putting those kinds of restraints on a vampire, let alone a Vrykolakas, was folly, but Vladec has his own way of doing things. It got to the point where Constantinos would attack women out of spite, then kill them."

"Sorina. I know." The vision of her mutilated body once again rose up before my mind's eye.

"Yes. Constantinos was just the means to the end. Vladec needed a protégée, someone he could remake in his own image, so when news reached Vladec of Stefan's parents' marriage, he focused all his attention on those poor unfortunates. I've no doubt he was somehow instrumental in throwing Ruxandra and Dragos into each other's company, if only to spite Florin's ghost. He was there for every birth, and six times he was disappointed, so that he gave up before he even knew Ruxandra was pregnant a seventh time."

"With Stefan?"

"Exactly. Vladec never did like to wait. If he had, he would have saved us all a lot of trouble...and a lot of innocent blood."

"So he never knew his prize was right beneath his nose."

"Ironic, no?"

"But what of the sisters?"

"Oh, he had his way with them in the meantime, except for one."

"You're thinking of Olga?" I asked, although I already knew the answer. "How do you know?"

"It's not important. She is one of the lucky ones."

On that point, Luc and I were in agreement. Whatever her fate had been after she killed herself, I knew she was better off dead. Life—or as close to life as an undead person could be—as one of Salei's cohorts was an unenviable fate. Yet, I thought ruefully, it was a fate Stefan had chosen. Maybe he truly had no say in the matter, but certainly when given the alternatives, he had gone along with the scheme more willingly than I would have thought possible. And even at this stage of the affair, I still could not bring myself to accept that he was lost, nor could I condemn him outright. Why was I still willing to think the best of him even after he had tried to kill me?

How does one start over?

The answer was simple enough. For us, this was the end. There would be no starting over, no new beginning. It would be nearly impossible to forget the last thirteen years of our lives...and the events of the past two months that had turned us from brothers into enemies.

Luc turned away and shoved his hands in his pockets. This was a greater strain on him than he was letting on, but it was almost as if he had no will to stop himself from telling me more.

"It happened during a journey to the Black Sea. Florin and Vladec and Vladec's father, Miroslav...*Miroslav*," Luc said, sighing. He was staring into the darkness at the end of the alley. I got the feeling he was not simply letting his eyes rest there by accident. "To think it could have ended there," he muttered.

It might have been my imagination, but I swore I heard a slight cough coming from the darkness Luc was staring into. Luc didn't seem to hear, or maybe his indifference was for my benefit. The cough could have been a signal given by someone or some*thing* cloaked within the darkness. Perhaps I was just becoming fevered again, which had been occurring all too frequently over the past few days.

"Sorry," Luc said, shaking his head. "Where was I...Oh, yes. Miroslav. They say he was a good man, a strong man, a man with purpose. He would have to be to have the fortitude to try and stake his own son after the Upyr attacked Vladec."

I gaped at the man. I don't know why I should have been shocked, given what I had been exposed to, but the thought of a father turning on his son seemed so abominable it made me shiver. There was something almost biblical about the notion.

Godly, brave Miroslav, the would-be murderer of his son. If only he had done the deed before Vladec turned the tables and plunged the stake into his father's heart.

The words came unbidden into my mind. I stared at Luc, who met my bewildered gaze unflinchingly.

He nodded, affirming my thoughts, although I had yet to share them. I tried to rationalize his knowledge, but this silent confirmation did nothing to allay my fears. I had no choice but to add mind reading to the list of gifts Salei and Company had bestowed on this wraith.

"Florin and Vladec were once the best of friends," Luc said, turning away again, "but after the incident, that friendship turned to hatred, at least on Vladec's side—hatred that Florin was still whole, hatred that Vladec had been turned instead. Maybe even a shred of remorse that Vladec had killed his own father, I don't know. Regardless of the reason, that hatred has festered and eaten away at Vladec for hundreds of years, especially since Florin was essentially the one that got away. And ever since, Vladec has made it his mission to destroy the lives of every single Istratescu he encounters. He has held a personal vendetta, however unreasonable, against Florin's family for centuries. It has literally been a blood feud. He fought it in the beginning, tried fanatically to cling to his father's side, his father's blood. Pretty ironic when you consider that he staked his own father moments after he was turned. But that's neither here nor there."

Again I heard a small scuffling sound from the back of the alley. This time, Luc heard it too, though he tried to shrug off his apprehension. "You see," he said, coming closer and lowering his voice to a tone barely above a whisper, "Ruxandra, Stefan's mother, is an Istratescu, and Dragos, as you know, is a Belododia. And therein lies the connection...Vladec is *also* a Belododia on his mother's side."

"But Salei isn't a Romanian name," I said idiotically. After listening to revelations of murder, depravity, and vengeance, Salei's surname was the only thing that struck me as being, I don't know, just the slightest bit off? I must have truly been three steps away from madness.

"Technicality."

"Maybe, but haven't you been in his service long enough to discover the reason?"

"How should I know?!" he exploded. "I can't understand his whims. I'm old, Eric, but I'm not *that* old. Not even *I* know all his secrets. But I do know this. Regardless of his surname, he is part of that family of killers, of knaves, of cursed ones. He tried to deny his heritage before the turning, but you cannot deny your own blood forever, and when the Upyr attacked, well, Vladec couldn't help but give in to his family's natural impulses. I was told he did fight against it for a while, but I suppose he realized it was useless to resist, and so he embraced his newfound bloodlust, and vengeance, wholeheartedly."

Bloodlust? An ages old vendetta that somehow involved my best friend's family? Hidden grudges and legacies of murder passed down through the ages? And an *Upyr*? What the devil was this thing, this Upyr, Luc kept mentioning? Things like this didn't happen. We were less than twelve years from the dawn of the twentieth century, the modern age, and here was this fool, talking to me of nonsense that should have died out in the Middle Ages.

How does one go on after doing such unspeakable things?

Stefan's words shot through my mind and my hands instinctively tightened around the sword I still clutched within my grasp. "Can Salei be killed?" I heard myself asking.

"Of course Vladec can be killed, but the only thing that can kill the Corcitura has remained a mystery. No one knows where it is. No one knows *what* it is."

"But if Florin only united his blood with Vladec's, how can it be of any use to Stefan, since the blood of Constantinos now flows through his veins as well?"

"There is a rumor that Stefan's sole surviving sister somehow obtained the blood of Constantinos once, when he dared to venture out of Greece to hunt down Vladec and the woman Constantinos had staked a claim to all those years ago."

So she was the linchpin. It all made sense to me now. He mistook Sorina for the woman he had lost to his enemy, the woman he wanted to exact vengeance upon for deserting him years before. "Leonora," I said quietly.

"Yes. And when they reached Brasov, Nadia stole the blood. What she did with it, I don't know, but she must have it stored in some secret place. She of all the sisters has shown the most courage. She would have to, considering what she must have gone through to get the blood of a Vrykolakas, especially one as vicious as Constantinos.

"The blood is her bargaining chip, and it is her threat against Salei, for the blood can somehow kill the Corcitura. And there is the paradox. As long as the blood is in her possession, she is safe. Without the blood, she is as good as dead. So what does she do? She saves it, hides it away, keeps it at hand in case of an unexpected visit from her ancestor, and when the time is right, she seizes her chance and uses it to kill the one who has been turned, giving him not life, for there is no cure once he has been bitten, but rest, eternal and peaceful—and saving him from an eternity of feasting on humanity. It is her task to make sure he will never rise again once he has been laid in the earth."

What could I say to such revelations? Luckily, Luc didn't allow me the luxury to ponder over a suitable response. He was not yet finished unburdening himself of the history I was certain he had shared with only a few other souls. Knowing what I now did of Salei's methods, I thought it highly probable that those few had been done away with or welcomed into his congregation of the damned long ago.

"Vladec's ransacked that house time and again, and each time he's come up empty-handed. He cannot sense it, he cannot trace it. She has kept it hidden, out of reach, yet tantalizingly close. He knows if he tries to force her to reveal it, she'll use it against his precious creation. He fears her. I bet you thought there was nothing that could scare him. Well, that slip of a girl can. She holds the key to the destruction of all his plans. She is the last untainted member of the Istratescu-Belododia line, the last one who can kill Stefan, Vladec's final hope. If Stefan is killed, the dream of a Corcitura, a new, invincible species, will die with him. Salei is obsessed with finding that blood. He cannot live with the idea that he does not hold all the cards, that he cannot possess the blood, if only to destroy it so no one will ever be able to kill his hybrid. Knowing she has it and will never reveal its location eats away at him little by little every day. If I were in his position, I would have torn Nadia's head off ages ago, the blood be damned. It's not as if someone is going to waltz into her house and find it after she's dead and automatically know it can kill Vladec's creature. But try telling that to Salei. You'd think with all that occult and forbidden knowledge he has amassed throughout the centuries, he would find a way to do her in, wouldn't you? But that blood is her life, her protection. I can't explain it, but as long as she is its possessor, he is unwilling to harm her and has no power over her. He's tried all his tricks, but she is immune to his charms, to everything. Sorina gave her a nickname once: Vladec's Bane. Mademoiselle Boroi was quite right, no? Nadia is truly the thorn in his side. I can't help feeling that one day she will be his downfall. The blood gives her a power he cannot control."

There was something in his logic that didn't make sense to me. Who was I fooling? *None* of this made sense and never had. But I was too overtaxed—mentally, spiritually, physically—to try and decipher riddles that had kept smarter men guessing for hundreds of years.

Luc shuffled away a pace and crossed his arms, staring off into space once more. "In a vial somewhere, the blood of Vladec, Constantinos, and the untainted blood of Stefan's ancestor, Florin Istratescu, has been united. If Vladec has succeeded in turning Stefan, which it seems he has, there can only be one way to kill Stefan. And that way is to be found in Romania...with Nadia Belododia. I wish you luck in discovering where she keeps it."

I closed my eyes and remembered the sideboard, the drawer, the cross hidden away in the back—and Nadia Belododia's face clouded over with apprehension as she slammed the drawer shut.

Of course.

The cabochon was not a ruby. It was the combined blood of two vampires and a pure-blooded Istratescu. And Nadia was keeping it hidden, even from the one who needed it most. I knew her more thoroughly in that moment than I had when I was in her presence. Luc was wrong, dead wrong, only he hadn't realized it yet. He maintained the Corcitura had to be male, but I knew that wasn't the case, and apparently, Nadia did, too. She must have hidden the cross to protect herself in the event that Salei did find a way to break through her defenses. If he failed with her brother, he would come after her, and she wasn't willing to waste the blood on Stefan. Luc talked a good deal about the power of the blood, but what if Nadia were careless? What if she were away from it for too long? I didn't believe in its supposed protection. If she weren't careful, there would come a day when Salei would catch her unawares. With Constantinos in the offing prepared to do his part, they would turn her into the hybrid Salei sought so madly to create. She knew all this and knew it well. Death was a constant threat for her. With that blood, she would not have life, but she could save herself from the plague of being a walking, blood-sucking corpse for the rest of her existence. She'd use the blood if given the chance. I'd stake my life on it.

Help. I laughed bitterly at the memory of her words. What help could she have given us? She knew Stefan was already too far gone. Her intention was never to help him, or to even kill him, for that would mean the use of the blood. She was going to save her own skin for as long as she could, at the expense of her brother's life. She had sacrificed us to Vladec Salei. She was the one who had turned a blind eye when they spirited us away to Castle Bran for Salei's midnight ritual. The Belododia streak of self-preservation ran through her more strongly than all the rest. No matter what he had tried to do to her, in the end, she had become exactly like her father.

"What are you thinking, Eric? You know something, don't you?"

Read my mind and find out, you abomination, I thought, then shut my mind against Luc. "No," I lied, turning away. The secret of the cross was the one thing he did not know. I didn't want him to relay my suspicions to Vladec Salei. I would never see the cross or Nadia again if that happened. Maybe Vladec was powerless in the presence of the blood, but *I* wouldn't be. "Why haven't you fought them, Luc?" I said, intentionally becoming furious and changing the subject to throw him off the scent of my former thoughts. "Why don't you stand up to them?"

"Why don't I stand up to them?" he asked, laughing derisively. "Have you ever tried standing up to a vampire?"

"Yes, actually."

"It's not a pleasant experience, is it?"

"Not in the least."

Again, I heard a noise. Luc heard it, too, only this time he couldn't deny it. A crash sounded behind the alley wall. I had half unsheathed the sword, but found that I couldn't pull it out any further, for Luc had grabbed my hands and hurried me to the mouth of the alley.

"Listen to me, Eric. I have a wife and three daughters. If I don't do exactly what Salei and his minions tell me to, they will turn us all."

"Luc, I'm sorry, I..."

"Which is why I have to tell them you're here."

Cold dread gripped my heart. The world began to spin. In spite of my desire to be as far away from him as possible at that moment, I clutched Luc's shoulder to steady myself. "Luc, I'm begging you, please."

"But I don't have to tell them *yet.*"

I thought I hadn't heard him correctly. My luck wasn't running this way of late. I must have been mistaken. But when I saw that he was regarding me intently, I knew he was serious.

"You're looking for Lady Guildford's. It's 64 Boulevard Montmartre. Eric, hurry, *please.* I can keep them off the scent not longer than a few hours. Then they will find you. And I will be powerless to stop them."

All sense of urgency seemed to have deserted me now that I needed it most. I pulled the card from my pocket and stared at it blankly. The numbers were so blurred, it was a moment before I realized that the sixty-four had been smudged so that it now appeared to be a fifty-eight. I looked at the card, then at Luc, then back at the card, and would have probably stayed in this state of shock had Luc not slapped me across the face. "Get on with you, now, you fool! *Go!*"

I didn't need to be told twice. I nodded toward Luc, then sped off down the boulevard as fast as my feet would carry me.

I had not traveled more than a few feet when I heard an angry string of curses, followed by a noise that sounded like a fist connecting with someone's jaw. I should have gone on, should have kept running, but the temptation was too great. Despite the danger, I halted to look back.

Luc was sprawled on the pavement. Looming over his unconscious form was Vladec Salei.

They had found me.

I glanced up the street, the sword shaking furiously in my hand, as I tried to come to terms with the fact that Salei had somehow not noticed me standing directly before him. He was glaring down at Luc, muttering something and looking pleased with whatever it was he was saying.

I knew better than to begrudge my good fortune. I was two doors from Guildy's flat. If I made a run for it now, I might make it through in time, assuming she was in. I had a vague memory of reading something about their kind not being able to enter your home unless you invited them in, but that seemed so much superstition to me now. I doubted Salei would let a few vampiric guidelines stop him from getting what he wanted.

I backed away slowly at first, then turned and broke into a run. Reaching Guildy's door, I pounded furiously upon it, not knowing any other way of making my presence known, and certain it would only be a matter of moments before I attracted Salei's attention.

I was right.

In an instant, he had covered the distance between us. I felt his suddenly elongated nails scraping against my back and redoubled my efforts on the door, but instead of the wood I had been pounding on, there was no longer anything but air. I sailed through the newly opened doorway and crashed to the floor. Something pushed at my legs, sending me sliding down the hallway. Before I could recover enough to stop whatever it was that had shoved me, I heard a shriek and looked back to see a stocky man standing with his back against the now closed entrance I had fallen through.

Salei, and who I assumed to be either Stefan or Augustin Boroi, for surely Luc was still unconscious, pounded so violently against the door that it and the man standing against it shook with each blow. Yet the man did not abandon his post, he did not even flinch, regardless of the screeches and clawing that were separated from him by mere inches of wood. There was something of the British Bulldog spirit in him that gave me hope I would make it out of this affair alive.

The shrieking continued, but was no longer my main concern. A shadow had fallen across me. I looked up to see Guildy standing on the threshold of the sitting room. "Ambrose, what in the name of all that is holy...Good Lord, it's Eric!"

We stared at one another, uncomprehending. Oddly, the first thing I noticed was that her hair was no longer the shocking shade of purple it had been the night we met at the opera.

"Thank God," I said, rising to my feet.

"Don't you look a sight. Here for a quatre-cinq, are you?" she asked mischievously, her eyes twinkling in jest.

Ordinarily, I would have found her amusing, but her joking just set my already frayed nerves even more on edge. I couldn't fathom why she was so calm, why she wasn't making a fuss about the sounds emanating from outside the door...and then I realized that I no longer heard them either.

Something shinnied past the window on the opposite side of the door. The way it moved made me wince, for the thing that had skimmed up the side of the house seemed decidedly unnatural—decidedly *inhuman.*

I scanned the sitting room for any means of entrance. There was a fireplace in the center of the wall, but I didn't believe our vampires would take it into their heads to try a Father Christmas approach. There was a door that led off into another room and of course the entrance to the hallway. No need to worry on that front, what with Ambrose guarding the main door. The rest of the room was furnished with overstuffed divans and small occasional tables, plus one large escritoire with writing implements strewn about on its open top. No doubt Guildy had been penning letters when I barged in.

"Eric, what on earth's the matter?" asked Guildy, coming in from the hallway. Her entrance drew my attention back toward the windows. There were three of them, floor to ceiling in size and each of them uncovered—leaving us on display to the hunters lurking outside. I raced over to the windows and quickly drew the heavy, brocade draperies across them, so that nothing from without could see what was going on within.

"What on earth are you doing?"

"Don't argue with me, Guildy. Do you have another entrance to the upstairs?"

"There are the back stairs outside, but why would you need to use them?"

Now was the moment I had been dreading, yet I could do nothing to sugarcoat the facts. "How well do you know Vladec Salei?"

She hesitated, as if puzzled by the question. "I pride myself on being a good judge of character, but there are times when I've doubted Vladec's...motives. Why? What's happened to you, Eric? And where is your friend?"

I would have told her everything if my eyes hadn't strayed to the ormolu clock above the mantel. I could not focus on anything else. It wasn't so much the time that captivated me, but rather the date—August eighth. In two weeks' time, I would turn nineteen...*again.*

"Eric?"

I felt Guildy's hand close around my arm. I turned to look at her. She seemed older, concern creasing her brow. Lines I had not noticed before were etched into her face, drawing her mouth downward into a worried frown.

I *had* to tell her all that had happened, all I now knew, no matter how ridiculous it sounded. "Guildy, brace yourself," I said. "This is going to sound insane, but Salei turned Stefan into..." Into a what? I stumbled, trying to find some logical way of explaining. There was none. I knew Stefan was much more than a vampire, yet I couldn't put into words what I fancied being a Corcitura consisted of. "Stefan is...Stefan is..."

"A vampire."

I grabbed the back of the divan to keep from tumbling to the ground. Guildy remained emotionless. I had expected her to take me for a fool. Now she stood before me, so calm that there could be no doubting her certainty, and I was the one left gaping at the awful, unbelievable truth.

"How do you..."

"I told you I've always suspected him of something. The operas...I knew there was more to them than what they seemed, this last time especially, with what happened to poor Nanette. And then there's his age. I once told you he didn't look it. I've learned that's truer in a more horrid and unnatural way than I could have guessed."

"Luc told you."

"No, it wasn't Luc," she said, her eyes narrowing as she turned away. It was as though a shutter had come down over her face, shading her true emotions, but I had seen something, a flicker of apprehension in her eyes before she walked away. She knew more than she was letting on. She was hiding something, protecting someone. "It was...someone else...someone who I know I can trust, who would never harm me the way Vladec would if he knew I was privy to his secrets. And that's all I can say."

So she *was* keeping secrets from me. "Guildy, if you know something, some way to get me out of this...."

"I know a way..." she said quietly. I waited for what seemed like an eternity, unable to breathe, holding out hope that she had concocted some master plan to help me escape.

"Run."

In her eyes was a look I couldn't read. What was the emotion? Resolution, resignation, terror? And then I realized she wasn't looking at me at all, but past my shoulder toward the windows. The curtain was fluttering, yet there was no breeze...and why would the curtain be moving when the window was closed? I looked down toward the bottom of the window and noticed that the brocade curtain had been drawn back.

And that's when I saw the hand.

A circle had been cut in the glass—a perfect sphere through which a dead-white hand was pushing. Filthy, yellowed, foot long nails tapped the glass impatiently. The hand snaked through, its skin catching on a chip of glass. Blood pooled from the wound, streaming down the fingers in rivulets. The hand slid back through the hole, only to reappear moments later as clean and sound as if there had never been the hint of a scratch.

I watched in mute horror as the razor-tipped fingers passed completely through the hole. If it were possible for fingers to convey expression, the ones attached to this hand could have been described as self-satisfied as they dug into the thick pile of the carpet beneath the window.

A harsh intake of breath from Guildy drew my attention away from that disembodied hand. Guildy was all resolution now. Her hand was clutched so tightly around something hanging on a chain round her neck that her knuckles were stretched and white to the point of appearing bloodless. Through her clasped fingers, I saw the four points of a cross.

"The library," she said, her jaw tight. "Upstairs. Hide there. I can handle this."

An army of men couldn't handle Vladec Salei, let alone one aging woman. It was insanity, and I told her as much, but she was adamant. "I can handle this, Eric," she said, her voice as hard as iron, "go."

I backed out of the room, my eyes flitting between Guildy and the nails making a deeper and deeper hole in the carpet. I nearly collided with Ambrose when I passed through the hall. As I backed up the staircase, I saw him enter the sitting room, a rifle cocked open in his hands. He was loading the gun with bullets.

I hoped they were made of silver.

I charged upstairs and stumbled into three rooms before finally finding the library. The room was in shadow, save for a sliver of light peeking through the curtains drawn about the room's only window. I peered into the darkness, my eyes throbbing from the strain, until I finally discerned the shape of an oil lamp resting on a desk in the corner of the room. I fumbled around till I found some matches, then lit the lamp. A feeble light pooled around me. I held the light before me to penetrate the gloom and stumbled back in surprise, colliding with the desk and losing my grip as I saw what the lamp had illuminated. Heat burned my fingers as I felt the glass slip from my grasp, but I caught the lamp in time to save it from shattering to the floor.

I clutched the base of the lamp and turned the flame up as high as it would go.

I was not alone in the room.

A woman was seated in an armchair in the nook where the floor to ceiling library shelves met. Her face was cloaked in shadow, but I had the distinct impression she was watching me out of the corners of her eyes. A slim, elegant white hand emerged from the darkness and placed a book upon the table by the chair. Alongside the book in a glass bottle were several dark purple tablets. I narrowed my eyes and discerned the title of the book, stenciled in gold filigreed letters along its spine: *A History of Hematology.*

Not exactly what I would classify as light reading.

"I knew our paths would cross again eventually, Eric."

"I can't say I'm surprised to see you here, Leonora." Falser bravado had never before been spoken. I was stunned to my core to find her here. "You were the one who told Guildy everything."

She hesitated a moment, then reached for the pill bottle and uncorked the stopper, dropping two tablets into the palm of her hand. "Yes."

Elaboration? I knew I wouldn't get her to share more information with me willingly, but I also knew I had to tread carefully, for I had already begun to believe she was not as innocent as she seemed. I noted that she still wore white. I assumed it was her favorite color, something to remind her of the days before she became sullied and inhuman. I was still wary of her, though I knew if she asked me to, I would crumble and do anything she wished, and this weakness terrified me.

The sight of her shaking fist—the pills clutched within her palm—didn't do anything to ease my apprehension. Suddenly, I remembered what Luc had said about Leonora and Constantinos, and it was as though a veil had been lifted. Sorina had mentioned it in passing, and spitefully at that, so I had paid it no never mind when I heard her speak of iron tablets. But now the truth was brought home to me, confirmed by the study of hematology Leonora had been reading. I knew what the pills were. I knew that she was self-medicating, trying to resist the urge to feed on humans.

Her palm stopped halfway to her mouth. She stared at me, her hand no longer shaking. "For my anemia," she said, downing the pills without the aid of any water. "I suppose there's nothing I can tell you about Vladec that you already don't know."

"Oh, I'm not so sure," I said casually. I didn't like the way she had crossed her arms over her chest, almost as though she were caging herself in. She stared up at me through her lashes, her pupils huge and obscuring. Something was very wrong with her. She seemed to be putting on a facade of indifference to mask her true feelings—or urges.

My eyes strayed to the pill bottle. I couldn't help wondering who supplied them, wondering if she knew I was suspicious. Something in my manner must have betrayed my concern, for I felt a heaviness in the air, almost as if she sensed I knew the truth.

"My pills, I need them," she said distractedly, reaching once more for the bottle.

"Who do you think you're fooling, Leonora?"

"I don't know what you mean," she said, her voice catching. She laughed uneasily and rose, taking the lamp from my hands and setting it atop the hematology book. She reached for the bottle, but then her hands recoiled and balled up into fists. Her lips began to move, as though she were muttering to herself. Her eyes were glassy when she turned to me.

"Leonora, I know about Constantinos."

"You..." She broke off, her eyes widening. She lunged madly for the pills...and so did I. She must have thought I only knew about Vladec and Stefan, not that Constantinos had turned her, too.

"Leonora, stop it, *stop it*!" I said, knocking the bottle from her hands.

"No, I need them!" she shrieked, breaking free from my grasp and dropping to the floor, clawing at the spilled tablets like a madwoman.

"Leonora, enough," I said, grabbing her and dragging her to her feet. Something feral flashed across her face, but the moment passed as quickly as it had come, and I was shocked to see that she was crying.

"Do you not understand? Those pills grant me my last semblance of humanity."

"There is no need to hide that from me, Leonora. I know what you are."

Her shoulders tensed as her head snapped up. She looked more like an animal than a woman. "What? *You* know what I am? And what is that? A mother who murders her own child?"

"What?!" I should have backed away from her, any sane man would have. But I'd lost my reason the first day I set eyes on Leonora, and I wasn't going to abandon her now. "I don't believe you. This is a trick. You couldn't have."

"In the state I was in after the turning, I could have murdered half of Greece. My child suffered because he was closest to me. And for that, I will never forgive myself."

I finally let go of her wrists. My hands fell to my sides. It was as though the wind had been knocked from my lungs. This woman, this beautiful, hunted, undead woman, was a child killer. No. Not Leonora, I warred with myself. It wasn't possible. I would have believed it of Constantinos. I would have believed it of Vladec Salei... *Vladec Salei.* A man to whom murder was second nature. "How?"

"*How*? You have the temerity to ask me how? How do you think?" she said, more anguished than enraged. "Aren't you satisfied that I admitted my sin, Eric? What more do you want from me?"

"I want you to tell me what happened. Every last detail."

"You're sicker than Constantinos," she said, her mouth twisting in disgust. "What good would that do for anyone?"

"It would get to the truth."

"I've told you the truth!" she bellowed.

"Your version, Salei's version. I don't believe you could kill your own son."

"Clearly, you've never witnessed a vampiric rebirth."

Despite my resolve to wrench the truth from her no matter what, I faltered at the thought of such a horror. "Regardless," I said, pressing on, shoving the visual from my mind, "Tell me what happened, truly. That is, if you can remember."

The change that came over her revealed everything. Her eyelids fluttered, her brows relaxed, she looked around her as though she didn't know where she was. "I..."

"Yes."

"I..."

"Go on."

"I can't."

"Exactly."

"Constantinos destroyed my life and the life of the one I loved most."

"Mattias."

"Yes."

"And your son..."

"I did that," she said, without a shred of conviction.

"No. That's what *he* wanted you to believe," I said, taking her hands in mine.

"I was not myself, I killed my son."

"Leonora, please, stop believing his lies. Don't you see it was his way of controlling you? He knew your supposed secret. He could tell it to the world whenever he chose."

She nodded absently. I knew my wild speculation was no longer just that. The seed of doubt had taken root in her mind. "I was robbed of air for too long. My memory was never the same after that night. But how, Eric? How could he convince me I was a murderer?"

"Suggestion? Hypnosis? You know him better than I do."

Her black eyes looked up at me, imploring me to explain away her guilt, to absolve her from the sin of a crime she never committed.

"All obstacles were eliminated," I said, speaking my thoughts, following my suspicions to their conclusion. "Constantinos did away with your husband, and Salei did away with your son."

"No..." she maintained weakly.

"And now, they are fighting for you."

"What?"

She was genuinely startled. She shook her head in disbelief. Surely she knew Constantinos was still alive?

"That is why he sent me away..." she said, almost to herself.

"Who?"

"Vladec...he couldn't be so mad. He knows better than to get himself tangled with Constantinos. Oh, what a fool I have been." She broke away and began pacing. I watched for any sudden movement toward the pills, but she was in her own shadow world now and paid no notice to anything or anyone. "Of course Constantinos isn't dead. I should have known better than to believe Vladec. And if Constantinos is alive... I wonder...Zigmund...no, I would have felt his presence. *That*, I know, is too much to hope for."

Zigmund, there was that name again. The name Constantinos had obsessed over, the name that had caused Stefan to be turned. If I ever found out this Zigmund character was still alive, I'd kill him.

"He used me," she said bitterly.

"Why has Salei never turned you?" I asked, finding this fact inexplicable.

"He wouldn't dare. He knows what Constantinos did to me. He dares not trifle with the power of a full-fledged Vrykolakas." I thought of the barbed tongue, the sores, the rampant stench of evil that followed Constantinos wherever he went. Leonora could not possibly turn into such an abomination when provoked? I hoped that whatever goodness she had possessed while still human had transferred over to her when she became one of them.

Something still did not make sense. The question, "Then why else do you stay with him?" was on my lips. He had designed a fabrication to keep her under his thumb, but if she'd really wanted to, she could have fled. She looked so utterly defeated that I couldn't bring myself to torment her further. Her arms hung loose by her sides, and that's when I noticed the blood spotting the lace of her sleeve and the hole in her wrist. A slight hole, as if made by a needle or syringe. That sight told me everything. I knew what Salei's true hold over her was. He was her supplier. Without him, she would die.

"Don't look so scandalized, Eric. Would you rather I tore open throats? It's been a struggle all these years, since I will not feed, much to Vladec's dismay. He even tried to force me to take part in the little turning productions."

"Productions?" I asked, surprised by the term.

"The operas. The Borois' operas. Or rather *Boroi*, now." A slight smile lifted the corner of her lips, but quickly vanished. Warring sides of her nature: joy that Sorina Boroi was dead, yet an inexplicably human sadness over the loss of life. She wasn't as far gone as I had thought.

"So, the operas are not Salei's doing?"

"Vladec was Augustin and Sorina's mentor. Something of a father figure to them. To Augustin, at least. To Sorina, well, you and I both know she had other ideas. Vladec never felt anything but a filial regard for her. He taught them everything he knows, took them in after they had been turned. The operas were a creative outlet for them and also a means to obtain fresh meat."

I shuddered at the casual tone her voice took on as she described the calculated trapping and killing of those young girls. I thought of Arabella: innocent and terrified on that stage and then lying in the middle of Castle Bran, sucked dry of life by Boroi and Stefan's sisters.

"It was no trouble to lure them, poor unsuspecting innocents that they were," she continued. "None of them could resist Augustin's charms or the promise of fame on the stage. I turned a blind eye to them all, tolerated them, even, but this last time with Nanette Monteau..."

"Arabella?" I questioned.

"Arabella, yes...that was different. The story was familiar, *too* familiar. It was just the kind of tasteless thing Sorina Boroi would have dreamed up to torment me...and Vladec sanctioned it."

I remembered Arabella's terror at the sight of the cloaked figure, who I now knew was meant to represent Constantinos.

"The pain was still too raw. When I saw that...that...atrocity on stage..." She looked up at me with an expression that melted my heart. I wanted to reach out to her, to take her in my arms, to save her from this death march the rest of her existence would be.

"When I saw what Constantinos had done to me, I panicked," she said, reliving the past once more. "And then Vladec materialized. I told you once he saved me. I'm not so sure of that now."

She turned away, lost in remembrances of things I was sorry I'd forced her to recall. "I must have felt affection for him once. He had the answer to my needs. It isn't human blood, if you were wondering. There's a butcher he knows, somewhere, he won't tell me where, for obvious reasons, that supplies him with the blood of slaughtered animals."

She paused, allowing me time to let these facts, along with the presence of the iron tablets, sink in. "I turned a blind eye to his pursuits all these years," she said, her voice strained, "and I will have to atone for my complicity one day. But now this? The devil used me. I shouldn't be surprised," she said, her tone changing yet again as she lapsed into a fog of oblivion to my presence. "He dangled the prospect of seeing me again in front of Constantinos like a slab of meat in front of a starving wolf. A wolf, that's rich," she said, and laughed as though she knew more than she was ever going to tell me. "Vladec may be a lot of things," she continued, "but a fool he is not. But this...this is *madness* and can only mean one thing. Listen to me, Eric," she said, rounding on me, gripping my shirt collar. "If Vladec has conscripted Constantinos, it can only mean that he has gone through with that idiotic plan of his, to turn Stefan into a..."

"Corcitura, I know."

Her brow furrowed. "How would you know? He has only ever shared his intentions with me..."

"And Luc."

"Sciocco," she muttered. She sighed and looked at me as though I should know what this meant.

"You cannot mean Luc will suffer for this?" I asked.

"Yes, sooner or later Vladec will kill him. To possess such knowledge is a death sentence for Luc. They've made him their lackey, their gatherer. Their wraith is what they call him. He has sight, knowledge, whatever you want to call it. He would have been better off if they'd turned him. It's unnatural, the things he knows and is capable of. And now they will make him pay for sharing his knowledge with you. I *do* pity him," she said, as if this admission surprised her.

She had mentioned *they*...she couldn't mean Constantinos? I had thought Salei had been truthful in that respect at least. Salei had tainted Stefan's scent like he said he would. I had witnessed it. Leonora could only have been talking about one other person, or vampire, I corrected myself.

"Augustin Boroi."

She didn't say anything, but her eyes confirmed it. "Eric, you must run."

Somewhere within the house, glass shattered. Gunshots reverberated downstairs. An inhuman shriek snaked up through the floorboards. I heard Guildy screaming, then Ambrose fired again and all was silent.

I was in a daze, unsure of what had just happened. It was quiet now, too quiet. I started as I felt Leonora's hand on mine. I looked down and uncurled my palm, exposing a roll of pounds.

"It's enough to get you home and start you out in a new life, far away from everything you've known...somewhere where you'll be safe."

"Leonora, I can't."

"Just take it...please."

I stuffed the money in my pocket and turned to leave, but she held me back.

"Promise me you will return to me if I need you," she said, clutching at my arm, her eyes fevered, desperate.

"Leonora...I..."

"Promise me, Eric! Don't leave me without hope. I can last out on my own, I know, but if I ever need your help, for myself or one who is dear to me, promise me you'll come? I have no one else I can trust."

Her words ripped at my heart and left me speechless. What could I do for her, save love her? At that moment, that was all I had to offer. I knew this could very well be the last time I would see her, although I railed against that reality, holding out hope where no hope existed.

A crash sounded below. My time was running out. This was my last chance to do what I had been wanting to ever since the first day I saw Leonora.

I took her face in my hands and kissed her.

Her lips were cold as ice, her face, equally frigid, but as the kiss deepened, I felt the warmth of my own lips transfer to hers, and I felt something else, too. I pulled away, my lips pricked, a small speck of blood left where her incisors had grazed me.

"Now you know what it feels like to kiss a Vrykolakas," she said quietly, her teeth retracting. "Go, and God protect you."

I wanted to stay, to kiss her again, to feel the electric heat her lips sent through my body, yet I knew if I did, there was no telling what she would do in her state. It was with great control that she had only let her fangs brush against my lips. If I stayed, she might do any number of things...and I'd let her get away with all of them.

I squeezed her hand, then fled the room. I looked back before descending the stairs and saw that she had dropped to her knees and was gathering her pills back into the bottle. If she needed me, I had promised I'd be there. As I watched her shaking hands and worried face, I knew that no matter the danger to myself, I would stay true to my word.

The sitting room was in a shambles by the time I crossed the threshold. All the tables had been overturned. Even the escritoire, which no less than two or three men could have lifted, was lying on its side.

Ambrose stood, gun at the ready, by the shattered windowpane, and Guildy, thank God, was still in one piece. She was leaning against the divan, her hands still clutched around the cross, her eyes vacant and staring fixedly at the gaping hole where a window used to be. At her feet was the sword I had dropped in my haste to flee upstairs. I hadn't even noticed I'd left it behind.

I kicked the scabbard aside and knelt before this woman who had not flinched when death came to call. "Guildy, *Guildy*," I said, slapping her face gently.

She looked at me with unseeing eyes. "Eric? Eric, what are you still doing here? They will be back. You must run. Go, *now!*"

I grabbed the sword and rose, tripping over one of the tables as I backed toward the front door.

"Not that way, you foolish boy," she chided, rising to her feet. She was shaking, but putting up a good front for my sake. "Go through the back. They will be in the front, waiting to ambush you. They really *are* vampires."

"Guildy, please..."

"No," she said, placing a hand to her forehead to stop herself from shaking. "Don't tell me any more. I feel mad as it is. They will not harm me, at least the true ones won't. I can't be sure of the new blood." She stopped on the threshold, laughed spasmodically, then led me toward the back of the house.

So Stefan was indeed with them. Augustin Boroi, Vladec Salei, and Stefan Belododia—an unholy trinity of newly minted blood brothers. And here I was with nothing but the blasted sword to protect me.

Guildy opened the door a crack and looked out. Once she had assured me there was no threat, she shoved me through the opening.

"You will always have a friend at the ready in me, old toff," she said, rallying somewhat to ruffle my hair. "Pray, don't ever show your face in Paris again. But if you need me, I'll be there. I expect you to write often, but do it through a third channel, Eric, I beg you. I cannot bear to think what they will do to you if they find you."

"But what about you?" I asked. They didn't have short memories. They would not forget her stand against them.

"They don't frighten me," she lied. "In honesty, Eric," she said, taking my hand, "their interest is in you, not an old woman who is bound to die in a few years anyway."

"Guildy!"

"No, Eric, listen to reason. I am not their concern. They would have reacted exactly the same way had you popped into the house next door."

I swallowed hard. She was right.

"Now, get on with you. You can catch the last train to Calais if you hurry. Be careful, my dearest boy."

I wanted to linger, to stay with her, make certain she would be safe. "There's nothing you can do or say that will make me feel better, love," she said. "Go, now, before it's too late."

I kissed her on the cheek then slinked off, careful not to draw attention to myself, which was rather hard, considering the sword and my lack of protective covering with which to conceal my face.

Corcitura

As I rounded the corner, I saw Salei in front of the house, right where Guildy had suspected he would still be—lurking underneath the shattered window. He was keeping guard, but there was no sign of Boroi or my erstwhile best friend.

I flattened myself against the wall and watched them, waiting for some sign or signal as to their next move. Something fell atop my head and I brushed it away. A raindrop, most probably. As I turned my attention back to the front of the house, I goggled at the sight before me.

Dangling directly outside the window of the room in which I had been with Leonora not ten minutes before, was Stefan. There were no handholds or footholds for him to grab onto, but he hung there nonetheless, seemingly affixed to the side of Guildy's house. I wondered how long he had been hanging there, how much he had heard of our conversation, if anything. Without thinking, I took a step in his direction. I don't know what I thought to do, or what defense I could have offered myself, save for the sword, which I was certain was powerless against him, but the idea of Leonora being threatened filled me with a rage that drove all rational thought from my mind. Only after I had gone a pace did I realize the danger I had placed myself in.

In a flash, Stefan somersaulted off the window and landed, catlike, on his feet on the pavement below. I stopped dead in my tracks and flattened myself against the wall again, hoping they had not noticed me.

Something struck my head again. I knew it couldn't be rain this time, for the sky was clear, with not a single cloud on the horizon. Another drop hit my head and I looked up angrily.

It wasn't rain.

Augustin Boroi, his drool-flecked fangs fully extended, was perched on the wall like a spider, his mouth inches from my head.

I bolted like the devil was on my heels, which was closer to the truth than I liked. The streets were empty, something I found a little too convenient. Salei and Company must have orchestrated this, too, curse them. I had not even the slightest inkling how influential they were in Paris. I was on my own, with not even a passerby to help me.

Although there were no people about, there were objects, and I intended to use whatever I could to stop Augustin Boroi. Everything I passed, I pulled down—wastebaskets, newsstands, whatever I could get my hands on—in the hope that it would trip my pursuer up. But he came on doggedly, chasing me on all fours, loping like some wild beast after its prey.

I rounded a turn and momentarily lost him. Panting, I halted in front of the Musée Grévin. A huge crowd swelled around the entrance. Posters advertising the new, "Thrillingly lifelike!" waxwork of the Austrian illusionist De La Mano were plastered all over the front of the facade. Patrons pointed and laughed and speculated about the man being resurrected in wax, since no one really knew if he were alive or dead, being that he'd vanished six years before. *Bloody macabre*, I heard someone say.

I had to laugh at this bit of unaccustomed luck. Salei could clear the streets, but a museum was an entirely different story, especially one as popular with tourists as the Grévin. Besides the crowd milling about the entrance, there was an equally large mob within. This would provide the perfect cover.

I reached into my pocket, pulled out the ticket fare, and disappeared into the throng. I was halfway through the lobby when I saw Augustin Boroi pacing outside. I ducked down, but the crowd was too thick for him to get through, and the ticket man was just closing the doors to shut out any more visitors. The hour must have been later than I thought.

I breathed a sigh of relief and wandered along into the rotunda. The Grévin reminded me of a mix of a Venetian palazzo and the Opéra Garnier, with all its marble, heavy gilding, rich red hangings and velvets, and baroque architecture. Up in one of the balconies surrounding the gallery, I saw a mannequin perched cross-legged on the ledge. He resembled Pierrot the French Clown from the old French Pantomimes. I shuddered at the sight of him. Ever since I was a child, I had loathed clowns, and the heavy, kohl-lidded eyes and moue of surprise on this one's face seemed somehow sinister to me. He was chalk-white from head to foot, his face as pale as alabaster, save for the black paint they had used to highlight his eyes and lips. His brows were arched and as raven black as his hair. He would have looked like a ghost if not for the few black poufs on his costume and shoes.

As I walked through to the dioramas, I couldn't suppress the feeling that the clown's eyes were following me, watching me with an interest I found frightening, all the more so because I must have been imagining the whole thing. Ridiculous. It was a mannequin, nothing more, nothing less. I was letting childhood fears get the best of me. Augustin Boroi was long gone, and Salei and Stefan with him. All I had to do was bide my time until night fell and then make for Gare du Nord and catch the train to Calais. After all the running I'd been doing over the past week, it would be a relief to relax and have a few hours of peace before I was forced to become a fugitive once again.

I wandered about for an hour or more before finally coming to what I had heard people in the museum say was the "pièce de résistance" of the dioramas—Marat's murder. I heard gasps of astonishment and disapproving comments regarding the "gauche realism of the French" from a few English ladies who were standing about, yet they did nothing to spare themselves from the sight, and instead remained gawking like schoolchildren, unable to tear themselves away. As I took in the scene, I noticed an Englishwoman and her beau standing next to me. He was looking on with a decidedly diffident eye, but she appeared to be on the verge of succumbing to some sort of fit.

"How shocking, Alistair," she said to the disinterested man, "it looks like real blood."

"Nonsense, Judith, don't be hysterical. Anyone can see it is synthetic."

I wasn't sure I agreed with him. I could tell Judith wasn't certain either, but they passed on and I forgot about them as I stepped closer for a better look. Marat lay in his bathtub, his lower body submerged in a pool of the "synthetic" blood.

A few feet away, Charlotte Corday, still clutching the knife, was being hauled away by the gendarmerie. In front of the ghastly scene, a sign had been posted, letting the public know that this was the actual bathtub in which Marat had been stabbed, with the knife being real as well. Having had more experience with blood than I thought I ever would, I wanted a closer look. I was about to stick my finger in the tub, when the next group came through and shunted me along.

I walked on past several more dioramas before coming to one that caught my eye and held my interest. In front of me unfolded a magnificent tableau of Henry VIII and his six wives in one of the staterooms at Greenwich Palace. Bluff King Hal was resplendent and imposing in his cloth of gold and slashed doublet. A regal velvet cape trailed from his massive shoulders and a feathered cap was poised atop his head at a jaunty angle. He was posed in his usual arms akimbo position and dominated the entire scene. The wives were no less impressive. Katharine of Aragon, Anne Boleyn, and Jane Seymour flanked his left, while Anne of Cleves, Katherine Howard, and Katherine Parr stood in a line to his right.

I thought it would've been in keeping with the bloodthirsty example of the Marat diorama if the tableau designers would have had Anne Boleyn and Katherine Howard holding their heads instead of doing things the dull and conventional way and keeping them attached to the queens' necks. Regardless of the historical inaccuracy, I found all the wives lovely, but Anne Boleyn was the one I decided to study closer. I'd always had a soft-spot for Anne Boleyn. I suppose this was engendered in me by my mother, who never did give credence to the incest and adultery rumors and had regaled me with the history of the doomed queen from a young age. As I admired her French style black dress with the longer, characteristic "Anne Sleeves," I noticed something wrong with her signature *B* necklace. It wasn't a *B* at all.

It was an *L*.

The same *L* attached to the necklace worn by Leonora.

Corcitura

I nearly snatched the necklace from around her neck. I tried to convince myself this was a logical occurrence, but there was nothing logical about the presence of Leonora's necklace in a wax museum. I thought back to our encounter in Guildy's library. There had been nothing around Leonora's neck but a thick choker of velvet. I remembered the feel of it beneath my fingers, for I had let my hands stray to her throat when I kissed her. How long the necklace had been out of her possession, I wasn't sure, but I hadn't set eyes on it since that night on the boat to Greece.

Its presence was no accident.

It was a message from those who were hunting me.

I raced back to the rotunda, looking up at the clown as I hurried through the room. He was still casually perched on the balcony ledge. Something about him seemed wrong, but I hadn't the time to worry over a mannequin.

I was expecting to find a crowd, but not a soul was in sight. What's more, it was black as pitch outside the doors—doors which were locked and would not budge no matter how hard I pushed against them. I pulled out my watch. It was half past nine already. Where had the hours gone?

I backed away from the doors. This couldn't be happening. Not again. I would have to find another way out or spend the night amongst the waxworks.

The prospect of keeping company in the dark with all those leering faces did not appeal to me in the least.

*Leering...*the word struck me cold, for it reminded me of the mannequin. And when I looked up toward the balcony, I saw that the clown was gone.

A ghostly, reedy sound drifted toward me. As it wafted through the rotunda, I realized it was a voice—a voice calling my name.

"Eeeeeeeeric."

The voice called out again, ending on a mad cackle that ricocheted through the hall. So the clown was playing its part to the hilt, except it wasn't a mannequin suddenly come to life through some black magic trick.

It was Augustin Boroi.

And he was hunting me.

‡

I skidded on the marble floor, throwing my arms around a pillar just in time to stop myself from crashing into a freestanding candelabra. I tried not to move, slowly drawing my foot away from the feet of the stand. The candles flickered as the stand rocked and finally settled back into place after a moment that seemed to drag on forever. All I needed was for the candelabra to tip over and set this whole bloody place on fire.

I crouched low and slid back against the pillar. This was a good hiding place.

You think so? My heart sank when I looked across the way and saw myself reflected in the floor to ceiling mirrors that surrounded me. To the right, it was no better, nor up above. Mirrors on the ceiling, mirrors on the walls... I was trapped in a blasted mirrored box.

Which meant I was as good as found.

I froze as I heard the slow, deliberate sound of footsteps marching up the corridor.

He was here.

I looked around the pillar. Augustin Boroi, or rather Perrot the Demonic Clown, stood in front of the waxwork of De La Mano and his assistant Lucinda. Boroi was engrossed in reading the plaque in front of the tableau.

"Child's play," he said. I saw his painted lips curl in derision. "What a farce. What *amateurs.*"

He tossed something back and forth between his hands, something that threw light against the face of De La Mano, distorting the waxwork's features. The air around that little orange ball seemed to be sucked into it every time it arced through space.

I heard something that sounded like kindling. Again, I looked at the ball.

Fire. What the devil was he playing at? I knew he was overly theatrical. Anyone who saw him act would know that. But a magician? That was the only explanation, for how could his hands not be singed by that flickering ball of flame?

I tightened my grip on the sword. This was the first time I had witnessed his skills at legerdemain, and I hoped it would be my last. One of us wasn't getting out of here alive. I was determined to do everything a human being could to ensure that I walked out of this place in one piece.

Laughter, low and threatening, snaked through the corridor. I put my hands over my ears, but that didn't do anything to stop the laughter from burrowing into my brain, jarring it as it shook the parquet floor.

I looked around the pillar as the laughter stopped. The ball of fire hung suspended above Boroi's upturned palm.

Sparks suddenly flew upward. Boroi snapped his fingers and the ball of flame disappeared. Again the corridor shook with his laughter.

Something was happening to the waxworks. De La Mano and Lucinda folded in on themselves, their wax skin melting grotesquely. Noses caved in, leaving gaping black holes. Eyes grew runny at the corners, the dye cascading down their faces making the figures look as though they were crying blood. It was ghastly, but I couldn't turn away. Rivulets of fire trailed up their bodies, devouring every last bit of wax and cloth and jewel. The pearls on Lucinda's costume exploded as the fire touched them. I slid my feet under me, leaning against the pillar to dodge the shards that rained down.

Boroi walked on past tableau after tableau. Every figure he glanced at was immediately reduced to a puddle of goo. A fleeting thought that this would happen to me if he looked my way nearly caused me to bolt like a maniac from where I sat. But that would have done me no good. I had to stay calm...

...which was nearly impossible when I saw the fire streaking out behind Boroi's feet.

Two lines of flame flowed in his wake. He lifted one foot, then the other, and after each step, tongues of fire sprouted from the surface of the wood.

"One two three, let me see, how shall I dispose of Bradburry?"

Calmness be damned. To wait any longer was suicidal. I scrabbled across the floor, bounded to my feet, and ran from the room.

I pulled up on the threshold, winded, completely lost. The room was dark, but I could just make out the tableau in the corner—Marat's death scene.

How fitting, I thought grimly.

"Three, four, five...how long will he stay alive?"

Oh, shut up, you demented clown.

I ducked behind the gendarmerie and covered my ears with my hands. I couldn't take much more of his Carrollian babbling, nor the way he was toying with me. As long as his patience and sadistic streak held out, I had time, but once he tired of the game, I would be dispatched—mercilessly.

Just like Marat.

Of all the dioramas I had to find myself in. And yet... I saw the knife in Charlotte Corday's hands and remembered the blade I held in my own. The sword was silver. Augustin Boroi was no Corcitura, after all.

He'd had the chance to be puppet master. Now it was my turn, my chance to toy with him as cruelly as he was toying with me, to get back at him for everything—for Stefan, for thinking I was the one who killed Boroi's bally witch of a sister. Bait him, that's what I wanted to do.

"I suppose you'd like to know how your sister died."

"You killed her, burned her, *wretch*!"

The voice was much closer now, much closer than I had expected. So close, in fact, that I could almost feel the force of his anger. I knew he and Sorina had committed worse abominations than incest, but it was the most inflammatory accusation I could think of at the moment. And besides, there must have been rumors circulating that they were more familial than they cared to admit. "You loved her, didn't you? But with what kind of love? It's a good thing she died before you had the chance to express yourself any further."

He swore in French, which was odd. I didn't know he even spoke French. But when he continued spewing hate at me, I guessed he'd chosen French for my benefit, since it was one of the languages I understood. He called me the filthiest names and heaped curse upon curse on my soul, so that I was certain if I didn't make it out of this alive, I would be damned for all eternity.

Corcitura

All the more reason to get out of here...now.

The waxwork of Charlotte Corday began to totter. A low, savage growl seemed to be coming from the statue, or rather from the figure behind it. I braced myself for the impact as Augustin Boroi flung the waxwork aside and pounced on me.

He lunged for my throat. I raised the sheathed sword, using it as a barrier between us—he holding onto one side and me clinging with all my might to the other. He clawed at the sheath, trying to rip the sword from my grasp, but I'd had enough of him and was not going to let go.

He still wore the white, ruffled garb. The death white face paint had turned a mottled grey color, and the kohl around his eyes had been smeared by the perspiration beading down his brow, so that his face now looked as though it had been streaked by black tears.

I kicked him in the leg, but he held firm, the blow only loosing his skullcap and exposing his wild curls. The motion distracted me, but only for a moment, for he hissed and all my attention focused on his eyes. It was the first time I had seen Augustin Boroi in his true state. Not even the glimpse of him on the wall of Guildy's house could have prepared me for the full horror that was now nearly nose to nose with me.

His eyes had gone completely black, the pupils elongating into vertical slits that seemed almost reptilian. His fangs were fully extended. Drool spattered against my face as he spat out more and more vile curses in French.

He leaned closer to my throat. I tore at his sleeve, ripping the fabric to reveal his bare arm underneath. A bullet was lodged in his shoulder, blood dripping from the fresh wound.

Ambrose's handiwork.

Yet Augustin was not dead, not even inhibited, because Ambrose had not aimed for the beast's heart.

He yanked at the sheath, but I pulled it back, causing us to roll over and collide with the fallen statue of Charlotte Corday. The knife in her upraised hand bobbled above his head. I wished it would fall and impale him, though it wouldn't do anything more than stun him momentarily. The collision was enough to distract Boroi and make him loosen his hold. I seized my chance, latched onto the hilt of the sword, and unsheathed the blade. I slid back on the floor to gain purchase, then kicked my legs into his chest as hard as I could, knocking him backward. He was winded and more than a little shocked, which was exactly what I was hoping the effect would be. I scrambled to my feet and got ready to strike the blow that would either save me or simply delay the inevitable.

Boroi righted himself and glared at me. "A sword, silver perchance?" he asked mockingly. He wiped the foam from his mouth. I saw that his nails had grown longer over the past minute. He was transformed even more now. His fangs were more pronounced, his eyes, if it were possible, had turned an ever deeper shade of black, and those nails...those nails were more like talons than anything a human being should have possessed.

I gripped the hilt so tightly I could feel the silver digging into my palms. I knew I could face him, yet his confidence unnerved me, especially now that he was circling me as if he were moments from lunging in for the kill. The attack would be swift, my death slow and painful, and then, if he deemed me worthy, which I doubted, I'd become one like him. I raised the sword higher, protecting my throat from the coming attack as best I could.

"I wanted to burn you, make you suffer like Sorina. You left her to die in that accursed hellhole," he growled. As he spoke, I felt heat travelling up my arms, felt my hands burning, and knew the godless wretch was using his tricks on me. He was insane if he thought I'd melt as easily as the waxwork of De La Mano.

"Enough with your parlor tricks," I said, shaking the flames off. They disappeared as soon as I focused my attention on them. It couldn't have just been a trick. I felt the heat, but they were gone, and my skin showed no signs of having been burned. Had it all been in my mind? Was he trying to drive me insane?

No, just to distraction. Enough so you'll drop the sword.

I backed away in alarm, for he'd somehow inched closer to me without my noticing. I raised the sword. "Fight me fairly, like a man, if you still consider yourself one." *Well, that was powerful, Eric. Absolutely terrifying.*

"You amuse me, Bradburry. In another life, maybe you would have felt differently. I could have taught you great things."

"Stop parroting Vladec Salei."

All his amusement vanished. His face became like a mask, his eyes narrowed to slits, his mouth turned down at the edges.

Prey was only amusing when it didn't talk back.

"Very well, then. We will do things the way they are done in Wallachia. Or at least the way *I* do them." He laughed—a hollow grating cackle that shivered my spine—as he advanced on me, his fangs so long they covered his lower lip.

I braced myself. He lunged, flying through the air. His screech did not shake my resolve, for my scream was even louder. I fell to my knees and struck out with the sword.

The force of the impact slammed me into the floor. By some miracle, I was alive. I hadn't yet opened my eyes. If anyone knew how to cheat death, it would be Augustin Boroi. I wasn't ready to face the possibility that I had missed. I was shivering uncontrollably, my hands clamped onto the hilt so fiercely I'd probably have the imprint permanently impressed upon my palms.

I couldn't go on like a statue forever. My head was still firmly affixed to my neck, which was a good sign. That decided me. I finally forced myself to open my eyes. The sight before me made my heart lodge in my throat.

I hadn't missed.

His breath hissed through his teeth as he tried to cling to his last moments of life. His fangs were still extended, spittle dripping off them and onto my shirt, mixing with the blood that had already fallen there from his wound. His eyes shrunk to normal size as the life drained from them and they became nothing more than hollow black pools. He twitched convulsively one last time, his incisors receding of their own volition, for Augustin Boroi was very much dead—impaled straight through the heart by the silver sword.

Even in death, he was a heavy beast. I flung him off me and slid the sword out of his chest, wiping the blood on a towel hanging on the ledge of Marat's bath. *Realism,* I reminded myself—they'd think it was part of the diorama.

Marat wasn't hard to lift. It only took me a few moments to hide the body.

I walked back to Boroi, rolled him onto my shoulders, and headed for the tub once more. Why I should have feared he would reanimate was beyond me, but I wasn't clear on all the characteristics of his vampiric type, so I made sure to keep his head away from my throat. It was the work of a moment to drop him into the tub and arrange him in the position Marat had occupied.

I stepped back to survey my handiwork, undisturbed that I had just taken a life. Boroi wasn't a some*one*, he was a some*thing*. I couldn't find it in my heart to be remorseful when I knew I had done the world a service by dispatching such a devil. And if not the world, at least the entire female population under the age of fifty—and more importantly, Leonora. His lusts would have fixated on her eventually.

As I stepped back, I bumped into something that made me screech. Turning round, I saw it was Charlotte Corday, knife still in hand.

Why not?

I righted the waxwork, wrenched the knife from her grasp, and slid it into the slot in Boroi's chest. Best to make it look authentic. Let them think some mad anarchist had stormed the Musée and killed someone in the manner of Marat. The political establishment and the gendarmerie would have their hands full solving this one. Especially when they realized the victim was dead twice over.

I retreated through a tableau showing the Field of the Cloth of Gold, then passed Henry and his wives, making sure to retrieve Leonora's necklace from around the throat of Anne Boleyn.

I had to find a way out. I hoped I would find keys behind the ticket counter. Failing that, I would have no choice but to break through the glass doors at the entrance. A place this large and popular was bound to have some sort of anti-burglar system. I would be taking a great chance by shattering that glass, but what other option did I have? Besides, it was meant to look like a crime, after all. And there was no way I would spend the night amongst the leering waxworks, nor the specter of Augustin Boroi. Seeing one mannequin come to life was quite enough for me.

I reached the rotunda and made straight for the ticket counter. After a search, I came up empty. There was nothing for it but to break out. I seized a stool and chucked it through the glass. As I had suspected, a tremendous clanging of bells erupted once the glass was shattered. Thankfully, it was dark enough outside to provide me cover, and as the bells continued to peal, I bolted through the opening and hightailed it down the thoroughfare.

The facade of Gare du Nord soon loomed into view. I stopped to consult my watch. Half past two in the morning. In six hours' time, I would be on the train to Calais. Concealing myself until then would be an adventure.

I took a seat on a bench near the entrance to the station. The previous day's *L'Observateur de Paris* was bunched up in the corner. That would do as a good disguise and also as a means to entertain myself until dawn arrived. I read over an article about the exorbitant price of imported fish, then turned to the gossip columns where I read about a woman named Manon Larue being linked in a scandalous way with some Russian count. Typical music hall gossip. After a while, I tired of reading, but kept the paper open to hide my face.

An hour passed. I felt my eyes closing but would not give in to sleep this night. Something ran past the bench. I jolted up, fearful of seeing Salei and Stefan, but it was only two lovers playing a game of tag.

I settled in and watched the wind blowing through the trees until around six thirty, when I heard Gare Du Nord waking up behind me. Stretching my legs, I put the paper down and rose from the bench, only to be nearly collided with by two eager young chaps chuntering on about the discovery of a body in the Marat diorama at the Musée Grévin. Those blasted alarm bells had done their job right quick.

I left the lads to their own suppositions and hurried into the station. By seven, I was settled into a cabin aboard the train bound for Calais. Now that I was safe, I allowed myself some rest, waking when I felt the train pulling out of the station. I was heading home, but even though I had left my pursuers behind me, I was still troubled by one thing.

What was I going to tell Stefan's parents?

The Ratliff Horror

s I stepped off the train at Euston Station, I suppressed the urge to bend down and kiss my native soil. There were times during the past two months when I thought I'd never live to see London again. For two months, I had been fighting against things I didn't understand, and now here I was alive, for the moment.

As I passed through the crowded station, I looked about for any sign of my pursuers, and sighed when I did not see them. It was a sigh of relief, but also of disappointment. To feel this way bordered on the suicidal, but the fact that I had passed through Calais and then on to London undetected made me suspicious. It would have been better if I had at least known they were not too far behind. What was that old adage? Keep your friends close and your enemies closer. Well, not too close, but close enough that I could be one step ahead of them.

In ten minutes, I was on my street. In another two, I'd be home, but I couldn't make myself take any more steps, not yet, not when I had no idea what I was going to say to my parents, let alone Stefan's later that night.

I stood before my home, staring up the steps at the red door and brass knocker, wondering what Mother and Roderick would say when they saw me back so soon—and noticeably alone. We'd promised to come home together, to gush mutually to our parents about our adventures and experiences, but that was definitely not going to happen now.

I had purchased a coat in Dover and now had the sword concealed within it, but the moment my mother hugged me, she'd feel it and then I'd have to make up some half-baked story to cover the truth. The simplest solution would be to tell them that I had dropped Stefan at his parents' home. I decided to lead with that until rest and a sound mind allowed me to think of a way of telling them what really happened. I doubted they'd give credence to that version of the story when the time came, but one look at Stefan in his new incarnation would be enough to make them believers.

I walked up the steps and raised my fist, but the door swung open before I could even knock.

"Eric, thank God," my mother said, taking me in her arms. "We feared the worst. Poor Stefan must be devastated."

"Poor Stefan? What do you mean?" I demanded, breaking away from her.

"I can't bear to repeat it," she said, overcome to the point of tears. "Roderick's gone to see if there's anything he can do to help. It's dreadful Eric...*horrifying*."

"Mother," I said, taking her by the shoulders. "What's happened?"

All she could manage was a shuddering gasp before she collapsed on the settee, not quite fainting, but very close to it.

"Jameson," I shouted. "Jameson, come quickly." Moments later, Jameson, our butler, appeared, carrying a tray on which rested a cup of tea and a copy of the *Daily Telegraph*.

"Here, Mother," I said, putting the cup to her lips. "Drink this."

"It's best I go upstairs," she said weakly, taking the tea with her and rising unsteadily to her feet. I watched her totter up the stairs before turning my attention back to Jameson, hoping he could shed some light on what had happened.

"A big to-do about all this, what?" I said lightly, trying to alleviate the sense of foreboding that had settled like an incubus on my chest.

Jameson looked at me steadily, but didn't answer.

"And Roddy's gone off to save the day, I hear?" I asked, trying once again to elicit some response from the butler.

"A pressing matter has called him away, sir," he said officiously. He had an ill-favored look about him that told me he knew more than he was letting on. "I shouldn't suspect he will be returning anytime soon," he continued hastily. "Now, if you will not be needing me any longer, sir, I shall leave you to rest. Sir...Sir, I say, is something the matter?"

It was no longer in my power to pay any heed to Jameson, for my attention was focused solely on the enormous black letters glaring up at me from the front page of the *Telegraph.*

Millionaire Philanthropists Found Dead

I snatched the paper off the tray and held it before my eyes, foolishly hoping the millionaire philanthropists of the headline were not the same ones I had been acquainted with since the days of my childhood. The headline danced before me, blurring in and out as I read over the words again and again, too scared to look at the report and have all my fears confirmed. Finally, I looked away from the headline and forced myself to read the article below.

London, Monday, 13 August 1888—Late last evening, David and Marishka Ratliff were found brutally murdered in their home in Westminster. Scotland Yard inspectors immediately questioned Mr. and Mrs. Ratliff's servants and neighbors, but all were cleared of any involvement in the crime. The inspectors have noted that the modus operandi matches that employed in the murder of a woman, Martha Tabram, who was found stabbed to death in Whitechapel nearly one week ago. Although the authorities had ruled that the Tabram murder was an isolated incident, this new crime has made them reconsider. Do we have a killer in our midst?

The authorities seem to think so. As with the former victim, the bodies of Mr. and Mrs. Ratliff were covered in stab wounds, but in this case, the killer has added an additional weapon to his murderous arsenal: slashing throats in a particularly savage fashion with what the Americans call Devil's Rope. Upon further inspection, it was determined that Mr. and Mrs. Ratliff's throats had been savagely ripped open by a piece of barbed wire. Authorities had thought the killer to be from Whitechapel, but in light of this recent crime in Westminster, it is feared that the murderer has taken up residence in this district and will begin to perpetuate more atrocities in this part of the city. They caution against widespread panic, but one cannot help wondering when the next ax, or piece of barbed wire, as we now have it, will fall.

I ignored the last line for the sensationalism it was and turned the page. A photograph of David and Marishka with Stefan as a child took up half the page and underneath it ran the following:

Mr. and Mrs. Ratliff were well-known throughout Europe for their care of and generosity toward Romanian orphans, many of whom they brought to London to be educated. They are survived by their son, Stefan, who was not home when the murders were committed and is not a suspect in his parents' deaths. Mr. and Mrs. Ratliff's only son and heir, who was overcome with grief when given the horrible news, has asked that we print the following in memory of his beloved parents:

In Memoriam

As they were loved in life, so they shall be loved in death.
They will be sorely missed.

My entire body was shaking. Rage coursed through me. If Stefan had been in my presence then, Corcitura or not, I would have killed him with my bare hands. My one consolation was that he had *only* killed his parents, as horrible as that rationalization seemed. It was a small victory for their souls, for Stefan had not sought to make them members of his undead cadre. I couldn't think of any reason for him to murder yet another set of parents, but then again, that parricidal tendency had plagued the Belododia family for generations. Was it really an urge too strong for any of them to resist?

Forget them, and start over...with us, your true family, my Corcitura, my own...

The words spoken by Stefan in Vladec Salei's voice ricocheted through my mind. Salei was Stefan's father now, his nearly half-millennium old ancestor who would become his mentor and assume control over Stefan's life now that his adoptive parents had been done away with. And if that were the case, the role of Stefan's mother would fall to...*No.*

I threw the paper down and stormed away from the bewildered Jameson. What could I do about it if it were true? Who was I fooling now? She was the logical figure. She had no choice. Leonora would go along in the bargain, serving as Stefan's protector...or worse, a bride...no, Salei would never let Stefan take that much control away from him. Yet did Salei truly understand the monster he had created? A Vrykolakas, an Upyr—concepts that were still so alien to me—along with the volatile bloodline of the Belododias. If it weren't so awful it would have been comical, for I was certain Salei had no idea what he had done. And if it were in my power, I would be there when he discovered his mistake.

I picked up the paper and stared at the memorial once again. "Sorely missed by everyone but you, that is," I grunted, my teeth clenched in anger, my heart appalled by such blatant hypocrisy.

I reread the article and decided I had to act immediately. I had to find him before he fled the country with Vladec Salei. God only knew where they were headed. Maybe back to Greece, since there was no longer any need to keep up with the pretense of the operas. The spectacles would be missed, but I had a feeling all the mothers and fathers in Paris would sleep better knowing their daughters were safe in their beds and not being dragged like lambs to the slaughter beneath the opera's stage.

Or maybe they'd head to Romania and seek out Nadia and the blood. I made a mental note to make inquiries and track her down as soon as I could, no matter the obstacles or danger to herself. I had no delusions about her motives any longer, so danger be damned. If she were compromised, all the better. She had chosen to save her own skin. Let her fend for herself if the need arose. She was already quite good at self-preservation.

Then there was the question of the money. I didn't think Vladec Salei needed any more, but several million pounds wouldn't hurt, especially when it was all left in Stefan's name. He'd need a legal guardian until he came of age and who better than his own ancestor? Of course, that small detail would have to be kept out of the papers, but if there was one person who never let technicalities hinder him it was Vladec Salei.

I unhooked the sword from the belt loop at my back and affixed it to one on my left side, making the blade ready for quick unsheathing in case the need arose. The action exposed the sword to view. Jameson's slack-jawed surprise made me turn away. If I told him what I was planning, he'd do everything in his power to detain me. Jameson and I had always shared an uncanny bond. He had stopped me from making a fool of myself on many occasions, but this was different. He had been with our family for years and honestly felt more like an uncle to me than just a butler. I trusted him implicitly, but in this matter it was best he didn't know what I was planning to do.

"Keep an eye on Mother, Jameson," I said, still not meeting his eyes. "I'll be back as soon as I can."

"Master Eric..." That was a bad sign. Whenever he called me "Master Eric," it usually meant either a lecture was to follow or an all-out argument, in which I was usually the loser. "Whatever has happened to Mr. and Mrs. Ratliff, is it worth risking your life to find out the truth?"

I stared at him, wondering if he knew more than he was letting on. But how could he even begin to suspect? "Jameson," I said gravely, "I know what I must do. I have no choice. Take care of Mother until I return, and don't let anyone except Roderick into this house. Trust me...I know what I'm doing."

The truth was, I hadn't the slightest idea if what I was doing was right, or if it would do any good whatsoever. I only knew I had to do it. To let Stefan off scot-free, to let him live with the delusion that no one suspected him of murder, was something I could not allow.

Without waiting for a response, I squeezed Jameson's outstretched hand, pulled the coat around me, and set off, making sure to secure the front door behind me.

I had thought I'd be sweltering in the heavy overcoat, but the air was unseasonably frigid for an afternoon in the middle of August. I turned up the collar of the coat to shield my face from the bitter wind that felt like daggers as it pricked my skin, but the pain was the least of my worries. All I could think of were the cryptic words Vladec Salei had spoken through Stefan on that night in Venice. I cursed myself for not understanding their hidden meaning. If I had taken the time to puzzle over them, I might have been able to somehow prevent this horrible act of parricide. However painful these thoughts might be, I realized that hindsight would solve nothing now. The only thing that mattered was getting to Stefan before it was too late.

I didn't know what I expected to find at the scene. My mind raced over images of what I thought I'd be confronted with when I arrived, each scenario more gruesome or preposterous than the last. A coven of vampires crouched over the dead bodies of Stefan's parents? Highly unlikely, of course. Stefan, overcome with remorse, on his knees confessing to the police? That was an even remoter possibility. But the scene I saw when I arrived at the Ratliff mansion was more disturbing than all the pictures my thoughts had conjured. There was no blood, no dead bodies, no vampires...there was nothing amiss at all. If not for the presence of some Scotland Yard inspectors and a small crowd of onlookers that had gathered, there would have been no evidence that a violent crime had been committed here the night before.

The most unsettling aspect of this tableau was Stefan. He was sitting apart from the other players, as far removed from the action as he could be. He was perched on a bench on the side of the street, legs crossed, arms spread out along the top of the bench's back, his eyes staring out at nothing in particular with a vacant expression I could not read. I walked around his line of vision, seeking to take him by surprise. My skulking might have been unnecessary for all I knew. He probably sensed me and simply chose not to let on.

I never took my eyes off him as I circled behind, and it was with great effort that I suppressed my desire to run him through with the sword when I saw the small smile that lifted the corner of his lips. It was a smile of quiet triumph, as much of a celebration as he would allow himself to show in the presence of the authorities.

He was still sitting casually, reveling in his success, when I came up behind him and placed a hand on his arm. The muscles tightened beneath my hand and his shoulders stiffened as he uncrossed his legs and sat up as straight as a rod.

So my skulking had not been in vain. I *had* taken him by surprise after all.

"Bradburry...I thought you'd learned your lesson."

"You know I was always a slow learner," I said, continuing the banter as I reached for the sword.

"Slow to take a hint...yet not slow to react. Poor Augustin."

"I did what I had to," I responded, feeling the reassurance of the hilt within my grasp.

"And so did I," he said quietly. His shoulders went limp. The side of his face grew taut with an expression that almost conveyed remorse. If I didn't know better, if I hadn't seen him dangling outside Guildy's window looking like a ghoul just risen from the grave, this contrite demeanor would have taken me in.

"You've become an adept little chameleon," I said coldly. His mood instantly reverted to the tenseness of before. His eyes were narrowed and cunning as he turned and looked up into my face. "How did you do it, Stefan?"

"Do what?" he asked, blankly.

"You don't expect me to believe you know nothing?" He'd just admitted his guilt to me not two minutes before.

"I have no notion of what you are referring to."

This was preposterous. Did he take me for a fool? "Where were you last night, Stefan?" I said hotly.

"I was with a friend."

A tidy little alibi. "And would this friend be Vladec Salei, or have you taken up with a new troupe since you arrived back in London?"

"No!" he snapped, revealing more of his teeth than I thought prudent, given our surroundings.

I stepped back and let my coat close around the sword, not wanting to reveal my hand quite yet. He glanced at my side and his eyes flickered up to my face. He was startled, but he hadn't seen what was concealed underneath my coat. Apprehension clouded his eyes, but only momentarily, for he quickly regained control and once more assumed that suave, unflappable air he had learned so well from his mentor.

"Who, then?" I asked.

"It is none of your concern whom I choose to spend my evenings with, *Bradburry*."

I let him glare and sulk and think he had frightened me, which was not far from the truth. I did not like the way he glowered at me when he had called me Bradburry, something I still couldn't get used to coming from him. His face was fixed into the same look of hatred he had shown me in Venice, the same expression of malice I had seen him assume whenever there was any talk of Vladec Salei. In fact, it was almost as if Salei was staring out of Stefan's eyes at me now.

He seemed content to glare at me for the rest of his life, but I wasn't going to let him get off that easily. I wanted answers and I wanted justice. I was about to bait him further, when his contorted features relaxed and a look of cool detachment entered his eyes.

"Why do you plague me with such questions?" he asked calmly. "Can you not see that I grieve?"

Grieve? I nearly burst out laughing. Did he think I was suffering from amnesia? Had he forgotten all that had occurred since our arrival in Paris? Did he expect me to selectively forget everything I knew of him, especially that telling, hateful rant about David and Marishka that he indulged in when we were in Romania? And what about the revelation he had kept hidden from me his whole life—that he was a murderer? He must have thought that little time distorting jaunt they took me on did something to dull my senses and shatter my memory.

"If I truly believed your mourning to be sincere, Stefan," I said, my rage mounting, "I would have never questioned you to begin with. As it stands, I see no reason to repent for transgressions I have not committed. To do so under the present circumstances would be a grievous injustice to your parents' memory, for I would *never* apologize to their murderer."

My accusations had stunned Stefan so mightily that he staggered forward on the bench. "*Murderer?*" he gasped, color rushing into his pale face. "How could you, my supposed best friend in the entire world, even think such a horrible thing? Give me one good reason why I would want to kill my parents, for your logic is beyond my comprehension."

"Oh, I can think of plenty of reasons," I continued, anger at his falseness overwhelming me, "three and a half million reasons to be exact, and they're all sitting in the Bank of England."

"Are you actually suggesting that I killed my parents for their money?" Stefan asked, his tone quavering with horror that was badly feigned, even for one as skilled at dissembling as him.

"I'm not suggesting, Stefan. I *know*."

"No, you do not know me at all," he said darkly. "That's the problem. You never did."

"And why is that? Because you kept secrets from me, turned against me the minute someone else paid you any attention, and then threw in your lot with some wretched ghoul the moment you clapped eyes on him? It might not have been the money, Stefan, though I've no doubt that was an incentive. But it was something deeper in your heart. You made the choice, no matter how persuasive Vladec Salei was. It was *you* who chose to kill them in the end."

My words had come out in a rush, and as I stopped to catch my breath, I was stunned to see Stefan smiling. His head was bent and he looked as though he was studying his shoes, but I knew better. I had wanted to ask him if everything we had been to each other was a lie. All our years of friendship, our brotherhood...was that just a charade, too? I had wanted to ask him a million things, to discover what had turned him so black-hearted, but at the sight of his smile, all my questions faded and what I wanted most was to cut that blasted smirk off his face.

I unhooked the sword.

"A sword?" he cried, looking at the sheathed blade in disbelief. "Oh, very *Three Musketeers*. And where are your seconds, Monsieur D'Artagnan?" He covered his mouth with his hand, indulging in a laughing fit. But that abruptly ceased when I unsheathed the blade and he saw that the sword was the one I had stolen from him in Venice.

"*Give that to me,*" he growled.

"Your powers of mesmerism need work," I said wryly. "You are no Sorina Boroi."

"I...I..." he stuttered, visibly flustered. His mouth snapped shut and he smoothed his waistcoat, rising from the bench and drawing himself up to his full height, which was still four inches shorter than I was. "You will make a fine barrister one day, Bradburry," he hissed, "but do *not* play judge and jury with me!"

Before I could raise the sword, Stefan lunged over the bench and pinned me to the ground, crushing me under his seemingly frail form. The sword was knocked away, my grasping hand nowhere near reaching it. I struck him with my fists, but no matter how many blows I dealt, he would not budge. He did not even flinch. It was as though he felt no pain. Nothing I did could induce him to relent.

He reached for my neck, his fingernails suddenly turning a deep purple hue before my eyes. I intercepted and thrust out my palm, wrapping it around his ice-cold wrist. Everything about him seemed to be dying away except his unconquerable strength, which was rapidly sapping my resistance.

My strength finally failed me. I let my hands fall back against my chest. I felt more than saw him seize my shirt collar and tear it away, leaving my throat exposed. His breathing was labored and feverish as he leaned down toward my neck. Through my bleary eyes, I saw what appeared to be a tiny barb protruding through his parted lips. *So he'd inherited his tongue from Constantinos*, I thought grimly. I should've concentrated on the barb that was about to rip open my throat, but in my last moments of consciousness, I suddenly noticed his eyes.

"Your eyes!" I shrieked in horror. "They have no pupils!"

"Of course they have pupils!" he shouted, releasing me from his death grip and shielding his translucent eyes with his hands.

I sat up on my elbows and eyed him through narrowed lids.

"No, not yet," he whimpered. "It can't be happening so soon. It wasn't supposed to be this way. He told me I had nothing to fear. Liar! Curse him!"

The sight was impossible to bear, mainly because I didn't know if his mood was sincere or just another ruse to trick me into letting down my guard. He drew his knees up to his chest and clutched them tightly, rocking back and forth and mumbling to himself incoherently.

He looked utterly pathetic and so unlike the Stefan Ratliff I had known since childhood. I advanced toward him cautiously, mulling over memories in my mind: all our days at school, all our adventures, every word that could be construed to mean something different, now that I knew the secrets he had kept hidden. I was searching for some sign, some clue as to how he could have concealed his past from me, but my searching was in vain, for I could not recall a single instance in which he had betrayed himself in any way. He had either intentionally set out to deceive me or I had simply been blinded by the charming front he had presented all these years. Yet something was not right with either of those scenarios. I could not resign myself to having so badly misjudged his character.

Maybe I had never seen anything because I had never wanted to admit that he wasn't as perfect or as true a friend as I had always believed him to be. Looking back, I now felt like a fool for allowing the disillusionment to go on this long. In public, he'd always been the charmer, the popular one, the most caring and compassionate—the one everyone gravitated to. Yet in moments when it was just the two of us, he displayed a weakness that threatened to consume him, almost as if the charming act were too much of a strain to keep up in front of me, as if around everyone else he was holding back his true nature and feelings and with me he could forgo the pretense and be himself.

He was my best friend, yet the friendship had always seemed one-sided, now that I thought about it. I was the one who always had to be there to listen to his complaints, to bear him up when he was feeling low, to give in so that his plans could go off without a hitch, while all my ideas and schemes were forgotten, all my hopes and dreams given the requisite moment of attention but then pushed to the background in favor of his wants and needs.

He had the ability to infuriate me and make me hate him, but I would always forgive him—too quickly for my own good—because he had no one else who understood him the way I did, and neither did I. It was a symbiotic friendship. As I drew closer to his shuddering body, something in my mind clicked into place, and I had a blinding moment of clarity. Thirteen years of friendship had bonded us together more thoroughly than if we had been born of the same mother. Even at this late stage, I was unwilling to let him go.

"I forgive you, Stefan. For every crime you've committed, for everything you've done, I forgive you. We can get through this."

"I'm past redemption, Eric. What good is forgiveness to me now? I'm too far gone."

"No, you're not. Don't do this, Stefan. Don't give in. Fight it!" I said irrationally. He was standing on the precipice of a transformation that would debilitate him and turn him into something he had no control over, and I was asking him to deny it. This was my last hope, my final chance to save him, and I was asking him to do the impossible.

"Fight it, are you mad?! Fight bloodlust, the uncontrollable thirst, the desire I feel right now..." His fingers flexed convulsively as he struggled to continue. Anger, hatred, confusion, fear...all of these emotions warred in his eyes at once, darkening them, taking away some of the unnatural translucence. He looked away from me for an instant, then jerked back around. When he lifted his face to mine, I hardly recognized him. "Can you expect me to deny the hunger I have for your blood? The urge to tear off your head at this very moment? No, Eric. It's too late. I'm marked. I've already killed, and I will kill again."

He bent his head, fixing his vacant eyes on the pavement. I noticed that his teeth had extended a little. They were still canine-like and shockingly white, yet they appeared to be sharper, now, almost serrated.

Perfect for tearing into flesh.

Vladec Salei's nearly indestructible killing machine was sitting by my side, yet no matter how terrifying the thought that Stefan could lop off my head at any moment, I couldn't make myself move away from him. It was almost as if he were exerting some influence over me, just as Sorina Boroi had done to me in Paris.

"By nightfall you will no longer recognize me," he said in such a low voice I had to strain to hear the words. "What you saw outside Lady Guildford's house was only a preview of the monster I will become. I'm almost fully turned, Eric. I haven't much time left. Soon I will become a greater beast than those my countrymen have feared for centuries and then nothing will be able to stop me...not even myself. Swear to me, Eric," he said in a feverish voice, his eyes suddenly very dark and wild. "Swear to me you will do what I ask."

"I swear it, anything," I assented without thinking.

"Kill me."

"You know I can't," I said, more out of practicality than from any desire to not end his life.

"Kill me before it's too late," he insisted.

I leaned away from him. I sensed he was becoming hysterical again. I didn't have the strength to fight off another of his attacks. "Stefan, this is madness...you know I don't have..."

"Then you have condemned me to a fate worse than the death I am begging you to inflict upon me!" he shouted, causing the Scotland Yard inspectors and newly gathered police force to shoot alarmed glances at us. "My parents were only the start," he whispered. "If I am allowed to live, there is no telling what further atrocities I will commit. I can't be held responsible for what I will do."

"Stefan..."

"Why don't you call me what I am? I do not deserve to be called Stefan any longer."

Was it genuine remorse or just another one of the masks he had become so adept at wearing these past months? I searched his face for the contrition of a moment before, but there was no sign of it. Instead, he now had a strange look in his eyes, as if he couldn't believe he had just said something so contrite. And that's when I knew that whatever I had seen had been his last display of human feeling. Though his outer transformation was not yet complete, the corruption of his soul had already started to take place. He was toying with my mind. I had been a fool to believe I could save him.

"So help me God, Stefan, I would kill you if I could. Even if it meant having your blood on my hands."

"Not my blood, Eric," he said, his voice clam, menacing. "The blood of my victims." His lips twitched into a smirk so horrifying in its lack of warmth that I shuddered as though I'd been showered with ice. "You have made your choice, Bradburry, and I have made mine. Guard well the ones you love. It is for them that I shall come first."

I felt as though the wind had been knocked out of me. I couldn't speak, I couldn't breathe. Images of my mother, Roderick, my Aunt Roberta in America, Guildy...*Leonora*...pictures of all the ones I loved most flashed through my mind. Hot tears pricked my eyes, but I would have died before showing weakness to the monster glowering at my side. After a moment, I must have regained my resolve, for I heard a voice start to mumble, and I realized it was my own. "Half Vrykolakas...half Upyr..."

"All indestructible..."

"Almost." Anger, revulsion, and hatred surged through me. I dropped to my knees and rolled over on the ground, grasping the sword. Maybe it would detain him, slow him down, stop him long enough for something to be done to incarcerate him. Or maybe he'd find it humorous and use it to kill me instead. It was a chance I had no choice but to take.

I clutched the hilt and rammed the blade so forcefully though his chest that the tip came out his back.

His eyes bulged. For one hopeful moment, I thought I really had killed him, despite all Luc had told me to the contrary about conventional weapons being useless against him. He looked down at the blade in disbelief, then back up at me, his eyes widened in shock. Slowly, he raised his hand and grasped the hilt. Just as he was about to extract the sword, his other fist shot up and closed around his hand, gripping so tightly I expected the pressure to crack the skin and draw blood.

Blood...

I had been so preoccupied with Stefan's reaction that I had not noticed this simple fact. There was no blood anywhere. Not on the blade, not on the ground, not spurting out of the sizable gash the sword had made in Stefan's chest.

With one hand he pulled at the sword, while with the other, he shoved it in deeper. He was gibbering in a language I couldn't understand. As the spectacle wore on, I realized that Stefan's voice had split into two separate and distinct voices.

Salei was controlling him again, warring with him internally, just as he had done that night in Venice.

One instant, his eyes shone with a feral light. The next, he tucked his chin as though shying away from an aggressor. His eyes narrowed in fear and he whimpered, raising his shoulder slightly as though he were trying to ward off a blow.

I watched in mute fascination as the struggle for supremacy escalated. I forced myself to look away from his writhing form for a moment to see if the commotion had caught the attention of the constabulary. It was with great relief and simultaneous fear that I saw them staring at us. I felt like shouting to them, calling them over to clap Stefan in irons, but before I could, I heard an accented voice shout in English, "It cannot harm you, it is *mine!*" and my attention immediately returned to Stefan.

He had crumpled to the ground, his arms clutched around my legs. I felt him shaking against my knees and looked down to see his shoulders trembling. I believed he had won out over Vladec Salei. This shuddering was caused by him crying in relief that he had somehow—miraculously and beyond my powers to ascertain just *how*—set himself free. But then I understood. He was not crying.

He was laughing.

The laugh gurgled low in his throat. My legs shook of their own accord, for I'd heard that laugh once before.

In Greece, cowering in the dark, when I was hiding from Constantinos.

The sword quivered back and forth, twanging almost musically with each convulsive laugh. He had grown as pale as I'd ever seen him. Lifting his head, he smiled at me with a mouthful of serrated fangs.

"Oh, Eric, really," he said, looking down at the sword and laughing again. "You always were so gullible."

In one swift motion, he ripped the sword out of his chest and jumped to his feet. I was stunned that he was now on eyelevel with me. He had always been shorter, yet now his eyes bore directly into my own. They were no longer the translucent, sightless eyes of a corpse. These were deep and dark and deadly...the eyes of an animal, a hunter, a beast who fixes a stare on his prey just before he devours it.

And I was as paralyzed as a mouse before a cobra.

"Thank you," he said casually, weighing the sword in his hands. "I've been meaning to reclaim this ever since Venice. Vladec will be so pleased. And now, what shall I do with you?"

I envisioned myself sprawled on some sacrificial altar, surrounded by vampires all hungering for my blood. I saw myself shriveled, or worse, turned into one of them—an insatiable beast with no control over its impulses. This last visual was too much and jolted me into action. Not fully considering the risk I was taking, I seized Stefan by the collar and brought his face close to mine.

"All I have to do," I said, my voice trembling with anger, "is say one word and they will come running."

I expected him to laugh, but he grew serious. "And what word would that be?" he said almost fearfully, darting a glance at the gathered constabulary.

"Oh, Stefan, I believe you already know." Something flickered across his face. Fear? Maybe, but it was too late. I'd already shouted the word: "*Murderer!*"

There was a flurry of arms and legs and then a high, keening wail that reminded me of train wheels braking to a halt. Before I knew what had happened, twelve officers of the law had fallen upon Stefan and were dragging him into a patrol wagon. He resisted mightily, but I was quick to note he did not bare his fangs or otherwise show any signs of the creature he had become. It was almost as if he wanted to be hauled away.

I felt no pity in my heart, neither was I struck with any pangs of remorse for what I had done. Instead, I felt a great sense of relief, although I wasn't entirely certain I had seen the last of Stefan...or if the bars of the patrol wagon would cage him in long enough to let justice be done upon him.

As I walked away, I spotted a Scotland Yarder lingering off to the side, obviously waiting to interrogate me. "Sir, a word," he said officiously.

I looked back to see Stefan struggling against his captors. It was taking all twelve of them to hold him down and keep him from escaping. I hoped they would make quick work of getting him into the wagon, but I didn't hold out much hope for their chances, judging from the way he was fighting against their restraints. "He's dangerous, he must be locked up," I said rapidly. "An asylum, a mental institution, somewhere where he can do no harm to himself or anyone else. You *must* do this."

"But, Sir..."

"Trust me!"

"All right, all right, calm down," he said soothingly, probably thinking I was on the verge of a nervous collapse. "You say he's a murderer. I'm supposing you mean he's responsible for the murder of his parents? I suspected as much. Much too cool and collected, that one. Tell me what you know."

Thus prompted, I rattled off my lie, telling him how Stefan had confessed outright the moment he saw me, but then had decided to flee once I told him I would take the confession to the authorities. The inspector considered this for a moment, then seemed satisfied with my story, although I feared he wasn't entirely convinced of my own innocence. It was obvious he didn't fully trust me, yet he let me go nonetheless, but only after he had secured my address and a promise to be at the inquest on the morrow, stressing I would be arrested if I didn't make my appearance.

My part in the Ratliff Horror had come to an end. I could still hear Stefan making a big show of being dragged away, but I cared not a whit whether he rotted to death in prison or was hung within a fortnight. Neither of those means of execution would do him any harm. I inwardly cast my vote for a return to burning at the stake. Incineration had worked against Sorina Boroi. It seemed to solve the problem of permanently dispatching their kind.

I had traveled a few feet, trying unsuccessfully to ignore the shouts of "Traitor!" Stefan was hurling at me, when I caught sight of a tall, slender young man. He had apparently also noticed me, for as soon as our eyes met, he began walking toward me. I was in no mood to talk with this stranger, whoever he was, and turned onto another path, but the stranger was too quick and intercepted me, grabbing me by the arm and pulling me into a corner. He removed his hat and handed me a small card.

Good God, what had happened to this man's face? Five gouges marred the perimeter of his face, the unnaturally smooth pink flesh stark against the paleness of the rest of his skin. The deepest gouge was directly beneath his right eye, so close to the eyeball, in fact, that I was shocked he hadn't been blinded.

"I know of the creature that did this to your friend," he whispered with great urgency, his English nearly flawless save for a slight German accent. "I have been hunting him for thirty years."

"That's not surprising," I said. His words should have shocked me, especially since he looked so young, but I was too jaded to be surprised by anything anymore. "But I'm afraid you are mistaken. It wasn't only Vladec Salei who did this to my...friend. There was another."

"Another..." he said, choking on the word. He looked above my head toward the fray, as if trying to find an answer there. "What do you mean, Vladec Salei? Who *is* Vladec Salei? You must mean Constantinos."

"Apparently, you don't know all you think." It was a spiteful thing to say to one in such a state of confusion and distress, but I was in no mood to be detained by this man any longer. I handed him back his card, but he closed my fist around it.

"Listen to me," he said, taking me by the shoulders. "We cannot go into details here. We are not safe. Be at the *Shetland Arms* tonight at eight o'clock, and I will tell you what I know."

"What could you possibly know that I don't already?" I said angrily, trying to shrug him off.

"Trust me." I wanted to get away from him, to hurry home and lock myself within the safety of my parents' house, but something about his eyes and the sincerity of his voice made me want to know more. In spite of my resolve to dislike him on sight, I couldn't help being intrigued.

"Be sure to tell no one," he continued. "If Constantinos discovers my whereabouts, it will be the end of us. We may still be able to, if not save your friend, then end his life before he kills again, but secrecy is of the utmost..."

I looked up, for he was a good head taller than me, expecting him to resume, but his mouth was agape. I thought he was just momentarily overcome by the news I had broken to him, but when he continued to stare, fear dilating his sapphire-colored eyes, I knew something had gone terribly wrong. It was then that the cacophony broke out behind us.

I looked around. The patrol wagon lay feebly on its side, its roof ripped open, its wheels shattered to bits. Six constables lay crushed beneath its weight, while the other six struggled to lift the massive wagon off their fallen comrades.

"What in the name of God..." the stranger breathed.

"That had nothing to do with God." It was the last coherent thought I had before dread seized hold of me, and I began to tremble as I stared at the dismantled wagon, its door swinging on its hinges, exposing the bare compartment within.

Stefan was gone.

I fell to my knees and retched onto the pavement. Now, it was only a matter of time before the carnage began. The one thing I thought of that moment was the sword. He had been stripped of it when the constabulary set upon him, but as I scanned the police, I saw no sign of that blasted sword of Vladec Salei's.

"If only I could have killed him when I had the chance," I said miserably.

"I don't believe you have the power to kill him." I drew my sleeve across my mouth and looked up to see the strange young man standing beside me, his face now calm where a moment before it had been contorted by fear. I didn't have the strength to rise just then, so I let him place his hands under my arms and help me to my feet. "Not if what you say is true. It's too fantastic. Two of them attacking the same person. All you can do now is run."

"*Run*?" It was the answer everyone I went to for help gave me. I was sick of hearing it. Was there no other solution? Could I not stand and fight? No, I knew I could not, for I had tried too many times before and failed.

"You have become the hunted. If you value your life, you and all those dear to your heart will leave this country at once. Do not tell anyone where your final destination will be. Sever all ties. Abandon everything and every place that he was familiar with. He must never be able to find you."

Despite all arguments to the contrary, and the knot of fear in my stomach, I knew he was right. I had no other options now. No matter how painful it would be, my family and I now had no choice but to forsake our home. We could start anew in a different part of the world easily enough, I hoped. Possessions come and go; lives are another matter, and the salvation of ours depended on my swift action.

"Time is of the essence," the stranger said. "You must leave before nightfall. May God have mercy on you."

"Wait! How will I find you again?" But it was no use. Before I could say more, he was gone.

He had left me with a head full of conflicted thoughts and nothing more. No, that wasn't true. I remembered the card. As I uncurled my fist and looked down at the small piece of paper, I saw that it bore nothing more than a name.

Zigmund Fertig.

‡

I stood as if frozen. *Zigmund Fertig. Zigmund,* the name of the one whom Constantinos had mistaken Stefan for. The name of the person I had vowed I'd kill if I ever chanced to run across his path.

The name swam before me as I tried to come to terms with how any of this could be possible. It must be a mistake, another Zigmund Fertig, yet that was a ludicrous assumption and I knew it.

I stared at the letters, reading the name again. The chances of a coincidence were too great to even be entertained as a plausible explanation. I'd known since her half-confession in the library, since she had said he might still be alive.

There was only one truth: he was Leonora's son, the son who had supposedly been killed. *Leonora's son*—alive and well, and from the looks of him, over thirty years of age.

Even though I had learned she was a vampire, the remembrance of her youthful face made it hard for me to accept the truth. If her son was that age, then Leonora was...far older than I could have ever imagined. Fifty at the least, though she looked no older than the twenty-four-year-old I had taken her for.

I winced as pain throbbed behind my eyes. That stabbing sensation was always a prelude to a migraine. I couldn't afford to be incapacitated now. If I stayed standing here, trying to make the illogical seem logical, I'd lose my senses. Time was waning. Each moment I wasted was a moment gained for Stefan. I couldn't tarry over Leonora's past when the present could end for me any minute.

I shoved the card into my pocket and raced home on foot, not even bothering with the pretense of a cab. By the time I got there, the sun was already low in the sky. In a few hours, it would set. That was not good. They were formidable in daytime, and at night they were even worse. Stefan was fearsome at all hours, but Vladec Salei...well, I had seen what mischief he excelled at working once the moon rose.

I raced up the steps and threw open the door, nearly colliding with my mother as I entered.

"Have you heard the news, Eric?" my mother asked breathlessly as she followed me into the drawing room. "The authorities now believe Stefan murdered David and Marishka! It's completely absurd!"

The gossipmongers had outdone themselves this time. "We must leave at once," I panted, my frantic dash catching up with me.

"Leave?" she gasped. "What do you mean, *leave*? Why...what's happened...Eric, good Lord, what happened to your shirt?"

It was the first time I had bothered to take in my appearance. I looked down at my collar and saw that I had none, remembering that Stefan had ripped it away. "I will explain once we are safe in Brussels." It was the first place I could think of, and now that I had said it aloud, it seemed like the best idea. "Where's Roderick?" I asked, pushing past her.

"Brussels!" she shrieked. "Who said anything about going to Brussels? Eric, my love," she said, placing a hand upon my forehead. "Are you feeling well? The shock must be getting to you. Come, sit, and I'll have Jameson bring some tea."

"No, Mother!" I sputtered, brushing her hand aside. "We haven't the time. Tell Roderick we must leave at once. Only pack what you can carry without burdening yourself. We'll buy new things once we reach Brussels. Now..."

A noise at the door silenced me. Standing outside, behind the etched glass on either side of the entrance to our home, I discerned a familiar profile. I bit down on my tongue to keep from screaming. Mother recognized him, too. She was halfway to the door when I grabbed her, dropped to the floor, and dragged her behind the settee.

"Eric, what on earth is wrong with you?" she protested. But all she received for an answer was the warning finger I placed to my lips, for I was not about to reveal our presence to the thing standing on our doorstep. My breathing was so labored and heavy that I was surprised he couldn't hear me through the door. He would rip it off its hinges and discover us any moment now. I had run out of options. This was the last stand. I had nothing left to fight him with. I could feel myself being drawn to the door, wanting to open it, yet knowing that would be certain death.

I shut my eyes and tried to shake his hold from my mind. He *had* to be the one making me think these suicidal thoughts. I had told him his powers of mesmerism needed work. Well, in the time since we parted, his powers had grown remarkably strong and were chipping away at my resolve.

I'd be opening that door if something didn't happen to break the hold and that's when Jameson suddenly entered. He looked down at us, then at the form standing outside, then at us again.

"We are not here," I mouthed, shaking my head from side to side. Jameson had become my focus. The thoughts of a moment before vanished as I concentrated on his solid form, his kind face, his faithfulness to my family. Thankfully, Jameson understood, gave a curt nod, and headed to the door.

"Mr. Ratliff," I heard Jameson calmly address Stefan. "I'm terribly sorry, but none of the family are home at present. If you would call again this evening..."

Jameson's voice was hard as flint. There would be no trifling with his mind, no matter how potent Stefan's powers.

I heard nothing for what seemed like forever, during which time I felt as though Stefan's eyes were aimed directly at the settee. "Very well, then," he finally said, "I shall call again at eight o'clock. If Mr. Bradburry should return, please give him this card. Good day, Jameson."

"Good day, sir."

Only after I heard the turning of the door's lock did I feel it was safe to breathe. I cautiously raised myself off the floor and walked over to where Jameson was standing, the card he had been given clutched in his grasp.

"Jameson, you're invaluable," I said, squeezing his shoulder affectionately. "Pack your things. You're coming with us to Brussels. Now, all we need is to find Roderick..."

"Mr. Ratliff's card, Sir," Jameson whispered, stuffing the card into my hand. I was still exhilarated from our narrow escape. Why on earth did Jameson not feel the same way? He did not share my relief. Neither would he look into my eyes. It was unfathomable to me that he should seem so somber, yet as I glanced down at the card, I understood the reason.

The name on the card was not Stefan Ratliff.

It was Roderick Caldwell.

A dark red line had been drawn through my stepfather's name. It seemed that the viscous substance had not completely dried. I touched my finger to it and raised it to my lips, but could not make myself taste it. Nor did I have to. The pungent, coppery smell told me what the substance was the moment I had raised my hand to my face.

There was a small arrow, drawn with the same liquid, at the bottom right corner of the card. I flipped the paper over and clutched Jameson's arm for support. There, written in that same horrid crimson substitute for ink, was a message from Stefan:

The first has fallen. So it has begun. Roderick's blood is on your hands. I am blameless. The rest will soon follow:

2~Laura Caldwell
3~Gerard Ives
4~Roberta B. Ives
5~Daniel Jameson

And on the day we meet again...

6~Eric Bradburry

    S. B.

I should have been terrified beyond reason, yet I felt nothing. It was as though my insides, all my emotions, had been carved out of me. I felt hollow, and I knew I would never feel the same again. Something had died inside me with the reading of that card. Everything that had happened to me over the past two months seemed to recede, and a sense of iron determination took hold of me.

"Order a cab, Jameson," I commanded.

"Immediately, Sir."

"But we must wait until Roderick comes back," my mother protested.

"Roderick is not coming back, Mother."

"Wha...what do you mean?" she asked frantically.

I took her hands in mine and drew her into my arms. *Dearest Mother.* The pain I was about to inflict on her would be too much for her to bear. "He's been murdered."

She let out an anguished cry before collapsing. I bore her insensible form to the settee, and as I laid her down, I thought I heard a laugh. Either my mind was three steps away from snapping, or Stefan had somehow heard her shriek.

I looked toward the door, but it was shut and we were alone in the room. Wherever he was, he was enjoying this. Well, let him take pleasure in the suffering of others while he could. One day, the tables would be turned, and I'd be there to see it.

Corcitura

I didn't want to leave her alone, but I had no choice. I hurried upstairs to gather just enough to see us through the journey. As I passed Roderick's study, I succumbed to the grief I had repressed after reading that wretched card. As much as we had differed in opinion over the years, he was the closest thing I had ever had to a father. The days ahead would be worse for the loss of him. Until that moment, I had never truly realized how important he was to me, and, truth be told, how much I admired him and even loved him. It was my duty to avenge him one day, and I swore to him, as I crossed the threshold, that if it cost me my last breath, I would see that he had justice.

I looked around the study for some memento or other I could take with me. After a search, my eyes lit upon his pocket watch and the copy of Dickens' *Hard Times* in which he always kept a couple hundred pounds. I grabbed both these items and headed downstairs. I had already tarried longer than I should have.

I hastened through the door and bolted it behind me, knowing in my heart I'd never see this house again. Feeling a hand on my shoulder, I turned to see Jameson standing there, smiling that bittersweet smile that had comforted me and seen me through every grief I had ever experienced in my life. I looked past him to see our transportation waiting for us further down the walkway. Tears would serve us no purpose now, nor could there be any words of condolence to soften our mutual grief. I nodded to him, and he to me, and the two of us made for the cab.

"Euston Station, quickly," I ordered the cabbie, and he set the vehicle in motion.

We rode in silence, each of us supporting my still unconscious mother between us, and soon I saw the familiar terminus of Euston Station. Could it be that I had arrived at this very station some ten hours before? It felt like a lifetime ago.

I waited in the cab with my mother as Jameson bought our tickets. She was breathing stertorously. It would be a long while before she came out of her stupor. I caressed her forehead and held her hand, trying to give her comfort even though she was unconscious.

A knock on the window told me Jameson had returned. I lifted Mother into his arms and carried our meager baggage to our cabin, which was smaller even than the one Stefan and I had shared on this same train at the outset of what I had thought would be our greatest adventure. Then, we had been travelling on Stefan's budget. Now, we had maybe fifty pounds to our names, plus the money in Roderick's book that would have to see us through until Brussels. This was the result of yet another stupid mistake on my part. My coat had been covered in bile. I had rid myself of it, along with the roll of pounds Leonora had given me, as soon as I stepped across the threshold of my house.

We were traveling to Dover yet again. I was reliving my journey to the Continent, only this time, I wasn't at all excited about arriving at my destination.

Our circumstances were bleak, but I still couldn't resign myself to despair, even though I knew I should have. With a little luck, and some favorable winds, we would make a safe Channel crossing and reach Calais without incident.

I was mentally planning our journey to Brussels when I felt the wheels of the train lurch forward, pulling us out of the station...away from London, away from home, away from the life I had known ever since before I could remember.

"I'm glad you're here, Jameson," I said, looking out the window, watching London slip away from us. "Mother and I are going to depend on you greatly in the weeks to come."

"Don't you worry about anything," he replied. "I'll look after the both of you. You will find peace in Brussels, Master Eric, you'll see."

"No, Jameson. I will have no peace until Stefan Belododia is dead."

Book the First: The Narrative of Eric Bradburry Part II: 1894

The Personal Representative of
Mrs. Roberta B. Ives

*T*wenty-first June 1894. Today was the sixth anniversary of the day Stefan and I set out for France—and our lives changed forever. Six years had passed since I had last seen Stefan and Vladec Salei. Six years I had spent living with the memory of killing Augustin Boroi in the shadows of the Musée Grévin. Someone else might have been overcome with grief at taking a life, but I wasn't. Not that life, not when I knew he was nothing more than a hollow shell when I killed him. There was no life left in him by the time I got there and there hadn't been in hundreds of years.

I wish I could say our fortunes improved once we reached Brussels, but that would be a lie. We weren't in Brussels long enough to give our fortunes a chance. The morning after we arrived, the concierge at our hotel delivered a note to me, on which was written a single word.

Marked.

A red line of the same substance and color as the one on my stepfather's card had been slashed through the word. I had been a fool. I should've known he would not let me go as easily as that. He had sent the card, of course, or rather, he'd hand delivered it, for I had left him only a few days earlier.

Corcitura

The note was not sealed, had no return address, and had been entrusted to the concierge. Either Stefan was there, or he had spies in Brussels, neither scenario a comforting thought. If we'd stayed even a moment longer in the city, we would have been dead by nightfall.

Stefan could have been hiding in the room next to ours, for all I knew at the time, and so I had decided on a plan drastically different from anything I had thought up before then. I wouldn't go on ahead, fleeing forward with him always in pursuit. I'd double back. He'd never believe I'd have the smarts to retreat, and so it was to Bruges that I planned our escape. Another point in my favor was that the city was called the Venice of the North. Like me, I was sure Stefan had no desire to settle in a place so similar in appearance to the city where his plans had failed, and the life I had always known had come to an end.

The city would be perfect, or so I'd hoped. It was smaller than Brussels, less conspicuous, and utterly alien to every notion I knew Stefan had in mind as what I would select for a haven. Bruges was also near the coast, so if it came to that, we could have got passage back to England and fled at a moment's notice.

For a month we lived in what I can only call an almost frozen state of panic—too afraid to venture out into the streets of Bruges longer than was necessary and then only to procure what we needed to subsist on. We were paralyzed by fear that some spy had followed us, or worse, Stefan himself...with Salei in tow, or leading the charge, as the case might have been. But when we were not discovered, and time had passed sufficiently to assure us we were safe, we realized we'd been spared. Even though we no longer had the specter of the undead hunting us, we had an entirely new evil to contend with: penury.

The authorities at Scotland Yard had been unable to discover Roderick's body. In the face of this lack of evidence, or more aptly, their lack of desire to do anything further to resolve a situation that was confounding them beyond their capabilities, they claimed there never had been a murder. Roderick had apparently staged his own death to get away and leave us destitute. That was the "logical explanation," according to them. After all, where was the body? That gave them their lead, which opened the floodgates for dozens of "witnesses" to come forth. Some said Roddy had confided in them regarding his bad debts, others how the creditors were dogging his every step, but the one that was the worst, for Mother especially, was the prim little miss who came forward claiming she and Roddy had been having a torrid affair for over six years. Wild speculations the lot of them, each one going against everything Roddy believed in and stood for, yet the authorities, along with the papers, gave them credence. In a matter of days, thanks to a few articles in the *Telegraph* and *Times*, Roddy's reputation was in tatters.

I dreaded setting foot in England again, but they wanted to question me further, so I had no choice. The last thing I needed was for them to detain me there longer than was necessary, or worse, trump up evidence against me and charge me with aiding and abetting Roddy's murderer, no matter that they claimed my stepfather wasn't dead. I didn't trust them, nor did I trust to luck, for who knew if Stefan and Salei were waiting for an opportunity to catch me in transit and finish what they had started.

I was a day away from setting off, when I received an unexpected and not unwelcome surprise in the form of two Scotland Yarders come to question me. From the grim looks on their faces and their reserved manner, I believed they had arrived to arrest me and escort me back to England, but when they learned how ill my mother was—and she was in such an emotionally stricken state that her grief had begun to take a toll on her physical health and appearance—they, for whatever reason, decided there was no need to put us through any further strain for nothing more than what the head inspector admitted was really just speculation.

They questioned me again. After several hours of interrogations, they finally made up their minds to clear me of any involvement once and for all, yet they were still unwilling to believe my claims that Stefan was responsible for Roddy's murder. They pressed me for further proof, but what could I have told them? Nothing more than wild, outlandish claims that would have convinced them I was a madman and deserved to be locked up. Getting myself incarcerated in an insane asylum would serve no purpose to Mother and Jameson.

When I finally was able to present the card to the inspectors, it had lost all its urgency and value. The blood had long since dried and Stefan had vanished, not that they suspected him anyway. Even after they inspected the card further and read Stefan's admission, they still did not credit it, believing it to be just another hoax on Roddy's part—a trick to make his murder seem more convincing and place the blame on Stefan. Inspector Innis, the lead detective, even pointed to the fact that Stefan and I had only returned to England mere hours before the murder took place, which he claimed made Stefan's involvement seem almost entirely preposterous. *I* wanted to point out to Innis that *he* seemed to be conveniently overlooking the fact that David and Marishka—and most certainly Roddy, as well—had been murdered in a savage, clumsy fashion that could only have taken place in a moment of fury. He was making it out to seem that the murderer was a criminal mastermind who had been planning the crime for months.

No, not months...only since the night in Venice...

For one horrible moment, I had suspected Innis of collusion, but quickly realized that thought was ridiculous. I was simply searching for something sane to cling to.

It was then that I had forced myself to finally face the truth. I was struggling in a world where reality was dominant and there was no room for any other explanations that would not conform to the mundane. I could have shattered their illusions in an instant, but I knew they'd never believe me. They were content to live out their lives, not knowing death might be stalking their streets. Fine. Let them continue in their ignorance, while I dealt with the reality, *my* reality, that monsters were alive and well...and knew my name.

Innis must have known at least the train of my thoughts, for he had stared at me as though he was trying to read my mind. *Sorry, Innis.* I had already decided to keep the truth to myself. Confessing that a hybrid vampire and his equally bloodthirsty ancestor had followed me back to England would do nothing to further the "sanity personified" image I had been trying to project.

I remember glancing down at the card as Innis handed it back to me and realizing I had been a fool to think anyone would have accepted my words for the truth. Whoever saw it would think it an ordinary calling card. It didn't help that the blood now looked as harmless as red ink.

Even though they didn't credit the evidence I presented, I was lucky to no longer be a suspect. I had marveled over my unexpected good fortune for just about three seconds, when Innis delivered the final blow. As he turned to leave, Inspector Innis, his face grave, informed us that he was so terribly sorry—and here he'd looked pityingly at my mother—but since they could not find Roderick or any evidence of his body, we would not be allowed access to anything. The only way Mother would receive any of the inheritance was to be if Roddy's death was a proven fact. I had seen the worried look in Innis' eyes and knew he was thinking about the possibility of Roddy having a mistress. I'd blessed him inwardly for not making his thoughts known. Mother was already on the verge of fainting, and to hear once more the slander against her husband would have been too much to recover from.

The full import of Innis' words had struck me as I closed the door. I had nothing. Mother had some money she had hidden away in her reticule plus the money I'd taken from *Hard Times* before we fled. Adding to that Jameson's savings, our total finances amounted to just enough to get us better lodgings until the three of us could find employment and earn what we needed to buy a flat of our own—a goal that seemed a long way off, given that Jameson had always buttled, I had always been a student, and Mother had never worked a day in her life.

Regardless of our lack of experience, the three of us managed to eke out our existence in a drafty garret apartment overlooking the Minnewater wending its way through the center of town. The garret served us as best it could, although the wind rattled through the slats and made it colder than an icebox during the wintertime. And then there was the contingent of mice that entertained us each night by tapping a steady tattoo on the floor.

For all its failings, the hidden secret of the place was the view from our single window. Opening over the "Lake of Love," which was crowded with boats motoring across its surface on any given day, the view afforded us a glimpse of the towering brick steeple of the Church of Our Lady. I often found Mother sitting at the window in the early hours of the morning, a chipped teacup in her hands, looking wistfully through the trees toward the Gothic spire. She hadn't been to church since Roddy's passing. I hoped the sketch I had been secretly making of the statue of Michelangelo's Madonna would be enough of an incentive to convince her to enter the church and see the statue for herself. The important thing was getting her inside. Once there, I knew He'd work things out. She was past my help now. The comforting she needed only God could give.

Although the flat wasn't the best of places, it sheltered us for two years, during which time Jameson and I took the odd job here and there, and Mother surprised us all by becoming an academic. Well, not entirely, but she had taken to tutoring young children and almost becoming a governess to them—Jameson had started calling her *Mistress Eyre*, which cheered her immensely—and had built up a loyal clientele so that we had enough money for food, at least. What's more, she was so happy, and I knew the job was keeping her mind off other thoughts that would have sunk her into a depression had she not been otherwise engaged.

Though my business prospects weren't what I would have wished, I took comfort from my surroundings. Each morning, I strolled through the Beguinage De Wijngaard, often pausing to lean against the poplar trees whose branches shaded the walk. The little area was quiet and peaceful, with no more than a few fellow strollers wandering about admiring the flowers and row of houses that encircled the garden. It was at times like these, when my mind was free to wander where it would, that my thoughts somehow always returned to Vladec Salei. Maybe I had been making a greater monster of him than he really was, or maybe I was still under his influence, for I was certain that he wanted me to believe he was no more than a harmless man who happened to use vampirism to get what he desired. Some remnant of his mesmerism was still upon me. I had never been able to shake the feeling that he was tucked away in a corner of my mind, that he could read my thoughts, know what I was thinking. He had done something to me, but what that was, I had never been able to discover. All I knew was that the feeling had been with me since the morning I woke up and found myself in Venice.

Marked.

Stefan had written that on the card. I supposed I'd never truly know what he meant, and I was not enough of a fool to think I wouldn't be perfectly happy if it remained a mystery to me for the rest of my life. But Salei still troubled me, mainly because I knew he was just as sick and vile as Constantinos, no matter the appearance he tried to project. Underneath that urbane exterior beat a heart even blacker than that of the Vrykolakas. How could I have ever thought otherwise? And then, as if to drive home the point as thoroughly as I would have loved to drive that wyvern-headed sword into Salei's heart, the vision of him looming over Stefan in Castle Bran, the moonlight falling on his mouth—the mouth bathed in Stefan's blood—flashed through my mind. There could be no arguing against *that* horror that I had witnessed with my own eyes.

I would rest there, lost in thought, until I noticed that the garden was starting to fill, which signaled the end of my idling over memories I would never forget and situations I could do nothing to change. The garden never stayed empty for long, and as the morning waned, I knew I'd best set off back toward the banks of the Minnewater and whatever employment I had secured for that day. Since I had been in Bruges, this had been my ritual, this had been my peace, but it was always interrupted by the arrival of those Devil Birds, or as they were more commonly known, the Swans of Bruges, who dotted the banks and were quite protective of their real estate, which to them included practically the entire strip of land along the Minnewater. They were pernickety things, and loud, too. I'd already invaded their territory once and received a hole in my pants' leg for my transgression.

The birds could be peaceful, as long as you kept at least ten miles away from them. They'd bide their time, hiding themselves in the shelter of the green veil the weeping willow provided, as unsuspecting strollers drew near. Then before one realized one had traveled into enemy territory, there would be a flurry of white, a splash of foam, and the next sight one saw was a feathered gargoyle, its wings outstretched, running up the bank and honking for all it was worth as it bore down on its prey.

This was what had happened to me on my first sojourn down the bank. I had spotted a couple of them weaving in and out of the green curtain and a few more sitting peacefully along the bank. Little did I know these last were scouts. As I walked by one, I swear it raised an eyebrow at me, although that was ridiculous, because it hadn't any. Regardless, it was as though there were an invisible line in the grass, and once my foot crossed this, I was a dead man. You'd think that after all I'd witnessed, I wouldn't be so terrified of a stupid bird, but the sight of that thing bearing down on one like a fiend escaped from hell was enough to send even a man braver than William Wallace running for the hills.

And so I learned to keep my distance. I gave them sidelong glances as I passed by, and they did the same, the cagey devils. We had come to an understanding. Since those first few mornings when I had nearly been mangled by an animal with no teeth, relations between us had been relatively peaceful. I could almost imagine the swan inclined its head in greeting as I passed, but that was most probably a trick of the sun.

Luckily, I had found employment as an assistant to the head lace maker of Bruges, Madame Larange. She was a fine, robust lady of about fifty-five, who took me in and indulged me to a degree I found unfathomable, given that I had just met her. I suppose she took to me so quickly because she pitied my mother. When everyone else was making comments on Mother's sanity, Madame Larange always made it a point to ask after her, even if clients were around to hear it. She did not care what others said and even stitched a sampler for my mother's birthday and brought the framed product to our garret regardless of everyone's talk. She treated me as a son, but her lace came first in her heart, as I quickly found out during those first days when I had another encounter with one of those warmongering swans, who bypassed me and instead went for my parcel, ripping it to shreds. In that paper wrapping had been a lace tablecloth meant for the mayor's wife—a lace tablecloth Madame Larange had been commissioned to make, a lace tablecloth that had taken her *over a year* to complete. So ended my employment with Bruges' First Lady of Lace.

My next job saw me vending alongside one of the Liège waffle sellers in the city's center. This time, it wasn't a swan that ruined me but an urchin who looked about as destitute as I was. He'd been hanging around the cart, muttering pitifully about how his poor, old, sickly mama was at death's door and wanted nothing more than one of Monsieur DuClerc's famous Liège waffles...with an extra sprinkling of sugar, if I'd be so kind. It was her dying wish, the child said, looking up at me with tearful eyes. Of course, I had melted at the sight of this unfortunate, gave him three waffles for good measure, and was feeling puffed up by my good deed until I came across the same child a few hours later, larking around with his brother and crowing about how he had, if translated into my parlance, "ripped off a right good chump with that ghastly story about Mummy." Furthermore, the little brat was in city clothes, noticeably without the patches that had covered nearly every inch of his pants a few hours before, and his mouth was spattered with that "extra sprinkling of sugar" apparently meant for his mother, whose existence I now doubted.

I was ready to collar the little liar myself, and would have dragged him back to Monsieur DuClerc had not his mother, looking the picture of health, sauntered in and hauled him and the brother away before I had the chance. Shortly thereafter, I discovered they were the mayor's sons. When I explained this to Monsieur DuClerc, I found myself out of a job once again. Apparently, three free waffles were two waffles too many, even for the mayor's brat.

Back in England, I had always planned to study the law, but after all I'd been *through* with the law, I decided to have no part of it. If I were ever given the chance, I would study finance and maybe learn something that could help improve our situation, but with the scant funds we were earning, higher learning was a remote possibility at best. My emotions were so volatile during this time that I didn't know whether to give in and lose hope, or just shut my ears to the world and all the idle gossip and press on regardless of everyone's doubts. I was in such a fog that I almost succumbed to believing the screed they were spreading about Roddy, even going so far as to rail at him in my mind, only to stop a moment later and remind myself that I had seen his blood and knew he had died at the hands of my former best friend.

My employment options were running out, as was my money. My next job would be doing who knew what. I wasn't looking forward to starting the hunt yet again. I supposed I could try for a chimney sweep next, but I'd probably lose that job in a day after a fight with a crow, or push the sweep too far down as Father Christmas was trying to push his way up...or maybe I'd suddenly discover that ashes made me sneeze. Something outlandish was bound to happen, given my luck.

I was at my wits' end and didn't know where to turn, and that's when I received a present from Guildy. I don't know why she should have taken to me as she did, or what I ever did to deserve her, for that matter, but I received a letter from her informing me that my tuition had been paid and I was free to study at university whenever my time and circumstances permitted. To say that I was flabbergasted would have been an understatement. I had written to her through our solicitor immediately upon settling in Bruges, but having received no answer during those two years, I feared the worst. Guildy was my only lifeline to the past, my only real friend, and the thought that I couldn't find her terrified me, for I immediately suspected that Salei and Stefan had done away with her.

Guildy wasn't the only one I had tried to seek out. While waiting to hear back from her, I had also made inquiries regarding Nadia Belododia's whereabouts. I was determined to find her, to make her confess the truth, and, more importantly, convince her to give me the cross, but she had seemingly disappeared off the face of the earth. She wasn't in Romania any longer, or so I was told. In fact, they couldn't find any record of a Nadia Belododia even existing. She must have either changed her name and somehow erased all her records or bribed someone in charge of the files to conveniently forget she had ever been born.

I gave up on Nadia after that. She could be chained at the bottom of the ocean for all I cared. The cross could have been wild speculation on Luc's part, but I somehow doubted it. Still, what else could I have done without exposing myself?

I focused on Guildy, and only Guildy, after my failed attempts at finding Nadia. Shortly after bestowing her generous gift, I received another surprise in the person of the benefactress herself. I had always thought Guildy was my lucky charm, but I never even dreamed her coming would herald an event that would change all our lives.

Two days after attaining my majority, I heard from Inspector Innis. Apparently, he had believed me—though he had never given me any indication of this—and had been keeping up inquiries into Roddy's supposed whereabouts. After much investigation, the consensus was reached that Roddy had been murdered, but not by Stefan. It seems there was a fellow who had come on the scene shortly after Stefan had murdered his parents. Jack the Ripper, they called him. This man's methods seemed to match those used to murder Stefan's parents, and after Ripper had gone on his spree through Whitechapel shortly following the Ratliff murders, the authorities had been hard-pressed to deny that maybe, *just maybe*, Roddy had been killed by this Ripper fellow after all. It certainly took them long enough to make up their minds. Two years later, the Yarders finally declared Roddy dead. His income and all his holdings, noticeably free of bad debts, I might add, went to us.

We were saved.

Corcitura

Guildy stayed with us for a few months, during which time she helped us find a house steps from the Minnewater. Though it wasn't far from our old lodgings, it was a marked change from the poverty we'd lived in. It also reminded me of our old home in Mayfair. It had the same red door and etched windows, but this one had a little garden round back in which my mother loved to potter about. I feared for my mother's mind during that time the most, for she had no longer any reason to work. She had been kept occupied those past two years, thankfully delaying any further deterioration of her sanity, although some part of her mind had gone the day we left London. She never fully recovered from the shock of Roddy's murder, insisting that he was merely away on business and would return to her someday. And she believed me even less when I finally told her the truth about Stefan and that it was he who had killed her husband. Till this day, when I'd bring up the matter, she would laugh and tap my forehead as though *I* were the dotty one, saying she would have a word with the fellows at university who were obviously filling my head with nonsense.

That was the way she'd remained, flitting between a dreamlike state and occasional moments of clarity. Thank God for Guildy. I don't know what I would have done without her to help me through those days. She was my rock and quite the comfort to Mother, and so was Horace Guildford, who finally got himself out of that frightful indisposition long enough to pay us a visit and help us get started on our new path.

On this day, as I sat in the garden watching Mother tending her flowers, with Jameson standing in as her assistant and bringing her tools as she desired them, I remembered that everything that had happened over the last six years had always occurred on or around my birthday. The first of the lot was spent with Stefan and then Guildy, alternately in Venice due to Salei's treachery, and then two weeks before the date on which I was supposed to celebrate, on that day when time had stopped—and I had murdered Augustin Boroi. The next two had been spent nearly destitute, while the last three had seen a change, starting with the double good fortune of having a chance for further education bestowed on me and all our prayers answered. I wondered what this year would hold. I had begun to fear my birthdays for this very reason.

The way the light was catching on Mother's hair made me think of. *Leonora*, who I'd probably never see again. She had disappeared with Salei and Stefan, too. I had tried against reason not to contact her, to find out anything regarding her whereabouts, but my impulses won out in the end. The search had been fruitless, on Guildy's part as well.

As time wore on, the pain of not seeing her lessened. Despite my vow that I would never recover from the damage she had done to my heart, I did indeed find a way to live my life without her in it. Looking back, I realized that I had only been infatuated with her, *heavily* infatuated at that. I had not loved her as passionately and recklessly as I thought. But not even this realization could erase her memory from my mind. I would *never* forget her. She'd always have a claim, however small, on my heart, and if I could honor my promise to her someday, I vowed I would, but only as a friend.

Guildy told me she had only seen Stefan once more and Leonora had not been in his company. Guildy had thought he was alone, but his mentor had appeared moments later, and the two of them disappeared into Gare du Nord and out of Guildy's life. Thankfully, they had not seen her, and when I questioned her further about whether or not she had run into them on any other occasions, she seemed to withdraw into herself and would say no more.

When she visited us last, I noticed something peculiar about Guildy's face, something I had never seen before. Although she had tried to conceal it with cosmetics, I could still see a thin purple line snaking up the side of her cheek, close enough to her jaw to be unnoticeable to strangers, but not to me. It looked as though someone had raked a nail across her skin. And of course, that made me recall a vision I had tried to suppress for the last six years. Nails slicing a hole in the glass of Guildy's window, nails sharp as razors and encrusted with the filth of the grave—nails belonging to a dead man who was very much alive.

Corcitura

When I questioned her about the scar, she got flustered and changed the subject, and since the changed topic concerned Leonora, in spite of myself, I was interested. Although Leonora had not been with Stefan, Guildy had been surprised to receive a letter from her shortly after she had seen Stefan and Vladec Salei at Gare Du Nord. There was no address on the envelope, save for the markings that told of its coming from Prague, which led Guildy to believe that's where the Clan Belododia was making their home, for the time being at least. The letter stated no further particulars as to their whereabouts and nothing to excite curiosity in the reader, but rather that they were all well and happy. It ended with an admonishment to Guildy: if she valued her life, and Leonora's as well, she would burn the letter and never try to make contact again. There was a postscript that pertained to me, too: Guildy was to tell me nothing of the letter. There was no reason to endanger me further than I already was.

Well, there was no sense in Guildy *not* telling me, for I was bound to drag the truth from her one day. If it had to do with Leonora, I needed to know. I didn't give her words credence at all. Happy? I doubted it. How could she be happy in such company? New mother to one, mistress to the other, or so he believed. No matter how much I thought it over, I'd never be able to accept the idea.

I pushed the remembrances out of my mind and focused on my current position in life. With my new knowledge of finances, I had decided it was time to seek real employment. I wasn't going to become one of the idle rich, as Guildy called them, even though she was considered a member of that class. Yet there was nothing idle about Elspeth Guildford. One look at her and that illusion was dispelled instantly.

I had recently applied for a position with the firm of Danvers, Voorjit, and Snelling, and was waiting to hear back from them. I expected an answer any day now. Would the firm accept me? Well, why not? I had distinguished myself at university and had been called one of the brightest financial minds in the city. Of course they would accept me!

Two minutes later, I doubted myself again. I had had no real work experience, and what were the words of a few professors compared to one hundred and twenty-five years of combined financial expertise? To think I would have been hired had been folly.

"Eric, pass me that trowel, and for goodness' sake, lad, stop daydreaming! Whatever will the neighbors say if they see that blank look on your face? There's room for only one half-wit in our family."

I gaped at her. She couldn't be making a joke, could she? She hadn't shown any inclination to jest in the six years since Roddy's death. I had ceased to believe she even possessed the mental capacity for such an action. This was too much to hope for.

"Mother...I didn't..." I stuttered, falling to my knees beside her.

"Now, Eric," she said, leaning back on her heels. "You honestly didn't believe all that talk, did you? It was just about as bad as what they were saying against dear Roderick. Poor fellow. Oh, look! Jameson's returned, and he's brought you a present."

I turned my astonishment from Mother onto Jameson. She had mentioned a present, so I was expecting to see him carrying a huge bow-wrapped package, but all he held in his hands was an envelope.

My heart caught in my throat at the sight of it.

Leonora.

I tore the envelope from his hands, daring to hope it was from her, yet dreading what it would say...what she would require of me.

"Who is it from, love?" asked my mother. She had gone back to her tending, yet there was a half-smile on her face that made me instantly curious and a little suspicious as to how much she knew about this mystery note.

I looked down at the label, noticing that the address was from America. There was no name on the envelope, save that of the solicitors, but when I opened it and read the salutation, I knew who it was from. Only one person ever called me Braddie: my Aunt Roberta.

My Dearest Braddie,

Corcitura

I hear congratulations are in order! It has reached my ears that you are now quite the don of the financial world, or if not yet, you certainly will be soon, given your mother's praises. But before your head gets too swelled, and your mother risks being brought up on charges of perjury regarding your merits, I have a proposition to make you. You can tell Messrs Danvers, Voorjit, and what's-his-name they will have to wait.

Since your Uncle Gerard's death last winter, I have been in a terrible state with my finances. I have no head for numbers, and since you are such a natty financial wizard, what do you say to coming to live with your Aunt Robbie and becoming her personal representative in America? Does the idea appeal to your sensibilities, what? I will brook no dissension in this, and have already enclosed passage for you on the Campania, which sails...well, by the time you receive this letter, you will only have a few days left to make up your mind.

You remind me so of your father at that age, ready to set the world on fire. You have that fighting Bradburry spirit we all inherited. Think of all the trouble we'll get into, Braddie. By the bye, you might want to strike out that last statement before showing this letter to your mother. We must make certain to uphold a veneer of respectability.

Ever your loving Aunt,
   Robbie

P. S. When you write me back, don't you dare close with "a bien tot" or I'll cut you right out of my will. I know you spent time in Paris, but I'll not have you bringing any of those Frenchified ways to America. Get on with you, now, and give my love to your mother.

I sat back on my heels, stunned. *Go to America, me?* As Aunt Robbie's personal representative? I didn't have nearly enough experience or knowledge for her to want me in such a capacity, and as I looked at my mother, I realized the local ladies would have to revise their opinion of her. She was no simpleton. She must have been behind this scheme, regardless of how Aunt Robbie had tried to take credit for it.

I read over the astonishing letter again, trying to come to terms with the proposal. A change of scenery would do me good, and to get out of Europe would be even better, especially since the fear of Stefan discovering me had been my constant companion for the last six years. There was no incident more illustrative of this than what occurred last year at an All Hallows Eve ball.

The prospect of attending anything even remotely involving monsters, even if they were only in costume form, was repulsive to me. Not to mention that I had been terrorized by dreams of wax figures coming to life ever since I left Paris. The idea of being around so many masked faces filled me with dread. Yet Mother wanted to go, and so I relented.

I'd been idling by the buffet and had not been there more than five minutes when some fool wearing a black cape, beaver hat, and a death's head mask with a slit through which his fangs were visible, accosted me with the words, "I believe you are just my type...type O." For a moment I didn't know what to think. I knew he was neither Salei nor Stefan, and for one agonizing instant, I feared he was Augustin Boroi come back to haunt me. My hand clutched a butter knife. I'd been moments away from stabbing it through his heart, when he removed the mask, laughed in my face, then took his lady's arm and danced off into the crowd. Thankfully, the orchestra was playing loudly enough to cover the sound of the butter knife clattering to the floor, but not loudly enough that my mother, who was standing by my side, had not heard the stranger's remark. I'd reached out to catch her, but she had already fainted dead away, thus furthering the rumors that she was a superstitious, half-mad woman who couldn't handle a jest.

Soon after the ball, the rumor I had tried to suppress became common knowledge. The ladies of our circle didn't need an excuse to gossip, and Mother's display set their tongues wagging almost immediately. After a few days of rampant speculation, the entire story had come out. It didn't help matters, either, that Mother had been loose with information she should have kept secret and had poured out her grief and suspicions to anyone with a sympathetic ear. Everyone knew Jack the Ripper had supposedly done away with Roddy. That bit of news was harmless enough, yet when added to Mother's conjectures that Ripper was really a vampire in disguise, she and I and even Jameson had become the butt of every joke and ill-natured jab in the city. They all discoursed at great length on the possibility of there being such creatures, but I stayed silent. I felt no need to justify myself to them, nor did I feel compelled to share the recurring nightmare I'd been having in which Stefan had somehow populated the earth with an army of Corcituras, thereby virtually obliterating the human race by the dawn of the next millennium.

All the women were acerbic to varying degrees, but there was one who took particular delight in torturing my mother. This oppressor was Cornelia Danvers, the daughter of the man at whose firm I was applying for a position. Maybe I was developing a sixth sense, or maybe it was the way she'd looked me over from head to foot as if she were sizing up a piece of meat, but from the moment she clapped eyes on me, I could tell she'd marked me for a conquest. I had been deemed a suitable husband, now that I had inherited my share of Roddy's capital. She didn't seem to care that I hadn't shown the slightest inclination to be in the same room with her, nor had she noticed that every time we met, I paid my respects and always made a quick exit. I'm sure she thought I was trying to inflame her interest by appearing indifferent to her, which must have been a novel sensation, considering that half the eligible bachelors—ranging from ones fresh out of the nursery to others halfway to the grave—were falling all over themselves for nothing more than a glance from her green-flecked eyes.

There was one chap in particular who had completely succumbed to her allure. He fancied himself a poet and spent his days hanging out his window, waiting for her to pass underneath and praying that the sun would shine upon her head at just the right angle so he could capture her essence and write the perfect sonnet to her red-gold hair and upturned nose that he swore was bestowed upon Cornelia by Venus herself. *Pathetic milksop.*

The one time I had been forced to keep her company, she hinted that her family was so entrenched in Bruges they were practically part of the masonry. She then went on to tell me a wild story about how one of her grandfathers—I forget how many greats back he was—on her father's side had escaped the oppression of Richard III and fled to Bruges, establishing some guild or other, and the family had been part of the ruling class of the city ever since. True, we did live in one of the foremost capitals of lace making, but I didn't think that gave her carte blanche to embroider the truth so blatantly. As to the family being older than the bricks, I had my doubts. She spoke neither Flemish nor French, not to mention that her surname was *Danvers*. And then there was the fact that when she was in a pet, she could pop out a Norwich accent the likes of which I'd never heard equaled in my lifetime. This was brought home to me rather blatantly one evening when she screeched "Cor blarst me!" after spilling cordial all over her best gown. Good thing the poet wasn't around to hear his Venus at her most ungodly.

She had hinted several times that forming a joint partnership between us would help my cause with her father. I had no illusions. I knew that by joint partnership she meant marriage, and if she was trying to blackmail me into such a venture just to get employment at her father's firm, she was in for a disappointment. I'd rather take my chances with a hundred Augustin Borois than spend one second married to her.

I believe she thought me completely in thrall to her charms. Either that, or she took me for a dullard who wouldn't think anything of her constantly telling me how sorry she was that I had such a "dotard for a mother." I could have told her that besmirching the mother of the man you are trying to snare isn't a way to win his heart, but I wasn't as *charitable* as her. Whenever I chanced to catch her eye, I always saw her looking at me with an expression of pity—a look that made my skin crawl. No doubt she felt magnanimous by being so kind to the poor, unfortunate, grown-up version of Oliver Twist she took me to be.

One evening, we had gathered in her father's drawing room after dinner, and somehow the talk turned to the episode with the vampire at the masquerade ball.

The light was dim, made more so by the haze from Mr. Danvers' cigar smoke. It cast Cornelia in a lurid cloud of chartreuse that made her look greener than usual. "Dearest Laura," she began, her voice so sweet it made me wary. "Twas"—she always got medieval when she waxed bitter— "such a shame that rash of killings in London all those years ago. How some could think anyone other than the Ripper killed Roddy is beyond me."

"Stefan Belododia killed my husband as assuredly as Ripper ever could."

I had told Mother the whole story, not sparing any detail, and sometimes, as I looked back—and especially since she was so unguarded in what she told Cornelia—I wish I had just let her believe Roddy had run off with another woman.

"He was a vampire, you know," my mother said quietly, looking down at her trembling hands.

"A vampire, really, Laura," Cornelia said, tut-tutting for good measure. "Such folly. Eric, you must regulate your mother's reading. Sensation novels can be a very dangerous influence on one's mind, especially if one is already unsettled in the attic. Don't you agree, Father?"

"Brooom-hoom," coughed Mr. Danvers around his cigar. Cornelia seemed pleased with his assessment.

"It is the true version of the story!" my mother protested vehemently, her eyes growing wild.

"Yes, Laura, we are all familiar with *your* version of the story...the *bedtime* story. A vampire," she said, tittering behind her hand. "Really, Eric, this is too much."

"Yes, Cornelia," I'd said, endeavoring to remain calm, "for once you and I are in perfect agreement."

"Splendid!"

"It is rather splendid. Good choice of words. You've made up my mind for me."

"I thought so," she said, looking significantly at my mother. What did she think? Did she really believe I'd go against my mother to side with her? And that look...it was so smug, so knowing—almost as if she expected me to announce that I was committing my mother to an insane asylum on the morrow.

"Yes, it is all clear now. You've finally presented me with an opportunity to divest myself of something I have been wanting to be rid of for quite some time. Good-bye, Cornelia."

"Good-bye?"

"You've outstayed your welcome. And I have been tolerant far too long. I hope you will enjoy the rest of your life, for I have no intention of being a part of it. Good evening."

I stared at her in triumph, but after a moment, nothing happened. I had expected her to flounce out of the room, but instead she was still sitting there, looking shocked and bewildered. Hadn't she heard me?

"But, Eric, this is my house."

"Well, I don't see that that should make any difference!" And with that parting volley, I'd taken Mother by the arm and walked out of Cornelia's life.

In the six months since that evening, I had been spared the sight of Cornelia Danvers. She hadn't bothered with us, and we certainly had counted ourselves lucky to no longer be obligated to bother with her. I'd noticed a significant alteration in Mother's spirits, too. She was much happier and outgoing—changes I attributed to her no longer being under Cornelia's thumb, as it were.

Perhaps I'd been a fool to still think I had a chance of gaining employment with her father's firm after that incident at the party. I had hoped that with time, the remembrance of my outburst would diminish somewhat, and Cornelia's father would discover what a boil his daughter truly was. Perhaps he would understand that I had done what he should have— in his capacity as father—years ago. My actions had been exactly the kind of set down one with Cornelia's hoity-toity mindset needed.

Ha, what a lark, that notion! Apparently, I had received another letter this day that I had failed to notice when

Corcitura

Jameson gave me Aunt Robbie's. And, surprise of surprises, it was the letter I had deluded myself into thinking would never come. A letter from Papa Danvers himself, the gist of it being that my services would not be needed this day, nor tomorrow, nor if suddenly every other solicitor in the country was struck dead in the night. In short, I'd been rebuffed. So died all my hopes for a distinguished future with Messrs Danvers, Voorjit and Snelling.

Strangely, I felt relieved. And it wasn't only because I had another option resting beside me in the form of Aunt Robbie's offer. Office work would have most probably bored me to tears, not to mention that I would be forced to see that blight daughter of his on special occasions. No, Aunt Robbie's was the right path for me, and I was determined to take it.

The rustling wind and Mother's squeal of delight woke me from my reverie, which I was only too happy to come out of. Dwelling on memories of Cornelia always threatened to ruin my day.

"Eric, look, it finally grew!" For months, now, she'd been trying to replicate the Tudor Roses she'd had in her garden in Mayfair, but every time she'd try to grow one here, it had died. Maybe the soil was wrong for it, or the climate was not right, but nothing had ever bloomed until now.

She was bent over the rose, cradling the red and white bloom in her hands as delicately as if she were holding a newborn baby.

I turned her face toward mine, startled when I saw her cheeks dotted with tears.

"Mother, what is it?"

"Oh, Eric, I know all about Roberta's letter. I want you to go. To get away, start a new life. Don't worry about me, dear. This rose is like a revelation. I know it sounds ridiculous, but since Roddy died, this is the first thing I've done right. I cannot explain it, but I feel somehow reborn."

She took my hands in hers, squeezed them, and turned back to her rose, but not before I had seen the look in her eyes. I started, because for a moment, however brief, the look in her eyes was familiar...a look I hadn't seen in years. Certainty, calmness, acceptance...

Hope.

Not a single trace of the madness she had displayed ever since we'd left London remained. "Eric, love," she said, caressing the rose. "I want you to go. Go and start anew and mend your heart. I want you to return to me with the light back in your eyes."

Since reading the letter, I had wondered if I could ever leave Mother. If I left, I'd be abandoning her, yet in these precious moments, my mother had opened her heart to me as she'd never done before. Something within her, and myself, had changed. I'd had my doubts, but now that I had her blessing, now that I *knew* she no longer needed me to hold her up and keep her sane, I saw no reason to dawdle any longer.

After a few hours, everything had been settled. I was to leave on the following morning for Liverpool, via Paris. I wrote to Guildy, though I'd not be able to stay more than a few hours with her. I was just passing through Paris, nor would I want to tarry longer than was necessary, given my memories of that city and what I had done there. After Paris, it'd be a dash through London. I wasn't going to stop there at all, not even to visit my old haunts. Leonora's letter had made no mention of what had passed between Stefan and myself there, but I thought it better to take no chances. Even after all the years that had passed, I still looked over my shoulder every time I heard a sound. It was a feeling I would never be rid of.

My valise was packed and ready to go within an hour. Mother insisted I take a steamer trunk, and I obliged, though I saw no reason why I couldn't procure the necessary items once I reached New York. But seeing her so alive, so refreshed, as if she had come out of a dark sleep, made me agree to anything she wanted. It was almost as though she had risen from the grave fully revived, and I intended to further this new attitude as much as I could before I left her for God knew how long. I'd no doubt Jameson would be able to draw her even further out of the darkness now that she had already begun to emerge. He had become even more of a father to me over the years, and to Mother, well, there were no words to describe the support he had given her through her darkest hours when everyone had given her up for lost.

The day was half gone by the time I finished packing. Mother was busy in her garden again, with Jameson standing watch. I looked down at them from my window as I prepared to write a letter to Aunt Robbie. I'd probably reach her before the letter, but there was form to these things, as Roddy would have said.

Roddy...the remembrance stung me. I tried unsuccessfully to hold back tears. Moments like these had come more often over the past six years than I would have anticipated. It was the void he left in our lives, but also my inability to avenge him. How could I exact vengeance upon someone whom I feared and had no idea how to kill? And how would I find him and dispatch him when the time came?

I laughed morbidly as a thought entered my mind—I was lusting for Stefan's blood as thoroughly as he'd lusted for my own, yet the reasons for our respective bloodlust were as different as night and day. Frustration threatened to overwhelm me again as I thought of the impossibility of the situation. There were only three people in this world who knew my secret: Mother, Jameson, and Guildy, and since Stefan had disappeared, I doubted I'd ever be given the chance to prove my story true. Most likely, I'd take my secret with me to the grave.

I can live with that, I thought cavalierly, while at the same time hoping my trip to the grave would happen years from now and not tomorrow.

I blew on the ink to help it dry, pushing thoughts of Stefan from my mind as I reread my letter to Aunt Robbie. It was nothing too long, or too formal, for Aunt Robbie and I had never stood on ceremony.

I folded the note, tucked it into the envelope, and sealed it with the wax *B* stamp Aunt Robbie had sent me for my birthday. She never ceased to remind me that I was a Bradburry, whatever that meant. She was very proud of our heritage and never let me forget that it was from these great Saxons that we were descended. There was a time when she had insisted on spelling the name "Braidbury," which she claimed was the true spelling, ours being a variant, but the family had finally knocked some sense into her by pointing out that if she continued to alter the spelling, when her father died, the inheritance would go to her cousin William, who had no delusions of grandeur about his forebears. That had ended the debate rather quickly.

I chuckled as I wrote the address of the solicitor on the envelope. When ending the letter, I hadn't used *a bien tot*, but rather *au revoir*, followed by a string of felicitations and well wishes, not to mention several postscripts, in French. That would get her riled. I had a feeling she'd be waiting on the pier in New York, ready to box my ears for my insolence once I set foot off the *Campania*, but the thought of seeing her for the first time in more than a decade, and going to a place where I'd be safe and happy, would soften whatever pinch she might inflict on me.

The desk clock near my hand chimed four. I looked down into the garden and saw Mother and Jameson heading inside. This would be our last tea together. There was no use being sentimental about it. If Aunt Robbie had her way, I'd stay in New York forever, but I knew I'd return someday...if not for Mother and Jameson, then for Roddy.

A hybrid vampire and I had a score to settle.

‡

"Will there be anything else, Mr. Bradburry?"

"No, Dillard, that's all. Thanks."

"If I may, Sir, the view out of port is stunning. You can just make it if you hurry."

A blast from one of the smokestacks shook the cabin. I nodded to Dillard and walked out the door, making my way up the stairs and out onto the aft deck. The sun had already set, but I could still make out the lights of Liverpool behind us and the hands of hundreds of Liverpudlians waving to us from the pier.

I glanced down at the brochure, comparing the smokestacks on the paper to the huge ones silhouetted against the moonlit sky above me. Another blast signaled our departure, and I leaned against the railing, staring down into the sea.

Guildy's words on the platform at Gare Du Nord came back to me then: "Come, you silly toff, there's no reason for you to worry. You're going to America! Land of the free, home of the brave. All are welcome."

"Even those of us who once associated with vampires?" I had asked, half joking, half deadly serious.

"Now, now. You're no longer 'with vampire,' thank God. No one's going to hold that aspect of your past against you."

Six days from now, I'd find out. I wasn't planning to bruit my secrets about, but adjusting to life in a new country, with new ways, new customs, new faces—it would take some getting used to. As I settled against the railing, looking back at the lights of the city receding in the distance, I hoped within my heart that Guildy was right.

New York, Aunt Robbie, and The Millionaires' Ball

"*L*and, ho, Mummy. Land, ho!!!"

I looked down at the towheaded sprat next to me and smiled. He couldn't have been more than four years old, yet seemed to be a nice little British chap with a good command of nautical terminology and a rather stately, maritime bearing, especially given the pea coat he was wearing. I half expected him to shout "Hard to larboard, with ye, weasly dogs!" any minute.

"Lady Libby, Lady Libby!" he chuntered on, trying to fling himself out of his mother's stranglehold and into the water. "Ready for action, sir!" and here he gave a salute that would have made Wellington jealous.

His mother smiled apologetically at me. "His father's in the Royal Navy," she said by way of explanation. I smiled in return, then watched her and Little Welly move up the forecastle to get a better view of Lady Liberty as we steamed past her on our way into New York Harbor.

Cawing broke out above. I looked up to see seagulls weaving in and out of the smoke the stacks were puffing into the air. Another blast sent the birds fleeing toward the surface of the water, and I looked down to see a tug pulling up alongside us. A toot from the other side of the ship told me the tug's twin was moving in, which signaled that I'd better get myself presentable and ready to disembark. Aunt Robbie was surely waiting on the dock that was already lined with people.

I leaned down to pick up my valise, having already given orders that my steamer trunk was to meet me on the pier, and walked up to the gangplank that was just being lowered. A squeak and a "Disembark, *ho!*" met my ears, and I turned to see Little Welly and his mother standing in the line that had formed behind me. I waved good-bye to them, and the little sprat saluted me back. *Brace yourself, Royal Navy*, I thought as I walked off the ship.

In the distance, I saw an ornate building with glass windows. Ellis Island, which I was thankful I'd be bypassing, given Aunt Robbie's generosity. I thanked God I wasn't sick, nor had contracted anything during the trans-Atlantic voyage. All I had to do was clear Customs on the pier, and I'd be on my way.

The gangway was lowered for us. I heard shouts from below and noticed that hands and arms were waving out of the lower deck promenades. The voices and arms belonged to third class and steerage passengers, the majority of them immigrants looking to start a new life in this land of opportunity. A few years ago, I would have been among them. I knew the ins and outs of what would happen to those people, and I didn't envy them. A sheet of questions which you had better know all the answers to, and of course there were the medical inspections, which I'd heard were not pleasant, not to mention the indignity of having labels affixed to your clothes once you disembarked the ship. If you tripped up on any of the quizzing, or if you were declared consumptive or worse, it was back on the boat and across the ocean again, returned to wherever it was you came from.

Someone shoved me in the back, and I walked down the gangway, hoping my fellow passengers below decks would make it through without incident. There was nothing I could do for them but hope that the life they would make for themselves in this city would be better than the one they had left behind.

After being cleared by Customs, I headed for the receiving end of the dock, searching for Aunt Robbie.

I pushed my way through the crowd of passengers. All around me, people were laughing, hugging, and piercing my ears with their cries and jubilation at seeing their families.

"Lord, don't you look a sight!" exclaimed one woman.

"What a surprise to see you here, Alexander!" shouted another.

"Why? You told me to be here at ten sharp. I shouldn't think it much of a surprise that I actually showed up," grumbled Alexander. I chuckled at the woman's astonished face and pressed on, weaving my way through the sea of bodies and steamer trunks, receiving an occasional jolt in the ribs or an ostrich plume in the face for my troubles.

The preferred means of locating one's relatives seemed to be to just shout their name at the top of your lungs. *Well, when in New York...*

"*Roberta Bradburry Ives*!" I bellowed so loudly a man next to me jumped three feet in the air. "Sorry," I said, but he was already shrinking away from me as though I were a madman. "Aunt Robbie! Where are you?!" I shouted again. I stood up on tiptoe, scanning the crowd, looking for any sign of one of those large, plumed hats she favored. Of course, the last time I had seen her wear one of those creations was twelve years ago. Her style might have changed since then, though I doubted it.

I noticed the porter standing at the end of the pier. I figured I'd have a word with him and had almost reached him, when I felt a tap on my shoulder.

"Au revoir, good monsieur."

"*Au revoir?*" I thought aloud. Why would someone be addressing me with good-bye? Unless...

"Aunt Robbie?!" I turned and knocked right into that bloody plumed hat I knew she'd be wearing.

"Au revoir, eh, au *revoir*? Of all the cheek."

Her black brows were perfectly arched and set in an expression that was half smirk, half challenge.

Corcitura

"So, what do you think of your old Aunt Robbie? Has she held up well all these years?" she asked, twirling for my benefit.

I took a step back, stroking my chin, pretending to be appraising her critically. She wore a striking high-necked black and white dress and clutched a matching lace parasol. The plume on her hat must have been at least five feet in height, and fluttered precariously in the breeze. When I had finished looking at the plume, I noticed with a shock that her face was completely devoid of lines or creases, a fact I found unfathomable, for she was close to sixty-five. Her eyes were still the same Bradbury brown, that deep chocolate that was almost black, just like mine, and her hair matched the two-tone dress to perfection. It was still black as pitch with a few threads of white running through it. She hadn't taken any measures to hide these signs of age, but seemed rather to revel in them, which was typical of Aunt Robbie—she had always marched to her own beat.

"All right, all right, that's enough of the scrutiny," she said, waving her hand. "Now it's my turn. Let me have a look at you. Well, the nose can't be helped, nor the ears, Lord love you, but they're well hidden by that mop on your head," she said, reaching up to tousle my hair. "It was reddish the last time I saw you, but no, it's that same stubborn dark brown as your father's now."

She stepped back and looked me over from head to foot, her eyes crinkling at the corners when she saw the expectant expression on my face. I couldn't decide if she was amused or about to cry, and before I could ask her if all was well, she hooked her parasol over her arm and took my hand in hers.

"Twelve years really is too long, Braddie," she said quietly as she led me off to the waiting cab.

"An eternity," I agreed, meaning more than I chose to let on just yet. If she only knew what had happened to me six years ago, I think she would have sent me back across the Atlantic—loaded down with chains and in the company of a small army of policemen, or so my imagination convinced me—to be locked away once I set foot on English soil. There were a thousand questions I wanted to ask her, a thousand things I wanted to know, first among them why she hadn't come to visit or help us when we were destitute, but all I could think of to say was, "Is that our cab over there?" Those parliamentarians didn't know how lucky they were to have been spared my stimulating conversation.

"Yes, and that mountain of a man standing at the ready is..."

"Ah, Monsieur Bradburry!" Startled, I turned to see that the man who was accosting me in French was none other than my second steward from the *Campania*, Laurent.

I unlinked my arm from Aunt Robbie's and threw myself into conversation with Laurent. I laughed and chortled and parleyed with him in French, stealing furtive looks out of the corner of my eye to gauge Aunt Robbie's level of annoyance. It was right around five minutes into the conversation that I thought I could detect steam rising out of her nostrils, and knew it was time to send Laurent packing. I bid adieu to my steward, wished him luck in his ventures in "The New World," as he called America, and once more linked arms with my Aunt, trying unsuccessfully to keep my lips from twitching into a smirk.

"I suppose you find yourself amusing," she said wryly.

"*Highly*," I answered, stifling a laugh.

"After a few days with me, I'll get that French out of you."

British to her core was my Aunt Robbie and always had been, never feeling too kindly toward our neighbors across the Channel. I smiled fondly down at her and let her lead me along through the thinning crowd. "But priority number one is getting you into society, lad. Oh, by the bye, this is Jerrold."

I looked up several feet into the eyes of a man who was more brick than human. "Your bodyguard?" I asked.

"Very droll. Maximilian Jerrold," she said by way of formal introduction, "my valet and right hand, so I suppose that makes you my left?"

"Touché," I said, smiling as I extended my hand for Jerrold to shake.

Corcitura

"Your servant, Sir," he mumbled, quickly withdrawing his hand and letting down the step so we could climb up into the cab.

"Don't take his taciturnity to heart. Cat's got his tongue the majority of the time," Aunt Robbie whispered to me as we settled in. "Most people just get a grimace and a curt nod. You got three words, so you've practically become old chums in a matter of seconds!"

I shook my head as she gave the driver the address, and the cab set off. Aunt Robbie leaned over and lowered the window on my side, then settled back against the cushions, crossed her arms, and stared at me expectantly. I had no idea what she was waiting for, but then I heard it.

"FRESH FISH!!!!! Get 'em while they're cold!" That was a new one. Get em' while they're *cold*? Didn't seem like such a great selling tactic to me, but what did I know of New York business? The fishmonger's stall was crowded with people jostling each other to be first in line, their money-stuffed hands waving wildly. A loud honking noise nearly jolted me off my seat. When I shifted to the window on the opposite side of the cab, I saw a man furiously pumping the small rubber ball on the end of a horn and waving at us to get out of the way of his carriage. I was a bundle of nerves, but Aunt Robbie was leaning back against the seat comfortably, her eyes closed, a strange smile on her face. I was aghast at her calmness. Was this the same Roberta B. Ives who had tobogganed with me down the slopes of Cortina when I was eight years old, shouting "view halloo!" as snow kicked up around us and ensconced us in our own private blizzard? The same woman who had smiled calmly and made light of my mother's protests that we had nearly caused an avalanche? This sedate creature sitting across from me couldn't be the same person. *My* Aunt Robbie would have given that honking fiend what for by now.

"I know what you're thinking," she said. "But you get used to it after living so long in New York. It's a different way of life than the one you've led, Braddie. You can't be picking fights with every hothead that crosses your path or you'd never make it through the day in one piece.

"Look out there," she said, sliding over to my side of the cab. "Different faces, different sizes, shapes, colors...listen to them all. Languages you've never even heard before. That's the magic of New York. It's one giant cauldron of people. You can visit every country in the world without ever leaving the city."

I stared out the window in wonder, watching the crowds milling and bustling all around us. We wended our way down streets teeming with vendor carts and nannies pushing the little master or mistress along in prams. I saw fishmongers, costermongers, haberdashers, people engaged in veritably any occupation one could think of—they all found a home on the avenues and boulevards of New York City. I leaned closer toward the window to take it all in—the sights, the smells, a million and one different vistas opening before my eyes. I had thought I'd seen it all in the Portobello Road market, but this crowd parting before us made my home market seem like a flea circus.

"We're here!" Aunt Robbie chimed, startling me out of my reverie.

"So soon?" I asked, but she wasn't listening. She was so excited she nearly knocked off her hat as she bustled out of the cab. "Come and see your new home, Braddie. It's not as grand as what I'm sure you're used to, but it'll have to do until you make your first million."

"Not as grand..." I laughed, the words dying away as I stepped onto the pavement.

Two large stone lions flanked the steps leading up to the ebony shellacked door, in the center of which was affixed a huge gold doorknocker carved to resemble a lion's head. Although the entrance was massive and took up most of the space on the sidewalk, the exterior of the house wasn't as imposing, being tall and thin and made of brick. Once I stepped across the threshold, however, all that changed.

Not as grand indeed.

A long hallway stretched out before me and ended in a wrought iron spiral staircase that wound up for what must have been at least four floors. The steps were carpeted in rich burgundy velvet and the two bay windows on either side of the staircase were draped with matching velvet curtains. The windows let in a spectacular amount of light, which flooded the entire stairwell and glinted off the staircase's golden, acanthus leaf encrusted spindles.

From where I stood to the stairwell, the floor was completely covered in black and white checkered marble tile so polished I felt as though I were seeing my reflection in a mirror as I looked down.

At her prompting, I followed Aunt Robbie into the parlor to our left. I shouldn't have been surprised by the opulence, but it took me aback just the same. All the woodwork in the room was painted white. There was a white fireplace, white chairs with carved woodworking so intricate and frothy that it looked like frosting on a cake, white tables with glass tops, a white grandfather clock tolling away in the corner, and underneath it all, a shockingly red carpet that, combined with the excess of white furnishings, made the whole room look like a decadent trifle.

"Always reminded me of a wedding cake," Aunt Robbie muttered, waving her hand to encompass the entire room as she sat down, "but your dear Uncle Gerry's mama furnished the house for us as a present after we moved here, and when the old dragon came to live with us, my say in changing the décor was vetoed. I didn't have the heart to alter it after she died, what with Gerry being so fond of her and all.

"And to complete the illusion..." she said, looking meaningfully at the tea table. I followed her gaze and laughed when I saw the design of the room replicated in the form of two identical pieces of cake, topped with strawberries and cream, resting on plates in the center of the table. By their side sat two white, rose-festooned china cups filled with tea.

"So," I said, slapping both hands against my knees as I settled back into the chair across from Aunt Robbie, "what do you want to knaaaaaaa!"

"What do I want to knaaaa?" I heard her say. "What an odd question."

I struggled to raise myself up, for upon sitting down in the chair, I had sunk in about five feet, the cushion was so plush. Aunt Robbie's laughter grew louder as she reached down and helped me up.

"And what, my dear Aunt, do you find so amusing about the situation?"

"Nothing," she chortled, "old habits die hard, I suppose. It's just that you used to disappear into that very chair every time you sat in it when you came to visit me in Kent."

"Yes, I had forgotten. Do you remember that time...."

"Eric, wait..." She stepped back and once more took a seat, folding her hands in her lap. After a moment that seemed to stretch on forever, she finally spoke. "What really happened with you and Stefan?"

It was a question I had been dreading. I felt deflated as I looked at her face. The moment of truth was upon me at last.

"Exactly how much did Mother tell you of our situation?" I asked, stalling.

"That's not important," she said evasively.

I reached toward the table, gently lifted the teacup, and took a sip for courage. I wished it had had a shot of rum in it, because straight tea just made my stomach feel even worse.

I put down the cup and stared at my hands. "Stefan...*changed*..." I said hesitantly.

"In what way?"

This wasn't going to be easy. So much for the vague approach.

"He met...some people who had a bad influence on him, more than a bad influence, actually."

"So it wasn't the Ripper who killed Roddy, was it? It was Stefan."

"We believe so, or at least *I* do, anyway..."

"There's more, though, isn't there?"

I nodded, taking another sip to steel myself.

"But you're not going to tell me."

"Not now, at any rate," I said quietly. "Maybe later, when you've had time to judge the soundness of my mind."

"What do you mean by that?"

I looked up at her. There was concern in her eyes. She reached out her hand and placed it over mine. "Eric, let me tell you something. You know that whatever it is, how outlandish it might be, how insane and ridiculous, I'll believe it."

"Why?"

"Because I love you. And because I've already guessed the answer, I just need to hear you tell me yourself."

This was incomprehensible. How could she have known, *really* known, what Stefan had become, unless Mother had been more lucid than I gave her credit for?

"Go on, love," she coaxed.

"These people...they turned Stefan into something dreadful. Something that no one would believe if I told them..."

"Say it, Eric, *please.*"

Name the beast and fear it no more... She claimed she knew my secret, so why should I hold back any longer? "A vampire."

Aunt Robbie remained silent. I wondered if she really had known the truth, or had just been humoring me.

"And the worst part is," I hurried on, anxious to release the anger that was welling up in my chest, "he wanted to become one. It was almost as if he'd always known it was his destiny, as if he needed it to somehow make himself whole."

"Didn't he put up a fight?"

"For about three seconds."

"You seem resentful."

"Oh, just a *tad*," I said through gritted teeth. "You think you know someone, you are *sure* you know them inside and out, and then another comes along and subsumes them and they are dead to you forever. It makes you doubt yourself, wonder if you had something to do with it, if you somehow pushed them toward the decision that would destroy their life."

"Eric, *stop.* What happened to Stefan was not your fault."

"Wasn't it?" I asked, rounding on her, but the moment I saw her eyes, I knew she was right. How could I have known that pushing for the meeting with Leonora would result in all this? Yet although my family had absolved me from blame, I still felt a gnawing in my heart, like a maggot chewing on the remnants of a corpse—a guilt I'd never be rid of. Incessant, corruptive. "And how long have you known?" I couldn't reconcile myself to how reasonable she was being about the entire situation.

"About two months. I could strangle that mother of yours for letting you stay destitute for so long. She kept rambling on about your finding a card with my name on it, a threat of some kind, and so she didn't want to involve me. She's much smarter than you think, although incredibly hardheaded."

"Tell me Uncle Gerard died of natural causes," I demanded, suddenly afraid. With all that had happened, I had pushed the memory of the card from my mind, along with the memory of the threat scrawled across it in my stepfather's blood.

"The heart. It was always weak. Then one day it just gave out and he was gone. My loveable old Scotch," she whispered, her voice catching. She wrinkled her nose and sniffed, which I remembered was the way she pushed back tears and regained her composure. She was descended from those rugged, show-no-emotion Braidbury Saxons, after all.

"Silly chit!" she chimed, changing tack. "I could club your mother for keeping secrets all those years. Destitute and not a friend in the world, and yet she insisted on making her own way. I'd like to box her ears."

"She was just doing what she thought best," I said mechanically, still not understanding how Aunt Robbie could be so accepting of the fact that my former best friend was now undead. "You're not bothered by this situation at all? You don't think I'm daft?" This was a new sensation for me.

"I've always felt comfortable amongst the horrors. I married your uncle Gerard, after all."

Her eyes had regained their former spark, and her eyebrow was once more arched in that manner that was half challenge, half amusement. If she could be so calm and accepting of the situation, why should I stop her? Why was I clinging to the terror of the past, when a new future was staring me in the face? Of course, I knew there'd have to be a time for deep discussion, but then again maybe not. Why should I dwell on the past when I couldn't change any of it? I was starting fresh, and if Aunt Robbie could look the other way, why couldn't I? "Oh, Aunt Robbie, it *is* good to be here."

"It gets even better. You and I are going out on the town tonight. We've been invited to a millionaires' ball."

"A millionaires' ball?" I asked, shocked.

"Is there an echo in here?" she said, chucking me underneath the chin. "Yes, a millionaires' ball. It all sounds rather hoity-toity and highfalutin, but we shall liven it up a bit, I think. So," she said, pausing to consult her watch, "in about twenty minutes, we'll ride in style up along the Hudson in our coach and four. What do you say? It'd be good for you to get out and meet some other young pups. Your mother condescended to tell me of your troubles with that Cornelia excrescence...well, she's in the past, and good riddance. Fresh young blood, that's what you need!"

I winced at her choice of words. Stefan and Salei would have perked up at that proposition. I had to keep reminding myself that they were no longer my concern, but when the memories of them had been a part of my life and every waking moment for so long, it was hard to rid myself of the feeling that they were lurking just beyond my line of sight.

"Oh, sorry. Poor wording, eh?"

"Slightly," I muttered.

"Well, vampires be damned, which I think they already are, but that's neither here nor there. By the bye, I read up on some books about them, if you're interested. Once I found out, I thought you were all daft, but then your mother was so adamant, and I received confirmation from Jameson, plus all that nonsense about Roddy and the Ripper...I'm woman enough to draw my own conclusions, even when they fly in the face of all logic. I'll show you the books later, that is, if you're interested?"

I wasn't sure how I felt about that suggestion. I was prepared to do a lot to further this new beginning, but I wasn't certain I'd go that far just quite yet. Shortly after settling in Bruges, I had found some books regarding vampirism, but had only got a short way with them before the memories of Castle Bran came flooding back. My experiences were enough to give me nightmares. I didn't need to dredge up more memories by reading about the very things I was trying to forget. But now, after being removed from the situation for so long, I wondered if reading in the comfort and safety of Aunt Robbie's home would help me better understand what I'd gone through, or at least prepare me to face the danger if I were ever to confront Salei or Constantinos again.

"Why not? What harm can it do?" I said more cavalierly than I felt.

"That's the spirit, Braddie!" she said, slapping me on the back. In many ways, Aunt Robbie was just one of the lads, and I loved her for it. "Jerrold!" she bellowed.

The brick wall answering to that name suddenly materialized in the archway. "Yes, Mum," he muttered.

"Take my nephew's things up to his room and lay out the suit."

"Right away, Mum."

"Suit?" I asked, puzzled. "But I brought my own things."

"Pshaw! You can't make your entrance into society looking like a ragamuffin. I've got it all taken care of."

"How?"

"Didn't you know I read minds as a hobby? Don't look so bewildered, lad, I'm only joking. I got the measurements from your mother. Now, off with you, we mustn't be late!"

I couldn't help always looking bewildered, for that's exactly the reaction she engendered in me. I smiled what must have looked like a half-witted smile, then went upstairs and began dressing.

Ten minutes later, I was standing in front of the hall mirror, tying my cravat, when Aunt Robbie shimmered into view behind me.

"Share the wealth, lad," she said, shoving me aside. "Be considerate."

Some of her mischievousness had rubbed off on me in the time since we'd been reunited. I marveled at how quickly we had fallen back into our old bantering pattern. It was as though we'd never been separated.

I cast her a sidelong look as she primped in the mirror and patted her hair to make sure it retained its curls. "I *am* being considerate," I said lightly. "I don't know how I could be any *more* considerate. Consideration is my middle name."

"I thought it was Murgatroyd?" she mumbled as she pried open hairpins between her teeth.

"Ha ha, it is to laugh. Very funny, Aunt Robbie."

She righted herself and surveyed her handiwork. "Ah, yes, that'll do. So, are you going to stand there fussing over that ruff at your neck all night, or shall we go out and make a few conquests? I do not believe I am quite so old that I still cannot break a few hearts. And we *are* a handsome pair, are we not?"

I stared at her in bewilderment that quickly turned to mirth. How could I not love her? She was such a welcome change in my life and a reminder of the humanity I had so sorely missed these past years. "Shall we be off, then, Lady Godiva?" I jested, holding out my arm.

"Why tarry any longer, dear sir? But if you expect me to ride naked through Central Park, you've got another thing coming."

She elbowed me good-naturedly in the ribs and the two of us, laughing and acting like a pair of children, made for the cab and shut ourselves up inside.

I'd just made it through the door when I heard a heavily accented, disembodied voice boom, "Where to, Milady?"

"Don't panic, love, that's just Jack," Aunt Robbie reassured me. Who Jack was, I couldn't have said, but he seemed to be settled up top and in charge of the reins. "Riverhampton, driver. The Dennison mansion. You know it well."

"Oh, aye, Mum, settle in!"

And before I could get my bearings, I was thrown back against the seat as Jack shot the cab down the thoroughfare.

"View halloo," Aunt Robbie muttered.

This was going to be an interesting ride.

‡

"When you see this place, Braddie, you aren't going to believe its sheer size. The conservatory alone is probably three times as big as my parlor."

We'd been clopping along at a brisk pace for almost a quarter of an hour, during which time Aunt Robbie had been filling me in on all the details of the place I was about to visit.

"Mansions, Braddie," she continued on, warming to her theme, "veritable castles moments from the city. It's wondrous."

"I imagine they are much like the royal residences back in England."

"Some are, but not the one we're going to tonight. Riverhampton outshines them all."

"So, who is this Dennison fellow, really?"

"He's sort of a financial bigwig in these parts."

"I'm guessing this means all that palaver about the personal representative was just a load of gibberish?"

"A complete and utter barrel of codfish."

"Beg pardon?"

"Spend five minutes with Steven and you'll understand where I've picked up my new vernacular."

I didn't have time to ask her who this Steven person was, nor did I have time to process how I would feel meeting a man with almost the exact same name as my former best friend, because at that moment, a loud blaring sound shot through the cab and drew my gaze to the window.

"Aunt Robbie, put down the window," I said.

A small boat was steaming up the Hudson to our right. I leaned closer and discerned that the railing was dotted with women in long elegant gowns and young men dressed in top hats and tailcoats. The majority of the young men were clustered toward the stern. I narrowed my eyes and saw a plump little blonde creature cavorting amidst this group of what I assumed were her many suitors. She clapped her hands and twirled around and there was a great eruption of laughter, which I took to mean they were playing charades or some other game.

After her triumph, the pixie raced over to a bench running alongside the cabin and knelt before a woman wearing an emerald green dress. I could not see much of this mystery woman, for her parasol shielded her face from view. Whatever she said must have pleased the sprite because I saw her grab the woman's hands and press them before running back to her waiting beaux, where she must have related to them yet another joke, for they all burst out laughing once again. If I had been closer, I'm sure I would have seen the girl blush with pleasure. She was a little queen holding court amongst her swains—a veritable Katherine Howard with Jane Seymour's coloring, I mused.

I turned my attention back to the woman in the emerald green dress, but she was no longer there. For some reason, I panicked when I didn't see her, but then I noticed she had moved further down the bench. I must have had a puzzled look on my face, for Aunt Robbie peeked out the window and said, "Ah, the young ones. You'll meet them all soon enough."

My eyes stayed riveted on the woman. I wondered who she was and why Aunt Robbie had a smug, enigmatic smile on her face and would not answer any of my questions regarding the woman's identity. Instead, like a Cheshire Cat, Aunt Robbie kept smiling and said, "You'll learn all your heart desires in time. Patience."

I stared at the girl again, but all I could see were bare upper arms, long green gloves that matched her dress, and the occasional dark curl of hair falling past her shoulders.

"How much farther?" I asked impatiently. I wasn't sure why, exactly, but ever since seeing that little group on the boat, the idea of this millionaires' ball had become much more exciting.

"Not much longer. Sit back, dear, or you'll crease your trousers."

I settled back and did as I was told—feeling all of seven years old—and after what felt like a century to my agitated mind, the cab finally pulled to a stop.

The infamous Jack came around and opened the door. He was a bent old man with a large red nose, yet his eyes held the spark of youth. "Hop out, me lovelies," he said, twinkling. If I didn't know better, I would swear Jack had had one too many cups of tea before we left, but all thoughts of whether or not our driver was inebriated fled my mind when I beheld Riverhampton.

"So, what do you think? Bigger than Sandringham House, eh?"

I stared, open-mouthed, at the grand castle sprawling before me. "Bigger even than Buckingham Palace, I'd say."

"Now don't get ahead of yourself. We don't want to give the Americans that much credit."

I felt her link her arm through mine and pull me toward the door. She must have guided me through the throng of people, for my eyes were riveted on the mansion the whole time. I would have undoubtedly stumbled into one person or another had she not been directing my steps.

Massive did not even begin to describe the mansion. It was colossal, made entirely of redbrick and nestled back toward the edge of the bank, with a view of the Hudson beyond. A large rose window that reminded me of the one I'd seen in Notre Dame was set into the brick on the left side of the house. The glass of the conservatory gleamed in the moonlight as we passed through the crowd, and I heard the faint sound of string music floating on the air.

I tore my eyes away from the house and noticed we were walking up a tree-lined pathway. Brilliant light streamed from the hundreds of orange and turquoise Chinese lanterns strung between the branches.

"Roberta, how good of you to come!"

I looked around to see who had called to Aunt Robbie and was nearly bowled over by a large, bear-like man with a very poorly affixed toupee.

"Rrrreg, dahling," Aunt Robbie trilled, "what a surprise to see you here!"

"Surprise, pish-tosh! You surely received my card? I sent it a week ago."

"Card? No, I'm afraid I can't say I ever received it." I looked at her through narrowed lids. The big saucer eyes and innocent expression might have fooled Reg, but they didn't fool me. I had seen that very card crumpled up in the wastepaper basket in the hallway only an hour ago.

"Come, come, Roberta, you must need an escort for the evening?"

"*Ahem*," I shot in, loudly clearing my throat and pushing my way between Reg and Aunt Robbie. My intrusion caused a ripple. I noticed that Reg's hair slipped off his bald pate half an inch, although he didn't seem to think anything amiss. "You have no need to fear, good sir, for she already has one."

"Roberta, this is highly irregular. The boy's barely out of his combinations!"

"I like them *young*," she said tartly, and led me along, leaving Reg to sputter and gape after us.

"Aunt Robbie! Are you trying to ruin us both?"

"Oh, please, don't worry about that old penguin. He's harmless. I have to keep him at bay."

"And I suppose you also *have* to address him as 'dahling?'" I said, defending the memory of Uncle Gerard.

"He loves it when I call him that. He insists I roll the R's too. The old sot has been after me ever since your uncle died."

"He's in love with you?"

"He's in love with the half million dollars I have sitting in the bank." We had almost reached the door, when Aunt Robbie turned, all smiles, and waved to the still bewildered Reg, before pushing me through the entrance of the manor. "Come along, my rich young beau from across the pond."

The first thing I noticed was a chandelier—almost as grand as the one at Opéra Garnier—hanging from the middle of the foyer's ceiling. There was such a crush of people gathered here—the ladies divesting themselves of wraps and the chaps of gloves and scarves—that it was nearly impossible to move.

Suddenly, I was yanked through the crowd and dragged along the hallway until we reached a large archway that led into the grand ballroom.

And grand it was.

One corner of the oak-paneled wall was taken up entirely by what must have been a fifty-piece orchestra. Directly in front of us, a great oak and marble staircase fanned out from at least three levels up. The moonlight pouring in through the glass dome in the ceiling glinted off the crystals on the ladies' gowns and made the room sparkle with celestial magnificence.

"Ah, yes, I told you it was a sight, didn't I?"

I stood speechless, marveling at the grandeur of it all, until my reverie was interrupted by a pair of giggles to my left. I turned to see two identical, frizzy-haired girls swirl by me in a flash of tulle.

"A word of warning," Aunt Robbie said. "Stay away from those Hayward sisters. They're not called the Wayward Haywards for nothing."

"They sound amusing," I muttered, still staring at the bubbly pair as they cavorted in front of the orchestra, obviously tying to distract the handsome bass player. A loud twang a few moments later told me they had succeeded.

"Only if you want to get saddled with one of them and a dyspeptic vulture of a mother-in-law for life. No, when you see them coming your way, you take off in the opposite direction. I have greater things planned for you, my boy, than to be shackled to one of those boils."

"Duly noted, Aunt Robbie," I said. I had no intention of taking one of the Wayward Haywards for a wife. I was more interested in finding out who that mystery girl in the emerald dress was.

Suddenly, the hair on the back of my neck began to prickle. I felt as though I were being watched. I looked around, but no one seemed to be staring at me. I was starting to believe I'd imagined the whole thing, until my eyes lit upon the sprite-faced blonde creature I had seen on the boat.

"Ah! There's a girl for you," Aunt Robbie chimed, noticing the attention the girl was paying me. "Go on over. She won't bite. Her name's Margaret Colfer, in case you were wondering. Charming girl."

I thought this idea rather dodgy without being properly introduced, but I didn't have time to ponder the propriety of the situation. Just then, the orchestra struck up a lively number and I found myself being pulled out into the throng of couples.

"There, now we've met."

Corcitura

I looked down into the deepest green eyes I had ever seen.

The sprite had captured me!

"Um, I don't think this is exactly according to form," I protested halfheartedly. She had an infectious smile that made me feel silly and reckless all at once.

"Hang form! I've never held with it in all my twenty years, why should I start now?"

Saucy minx. She had just told me her age without meaning to, or without doing it blatantly, at the very least. She dimpled as I stared down at her. She was quite a bit shorter than me, but made up for the difference in our heights with a pluck I found enchanting. There was also a marked lilt to her voice that intrigued me.

"Where are you from, exactly?" I asked, feeling instantly at ease. Her manner was such that I felt as though I'd known her far longer than just a few minutes.

"Dublin, of course. You know that song that goes, 'In Dublin's fair city, where girls are so pretty?' Who do you think gave them the inspiration for the lyrics?"

"Well, alive, alive, oh, then, missy," I said in my best Irish accent, and laughed as I twirled her across the floor.

My winning Irish lass claimed my hand for most of the evening. Several of her suitors had tried to cut in, but she had deterred them by saying I was a long lost cousin who had miraculously shown his face after years and years away on the Continent, and, therefore, I had insisted on claiming all but two of her dances, which she was saving for "someone else." Who that someone else was, she never said, but that he was present that evening was obvious.

As I spun her closer to the line of guests chatting just beyond the ballroom floor, I noticed a young man staring at us intently. I couldn't decide whether to be wary of his expression or amused by it, for the look on his face was simultaneously fierce and indulgent. He was not very tall, maybe a few inches shorter than I, and a few inches taller than Molly, as my companion had whispered to me was what she preferred to be called. She claimed only her closest friends called her that name. After confiding this to me, she appraised me from head to foot so that I knew she was hoping I wouldn't be averse to joining that select coterie, though from the remembrance of the lads on the boat, that close circle seemed to be widening by the minute.

I glanced again at the young man and saw that he had moved to the foot of the grand staircase and was staring up it expectantly. Molly noticed him, too, and suddenly stopped dancing and led me to where the man stood.

"Steven," she said, linking arms with the young man, who seemed startled by her arrival, "this is Eric Bradburry. Eric, may I present Steven Bannon?"

The young man looked at her upturned face fondly for more than I thought was necessary—I was beginning to think there was history between these two—then extended his hand. "Charmed," he said. Though I expected him to be sarcastic, I was surprised to see he was sincere. "Poppy here told me you'd be coming."

"Poppy?"

"Molly, Poppy, Goddess Mine, they are all aliases I go by," she said mischievously, twinkling up at him. He positively melted at her look and tuned on her a twinkling gaze of his own. I no longer suspected that there was a past history between them: I *knew* there was, and, what's more, there was a very strong present between them, too.

"So," I said, clearing my throat and bringing them somewhat out of their trance. "How did *Poppy* know I'd be here tonight?"

"Oh, Aunt Robbie, of course." Steven had a slight Irish accent, too, though I would have pegged him for one of the bored residents of Mayfair from his style of dress, which was quite beau monde, and his dark curling moustache and hair. His bright blue eyes sparkled. I thought maybe the sheen had been caused by too much drink, but then I looked down and saw that his glass of brandy was full to the brim. Steven also had sort of a Musketeerish look about him. I found myself wondering if he ever gadded about town in the middle of the night wearing a cape and feathered hat. Molly's fancifulness was rubbing off on me...

"Well, so much for secrets," I said without rancor. "What is it you do, Steven?"

"I, dear lad, am a writer."

"A *great* writer," Molly chimed, which caused Steven to puff out his chest a little.

"Well, I wouldn't say that, lovey," he said, patting her hand, "but I do my best."

"And has any of your work ever been published?" I asked, almost certain I already knew the answer.

He hesitated and looked at Molly for encouragement. "At the moment, no."

"But it will be one day soon," the irrepressible Molly struck in. *Behind every great man...*

"And what are the themes, generally?" I asked.

"Man's struggle against nature, the great open outdoors, that old-time, rugged spiritedness."

"So you write westerns."

"In a manner."

"I think that's wonderful," I said rather weakly. Thankfully, before he could launch into a detailed description of his latest project, a hush fell over the crowd and all eyes turned toward the grand staircase.

I wondered why they were all staring at the man standing at the top of the stairs. This must have been Mason Dennison. He was rather imposing and reminded me strongly of Lord Nelson, although Mr. Dennison had his full complement of limbs. Yet I did not see why he should cause such awe in his guests.

And then I saw her.

The striking emerald dress, the china-doll skin, the dark curls... Standing next to Mason Dennison was the girl from the boat who had captivated me for reasons I could not understand.

She had to be his daughter, for she resembled him, especially around the eyes, and I didn't think he was the type to take a wife more than forty years his junior. I expected her to be haughty, given her privileged station in life, but her face was so open and inviting and friendly as she smiled at each of her guests in turn. I noticed that she reserved the most brilliant, and only teeth revealing smile, for Molly. If I deluded myself, I could swear she had looked the same way at me, but Molly was at my side, and I knew the smile had been meant for her.

I felt my hand going forward of its own accord to reach for Miss Dennison, intending to invite her to dance with me, but a large, bull-necked man nearly trounced me into the ground and claimed her first. The smile vanished from Miss Dennison's face as she took the man's hand and let him lead her toward the dance floor. I heard Molly cough. When I glanced at her, I was surprised to see such contempt in her eyes.

"James Calhoun, at it again," she nearly spat, her eyes casting daggers at his receding back. "Mr. Perceptive, my eye. The stupid fool's too dense to know when someone loathes his innards."

And with that very unladylike sentiment, Molly swished away in a cloud of violet silk and stalked off in Miss Dennison's direction.

"So, what is it that you do?"

I glanced to my left and saw Steven standing beside me. He'd procured me a glass of brandy, which he held out to me. I took the glass and thanked him. "I'm in a bit of a transient position now."

"Not employed?"

"Employed in a manner, I suppose. I'm really nothing but a glorified lady's companion, if you want to know the truth."

To my surprise, Steven seemed to find this comment highly amusing, and laughed until he was very red in the face. "Robbie was right about you."

"So everyone tells me," I said, my mouth twisting into a smirk.

"Since you are unengaged at the moment, I'd like to bounce a few ideas off you. I'm having a spot of trouble coming up with a name for my latest protagonist."

"I'd think that'd be the first thing you'd have come up with."

"I do have a few names I've been trying out, but I can't seem to settle on one or the other. What do you think of Rowan Ash?"

I goggled at him. Was he serious? "Is there a particular reason you want this tree motif?" I asked, hoping that would put him off the idea.

"Well, the West, ruggedness, toughness, you know the drill."

"I'm surprised you didn't call him Calamity Clark or Tombstone Ted."

"Calamity Clark?! *Calamity Clark*?!" he gasped, his eyes widening. "Genius!"

"Thanks," I said, bewildered. "Rowan Ash struck me as being a mite Gothic."

"Yes, you're right. Conjures up images of vampires and dungeons and shadowy corners. Definitely not what I'm going for. Too melodramatic for my tastes."

"Ah, ha ha," I laughed, or tried to at least. One more "ha" and I'd start to sound hysterical. I wished I was back at Aunt Robbie's house, or at least on the other side of the room, for I was certain Steven would press me if I gave him the chance, and I didn't trust myself to remain calm. I felt my throat closing up and willed him to take himself off after Molly and have done with our conversation. I studied the brandy in my glass, not daring to look in his direction. He'd take a glance as a sign of encouragement, an invitation to continue, and I'd lose my sensibility if he started in on the subject of vampires again.

After a few minutes of silence, I had begun to believe he'd gone, for he hadn't uttered a word. What had passed between us seemed to be the extent he was willing to go for conversation. One quick glance, however, revealed that he was still beside me, but he'd receded so far into himself that I was hard-pressed to believe Steven was actually there.

I heard him clear his throat and saw that he was staring at Molly with wide, glassy eyes. I knew he wasn't drunk. He hadn't touched his brandy, but the look in his eyes was not a healthy one. I couldn't help wondering what he was thinking. The subject of vampires was obviously far from his mind now, so, taking a page from Aunt Robbie's book, I decided to be candid. After all, we'd known each other for at least half an hour, which seemed to be the appropriate amount of time required to elapse before one felt comfortable sharing confidences with a complete stranger. That seemed to be the general consensus amongst this assembly, at any rate. Molly would have probably thought thirty seconds sufficient.

"I hope you shan't think me forward," I said tentatively.

"Not a-*tall*," he answered, his eyes still fixed on Molly.

"Well...are you and Poppy engaged?"

"Egad! Engaged to Poppy?" he sputtered. "I love the girl, yes, but I'm not the marrying kind. Why would I ruin what I have with Poppy by doing something foolish like marrying her?" he said, laughing as though I was mad for suggesting such a thing.

"It seems like the normal thing to do when you love a girl, don't you agree?"

"The idea *had* crossed my mind, but Poppy's still very young, so there's no sense rushing into these things, right? Give her a few years to get me out of her system, and she'll make a better marriage elsewhere."

I knew him in an instant then. That devil-may-care exterior was all an act. He knew he couldn't support Molly, and rather than drag her into penury, he was willing to give her up. I looked toward Miss Dennison as the wild notion of marrying *her* crossed my mind. I wondered if I could give her up. She was obviously far wealthier than I could ever hope to be. It was impossible, yet I knew I could never give in as heroically as Steven could. I was selfish. If I set my mind on marrying Miss Dennison, I wouldn't be put off the idea so easily.

"Don't you value Molly enough to let her make up her own mind?" I asked boldly, not really sure why I had taken an immediate interest in their affairs. I knew I shouldn't be prying, but Steven was making an ass of himself.

He sighed and looked into his glass of untouched brandy. "You think I'm being a fool, don't you?"

"In a word, yes," I spoke without thinking.

"And you're probably right. Maybe I'll change my mind after a few days. Or maybe Poppy will decide *for* me and make me an honest man. I don't know, but I'm fairly certain she'd be miserable if I asked her to marry me."

"And how do you know this?"

"Well...I don't, really."

"Then why don't you ask?"

He stared at me as blankly as if I were speaking a foreign language. "*Ask?*"

"That's traditionally how it's done," I said, smiling.

"I just, well, I always assumed she'd refuse me, that's all."

"Have you seen the way she looks at you? Are you blind, man?"

He glanced over at Molly and saw that she was staring at him in a most friendly and inviting manner.

"No time like the present, eh?" I said, urging him on.

"Here? No, absolutely not. I cannot do it." And before I could say anything more, he put the still full glass on a tray a passing waiter was carrying, and blustered out of the ballroom. I looked at Molly and saw her face crumple. Apparently, Miss Dennison had also witnessed the exchange, for she was at Molly's side in an instant, claiming her hand. They shared a few words, which I was too far away to hear, then Miss Dennison tugged playfully on one of her friend's riotous blonde curls, which caused Molly's face to brighten, and led her toward a cluster of young bucks all eager to take her mind off her troubles with Steven.

Since I now knew that the job of "Personal Representative" had been nothing more than Aunt Robbie's scheme to get me to America, I decided there would be no harm in acquiring a new occupation: namely, playing Cupid to Molly and Steven. The two of them were so obviously in love, it was senseless to destroy that just because Steven was too proud. I would talk to Aunt Robbie about his works and see if something couldn't be done to help get them to the world. Maybe he could do what Dickens did with many of his novels and serialize them. It was worth a try.

I quaffed my brandy and headed toward the dance floor. I was intending to claim Miss Dennison's hand, bull-necked suitor or not, but found myself caught up in Aunt Robbie's arms instead.

"Ah, lad, I see you've met Steven. Dance with me, Eric, I have a plan."

"Well, look who decided to materialize," I teased as I twirled her, the two of us growing ever closer to Miss Dennison and her suitor. "You have a lot of nerve showing your face after all my personal information has been bruited about, and by your own tongue, I might add, Mrs. Ives."

"Oh, stop being such a twit," she teased in return. "Spin me closer, quickly, before the chance escapes us."

I did as told, but my mind was preoccupied with something other than Miss Dennison, at least for the second. "About Steven, Aunt Robbie. Isn't there something we could do?"

"Of course there is. Don't think I've been idle all this time. Steven's first story is going into print in a month, only he doesn't know it yet. Molly and I have arranged everything, with Mason's help. Maybe he'll finally have the nerve to ask the girl to marry him before someone else does. Speaking of marriage..." she said, eyeing me saucily.

"What?" I asked defensively, my face growing hot.

"You approve of Madelaine Dennison, I gather?"

Madelaine. The name intoxicated me. I felt dizzy. "Who wouldn't?" We were now almost directly in front of Madelaine and her suitor. I was afraid Aunt Robbie would be overheard.

"Good, good, then you wouldn't be averse to dancing with her, I take it?"

"Of course not, but try getting between that bull and her to give me a chance."

"Leave it to me." She twirled out of my arms and tapped the bull on the shoulder. "James, luv, I'd like a word."

"Begging your pardon, ma'am," he said. I could tell he was striving mightily to keep the irritation from his voice. "But I'm engaged with Miss Dennison..."

"That's what you think," I heard Aunt Robbie mutter underneath her breath. I wasn't sure if she meant for the dance or for the future.

"I was just telling Miss Dennison how highly efficient I've been at business. Mr. Dennison was praising my perception," the bull crowed. I had a strong desire to knock this popinjay in the jaw.

"Really?" asked Aunt Robbie archly. "Then you'll perceive that I am out of punch. And you'll be efficient in going to get me some more."

Apparently, James had gone deaf and mute the moment Aunt Robbie finished speaking, for he just stood there gaping like a fish on dry land.

"Oh, goodness, lads these days," Aunt Robbie chided. "You have to take them in hand or they'll just stand around collecting dust. Here, lend an old woman your arm and be my preux chevalier. Come along, now, James. Maddie will be here when you get back...although whether or not she'll be *engaged* is beyond my powers to perceive."

"Engaged?!" he shrieked.

"In dancing, *dancing*, of course. Could there be any other meaning?" and here she winked at me over her shoulder as she led James away.

"Shall we dance, Mr..."

"Bradburry, Eric Bradburry," I said, taking Miss Dennison's hand. The moment her palm was in mine, I felt an electric shock jolt through my body. Why did I have this bad habit of becoming infatuated with women I'd only just met? I'm sure Stefan would have quipped that there was something clinically wrong with me.

The thought startled me. It was the first time in years I'd dredged up a memory of Stefan before he'd changed. It was jarring to remember that he had once been normal. What this thought meant, or what I would have taken it to mean if I'd had time to think it over, I would have to wait to uncover, for just then, Madelaine Dennison spoke.

"Remind me to thank your aunt for that."

"You don't like James?" I asked, hopefully. She'd have to be blind not to see my obvious anxiety over her answer to this question.

"That and other things," she said. "My father adores him. James has informed both of us that he is highly eligible and very much in demand. I once saw James cut himself on a sheet of the *Financial Times*. His blood left a huge blue stain on the paper, poor thing," she said, the corner of her mouth rising in a smirk that tipped up her left eyebrow as well. The effect was decidedly bewitching, and I nearly stumbled over the dance steps as I tried not to gape at her like an idiot. I couldn't understand why she was still starting at me expectantly, until my mind finally registered what she'd said, and I burst out laughing—and Madeleine heartily joined in.

I wanted her to talk more, for her voice thrilled me. It was a pleasant voice, not quite husky, but pitched lower than the average woman's. I laughed to myself at the thought, for Madelaine could never be classified as average.

Her voice was musical and melodious and enticing all at once; it had sent a shock through me when I'd heard her say my name. Hers was a singer's voice, I suspected, resonant and lovely. Her laugh was equally unique, being deep yet angelic at the same time. She was a walking contradiction. I didn't know what to make of her, but when I looked into her gold-tinged brown eyes, I saw in them honesty and perception, as if she could read my soul without my having to say a word.

"So, how do you find New York, Miss Dennison?"

"Find it? I wish I could leave it. I've been here all my life. Don't mistake me, I do love it, but I'd like a chance to go back to London, maybe even live there, if only for a little while."

I had to stop myself from telling her she could if she married me. Where was my mind tonight?

"You've been to London before?" I said instead. That was a sensible question, after all.

"Yes, once, when I was very young. My mother was English, well, half-English. She died when I was thirteen."

"I'm so sorry. Maybe you'll get the chance to go back someday?"

"You're English, after all...maybe you...oh, sorry."

Someone had bumped into us, causing her to break off. Her eyes lost their focus, and she looked around, startled, so that I was left wondering what she had been thinking, wondering if she had been preparing to say something about us. *Ridiculous...*

I shook my head to clear my thoughts and focused my eyes on her face, taking in every detail. Her lips were sculpted, with the lower lip being a bit poutier than the upper, which only made her look more fetching when she smiled up at me. She had perfect little white teeth that occasionally bit down on the corner of her lip when she was trying not to smile, or to be coy, I couldn't tell which. Yet I was learning that dimples peeped out on either side of her mouth when she was in a mischievous mood.

"I see you've met the irrepressible Poppy."

"Why do you call her Poppy, exactly?" I asked, glancing at Molly as we danced past. She waved at me over Steven's shoulder. I was glad to see that they were dancing, and Steven no longer had a face like thunder.

"Through all the years I've known her, her hair has alternately been red or blonde, not with the help of any form of dye, mind you. Her follicles just can't make up their mind what color they want to be. And then of course she is very fond of that blood red rouge for her lips, so she is even more of a Poppy to me now, although I will always prefer to call her Molly."

"You two must be very close."

"She's a sister to me in all but blood. I've never taken to a person as quickly as I did to Molly. I feel I've known her for ages, though it's only been a few years. I don't know what I'd do without her. And Steven would be wise to realize that he would be lost without her, too, but the clod is too stubborn."

I don't know why, but I felt the need to defend Steven. "He's just trying to find his way in life on his own, trying to discover his purpose, that's all."

"And what's your purpose, Mr. Bradburry?"

"My purpose?"

"Yes, what brings you to the house of the idle rich?" she said with a twist to her mouth that told me she thought the notion as ridiculous as I did.

"I'm here as my aunt's personal representative."

"Oh?"

I thought that would elicit more than such a terse response, and I found myself stumbling to try and keep the conversation going. "Um, yes, well..."

"And what does being a personal representative entail?" she asked, the corners of her mouth and eyebrow both rising once again in amusement.

"Well," I said, looking across at the orchestra to focus my thoughts, "to tell the truth, I'm not exactly certain."

I expected her to think me a dolt or lose interest in me completely after such a remark, but instead her brow relaxed and her eyes brightened. "That's the first truly honest answer anyone has given me in a long time."

"People lie to you frequently?" I asked, feeling more concerned than I really should have been.

"Practically ten times in every conversation. James, for one, has never told me a single truth in the four months I've known him. They see this," she said, gesturing to her dress and jewels and face, "and think there is nothing up here," she continued, once again removing her hand from mine, this time to tap her forehead. "I'm smart enough to know when someone is lying to me just to further his own cause with my father."

I was stunned and more than that. Admiration for her coursed through me. Why she was affecting me this way, I had no idea, but I felt dizzy and it wasn't because I had had more than my usual quantity of brandy.

"So your father is an influential man?"

"In our circle, yes. He's a banker and has some connections in the publishing world. He even thought of running for Congress, but I was able to talk him out of that scheme, thankfully. He's too good a man to be among those vultures. Of course, he claimed he didn't want to run because he had too many skeletons in his closet."

I couldn't tell if she was jesting, but I had a feeling she was, for Mason Dennison didn't seem like the type to attract scandal if he could help it.

"My so-called beaux try to impress him every chance they get, and I am the one lucky enough to be the beneficiary of their divided attentions and flattery whenever they come round. They're more interested in Father than anything else."

"In all honesty, my dear Miss Dennison, I don't see how that can be true. They must all be blind. If I were courting you, your father would be the furthest thing from my mind."

It was a scandalous thing to say on many levels. I expected her to shove me off for the obvious clod I was making myself out to be.

"I believe you and I are going to be great friends, Mr. Bradburry," she said, her eyes sparkling in what I hoped was pleasure. If I weren't mistaken, I could have sworn I saw a blush creeping up her neck, but she turned away, and I was left with my own conjectures. What's more, I realized that the music had stopped, signaling the end of a dance I thought had been far too short.

I watched her recede, praying silently that she would look over her shoulder. One little glance was all I wanted. That would be a sign she was interested, that she didn't find me as lumpish as I had appeared. She was drawing closer to Molly and Steven. I'd lost her, for that night at least. I started to turn away, but felt a hand on my shoulder and was stunned to see Madelaine when I turned around.

"Do remember that while you are in New York, you will always be welcome in my father's house."

Before I could say anything, she was gone again. I gazed at her retreating form, openmouthed. Her father's house...where she resided. She was careful not to expose herself to the scandalmongers, but still, I hoped her words meant more than they were supposed to convey.

For the rest of the night, I talked to Molly and Steven, or rather, I stood near them and pretended to be listening to their conversation, when I was actually watching Madelaine over the rim of my glass. I weaved in and out of a dream, but I was fully awake. My head was clouded, I could not focus.

Her words continued to ring through my mind. She danced with no one in particular, though James Calhoun tried to claim her hand on several occasions. Every time I looked at Molly and Steven, I felt a pang of jealousy. I couldn't say why, for I knew that Steven was devoted to Molly and she to him, and Madelaine Dennison was apparently devoted to no man. With a little time, maybe if I accepted the invitation she had extended...

"Oh, sorry old boy. I didn't see you there."

I felt the brandy soaking through the front of my shirt before I even looked down to see the glass's contents spilled all over me. James Calhoun was glowering at me, a smug expression distorting his ugly face.

"Damn and blast," I mumbled, only half angry that he had purposely knocked into me, for I saw Madelaine coming toward me, carrying a cloth in her hands. *Swallow that, you stupid beast*, I thought to myself with satisfaction as I turned a smirk upon Calhoun.

"Of all the childish things to do, James Calhoun," she said in a venomous whisper as she tried to remove the stain from my shirtfront.

"Come now, Lainie..." he whined. I heard a snicker and saw Molly quickly bring her hand to her mouth to cover her tittering. I made a scandalized face then winked at her, which I probably shouldn't have done, for now we both had to struggle mightily to keep from guffawing at Calhoun's sudden transformation from a bull into a wheedling little cat. "I was only trying to teach this upstart a lesson. He's taking liberties where he shouldn't."

"No, the only one who is taking liberties is you, Mr. Calhoun. And for the last time, my name is Madelaine, not Lainie, not Madda, not whatever other confounded names you think I'd like to be called." Her outburst chased all our mirth away in an instant. I was shocked, and so was Calhoun, but it seemed this had been brewing in Madelaine's chest for quite some time and could no longer be lidded.

"Lai...Madelaine, please, what will your father say?"

Corcitura

"My father will thank me for getting rid of a foul canker like you, you worthless snake, once I reveal to him what you really are."

"And what am I?" I moved to step in front of Madelaine. I didn't like the glint in Calhoun's eyes, but apparently she wasn't afraid of him one whit. Smiling as if nothing were amiss, she inched closer to him and whispered, "A conniving fortune hunter with a wife and three children tucked safely away in Maryland. Don't think I don't know about you, Mr. Calhoun. And don't for one instant think I'm afraid of you. My father will know all unless you leave at once. Get out of my sight. I never want to see you in this house again."

A wife?! Children?! This was too much. It had to be a mistake. But from the look on Calhoun's face and the way he was trying to swallow this accusation, it must have been true.

"I'm so sorry, Mr. Bradburry," she said, once again tending to the stain on my shirt. James Calhoun was already halfway out of the room and completely out of my thoughts. I was only too eager to return all my attention to Madelaine.

"Miss Dennison, please, you don't have to." I reached out to stop her from worrying over the stain and my hands locked around hers. I felt her stiffen. I hadn't meant to startle her by the contact, but I must have done, since the look she cast on me was one of shock, but also of something else, something I couldn't decipher. Anger, joy, hope? Whatever that look had meant, it was gone in an instant, and she quickly folded her hands around the cloth. I felt the color rising to my cheeks and wanted nothing more than to recede into the wall, but Madelaine was not yet finished.

"My offer still stands, Mr. Bradburry. Don't let this little incident scare you off. If there are two things I cannot stomach, it is liars and cheats, and I know for a fact you are neither of those. I'm sorry you had to see me this way, but it was necessary for the likes of him. I assure you, I don't bite...at least not my friends, anyway."

I was amazed, floored, shocked, and hopelessly smitten. And then I remembered what she had said...*friends*. She considered me one of them. And in time, maybe she'd consider me something more.

"Thank you, Miss Dennison, I won't lightly forget that offer."

With that, the clock struck one, and I watched her walk off into the crowd.

"We look forward to seeing you again, Eric." Molly tilted up and kissed me on the cheek.

Steven glowered, but his was a good-natured scowl. "Until we meet again," he said, extending his hand.

"Soon, I hope," I said, shaking it.

"From the look on Maddie's face, I'd say *sooner* than soon." Molly gazed up at me mischievously. If she knew her "sister's" heart better than most, then my prospects with Madelaine were on the rise.

I would have loved to stay there longer, but it was growing late and I needed to think. I bid them good night and headed for the door, searching for Aunt Robbie. After a moment, I saw her chatting up Reg. The man was like the plague.

"And so, Mason was telling me, dash it all, I wish I could remember the right way to say it..."

"Oh, bother, Reggg, that's what happens when you get to be as old as Methuselah. The mind is the first thing to go. La, man, here is my young escort."

"Ready, dahling?" I asked, enjoying the game.

"Yes, dear, let us be off. Ta, Regggl!"

Poor old Reg. It had been a bewildering night for both of us, but I was enjoying my bewilderment. I wasn't so sure about Aunt Robbie's would-be lover.

"You enjoy playing with that old sot's mind, don't you?" I asked her once we were settled in the carriage.

"It is an amusing diversion. And how did you enjoy the ball?"

"That's a ridiculous question."

"You sour patch, you didn't like it?" she teased. "Nothing was there to charm you out of your stuffy 'a pox on you, life!' outlook?"

I knew she was staring at me archly, and I also knew that *she* knew exactly what I meant, tricky little thing that she was.

"A thousand thank yous, dear aunt of mine, for launching me into society."

"That's better. I have a feeling we will be visiting the Dennisons frequently."

I wanted to press her as to what she meant by that comment, but I dared not hope just yet. Knowing Aunt Robbie, there was hidden meaning behind her words, but I wasn't entirely sure Madelaine felt the same way, so I held my peace. "I hope so, certainly."

"I *know* so, lad," she said.

"Hard to larboard with ye, now, ye scabrous dogs!" a voice shouted from above.

"Let me guess, Jack keeps a keg under the seat cushion?"

"How'd you know?" Aunt Robbie retorted. Though it was too dark to see her face in the carriage, I would bet my life her eyes were twinkling.

I settled back and lost myself in my memories of the evening. Some would have reminisced about the architecture of Riverhampton, others the glamorous clothing worn by the guests. But my musings consisted chiefly of Madelaine's face—the way the light had made her dark hair shimmer, the way her lips pouted and her cheeks dimpled when she was amused...the way her eyes gazed up into mine with that unreadable look I hoped I'd be privileged enough to see again soon.

"All right, everybody out! On the double!"

"Was he a military man in another life?" I asked Aunt Robbie as we stepped out of the carriage. I wasn't feeling too kindly toward old Jack for truncating my reverie.

"He's a little touched in the head. Sometimes he thinks he's Wellington at Waterloo, but that's never interfered with his duties. There's not much light in his belfry, but he's a lovable old thing, and your Uncle Gerard was very fond of him, as am I."

We'd reached the hall by that time and were in the process of divesting ourselves of our wrap and jacket.

"We'll talk more about our conquests in the morning, lad. It's time for me to get my rest. This face of mine needs all the help it can get."

I kissed her on the cheek and followed her up the stairs. In a matter of moments, I was changed into my nightshirt and lying on my bed, too excited to sleep. I stared at the ceiling, mesmerized by the moonlight reflecting off its surface.

My feelings for Madelaine were nothing like my infatuation for Leonora. And now when I thought of Leonora, I could barely recall her face. What did that say about me? That I had been young and foolish and infatuated beyond belief. But this, *this* was different. Madelaine made me feel alive and scared, giddy and unsure, breathless and wary, excited and fearful—of what, I did not know.

As I rested my head back against the pillow, I was certain of one thing.

I was falling in love with Madelaine Dennison.

First Love

*I*t is believed that the Upyr makes its home in Russia. There is no evidence to suggest that this particular specimen travels beyond the borders of its homeland to seek prey, and anyone who tells you otherwise is an outright fraud and should be locked away for a very long time.

Disgusted, I flung the book across the room and winced as the tome crashed against a table by the window, sending a vase of flowers tumbling to the floor.

"Spring cleaning?"

Startled, I looked up to see Aunt Robbie standing in the doorway.

"I'm sorry, Aunt Robbie. I don't know why you put up with me."

"Because I'm a glutton for punishment," she said, leaning down to help me with the mess. "Oh, sorry, you were asking a rhetorical question, weren't you?"

Her face wore that irrepressible expression of amusement. "I'm sorry, Aunt Robbie," I said again, picking up the last of the broken fragments of porcelain, "but I don't think reading is such a good idea for me now, at least not on *this* subject."

"Ah, so Professor Grigory Potsdorf is a bit potty?" she asked as she hefted the book up off the ground.

"Professor Potsdorf is most *definitely* potty. Give me ten minutes with the good professor and I'll blow all his carefully construed assumptions to smithereens," I mumbled angrily, tossing the shards of the vase into the wastepaper basket near the window. "This reading was a very bad idea. Just when I think I'm over all this, I stumble upon something insignificant—a flash of red that reminds me of blood, a dark shadow seen out of the corner of my eye, a passage in a book that flies in the face of everything I know, everything I *lived*— and all the memories come flooding back in. If I have to read one more quack discrediting as myth any theory they do not know how to explain, I think I'll shoot myself."

"I know what this is really all about."

"What?" I asked guiltily. She had on her Cheshire Cat look, which always boded ill for my reserve.

"I'm not so old that I cannot still recognize the effects of first love."

I sank onto the window seat beside her and exhaled in frustration. "I haven't seen her in three months. What if she's forgotten me?"

"I hardly think that's likely. Besides, she's not going to forget you anytime soon."

"But what if that wretch Calhoun has been around?"

"You obviously don't know Madelaine."

"I'd like to change that," I said sulkily. And then it hit me. "Aunt Robbie," I said, pulling myself out of a slouch, "what did you mean she's not going to forget me anytime soon?"

My aunt had wandered to the other side of the room and was now pouring us a drink. "Isn't it a little early in the day for that?" I asked impatiently, coming to stand by her side.

"Tosh! It's never too early for absinthe."

"Absinthe?!" I shrieked. "Aunt Robbie, you're becoming a Bohemian! And I certainly don't think absinthe will do anything to help my mood."

"Don't you know what they say?" she asked, handing me a drink as she swirled the stem of her own glass between her fingers.

Against my better judgment, I decided to humor her. "No, what?"

Corcitura

"Absinthe makes the heart grow fonder."

I'd heard about absinthe's ability to burn your throat, and thanks to Aunt Robbie's little joke, I got to experience this feeling firsthand. "Water," I gasped, trying unsuccessfully not to choke on my own laughter, "water, you barmy old bat, quick!" I grasped the glass she held out to me and quaffed its contents, feeling relief as the liquid coursed down my throat. "Don't you ever pull a stunt like that again," I said, venturing to sound serious, though I was still laughing.

"I was just trying to prove a point," she said with maddening calmness. "And apart from the burn, you'll live. It was worth it, though, was it not? It got you out of the doldrums, for the moment anyway. You've been depressing me these past months. If it wasn't because of Madelaine, it was because of the vampires, and honestly, if you're going to find fault with every book on the subject, why don't you just write your own?"

"I might as well just send a personal invitation to Salei and Stefan to come finish me off, not to mention that the rest of the world would think me mad. And you're forgetting, my dear Aunt," I added to drive home the point, "the fact that they would in all likelihood feel it their duty to off *you* and all of our friends as well, just to be thorough. No thank you, Aunt Robbie. And you still haven't answered my question," I said, pouring myself another glass of water, which I had come to think of over the last few moments as the elixir of life.

"Fine, you want the truth, I'll tell it to you. No one can stop you from courting Madelaine but yourself, so what say we down another couple of drinks for courage, on your part at least, and pop over to Chez Dennison to see if we can't get to the bottom of this?"

"Wouldn't that be irregular?" I asked weakly. I'd been wanting to do the exact thing, but the thought of going there and once again being disappointed was more than I could stomach in my current state. All summer long, I had pursued Madelaine Dennison, and all summer long, she had eluded me. I'd have had better luck trying to grab hold of a will-o'-the-wisp—it couldn't be done. She flitted just beyond my reach, and as the hot days of September gave way to the crisp autumn air of October, I despaired of ever seeing her again.

Not that I hadn't. On the off chance that I actually *did* see her, it wasn't for more than a moment, which was certainly not long enough to declare myself. The time I remembered most vividly—and the one that was hardest to decipher—had been a Tuesday afternoon when I had come upon her near the willows by the riverbank behind her house. She'd been decidedly rude to me, which is why I now feared that what I had taken for interest the night of the millionaires' ball was in reality just courtesy to the dunderheaded nephew of her father's friend. I hadn't been able to get that conversation out of my mind, nor the way she had acted. I didn't understand why she was being so standoffish.

"Oh, Lord, what are you doing here?" she said when she saw me.

I'd separated myself from the party and wandered down toward the banks, delighted to find her on her own.

"Can't a friend pay a call? I thought you'd be happy to see me, since I came to see *you*, of course. Have you forgotten your invitation?"

"No, I haven't," she snapped, not looking up from her book. "I said you'd always be welcome in my father's house, and as you can see, we are *not* in it at present. Now, if you don't mind, I would love to be left in peace. I have been neglecting this novel for too long. I have much reading to catch up on."

I leaned over and plucked the book from her hands. "*The Principles of Musicality for the Modern Day Violinist.* That's hardly a novel, my dear girl, and something that is more suited to the schoolroom than a lazy day on the riverbank."

"Well, it shows how little you know of my interests and of *me*," she said, rising and snatching the book from my hands.

That had stumped me for a moment, for I did not know how to proceed. Still, I wasn't willing to give up. "I suppose James Calhoun has something to do with this new attitude."

"New attitude?" she asked, snapping the book shut. That had got her attention. "James Calhoun could be at the bottom of the ocean at this very moment for all I care. Why are you making this so difficult, Mr. Bradburry, when you know it's hopeless? Why do you keep hounding me?"

That was a blow. "I should think it's obvious."

"Not obvious to me," she said quietly, yet I had the feeling she wasn't being honest. "If that's all, Mr. Bradburry, I really must insist that you leave."

"I came to see you," I repeated dumbly. "I came to know if I could escort you to the luncheon Molly planned for today."

"Did you really? How terrible for you, then, to learn I won't be able to satisfy the purpose of your visit. You see, I have a...a..."

"A what?"

"Other plans. Plans that don't concern you," she said, walking underneath the shade of the willow and turning her back on me.

I knew better than to press her further. Had I been mistaken? I couldn't have been, surely...

"I hope you will be more receptive of my suit when next we see each other, Miss Dennison. I'm sorry if this interview has sickened you."

How much further could I humble myself? But all she did was nod her head slightly and open her book once more, ignoring my presence.

That was my most vivid memory of our brief encounters, probably because it was the most painful. I'd been to Riverhampton nearly twelve times since the millionaires' ball, and nine out of those twelve times, when I inquired as to Miss Dennison's whereabouts, I was always told she was "out." What that meant, I hadn't the slightest idea, but I was never given any more information than that.

I settled onto the window seat and wallowed in more self-pity. I was actually enjoying it, to be honest, but after about three minutes of saying "woe is me" in my mind, I began to feel ridiculous for acting so pathetic. Aunt Robbie would have snapped me out of this black mood right quick if she had taken her eyes off the absinthe for more than five seconds.

I sighed and took another sip of water. It was time to be brutally honest with myself. I'd actually only been reading the books on vampirism to while away the hours in-between meetings with Molly and Steven. Yes, I wanted to hear the "experts' perspectives," but after reading page upon page of nonsense that would have made laughingstocks of those fools had the world known, *really* known, the true nature of vampires, or at least the ones I'd had dealings with, I simply couldn't take it anymore. There was no denying it: I was bored stiff, and the only way out of this apathy, the only cure for the soul sucking monotony of my life, was Madelaine Dennison. It troubled me that I didn't know if she was consciously avoiding me, or if her father was somehow behind our separation, but there was something not quite right about the whole situation.

"We have a standing invitation to come whenever we want. It's not my fault Maddie is intent on playing the coquette."

"Oh, surely that cannot be it?" I said defensively, thinking of how soundly she had rebuffed me at our last meeting. I didn't think she had a coy bone in her body.

"Be that as it may, if you are ever going to make any headway with your cause, you must get Mason to like you. He doesn't hold with 'foreigners,' especially Englishmen, but I think he's taken a fancy to you. So buck up, lad, and get going. I'm not wasting any more time watching you wither away like some brooding lover. It'll do you good to see your friends again, anyway."

I brightened at that. Although I hadn't had a chance to plead my case to Madelaine over these last three months, I had grown closer to Molly and Steven, who had become quite the literary sensation overnight when *Calamity Clark, Sheriff of Laredo* hit the press. The book was eaten alive by the public. They couldn't get enough of the rugged, scar-lipped, one-eyed cowboy with the soft-spoken manner who could shoot a penny off a horny toad's head from a thousand yards away. Did I mention our hero was also lethal with a lasso?

Then there was the press—oh, the press! The *Times* called Steven the "Second coming of James Fennimore

Cooper," though most of Dear Old James' stories were set in the Northeast. This was the press we were talking about, after all, so allowances must be made. Then there was the *Post,* which trumpeted the young author's "startling powers of description and intuitive understanding of the deep roots of American grit." I believe it was also the *Post*—in an effort to outdo the *Times* in its praise—that said only a *native son* could have conjured up such pathos and vivid imagery of the "Old West." Apparently, in their ebullience, they forgot that Steven was from Ireland.

For his part, Steven ate it all up, but fame had not changed him. In fact, he was still the same dotty fool, at least when it came to women. He had still not proposed to Molly and she had confided in me that she feared he never would. He was financially well-off—*incredibly*, financially well-off, to be truthful—and in a few months, his second novel, *Calamity Clark and the Terror of the West*, would make him even richer. Six months after that, his third in the series, *Calamity Clark Meets Buckshot Bill*, was slated to be printed as a serial, followed quickly by the "best of all," according to Molly: *Calamity Clark and the Desperados of Death Junction*. In short, Steven was set for life, yet he was still dragging his heels where matters of the heart were concerned. I couldn't figure him out, but I'd promised myself I'd try to intervene, if only for Molly's sake.

Molly, for her part, had told me very little regarding Maddie's whereabouts, a fact I found strange, since Molly had become like a sister to me during this time. I thought she'd be more forthcoming, since she knew how I felt about her friend. But I suppose she had her reasons. Maddie *couldn't* find me repulsive? Or maybe she sensed I was withholding things and didn't want any part of my past. She had said in no uncertain terms that she hated liars, and I most certainly did not want to go the way of James Calhoun. Something had to be done. I just didn't know what that was yet.

"Stop sitting there like the bloody ghost of Christmas Future and get up! Honestly, you look like a specter! Go make yourself presentable. We'll be heading out in half an hour. See if you can work a miracle on yourself by then."

Aunt Robbie was determined. I knew better than to argue with her after she'd imbibed stimulants. She was fiery enough on her own; add a little absinthe and who knew how explosive a cocktail you'd end up with.

I dashed out of the room and was already halfway up the first landing when I heard her call out from the foot of the stairs. "And Eric, love, don't worry. She's not indifferent to you. She couldn't be. I know it."

I found that hard to believe given our last interview, but nevertheless, those words made my heart soar. I had no way of knowing if Aunt Robbie's sixth sense was right, but I needed the encouragement badly and clung to her words. In half an hour's time, I might see Madelaine again. I'd better make the most of this opportunity. The way things were going, I might not get another one for a very, *very* long time.

Especially if Madelaine had her way.

‡

"I'm sorry, Mr. Bradburry, but Miss Dennison is out."

Foiled again! It was all I could do not to give that smug valet a swift kick in the rear.

"Eric." Startled, I looked to the side and saw Molly standing at my elbow. Where she had materialized from, I had no idea, but I was glad of her company just the same. "Would you join me in the garden? There's a new flower come straight from Ireland that Steven and I would like you to see."

I knew this was Molly's way of saving the valet and my wounded pride, but I didn't appreciate her intervention. I didn't want to be known as a loose cannon around Chez Dennison, though, so I followed her out into the sprawling, mazelike gardens behind the mansion without protest. We walked along the gravel path in silence until I spied a nattily dressed figure sitting on a stone bench beneath a topiary trimmed into the shape of a dancing bear.

"Hallo, Steven," I said, my ill-humor dispersing when I saw him.

"Well, look who's come to darken our doorway once more!" I took his extended hand and shook it, looking over his ensemble as I did so. He'd taken the press's fawning a bit to heart and was wearing a coat that would have made Calamity Clark proud in its rugged chic. I was surprised he wasn't wearing chaps and a ten gallon hat, but then I saw he *was* wearing a lariat necktie. "I see the fair Madelaine has decided once again to deprive us of her presence, eh, Poppy, luv?"

"Frankly, that's what I brought Eric out here to discuss. Sit down, Eric, it's time you knew the truth."

I swallowed hard and sat down next to Steven, who looked just as puzzled as I did. I expected Molly to launch right into her story, but instead, she paced back and forth for a good five minutes in silence. I was beginning to lose my patience. I was also starting to fear for her hands, for she had been worrying and ringing them the whole time. What's more, she must have thrown about a dozen or so fearful looks over her shoulder, as though she were afraid of being caught, by whom, I could not guess.

Come on, Molly, just tell us, I thought, willing her to forgo the indecisiveness.

"Stop stalling, lass, we're hanging on your every word, you know...and Eric here is not getting any younger."

Molly halted and gave Steven a withering look, then smoothed her skirt and stared me dead in the eyes. "I am so sorry to tell you that Madelaine is not *HERE!*"

I looked at Steven and he at me, and in our eyes there was the same wonderment. "Easy, Poppy, there's no need to shout. Are you feeling right in the head?" he said.

"Of course I'm feeling right in the head, you dolt! And I'm not shouting!" she shouted. "Eric, look at me."

I did as instructed, though I was beginning to wonder if Molly had taken leave of her senses. She was talking to me in such a rush and baffled me so badly by nodding her head when she was speaking in the negative. Several times, she made wide, expansive gestures with her arms so that I began to wonder if I was talking to a girl or a bird, then furtively pointed to a dormer high up on the far side of the mansion.

The most confusing moment came when she stared at me as though I was an idiot for not catching her hidden meaning.

"What exactly are you getting at?" Steven said, rising to stare off at the window.

"Shut-up, Steven, Eric knows what I mean."

"*He does?*"

"Of course he does, so sit back down and mind your own business." She shoved him playfully, and he made a great show of pretending to stumble back onto the seat.

I stared at the window until I heard an exasperated sigh. The next thing I knew, I was being pulled from my seat, clutched by the chin, and made to look straight at the window. "Men! Are you all so thick-witted? Honestly. Now, listen," Molly commanded.

"I don't hear anything."

"That's because you're not trying hard enough...OH! Mr. Dennison, how lovely to see you! Enjoying your walk?"

Molly released my face and shoved me away as Mason Dennison and Aunt Robbie joined our circle.

"Likewise, young Margaret. Ah, Steven," he said in a booming voice, "So good of you to come. I hear the book is selling well."

"Yes, Sir," Steven said sheepishly. He was like a lamb in Mason Dennison's presence. He still hadn't come to terms with the generosity of his benefactor.

"Steven is rolling in it, I hear," shot in Aunt Robbie.

"*Yes. He. Is.*" Molly said meaningfully, glaring at Steven with unconcealed interest, which he pretended to ignore. The blister couldn't very well put off buying an engagement ring for much longer. I'd have to talk to him about this in private, and soon, although I wasn't in any position to offer advice, given my current standing with the woman I loved.

"It's good to see you here, young Bradburry." If he was so happy to see me, his tone certainly didn't betray his excessive mirth. He sounded like a man on his way to the gallows.

"And is your daughter well?" I asked. A hush fell over our small company, but I was tired of this game. If Madelaine wasn't as averse to seeing me as I had originally thought, then it must have been her father's order that she not be present whenever I came to call.

"She is well," he said uneasily, "but she's not in, I'm sorry to say."

"She seems to be out quite a lot and always when I pay a visit to this house—this *house*, I might add, that I was told I would always be welcome in. And I don't think your daughter is the type to tell falsehoods. Not when she hates liars so passionately."

Molly gasped at my effrontery, but I kept my eyes riveted on Mason Dennison, daring him to meet my gaze. "There's no accounting for the whims of a woman," he said gruffly. A wiser man would have known better than to say such a thing in the presence of my aunt, but apparently, Mason Dennison was unaware of this well-established fact, or rather chose to ignore it. I noticed he didn't dare to look in my aunt's direction. If he had, he would have seen steam coming from her ears. The look she was giving him was pure venom, and if it had been in her power to smite him on the spot, he would have already been dead and buried beneath her feet. I took satisfaction in knowing he'd receive a tongue-lashing once they were alone. I wouldn't want to be in his place when the harangue started.

"She was just being charitable. You should have known better than to take her words to heart. Come, Roberta," he said, dragging my fuming aunt away, "I need a change of scenery. The air here is oppressive."

So saying, he stalked off, my furious aunt not waiting until they were out of earshot to barrel into him. I heard the terms *pigheaded*, *archaic*, and then an explosive sound that must have been Aunt Robbie sputtering, followed by the words *pompous old goat*, before they disappeared behind the privacy of a bush sculpted into an elephant playing croquet with a mouse.

"Bra-*vo*," Steven drawled. I didn't know whether he was funning me or being serious. When I saw his expression, I knew it was the former. "I've been wanting to put old Dennison in his place for quite a while, but gratitude forbids me, you know."

"Does gratitude also forbid you from buying the woman you love a ring?"

"Now, Poppy..."

"Um, I think I'd best be heading off," I said, edging away. I had no desire to witness a lovers' quarrel.

"Oh, no you don't!" said Molly, grabbing my arm. "We are not finished here. Don't for one instant think I'm going to let that old popinjay come between you and my sister. Where were we...oh, yes, listen."

I let her grab my face once again—I was putty in Molly's hands for some reason—and direct my attention to the dormer window.

And then I heard it...passionate, undulating string music coming from within.

The strains of a violin.

"Ah," said Molly, nodding at my realization. "Now you understand. Make a run for it while you still can. And don't worry about Mr. Dennison. Leave him to us."

I felt a shove in my back and was propelled forward on the path. Molly and Steven had abandoned me to my own devices and were already too far down the walkway to hear me when I finally came to my senses and turned to ask what to do next. Molly's glance told me everything.

I was on my own now.

Only a fool would have wasted such an opportunity. Stealthily, feeling like a burglar, I stole into the house. I probably would have attracted less attention from the servants if I hadn't been creeping around like an intruder, but that couldn't be helped.

Pausing underneath the stairwell to get my bearings, I listened for a moment until I caught the sounds of the music. It was louder than before, which meant I was getting closer.

I padded up the green carpeted stairs until I reached a long hallway with a dozen or so doors on either side. All the doors where shut, but the music was now so loud, there could be no mistaking that it was coming from the room behind the largest oak door to my left. The door gave easily as I pushed it open, for it had not been locked, as I originally thought.

Corcitura

The first thing that caught my eye was a fresco on the opposite wall depicting nymphs frolicking around a cupidon holding a lyre. The fresco was beyond beautiful—lyrical, classical, and a fitting background to a music room, yet it didn't hold my attention for more than a second.

I suppose I was torturing myself by not looking at her directly, but I couldn't bring myself to glance at her now, not yet, not after all the anticipation, after all the waiting. To do so would be to cheapen the effect. When I did gaze upon her, I wanted to drink her in, take in her every look, make a memory. And so I made myself turn away and focus on everything but her until the moment would be right.

A wizened little man with hair so white and fluffy it looked as though a cloud had settled atop his head was hunched over a grand piano, pounding out notes in such a flurry that I wondered how his fingers stayed untangled. To the right of the piano stood a beautiful music stand that must have been at least two hundred years old, so intricate and Renaissance-like was the filigreeing and craftsmanship. But I'd be lying if I said I paid it more than a second's notice. My heart was pounding furiously, and my tongue felt like lead.

The moment had come. It was no longer in my power to fight the desire to look upon her.

Madelaine was so different from the last time I'd seen her. Though she was dressed plainly and without adornment, she was even more beautiful than she had been the night of the ball. Perhaps this was because she was so focused on her music—she was unaware anyone was watching her.

Her brow was smooth, relaxed. I knew that look.
Freedom.

It was something I'd tried to achieve over the past six years but never could. And yet Madelaine had attained it through her violin, her music. She was pouring her very spirit into the notes, letting the bow travel across the strings and give wings to her soul. I stood there transfixed and would have sunk even further into that melodious haze if the little maestro behind the piano hadn't slammed his fists onto the keys and jolted me awake.

"Madelaine! What *are* you doing?!" he squeaked. An accent...German? I couldn't be sure.

"Cadenza ad libitum!" Madelaine crowed, pointing the bow at what I assumed had to be her music master as though it were a sword. "I *told* you the cadenza needed more spirit. Ad libitum, freer, ohne einschränkungen."

"Don't quote back to me in my own tongue," he said good-naturedly, picking his glasses up off the top of the piano and polishing them on his sleeve. "Without restrictions, yes. There's no need to be pretentious. I speak English quite well." He sighed as he donned the spectacles. "You shall be the death of me," he said, his eyes crinkling at the corners.

She'll be the death of me, too, I thought absently.

"Yes, I know. It is my mission in life," Madelaine said lightly. "It was what I was put on this earth to do."

"My dear, we are not alone," he said, suddenly looking up.

I swallowed hard and tried to compose myself, but those bespectacled eyes skewered me to the spot.

"Oh!" Madelaine gasped, backing into the piano. "I didn't hear...I didn't know."

"I didn't mean to startle you or intrude," I said hurriedly, stumbling as I walked backward toward the doorway. "I'll leave, if you like."

"*No!*" Her vehemence stopped me dead. Something about her was decidedly different from the last time we'd met. She seemed happier now, more at ease. Vanity made me think it was my presence, but in reality, it was probably her music. "Please, stay, there's no harm in listening. And I could use an audience."

She placed the violin and bow atop the piano and guided me to the sofa in the middle of the room.

"Sorry we don't have any refreshments, but we weren't expecting guests, so you'll just have to be happy with me."

I noticed the smirk playing about her lips...and I knew with certainty that she hadn't been consciously avoiding me these past months at all.

I had a strong desire to kiss her then, but that would have been beyond the bounds of propriety, even though she was flirting with me none too subtly. What had caused this change in her attitude toward me?

I tried to think up something witty to say in return, but my genius consisted of mumbling, "That's quite all right, Miss Dennison," and settling onto the sofa like an automaton. I couldn't help it, I couldn't even think. I was too mesmerized by her face, her lithe movements, her very being.

"You will see just how fine momentarily," the music master said with barely concealed pride.

"Please, Herr Ackerman, don't get his hopes up. I'm only an amateur," she said to me apologetically.

"Amateur my eye! Coyness does not become you, my dear. There's no need to tease that boy so. He's half in love with you already. Now cease with the false modesty and play! From the top! And one!"

I was beet red by the time he'd finished, but Madelaine hid her blush by withdrawing into her music. It was probably the first and last time I'd ever envy her.

The first strains drew me in instantly, so that I felt I couldn't have moved had I tried. The music was haunting, beautiful, untamable, and bewitching, much like Madelaine herself. I stared in wonder as her nimble fingers flew up and down the fingerboard, her bow gliding effortlessly over the strings.

"Feeling! FEE-LING! Make it mean something. Bruch is meant to be lived, breathed, felt! FEEL IT!!" Herr Ackerman shouted.

I bit my lip to keep from laughing when Madelaine made a wry face and winked at me as she blew the hair out of her eyes, her fingers not missing a single note in the process. She'd just completed a complex sounding passage of double-stops and was now entering a section that suddenly slowed and grew very dark.

I felt myself growing uneasy and couldn't to stop fidgeting with the tassels on the cushion beside me. The music conjured visions of dark woods, and within, dark creatures possessed of darker minds and evil thoughts. Thankfully, the mood didn't last long. The piece transitioned into a quietly melodious and soothing cadence, and I once more relaxed as

I closed my eyes and listened to Madelaine's fingers gliding up higher and higher, creating notes each sweeter than the last.

Suddenly, there was a crash that shook me awake.

The music was changing once more.

Madelaine had stopped playing and was holding the violin before her as Herr Ackerman pounded away on the piano, the chords and melody growing heavier—much more intense and dark.

In a flash, my mind reverted to my former vision. Again I saw the woods. This time, there would be no awakening from the nightmare. My chest felt heavy. As I looked down, I saw Stefan, half-dead, cradled against my shoulder...and behind us sounded that same gnawing, sniffing, tireless presence.

Constantinos.

Terrified, I lunged through the trees, not caring that branches were gouging my skin, ignoring the blood streaming from each tear in my flesh. The edge of the forest was growing closer. Freedom was within my grasp, though I knew I'd never reach those trees. Suddenly, I felt something crawling over my skin. I winced as a sharp pain stabbed at the already torn flesh, ripping open the wounds. My heart stopped. I knew what was happening.

Something was drinking my blood.

No, not something...some*one*.

It was not Constantinos who was pursuing me, it was his creation, the hybrid monster he and Vladec Salei had made their own. He'd finally caught me after all these years.

I knew what I'd see if I opened my eyes, yet I couldn't make myself give in to the force that was urging me to look. I had to, but if I didn't, maybe it would all go away, like a bad dream dissipating with the first rays of dawn. Then another crunch and a further stab of pain decided me.

Just as I'd thought.

Stefan, his barbed tongue working feverishly, was tearing at my wounds, drinking the blood that was pouring from my veins. I couldn't register what I was witnessing, couldn't wrap my mind around the fact that he was here, and for all intents and purposes, was *eating* me. A voice in the back of my head was prodding me, urging me to do something before he finished me off, but all I could do was stand there in morbid fascination as I watched my blood drain into his mouth. Suddenly, my heart lurched and I blinked rapidly, my mind finally snapping into action.

This was not someone else's blood being drained from his body. This was *my* blood. If I didn't act soon, I'd be as desiccated as Arabella.

Horror should have been my impetus. Instead, it was a furious will to live, a desire to prove I was not as weak as all the others had been.

I must live, I must get away. He is not going to do to me what he did to Roderick. I am stronger than that.

Mustering as much force as I could, I kicked him savagely. Stunned, he shot back from the blow to his stomach—a stomach that was as engorged as Constantinos' had been that night I'd saved Stefan from succumbing to the fate he was trying to inflict on me now—and raced for the safety of the clearing beyond the trees. Whatever I had done to stun him had apparently not been strong enough to overcome his lust for my blood. I could still hear him lapping at the pool of it that had gathered on the forest floor.

My fingers stretched out imploringly toward the line of trees. I was so close to escaping, so close to salvation. Something flew by my ear. I stopped to swat the air.

Only a fool would have halted.

I was that fool.

How had he overtaken me? Blinding speed must have been some vampiric trick he'd learned. But that was the least of my worries now. All my thoughts focused on his glistening, blood soaked fangs and the shockingly white, claw-tipped hands that were reaching for my throat.

I stumbled back, gasping for breath. He hadn't even touched me, but already I could feel his hands upon my neck, his cold fingers choking the life out of me, when suddenly through the darkness, a plaintive wail called my soul back from the brink.

Slowly, I opened my eyes and was shocked when I saw I had never gone back to that godforsaken forest in Greece.

I had never blinked. I had never run...I had never even moved.

I was still in New York in a mansion along the Hudson River, and standing before me was a vision of light. An angel had walked into the chamber of death and set me free, and I no longer felt fear or despair.

Madelaine was the balm to my savaged soul. I concentrated on her as fiercely as a drowning man clings to a life preserver.

The plaintive wail was coming from her, or rather, her violin, for she was playing it again.

I sat as one dead, unable to move, unable to tear my eyes away. My mind, my heart, my ears were hers, as the music slowly drew me out of my nightmare. The music was still minor, but was so different in its brilliance, its almost gypsy fervor, that I couldn't help being enthralled.

My heart soared as I listened, enraptured, while Madelaine finished with a flourish and held the bow triumphantly in the air. It took all my restraint not to applaud and ruin the moment.

I glanced over to see if Herr Ackerman had noticed her triumph, but from the look of him, I didn't think he'd seen a thing, so focused was he on playing his part to the letter. The chords he was playing were so drastically different now, so joyous, that I was nearly brought to tears. In the span of a few minutes, I'd experienced moments of terror that made me cringe in fear and moments of such searing beauty that the pain was almost unbearable and I finally allowed myself to cry, if only a little.

My thoughts were jumbled, my feelings still very convoluted, but one thing I did know for certain. Something had happened to me during her performance—a reawakening of the soul. I'd found my Angel of Light. Madelaine had guided me from the depths of terror into the sun. She was my polestar, my salvation. I wondered if she even had an inkling of my feelings as I gazed at her watching Herr Ackerman resolve the chords to end the movement.

"Oh, good gracious," she said, her brilliant smile fading when she saw my face. "Are you ill?"

Before I could answer, she was at my side, her cool hand resting against my face. A bigger man than I would have told her nothing was the matter, but I'd longed for her touch, longed to be given her undivided attention, so I stayed quiet and let her worry over my health for longer than I should have until Herr Ackerman came over and slapped me gently on the cheek.

"Yes," I said, swallowing with difficulty. "Yes, I'm fine. It's just the music. It transported me." That at least was the truth. It *had* transported me—right back to that terrible night in Greece. I reached for my neck, but they were both staring at me so intently I let my hand drop.

"That's what every *artiste* strives to do," she said, the laugh back in her voice.

"You succeeded admirably," I said like a sop.

"That's only because the best music comes from Germany, didn't you know?" She glanced over at her music master and raised her eyebrow in challenge.

The familiarity between them amused me. His answer would be something biting, yet playful, no doubt. I glanced at him, laughing inwardly as I saw him shifting in his chair, readying himself for a suitable riposte, but then Madelaine coughed and drew my attention away...and I knew nothing but horror.

The lace around her neck had come undone, exposing a horrid red welt beneath her jaw. I panicked. I hadn't seen something so raw looking, so *red*, since...since...

"Your jaw," I nearly shouted, "it's bleeding! It's red..."

"Oh?" she said, looking down casually.

What was wrong with her?! Didn't she understand?!

"It's nothing. Just a violin's kiss."

"A violin's kiss?" I repeated, bewildered, unable to stop my voice from catching.

"The chinrest presses against my skin when I play. It's sort of my battle scar. Nothing to be alarmed about. It'll go away in half an hour."

It was a logical explanation, and it mollified me somewhat because I couldn't think of anything to say—anything *sane*, at least—to counter Madelaine's claim. I settled back into the sofa and noticed that Herr Ackerman was staring at me.

"Ah, yes, and you'd do well to remember it," he said absently, referring to Madelaine's former comment about German music, the comment she'd made before my little outburst.

To my dismay, he made no move to leave. Was he intending to play the governess and chaperone our visit? All things considered, I shouldn't have been surprised, especially after my actions a moment before. Had I been in his position, I wouldn't have left Madelaine alone either. Still, the music master's presence rankled me.

Pulling a small bell from his pocket, he rang it primly. Moments later, a stout young woman materialized, bearing a tray laden with tea things.

"Three for tea, then?" she asked brightly.

"Yes, Libba," replied Herr Ackerman, looking directly at me. "Our young friend is most obliging to humor an old man. Now, Herr...oh, pardon, I haven't caught your name..."

"Eric Bradburry," I said, remembering too late to unclench my teeth. His first impression of me had been less than flattering, so why should tact matter now?

"Bradburry," he said, rolling the r's, much to my annoyance. "I noticed you were, shall we say, overcome when Madelaine was playing."

"Wouldn't you be?" I asked, not bothering to repress the harshness in my voice. I didn't like the gleam in his eyes. He was too perceptive.

"No, I think there was more to it than that."

"Oh, really?"

"Yes, I saw that you were clutching your forehead."

"That's certainly not an indictment of my playing, is it?" asked Madelaine jokingly.

"No, of course not, the music just brought back many memories, some of them...not so good."

"Oh, how dreadful," Madelaine said, laying her hand on my arm. My reserve began to soften at her touch, but I wrangled my emotions, to use one of Steven's favorite phrases. Herr Ackerman was still scrutinizing me.

"Hmm, I think there is some deep trouble in your past, Herr Bradburry, and I think you are unwilling to share it."

What was your first clue?

"Honesty is valued very highly at Riverhampton. I wouldn't want you to take our house rules so lightly."

"With all due respect, Herr Ackerman, I do not think my past, whatever it might be, and I assure you it is *not* blemished"—I had to swallow that hard—"has anything to do with the present conversation. Besides, it would bore you to tears."

"I agree," said Madelaine briskly. I noticed her brow was creased. Worry? Fear? Distrust? I could throttle that music master for putting doubts into her mind.

"Well, I *don't*, but that is not important...for now. I am sorry if my topic of conversation was distasteful to you."

I glared at him, but kept my tone level. "Not at all," I said sourly, looking down at my hands. The man annoyed me. There was intelligence in those old eyes, almost as though he knew I was hiding secrets. And then he had the nerve to sit and intrude on my plans. But really, why should I have expected this household to be permissive? I wasn't even supposed to be here, much less Madelaine, according to her father, so if Herr Ackerman wanted to supervise our conversation, I shouldn't really blame him. All that was left was for Molly and Steven to materialize, and my planned idyll would be completely ruined.

"Oh! Make that *five* for tea, Libba."

Speak of the devil.

"Ah! Young Fraulein Colfer and young Herr Bannon, how lovely to have such wonderful company to tea." Was he a German music master or a society grande dame? Just when I thought he couldn't grate on my nerves any further...

"*Entre nous*," Molly said in a stage whisper, sidling in-between Madelaine and me, "but Mr. Dennison is on the prowl, so I thought Steven and I would come here to make sure everything looks proper."

"I'm eternally grateful," I drawled, which caused Steven to guffaw.

"Was her idea," he said, tucking into a biscuit. "I was against it from the start. Hang the old devil, I say."

"Oh, *really*?" This from Molly, whose ire was just begging to be inflamed.

"Let's not start a row, please," said Madelaine. "We only have so few moments together, so why spoil them?"

Everyone, save maybe Herr Ackerman, who was busy reading his tea leaves, knew what Madelaine meant at once. Molly blushed, Steven had the grace to look embarrassed, and I could do nothing but stare at the woman I was coming to realize might never be mine.

And so the afternoon passed without furthering my cause one whit.

Aunt Robbie was silent the entire trip home. I think she knew better than to question me on how my overtures were received.

As I climbed the stairs to my room, intending to lock myself away for the rest of the evening and give in to a good sulk, I felt Aunt Robbie's hand on my arm.

"I wouldn't give up so easily, if I were you."

"What makes you think I'm giving up?"

She looked genuinely startled. "You mean to go back, then?"

"I'm doing more than going back. I'm initiating an outing."

"Oh, you are, are you?" she said, narrowing her eyes. I was already too far gone in this scheme to tell her I honestly had no clue what I was planning, but I pressed on all the same.

"Yes...." I said, stalling. "Ah! Yes, indeed, I have decided a picnic is just the thing."

"Have you?"

"Yes, a picnic along the Hudson, preferably on a day when Mason Dennison cannot join us."

"Very good, go on..."

"Molly and Steven must attend to keep things proper, and so will you, but that's it. No Herr what's-his-name, no Libba, no servants at all. Just the three of you and Madelaine and myself. If I don't get a chance to talk with her alone then, I don't know when I ever will."

"You would have made Sir Tavistock Braidbury proud, love."

"Beg pardon?"

"Oh, never mind. Off to bed with you. I'll make all the arrangements, don't you fret."

"What would I do without you?" I said, truly meaning it.

"Stop being maudlin and get off to bed. We have a big day ahead of us."

I had nearly reached my room when I heard her call out from below. "Oh, and Eric, you'd do well to remember the words of that immortal American Hero."

"Who?"

"John Paul something or other."

"And what were those words?"

"I have not yet begun to fight."

I smiled as I leaned back over the banister. Truer words had never before been spoken.

‡

I raised the window and breathed in the crisp air of a late October morning. The weather would require a coat today, so I grabbed the one Roddy had given me just before I set out for the Continent. I had forgotten to take it the first time around and spared it everything I'd gone through with Stefan. I rubbed the fraying collar and tried to suppress the memories of my stepfather and how happy he was the day he gave it to me. This coat was one of the last things I gathered before I fled the country.

Never mind that. I couldn't start the day this way, couldn't let the memories flood in, for then whatever plans I had would succumb to the gloom, and I'd be worthless around Madelaine. And I couldn't afford to be worthless, not now, not when I might never get another opportunity as perfect as this.

The picnic had been put off for a day or two, which suited me fine, since it gave me a chance to procure the bauble I now held in my hands. It was a gold bracelet with a heart charm. This charm was the main attractant for me, for within the heart was a lock, and within that lock, a key was turning. Buying the bracelet was a foolish thing to do, seeing as how I barely knew Madelaine, and sentimental in the extreme. She'd most probably be disgusted or outraged that I had taken her newfound solicitude of the other day as anything more than friendly concern. Still, I laid the bracelet on the little satin pillow within the blue box and shoved it into my pocket. I would not hold back if the occasion presented itself and I fervently hoped it would—today.

I shrugged into the coat and headed for the stairs. Aunt Robbie had arranged everything to perfection. She even boosted my sprits by saying that practically as soon as she had sent out a card, Madelaine had returned her response in the affirmative. I found that a little far-fetched, but what did I care for logic?

"Is that what you've decided on?" Aunt Robbie said with mock disapproval as I settled into the cab.

"What, too Continental for your Americanized tastes?" I retorted, handing her the hamper.

"No, well, I just know for a fact Madelaine will be the height of fashion. I wouldn't want you to feel like an escapee from Bedlam."

I was puzzled, but then again, what did I know of women's fashion? Mother had never put on such airs. "For a picnic?"

"Tosh! You have a lot to learn of young ladies, *young* man. Doubtless Molly will look like a duchess."

Molly *had* looked like a duchess at the millionaires' ball, but I hardly thought she'd choose to dress so opulently for a garden party, especially with the certainty of acquiring grass stains on her highly expensive hem. And Steven, well, there was no use hazarding a guess on that front because I hadn't the slightest idea what Steven would show up wearing. Some days he was sensible, others he looked like an outlaw from the O.K. Corral.

The picnic was to be held in the gardens behind Riverhampton. I had hoped for a more discreet, less

~352~

restricted place, but I suppose Mason had given his input and suggested his mansion as the ideal location for such an affair. No doubt so he could keep his eyes on me the whole time. Well, that couldn't be helped, and I'd just have to make the best of it and try to get Aunt Robbie to distract him somehow.

I wondered if Molly had selected a theme. I'd been told the Chinese lanterns at the millionaires' ball had been her idea—told by Molly herself, that is—so I wasn't certain if she was a decorating genius or had been hanging about Steven too long and was taking creative license and embellishing her own skills. When we pulled to a stop before the mansion, and I saw her—indeed looking like a duchess in blue silk and bouncing about like a mad thing amongst the riot of flower baskets hanging from the tree-lined walk—I had no more doubts as to her creative abilities.

"Eric!" she shrieked, pulling me from the carriage. "What do you think?"

Bows and flowers and little tea tables dotted the landscape, looking like something out of a Lewis Carroll story. I surveyed her handiwork, half expecting the March Hare to pop out and consult his watch. Despite the confectionary aspect of the scene, it was charming, and even more charming was the fact that I saw Madelaine Dennison waving to me over the hedge.

"Ah, I see where your true interest lies. I told you you didn't need to kill yourself over the theme, Poppy, darling. Eric is of one mind in these affairs."

Steven had joined us and was looking deuced proper and not the least bit like a gunfighter, I was happy to note.

"At least Eric appreciated my hard work for half a second, unlike certain other people who shall remain nameless but are in present company." So Steven had not yet proposed. I didn't need to look at Molly's finger to note the absence of any engagement ring. Her tone conveyed her still unfulfilled hopes.

I smiled, but they didn't notice, for they were glaring at each other. I sensed a row brewing. Honestly, what drew them together was beyond me, but that they were in love was obvious, despite all the bickering. I slipped away and gave Aunt Robbie a sympathetic look as she took the two lovebirds in hand.

I traipsed through the gap between the hedges and saw more of Molly's craftsmanship on display. Back here, even more tables had been set up. I found myself wondering uncomfortably just how many people were coming to this "intimate gathering."

So much for my five person picnic.

Several other couples had already congregated. I ducked behind a hedge when I saw Mason Dennison's imposing figure coming into view.

"Damn and blast!" I swore, sotto voce.

"What kind of language is that to use in the presence of a lady?"

I stumbled forward onto my knees and sunk into the wet grass, marring my trousers with those stains I had been so solicitous for Molly to avoid. Brushing off my trousers, I righted myself and found that I was staring into the golden brown eyes of Madelaine Dennison. "My dear Mr. Bradburry," she said warmly, "I am so very glad to see you again so soon."

"Dearest Madelaine, is there always to be such formality between us?" The words were out of my mouth before I could think them appropriate or not. I had been dying for a moment alone with her, and it was all I could do not to take her hands in mine.

I'd embarrassed us both, for my face was inflamed and she had instantly lowered her head so I couldn't see the blush rising to her cheeks. I was about to apologize when she suddenly turned and began to walk off toward the river's edge.

"Walk with me," she said urgently, not stopping to turn round.

"But what will people say?" Now was a fine time to think of the correct thing to do, when I wasn't doing anything to stop myself from following her.

"Hang propriety, just walk with me." She'd turned her head to whisper this furiously to me, and I caught a flash of red at her neck. I didn't understand why the sight of that color should fill me with dread.

"What is it you want me to say?" she asked, rounding on me when we were out of earshot of the garden party revelers. I found it mystifying how contradictory Madelaine Dennison could be. She was vastly different from and more forthright than any other girl I'd ever known, and I wondered if her father had even the slightest inkling of how fiery she actually was. "Why do you think I've avoided you so long? Why do you think I've been so cold with you until recently? I can't do it anymore. I won't. It is all so impossible."

She turned away from me and tore off one of her gloves in a movement that dredged up a memory of another woman I had once known. I pushed the vision of that red-headed harpy from my mind. She wasn't going to ruin this moment for me, not after I'd waited so long for it to come.

"You want me to throw over my father and declare my love for you, Eric? Is that what you want? Well, good, because I am very close to doing just that."

"Madelaine, you..." I couldn't breathe, I couldn't think. The one thing ricocheting through my mind was that she hadn't called me Mr. Bradburry. "You called me Eric."

"So I did. I also gave myself away, but you didn't seem to hear that." This was said without rancor and with a devastating smile.

"I've thought of you constantly these past three months," she said quietly. "That day in the music room was like an answer to a prayer. I knew I couldn't be indifferent to you any longer, even if I tried. One time after that horrible scene on the riverbank, I heard your voice and I fled from the room. I had to see you. I had to let you know I was sorry for what I'd done to you. I did not mean to be cruel, you see, but I couldn't help it. I hardly understood what I was feeling. Apparently, Father *did*, and he stopped me from going out to meet you. We haven't been on very good terms since then. He knows, now, that he cannot stop me from giving my heart to the man I choose."

"What of James?" I said, mechanically. This revelation was too much to process at once.

"James, thankfully, is gone. I told my father everything. I think he was relieved, actually, but he's very much a 'by the book' man. He would have been a perfect courtier during Henry the Eighth's time. I would have been married off to a man of his choosing by the time I was twelve. Ridiculous, you must be thinking."

I nodded dumbly, and she continued.

"He's always been very protective. I suppose it's because Mother died so early in my life, and Papa feels he needs to be both parents at once. He seems fierce, but once you get to know him, he's..."

"As harmless as a puppy?" I said, half teasing, half hopeful.

The corner of her mouth rose in amusement, a very kissable amusement, I thought. "No, he's still fierce, but you're used to it by then."

"Maybe I could give him a present?"

"So it's bribery, now, is it?"

"In a manner."

"He's very fond of tobacco, and he collects pipes, too."

"Meerschaum?"

She grew suddenly silent. I thought I detected a trace of sadness in her eyes, but when I lifted her chin, I saw that whatever had clouded her eyes was now gone.

"I think he'd adore that," she said, smiling that brilliant smile once more.

"Noted," I said, reaching for her hand.

"So, why *do* you love me?"

I dropped her hand and sputtered, at a loss for what to say in answer to such a question. "Because you're you," I finally answered. *Weak as water, weak as water.*

"That's an original answer," she said. Her tone had been jesting, but I knew she was serious.

"Because I do, I can't explain it. When I saw you, I knew you were real, not some dream I'd invented and fallen in love with."

"I think there is a woman in your past," she said, still teasing, "a woman you've never forgotten."

I didn't know what to say to that. Should I tell her of Leonora? Why was everyone so good at reading into my past? First Herr Ackerman, now Madelaine.

"There was never anyone else but you," I said, meaning it, willing my past to disappear. Leonora had only been an infatuation, after all.

"Very charming words," she said wryly, turning away.

I felt I was losing her. The string that had held us together in the last few moments would snap if I didn't speak soon, didn't say something to reassure her. "I loved you because I saw you for what you were."

"And what was that?" she asked, finally turning to look at me, her face inches from my own. I knew we were violating several rules of propriety by being so close, but I didn't care.

"My salvation." There, I'd said it. Let her think me an idiot, but that's how I felt.

I expected her to recoil, to shove me away, to run back to her father, but instead she shocked me by drawing closer, almost as if she intended to kiss me. I could feel her breath on my lips, could feel myself leaning in, until I looked down at her neck and felt my blood run cold.

Now I knew why I had dreaded that flash of red. They were nothing but rubies, but situated so close to her neck, so *unnaturally* close, they looked like droplets of blood dripping from a gash.

A ripped neck...

I'd seen such a sight once before—six years ago in that unhallowed pit in Greece.

Without thinking, I grabbed the choker and tore it from her neck. I couldn't stop myself even if I'd had the will to try. I had to get it off her, had to save her from the same fate of that other woman who had died in my arms.

I held the necklace, my hands shaking, and heard a faint cry of outrage, but I couldn't move. I was in thrall to the vision in those glistening rubies—Sorina, lying on the floor in her death agony, her throat slashed, her blood pouring onto my hands.

"How *dare* you! Are you mad?!"

The necklace was ripped from my grasp. I looked up dazedly to see Madelaine glaring at me over her shoulder as she walked away, her eyes wide with horror, her left hand wrapped around her neck.

The necklace still mesmerized me. I stood there like one struck dumb, watching it dangling from Madelaine's hand, the sun glinting off those blood red stones...and then I realized what I'd done.

How could I have hurt her so? She, whom I professed to love more than my own life?

And then I had a horrible thought. What if her father had overheard me? I turned around, but when I looked back, I was startled to see that we had traveled some distance from the gardens and were now far away from Riverhampton and out on the expanse of grass by the water's edge.

"Maddie, please," I begged, running after her.

"Am I repulsive to you?" she asked. I expected her to be angry, but her tone was more hurt than enraged. "What happened to all that talk of being real? I thought that's what you wanted?"

"Maddie, I can explain," I said feebly.

"I don't think you can." She came to an abrupt halt and stood before me, removing her hand. To my horror, I saw that when I'd torn off the necklace, it must have caught on her skin, for blood was seeping from a small scratch by her collarbone. I nearly lost my reason then.

The nightmare was happening all over again.

I reached into my pocket and pulled out a handkerchief. "God, Maddie, I'm so sorry," I said, still horrified by the sight of blood at the base of her throat. "Let me, please." To my astonishment, she didn't flinch as I dabbed at the blood, though I had been the one to inflict the scratches. I could feel the pulse in her throat, could feel it racing, and before I knew what I was doing, before I could stop myself, my lips were on hers and she was kissing me back—fiercely.

"That wasn't very conventional, was it?" she gasped as she broke free.

I turned away, overcome by a range of emotions I'd never felt before.

"It reminded me of...I don't even remember," I said evasively, turning from her touch. I needed to tell her, needed to lay the truth bare before her, but I couldn't. Not when I was so close to having her, so close to making her mine. She'd run from me if she ever knew my secret.

"Tell me the truth, Eric, please...I need to know."

"I saw my best friend's parents garroted by Jack the Ripper," I lied. That wasn't why I'd reacted the way I had, but I wasn't about to tell her I had held a dying woman in my arms—a dying woman who would have survived having her throat torn open if the police hadn't incinerated her first.

Sorina's blood was on my hands. Sometimes, in the dark of night, I'd wake in a sweat and actually see my hands bathed in red, only to truly wake moments later and realize the vision had been a nightmare.

"When I saw those rubies next to your neck...all that *red*...believe me, Maddie, I swear that's what caused it. I'll never forgive myself for what I've done, but tell me *you* forgive me, please. I can't bear it if you don't. I'd rather die than have you hate me."

She stared at me for a long while, suspicion in her eyes, as she pressed the handkerchief to the wound. When she removed the cloth, I was relieved to see that the bleeding had stopped. The gashes had lost their redness and were, in fact, not as bad as they had originally seemed. I still felt like a beast for what I'd done to her. I never wanted to hurt her, but wasn't I doing so by not telling her the truth?

"I believe you, of course I do." With relief, I noted that her tone had softened and her eyes had lost their fierceness. "But why didn't you ever tell me before?"

"Tell you before?!" I shouted, losing my composure. "How could I tell you when I've barely seen you these past three months?"

"Oh, stop blubbering and come here," she said, pulling me by my lapels and kissing me again.

I felt electricity every time I touched her skin. "Better?" she said, looking smug, while I'm sure I looked shocked and bewildered, which was becoming my natural state when around her.

"Much." I caressed the scratches at her neck and once again felt like a dog. "I'm so sorry, my love."

"Never mind. A little blood loss never hurt anyone."

"But a lot can kill you," I said, my voice quavering as I remembered Arabella's corpse. "Oh, Maddie, I'm so sorry."

"Are you angling for another kiss?"

"Well, if you insist," I said, and she complied.

"Now, no more of this ridiculousness. It's just a scratch. I'm more worried about you. You're not yourself. What are you keeping from me?"

"If you only knew."

"Then tell me. There should be no secrets between us."

I think I would have told her all had Molly not shown up and spoiled everything.

"Ah ha! Caught you two in flagrante delicto!"

"Could anyone have worse timing?" Maddie muttered.

Molly bounded over to us, her eyes twinkling mischievously. I gave her a withering look, but she, irrepressible as ever, just wiggled her eyebrows suggestively. Molly had no tact.

"Everyone's been wondering where you two went off to, but I've done a good job of keeping them off the scent, especially your father, Maddie."

"My father?" Maddie paled and pulled my hands from around her waist. She gave me a wary glance before peering over the hedge, where I knew she was looking to see if her father had noticed her absence.

"Don't worry. Aunt Robbie's got him firmly in hand. When I bustled off, the two of them were engaged in a debate about some law or other. No need to fear. However," said Molly, linking her arms with ours and keeping herself firmly between us, "I think it's time we get back. Wouldn't want to set the tongues wagging even more, eh?"

Reluctantly, we let her lead us back to the garden party. Our reemergence didn't attract any gawkers, thankfully. In fact, no one turned an eye on us, for Steven was engaged in a reading of his latest novel. I couldn't tell if the guests were rapt or had been frozen in time. They all stared, glassy-eyed and motionless, at Steven orating from the platform that had been set up in the middle of the garden.

"Hands off, pardner! That there lambie pie belongs to me!"

"Stunning use of dialogue, that," said Molly sincerely. I had no doubt she was blindly in love with Steven. You couldn't hear a line like that and not laugh hysterically unless you were wild about the man who had written it.

I slumped down onto the chair Maddie held out for me and shared a commiserating look with her. This was going to be just a *wonderful* afternoon.

‡

Several hours later, I was back home, hopeful yet frustrated that Maddie and I had left things unsaid. I felt firmer in my courtship—after kissing her so many times, how could I not?—but was still racked with guilt that I had betrayed myself so violently and she had seen me at my worst. I wasn't a brutal man, far from it—killing Augustin Boroi aside—but the thought of hurting her in any way filled me with shame. She, for her part, had been so forgiving of my outburst—too forgiving. I wondered if she knew more than she was letting on, for how could someone be so accepting of such aggression?

By the time I entered my bedroom, it was shrouded in darkness. I pushed open the door, reached for the lamp I'd placed on the wardrobe, and lit it. The light cast an eerie glow over the room, and my mood became even blacker when I saw the lump in the middle of my bed.

I was rooted to the floor, fear immobilizing me. I tried to swallow, but that brought no relief to my suddenly parched throat. Slowly, I moved toward the bed, dreading the confrontation with the fiend curled beneath my covers.

With a cry, I threw back the counterpane and felt like a fool. The lump had been nothing more than a book—a book with a note attached to the cover.

A little light reading. I'm not giving up on you yet. If at first you don't succeed, try, try...you get the idea. ~Aunt Robbie.

She couldn't have been less subtle had she beaten me over the head with a stick. This tome was authored by someone who called himself Doctor Nosferatu. I groaned. Another quack. What would I be subjected to from this so-called professional, this vampire hunter?

Suddenly, I remembered a face and a name....and a card that now seemed unbearably heavy in the back pocket of my trousers.

I pulled my wallet out and leafed through the papers I kept there until I found the scrap I was looking for. Six years and still I could make out the embossed letters, though they had begun to fade. The *Z* was slightly bent and the only thing left visible of his surname was the *G* at the end of it. But I would have remembered that name even without the card.

Zigmund Fertig.

He was out there somewhere, searching for the same thing I was. Or maybe more, for he still didn't know his mother was alive. Could I tell him? The address was obliterated. I doubted he was still in London, not after what had happened there. He probably returned to the hunt, if he had not become the hunted already. I was also not considering the fact that he could be dead and rotting in a grave, but I doubted that possibility. Though I'd only spoken to him briefly, I knew Zigmund Fertig was a survivor. You could tell from those scars. Anyone who could survive an injury that should have blinded him was a fighter. He was out there. Now, what was I going to do about it?

The chime of the clock on my nightstand startled me back to reality. For this night at least, I wouldn't do anything about Fertig, nor the book, nor Stefan and Salei, for that matter. This night belonged to Madelaine Dennison. I wasn't about to let shadows invade my dreams of her.

‡

Three a. m. That's what the hands of the clock read when I woke. I'd been feeling the throbbing in my arm for hours, but I couldn't bring myself to admit I felt any pain. To do so would be to give in to insanity. But now there was not only pain, there was...

I threw off the covers and looked in horror at my blood-soaked sleeve. I felt the wounds opening underneath the cloth, felt the searing pain down to my bones.

I put one foot on the hardwood floor and tried to stand up, then collapsed, exhausted, onto the bed. If I could just make it to the washstand in the corner, just divest myself of this shirt and look upon the lacerations, that would be better than sitting here in fear, agonizing over what lay beneath the sleeve, even though I already knew.

I couldn't go on like this forever. There was nothing for it but to try again. I swung my legs over the side of the bed. Though the pain that racked my body was unbearable, I fought through it and stumbled over to the washstand.

I tore off the sleeve and bit my tongue to keep from retching.

So this was what Stefan had meant by *marked*.

The skin on my forearm was ravaged. Deep, bleeding gouges crisscrossed one another and snaked up my arm. Had a doctor seen the wounds, he would have thought I'd torn up my flesh with a piece of barbed wire. His diagnosis wouldn't have been far from the truth, though it was a barbed *tongue* that had done the deed in my case.

I grabbed the wet cloth and pressed it to my wounds, wincing as the water stung my flesh. This was not working. No sooner had I applied the cloth than it was already soaked through. If I didn't find a better way, Stefan would get his wish. I couldn't lose all this blood and hope to survive.

I flung the cloth across the room and tore off the rest of my shirt. Ripping the other sleeve from its seam, I fixed the tourniquet around my forearm and tightened the knot with my teeth. Tearing off another piece of the shirt, I dipped it into the water and pressed it forcefully against the gouges.

All I could do now was wait and pray that the cloth would stanch the flow. After a few moments, I could tell it was working. I felt the blood stop gushing. When I looked at the cloth, I saw that it was mostly white, was no longer being saturated.

I sank back against the wall and gazed at my arm. The lacerations were disgusting, yet fascinating at the same time...all that blood...those deep gouges...

Stop this descent into madness!

The voice jolted through me like a bolt of lightning. I knew that voice, knew that tone, but also knew that to hear that voice was impossible, for the owner of it was thousands of miles away. How had her voice found me here? How had it woken me before I could succumb to the desire to drink my own blood?

My mind ranged over every action, every thought, searching for some conduit through which her voice had come to me. And then I remembered the necklace.

With great effort, I tottered to my feet and stumbled toward my nightstand. Within the false bottom of the drawer was Leonora's necklace, the one the waxwork of Anne Boleyn had worn—the one I'd retrieved the day I'd killed Augustin Boroi.

The pearls struck the sides of the drawer as I yanked the necklace out. I had every intention of throwing it into the fire in the hearth, but when I stood before the grate, my hands trembling, the pearls glowing in the firelight, I couldn't make myself chuck it away. Even after all these years, even after the horror that had happened to me just now, I was still her slave. If I had held onto it this long—not even countenancing the notion of selling it when I was destitute—what made me think I'd give it up now? No matter how brash and cavalier I had tried to be, I still could not let her go, though this necklace might be the source of her power. It was something of hers through which she could reach me—reach straight into my mind.

I let the necklace fall to the rug.

Rest...sleep...you need your strength for what is to come...

"As you wish..." I mumbled. My eyelids grew heavy. All I wanted was to sleep, to rest, to dream this nightmare away.

In the morning, there were only a few faint scars still visible. All the blood had dried, and the skin, for the most part, had healed completely.

It looked as though there had been no wounds at all.

"Longacre Square, you say?"

"Yes, Longacre Square, and then a trip to see the Christmas windows at Macy's."

I mused over this while leafing through the book Aunt Robbie had given me two months before, on that fateful night when I had discovered what it meant to be marked...and Leonora had called to me. My arm hadn't given me any trouble these past months. Sometimes, I wondered if I'd dreamt the whole thing. Or told myself I had, at least. It was easier to cope this way. And from where I now stood, I didn't want to remember the past or relive it at all, marked or not. It was easier to just forget, especially now that I had Maddie.

I shook my head and pushed the thoughts away. Reading Dr. Nosferatu's book, as I had expected, had been no grand revelation. There was nothing new to be found within its pages, but the doctor's hypotheses had proved intriguing, if a little laughable. I had chortled profusely at his assertion that breathing on a vampire after you had ingested garlic would strike it dead.

I'd been laughing more than I had in my life, actually, since Madelaine and I were now engaged, albeit clandestinely. Aunt Robbie and Molly and Steven had always been present to make sure our meetings were unobjectionable; but, thankfully, they gave us enough leeway to sneak away and enjoy each other's company and embraces and kisses during our stolen moments. I found it difficult to believe that Mason Dennison had not discovered our secret, but he seemed to be rather oblivious about this. I liked to imagine he was getting used to my presence and was even growing fond of me. He'd seen a lot more of me these past months, starting with the All Hallows Eve Ball that was much more successful than the last one I'd been to in Bruges. No fools in vampire masks had accosted me, nor did I spend the whole night in a state of panic, terrified that Salei and Stefan were haunting my every step.

Maddie chased the shadows away. When I closed my eyes, I no longer saw the face of the woman who had haunted my dreams since the moment I'd kissed her in Guildy's study so many years ago. Leonora was a piece of my past I'd never forget but was trying to store away. I fooled myself into believing I'd be able to forget her, but then I'd remember her voice in the night and feel the heaviness of that card, her *son's* card, in my trouser pocket, and it was almost as if I were back in Paris, staring at her through those opera glasses and losing myself in her black eyes. But with Maddie in my life now, those occurrences were mercifully growing rarer with each passing day.

"Do you think I'll have time to buy that meerschaum pipe for Mason?" I asked as Aunt Robbie flitted into the room again. She had been atwitter all morning.

"Oh, the bribe, you mean? Yes, I think you will have just enough time to procure your ticket into Mason's good graces."

"Good. I'll get him a year's supply of snuff and smokes as well. That should do the trick."

Aunt Robbie laughed what I would consider a mirthless one and went off into the hall. I heard her mumble, "You hope," but didn't let it dampen my spirits, which were incredibly high this morning.

The clock tolled nine. It was time to make for Maddie's.

‡

"It's windering today, Libba."

"Is it, Miss?"

"Yes. All things are bleak and dreary and depressing. I love days like this. Father says it's my 'dark soul,' inherited from Mother's Scandinavian side."

"I didn't know she was from the North."

"Neither did Father until after they were married. She was half English and half Norwegian. Considering that, you can't expect me *not* to love brooding days, when she raised me on stories of trolls popping out from under bridges to tear unsuspecting travelers' heads off, and witches spiriting children away into the forest where they would cook them until they were the consistency of suet pudding."

"Y-yes, Miss."

It was hard not to laugh aloud at the look on Libba's face. She was not suited for the role of confidante, so I guessed she was pressed into service out of necessity while Molly was probably off chasing after Steven and demanding to know where that engagement ring was.

I quietly stepped across the threshold. I was beginning to feel like a Peeping Tom, for I always seemed to come upon Maddie unawares. Today was no different. I signaled to Libba to look the other way and not say a word as I slowly crept up behind Maddie. She was sprawled on the floor, facing the window, a sea of books scattered about her. I took note of the titles—*The Woman in White*, *Bleak House*, *The Moonstone*—and smiled, but the last one made me stop dead in my tracks.

Carmilla.

The name was like a clarion call to my heart. It was fiction, yes, but it had been one of the first books on vampirism I had read after everything that happened. I don't know why I'd picked it up, but I had, and regretted the decision ever since. Not only did the female vampire protagonist with her ever-changing name remind me of Stefan's sisters, but also of the woman I was trying to forget and knew I never would.

"There, you see, Libba? The mood is destroyed. The nerve of the sun to peek out during a perfectly good thundershower. It ruins the whole effect. That's that, I suppose. Time to rouse ourselves. Oh!" she exclaimed, brightening at the sight of me. "Is it your preferred method of address to sneak up on the girl you are courting and catch her off guard?"

"The element of surprise makes her chances of running away less likely," I said as I took her into my arms.

"And why would anyone ever run away from you?"

"I have no answer for that."

"I do," she said, and kissed me.

"Tell me, Miss Dennison," I said, coming up for air. "Do you not care for baubles?" I still had not had the chance to give her the bracelet. Every time we were together, our minds were occupied with other things, but now seemed like the perfect time, especially since Libba was there to prohibit any further ardor on my part.

"I care nothing for jewels of that sort, Mr. Bradburry," she said, feigning hauteur. "Would you like to see what I *do* treasure?"

"By all means."

She led me out of the room and down a corridor to a door I had not encountered before. Taking a key from within her pocket, she put it in the lock and tuned it. With a little effort, she finally managed to turn the handle. The door swung inward after a good push, and I found myself standing on the threshold of a library.

The library in the British Museum didn't hold a candle to this one. Every inch of this room was covered in books. Shelves upon shelves reached up to the cathedral ceiling; ladders of every shape and size were propped against nearly all the bookcases; acres of jewel-colored leather-bound tomes swam before my eyes. Surrounding the upper reaches of the library was a minstrel's gallery upon which were perched various green upholstered armchairs and small tables, atop which sat elegant, etched glass lamps. This room was a veritable bibliophile's paradise.

And in the middle of it all stood Madelaine—*my* Madelaine—looking as though she were the richest woman in the world.

"These," she said, holding out her arms to encompass the room, "are my jewels, Eric. Austen, Collins, Dickens, Zola, Dumas, Alcott, Gaskell, Shakespeare, Dante...authors contemporary and long dead who have transported me to places I will never travel to in this lifetime. After you and my family, *these* are the things I treasure most in this world."

The bracelet suddenly seemed insignificant when compared to all this.

"But I would treasure the bracelet as a token of your love, if you have the courage to give it to me."

"What...how did you know?"

"You dropped it on the floor about three minutes ago."

"So I did," I said, reaching down to pick up the crumpled mass of gold. She pushed up her sleeve and held out her arm to me. I couldn't help letting my fingers glide across her flesh, and once again I felt that electric jolt course through my body. I fastened the bracelet then draped my arms about her, locking her in an embrace as she leaned up and kissed me— kissed me so long and deep that I was completely lost and didn't hear the strangled cry from behind us until it was too late to pull away.

"Madelaine!"

"Father!" she shrieked, pushing me away.

"So, this is how it is, then, Sir?" Mason Dennison spat. "I invite you into my home and you skulk about like a thief, taking liberties with my daughter."

"You didn't invite him, Papa, I did," Madelaine said boldly. "If it were up to you, he'd never see me."

"Madelaine, I will not tolerate..."

"Yes, you will, Father! Listen, please. I am not a child, I am not property. You cannot force on me whom I will love, nor whom I will marry. And I love Eric."

"And what of James Calhoun?" Mason was floundering if he had to bring up that snake.

"Father, *please*," was all Madelaine said. There was a pained look in her eyes, almost as if she couldn't believe her father would even consider that leech a suitable prospect for her.

I suddenly felt a surge of courage. If she could speak to her father that way, then maybe I, as an outsider—an intruding, skulking outsider—might have some luck as well. "And *I* love *her*. And I intend to marry her. And now, I am going to take your daughter out for a constitutional because that is what proper courting ladies and gentlemen do, and I will brook no opposition in the matter, um, Sir."

It was highly disrespectful and extremely foolish to say such things to Mason Dennison, but I no longer cared. From now on, I would probably only be able to see Madelaine through the bars of whatever prison cell Mason's friends would lock me up in, but it was time I stood up for myself. I hadn't stood up for myself in years. It felt good to give someone what for.

"It's about time you showed some backbone, boy." To my astonishment, Mason Dennison came over and clamped his arms around me. For a moment, I thought he was trying to strangle me, then I realized he wasn't trying to crush the life out of me, but was rather giving me a hug. Highly irregular behavior, this.

"That's the type of man I want for my daughter, one who's not afraid to speak his mind nor fight for what he wants. You've got pluck, son. I could use you in my business."

Was I dreaming? To have gained Madelaine and her father's blessing, and what's more, to be told of his hidden admiration for me, was too much to hope for. It had to be a trick.

"Don't look at me like that, boy. I'm not going to throw you out on your rear. I'm serious." Not only was he serious, but that was the most jovial and the *most* Mason Dennison had ever said to me. "Now," he said, not giving me time to recover, "you mentioned taking a constitutional. I think that is a splendid idea. I shall join you both."

"Molly and Steven are coming as well," Maddie said cheerily.

"The more the merrier, I always say!"

"You do?" This from me.

"Of course," he responded in his newly cheerful voice.

"And Aunt Robbie, too," added Maddie.

"A queen amongst women."

"I couldn't agree more."

We all turned to see the queen amongst women standing in the doorway, smirking that self-satisfied smirk she always wore when she was in one of her mischievous moods. "Why are you all standing there goggling like idiots? Oh, to sing my praises no doubt, Mason, old thing. But still...the hour is growing late. You don't want to have to fight the crush of spectators, do you?"

The unofficial cicerone of our group having spoken, we peons dutifully bustled out of the room and followed her to destinations unknown.

"I love your aunt, you know," Maddie said, squeezing my arm as we walked a few paces behind the elder members of our group.

"As much as you love me?"

"I wouldn't go quite that far."

"Come along, Madelaine." I could tell Dennison was being magnanimous, but we didn't want to press our luck before the wedding. *Wedding...*

"You do realize that when I said I intended to marry you, I meant it?" I asked.

"Certainly I do. I know you'd never lie to me."

"Of course not," I said, swallowing hard. I hadn't exactly lied about my past. I'd just not given her a detailed account.

"Just make sure you are there to meet me at the altar. I have no plans to be a jilted bride."

"As if I would ever do such a thing."

"Just in case."

There it was again, the frown behind her smiling eyes, the serious tone underneath her mirth. Somehow, she knew I wasn't being completely honest, yet she masked her apprehensions well.

I felt a pang of guilt as we walked out into the bustle of another New York morning. What was I doing to the poor girl? Why couldn't I bring myself to be a man and tell her everything?

Because she'll run away screaming, and you'll never see her again...

My conscience was so helpful. Of course that was the reason, but now, with my heart so thoroughly engaged, and, more to the point, with the unexpected blessing and near-fawning acceptance of Mason Dennison, there could be no breaking of our troth...not that I wanted that to happen anyway.

Selfish, selfish, selfish, I scolded myself. When picturing the typical, straitlaced Victorian father, one needed to look no further than Mason Dennison. He fit the mold perfectly, so for him to accept me so easily, so willingly, so *gladly*, made me suspicious. I couldn't rationalize this drastic change in attitude. Had he really always been fond of me? Or had someone sung my praises to him? I suspected my aunt's hand in this. Yet then again, maybe it had something to do with Madelaine's mother's death. She'd said he'd had to be both parents to her. Was it guilt that she had been deprived of a mother's care and love at such a young age that made him consent? Or had he wanted to test my character by keeping me away and had then seen that I was not some flash in the pan but loved Madelaine with all my heart? My mind was reeling with suppositions. Good fortune wasn't a friend to me, so reconciling myself to this windfall was proving quite a task.

Just because we were now openly courting didn't mean I suddenly had favored privileges, nor could I ride in the same carriage as my betrothed. Molly—she was getting on my nerves more and more lately—clambered in with Maddie, while Steven, Aunt Robbie, and I were shut into the brougham behind Maddie's conveyance.

"Ah, good morrow, good morrow, good morrow!" said Steven.

"It would be an even better morrow if you were Madelaine."

"'Fraid I can't do that, old chap. Something to do with anatomy, I daresay. Besides which, I'd make a lousy woman."

I bit my tongue, wanting to say several things, but I had a feeling Aunt Robbie would take up the gauntlet against me if I uttered anything disparaging against persons of the feminine persuasion. I stared out the window in silence. It wasn't that far to our destination anyway, and Steven was prattling along good-naturedly enough.

Maddie's carriage shot ahead. It must have been driven by someone more sober than our Jack, for the brougham was already fading from sight. I reached up to bang on the roof, but Jack must have read my mind because no sooner had I done this than we lurched forward and pulled up alongside the girls' carriage.

"Can I help you, Sir?" said Maddie with mock arrogance as she put down the window.

I reached out my hand, trying to touch the tips of her fingers, only to be jostled back inside as Jack lumbered over a pothole, making us lose pace yet again.

"Lor' luv a duck!" I heard him slur from up top.

"Oh, never mind, lad," said Aunt Robbie. "We'll be out and about in no time."

Our first stop would be that tobacconists' shop, where I'd have to invent a story about an uncle on my mother's side always wanting a genuine meerschaum pipe. No sense in spoiling Mason's surprise on Christmas morning. Then it was off to Delmonico's for lunch—Aunt Robbie's idea—followed by visits to whatever other haunts the girls had in mind, and then finally to see those famous Macy's windows.

"Oh, Good Lord, Steven, must you really?"

I followed Aunt Robbie's horrified gaze and saw Steven drawing a book from his pocket...a fat book, I might add. I had no idea how he'd managed to stuff it into his waistcoat.

"Have to read it aloud to make sure the dialogue sounds authentic. Wouldn't want it to make people laugh in places were seriousness is called for, you know."

"Of course not," said Aunt Robbie, looking wry.

"Come, come, it won't be much longer. And you'll like this bit. Clark is up against a pretty slimy octopus in this chapter."

"What, *literally*? Have you gone Jules Verne on us, Steven?" teased Aunt Robbie.

"*Ahem*, the high noon sun glinted off Calamity Clark's Stetson, casting a long shadow behind him as he walked into the deserted town. The wind whistled through the empty streets, the eerie wailing rattling the shutters and kicking up a dust storm. Not a sound was heard, save for the beating of the hearts of the prairie dogs burrowed underfoot, but our hero had no doubt the desperadoes hiding in the safety of the saloon were quaking in their boots. As a tumbleweed rolled past, the rugged gunfighter eyed it with dread. This bit of bramble was an ill omen, a harbinger of death. Clark was certain it spelled his doom..."

I sighed and shared a commiserating look with Aunt Robbie. There was a deep furrow between her eyes; she was biting her lip. Poor thing. She could barely contain herself.

I shut my eyes and imagined what fun the girls must be having in the next brougham. Trying to endure wasn't easy with Steven droning on and Aunt Robbie doing her best impersonation of a leaky steam pipe.

We rattled over another pothole, which granted us a momentary reprieve, then Steven set to again. Barring the possibility that he might suddenly become mute, the drive threatened to drag on forever.

"Cheer up, lad," Aunt Robbie whispered. "We've only got seventy-seven more blocks to go."

"That makes me feel *so* much better."

"I thought it might."

☦

The man clad in the black roquelaure ducked into an alley. He'd been tailing us for fifty-seven blocks. I had no idea who he could be, but his presence was disquieting. Perhaps he was just visiting the same sights we were, even the tobacconist's shop.

Go right ahead, Eric, keep deluding yourself. The man was following us, or more aptly, *me*. There was something familiar about the way he carried himself, but I could not place him, no matter how hard I tried. I looked long and hard at the alley, willing him to come out and show himself, but nothing happened, and when I walked over to the mouth of the passage, I saw that it was empty. I could not have imagined him. God help me if I had.

I walked back over to my party, vowing to forget the unpleasant incident. They hadn't noticed anything was amiss, so I saw no reason to trouble them with my worries.

"What exactly is the theme supposed to be this year?" I asked, drawing Maddie's hand out of her muff and clasping it in mine. The visit to the tobacconist's had been fruitful, as was evidenced by the small wooden box containing the meerschaum pipe that I clutched under my arm. And lunch at Delmonico's had been pleasant enough, until Molly took it into her head that Steven had put an engagement ring in her glass of champagne and the waiter had obviously pinched it. She was getting desperate.

"Gothic tales and old Scandinavian legends," said Molly, traipsing along in front of us with Aunt Robbie. After Steven had cleared the waiter of wrongdoing, Molly had vowed not to speak to Steven ever again and was holding true to this promise. She hadn't uttered one word to him since we left Delmonico's.

"Tailor-made for me," said Maddie, her eyes shining mischievously.

"Dark stories of the North," Molly said over her shoulder.

"Oooo," whispered Maddie, shivering for good measure. She was a good sport, this girl I had chosen to throw my lot in with.

"And here we are!" This from Aunt Robbie, who had become the leader of our little expedition. We pulled up before the glass and ooo-ed and ahh-ed at the sights contained within. The thing I noticed first was the realism of the figures. It was almost as if a wizard had frozen actual people and shrunk them, reigniting the spark of life again once they were safely ensconced behind the glass.

We moved down the line, passing one scene after another. Each had its own distinct brand of subtle horror. I thought the worst and most terribly realistic was the scene from Hoffman's *Sandman*. There stood Nathanael, looking crazed, trying to push Clara from the steeple. I could hear him shouting "Spin, wooden dolly, spin!" in my mind. The scene was horrifying, yet wonderful at the same time, and I found myself wondering why Christmas just wasn't Christmas without a bit of horror thrown into the mix. I think Dickens must have started the trend with Scrooge and his ghosts.

Snow was flurrying everywhere in the next window, which was a scene depicting *The Snow Queen*. She looked fiercely beautiful in sparkling silver, her white hair flailing out behind her as the two children cowered beneath her haughty gaze. I was trying to figure out how they made the icicles on the bare trees look so authentic, when I heard Molly squeal. She and Steven, reunited in their curiosity, were peering through the glass of the next window, their brows knitted. Something about their expressions made me uneasy, but I brushed my misgivings aside.

"Oh, you two, why the long faces? It's only a window..." Madelaine broke off with a gasp. She was now staring at the window with the same expression.

"So now it's you *three,* is it?" I laughed, but became as comatose as my companions when I saw the scene separated from me by only a thin layer of glass. That scene was not a product of someone's imagination.

That scene was from my life.

A full moon rose above a castle courtyard. There was the well, there were the sisters, and there was I, clasped in Ruxandra's stranglehold. In the center of the courtyard, where I was expecting to see Augustin Boroi and Vladec Salei towering over the dead body of Olga, there stood a single figure completely dressed in black. I knew him at once. His shock of red hair could not be denied.

Stefan.

"That is in exceedingly bad taste, but very cleverly done," said Steven. They were chattering, but I couldn't make sense of what they were saying. My mind was slipping. I could feel myself losing my reason. I clutched the wall to steady myself and shook my head at Maddie's concerned glance.

"Look, the automaton with the red hair has a banner!"

Shut up, Molly, shut up!

"Oh! He's going to unfurl it! There's something written on it, but I can't quite make it out just yet. Give me a moment..."

This can't be happening...

"*Marked,* how curious."

"Eric!" Madelaine screamed my name, but the darkness had already taken hold.

The floor was getting closer. I wondered why this was happening. Then a pain shot through my body, and I realized I had collapsed to the pavement. Nothing mattered, not the pain, not my friends fussing over me. All the years washed away—my feelings of safety, my conviction to start a new life...all gone in the space of an instant.

And then my arm began to throb. As my fingers clamped over it, I felt the wetness again and knew the wounds had reopened.

Marked indeed.

He's found me, he's found me...

He's here.

‡

"Quiet, now, he's stirring. I think the worst has finally passed."

Bleary shapes weaved before me as I opened my eyes.

"Thank God." My heart thrilled at the voice, for I recognized it as Maddie's.

"We feared the worst, old boy." I still couldn't make out his features, but I knew the voice was Steven's. Someone was babbling on about how she had been prepared to make my funeral arrangements. It took me a moment to place the voice as Molly's and another half second to realize I didn't care about any of the other people in the room. My vision had cleared. Maddie was at my side, her hand clasped in mine, our eyes locked on each other to the exclusion of all.

I wanted to tell the others to leave us in peace, when a shadow fell across my bed. The imposing form of Mason Dennison—arms crossed, his face an undecipherable mask—loomed over me. In spite of his approval, I let my hand slip from Maddie's. The stare he was giving me was enough to make me believe that I had dreamed the whole thing—that he had never been so welcoming of me after finding me affixed to his daughter's face in the library. No father could be that open-minded. I know *I* wouldn't have had I been in his place.

"All right, the lot of you. Clear out. Give the boy some air." He didn't shout the orders, nor did he raise his voice, but the command of his tone sizzled through the room and everyone sprang into action. Seconds later, after I cast a last pleading glance toward Maddie as she shut the door, Mason Dennison and I were alone.

"Now that you've awakened from your fever dream, we can finally have a nice, long chat about your future."

If he continued in this quietly menacing fashion, I didn't expect to have a future for much longer. I swallowed hard several times and ventured to speak, only to be silenced with a warning finger.

"Lie quiet, now. You need your rest. I'm the one who needs to speak. Maddie told me of the horrors you witnessed. Jack the Ripper, your friend's parents murdered...a dreadful business. I can only guess that those blasted macabre windows were too much and sent you over the edge. And also...I feel I need to explain myself. I suppose you're still trying to come to terms with my consent."

"Yes, actually," I managed to choke out.

"Well, boy..."

"Eric, please," I said quietly.

"Eric, then. Son..."

I started up in bed. Son?

"It seems my daughter is quite taken with you. I've always known my Maddie to be constant in her affections. Once she sets her heart on something, it is virtually impossible to dissuade her from her purpose. She hasn't left your side all these days. I have never seen her affected this way by anyone. Any man, at least. Usually, she treats them as though they were infected with boils and sores. I needed to see how she was with you, how she really felt about you, to make sure it wasn't a passing infatuation on either of your parts. Now I see that it wasn't. And I can't help but be happy about it. And, son, I saw myself in you."

This was too much. "What are you saying?"

"I'm saying that she's yours. I've no objections."

If I hadn't been lying in bed, I would have collapsed in a heap on the floor. How could he be so trusting, so willing to part with the treasure that was his daughter? My thoughts must have shown on my face, for he smiled and said, "You remind me so much of me and Maddie of her mother. And when I saw the two of you together, I knew I couldn't fight it. And then I realized...I had turned into my dead wife's father.

He hadn't approved of me because I wasn't British, and I was disapproving of you solely because you weren't an American.

"I'm going to tell you something that I never want to hear pass your lips. Not even my own daughter knows the whole story, though I usually tell her everything. Do you understand me?"

I nodded.

"Good." He breathed in deeply and stared at the ground for so long, I feared he had fallen asleep. As I was reaching out my hand to shake him awake, he lifted up his head and began. "Madelaine's mother and I eloped. When her father discovered that we were engaged, *secretly* engaged, he flew into a rage and would have beaten her to death had I not intervened. That was the last night she ever saw him. The next day, we married and fled the country. And then, a fortnight later, we received word that the old man had died of a laudanum overdose, leaving Madelaine's mother penniless. He had made a new will the day after we fled. So, there we were, without so much as a dime to our name. Things remained that way for a while, until I got on my feet and found out I wasn't alone in the world as far as friends were concerned. Wonderful things, friends."

I thought of the person I used to call my brother and clenched the bedclothes in anger. Then Guildy flashed through my mind, and I understood Mason's point.

"After Madelaine's mother died, Maddie was all I had. I couldn't stand the thought of someone taking her away from me one day."

"I would never do that, Mr. Dennison..."

"Please, let me finish. I became a tyrant and so obsessed with her marrying someone of my own choosing that I almost pushed her into marriage with a man more abominable than any I'd ever met in all my sixty-five years on this earth. The same scenario was happening again a generation later. I knew my wife always felt a twinge of guilt for disobeying her father. There was nothing I could do or say to change that. I never forgave myself for it. I know she loved me. I know she would have followed me anywhere, but I *know* she never recovered from the shock of his death, nor the guilt of what we'd done, though that old beast had pushed us to it. It wore on her...and finally, it killed her. I didn't want the same thing to happen to my daughter. And that made me see what a fool I'd been. I certainly wasn't one to talk of propriety, not after what had happened between Madelaine's mother and me. I suspect you were surprised by my consent after that display of yours in the library?"

"Shocked, would be more apt."

"Yes, I expected you would be. You passed the test admirably, son."

"Thanks," I muttered.

"And as if I needed any more assurance of your *sterling* character, I've heard your aunt raving about what a good sort you were for years. I trust Robbie with my life. In fact, I do believe I love that old trout."

"Do you, Mason? How kind of you to admit it so tenderly."

Startled and red-faced, Mason Dennison turned to see Aunt Robbie standing behind him, for once smiling instead of smirking maddeningly.

Rallying, I reached toward the nightstand beside my bed and hefted up the package that someone, no doubt Maddie, had left for me. "I suppose I don't really need to give you this to gain your favor, now," I said, holding out the small wooden box to Mason, who seemed surprised by the gift. "But I want to all the same...Father."

He extended his hands and opened the box, gazing down at the meerschaum pipe I had purchased for him in the city.

He looked at the pipe, then at me, and then back at the pipe. I could see he was struggling to stop the tears from betraying his true emotions.

"It's only a pipe, Mason. You have thousands of them," said Aunt Robbie.

"No, it's not just a pipe. It's a bridge to the past. The past I was burying but shouldn't have been. Thank you."

It was unnerving to see a man of his stoicism in such a state. I blessed Maddie for telling me that day in the shop the real reason why she had started when I told her I'd wanted to purchase the meerschaum, why it was the perfect gift for her father. I'd thought of it unexpectedly, considering it a suitable present for him, yet little knowing how dear this thing was to his heart. The week before their fourteenth anniversary, Madelaine's mother had purchased a specially carved meerschaum pipe for Mason. The carving depicted a woman standing at the edge of a cliff, and behind her was a man reaching out his hand, entreating her to come away with him. Engraved on the side of the pipe was the following message: "To the man who wouldn't let me jump, who never gave in...the man who set me free." Three days later, Madelaine's mother was dead. Mason was so overcome with grief at her passing, he couldn't bear to have the pipe near him and it had been interred with his dead wife.

Mason smiled at me through his tears. That was all the thanks I needed.

‡

"I still don't understand why you won't let me read an excerpt from *Calamity Clark and the Revenge of the Revivified Rattler* at the wedding breakfast. The guests would love it."

I rolled my eyes and tried to remember we were in a church, and what a church at that—St. Patrick's Cathedral— and stilled my tongue. "Snakes and wedding breakfasts aren't exactly the best of bedfellows, old boy." There, that was civil enough.

I peered down the nave and caught sight of Molly bustling around in the vestibule. She was a vision in her lavender taffeta, flaunting her saucy avoirdupois, which went unnoticed by no one, not even Steven. He was paying much more attention to her these days. I knew his resistance was weakening. That much longed for proposal would happen any day now.

By necessity, Steven was best man. Steven, *Stefan*...it should have been him. This day of all days, when I should have been higher than a kite, I kept thinking of those who were dead to me. Why was that? Was it because of the diorama in that shop window and its undeniable message?

Or was it my own sick fancy that just couldn't let go, even after all this time?

Cautiously, I felt my arm. It was whole and dry and not paining me at all. What did that mean? That I was being granted a reprieve on my wedding day? I doubted it.

The organ began to play. In moments, Molly was standing across from us, ogling Steven. She was the maid of honor, of course.

And then came Maddie. The breath was knocked out of me at the sight of her. She was all in lace, all in white, just as another had once dressed. I pushed the vision of Leonora from my mind. To be unfaithful to Madelaine was to me a crime worse than murder. I'd already committed that. I wasn't about to start our life together unclean.

Mason lifted Maddie's veil and placed her hand in mine. I linked my fingers with hers and felt the coolness of her skin against my own. My palms were sweating profusely, but Maddie was calmness personified. I was in a daze, in thrall to her ethereal beauty, and couldn't take my eyes off her. I also couldn't understand why she was squeezing my hand, until I realized I had forgotten to say "I Do" for the third time.

"I do," I finally said.

"Good. For a moment there I thought you *didn't*," said the priest. I heard Steven stifle a guffaw.

Now that my part was over, I could return my gaze to my wife, or the woman who would soon be my wife if the ceremony ever ended. I expected her to be crying, to show some sign that she was on the verge of tears, but she looked so radiant, so blissfully happy, as though she were content and had no doubt she was making the right decision—to throw in her lot with a man she thought she knew. Why was I torturing myself with this? Was this grounds for divorce if she found out I hadn't told her all? I was no James Calhoun, but still, if she discovered that I had deceived her, had kept secrets that would have chased any sane woman away, what would she do? I never wanted to find out. So why should I not keep my own counsel? Why should I tell her?

Because you love her, that's why.

Corcitura

I glanced around at the congregation, searching for that voice that only seemed to come to me when I was on the verge of losing my sanity. I loved Madelaine, of course I did, more than I'd ever loved anyone or anything. But the only way she'd ever know the truth would be if Stefan told it to her himself, which I knew would never happen. No one would ever drag my secrets from me willingly.

I slipped the gold band onto her finger and took both of her hands in mine. I vaguely heard the priest intone the final blessing, and the next thing I knew, Maddie and I were kissing and facing the cheering guests for the first time as Mr. and Mrs. Eric Bradburry.

Whoever gave rice to the guests inside the church—and I confess I suspected it to be either Aunt Robbie or Molly—should've been shot. A couple of overeager congregants—friends of Steven, I noticed—decided to launch the grains at us while we were walking up the nave. After getting pelted in the eye six times, I couldn't take it anymore and grabbed Maddie's hand. She, for her part, was laughing hysterically and encouraging them to "do their worst" as we raced for the doors.

The ushers threw open the doors, and Madelaine and I stepped out into a sea of white. Mounds of snow blanketed the steps below us and delicate puffs rained down on our heads. For a moment, we just stood there staring at each other, our breath making mist between us. She was so beautiful, so real, so pure, so different from everyone else...and she was mine, however undeserving I was. I kissed her long and tenderly and felt my doubts melt away.

"Oi! M'lady, your lor'ship, your carriage awaits!"

I would've known that voice anywhere. Old Jack pointed to the carriage. It was completely white and so was the horse, so that if our driver hadn't directed our attention to it, I doubt we would have been able to see it for the snow. I had suggested we put up at the new Waldorf Hotel, but Maddie wanted to stay the night at Aunt Robbie's. My wife was a sentimental thing, I was learning. Besides, in this weather it wasn't the best idea to travel very far, and we'd be having the wedding breakfast at Aunt Robbie's anyway, so it was a logical choice.

Jack shunted us in and drove off. Fortunately, he could not go at his usual breakneck speed, for there was a fair amount of carriage traffic for a Saturday morning. That suited Maddie and me just fine. I was very fond of kissing my wife and she of me, so we were more than happy to amuse ourselves in this manner until we reached Aunt Robbie's house. Jack could have taken ten years to get there for all we cared.

Apparently, everyone else had taken a less scenic route. They were all congregated on the steps and threshold of my aunt's home when we arrived.

I guided Maddie through the press of bodies. As I carried her over the threshold and placed her down at my side, she clutched my arm and gasped and so did I, for we were astonished at the magnificence that surrounded us. Aunt Robbie had outdone herself with the décor. There were white silk ribbons draped through the railing of the staircase and covering every available bit of ceiling space. The place looked like a trifle before, but now it looked so fluffy and icing-like that I was really beginning to believe we were somehow inside a wedding cake. And the wedding cake, Good Lord! Seven tiers high, filled with lemon curd and vanilla custard, and, according to everyone there, including myself and Maddie as soon as we fed it to each other, "heavenly."

All morning long and well into the afternoon—it had become a Wedding Lunch and was threatening to turn into a Wedding Supper—my bride was passed from one guest to another, going round to each aunt, uncle, or cousin, and receiving congratulations and the occasional reprimand that she was much too young to marry and especially someone of foreign extraction like myself. Usually, when someone back home mentioned "foreign extraction," it meant French, which was about the worst insult one could level at an Englishman, but I was taking it all in stride.

As the hour grew later, I wandered into the hall, intending to drop subtle hints about time and tide waiting for no man to whoever would listen. My efforts had met with smiles and puzzled looks and several comments—sotto voce, of course—about English eccentrics, but no one seemed to get the hint that I wanted them gone.

And so I was idling alone when I heard a loud female voice say that ours was an unequal marriage. Startled, I looked into the drawing room to see that the speaker of this jibe was a corpulent sot whom I had seen at several of Mason's parties. I think she wanted the old codger for herself. Well, I wouldn't stand for such remarks. This woman needed to be given a set down, and I had every intention of doing so, until I realized she wasn't talking about money, which Maddie and I both had in spades. She was talking about how Maddie was too good a woman for the likes of me. What she meant by "the likes of me" I'll never know, but it made me uneasy to think she could see my defects so plainly. Of course, she might have just been jealous of two young people so much in love. I had heard she was a confirmed spinster no man in his right mind would go near.

"Don't waste your time on her. She's a rather pathetic excuse for a human being."

"Jealous, are we?" I said, accepting the glass of champagne my aunt held out to me.

"Of *that*? Pshaw!"

I laughed and took a sip. "It should really have been a double wedding, you know."

"Molly and Steven?"

"No, you old bat, you and Mason."

"But then I would have been your mother-in-law, and I don't want those duties added to my already extensive list. Aunt suits me just fine, and it's your aunt I will stay."

"Well, all right, then. Just don't hold off because of me. I've seen the way the old blister ogles you."

"Have you really?"

"Aunt Robbie!" Honestly, she could be so obtuse when it came to matters of her own heart.

"That's all well and good, but I think you'd best concern yourself with the affairs of your two young friends."

I looked across the room to see Molly crying into her champagne. Well, not exactly crying, but looking as though she was about to break into a flood of tears.

"Go on, I'll mingle about."

I set down my empty glass and made for Molly.

"Poppy, what's the matter?"

"That *clod*. He's rolling in it now, so why won't he propose?" Her lips were trembling. I wondered how Steven could be so blind. In fact, I was starting to wonder if Steven deserved her at all. I had spied a few chaps who were dying for Molly to notice them. It was my duty to steer her toward them, and I was about to do just that, when Steven loomed up before us. He wasn't drunk, though he had a silly grin on his face. His fist was closed around something. In a flash of understanding, I knew what he was about.

"Margaret, luv, we need to talk."

"Talk to yourself, or better yet, to your precious editor, who you apparently enjoy spending all your time with."

"Now, now, don't be childish, lass. I have something to ask you."

Molly's eyes bulged out of her head. "*Yes*?" she asked breathlessly. I was going to excuse myself from this tête-à-tête, but she held my hand in a vise-like grip, and I was afraid she'd yank it off if I left her side. I glanced across the room and saw Maddie watching me with an amused expression. It was clear that she, too, had guessed what was about to happen.

"Margaret, I love you."

"Yes..."

A pregnant pause.

"Margaret, I love you."

"You said that already," said Molly, exasperated.

"I know, I know. Give me a minute."

A waiter was passing by at that moment—since when did we have waiters?—carrying drinks on a platter. Molly grabbed the glass and handed it to Steven, who drank it rather absentmindedly.

"Thanks," he said, handing the empty glass back to her.

"Now, you were going to ask me something..."

"Don't rush me, lass."

"If I don't rush you, I might be standing here for the rest of my life!"

"Fine! Eric, would you ask her?"

"I most certainly will not! Besides, I don't truck with bigamy, and I've just got married myself, so it would be highly irregular."

"Fat lot of help you are," Steven muttered, but I saw he was smiling. It would happen any moment now, if only he'd buck up the nerve.

"That's it. Steven," said Molly, taking his hand, "If I wait for you any longer, I'll be waiting forever. I don't know why you are so afraid to ask or what sort of imbalance there is to your mind, but I'm tired of waiting. Steven Bannon, will you marry me?"

Well, what could he expect? Now he was standing there goggling and sputtering like a beached fish. Any sensible girl would have thrown him over for someone else, but not Molly. She wanted him, and now she'd *got* him, poor thing.

"Yes, I say *yes!*" he shrieked, causing everyone to look in our direction. The two of them were sobbing hysterically as they fell into each other's arms, and if Aunt Robbie hadn't intervened with calls for a toast, I've no doubt they would have gone on blubbering like fools forever.

"As Calamity Clark would say, 'What a pair of cockeyed codfish.'"

"But honest cockeyed codfish, nonetheless." Maddie stood at my side, smiling up at me. Thank God I'd got a woman with not only a beautiful face and demeanor, but a brain in the bargain. Those two ninnies would give each other quite a life, but they'd manage and be happy, if they didn't drive each other mad within the first few hours after the ceremony.

Little by little, the guests began to make their departures. We received many compliments, well-wishes, and blessings—save from that fat creature who had designs on Mason—along with hopes for the future and several invitations to dinner parties when we returned from our honeymoon.

By the time the last guest departed, it was nearing nine o'clock in the evening.

"Don't worry about me popping in, loves," Aunt Robbie said as we kissed her goodnight. "I've much to occupy myself with."

I gathered Maddie up into my arms and mounted the stairs. Something caught my foot and I stumbled, knocking into the wall and sending some of Aunt Robbie's pictures scattering.

"I think I must have put on some weight at the wedding breakfast, since you seem to be having trouble carrying your bride, my own love," she said, laughing that gorgeous laugh that thrilled through me every time I heard it.

I kissed her and tightened my arm about her waist. We would share my little room tonight and soon we'd settle in at Riverhampton—where Mason had already given us a separate wing—until we decided what we wanted to do with ourselves. Maddie was very attached to her father, but I sensed a wanderlust in her that matched my own. I didn't know if I'd chance an excursion to Europe, though Maddie had been professing her ardent desire to meet my mother. I knew I wouldn't be able to put her off the idea for much longer.

But those were thoughts for other days. Tonight was for us. Maddie was my life now, my own love, and very shortly, we would become one. No more thoughts of Leonora, or Stefan, or Salei, or the nagging feeling that they had done something to forever change me. For tonight at least, I could forget. For tonight, at least, I was complete.

This night, vampires would be the last things on my mind.

Book the First: The Narrative of Eric Bradburry Part III: Marked—1894-1895

The Letter

"Ah, I see married life suits you well."

I gave Aunt Robbie a wicked smile as I walked into the drawing room to join her for tea.

"Oh, don't look so smug so early in the morning. What that young wife of yours sees in you, I'll never know."

"Is this your post wedding night set down, dear Aunt?" I said, still smiling as I sipped my tea and accepted the biscuit she offered me.

"No, no, just telling you how I feel. By the bye, a letter came for you this morning."

"A letter?" Why should this bit of news make my heart jump?

"Yes. Most probably a billet-doux from a former lover. It's on the table in the hallway if you're so inclined."

I knew she wouldn't let me have a moment's peace until I opened the letter. I found it where she said it would be. The envelope was facedown, concealing the address, but giving a clear view of the large, red, bloody looking Gothic wax B that seemed to me a perversion of my own seal. Who did I know whose surname began with B? It could have been Steven, but no, for I remembered his seal had an S entwined with the B. I racked my mind, but couldn't for the life of me think of who might have sent me this letter.

And then it hit me and I stood paralyzed, not daring to overturn the envelope, willing it to dissolve where it rested.

"Sent it to yourself, did you?"

Her words seemed to come to me from a great distance. I felt as though I were in a fog, mostly because I had no idea what she meant. It took me a moment to understand she was referring to the seal looking similar to the one she sent me years ago as a birthday present. Dumbly, I shook my head. My heart was throbbing. I prayed my arm wouldn't start throbbing, too. No one had discovered my secret wounds, and I intended to keep my own counsel for as long as I could.

"Aren't you going to open it, love? You'll stay standing there like a statue forever...unless, of course, you've perfected the skill of reading through paper?"

I lifted the envelope off the table. The paper felt like a ten-ton weight in my hand. Slowly, dreading the address, I turned it over.

The letter was from Leonora...Leonora *Belododia.*

I broke the seal and let my eyes rove over the page.

My Dearest Eric,

You are probably stunned by the words you are now reading. Given what you went through, if I were in your place, I would have burned the letter on sight. Yet I'm hoping surprise and not anger (or worse, hatred) is what you feel now. Surprise that I've thought of you after all these years. Surprise that I'm writing to you or have the nerve to write to you, you might be saying to yourself. I vowed to never have any contact with you ever again, but I cannot hold to that promise any longer.

Eric, things have happened over the last six years that I never thought could. For one, ~~you have probably noticed that~~ *I am married now to Stefan. No, I will not be coy about it. Of course you noticed. It was probably the first thing that struck you. I beg you to understand my position. It is not a love match, nor could any marriage have ever been a love match for me, save one. But I was overruled. The match suited everyone. By some miracle, we haven't murdered one another, but I haven't yet ruled out that possibility. Changeability was* always Stefan's prerogative. His character is like an emerald—multifaceted and enhanced by inclusions. Add to that the volatile mix of bloodlines and his quick alterations in mood are something I have had to learn to live with.

But why should I explain all this to you? My words are just that: words. They mean nothing. If only I could make you believe me, Eric. I hope this letter convinces you, although I see that I have done a poor job of pleading my case so far. If you ever trusted me, then trust me more now.

He's changed.

He's changed so much you wouldn't recognize him. I might even venture to say he's learned to master the warring sides of his nature, but I gave up such foolish hopes ages ago.

There is no possibility of change for me. There is no cure for my "affliction" but a stake through the heart or an assignation with an ax. And for Stefan...who can say? No one has yet discovered how to send him from this world. I don't believe anyone ever will.

Forgive me for rambling. It has been happening more and more lately, now that I have so much time to reflect on all that has passed. As for Stefan, I know not how, I know not when, but he is not the same person you last saw in London. He is not a beast; he is not obsessed with the bloodlust Constantinos gifted to him, or the vengefulness he received from his other father. Believe me when I say this. He is not what he once was. He has changed. I think it is due in some small part to my influence—I, who have had to be mother, father, wife, sister, brother, all things to him—but more so to the absence of one who controlled him. Yes, Eric, he is gone. I have not seen Vladec Salei in close to seven years.

I don't expect you to believe any of this, given what you've experienced, what we've all experienced, but I hope you will think of me and remember how I'd never ask you to do anything that would endanger you without giving you a good reason. I loved you, Eric. I still love you, in my own way. Remember that. And never forget: you have been kissed by a vampire and that is life changing, as I'm sure you have noticed. You cannot keep company with our kind and hope to remain unscathed.

Corcitura

Once marked, forever marked.

You cannot hide from your past forever. There will be a time to face your demons and that time has now come.

I've burned my bridge at both ends, Eric, and I'm standing alone in the middle.

No, that is yet another lie. I'm not as alone as you might think.

Eric, there is a child.

There, I've said it, it is done with. Now you know the reason, now you know my real purpose in writing this letter.

Come as soon as you can—and alone. Tell no one, especially not your wife. The less involved the better, for her sake and yours. A guide will be waiting to take you to Château Belododia. Meet him in the shadow of St. Vitus Cathedral. He'll know what to do.

I need you here now. Greydanus, my son, needs you more than he knows. And most of all, Stefan needs you, as unlikely as that may seem. Please, Eric. Do not forsake us as we have forsaken you.

Yours Eternally,

Leonora

My eyes had lost their ability to focus. For a change, my head was throbbing instead of my arm.

"Bad news, I take it?"

The letter was trembling in my hands...no, that wasn't right. My *hands* were trembling. The letter was perfectly still.

"No," I croaked, my throat suddenly very dry. "Just unexpected." I prayed that would satisfy my aunt. I couldn't be bothered to answer questions, not now when my mind was whirling.

What was I to make of this letter of contradictions? How could she be mine eternally, when she was bound to Stefan? Belododia, Belododia, Stefan *Bloody* Belododia. How could she have married him? Stefan needed me. Ha! Stefan needed me, as what? His next meal?

Once marked, forever marked. It was a threat and a warning. I'd known this day would come, even more so since the incident with my arm. I'd been a fool to think they'd ever let me alone.

This letter was full of lies, but I had made a rash vow, and now I was being held to account. The pull was too great to resist, as were the consequences of my inaction. I did not even want to consider what they would do to Maddie or Aunt Robbie if I didn't follow their commands. That decided me. I was being summoned to the devil's den, but I would go willingly and of my own free will. Maybe that would break some of their hold over me.

Stefan needed me. I still couldn't make sense of that little bit of information. It had a thousand and one interpretations, all of them undoubtedly fatal to me.

I balled my hand into a fist and pressed it against my forehead. None of this made sense. For all those years, she had been Salei's wife in every way but legally and then Stefan came along, a mere snip of a boy, and she married him and bore his child. It couldn't be true. It was all too disgusting, too surreal, to be true.

Marriage, I thought again, shaking my head. Vampires, married? It was laughable. And ironic, that on the very day after my own wedding, I should get a letter mocking the institution. What dammed ceremony must they have gone through, I wondered. Exchanging blood instead of rings? Oh, yes, that was lovely. I wanted to march into the drawing room and throw the letter into the fire, but something stayed my hand.

Greydanus.

The child of their union. What if there was hope for him and what he could do? In all my readings, not one of the doctors had ever outlined how to dispatch or deal with a child of two vampires. What of him, then? What part did he have to play in this macabre opera? And why did the mere saying of that name fascinate me so?

Greydanus...

"Good Morning, Aunt Robbie."

Don't bring your wife. How the devil had she known I was married? Ah, yes, how could I forget? I was marked. That meant that Leonora apparently had knowledge of everything.

My arm was definitely not a dream. I glanced down at it, expecting to see blood seeping through the fabric of my dressing gown, but there was none, thank God.

I hadn't known Madelaine was with us until I felt her draw her arms round my waist and rest her chin on my shoulder. Only then did I realize the voice that had wished my aunt good morning a moment before belonged to my wife.

"Dearest," I said, half-turning to kiss her forehead, "And how are you this fine day, Mrs. Bradburry?"

"Sleep-deprived. But more importantly, what is that?"

"This?" I asked, holding up the letter. "Oh, why, you remember that old school friend I told you about...Stefan?"

"No."

"I never told you about him?" I asked as casually as I could.

"Not that I can recall."

"But you did tell *me*."

Aunt Robbie stood before us. The expression in her eyes terrified me, for I knew that if I didn't tell Madelaine the truth, *she* would. How could I bring my wife into this? Yet how could I not?

"Well," I continued, "it seems he is married now and living in Prague and there is a child, a child who is unwell," I added hastily—for all I knew, this might have been the truth—"and since I am Stefan's dearest friend, he wants me to be at his side during this time."

"I don't see what you can do about it, my love," Madelaine said absently, no trace of resentment in her voice, "you're not a physician."

"No, but I'd feel better being there all the same."

She brushed the hair out of her eyes and yawned into her palm, then stretched her arms behind her back. Now that all traces of sleep were gone, I started to worry. She had on that look I had come to learn was her decisive look, which meant she'd brook no dissent. "Well," she said, brightening, "all right. When shall we be off?"

"*We*?" I paled. I must have done. If I'd been before a mirror, I wouldn't have recognized my pallid reflection.

"You certainly don't expect me to let you go off on your own? Eric!" she said on a laugh. "And we can easily honeymoon in Prague. I've always wanted to go there anyway. There's something so mystical and creepy about that city."

"Yes," I said slowly, letting her words sink in. She was excited and innocent...so innocent.

What was I doing to her?

"What is it, dearest?" she asked. Her face was so angelic that I felt like a monster for dragging her into this. Yet drag her into it I would. And if she were with me, I could watch her, protect her, keep her safe. *Really, Eric*, I said to myself, *how illogical is that?* Keep her safe? By forcing her to keep company with the monsters that wanted us both dead? Impossible...yet I needed her with me, needed her to keep me sane, to fight against the darkness within and without. I didn't possess the courage to face my demons alone.

"Nothing, I'm just happy you agreed so quickly," I lied.

"Then it's settled," she said, kissing me lightly on the lips. "I'll send word to Father and tell him our arrangements have changed."

I marveled over her compassion and cringed at my duplicity. My eyes were riveted to her as she made for the stairs, her robe billowing out behind her as she hastened her pace. She reached out her hand for the banister, then paused and turned round to face me. A strange light illuminated her eyes. For one sickening moment, I thought she'd found me out. Somehow, someway, she'd discovered my treachery. "I think I'll bring my violin along, too," she said. "The little fellow will need some uplifting, I daresay."

What good would music do in that abominable place? She'd be better armed with a sword and silver bullets.

"Eric, you can't do this."

"This is none of your concern," I said gruffly, pushing past my aunt and retreating to the drawing room. "I need her with me."

"No, you don't! Stefan, there can only be *one* Stefan. How can you even think of involving her in this?"

"Aunt, I...the letter. It's from Leonora."

"Damnation take Leonora! You're married to Madelaine now. Enough with that harridan who has such a hold over your heart! You don't even know if that letter is authentic! It could have been written by him."

I stared down at the paper, the black lettering running together and looking like great globs of nothingness. I hadn't even considered the possibility that the letter might be an out-and-out forgery. My conviction wasn't strengthened when I remembered that I'd never seen a scrap of anything written by Leonora. Surely this elegant script had to belong to her?

My aunt was still chuntering on, but I no longer heard her, for I'd recalled a memory.

Red lettering, viscous ink, not yet dry...a spidery scrawl.

"Answer me that, Eric. Can you say for certain that he did not disguise his handwriting? Can you swear on your life that that letter is real?"

The red script glistened in my mind's eye like a curse—a reminder I'd never forget. "This isn't Stefan's writing. I'm certain," I said, my voice like iron. "I have no choice. I must go."

"Then you will go without Madelaine. I will not have you ruining that dear girl's life as well."

"She is my wife, Aunt. Her place is by my side."

"Then you have condemned her to death!"

"You don't know that," I said, my voice catching.

"Oh, yes, I do."

"Well, it didn't happen to *me*," I said defensively, shying away from her.

"Can you be so sure of that?"

As if in answer, a flesh-searing pain tore through my arm and I doubled over in agony. I clutched at my arm, spasms knocking the breath out of me, and staggered against the fireplace.

"Good God, Eric, what the devil is this?!"

She'd ripped my hand away and torn my sleeve, revealing the secret I'd fought so desperately to keep.

"A wet cloth, quickly," I panted, "and for the love of God, be quiet about it! Madelaine does not yet know."

My mouth contorted in a rictus of pain as my vision began to blur. I banged my head back against the wood, willing myself to focus and master my emotions, for the clouding of my vision had been caused by tears. I couldn't give in to weakness now. That's exactly what *he* would want.

I winced as another fireball of pain shot up my arm. I could feel the sweat pouring into my eyes. I bit my lip and tightened my grip, my fingers making a tourniquet. The pain was unbearable. It felt as though someone had stuck a hot poker beneath my skin and was trying to rip it out through bone and flesh.

"Hurry, please," I whispered to my aunt as she knelt down beside me, damp cloth in hand. The second the cloth touched my wounds, I felt coolness spreading through my body.

Relief, salvation.

My vision cleared. I looked down tentatively, expecting to see the usual ghastly sight, but instead the skin was closing. Only faint, raised marks could still be seen. I was whole once more.

"Incredible." Aunt Robbie was looking at my arm in wonder. She reached out her fingers, then must have lost her nerve, and pulled her hand back. "It makes you wonder if they were ever there in the first place or if it was just a hallucination."

"Trust me," I said, performing the ritual of wrapping then knotting the other washcloth around my upper arm, "it was no dream. You remember that day before the windows? That little automaton with the banner? *Marked*, if you recall. Well, that was no accident. I don't know how, but that was Stefan's doing. And so is this."

"The wounds looked like they had been made by barbs."

"The barbs are a gift from his Grecian father," I said grimly, as I regained my strength. "A peculiar family characteristic I wish he hadn't inherited."

"He did this to you," she said slowly, her eyes darting back and forth as if she were trying to form her argument in her mind before speaking it aloud, "and yet you want to go to him? With Madelaine? Why, Eric," she asked, finally putting her hand on my arm, "In God's name, *why*?"

The time to face your demons is now. "Confronting him may be the only way I can stop this," I said, pointing to my arm. Aunt Robbie's eyes were fixated on my bare, no-longer-scarred skin. I carefully rolled down my sleeve and fastened the button at the cuff. Yet still she stared. It was obvious she was having trouble rationalizing the horror she'd just witnessed.

"None of this makes sense," she said, her voice an awed whisper. "You'd walk into the house, *stay* in the house, of someone who wants you dead. Someone who did *this* to you. I don't understand it."

She was right. I'd escaped Stefan and Salei by the skin of my teeth more times than I cared to dwell upon. I was also conveniently forgetting that Stefan had tried to kill me on several occasions. Why the devil *did* I think I'd be safe in his house?

Leonora.

I had to stop thinking about her. She would drive me to commit irrational acts, to place those I loved most in this world in situations that could only end in tragedy or death. I had to think clearly.

There is a child.

Well, if clear thinking produced *that* thought, then clear thinking was highly overrated. I knew I had no choice. They'd called to me and I would answer the summons...in the flesh.

I raised myself off the ground. I still hadn't got my sea legs, but I was steady enough to walk.

"Eric, please, think, reconsider." She must have seen the determination in my face, yet still she begged—pleaded, though both of us knew no amount of wheedling could deter me now.

"I've made my decision."

"Then you've made mine for me."

"What?" Something in her tone sent a thrill of panic through my chest.

"I'm telling her. Everything."

"Aunt Robbie, no, you mustn't. You'll destroy her, you'll destroy *us*."

"Yes, destroy her emotionally, not physically. Only Stefan can do that. At least Madelaine will still be alive, will still *have* a life to live after you...after you've...oh, confound it all!"

She was crying hysterically, the sobs racking her body so that her shoulders shook convulsively. I'd never seen her so fragile. The sight of her completely unhinged shocked and stunned and terrified me.

"Aunt Robbie," I said, taking her into my arms. A loud gasp escaped her and she tried to pull away, but I held firm. She beat against my chest, vainly endeavoring to break free, but finally gave in and slumped against me, defeated, when she realized I wasn't going to let her go.

"Eric, no. Please."

"I must do this. For us."

"For *her*."

"Madelaine?"

"No, Leonora. That's why you're doing this."

"No," and for the first time, I knew that to be the truth. It wasn't for Leonora and neither was it for the child. It wasn't even for Roderick or Mother or Jameson or Aunt Robbie. It was for Madelaine...and me...and in some terrible way, for Stefan as well. If I was being given the chance to not only save ourselves, but to stop whatever reign of terror Stefan had unleashed, or would unleash on us and the rest of humanity, I knew I had no choice but to take it.

"God help you, Eric. God help you both."

I prayed He would.

‡

Six weeks later, we were ready to go. Thankfully, I didn't need to think up an excuse to beg off visiting Guildy, for I'd never told Maddie of her existence. Thinking up a reason for not calling on my mother, however, had been another matter entirely, though not as impossible a task as I had feared, once I'd convinced Aunt Robbie to go along with my fiction. I just hoped my wife would believe the story of my mother's sudden holiday to Baden when I told it to her, which I planned to do once we were safely aboard the *Campania*.

The days had passed in a flurry. So much was going through my mind that I was only vaguely aware of plodding through every hour, but I *do* remember spending quite a lot of time with Molly and Steven, now the picture of near-wedded bliss. They were with us now at the edge of the pier, sending us off to what Molly called "locales unknown."

"Now, don't forget, you must be back in time for the wedding in three months."

"Wouldn't miss it for the world," I said, kissing her on the cheek.

"Bring me back a marionette," said Steven, extending his hand. "I hear they specialize in them in Prague."

I shook his hand and sighed inwardly. Steven *would* be the one to mention marionettes. Stefan's little automaton flashed through my mind, but I wasn't going to bring him up. Not when Madelaine was in such good humor.

"Of course, and when we return, I shall expect to be reading *Calamity Clark and the Demon of Death Valley*."

"Oh, well, yes, you know, onto the next and all that." Steven blushed and hooked his arm around Molly's waist.

I took Maddie's valise and turned up the gangplank after my wife. Suddenly, I felt a hand on my arm. When I looked back, Molly was standing there, her face troubled.

Good Lord, she's found out about the letter.

She and Steven had been kept in the dark. They still thought this was a honeymoon and nothing else. In fact, the only ones who knew the truth, the *real* truth, were Aunt Robbie and I.

Molly frowned at me and clutched my arm tighter. "Take care of her, Eric. She's never been abroad without her father before. You're all she's got."

"She's all I've got, too, Molly."

If you only knew.

‡

Three days out from New York, I finally told Madelaine about Mother. We were up on the aft deck watching the sunset, which had become tradition for us these past few days.

"The *Campania* is a beautiful ship," Maddie said wistfully. She was dressed all in black and looked striking against the orange glow of the setting sun, her hair loose and blowing in the wind. I gazed at her and felt uncertain about everything I'd done up to this point. This wasn't the first time this had happened. She'd always had the ability to disarm me with the least amount of effort. Sometimes, I felt like I'd known her my whole life, and at others, I felt I didn't know her at all, nor she me.

"This is the ship that brought me to America, you know," I said, wrapping my arms around her and resting my chin atop her head. "She won a Blue Riband for speed last year, so we should be in Liverpool in no time."

"Less than six days, yes. But let's not rush. This is part of the honeymoon, too. And once we get to Prague, I'll have to share you with our host."

I didn't like her phrasing, but I let it pass.

"I'd so hoped to meet your mother, Eric. Of all places to run off to, Baden, and on such short notice."

"Oh, not at all," I said, laughing nervously. "Apparently, she's been there for months. Mother's always wanted to travel and now that she has means, she's set her mind to it. The big attractions were those famous hot springs there, not to mention the casino. And she's gone off with friends, so there's no need to worry. She's quite cosmopolitan now."

My wife looked back at me quizzically, her eyebrow and the corner of her mouth doing their little simultaneous lift. That look never ceased to make me feel as though my mind were laid bare before her. Instantly, I tried to clear my head and think about anything but what had been occupying my every waking moment since I got the letter. Maddie was supposed to be the one I could share anything with, yet here I was putting up a barrier between my wife and my innermost thoughts. Our whole married life was a lie, I thought miserably. I suddenly felt as though I had a barb in my heart, so forceful was the pain. Yet I knew it wasn't anything physical nor any torture of Stefan's devising. Maybe it was my conscience, or some other unnamable prompting, but as soon as I banished that vile thought, the pain subsided.

It was no lie that I loved her. That in itself was truth enough to give me strength.

"Hmm," said my wife, her brow relaxing. "Are you sure you're not just protecting me from your mother? She doesn't have a prejudice against American girls, does she? An American, oh, Eric, the *horror*." She shuddered theatrically and nestled back against my chest. Guilt tore at my heart. I felt even worse than before. Maybe Aunt Robbie had been right. But I *needed* Maddie by my side. She was my rock, my sense in a senseless world. The lie about Mother was necessary, I kept telling myself. And besides which, I couldn't risk exposing Mother and Jameson to danger.

No, you only do that to your wife.

Oh, shut up. I was beginning to hate my suddenly vocal conscience.

"I think we should retire," I said wearily.

"Oh, *you*," she said, laughing and punching my arm playfully. I looked down at her, bewildered. I had meant something entirely different, and as I searched her upturned face, I felt a stinging behind my eyes. I couldn't fight it. My throat closed, and I felt hot tears burning my face. "What would I do without you?"

"What a soppy thing to say," she laughed, but her merriment died away almost immediately when she looked up at me. "You are not yourself," she said, her eyes grave, her voice barely above a whisper yet hard as flint. "In fact, now that I think of it, you haven't been yourself for days. You always seem to have a harried look, as though you fear someone is hunting you."

I glanced at her through narrowed lids, dreading the question I knew she'd ask next. "Why exactly are we going to Prague?"

"Why? You know perfectly well *why*." I hadn't meant to be harsh, but even *I* flinched at the venom of my tone. I felt Maddie stiffen in my arms and watched in uneasy silence as she pulled out of my embrace.

I ran my fingers through my hair and avoided my wife's eyes, which was completely unnecessary, seeing as how she'd kept her back to me and didn't seem inclined to ever look at me again.

Nonsense. A fever dream while awake.

I breathed in deeply and tried to calm myself. I was being melodramatic, yet my fear was real. It was a fear I'd had ever since I met Madelaine—wanting to possess her body and soul, yet terrified of losing her. I didn't need any help on that front. I was doing a fine job of pushing her away on my own. Over the past few days, I had been wondering if she were regretting her decision to throw in her lot with one as unstable as I was beginning to seem. Her silence now was convincing me that my surmises had been correct. I wanted nothing more than to protect her, which seemed ridiculous, given what I was doing.

What *I* was doing...*my* doing.

If anything happened to her, it'd be on my head. Her death would be my fault, the guilt my curse to live with, if I lived at all. How had I ever convinced myself this was a good idea?

"I can't do this, I can't do this."

"What can't you do?"

Had I spoken aloud? I looked at Maddie, whose face was a mask. Alarm and concern warred for supremacy, yet her voice had been as cold as ice.

"Nothing. Nothing at all. Your husband is letting the sea give him obscure and sick fancies." From the bewildered look on her face, she obviously didn't understand why I was speaking in the third person, and to be truthful, neither did I. "Come to bed, Mrs. Bradburry."

I held out my hand to her. It hung in midair for what seemed like an age before she finally, cautiously slipped her palm into mine. I tightened my fingers around hers, trying to impart some warmth to her frigid hand. I didn't know whether her coldness came from the climate or from the shock of what had passed between us—the scene I wished I could strike from both our memories, the harshness I somehow knew my wife would never forget.

Corcitura

As soon as we touched, I felt the tension, the resistance in her grasp. As I chafed her hand, her reluctance subsided somewhat and she allowed me to put my arm around her shoulder and guide her down the promenade. I prayed she wouldn't ask me any more questions, unknowingly forcing me to tell any more lies. I wanted to hold onto this semblance of unity for as long as I could. Even though our harmony was a facade, a shambles, a *lie*, I still felt safer with her near me.

Why should I not be granted a moment's peace before our world imploded?

☦

Twilight. A field in the gloaming. Dark clouds scuttling across the sky, obscuring the setting sun.

I stepped through the rippling grass, noticing with surprise that my feet were bare. I knew not where I was headed, only that I was being pulled toward whatever it was I was meant to see.

A round tower shimmered into view. I squinted my eyes and made out that it wasn't a round tower at all, but a rectangular one with four pointed, sharp-looking spires and a third broader one topping the roof. Dark brickwork covered the tower's entire front. Within the center, close to the ground, was a single wooden door. Bits of splintered wood hung from its frame and lichen had begun to grow up from the earth to cover the entire bottom half of the door. Clearly, no one had passed this way for ages.

I sensed that the door would take me somewhere I had no desire to go, yet I kept walking toward it, unable to resist. The padlock and chains hanging on the door looked impenetrable, but they fell away as soon as I stretched out my hand. Thunder roiled through the night sky. The ground shook as lightning sizzled through the air and struck a tree near me, setting it afire. Wind whipped round me, tearing at my clothes. For the first time, I noticed I was dressed only in a thin, unbuttoned shirt and breeches.

Like the beating of an overstrained heart, the throbbing shot through my arm, but I ignored it and the blood that was beginning to seep from the reopened wounds.

Just one little push...

I brushed my fingers against the wood; the door gave way.

Inside, there was darkness so thick it hurt to stare into its black depths. There was nothing within, nothing...

...but a pair of pupilless orbs staring at me.

Stefan.

No, it was not him.

It was me.

Or what used to be me.

Soulless eyes, bared fangs...a thing no longer of this earth.

"Welcome to the house of the undead."

‡

"*No!*"

"Eric, *Eric*, what is it?! Wake up, you're having a nightmare!"

I was soaked in sweat, but instead of finding myself in that godforsaken field, I was here, safe, in my bed in my cabin aboard the *Campania*, my wife lying at my side. It had all been a dream, a nightmare, except that a dull pain in my arm still remained, but there was no blood, no evidence, thank goodness.

Maddie stared at me. I shrank from her gaze. Her eyes were so piercing, so knowing.

"You must be cold," I said huskily, pulling the blanket around her bare shoulders. "Go back to bed. It was only a dream, I assure you. Nothing more."

She was still staring at me as though she didn't believe a word I said. Gently, without taking her eyes from my face, she reached out and closed her hand over my arm. Her fingers felt cool on my hot skin. The sparks I felt whenever we touched shot through my body. I leaned down to kiss her, but suddenly she tore away, holding her finger to her mouth.

"What is it?" My throat had gone dry. I could barely croak out any words. She hadn't merely put her finger to her mouth. She was sucking at a wound, a wound I'd somehow caused.

"When did that happen? And what did you get sutures for?"

"Sutures?" I felt the room beginning to spin. Absently, I looked down at my arm. Either I was hallucinating, or Stefan was growing impatient and becoming more generous with his gifts. A barb, so tiny that it appeared to be nothing more than a black speck, was protruding from the opening wounds in my skin.

"I think I need some air." I grabbed my clothes off the floor and hastily threw them on. As soon as the door shut behind me, I was off, racing down the corridor like a man possessed. In some ways, I suppose I was. You couldn't have an undead man gnaw on your arm and expect to get away scot-free.

The sea air struck me hard in the face as I burst out on deck. I raced toward the railing and leaned over, not caring that I was dangerously close to toppling into the ocean. I sniffed in the salt air, willing it to somehow turn sanctified and cleanse me of my demons.

"Tell me more about Stefan."

How long had she been there? She looked so solitary and remote, dressed all in black from her head to her slippers. Yet the color of her clothes was not the only reason for this. Her face showed no warmth either. Everything about her was forbidding and closed off, as though she wanted nothing to do with me. Could I really blame her? My actions had given her just cause to doubt my character, not to mention my sanity.

Her dark hair was still loose and fell over her arms, which she'd crossed, hugging herself. Normally, she would have been hugging me for warmth, I noted bitterly. I saw she'd bandaged the finger I'd cut. I couldn't help looking at the white cloth, couldn't stop myself from staring at the red blot where the blood had left its mark. Hastily, she tucked in her hand and hugged herself tighter, making no move to come to me for comfort.

"Tell me more about him," she said, rubbing her arms and not moving an inch closer to me. "I feel I should know something about our host, don't you think?"

"He was nothing more than an old school friend. That's all."

"Then why rush to his side?"

"The child, his wife's child, and his as well...they want to christen him"—God forgive me this blasphemy—"and I'm to be his godparent."

"I don't recall you mentioning that," she said, her voice still hard and cold, her eyes narrowing suspiciously. "I thought the child was ill."

"It must have slipped my mind, what with all the other things I had to think of." The last thing I wanted was to sound defensive, but that's how I came across. "Besides, the child is ill, so it makes sense to christen it now of all times, does it not?"

"It just seems odd he'd call on you after all these years."

"I know, but Stefan was always an odd sort."

"Yes, he must have been. Tell me more about his wife, the mysterious Leonora. She seems quite an enigmatic figure. Always flitting in and out of your narratives. She seems never to stay in place quite long enough for me to get a straight answer about her character."

I had no response to that accusation. What could I say that I hadn't already? How many more lies could I tell before Madelaine shattered them all and discovered the truth?

"I can't help feeling that you and she were more than just mere acquaintances."

"I met her a few times, that's all. Nothing more."

"Do you not trust me, Eric?" she said suddenly, her eyes flashing in the moonlight.

I was stung. Of course I trusted her. How could I not? She'd never done anything to endanger me, never given me any reason to doubt her. "Dearest, I trust you with my life."

"Yes, but who can I trust with mine?"

I felt as though I had been stabbed. The pain that shot through my heart was more piercing than the bite from any barb had ever been. If she doubted, that meant she knew. She might not know *all*, but she knew I was keeping secrets—lying.

Treachery. Her husband was using her, of that much she must have been certain. I knew not what to say, nor what, if anything, could calm her fears. I wanted nothing more than to kiss her then, to hold her to me tightly, to make her understand why I was doing this to us. But she wouldn't come to me of her own accord, and I didn't have the courage to act on my desires.

She shook her head and bit her lip and turned on me a look I will never forget. The look in her eyes wasn't anger, nor fear.

Disappointment.

I'd let her down. I'd failed her, and I didn't know if I'd ever be able to regain her trust. She'd given me one last chance, one last moment to come clean, to tell her everything, and I'd lied yet again.

Silently, she turned and walked down the promenade, leaving me alone in the dark...alone with my fears, my doubts, my guilt.

I should have burned that damned letter when I had the chance.

‡

Ten days later, we found ourselves in Prague. Over Nuremburg and into this most mysterious of Eastern capitals. That had been the plan. I hadn't taken any chances. I didn't want to come anywhere near the route I'd taken on that cursed trip that had changed my life. Nor did I have any desire to visit the countries I had been spirited through while unconscious. My one saving grace was that I clung to the urgency of the note, which mollified Maddie. She hadn't protested when I told her of my plan to reach our final destination via an uncommon route, nor had she complained when I dissuaded her from staying in Paris. In fact, we'd bypassed Paris completely and she'd not said a word.

Something had happened since that night on the ship. It was almost as if she'd retreated into herself and was just going along with me to keep the peace. I hoped that wasn't the case. The thing I loved about her most was her fiery nature. I would hate myself forever if I'd been the one to extinguish that flame.

I had also feared she'd insist on separate cabins after what had passed between us, but she'd not made that demand. In some ways, she'd become listless when it came to our traveling. On several mornings, she'd even woken up rather unwell, but when I'd asked what was wrong, she said it was just that she wasn't used to the movements of ships or trains or the other conveyances we were taking. The one thing she did insist on was getting to Prague as quickly as possible. At every stage, she made clear her desire that we hurry on for the child's sake. I think she feared he might succumb to his illness if we tarried. I didn't have the heart to tell her that his sickness was of the phantom variety. She was all solicitousness for Greydanus. It was strange how she'd taken to the idea of the child so strongly.

The idea of the child...I'd never thought of that before.

What if the child didn't even exist?

What if Aunt Robbie had been right and this had all been an elaborate ruse to entrap me?

No, not Leonora, she wouldn't be so duplicitous. She *couldn't* be. Yet what did I know of her, *truly* know of her?

Nothing, I realized, my heart sinking. Naught but my own ideals and fancies.

I was driving myself insane with these thoughts. Hindsight would do me no good now, not when I was in their territory, their adopted homeland, as I'd come to think of this city. It was strange how much it affected me to be here. On crossing the border, I had felt somehow even more apprehensive, if that were possible. I was more on edge, as if I expected every single person I passed of having vampiric tendencies. Who was to say they didn't masquerade as the living during the day, then transform into something nightmarish when the moon rose? Absurd notions, the lot of them, yet I couldn't shake off the feeling of familiarity, of kinship to this place. I think it must have been because Prague reminded me so strongly of Brasov, only on a grander scale and far more cosmopolitan. It possessed that same air of mysticism, that same unsettling feeling that a presence lurked just below the surface, waiting to pounce.

I breathed in deeply, letting the scent of Prague fill my lungs. *Prague*, with its Gothic spires and marionette shops, its *leering* marionettes, I thought, grimacing as I passed a shop chock-full of the smiling wooden devils. I remembered Steven's request and pushed it out of my mind. When I was in a better state, I'd venture into that shop and buy him his souvenir. But not now, not when I was having trouble distinguishing reality from nightmares.

We rounded a corner, and I stopped so suddenly I heard the bones in my knees crack in protest. Looming before me, solid, imposing, towering, was a sight I thought I'd never see with my waking eyes.

Everything was the same. The five-spired top, its turrets jutting into the sky. An exact replica, save for the gaping archway where the padlocked door had been.

It was the tower from my dream.

"Aren't you coming?"

I glanced through the archway. Madelaine was already halfway across the bridge. If there had been a way for me to cross over without going through that tower, I would have taken that route in a heartbeat.

My mind was still reeling as I tried to make sense of this apparition. I'd seen paintings of the entrance to Charles Bridge before. That must have been it. That *had* to have been it. But why it should have taken on another aspect, a hidden aspect with that padlocked door, in my dream, I could not say.

"Eric, the guide, I'm sure he's waiting. What's the matter?"

"No, stay there, I'm coming over." Slowly, cautiously, I walked underneath the arch, and breathed a sigh of relief as I crossed to the other side. I don't know what I had been expecting. Maybe some unseen gargoyle hurtling stones at me from within as I passed through? I needed to control myself. My wife already suspected me of being unhinged. One more sick fancy and it would become a self-fulfilling prophecy.

I accepted Madelaine's arm and latched onto the stone railing of the bridge for support, catching sight for the first time of the little boats motoring along the Vltava. Now I knew yet another reason why I felt so uneasy. This place reminded me so much of Venice...*too* much.

As we walked along, we passed dozens of statues. I was grateful for the distraction these provided, for with each step we took, we drew nearer to St. Vitus's looming hulk—and our guide. I didn't even want to think who or what this might be.

But the statues held my attention, for how could they fail to? There were so many of them spaced evenly along either side of the bridge. I stopped counting after the first twenty. At one point, I recognized St. Francis of Assisi, flanked on either side by angels. And at another, there was the commanding figure of Christ on the Cross.

The moon had risen by the time we reached St. Vitus. Had we been walking so long? Or had I just let myself become so enthralled by the statues that I had lost all track of time?

I gazed up at the cathedral, craning my neck to see the top, which was impossible, given the gloom of the sky. Massive and mightier than Notre Dame was St. Vitus. It had a rose window, but that's where the similarities ended. Its spires pointed straight up into the blackness of the night, infinitely high, like two spears reaching toward heaven. I knew this cathedral wasn't older than its sister in Paris, though the original, smaller St. Vitus had been constructed first. Even so, it *seemed* older, both in appearance and something else. It *felt* old, as though it had stood at this spot, a silent stone sentinel, for all eternity. I shivered and pulled my coat in tighter. Reaching for Maddie's hand, my palm closed around air.

Frantic, I glanced up and saw the statue of St. Michael spearing the devil. What I wouldn't give to be able to arm myself with that spear right now.

God, no, no, not my wife. It was happening already. They'd come for her.

Desperately, I hunted around the square, white spots dancing before my eyes in the darkness. Nobody was there but a few passing worshippers and some milling policemen.

Maddie was nowhere in sight.

I could feel the panic rising in my throat, threatening to turn into a scream, when I heard a laugh.

Maddie's laugh.

There could be no mistaking that sound I loved. Suddenly, she was before me, several feet off, talking to a man whose face I couldn't see. He was all in shadow, a black clad figure wearing what looked to be a roquelaure—a black roquelaure identical to the one I had seen draped around that man who had disappeared into an alley in New York...disappeared into an alley almost immediately before Stefan had revealed himself to me.

My heart was hammering. Who this man was or what he wanted with my wife, I didn't know, but I was going to put an end to their little conversation regardless of his intentions.

I set off at a brisk walk, which didn't take long to turn into a run, and in a moment I was at her side.

"Eric! You'll never guess," she said. I was so relieved to hear the happiness in her voice that I allowed myself a smile. "I've found our guide."

"Fancy meeting you here, Monsieur Bradburry."

I felt as though a dead hand had reached up from the grave and squeezed my heart till I could no longer breathe. I knew that voice. The Gallic lilt, the harried tone that had not changed in nearly seven years.

Luc.

"Should I say Mademoiselle, or is it Madame?"

"Madame, yes. Madelaine Bradburry. Now, what did you say your name was again, Monsieur..."

"Luc. Just Luc."

Monsieur Sans-Surname, resurrected from the dead to infect my life once more.

I stared at this phantom of my past. The last I'd seen of him, he was sprawled on his back at the feet of Vladec Salei.

I'd given him up for lost and now here he was, grinning that lopsided, self-satisfied grin that had once infuriated me. He looked the same, though there was a vacancy to his eyes that hadn't been there before and lines around his mouth. Frown lines. I expected he no longer had any reason to smile.

"How is your family?" I asked, extending my hand.

"No longer troubled by the cares of this world."

That was all the answer I needed.

"Shall we be going, then?"

He took Madelaine's valise and violin case and held out his hand toward a coach and four that I had not seen there a minute ago.

Vampiric magic? Who knew?

"How long have you been with the Belododias, Luc?" asked my wife. She had livened up considerably since encountering our guide. I didn't know whether to be happy about that or not. Maddie naturally took to people, but what if her sudden cheeriness was the result of Luc exerting one of his *gifts*? A wraith, he'd once called himself. *All the symptoms but none of the perks.*

"It feels like forever sometimes."

Maddie shot me a worried look. I commiserated, but kept walking toward the coach.

"Surely, that can be a good thing?"

"Here we are, Madame," said Luc, not meeting her eyes. He let down the step and helped her into the coach. "We are about an hour's journey out. Settle in for the ride, Madame et Monsieur. It will be a long one."

I expected Maddie to be bursting with questions, but the curiosity she had displayed in Luc's presence vanished the moment she settled into the coach. She was silent and reserved once more and spent her time gazing out the window at the never-ending line of trees we passed.

I was growing restless and wanted nothing more than to be out of this coach. The forest had grown thicker the deeper we traveled into it, darkness closing in around us oppressively. Occasionally, flashes of light brightened our windows as the moon fought through the tangle of trees, but these moments were fleeting.

Luc, for his part, was silent, too. Twice I stuck my head out of the window to make sure he hadn't betrayed us and fled, and twice I had seen his hunched, cloaked form sitting up on the box. He was cowed and bent and looked a hundred years old from this vantage point. What the devil had happened to him since I'd seen him last?

The devil had happened to him.

It was her voice once again, louder this time because I was getting nearer. I shifted my weight and felt the pearls of her necklace pressing into my side. I shoved my hand into my coat pocket and tightened the strings of the bag I'd stored the necklace in, cinching it closed. As soon as the moment arose, I'd give her back this cursed trinket that I still believed had something to do with Leonora's hold over me.

I put my arm around Maddie's shoulder and drew her close, feeling warmer the moment I touched her. For the thousandth time since we left New York, I doubted my course of action. Why had I brought her? I should have listened to Aunt Robbie, should have let her take Maddie somewhere safe, for *they* obviously knew where to find my aunt if they'd found me so easily. Yet here I was, moments away from thrusting us into hell, and I had no one to blame for the consequences but myself.

A loud rapping jolted us both. Maddie jumped in my arms. She was just as apprehensive as I was, though she was putting up a brave front. She knew there was something wrong with this whole situation, yet she hadn't said a word in protest. She was either incredibly trusting—which I knew not to be the case—or she kept her own counsel and made her own plans, which was the more likely scenario of the two. My wife was no simpleton, but her judgment was clouded when it came to one thing.

Me.

"We are pulling in now," said Luc through the window. I hadn't even noticed there was a tiny pane of glass near the box, for black curtains had covered it. Now I saw his shaggy head peeking through and noticed something unnatural in his eyes.

He slid the window closed as the coach ground to a halt. I had clasped Maddie's hand and was holding it so tightly I was surprised she didn't twist out of my grasp. But then I felt a return pressure. She was clinging to me just as fiercely as Luc threw open the door and waved us out.

"Here we are at last. The keeper of the castle awaits."

"A castle in the forest," I heard Maddie whisper, her tone freezing the blood in my veins.

The vista spreading out before us was simultaneously breathtaking and dreadful. A massive grey stone castle dating from at least the thirteenth century sprawled across the lawn. A large, triple-spired clock tower shot up from the center of what I had come to think of as the fortress, looking forbidding and medieval in the moonlight. The tower was imposing and impossibly high and looked quite similar to the entrance to Charles Bridge back down in the city, which felt like a world away. It was so isolated here in this castle in the forest. All my fears of Prague suddenly seemed ridiculous. I wished that I could be back in town, hiding in that marionette shop. Anywhere would be better than this place.

Luc mumbled something and led us on. I looked once more at the bulwark and the dozens of fir trees growing rampantly around it. Several large creepers had already snaked up the bricks and embedded themselves between the mortar. Wild thoughts were going through my mind then, for I envisioned myself using these vines to escape from the highest windows.

Eric, get a hold of yourself. I couldn't think like this. I needed to be strong, needed to stay focused. Sanity was now my only defense.

We rounded the castle and came to a halt. Before us was a chapel in ruins. I felt something grab my hand and turned to see Maddie staring straight ahead. The look in her eyes terrified me. I hadn't seen what she had, and I didn't want to.

As I passed the chapel, I looked through the crumbling stonework at what was within. A white stone iron maiden had been propped in one corner. A large catafalque took up the breadth of the center of the chapel. Something was crouched on the bier, something that squawked and flapped leather wings.

"Eric, are those..."

"Vultures. Come along, Madelaine." I wasn't going to tell her what I'd seen. I didn't even believe it myself. I *had* thought they were vultures, carrion birds, eaters of the dead. That would have been fitting, but the creatures I'd seen belonged to the fog-shrouded confines of myth.

I'd seen these beasts immortalized in the golden necklaces worn by Stefan's sisters and in the head of the staff that could kill Vladec Salei. These were the living representations of his emblem.

Wyverns.

There were four of them, small yet vicious. They were tearing something to shreds, fighting amongst themselves for the largest portion of their spoils. I swallowed hard and passed on, hoping whatever it was they were devouring had died quickly and had not been human.

I glanced at my wife to see if her terror had subsided, but she was staring straight ahead with that same wide-eyed look of fear.

"The family that sins together *dies* together," I heard Luc mutter. I didn't have the slightest idea what he meant, until I saw that he, though weary, had the same terrified look in his eyes that my wife did. So Luc was not as jaded as I'd believed.

A hill rose to our left. Dotting its sides and crowding every available bit of land underneath it were headstones— large ones, squat ones, black ones, and stark white ones. Every manner you could imagine—thousands of them all in our backyard. Atop the hill was a crumbling wreck of round stone that must have once been a mausoleum.

What a lovely view we'd wake to every morning.

If there was one blessing to be found this night, it was that we didn't have to traverse this land of the dead. Luc beckoned us to follow him. We were only too eager to leave behind this macabre tableau.

I was regretting my decision to come here more and more. There were so many of them, those headstones. I couldn't get them out of my mind. I wondered if this really was Stefan's ancestral home or if he'd just robbed someone of it, then set about filling that graveyard with victims over the years. That was giving him too much credit, though. I doubted he'd take the time to bury his dead, let alone mark their graves.

We marched through the verge and undergrowth. After a few moments, we had walked the breadth of the castle and had come upon a new section. The lawns were just as overgrown here, but they were somehow beautiful in their chaos. A large lake, whose grey water was pocked with algae and lichen and a sickly yellow blooming flower I could not name, covered almost the entire lawn. As I looked at the castle, I realized we had come upon it from the back and were now finally standing at its front. I spied several more turrets as we made our way around to the entrance. Tessellated brick ran along the roof and dormer windows were tucked underneath nearly every gable.

As we walked on, I caught sight of a semi-circular tower with a small balcony at its top. It was tucked back from the main part of the house and would have been beautiful had it not been so precariously high and shrouded in gloom. Underneath this tower, there was a large bay window. My eyes were drawn to it, why, I could not say. There was nothing remarkable about the window, nor the tower, nor anything, really, but I was mesmerized. Maybe it was another fancy or maybe it was her in truth, but I was sure I saw a dark-haired figure at that window looking down at me.

"Absurd," I muttered.

"Is it?" Maddie's eyes were still wide, but they had lost their terror-stricken look. She was adjusting well to the situation, much better than I was, but there was no denying the reproach in her voice, nor the fear that had made it crack. Things couldn't get any worse this night, I thought to myself.

And then it began to snow.

"Lovely, just lovely."

"I've always thought so. Nothing like a little blizzard to ensure you can't escape, eh?"

Corcitura

My mouth hung open as I watched Luc saunter off. He always said the right thing. As if my nerves weren't already frayed enough.

We reached the main door. I couldn't help breathing a sigh of relief. I'd been expecting an iron door studded with spikes. That iron maiden in the chapel had put me in mind of a torture chamber, so why should the entrance to this place be any less forbidding? I was shocked it wasn't a portcullis.

The door was by no means unimposing, though. It was at least thirteen feet high and made of wood so smooth I could see all three of us reflected in its surface. I looked up and had to force myself not to stumble back. I hadn't noticed the knocker until then. I balled up my hands into fists and made myself stay steady. I couldn't give in now, not when I was on the threshold of my worst nightmare.

Stay strong, stay focused. They cannot harm you unless you give them your consent.

The shape of the knocker was even more familiar to me after the refresher I'd been given not five minutes ago. It was the selfsame wyvern's head that had adorned the sword I'd stolen from Stefan in Venice, the sword that had drawn no blood when I'd stabbed him with it.

"Maybe we should stay somewhere else." It was an asinine thing to say, but I couldn't think up anything that would have sounded reasonable at such a moment as this.

"Why on earth are you whispering?" Luc asked gruffly. Before I could stop him, he reached out and banged the knocker three times. The booming shook the frame and clanged horribly through the stillness of the night.

"Loud enough to wake the dead," I heard him say under his breath. I stared at him, my heart beating furiously, and waited...*waited*...for what, I didn't know.

"Maybe no one's home?"

"I assure you, Madame Bradburry, they're here. They know you're coming. They've been waiting for you."

As if in answer, I heard something moving behind the door. Footsteps so soft it defied logic that I should hear them. But hear them I did, and I wasn't the only one. Maddie was straining to hear, too.

One of the round bronze handles began to twist. It creaked and grated and protested until it could no longer resist. I shuddered as the door slowly opened. My heart was in my throat. All I could think of was the dream, the nightmare, and my own sightless eyes staring out at me from the darkness.

Welcome to the house of the undead.

With a scrape and a moan, the door was pulled inward. My eyes roved over the opening, searching for the one who had unlocked the door. I was expecting to see Stefan, yet there was no one there. But wait...I was mistaken. There *was* someone there, only he was very small and very grave.

And he looked *exactly* like me.

Greydanus.

"Welcome to my father's house," he said, his black eyes staring straight ahead. "Welcome to Château Belododia."

The Tightening of the Noose

"*I*'m sure there's a perfectly rational explanation for why that child looks *exactly* like you," my wife hissed as we followed the boy inside."

"Honestly," I said, my eyes glued to the child's back, "I'm just as stunned as you are."

"That's very reassuring."

What a fool I was not to understand her anger until this moment.

"Maddie, please, you cannot think, you cannot imagine..."

"I don't know what I think, Eric," she said wearily. "I'm not sure if I even know *you*."

"Madelaine, don't say that, *please*."

"Save this talk for a later time."

"But I want you to believe me. We cannot let this go unresolved."

"Oh, don't worry. I have no intention of letting this go. But we can't talk here. And besides, look." I followed her gaze and froze. "It seems our host has come to greet us."

I might as well have been back in London. For all the years that had passed, the minute I set eyes on him I felt as though I'd not been parted from him for a single day. There was something so uncannily familiar about him, as though he still retained some semblance of the old Stefan, yet I'd be deceiving myself if I said he hadn't changed. He *had* and not for the better. His hair was longer and slicked back in a fashion he'd never adhered to when I'd known him. His attire was darker and more formal and his eyes, though now almost fully translucent, save for the black pinpricks in their centers, were somehow older, hungrier, crueler.

"Eric, *Eric*, it has been too long." His accent was less pronounced than it had been that night in Venice after his first feast of blood, but there was a cultivation to his voice that was not his own.

I had to check myself. I had almost said, *You have become Vladec Salei.*

"Indeed, much too long," I said, extending my hand. The coldness of his grip stunned me, but I rallied before Maddie could notice my discomfort.

"My brother," he said, those clear orbs boring into me. We were locked in a silent war, my former best friend and I. Unspoken curses, threats, accusations, passed between his eyes and mine. I tightened my grip and so did he, and if not for him suddenly taking note of Greydanus, I've no idea how long we would have stood like this.

"Ah, so my son has seen fit to play butler tonight," he said, releasing my hand as he turned to the child. The look he gave the boy was pitiless, filled with scorn. The child stood with his head bowed, his hands clasped before him, not meeting his father's eyes.

"Come here, boy," said Stefan, snapping his fingers. The boy's head darted up, his eyes like a startled rabbit's, and he came forward, bowing his head once again as he walked. Stefan laid his hands on the child's shoulders, digging his fingers into the red fabric, digging deeper than was necessary. Had I been Greydanus, I would have flinched, cried out in pain, shown *some* sign of life, but all the child did was stare at me. I saw his lip tremble slightly, but then he bit it to hide this betrayal of emotion.

What had Stefan done to this boy?

"I wonder where your mother's run off to, Grey? Where *can* she be? I would have thought she would be the first one to greet our guests. Oh! Wait! I do believe I hear her!"

"Has he always been this theatrical?" Maddie whispered to me. I shrugged my shoulders, for this new attitude was beyond baffling, not to mention unsettling. He was acting so odd, so alien to that quiet, albeit *vindictively* quiet, man he used to be that I wondered if this was what Leonora meant when she said he'd changed. Still, that unnaturally raised voice, the fervid gleam in his eyes—it was all too much, too false, too staged, as if he were trying too hard to convince me he was different.

"Darling, our guests have arrived."

I hadn't paid any attention to our surroundings until I saw her standing at the top of the double winged, black stone staircase. She was still all in white, still a living statue of alabaster. Her lips were blood red, her eyes just as black as her hair, save for a stark streak of white that trailed out from the middle of her scalp. What had caused this? Shock? Yet what could shock a vampire?

She blinked at me, breaking my trance. I refocused on her face. She hadn't aged a day, but really, why should she have when she was no longer bound by the strictures of mortality?

"Eric," she breathed. Was it traitorous for my heart to leap at the sound of her voice?

"No kiss, my love?" Stefan grabbed her wrist and pulled her toward him, while with the other hand he dug his fingernails so fiercely into his son's shoulders that Greydanus finally did wince and let out a squeal. What a happy family picture they presented.

"Displays of affection should be left for behind closed doors, *dearest*," Leonora said. I saw something feral pass before her eyes. Stefan must have seen it, too, for he dropped her wrist and let her pass.

Ignoring Maddie and her son, she held out her hand to me. I took it, disregarding its coldness, but would not kiss it. Maddie had been betrayed enough already. I wouldn't add to her pain.

As she drew closer to me, I was startled to see her eyes shining with tears. I was reminded of that night on the boat to Greece, the night I'd held her in my arms.

"I had forgotten your kind could cry. It always seemed so impossible to me."

"All things are possible if you believe they can happen. And I am much more than a vampire," she whispered in a tone only I could hear. I didn't know what her words meant, but they comforted me. She pulled away and smiled at me warmly. When she caught sight of Maddie, the smile disappeared.

I saw the alarm in Leonora's eyes and turned away. I'd failed them both—Leonora, who'd warned me not to bring my wife and Maddie, who was still oblivious to my treachery.

"Leonora," said Maddie. Before any of us knew what she was about, she'd walked up to Leonora and wrapped her arms around her. It wasn't an affectionate hug, but I could tell it stunned Leonora all the same. She stood with her arms hanging by her sides, looking more statue-like than ever, until it was done.

"We are delighted to be here, *my* husband and I both." You'd have to be an idiot not to take her meaning, and Leonora was no idiot. I saw her lips flick up a notch at the corners. The boundaries had been made clear. There was no longer any question whom I belonged to.

"What a pretty pair you two are." Stefan's touch made my flesh crawl. Though I was heavily coated, I could feel the coldness of his fingers down to my bones. As casually as I could, I shook his hand off my shoulder, swallowing hard when I noticed the look on his face. Apparently, I hadn't been as casual as I'd hoped.

"You both must be *starving* after such a long journey. Come, come, leave Luc to deal with your bags."

I had forgotten Luc's presence, but he must have been there the whole time, keeping to the shadows. He was quite good at that, I reflected ruefully, thinking back to New York. That's the way he'd found me, after all.

He hefted the valises and receded into the darkness without a word. There were so many things I wanted to ask him, so many secrets I wanted him to reveal, but Maddie was pulling me away. I looked over my shoulder, hoping to catch sight of Luc and give him a sign that I wanted to meet with him, but he was gone, so I let Maddie lead me toward the staircase.

I was puzzled that we were ascending to the dining hall, but then I realized that the foyer was just one big room with no doors leading off it. The alcove we'd been welcomed into had been so dark that the sudden brightness of the foyer was almost too much. I'd seen the glow behind Leonora as she dismounted the stairs. Now that I was fully exposed to it, the brightness was so fierce that it was almost painful to keep my eyes open for more than a few seconds in this place. Several sideboards and chests circled the edges of the room. On every open space—window seats, recesses, shelves—multi-branched candelabra were blazing with an unnatural brilliance.

Weren't vampires supposed to hate sunlight? But candlelight was artificial. Maybe some part of them did long for light, but they had to settle for the substitute, since the real thing was deadly to their kind. Leonora had never had any issues with this that I could recall, and Stefan...well, what rules applied to him? This overabundance of light must have been some quirk of his, some secret way of flaunting his superiority over the strictures of his less fortunate brothers. I shook my head and passed on, thankful for the gloom that enveloped us as we traveled higher and higher up the stairs.

"So, I suppose that was another lie."

"What?" I'd been concentrating so hard on the radiance below that I hadn't known Maddie was talking to me.

"About the child," she said, sighing. "He doesn't look sick to me."

I stared at Greydanus's back as he led us on. My wife was right, but I was not going to admit to yet another lie. "Look at him," I whispered, "he's wasting away. Anyone can see that." I didn't believe this for an instant. Apart from a natural paleness and the gravity of his character, he looked remarkably healthy for a vampire.

"Those blood red lips say otherwise."

She unhooked her arm from mine and caught up with Greydanus, trying to engage him in conversation. She was right. He'd inherited those blood red lips from his mother...and I prayed that color was indeed due to heredity.

"Not much happens around here. I'm glad you've come." The child's mouth rose at the corners as my wife smiled down at him. There was something odd about that child. Well, *obviously* there was something odd, but I wasn't talking vampiric-wise. He seemed somehow different, uncorrupted. How on earth could such a child belong to Stefan?

"Don't talk to your elders, boy, when they haven't asked for your opinion." Stefan glared down at his son, the child shrinking back from his father's eyes. "Now, shall we?" Stefan said, turning those crystal clear orbs on us. "I've a splendid feast set out for you both."

With one hand he pushed open doors that would have given Samson difficulty and ushered us into a long, ill-lit room.

Dangling from the raftered ceiling were a brace of chandeliers, their candles nearly burned to their wicks, dripping wax hardened over gold that once must have shone as brilliantly as the sun. The contrast between this room and the foyer was stark. My heart began to throb. I didn't understand why, until my thoughts reordered themselves and my mind raced down a different road. What if the reason for this darkness was to hide something? What if they did not like to see what they ate?

I saw that there was nothing on their plates. In fact, there were no plates at all, nor goblets, nor utensils. *Nothing.*

Yet the table was not completely empty. At the far end of the table, laid out before a pair of high-backed chairs, were two pewter plates.

Our dinner.

Meat looking like it had been just torn off the bone and globs of something white that must have once been potatoes were drowning in a thick red sauce that I could only hope had been made from red wine.

I suddenly lost my appetite.

"Aren't you eating?" asked Maddie as I pushed her chair closer toward the table. She was trying to keep from looking at the plate.

"We take our meals later than most," Stefan answered.

"Father's had bad hunting of late."

Was I mistaken or did I see a gleam of triumph in the child's eyes? Stefan paled, or became paler, as it were, and ignored the boy's remark. Frankly, I didn't understand why the child was being allowed to join his parents for dinner. Stefan certainly didn't seem like a permissive father.

"Just last night you said that food tastes like ash and has not satisfied in ages. That's why you're here," he said, turning a smile on us. It was simultaneously the most angelic and hellish thing I'd ever seen in my life.

"Confound it all, Greydanus," Stefan thundered, crashing his fist against the table, "you will not speak unless spoken to!"

"What does he mean?" Maddie's voice was thin, shaking, terrified. I didn't trust myself to speak, for my voice would have sounded the same.

Too late I was realizing this had all been a trap.

"You will bring him luck, that's all he meant." Leonora's black eyes stared out at me from the gloom at the opposite end of the table. I found no comfort in her look, and her words did nothing to dispel the foreboding in my heart.

Her voice had been reedy, too.

"Come, come, we've so much to reminisce over without this brat spoiling everything."

"Run along to bed, Grey. I'll be up to tuck you in later." The child's eyes were riveted on Leonora as he pushed back his chair and slowly walked toward the door.

"And I to have a word about this little incident." Greydanus cast a worried look at his father, but remained silent as he walked away.

I turned back to my meal, determined to make some headway with the mash on my plate, when I heard a horrendous scraping sound. Stefan's chair was pushed back nearly toward the door. His hands where clamped around his son's arm. It almost looked as if he were trying to wrench it off.

I rose from my seat, but knew at once there was no need to get involved. This was a private battle—and no longer physical.

If they could have killed each other with their eyes they would have. Greydanus, his jaw working silently, stared into his father's face, and Stefan stared back. In their eyes was hatred like I'd never seen before. For those brief minutes, Greydanus wasn't a child of God knew what age—he was a man, old before his time. When he blinked, Stefan released his grip and slumped back in his chair, and I was left wondering what had just happened.

"Well," Stefan said, his voice ragged, "now that *that* unpleasantness has passed." He shoved his chair back toward the table and resettled himself as though nothing had occurred.

"How could you treat him so cruelly?" I thought Maddie was on the verge of tears, until I looked at her face. There was no sadness there. I'd never seen my wife so furious.

"What, that horrid little boy? I hate the sight of him. If it weren't for his unusual gifts, I'd swear he wasn't even my child. But there's no denying he inherited his father's unique skills, if you take my meaning."

Maddie looked at me with wild eyes, but I just shook my head. I'd face a barrage of accusations and questions once we were alone.

"Frankly, my good son, I never thought I'd see you again, much less here, especially after what happened between us."

Another burning look from Maddie. "What would that be?" she demanded.

"Eric knows what I mean." Where it came from, I don't know, but suddenly a tall crystal chalice was before him. I bit my tongue to keep from retching. The same dark viscous liquid swirled within the glass. I had seen that substance before, one night long ago in a vampire den in Venice.

Sangue di Vita.

Stefan lifted the glass to his lips, drank long and deep. "I see that's caught your attention."

I turned to Maddie and said in a whisper, "Let's just say Stefan and I didn't have the best of partings."

He snorted so fiercely, I was surprised the liquid didn't spurt out of his nose. "Well, *that's* an understatement."

Shut up, Stefan, shut up.

I intend to do nothing of the sort.

Where had his voice come from? He was sipping from that blasted chalice, so how could he have spoken? I looked up at Leonora, whose face was unreadable. Maybe she'd taught him that little trick. I tried to close off my thoughts, but I could still feel his presence. What a horrifying feeling it was not even to have privacy in my own mind.

"The years have been kind to you, old friend. And have you made new acquaintances?"

"Yes, several," I said uneasily, picking at my food, trying to keep my mind blank. I didn't like where this conversation was heading.

"Ah, but no one like Sorina, I'd wager."

My fork clattered against the plate. "Of course not."

"*Sorina?*" The accusation in Maddie's voice was undeniable. "And what happened to *her?*"

"Poor girl, she lost her head in Greece. We never did hear from her again. She just went poof, as they say. I expect she's in warmer climes now, wouldn't you agree, Eric?"

I watched him sip that redder than red liquid. Oh, yes, he was pleased with himself. No one could fail to see that, not with that smirk plastered on his face.

He set down the glass and tented his fingers. I couldn't help staring. How could I not have noticed them when he'd nearly stabbed them through his son's shoulder? There could be no denying them now. They protruded longer than any normal ones should have—long, sharp, brittle, yellowed with an age their master had not yet attained. They reminded me of a pair I'd seen before but had tried to forget. Razor sharp nails—just like his father's. I curled my fingers into my palm, suddenly feeling disgusted.

"I'm not fastidious by nature," he said, looking down at his hands. "If you'd stayed around longer, you would have learned this. But enough about me. Do you remember that day in Paris?"

"When you and Luc went off to degrade yourselves," I said with the ghost of a smile. Maybe he'd given up on the former path and just wanted conversation.

Hardly.

"No, no, not that time. I mean that day you flitted off to the Musée Grévin. What fun you must have had amongst all those waxworks. I believe that was the day you sent my Romanian friend packing. What was his name again? Ah, well, easy come, easy go."

"And what of you?" I was desperate. I had to say something. I couldn't sit by and let him pummel me with insinuations. "Have you been enjoying your new friends? You should be. You threw over a friendship of a lifetime for one of no more than a week. Have you no witty comment to justify that?"

"No," he said, shrugging. "You got boring, Eric. You didn't want to help me find what I was seeking. What else did you expect me to do?" He reached for the glass, which had somehow been refilled, and downed it in one draught.

I shifted in my chair. "Stop looking at me like that, Madelaine," I said gruffly, hoping no one else would hear.

I was wrong.

"Eric! You must not be so unfeeling to your wife. Women are delicate creatures. They must be nurtured, loved, caressed."

"That's rich coming from you."

"Ah yes, because you would know so much more about that than I would, eh? Since you and my wife have such history. How could I forget that oh so informative rendezvous in Lady Guildford's library?"

Madelaine threw down her napkin and pushed back her plate, the pewter scraping loudly against the tabletop. I didn't blame her for not wanting to hear any more about my past dalliances.

"No need to be upset, my dear Mrs. Bradburry. All that is in the past. It happened long before he lost his heart to you."

If it had been in my power, I would have killed him then, regardless of whatever rules and regulations pertained to his kind. After what I'd seen in Greece, I was willing to bet even *he* couldn't regenerate if I lopped off his head completely. *One clean swipe of a blade across the throat...*

What was I thinking? I'd heard similar words before in a tavern in Brasov, when Stefan admitted to killing his own father, his *real* father. Stefan was in my head again.

Get out.

No, thank you. I quite like it here.

"Ah, yes, Eric and I had good times. Especially in regard to my fathers. I don't suppose Eric has ever told you of my four fathers?"

"No, but there's nothing surprising about that. What makes yours so special? We all have forefathers," my wife snapped.

"No, no, my dear, not *fore*fathers. *Four* fathers," he said, holding up four fingers so the meaning could not be lost.

"Oh?"

"Yes, most are lucky enough to only have one, at most two. I had four. Two who betrayed me and two who gave me new life. You remember those two, don't you, *brother?*"

"How could I forget?" That pestilent, black-shrouded fiend and his suave yet equally deadly counterpart. I'd never forget Stefan's creators.

"True...it's a pity they aren't here now. I know you'd like to see them again someday."

"Not especially, no."

"Oh, that's right. You never did get on with them, now I remember. See what happens to the mind over the years? Details slip. You forget things you should have never forgotten, important things, *life*-threatening things. Well, I do hope you enjoy your stay here," he said, rising and snapping his fingers at Leonora. Before I had time to blink, she was beside him, slipping her hand into his. His earth-encrusted nails closed over her milk-white flesh, encircling her hand, possessing her.

How could she be so submissive? He must have been holding something against her. He *had* to be. I had seen hatred in her eyes not so long ago. How could she have let that go so quickly?

Melika Dannese Lux

"It is *so* good to see you again," Stefan said, eying Maddie. I'd put an end to that quickly. He'd have to learn to be happy enough with one bride because I had no intention of giving him mine. "Just follow the stairs till you reach the top. Yours is the first room on the right, the tower room. Good night."

A chill wind whistled around our heads, snaking toward the ceiling and extinguishing the candlelight.

"Eric..."

The night seeped in through the open windows, moonlight illuminating the empty space before us.

Stefan and Leonora were gone.

"Eric..." my wife said again. Her voice had sunk to a whisper. Her hand, when I took it in mine, was as frigid as Stefan's had been.

"Come," I said, guiding her through the doorway and up the stairs.

She seemed to be walking in a daze, letting me lead her on. We had almost reached the landing when she broke from my grasp.

"This child..."

"Shh, not here."

"Why? Because the walls have ears?"

"Don't be sarcastic, Maddie, it doesn't suit you."

She bit her lip and walked on ahead the last few steps, shoving open the door and passing over the threshold.

"Now do I have your permission to speak?"

The valises were on the bed and the lamps were lit. As I looked around, I had the distinct feeling that I had seen this room somewhere before. And then I remembered Stefan's words.

The tower room.

The dark-haired figure appeared in my mind's eye. I was sure it had been Leonora I had seen watching me from this very room—this room that I was slowly beginning to hate. Everywhere I looked, I saw red. The walls were covered in red velvet, with a shimmering fleur-de-lis pattern embossed upon the fabric. That, too, was red, but a red so dark I mistook it for black at first.

The carpet was a deep crimson—plush underfoot, even through my shoes. Gold thread snaked through the red damask draperies of the lead-paned window, and the same pattern was repeated on the curtains encircling the massive four-poster bed. The only thing that wasn't red was the jet-beaded chandelier hanging from the middle of the ceiling and also the black-stained wood of the bed frame.

The room was opulent, yes, but not in the least comforting. *So much red...* I was relieved to see that the pillows were stuffed into cream-colored cases. Thankfully, there was something to break up the bloodiness of the room.

The rest of the furniture followed the scheme of the bed—dark wood, heavy, oppressive. An ancient-looking sideboard took up one wall. Above it rested a large, gilded mirror. In fact, now that I was able to focus on something besides the overpowering red décor, I noticed that there were a number of mirrors in this room. Two floor-to-ceiling ones flanked either side of the bed and above the spinet hung an oval looking glass which found its mirror, quite literally, in the one above the gilded fireplace at the opposite end of the room. The owner of this room, whoever he might be, certainly enjoyed looking at himself. I was surprised there wasn't a mirror on the underside of the canopy.

Maddie was unpacking her valise. She tossed something across the bed toward me. I picked it up, realizing it was a piece of the baguette we'd bought upon reaching Prague. It tasted stale but satisfying, such as it was.

"I noticed you didn't touch your dinner," she said, tearing off a piece and eating it. "It's the best we can do for now. I've no intention of eating more than I can help while we're here. There's something wrong with that food, Eric. I don't know what, but I've no intention of testing it to find out."

I sensed she wanted to say more, but she remained silent. She'd stopped fiddling with her clothes and was staring straight at me, biting the corner of her lip, stalling, as if she were unsure of whether or not she wanted to go on. "There's something wrong with all of this, Eric," she said finally. "When you said child," she continued slowly, carefully choosing her words, "and then mentioned the christening, I was expecting a baby, not a child of six. There is something terribly wrong here," she said again, firmer this time. "That child is terrified of his father and no wonder."

Yes, that was true, but she hadn't seen what I saw in Stefan's eyes—that mortal terror of his six-year-old son.

I stared down at the piece of baguette and broke off another bite. I couldn't hold out much longer in the face of her suspicions. I'd have to tell her the truth—soon.

"Aren't you going to say anything? Or are you too busy worrying about *her*?"

"Maddie, please..."

"I should have never married you."

The bread fell from my hands. "What did you say?"

"You heard," she said quietly, refolding clothes she had unfolded a second before.

My heart felt like a dead weight in my chest. "You can't mean that."

"Can't I? Oh, Eric, I don't know what I mean anymore. I thought I was doing what I wanted...I thought marrying you was right, even Father agreed, which shocked me, but now I'm not sure. I'm not sure of anything. And now we're here and have to deal with this, whatever *this* might be." She crumpled up the nightshirt and tossed it back into the valise. "You've always lied to me, Eric. I don't know what's real and what isn't. You could have lied about loving me, for all I know. How could you claim to love me and subject me to...to...to God knows what's going on here?!"

"Maddie, no," I said, stretching out my arms, wanting to hold her and never let go, wanting to reassure her that she never needed to doubt my love.

"No, Eric. No." She backed away from me, her hands up as if warding off a blow. "Not now. Just...get away from me."

My arms fell to my sides. I felt lifeless, as desiccated as a corpse, but angry as well. I didn't know who I was furious with, but it wasn't my wife. I'd never seen her like this—so cold, so defensive, so unloving, but how could I have blamed her?

I sat back on the spinet bench by the window and glared into the fire burning in the grate beside it.

"If you won't tell me the truth, I'll find out myself. Don't cross me in this, Eric."

"I have no intention of crossing you. But if I told you the truth, you wouldn't believe me."

"For once in your life be honest with me." I know she wanted me to speak to her, to say something to restore her faith in me, but all I could do was stare at the book she was now holding in her hands. Of all the novels she could have brought, why had she chosen that one? That tooled leather cover as red as blood. The illustration of the she-devil on the front. The knife-like sharpness of the Gothic lettering.

Carmilla.

I grabbed the book from my wife's hands and threw it into the fire, relishing the sight of the flames devouring its pages.

"What's *wrong* with you? Eric..." She was staring into the fire, the glow reflected in her eyes, magnifying the golden flecks. Slowly, she turned toward me, and the look on her face told me everything.

She knew.

"But you can't mean...Eric, that's ridiculous! It can't be...*can it?*"

I nodded, feeling very old, very weary, but also relieved. It was as close to a confession as I'd get.

"Eric, what have you done?"

"You have to believe me...what was that?"

"I heard it, too."

Voices, low and melodic, ululated below the window. We strained to hear more: the voices were speaking French and something else—a language I hadn't heard in years.

Romanian.

I padded to the window, Maddie close on my heels. The glow of a gibbous moon reflected eerily against the snow-covered ground, illuminating the figures below.

They were all cloaked in black, but the hoods did not conceal their faces. Seven years was a long time, yet not so long that I couldn't still recognize that translucent skin, the blue veins spidering beneath the surface. Nor could the hoods hide the wyvern necklaces shackled around each feminine neck.

Ruxandra, Magdalena, Dacia, Irina.

I'd know them anywhere.

Stefan's sisters.

The ones who were left...the ones who'd let Vladec Salei turn them.

The leader of the group, undoubtedly Stefan, shouted something I couldn't understand. An almost palpable tremor went through the ranks. As the sisters parted to make room, a small, black-cloaked figure bobbed into their midst.

Greydanus.

The child glanced over his shoulder. I pressed my hands against the frozen panes and leaned closer, trying to catch a glimpse of who he was looking for. Was it her? His mother, come to take him out to hunt?

No, it was a man. It had to be Luc. His shaggy head looked wolfish and unkempt in the moonlight. He stepped forward, reforming the circle, the group that now numbered seven.

Stefan pointed at Luc, then at Greydanus, and stalked off, followed by his coven. The boy and Luc stared at one another in silence, for I heard no more voices, nor did their lips move. Then Luc led Greydanus forward, and the pair set off toward the line of trees.

"So, they're using us as bait..."

I hadn't the heart to tell her, "Oh, no, darling, we're the main course." I wasn't even sure why we were here yet myself. There was no sense in making her more terrified than she already was.

"They're after us," she continued, trance-like. "Of course they are. They just haven't figured out what to do with us...yet."

This was worrisome. Well, *more* worrisome. I expected her to look feverish, crazed, but she was so calm it was uncanny—standing there staring out the window, her hands folded across her stomach.

Greydanus and Luc had still not reached the woods. I wondered why they were making such slow progress. Maybe it was because of the snow or more likely it was due to Greydanus's lack of enthusiasm for whatever his father had planned.

Suddenly, the little black-cloaked figure halted. I shivered, feeling as though someone were running their frigid, wispy fingers down my spine. The child turned slowly back toward the château. I shouldn't have been able to see him so clearly from such a distance, but I did. His eyes were glowing. Two black orbs that stared straight up at me...

"I'm with you, Eric."

For a moment, I didn't know who had spoken, Greydanus or my wife. But the child was no longer there. The voice had been Maddie's, yet somehow, someway, Greydanus had said those same words.

"You're not going to leave." It wasn't a question.

"How can I? You could be my only hope for survival." I detected the hint of a smile in her voice, though her face was still grave. I thanked God that she was here with me—my angel in hell.

"We're all we've got, unless you trust that man to help us."

I remembered Paris. Luc had helped me then. But things had changed.

"No, I can't trust him. It's just us."

"A fine pair."

"None better."

In the darkness of the room, she nestled closer to me. Even after all my deceit, she was still here, still willing to see me through this, and I her.

I'd never lie to her again, never abandon her to whatever forces were at work here. Tomorrow morning, I'd tell her everything. It would make us stronger, we'd heal, we'd be united in our stand against them.

We still had one thing precious to us, something they no longer possessed. We still had *life*.

And that, I realized, was something far more meaningful than empty words.

‡

Maddie lay as still as death. By the time she'd nodded off to sleep, it was past three in the morning. Even though she was at rest, I could see she was troubled. Her eyes were shut tighter than they should have been, and her brows were creased into an expression that almost looked pained. The counterpane was bunched tightly in her fists and pulled all the way up to her chin.

I kissed her lightly on the forehead and shrank back when I felt the heat. All she needed was to have a fever in such a place. Maybe the burning I'd felt was due to the fact that she'd swathed herself in the blanket. Gently, I eased the covers lower and nestled her back into the pillows. I laid my hand against her forehead. Either the heat had lessened or I'd made myself believe it had, for her skin felt cooler to the touch.

By the time I slipped out of the room, it was a quarter past six in the morning. I had things to do, "gifts" to return, and someone I needed to talk with. She was the only person in this house who could give me the answers I was seeking.

I paused on the landing and shrugged into my coat, patting the pocket to make sure the necklace was still there. The house felt unnaturally cold that morning, but then again, it had felt unnaturally cold last night. As I was folding down my cuffs, I caught sight of something moving down by the now frozen lake. I stepped over to the window and looked out.

Perched on the edge of the ice was an enormous white dog. But that couldn't be right. It was too huge, too fierce looking to be merely a dog.

I leaned in for a closer look, nearly upsetting the casement.

I had been right. It was no dog.

It was a wolf.

A searing memory shot through my mind. The last time I'd seen a creature so large, so powerful, had been in Bulgaria.

A beast with red-rimmed eyes.

A beast I somehow knew was not a wolf at all—a beast that had once been a man.

I heard a loud creak and realized that I had leaned against the casement, pushing the window open.

The wolf lifted its head. Two large black eyes stared out at me from all that whiteness with an intensity that was unnerving.

"Don't run away," I said into the frigid wind. Without thinking, I dashed down the stairs. I had no idea why I was racing to confront a beast that could have killed me with very little effort. I just knew I had to catch a better glimpse of the creature before it vanished.

Too late I reached the lake. The wolf was gone. Paw prints marked the snow that had fallen across the frozen surface. With a shock, I realized the wolf had been sitting in the middle of the ice. How it hadn't broken through was unfathomable. The creature must have weighed at least two hundred pounds, maybe more.

Tentatively, I set my foot on the frozen surface and immediately drew it back. Small cracks spidered outward across the ice, creating a hole right where the paw prints had been.

"Whoever you are, you are certainly light on your paws, my friend," I said, shivering and buttoning up my coat. I didn't know why, but I felt defeated. What had I hoped to accomplish by confronting a wolf? Still, I felt as though I'd missed an opportunity.

So now I was out here in the freezing cold, and what did I have to show for my troubles? I hadn't found Leonora, and I hadn't got any of the answers I was seeking. I'd spent too much time chasing after a wolf that could have been a figment of my imagination for all I knew.

Disgusted with my foolishness, I had half turned toward the château, when a figure emerged from the edge of the forest. She was wrapped in a long, white fur coat. Her black hair hung loose and was dotted with snowflakes, the white streak running down the middle of her scalp looking starkly out of place. Blood red lips drew even more attention to the fair alabaster shade of her skin, and her eyes, those black eyes I'd know anywhere, were unnaturally bright.

Leonora.

I am much more than a vampire.

Impossible.

I pulled the necklace from my coat pocket and held it out to her. "I believe this is yours."

She started at the sight of it. "Where did you get that?"

"I think you already know."

She had the grace, or skill, to look abashed. Oddly, though, I couldn't shake the feeling that she really had no idea where I'd found the necklace.

I sighed. I couldn't keep up a pretense with her, no matter how angry I was. "In the Musée Grévin."

"The day..."

She knew *that.* "Yes, there is no need to go into it all over again."

"Yet you kept it all these years."

"I had no choice."

"You could have destroyed it."

"I didn't have the courage to...*then.*"

She looked startled. "Keep it," she said with finality. "As a gift."

"It is a gift I want no part of." She was no longer just some memory I'd tried to unsuccessfully suppress all these years. Facing her now, in the flesh, I felt my will strengthening. Madelaine's resolve, her love, had given me courage I thought I'd never be able to maintain in Leonora's presence. Whatever hold Leonora had had over me, necklace or not, was broken.

"Then keep it as a part of me. A reminder..."

"Of what? Murder? Deception?"

"As a reminder of what we shared."

I knew she bore me no ill will, but I would not give in. This was a last desperate attempt to control me, to dissuade me. "I will not divide my loyalties, Leonora. I know where my allegiance lies."

I shoved the necklace into her hands. She curled her delicate fingers around the bauble. Instantly, I felt release, as if a shackle had been removed from my mind.

"You *are* stronger," she said, half to herself. She tucked the necklace away into a pocket of her voluminous fur coat.

I felt free, but there was still so much to be done, so much I still didn't understand.

"We need to talk," I said with effort. My voice felt like dry leaves in my throat.

"About what?" she said abstractedly, guiltily.

"Oh, I don't know, maybe why your son looks *exactly* like me?"

"Zigmund is dead. Do you not remember? I killed him. You cannot know what he looks like."

"Neither you nor I believe you murdered him. And don't be smart, Leonora. You know what I meant." I wasn't going to tell her I *did* know what her son looked like. I didn't trust her with the secret that Zigmund was alive, or had been seven years ago.

"Do not ask me to reveal that."

"Did you steal Greydanus? Is that it?" I pressed on relentlessly, trotting after her, for she had begun to walk back toward the château. She seemed so remote, so imposing, so much stronger than I—so cold and powerful in that white coat that kept billowing about her like a cape. And her eyes...the intensity in them was almost savage. "You found a child who looks exactly like me, for whatever reason, and you stole him?" I demanded, desperate to know the truth.

"*No!*"

"Then why does he have my face?!"

She rounded on me with such ferocity that for a moment I didn't recognize her. A flash of fangs, a dark gleam in her blacker-than-night eyes. It was the most vampiric I'd ever seen her.

"Because I pretended it was *you* who I was making love to!"

I winced, feeling as though I'd been struck. Leonora's hands flew to her mouth. I was horrified by what she'd just revealed, and apparently, so was she. She shook her head and backed away from me. "It was the only way I could endure it."

I had never heard her speak so quietly before. She wasn't hysterical by any means, but her tears choked her words, muffling them. I watched her silently, not knowing what to say and certainly having no intention of comforting her. How could I? I wasn't sure what to feel.

I stood stone still as I watched her warring with herself. Suddenly, it was as though she regained control, for her entire demeanor changed—dramatically so. Her arms fell to her sides and her fists clenched. She seemed more enraged than sorrowful. As she turned her eyes on me, I shrank from the look of unconcealed hatred I saw in those twin black orbs. "Have you *any* idea the torture I suffered to give him that child? The humiliation I endured while he expended his lust upon my body? Scars inflicted by the barbed tongue of a Vrykolakas never heal, Eric, not even for vampires. I will carry them with me forever, these marks of his passion."

Before I could tell her I had no desire to see these scars, she opened her coat and lifted up her bodice, revealing her stomach. A ragged, red gash, looking remarkably fresh, snaked across her skin from just under her ribs to her navel. I felt bile rising in my throat.

I could have been looking at my own arm during one of my attacks. The gash was identical.

I reached out my fingers to touch the mangled flesh, but she pulled away and lowered the bodice before I had the chance. "Small comfort the child looks like you."

Scars inflicted by the barbed tongue of a Vrykolakas never heal.

I remembered her neck and the necks of the others the Vrykolakas had attacked. I swallowed hard, willing myself not to look away. Encircling her neck was a ghastly scar—a laceration so deep, I was surprised I couldn't see the bone beneath the gouged flesh. The angry red furrows stood out dramatically, heightening the pallor of her too-pale skin.

She had never let me see these scars before, but now, at least for this moment, I suspected she was tired of hiding what she was. After she was satisfied that I understood the suffering she had endured at the hands of these beasts, she retied the small black velvet choker around her neck, and I was spared from gazing upon any more horror.

Corcitura

This was all too violent to comprehend. First Stefan, now this. What had she been through, and why on earth had she let Stefan do all this to her?

Salei. Who else could have designed this torture?

"Is Salei dead?" I asked, taking a step toward her.

She didn't answer.

"Leonora, is Salei dead, or was that another lie?"

"Vladec Salei is very much alive, in his own way. And if you are wondering why I did it, and I know you are, there are two reasons. I let Vladec convince me I had killed my own son. I was a fool, Eric. I didn't know who to believe, so I listened to the one who had always been there to protect me. I craved another child. I missed the feel of his sweet, soft skin, the smell of him just after I'd given him a warm bath. I wanted another son to replace the child I had murdered. And then there is the other reason."

"Which is?"

"Vladec can be very persuasive, violently persuasive. My having Stefan's child was Vladec's wish."

"Why?" I didn't want to know, but I had to.

"Because Grey would be the perfect specimen, so perfect that Stefan tried to kill the child before it was born. I've another scar from that encounter, but I've no intention of showing it to you."

She turned back toward the lake and stared into the forest. "Stefan knew he was losing favor with his father. If Grey lives up to his potential, he will be Vladec's greatest creation, greater even than Stefan."

"How so?" I was fascinated in spite of the horror this revelation should have filled me with.

"Greydanus is a Born Vampire, we were made. Even Stefan, for all his novelty, isn't stronger than his son. Greydanus is more powerful than either of us, and he doesn't even know it yet."

"So the meetings in the forest?" I let the question hang in the air.

"His training. Eric," she said, turning toward me, her eyes pleading, "I cannot let him corrupt my son. That's why you're here."

"What, to be the bait so your precious boy will live? He's already a vampire, Leonora, I'm *not*."

"You're marked."

"So what if I'm marked?! You think I want this? It might seem morbid, but I want to die one day. I don't want to linger, ageless, forever."

"Don't look at me like that, Eric. I'm not a monster."

"No, but I never thought you'd give in so easily."

"Do not judge what you don't understand," she spat, her voice filled with contempt.

"Fine, I won't, but don't expect me to be a willing sacrifice. I'm not going to give up my life for your child, though he looks like me, though you *say* I was in your mind when he was conceived. I have Maddie now. Though she might never forgive me for bringing her here, never want to have anything to do with me ever again, I intend to get both of us out of here alive, with or without your help. I came here for you, Leonora, for *you*. Everything I've done to endanger our lives has been for *you*. I see now that I was wrong. God forgive me for being such a fool."

"Eric...my son, Zigmund."

She'd seen it in my eyes. In my weakened state, I must have given the secret away. She could read me so easily, even without the aid of the trinket I had returned to her.

She knew.

I reached for my wallet, intending to bring out the card with her son's name on it. What good was keeping him a secret any longer? When I opened the wallet, the card wasn't there.

I patted my pockets, turned the wallet inside out, but I couldn't find that blasted card, or anything else for that matter. Somehow, between here and the bedroom, my wallet had been completely cleaned out.

Maddie.

I rushed back to the château, hoping Maddie was still asleep, hoping she hadn't been the one to find the card. When I burst through the door of our room, she wasn't there.

All that was there was the evidence that she was the one who'd pillaged my wallet. Notes here, money there, bits and bobs strewn about the bed.

But no card.

And no Maddie.

"Why didn't you tell me he was alive?" Leonora asked me as soon as I came out onto the grounds again.

"How could I? I wasn't going to betray my position just so you could clear your conscience. Besides which, I don't even know if he *is* still alive. For all we know he could be dead. That was seven years ago. *Madelaine!*"

I called and called and Leonora concentrated, but maybe being unmarked was Maddie's salvation, for Leonora could not get a bead on where she was, and, hopefully, neither could Stefan.

"How could you not know he was alive?" I asked, pulling up to catch my breath. We'd reached the outer limits of the château and were heading for the graveyard, the last place we had left to look. I didn't want to think about the hidden passageways or subterranean vaults still within the house. I dreaded what I might find in those dank, dark places. "You could get inside my mind but you can't get inside your own son's?"

"Eric, I haven't seen my son in over thirty years. But that's not it," she said, shaking her head. "I don't understand. Unless he *is* dead."

"He can't be dead," I said firmly. He couldn't be. He *had* to be alive.

"No, he must think *I'm* dead. He's shut me out. I'm dead to him, as he was dead to me all this time because I thought I'd killed him. That's why it's not working."

Exasperated, I left her side and walked off toward the cemetery.

"*Eric...*" Her voice chilled me and stopped me dead. I followed her gaze to a point in the distance and could just discern a small dark figure. "She's in the graveyard. Hurry."

I ran. I slipped on snow and tripped over graves until I finally reached her.

Melika Dannese Lux

She was sitting on a bench in front of a black granite tombstone topped by a headless stone angel. Her head was bent, her loose hair veiling her face, creating a black waterfall to hide behind. My heart seized within my chest. She looked so lifeless.

"Maddie," I said, shaking her by the shoulders. Slowly, her head rose. I don't know what I expected to see, hollowed out eyes, maybe, but she was unharmed and in complete control of her senses, which was more than I could say for myself. She rested her elbows on her knees and held out her hand.

Clutched in her fingers was a card.

The card.

The card with the name Zigmund Fertig embossed upon it.

"Care to explain *this*?"

"It's just a card like any other."

"Stop lying to me, Eric! You kept saying his name over and over in your sleep. What does it mean, and what does *she* have to do with it?"

"Zigmund Fertig, Professor of Antiquity and Folklore with an emphasis on Slavic Studies. Currently residing in Munich and teaching at Ludwig Maximilians University."

Startled, all three of us looked around to see who had spoken.

Luc leaned against an obelisk marking a grave. His eyes were dark. Black smudges underneath them betrayed that he hadn't slept in God knew how long.

"How could you read that?" I asked him, taking the card from Maddie's fingers. I turned it over and over, marveling at the transformation that had taken place. When I'd last looked at the card, the lettering had been barely discernible, but now the name was more legible than it had been in years.

"I didn't have to read it. I know."

"You knew my son was alive? How could you possibly know when even I didn't?" Leonora glowered at Luc. She managed to somehow look amazed and hateful simultaneously.

"Your lover gave me gifts. He never put restrictions on what I could do with them. So I did a little digging."

"How could you not tell me?"

"I judged it best to keep up the fiction, given your tendency to lash out."

"You judged it best? You thought it best to keep up this *fiction*, this fiction that I had killed my son? *You* decided? When did you become God?!"

I grabbed her before she could rip into Luc's throat.

"See?! *See?!* This is why I kept the secret."

"Steady, Leonora, steady," I said, struggling mightily to keep her arms pinned to her sides. If she wanted him, she could have taken him. It was no force of mine that was holding her back. After a moment's struggle, I felt the fight go out of her and released her.

"How long have you known he was alive?" I asked.

"For a while."

"Yet you never told me, you monster," Leonora spat, her eyes narrowed, resentful.

"That would have been a fine sight. Oh, yes, tell you and then you'd get hysterical—like you did just now—rampage off, and confront the poor man, probably striking him dead from the shock of seeing you after all these years. Bah! No, *you* stay here. We have to give him time to let the truth that his mother, whom he thought was dead, is very much alive, so to speak."

"I wouldn't have got hysterical."

"After that display, do you expect me to believe you? Apart from this little incident," he said, waving his hands, "I've seen you with Greydanus. I know how you are."

"So, what are you?" Maddie interrupted, addressing Luc.

"Tracker, hunter, wraith, call me what you will. I am not a vampire nor am I omniscient. I'm just good at finding things."

"And people," I said, grimacing.

"And people," echoed Luc, smirking.

"I'm coming with you," I said.

"No, you are not. We cannot have anyone intimate with Stefan in any way coming along and fouling our plans."

"Plans, that's rich. You're going after someone who might, I repeat *might,* be able to help us, but we really don't know for certain one way or the other. Not to mention that your entire plan is contingent on him believing you. If I were him, I'd take you for a complete lunatic. This 'plan' of yours has a million and one holes in it."

"Then it's a good thing I've got a million and one plugs," he said savagely.

"And what about you?" I protested. "You've been Stefan's right hand." My common sense was wasted on them. I was in the minority; I knew my reasoning wouldn't make any difference when all three of them were in such a frenetic state.

"I've not been specially chosen nor have I given him a child," Luc answered, maddeningly self-assured.

"Your gifts..." I had no other opposing reasons to cling to.

"No matter. I know tricks you don't. And I've lived longer, much longer." He sighed and ran his fingers through his hair. He'd once told me he was thirty-six—thirty-six when the near transformation had happened. He might have been several hundred years old for all I knew. I looked at Leonora. She would forever be twenty-four.

"If Stefan doesn't know already, he'll be suspicious if both you and Leonora disappear. No, I'll go. The three of you stay here and work things out as best you can."

"How do we know we can trust you?" I asked. I'd never trusted Luc. Why should I start now? "What's to say you won't bolt as soon as you're free?"

"I didn't bolt when I was in New York, if you'll remember," he said, looking me in the eyes with infinite sadness. "The outer world holds nothing for me anymore, Eric. I'll go."

"You'd better hurry."

I turned at the sound of Maddie's voice. She was staring at the grave next to the one beside the bench.

"None of these graves are marked, Eric. Except for this one. Read the headstone."

Madelaine Bradburry, Beloved Wife and Mother

Eric Bradburry, Jr.

"Junior?!" I exclaimed, looking at her wildly, my eyes roving over her face. "What does it mean, *Junior?*"

"What does it mean?! *What does it mean?!* Eric! Who cares what it means! Why is it even here?!"

"You're pregnant?!" I asked idiotically.

"Look at the date."

I turned back to the headstone, thinking nothing could be more bizarre than what I'd already seen. I was wrong.

B. 27th Oct., 1872 D. 13th Jan., 1895.

"That's ten days from now."

I slumped against the stone, my mind reeling. She'd been brought here to die. *I* had brought her here to die. And now that we were to have a son...

Vaguely, I heard a voice. When I looked up, Maddie was kneeling beside me, her hand on my arm.

"Tell me the truth, Eric. Why have I been brought here to die? And what does Stefan want from me?"

"Nothing," said Leonora. "He wants nothing from you. It's Eric he's after. And I'm afraid I've led you straight to him."

The silence around us was disturbed by the rustling of wings...large wings, by the sound of it. I looked up, expecting to see the gaggle of miniature wyverns I'd seen the night before, but there was nothing there.

"I'll leave at once," said Luc, shouldering a rucksack I hadn't noticed before. "And no buts about it. We're running out of time."

"Why so suddenly? Why is all this happening now? Why hasn't it happened already?" I asked, cradling Maddie. She was trembling, though not with fear. If I weren't mistaken, I'd say she was enraged.

"Because you're here. You're the catalyst, Eric. You always have been."

"There must be some other reason. What if I had said no? What if I'd stayed in New York?"

"Don't trouble me with technicalities," Luc said evasively. "Madelaine." Luc took my wife's hands in his. "You might want to look up Zigmund's book."

"What for?" she asked sharply.

"Enlightenment," he answered, spreading his hands in that maddening Gallic gesture that suppressed any dissent. "Try the libraries here in Prague. Start small at first, then work your way up to the university. There's bound to be a copy of *Fertig's Lexicon of Nosferatu* somewhere in this city."

"I wish you luck," I said, extending my hand. "For all our sakes."

Luc's hand was as cold as ice. I had to fight not to shrink back from his touch. Why should he be this cold if he claimed he wasn't a vampire?

"I will see you again...soon."

Something in his voice made me shudder. And his eyes...I'd never seen them so alive.

Unnerved, I left Luc and Leonora to cement the remaining details of the plan and guided Maddie back up to our room.

"Rest, my own love. You're going to need it."

I sat her on the edge of the bed, then busied myself securing the door. After seeing that writing on the grave, I didn't know how else to react. I pushed one of the lowboys against the door and glanced over my shoulder at Maddie. She was right where I'd left her, staring into the grate at the ashes of *Carmilla*.

Suddenly, she bolted to her feet. "I don't care what they say. I *know* he means to kill me, too, but I'm not going to sit by and wilt away waiting for death to come for me."

"What're you doing?" Her sudden activity alarmed me. She made for the desk in the corner, drew out some paper, and sat down with purpose.

"Writing a letter to Zigmund."

"What on earth for?"

"Because they do it in all the best Gothic stories. What do you think I'm writing it for, Eric?" she said, looking at me in exasperation. "He needs to know the circumstances. This could be Luc's letter of introduction. A setting out of the facts. It might help him to better accept the situation, since we're asking him to come to a place he has no idea about, where his mother is still alive."

"Do you think it wise to mention her?"

"I'm not mentioning her. Zigmund's a professor of esoteric knowledge. I'm sure he's familiar with the ways of vampires. With any luck, he won't think us completely crazy. You heard what Luc said. He thinks it would be disastrous to even mention Leonora."

"Oh, so now it's 'what Luc says,' eh?" It was a pettish thing to say. I hated myself for saying it aloud.

"Yes," she continued, her eyes focused on the paper. "He's been truthful with me so far, which is more than I can say for some people."

I knew better than to argue with her now. Both of us had received our fair share of shocking news for the day.

I walked over to the spinet and noticed that a piece of sheet music had been set out atop it. Chopin's *Posthumous Nocturne in E flat major.* It was a lovely piece, but I'd no talent for the piano. Perhaps Maddie could play it sometime, I thought absently.

What was I thinking? I didn't even know if we would last the night. And who in their right mind would want to idle over the spinet at a time like this?

I wandered to the window and sat down on the seat. Snow was falling heavily outside and showed no signs of abating. The cracks I had caused in the pond not so long before were already almost frozen over again.

I thought of Luc out there amidst the drifts and mounds and all that blinding whiteness, and wondered just how he was going to reach Zigmund in time...and if reaching Zigmund would help us at all.

I rested my forehead against the glass. I'd begun to doze off when a sight at the edge of the trees drove all thoughts of sleep from my mind.

A small, brownish-gray wolf padded back and forth, looking skittish and unsure of where to go or what to do next. He glanced back toward the trees, then toward where Leonora and Luc had been standing.

I unlatched the lock and pushed open the window, leaning out to catch a better glimpse of the creature.

The snow beneath the wolf's paws was spotted with blood. The creature had obviously been attacked and was injured, for its front left leg was curled up near its chest. The wolf darted another panicked glance toward the trees and made as if to move, but something stayed it. It looked so unsure and helpless. Even though I was some distance away, I could just make out its faint, pitiful whimpers through the sound of the wind.

The presence of wolves around the château boggled my mind. The house and its grounds were like a magnet to them somehow. First there had been the enormous white beast I'd seen this morning and now this tiny dun creature. Where had they come from? What did they want?

Again I heard that flapping of wings and so did the hunted little animal down below.

I thought it was going to bolt for certain this time, but instead, it raised its muzzle and took a step toward the château.

And then it looked at me. I knew in an instant who that wolf really was.

Those eyes could not be denied. Those huge black eyes, radiating eyes, eyes I had last seen in a small, grave, childish face.

I shut my eyes to break the contact, the intensity, the pull of those eyes that should not have been inside the head of a wolf.

When I looked back, he was gone.

He...*yes*...I could think of him in human terms, now that I knew the truth.

The wolf was Greydanus.

My search of the grounds was fruitless. I returned indoors, disheartened. I'd no desire to ransack this mansion in search of that wolf that was a boy who just somehow happened to also be a vampire. My mind still reeled at the thought. A vampire, a wolf, a Corcitura's child...

Was this what Leonora had meant about the child not knowing just how powerful he was? Surely a creature that had three opposing sides of its nature would prove formidable, even for an adversary such as Stefan.

An adversary that was this creature's own father.

If I continued to dwell on those thoughts, I'd stay rooted to this spot forever. I wasn't safe standing here exposed, but at least I didn't have to worry about Madelaine. I'd made sure that she bolted the door once I'd left. I prayed she hadn't opened it since. Still, I couldn't help worrying. I was accomplishing nothing here. It was time I was back where I belonged.

Where I belonged. I belonged in New York at Riverhampton, safely ensconced with my wife and our child.

Our child. I was trying to solve the mystery of Leonora's child. Too long I'd neglected to take care of those who mattered most. Madelaine, our son. There was no room left in my life for Greydanus and Leonora, as regrettable as it was to realize this now that I probably had no way of escaping this situation alive.

I quickened my pace, anxious to get back to the relative safety of our tower room. I needed to see that Madelaine was safe. Until then, I couldn't rest easy.

My footsteps seemed unnaturally loud as I sprinted past the closed doors of the passageway. I rounded the bend of the third landing and pulled up abruptly.

The door at the end of the hall, the door I had to pass by in order to reach the stairs, stood open. Light streaked out, illuminating the threshold of the room.

Stefan's study.

"Is someone there? Leonora, dearest, is that you?"

The voice, so deceptive in its innocence, sickened me. He knew I wasn't Leonora. He would have known for a mile or more that it was me coming, not his wife.

Short of leaping across the divide, there was nothing I could do but pass that doorway and perforce answer his summons.

"No," I said, appearing in the archway.

"Ah, Eric." He glanced up at me briefly, then turned his attention back to the ledger he was writing in. "Do come in," he continued as he scribbled away. His face was clouded over, but I got the feeling that even though he pretended to be concentrating on his work, he was acutely aware of everything I was thinking. The quill flew across the paper as though it were possessed. I'd never seen anyone write so rapidly.

"Have a seat, won't you?"

"I prefer to stand."

"Making it a brief visit, then?"

"If you please."

"What if I *don't*?" My heart burned, for he looked up at me, focusing all his attention on my face, yet the quill continued to fly across the page. It was as though someone else was controlling the pen.

"Sit, Eric."

I had no will to resist. I pulled out the chair and settled into it, dreading what was to come, what he'd do to me. I felt as though I'd lost any power over myself once those piercing eyes were turned on me. They pinned me to the seat.

"How is your little *wife*?"

"I should think you'd know how well she is," I said testily, remembering the tombstone.

"Ah, yes, quite," he said, his head bowed, but not lowered enough so that I didn't see the smirk twisting his lips.

"Why do you delight in toying with me so?"

"Because you are so bloody readable, Eric. You've never learned to hide your emotions. It is the one thing I do not regret losing when I came into my own."

How easily he talked about his transformation. How easily he had let go of his former life, his *human* life, the life that had given him a soul. Of all the things that had mystified me the most, his blind acceptance of Vladec Salei's "gift" had always been the hardest to swallow. "How can you be so cavalier?" I asked before I could think it wise if I should speak or not. "How could you give up your life so easily?"

"You call that husk a life? I do pity you, Eric, even after all these years," he said, amused.

"You didn't even fight it, Stefan." This had always been my linchpin argument.

The pen suddenly stopped moving. Stefan rested it in the inkwell and blew on the page. Curious, I leaned forward, but he moved the book closer to him so that I could see no more. "You expected me to fight something that had been in my blood for years," he said in all seriousness. "It couldn't have been done, Eric. Not even if I had wanted to."

"That's the trouble. You didn't want to. You accepted it with everything you were worth."

"So what if I did?" he said, his voice maddeningly devoid of emotion. "When this curse runs through one's veins, it is only a matter of time before one succumbs. Our family was doomed from the start."

"I don't believe that."

"Then you are a fool."

There was no acerbity in that statement. Looking at him now, a small part of me wanted to believe that he wasn't past saving. Maybe this was what Leonora had meant. And maybe I was still holding on to something that had died years ago.

"There is no denying this legacy of blood, Eric," he said, once again picking up the pen. He poised it above the page, but did not press the nib to the paper. "Ancestral spirits. Sins of the fathers..." he whispered, seemingly oblivious to my presence. His eyes roved over the pages he had filled with his spidery scrawl. There was fever in his eyes—fever and something I had not seen in years.

"Stefan..."

"No. I'm the fool, Eric. I'm the fool. Your coming has made me see that. It has decided me."

I didn't like the sound of that. Decided him on what?

The look that I had thought I'd seen—the look of hope, pleading, a last cry for salvation—vanished, and his eyes were hard once more. He pressed the pen so hard into the page that the nib slashed a hole in the paper as he began to write.

"How clumsy," he said quietly.

I watched him tear out the page and place it in the flame of the candle resting atop his desk. The paper crackled as it caught fire, then Stefan turned and tossed it onto the blazing logs within the hearth. I thought the double burning excessive.

"No sense in being careless about these things."

"Just what exactly are you writing?"

"Curious. I like that. It's not like you to be curious."

"People change."

"That certainly is true," he said with a terrifying smile. I did not need to ask for clarification on what he meant.

"This," he said after a moment, "is an illustrious history of our family. Our sadists, our murderers, our rogues' gallery of wretches. Charming work. Father commissioned me to write it, but I admit my mind has wandered to other things. To other plans..."

A far off look entered his eyes. I crouched lower in the chair, shrinking from his gaze, and more so from the thoughts that were whirling through my mind. What exactly were his plans? What did he have in mind? And why did I need to be here to witness them?

"How do I figure into these plans of yours?" It was a reckless thing to say, but I needed to know.

"You are the catalyst, dear boy." The same thing Luc had said, though from the look of Stefan, there was much more he was not telling me. "I'm afraid I can't say anything else without ruining the surprise."

"Surprise?"

"Oh, yes, I love surprises."

"You never used to."

"That whole changing issue again?" he asked, his eyes mocking me, the uninitiated. "Now your mind is on the right track."

I cursed myself for thinking that word. I intended to remain uninitiated for as long as there was life left within me.

"And what of my wife?"

"I have plans for her, too."

I rocketed out of my chair and snatched the book out from underneath his hands, sending both pen and inkwell flying across the room. The ink splattered and ran down the wall in great globs that looked like old blood.

"I'll have that back, if you please," he said, holding out his long-nailed hand. I was shaking, anger choking me so that my breath came in pants. I stared down at the book, contemplating whether or not to tear out the pages or chuck the entire thing into the fire. I did not understand why he was so obsessed with it.

Until I saw the names.

Ruxandra Istratescu. Magdalena Istratescu...

Line after line was filled with the names of Istratescu women. Beside each name was a small symbol that I at first took for an asterisk. As I looked closer, I saw it for what it was.

An openmouthed wyvern's head.

Stefan was staring at his hands, though I felt as though his eyes were on me. When I turned my attention back to the book, I saw that there were only a few pages left. I leafed through to the end.

Nearly five hundred years to the day. One more obstacle needs to be eliminated. Then the way will be clear for the last blood sacrifice that will make Father's transformation complete—secure—irreversible.

Beneath this cryptic scrawl, a new symbol had been drawn beside the last two names written in the ledger. The symbol was a death's head with the eyes and teeth of a wyvern and the barbed tongue of a Vrykolakas.

And the two names were mine and my wife's.

So this was what he had in mind for us. This was what I had traveled halfway across the world for—to be sacrificed to a monster I had spent the last seven years running from.

I realized now that I was very near to the end. If it came to it, I'd fight to the death before letting him have his way with Maddie.

I closed the book and shut my mind, willing myself to be strong.

"Fascinating reading," I said, matching his cavalier tone as I handed the book back to its owner.

"I thought it might be."

"Good night, Stefan," I said, backing away.

"I'll be expecting you at dinner."

"I don't think I have the appetite for it."

I expected him to protest, violently if necessary, but he just folded his hands across the ledger. "So be it. We'll have time enough to talk in the future. We have all the time in the world."

I backed out of the room like some toady exiting the presence chamber of a king. No matter that I had an ally in Luc, who was hopefully well on his way toward Zigmund.

"Wise choice, brother." The words came to me in a whisper just before I closed the study door.

Regardless of my bravado, I had not been able to turn my back on Stefan.

So how in my right mind did I still believe I could defeat him?

‡

"Do you think he believed the excuse?"

After first bolting the door and shoving a lowboy in front of it, I'd told her everything that had passed between Stefan and me in his study—everything except what I'd read in the last pages of his family chronicle. Yet even with all the implications behind his words, Madelaine didn't seem as terrified as I was. She'd been acting more resigned to everything since Luc left, which worried me. Hope sprang eternal for her, but I was beginning to see more and more that our hope was that of a fool's, as was Luc's errand.

"I really don't care if he believes us or not," I answered. "Stefan probably already knows what I'm thinking before I say it anyway. The perks of being *marked*, my love. I don't suppose you've got any more of that baguette?"

Maddie tossed me the last of the pieces we'd been living off since yesterday.

"Let's hope one of Luc's gifts is speed," she said between bites. He'd taken her letter and left six hours ago. There was a very slim chance he'd make it back before the prophecy of that stone was supposed to come true. If he didn't, I'd have to find a way to hide Maddie or get her away from here until Luc returned. I'd need Leonora's help with this and her son's as well. One of her sons. I prayed Zigmund would believe us, otherwise...

"We haven't got much time left," Madelaine said quietly.

"I'm not worried," I lied. I was sick with terror over the thought of losing her. But I couldn't let on. Not now. I felt as though I had no control over my own thoughts in this place. I couldn't keep Stefan out unless I concentrated, and I was struggling mightily to do just that.

"I'm worried...about Leonora."

My heart dropped into my stomach at this admission. She'd only ever been suspicious of Leonora, treating her as someone to be tolerated but never trusted. "How so?" I managed to finally say as I sat down beside her.

"I don't know what she's going to do when she sees Zigmund. It frightens me. How would you react if you thought your child was dead, then found out he was alive after so long?"

"I hope I never have to go through that," I said, placing my hand on her stomach. She put her hand over mine and kissed me gently on the lips.

"I hope not either." There it was again—the worry, the unspoken fear, but she damped it down and began to change for bed.

"When are you going to start looking for the book?" I asked as I slipped into my nightshirt.

"Tomorrow. I'm beginning the search tomorrow. We can't wait any longer. The days are running out...soon it will be the last day...the last day..."

"Never," I said firmly. "I won't let that happen."

She smiled at me sadly, which made me doubt my own courage. I hated feeling so vulnerable, so powerless to defend those I loved.

"I don't know what I'll find in that book," she went on, "but maybe it'll help us understand things better."

I smiled at that. I understood things perfectly well, that was the problem. I was marked; my wife had been singled out for death; Leonora wanted me to sacrifice myself to save her son, whom I had seen in his true form beneath my window...and Luc? Well, what of Luc? I hoped he was telling the truth, was who he claimed to be. I didn't feel easy entrusting such a monumental task to him.

"Luc will be back soon...with Zigmund." I had to believe it. The alternatives weren't acceptable.

"Did you notice anything strange about Stefan when you spoke to him?" she asked.

I swallowed hard and turned my face away, hoping she wouldn't discover my treachery in keeping our death warrants a secret. "Strange? You mean strang*er*?"

"Well, considering."

"You wonder if he knows that we discovered the tombstone?"

"I wonder just how aware he is of all this, of our knowing anything at all about him."

More than you can know, my love, I said to myself, feeling a traitor for not telling her. But I couldn't. There was no reason to send her out of her mind with terror. Not when I was still alive to do something about saving us.

"I can't read him," she continued. "We only have a short time till whatever is going to happen *happens*, but he seems unhurried. As though he has all the time in the world...which troubles me."

"Me as well," I said, cringing inwardly over her choice of words.

All the time in the world...

I pulled her into bed and drew the covers over us. "Whatever it is, he is not going to hurt you. I'll kill him first."

"You can't." She'd taken this bit of news to heart most fiercely when I'd told it to her this afternoon. "The cross is the only way, you said. So how can you?"

"I don't know, but I'm willing to try anything. And maybe he just did that to scare you," I offered weakly.

"What...the etching on the grave? I don't think so."

"I don't think so either," I admitted. Somewhere in my mind, I heard a laugh.

Stefan's laugh.

I clutched Maddie to my chest and kissed the top of her head, tightening my arms around her, wanting to make her feel safe. I doubted either of us would sleep at all this night...this night that might be our last together on this earth.

What a morbid mind you have, Bradburry.

He'd crept inside again, invading my thoughts, no matter how hard I'd tried to lock him out. I shook my head and nestled my face into Maddie's dark hair, breathing in the warring scents—snow and leaves and the lavender water I'd given her as a present last Christmas. She smelled clean and wholesome and alive—so unlike anything else in this tomb.

I clung to her. I'd once told her she was my salvation.

Now, I would be hers.

Keep lying to yourself, brother.

‡

His hot breath tickled my neck. The mirror reflected him, which I found uncanny, for some of his kind were not supposed to have reflections. Then again, I'd no idea what he truly was. I'd never heard of a creature that could change into a wolf at will yet still possess all the traits of a vampire.

His small hands, miraculously no longer injured, were raised to his shoulders, his fingers convulsing every time he made the choice to move in closer, then suddenly moved away just as quickly. I'd been watching him do this for what seemed like forever, but from the hands on the clock on Maddie's nightstand, it had only been five minutes. He looked so vulnerable, so childlike, except that what he was about to do was anything but innocent.

I lay perfectly still, thankful that Maddie was turned on her other side. If he looked in the mirror, he would see my eyes on him, yet he was so focused on the exposed flesh of my neck that he didn't notice anything else. His eyes were black as jet beads, his face a mix of warring emotions—anguish, panic, fear, and finally...defeat.

His hands unclenched and dropped to his sides. I saw a shudder pass through his body as he slowly made his way to the door. I felt his fear, I knew his dread. I would not want to face the person who was undoubtedly on the opposite side of that door either.

Softly, the door opened, and just as softly, I heard it click shut.

I slipped out of bed and padded over to the door. I held my breath and slowly turned the door handle, hoping it wouldn't creak or give resistance. Thankfully, it opened easily and without a sound. My breath escaped in a hiss as I peered through the crack.

It was just as I suspected, though the sight of him so near still set my nerves on edge.

"Worthless, so incredibly worthless. Such a waste of time and energy," Stefan said, his mouth twisted in disgust. "I don't know why I ever listened to Vladec. If I had known I'd have been getting damaged goods, I would have never bothered. Any other harlot would have served the purpose better than your mother."

Greydanus looked up at his father. I shrank back. The look in those eyes...

"Why are you staring at me like that, you wretched child? It's not my fault you are so weak."

"I am not weak." His voice did not tremble, it did not waver. It was like steel, and it sent a shiver through my body.

"*Really?*" I stifled a cry of anger as he grabbed the child's arm and squeezed, squeezed so hard that even Stefan's pallid hand grew purple from the pressure. But Greydanus did not cry out, he did not even blink.

"I should have killed you before you were born," Stefan said, flinging the child's arm away.

"Yet you couldn't. More fool you."

Stefan whipped around, his jaw hanging open. I smiled to myself. It felt good to see him unnerved.

"You wanted me to be born, though you were jealous. I was to be your progeny. Your son, the child of your greatness. Grandfather commanded it."

"Well, Grandfather isn't here now, is he?"

"He will be."

"Don't stand there like some omniscient little god." His voice was very nearly a shriek. "That's what you fancy yourself? Of course! Preening and lofty little dog that you are. Some type of god? *I* am the only god you will ever know. *I* am the one who gave you life, and I can take it away whenever I choose."

"You cannot."

"Yes I...what's this?!"

His fingers closed around Greydanus's neck. This was the end. He was going to strangle the boy. But I'd been mistaken. Stefan wasn't trying to choke the life from his son. He was reaching for something hanging around the child's neck.

Greydanus clutched his neck and glared at his father, who in turn was glaring at what he'd just ripped off his son. Dangling from Stefan's fingers was a golden chain, and on the end of that chain hung a crucifix.

"Making idols of dead gods?! I told you never to bring this into this house again!"

"You are the only idol here. You are the only dead god," he rasped, his hands still encircling his neck. "My God is not dead. Nothing you can do will kill Him, no matter how hard you try."

I felt a surge of pride. Who would have thought? A vampire with a soul. It was impossible, yet it gave me a hope so intense I nearly cried out in joy.

"One day soon," Greydanus continued, his voice low, "I will come into my own. Neither you nor Grandfather nor even Mother can stop me. I will make all things right. I will free everything you've created. I will turn back the tide on your destruction. And then, when you have seen everything made new, I will kill you...*Father.*"

"That's the way, Greydanus," I whispered. Finally, the child was standing up to his father.

The floor suddenly felt very cold. When I shifted my feet beneath me, I don't know how it happened, but I slipped—slipped right into the door and slammed it shut.

I scrambled to my feet. Just as I had regained my legs, I was knocked to the ground. I had cheated death so many times before, but this was beyond absurd. How could I have thought I would go unnoticed?

The door flung open. I lunged against it, using my weight to try and force it shut, but my strength was no match for Stefan's. I glanced over my shoulder, wondering frantically why Maddie wasn't awake after all this commotion. There had to be some devilry at work here, for she should have been roused ages ago with all this noise.

The door swung inward again, colliding with my head and knocking me almost senseless. I scrabbled for the bed, lifting myself up just enough to catch a glimpse of my wife. Her arms hung limply over the side. She seemed somehow even more listless and comatose than before.

Drugged.

My legs were yanked out from under me. Pain seared through my body. I bit down hard on my lip as nails raked across my back. A hand encircled my ankle. I clawed at it, trying to rip the hand away, but the grip was like iron.

And then the world suddenly turned upside-down. I landed on my back, my shoulders crashing against the floor. Every bone in my body felt as though it had been shattered.

My strength was failing, yet I had to try, had to do something to resist. I kicked at my attacker, but his hand was still wrapped around my ankle. Vainly I tried to reach for the bed frame, but a sharp pull sent me reeling, knocking my head against the end of the bed and causing my vision to blur.

"Oh, Eric, you've been eavesdropping," Stefan said in a maddening, singsong voice. I glared up at him through bleary eyes. He reached out a long-nailed finger and wiped the blood from my lip. I gagged as I watched him stick his finger in his mouth, savoring the blood, *my* blood, his eyes growing brighter as he licked the last vestiges off his skin. "We can't have you poking about, can we? This game has gone on long enough. It's time I freed you from your corruptible state."

Stefan grabbed me by the hair and dragged me to the door. I clawed at his leg, trying to raise myself, scratching at his hands, at anything, but I gained no purchase.

"Stop fidgeting, will you!"

I reached up once more...and then all I knew was pain—dark, searing pain—and Greydanus's bottomless eyes staring into my own.

‡

Voices ricocheted in and out of my mind, but this time they were *real* voices, belonging to *real* people standing close to me. One I could see, the other must have been in the shadows, which were legion.

My head still throbbed from Stefan's blow. I swiveled my eyes about, trying to make sense of where I was. The room appeared to be circular—slate floor, stone walls, and at the far end, an opaque oval that told the time.

The clock tower.

The hands pointed up toward twelve—midnight.

"Be it ever so humble, there's no place like hell."

"What have you done with Greydanus?" It was the first thing that came to me, the first memory I recalled before being struck and brought to this dungeon.

"He's resting."

"Dead, you mean."

"Of course not! Would I kill my own son? I'm not a monster, Eric, regardless of what you think."

Truth be told, I was thinking of his parents and Roddy and just how monstrous he'd been to them.

"I brought you here for many reasons, one of them to be Greydanus's first turn, but he's failed that, so we will have to tread slowly. He is young yet. I'm not worried. I've all the time in the world, Eric, as I told you before. That's one of the many perks of being immortal."

"You're not immortal," I spat.

"Close to it." He smirked at me over his shoulder. "No, Eric, no. When you meddle with the dark, sooner or later it will claim you. That is why you are here. You got rather fond of dark things, did you not? You've seen too much. You know things you shouldn't."

I felt as though I was choking on my tongue. "So, you're going to kill me," I said, the words sounding hollow in my throat. In the space of a moment, I'd seen what was before me—seen it and resigned myself to my fate. "Better to serve in heaven than burn in your hell."

"A perversion of Milton's great hero's words, how quaint. But alas, wrong. How wasteful would that be? I see great potential in you, Eric. I meant what I said before. All eternity awaits us, and I've no intention of being damned alone. Besides, if Father has his way...but no, that is for a later date. You will come into that in time, a few days' time. But until then, you are *mine*. As for your wife...well, she should provide me with a few hours' amusement and then I'll let my sisters do what they will with her."

I tore at my bonds so savagely that I felt the rope biting through my skin, drawing blood. I strained again and again, not caring what happened to my body. I had to survive to warn Maddie. I had to survive for our child.

Why wasn't I free of these bloody restraints?! I looked down and felt as though I was standing on the brink of an impassable chasm. I knew then for certain that I wasn't getting out of this alive, for I wasn't bound at all...except by the power of Stefan's mind.

"Good, good, rage is good. I see you're willing to kill to save her, but let's be serious. You cannot kill me."

"I can try."

"Haven't we already done that? Have you forgotten our little incident with the sword in London?"

I bit my tongue, forcing myself to remain calm.

"I thought not. So you see, there is no way."

"There is always a way. The cross."

"The cross?" he shrieked. "*The cross*?! Please! Don't insult me. Even if you found it, which you won't ever, my sister would never let you take it alive. Nadia won't ever betray me. She's not suicidal."

He circled me, his hands clasped behind his back. His paleness had never seemed as extreme to me until this moment. Now, dressed all in black, from the high-necked tunic that hid the marks of his transformation to his shining knee-high boots, he was as pale as a cadaver, save for that shock of red hair atop his head and the unnatural sheen of his nearly translucent eyes.

Those eyes were now level with my own as he stooped to one knee and stared into my face. "You've always been rather pallid, so you should fit right in."

Something was gnawing at the back of my mind. Something important. Something about Greydanus.

And then Leonora's words came back to me and made more sense than anything I'd ever learned in my entire life.

Greydanus is a Born Vampire, we were made.

"He's pure," I gasped, speaking more to myself than him.

"What?"

"Greydanus...he's pure. He's what Salei wanted all along. That's why he sacrificed you. That's why he used Leonora. Don't you see? You were both just means to an end."

Greydanus is more powerful than either of us, and he doesn't even know it yet.

That would explain the fear Stefan betrayed every time Greydanus looked at him a certain way. As long as Greydanus remained ignorant about his powers, Stefan retained control.

"Stop blathering on! *My* son?! That shrinking, detestable boy? Impossible." But I knew I'd got through. He was wavering. I could see it in the way his shoulders tensed, the way his long-nailed fingers were trembling. "My father would never do such a thing to me."

"He's not your father!" I couldn't help screaming. How long was he going to persist in believing Salei's lies?

"You're not in a position to be smug," he growled, slapping me so hard my world momentarily went dark. "Just because my son looks like you doesn't mean you know anything about him."

I licked the blood from my lips before he could claim it for his own. The bitterness of his tone gave me hope.

I'd struck a nerve.

I could see the worry in his eyes, the uncertainty. He knew much better than I just how treacherous his father could be. I'd planted the seeds of doubt; I only hoped they would take root before he could finish me off.

"I want the world to burn, Eric," he said, his voice dreamy. He'd regained his calm, curse him. "When everyone has suffered the way I have, when they have endured what I have endured, then they will be whole and I will be satisfied."

"But by then it will be too late!" I had no idea what he was rambling on about, but knowing him, it would be vile.

"That's the idea. That's what Father is planning. And they will pay."

"They, whoever they might be, weren't the ones! Some rogue Upyr ruined your *father's* life. And now the world has to pay?"

"Life is not fair. The innocent suffer with the guilty. I can't help that. Soon, one day, everyone will be like me, everyone will suffer what I have, and you will help me accomplish this."

So that's what this was all about. I was to be his right hand in destruction. Images of rogue Corcitura raced through my mind. I saw them running rampant through the streets, turning all in their path, creating a new species that would become the dominant race of this earth. It was as though Stefan were letting me see his thoughts, his plans.

"The innocent will suffer alongside the guilty," he repeated, his voice sounding miles away. And then, as if on cue, my arm began to throb. I clenched my teeth, trying not to scream, for the pain ripping through my flesh was the worst I'd ever endured.

"I may be damned, but not so thoroughly that I don't remember the scripture they drilled into me during our school days. What was it St. Paul said about thorns?"

"A thorn in the flesh..." I whispered, the words making me tremble.

"Yes, I do believe you're right. 'There was given unto me a thorn in the flesh, a messenger of Satan to buffet me, in order to keep me from exalting myself.'"

He knelt before me, his hands pinning down my unbound arms. I blinked rapidly, the sweat trickling into my eyes, mixing with my tears. He was corrupting scripture, interpreting it to suit his own diabolical devices. And I could do nothing to stop him.

"I am that messenger, Eric."

I screamed as he dug his fingernails into my flesh and plucked out the barb, *his* barb—the barb that had been left behind after he'd attacked me...in my dream. He inspected the barb, turning it over in his palm, and glowered at me through half-closed lids.

"I have not tried to exalt myself," I panted.

"Oh, but you have been happy, haven't you? Isn't that the same thing? Are you not exalted by those you love?"

"I have nothing to atone for."

But it seemed I had. I couldn't believe my eyes. He was supposed to be dead. I'd killed him nearly seven years ago, but logic didn't matter now.

He was there, no matter how hard I tried to deny it.

That soot-black hair, that olive-tinged skin, those eyes...*those eyes...*

Augustin Boroi, skewered on the wyvern-headed staff, lifted his head and winked at me.

The tower filled with screams. Not until I closed my mouth did I realize that the screams had been mine.

When I looked back to where Augustin had been, no one was there.

A dream? A nightmare?

Justice.

I knew that voice. I remembered her, oh, very well indeed. She'd tried to seduce me once.

"You have nothing to atone for?!" Stefan shrieked, startling me, tearing me away from the ghosts of the past. "If not for you, I would be whole. I would be a man like any other! If not for your insatiable lust for my wife, Vladec Salei would have never found me."

"That's a lie! He was hunting for you for years!" I looked around the room, casting about for something to hold on to, someone to come to my aid.

And then I saw Luc, his hand resting on a lever I had not noticed until now.

What did that lever open?

I screamed at him, begged him for help, but he remained impassive, his eyes looking like two burned out lumps of coal. "Luc, tell him, I'm begging you!"

"Luc obeys no one but me."

I remembered the graveyard and Leonora and Maddie and the blind faith we'd placed in this man I had always known I could not trust. "You lied to us?!"

"Of course he lied to you. The instinct of self-preservation runs deep in Luc's veins. Just ask his wife and daughters."

No, this could not be true. Not even Luc could be so base...could he? "You killed them to save yourself?!" He did not deny it, but just continued to stand there as though he were a part of the stone wall, as though he no longer had any will of his own. "You monster! You *murderer*!"

"Save your breath, Eric, it'll do no good. No one can hear you now."

He was right. He was incredibly, undeniably right. I was alone. Luc was a mindless drone, Maddie—God protect her and give her strength to deal with what was to come—was who knew where, fighting against who knew what, and Leonora and Greydanus...I had no idea where they might be, or if they were even still alive.

The only one who could help me now was Stefan. As insane as that notion was, he was my last hope. I had to believe there was still some humanity left within him.

"Stefan, please! This is me! Your brother. You cannot have forgotten what we meant to one another, even through all that's happened. You *can't* have forgotten!"

My heart soared. I was getting through. His eyes beaded back and forth, searching my face. For one, blinding instant,

I saw recognition, as if something of his old self were trying to break through.

And then he started to laugh.

"Bravo, old son, bravo," he said, his lips twitching upward so that I saw his serrated incisors elongating. "That was really a remarkable piece of desperation. No, alas, I'm sorry to have to disappoint you yet again...what am I saying? I'm not really sorry at all."

I strained against my phantom bonds, desperately trying to free myself, but it was useless. I watched in horror as he pushed Luc away and wrenched the lever down himself.

My chair rose up. For the first time I saw that the back of the chair was attached to a long chain depending from the ceiling. Metal scraped against metal. The grate the chair had been resting on, the grate I hadn't seen because it had been covered till now, began to retract.

"I've grown quite fond of this room," Stefan said, his voice sounding so cheery. "My father used to come here to get away from it all, to entertain his guests, you might say. They always had a screaming good time."

I heard the first screams then. Horrid, flesh-crawling screams—charnel house screams.

And then I looked down...and all was lost. Inside that pit were thousands of souls crying out for my blood; thousands of souls, gaunt-cheeked, hollow-eyed, dead for generations, clawing upward, ripping each other to pieces in their haste to reach me.

Hanging like a worm on a hook, I gazed down into the very depths of hell. The chain hitched lower. I retched as the stench of rotting flesh overpowered me.

I scanned the faces, but they all looked the same—dead, decayed, damned.

And then I saw two I recognized.

One I'd just seen, twitching on the end of a sword.

The other I'd know anywhere. That blood-red hair that was almost black.

Sorina.

Soot-blackened, charred, yet still ghastly beautiful. She was waiting for me, her arms outstretched, her neck torn open in a great upturned red gash that mimicked the smile on her blood-flecked lips.

"Welcome to the house of the undead."

Book the Second: The Narrative of Madelaine Bradburry 1895: Alone

Belododia's Belfry

My husband is gone. I cannot find him anywhere. When I went to sleep last night, he was by my side, but now, as the first rays of dawn break through the window, I know for certain he is gone. His side of the bed is cold—as cold as if he has not slept there at all. The door is bolted. There is no trace of him.

I have ransacked this room, torn it apart, and still it is as if he never set foot here, never even existed. I feel a heaviness in my limbs this morning, though I suppose it could just be the baby within me. When I look in the cup from which I drank my tea last night, I notice a residue, a filmy white liquid on the bottom. I dip in my finger and put it to my lips, tasting something sickly sweet.

I know I have been drugged.

I must go out into this desolate house; I must leave the safety of this chamber that begins to feel more and more like a tomb. I must find answers. Yet I am afraid, terrified even, of what will happen if the master of this place finds me alone. I have a mission; I know that, now that Eric is gone. My heart aches to admit it. I pray he is still alive, but if he is alive in a different form, will he still be the man I love? *Can* he even love in that state? I cannot think of these things now or I will go mad.

Corcitura

I must find Professor Fertig's book, though I do not know what good it will do me. It is only a book, just an insignificant book. Luc has gone to find the author, but even so, what can he tell us? Eric knows Stefan more deeply and truly than any of them. Now that he has disappeared, I cannot help but feel that all our chances for survival have disappeared with him.

Before he vanished, Eric told me many things, but many still he kept hidden. All I know for certain is that Stefan is some new form of vampire, a super vampire, or something along those lines, and he cannot be killed by ordinary methods. Several times, my husband mentioned a cross, a silver cross with a blood cabochon. It is in the possession of Stefan's sister, Nadia, though whether or not she is still alive is unknown. The last time my husband saw her was in Romania, but that was nearly seven years ago. What this has to do with the book, I do not know, nor why this book is so important, but I know I must find it. *I must.*

The only one I can count on is myself. I do not trust Stefan's so-called wife nor that son of hers who bears an uncanny resemblance to my husband. And though it pains me to admit it, I cannot trust Luc, *least* of all Luc, though he swears he will be able to bring Zigmund back.

I walk toward the door and reach for the handle. I breathe in deeply, steeling myself. Father did not raise a coward. Mother would not allow me to fear the dark. How could I fear the dark when I've been surrounded by it my whole life? I've always been drawn to things that make other women scream.

I press down on the handle and step out into the corridor. I don't know what I am expecting to see, maybe a bevy of vampires rushing down the hallway, but there is nothing. Darkness, silence—the corridor is empty.

I am nearly at the bottom of the steps when something calls to me. I know it is not *his* voice. Eric said only those who were marked can hear him in their minds. Still, whose voice could it be?

The voice draws me back up the staircase, leading me on, its soft, wordless timbre guiding me toward I don't know what. Finally, it ceases. I feel somehow bereft, even more alone without it, until I see where it has led me.

I am standing before the door leading up to the turret above our room. I noticed the turret the night we first arrived. How could I not? There is something dark about it, something mysterious, something unknown that frightens me. I have tried to convince myself I did not see a figure flitting up there that first night, but I cannot deny what I saw. Was it Leonora? Or something else? I have never ventured there on my own, but now I have no choice. The pull is too insistent.

I push open the door and once more the voice starts to call. I cannot make out what it says. All I know is that I must go to it, must answer its summons.

The steps are narrow and made of stones so ancient I am afraid they will crumble if I put too much weight on them. There is no light in here, no air. I feel choked and am thankful when I finally emerge onto the balcony. Tendrils of morning fog wisp through the railing, which is decaying, I notice with alarm. I dare not go near it. One false move and over I will go, which I'm sure will make the master of the house very pleased, since he has me marked for death already.

"Such a fine morning, my dear Mrs. Bradburry, is it not?"

I have tried my hardest to avoid him, yet he has found me regardless of my efforts. That voice *was* his, I am sure of it now, so why am I still hearing it if its owner is in my presence?

The breath catches in my throat as I look into his eyes. His dark-rimmed pupils are larger than I remember, the rest of his eyes so colorless as to be nearly white.

"It's a bit chilly," I say. He seems amused by this. His eyes crinkle at the edges and he buttons his coat, though I know it is just an act for my benefit. He has no pulse. How could he be cold?

"You know much, my dear, but what do you really know about vampires?"

His question startles me. I bite the inside of my cheek to keep from betraying my fears to this creature. "Naught but what I've read in Polidori and Le Fanu," I answer. I remember the ashes of *Carmilla* and the terror in Eric's eyes when he saw me holding the book. All I know of vampires, I have learned from a handful of novels, but what good does fiction do me when I have a damned soul staring me in the face?

"Ah, yes, but those are fairy tales," he says, waving his hand dismissively. "Pure fantasy." He pauses near a waterspout carved into a devil's head. It is meant to portray a gargoyle, but I have never seen one so ugly and diabolical-looking, even by grotesque standards. I shiver, but not because I am cold.

"What do you know about...*real* vampires?"

"Not enough to kill them." The boldness of my words surprises me, but he does not flinch. "What have you done with my husband?" I have spoken before I can stop myself, but then I realize I *don't* want to stop myself. Something has changed in the air between us. I'm no longer as afraid as I was.

"Eric?"

No, Faust, I think furiously to myself.

"I haven't the faintest idea. Was he not with you this morning? I should think you would know his whereabouts better than me. Or is there already strain in your too-brief marriage? Does he not want a child so soon?"

"Of course he wants..." I cut off the words, biting my tongue in the process. His eyes are gleaming, his lips parted in anticipation. He is staring at me as though he wants to devour me...me and the child he already knows I carry. "I beg your pardon, Mr. Belododia..."

"Stefan." The name slithers off his tongue.

"*Stefan*," I say with effort. "I expected Eric to be with you at the bedside of Greydanus. I must say the boy is doing remarkably well, considering that he was supposedly at death's door, hence our presence here."

"Ah, yes, my son..."

"Your son, who shares so many characteristics with my husband."

The words make me sick to say. I fear them too much, fear the implications, though Eric claimed he'd never known Leonora in that way.

I feel as though my words have erected a barrier between us—*more* of a barrier than there already was. He reaches out and brushes the leaves off the railing. I see his shoulders tense, his whole body becoming rigid. I take a step toward the railing and stare down at what he's looking at so intently.

A small, brownish-grey wolf prances about the frozen pond. Something about that wolf strikes me as familiar. I lean against the railing, causing bits of gravel to slip through the spindles. The wolf must have exceptional hearing. That small sound has alerted him to our presence.

The wolf ceases his wild gamboling and stares up at us. I find it hard to concentrate on anything else. The wolf's eyes are so radiant, glowing almost, yet black as night. Idiotically, I reach out my hand as if I could stroke the wolf's fur from such a great distance. I stare dumbly at the wolf, until I am jerked back to reality by the feel of a vise closing around my wrist. I cry out as I look down at my arm.

Stefan's ice-cold hand encircles my wrist, crushing it. "Do not be attracted to things you don't understand," he hisses. Is he talking of himself? I can soundly disabuse him of this notion in a matter of seconds. I am *not* attracted to him, though I do not understand him any more than that wolf down below.

He releases my wrist. There is a blue mark discoloring my skin where his hand used to be. I rub it fiercely, trying to instill some warmth, but it is no use. I wonder if I am now marked, too.

He seems to have forgotten me. He is still staring at the wolf. There are worry lines between his brows, and his mouth is drawn down at the edges into a scowl. "It appears we still have a wolf infestation. If you'll excuse me, I have business to attend to. I hope to see you again for dinner?"

"Yes, of course," I say abstractedly, watching the wolf run off into the forest.

"I wish you good hunting today, my dear." Before I can snatch it away, he takes my hand in his and kisses it. Ice shoots through my body and weakens my knees. I feel as though I have been kissed by death.

I am alone once more, on this the highest peak of the château. A chill wind lashes through the trees, sending snowflakes fluttering to the ground. Dark strands of my hair whip across my face, obscuring my vision, but not completely, not enough so that I am no longer incapable of watching Stefan...

...watching Stefan watching me. *He* is not alone, standing now at the edge of the forest. There is a woman at his side. She is not the woman I expected to see, the woman I mistrust. This woman's beauty terrifies me, mainly because it is so perfect, so inhuman. Her lustrous blonde hair flows freely down her back. She turns, and I can see her eyes—green and glowing and brutal. Her lips are redder than blood and her skin as pale as the snow she treads upon. I know she sees me, but whether he tells her not to acknowledge my presence or she decides to ignore me of her own accord is a mystery. Her eyes remain fixed on the wolf tracks at her feet.

He takes her hand and guides her toward the trees, and I am left with a memory of her face. I know I have seen her before.

Something slithers beneath my feet. I look down, expecting to see a snake or some other creature. Instead, there is nothing but a rose. A dead rose, its petals black and brittle. Affixed to the stem, threaded through a frayed black ribbon, is a small band of gold.

Eric's wedding ring.

This is all the impetus I need. I am down the staircase and making for the stables in an instant. I feel panic in my chest, but I damp it down. Hysteria will do me no good now. This is a clue. I know it is, though it is meant as a taunt. In my heart, I feel he is alive.

I must find that book.

കൃ

My driver has vanished like all the rest. I expected him to do as much, but not so soon. I wonder if he has gone back to report my whereabouts to his master? I am expecting Stefan to come for me or send the coach back. Whatever the circumstance, the driver will return to take me home. After all, death has asked me to dine with him this evening, and I do not intend to disappoint.

My search has proven fruitless so far. Peddlers, librarians, merchants—they all look at me askance when I ask them for *Fertig's Lexicon of Nosferatu*. I feel a fool even speaking the title, though I know they believe in the *vampyre,* as they call it in these parts. Yet no one seems willing to help.

I pause beneath the Astronomical Clock. It is already well past noon, and I have nothing to show for my efforts. My time is running out.

During my search, I have thought of little else than the book. Now, as I cross Mala Strana and head for the University, I cannot stop thinking of my husband. It is for him that I am doing all this. When I first met him, I knew I wanted to be with him, wanted him fiercely, but was that the only reason I loved him? It was a whirlwind, a dream, but was that all it was? A dream? Of course it wasn't. I fell in love with him for who he was. I saw in him the mirror of my own soul. We were so similar, held so many of the same desires and hopes, so many of the same dreams that polite society would look down upon. Yet even through it all, I felt something eating away at my happiness, as if I had always known it would come to this.

I think of my father now. I know he is not to blame. If anything, he brought us together. Father loves Eric, too. I loved Eric; I *still* love him, though I shouldn't after what has happened.

The snatches of myth or truth, as I now know them to be, that Eric has told me war within my mind, and I fight to keep from forgetting all the players. Constantinos is from Greece, Vladec Salei, the one who started it all, is a Russian, and Zigmund, somehow Leonora's son—though she doesn't look old enough to even be the mother of Greydanus—is the one who supposedly has the answers. And I have come to find his blasted book.

I walk on, musing, not seeing the entrance of the University until I am upon it. A man exits just as I am about to enter and holds open the door for me. I thank him and push on hurriedly, not wanting to be detained. My boot heels clomp nosily on the stone floor. I feel as though everyone's eyes are on me. They know I do not belong here.

I try to blend in and seem to succeed. The novelty of my appearance has worn off. No one has time for this young American woman wearing the hunted look. I am grateful for their disinterest.

I round a corner and stop on the threshold of a cavernous hall. High arched windows let in the sun, which reflects off the light stone of the walls. Students mill about; professors, their noses in books, dodge between columns. I am reminded of my tutors and allow myself to smile at the happy memory.

I do not read Czech, but I know how to find the library. I wait beside a column and watch the students. Two go in, empty-armed, through the massive wooden double doors. I wait. Ten minutes later, they come back out, their arms full of books. I go through the doors and am finally in the place I have been seeking.

Row upon row of freestanding, floor-to-ceiling bookshelves fill the raftered room. At nearly every desk is a student with a mound of books piled up beside him. I walk further in, the silence shrouding me, weighing me down. The air is very close in here, oppressive. My mood does not lighten as I see the face of the man sitting behind the main desk.

"Excuse me..." I whisper.

"Shhhhh!"

"Sorry." I drop my tone even lower. "Could you please direct me to the section concerning vampires?"

A few chairs scrape against the floor. I try to ignore the students now looking in my direction.

"The fiction section is over there," says the librarian derisively, his tone even more sour than his face. His English is heavily accented, but thank God he speaks my language, and I can just understand him.

"No, I meant the non-fiction section."

He narrows his eyes at me. This is where I get thrown out, I expect.

"Have an interest in the occult, do you?" he asks, rising.

"Morbid curiosity, really."

"Well, follow me."

I follow him past the main shelves and collections, down through a corridor, and finally out into a large room with vaulted ceilings and tapestries on the walls that do not contain bookcases.

"Here is our non-fiction section. You will find all you need on that caddy over there," he says, pointing to the largest bookcase I have ever seen. "We provide ladders to your right," he continues cheerily. "Happy hunting!"

Why is everyone wishing me that today? It's as though they all know I'm not going to find what I so desperately need.

I watch his receding form just as sourly as he'd watched me. Too late, he is gone, and I realize I have not asked him if the library even has Fertig's *Lexicon* in its collection. It can't be helped now. If I were to press him further, I know *he* would not be willing to help, either. I consider myself lucky for getting this far, especially after having come up against brick walls the entire morning.

The bookcase towers above me. I'll be here for the rest of the afternoon, but hopefully, I'll have something to show for all my troubles. I must find that book. I feel it calling to me, compelling me, driving me forward.

A ladder to my right beckons. I climb up and begin searching through the section marked *F. Falbright, Fernig, Festus...*

I look over the names again, but I was right the first time. There is no Fertig here.

Wonderful. Where else could it be listed? I move down the ladder, reaching the section marked N. Maybe they misfiled it under *Nosferatu.*

A hundred books are before me. I pull out one with a pebbled leather cover. The picture on the front startles me so severely that I nearly drop the book. It is a painting of a man with a squat forehead and heavy-lidded, protuberant eyes. His long, dark tresses fall past his shoulders. His mouth is unsmiling and sensual and makes me shiver. I have seen the set of those lips hundreds of times before in other men, and I know what it betokens—cruelty. This fellow might have been a tyrant or even a vampire in his day, but I can put my mind at ease. I know now, *definitively*, that my host is not the reincarnation of Vlad Tepes.

I place the book back on the shelf and move further down the line, but none of these books is the one I need.

Abandoning the ladder, I move down to the last shelf, the one marked *Z*. If the book is not here, I do not know where else I can turn. My fingers travel over the spines, the names: *Zabwich, Zbdorsk,* on and on...

And there it is.

Zigmund Fertig's Lexicon of Nosferatu.

I remove it from the shelf and heft it to my breast. It is weightier than I have expected and older-looking as well. I've no time to search for a desk to sit at nor do I want to be near anyone now.

I sit on the floor, cross my legs, and open the book.

Bypassing the preface, I make straight for the index. I know the vampires I am seeking. Strangely, the index is not alphabetical, and the ones I seek are listed in a separate section devoted just to them. I flip to the page and stare in wonder.

A man—tall, fair-haired, high-cheekboned, exceedingly handsome—stares back at me. Underneath the painting, there is a caption:

Do not be fooled by his suave appearance. The Upyr is one of the deadliest vampires on record.

I turn the page and gasp. I can still recognize the man, but only slightly. His skin is even paler, his eyes so hellish I cover the painting with my hand so I will not have to look at them. Still, I cannot forget those eyes or those extended fangs—and all that blood dripping from his mouth.

I focus on the text below the picture.

Upyr: An extremely vicious Russian vampire. It rests during the day and feeds at night. I have not had dealings with this creature, but a lead put me on the scent of one that is particularly fearsome, one that goes by the name Vladec Salei.

I close the book, keeping my finger within it to mark the page. If Zigmund knows of Vladec Salei, then surely he will know how to help us. I feel giddy and terrified all at once. I look around to make sure no one has noticed me sitting on the floor like a vagabond before I reopen the book.

This vampire is to be avoided at all costs. Its powers of mesmerism are uncanny and nearly impossible to combat for the weak-minded. Kill it if you have the chance, for it will not spare you. The best method is either a stake through the heart, or, more thorough and less likely to fail, to cleave its head from its body.

I swallow hard, but press on. Yes, it is grisly, but grislier still would be getting attacked by such a beast. I have no intention of becoming a statistic.

The next picture is ghastly, but somehow not as frightening as the Upyr. I can see this creature for what it is. The Upyr is a mystery. That very fact terrifies me more than I can even understand.

Vrykolakas: Once thought to denote a werewolf, the name has since become synonymous with one of the most fearsome vampires in the canon of Nosferatu. Indigenous to Greece, it has been known to leave its surroundings to hunt for food. I have had dealings with this creature and almost did not survive the encounter. My mother was not as lucky.

If you find yourself in its hunting grounds and hear a knock on your door in the middle of the night, do not call out, for the Vrykolakas will come for you. It is also believed that the creature can crush the life out of its victims by sitting atop their chests until their lungs collapse.

The smallest sounds disturb this beast, but large noises do not trouble it overmuch. Plague-like in appearance and armed with a savage barbed tongue, the Vrykolakas possesses the ability to regenerate from any wound inflicted on itself, save for complete burning or decapitation. It loathes fire with a hellish passion. If you encounter the beast, subdue it any way you can, then burn the body or cut off its head. Those are the only ways of ensuring it will never rise again.

Corcitura

Only one more entry remains. I stare at the term, not sure how to pronounce it.

Corcitura: The created progeny of a Vrykolakas and an Upyr. Not progeny in the usual sense, but in the made sense— made well after being born. A person bitten by a Vrykolakas and then an Upyr on two separate occasions will turn into this hybrid, mongrel, half-breed vampire, the strongest form of the species I have ever encountered. The combination of two such volatile forms of vampirism is catastrophic. I have spent the better part of the last decade trying to track this creature down. It is indigenous to Europe. I have seen it in action once, nearly seven years ago in London, where I witnessed it single- handedly destroying a police wagon. Its strength is unmatched, as is its cunning, and its bloodlust, though controlled, is insatiable.

I know of no way to kill it, save for a theory that my colleagues have taken great joy in deriding. If the creature has a blood relative, close kin, a sister or a brother, perhaps, this person will have to be the one to do the deed. The Corcitura's blood is so intermixed as to make any conventional way of killing it impossible. Neither holy objects nor silver nor sunlight nor the laughable garlic technique will have any effect on this creature. Only blood—the blood of the ones who turned it and the pure blood of one Florin Istratescu—can destroy this abomination.

My legs tingle from lack of use. I lean back against the bookcase and stretch them out from underneath me, the book turning over in my lap. Suddenly, my legs are forgotten, and all I can do is stare at the back cover of the book, not believing what I see.

Fair hair combed neatly back from his forehead, a pair of deep-set eyes obscured by wire-rimmed glasses, lips set in a grim line—Zigmund Fertig. He is young, much younger than I was expecting. And he looks nothing like Leonora. But none of that is important. I can scarcely breathe as I read the text beneath the photograph.

Professor Zigmund Fertig, 37, a native of Munich, now teaches Folkloric and Slavic Studies at Charles University.

He teaches at Charles University.

Melika Dannese Lux

I am sitting *in* the library of Charles University.

He is here.

Then who was it Luc went to find?

My mouth is dry, my heart beating wildly. I tuck the book under my arm and walk rapidly out of the library.

A thousand questions race through my mind, first among them, where is Luc? Why did he lie? And what does he gain by bringing about our destruction? That is the only explanation I can think of for his treachery.

I stop a man and pray that he speaks English. He looks at me as though I am not human, so I switch to German. Still he does not understand, but his companion does and directs me to the faculty offices. I travel up a wide, marble staircase, shuffling past more scholars and students before finally coming to a desk behind which a man is perched. He is engrossed in a novel by Goethe. Once again, I speak in German, enquiring if the Professor is in. The man says Professor Fertig is out, but should be back soon, and would I mind waiting?

I want to scream at him that *yes* I would mind waiting, but I hold my tongue and tell him I'll wait by the professor's office door. He returns his attention to his novel, and I slip down the corridor.

A small bronze plaque reading *Professor Zigmund Fertig* is affixed to the door. A shaft of light shines through the jamb. I push against the door and it lurches inward. I am desperate. My time is running out. I cannot afford to wait for him to return.

I step across the threshold, noting the state of disarray the room is in. Books lie face down upon a large rosewood desk. Even more tomes are scattered on the floor or have been strewn helter-skelter on the shelves that line the walls. A carved fireplace dominates the far wall of the room, abutting a window seat that reminds me of my favorite one back home in Riverhampton. I am flooded with the memories of sitting in my little nook, whiling the hours away, absorbed in one of my favorite books, which somehow or another always dealt with the dark and unexplainable.

Even in my wildest imaginings, I never would have thought I'd be living out one of those stories.

I have forgotten myself. What good will memories do me now? I wander over to the desk and look at the books. They are all about vampires, not surprisingly. I feel slight relief but also alarm because there seems to be a theme here. Pictures, drawings, woodcarvings—all show vampires in their most demonic states.

Writing is scrawled across the pages. Scribbled in the margins and on every available scrap of paper are notes, theories, and words in languages I cannot decipher. A twinge of fear shivers up my spine, and I wonder if it is such a good idea to be here. I am beginning to believe Professor Fertig is obsessed.

"I beg your pardon, Madam, but can I be of service?"

I cannot help staring. The picture in the back of his book revealed nothing of the scars. From his right cheek to his lower left jaw, arcing across his face in a half circle, five indentations scar his skin, the deepest gouge under his left eye. How did he not lose that eye?

He clears his throat and steps across the threshold. I am still surprised by how young he looks. He is close to forty, but looks no older than Eric. His demeanor is severe, making him seem older than he actually is.

I put my hand to my heart to steady its beating. "Professor Fertig, please forgive my intrusion, but I come on behalf of one whom I love."

"My dear lady, there is no need to be sorry," he responds in near perfect English. "Please," he says, pointing me to the window seat. "Wait, sorry," he says, picking up a book. I catch a glimpse of an illustration of a devil inside the front cover. That face seems somehow familiar, but he closes the book before I can see more. "Please, be seated."

He settles atop the desk, pushing his spectacles up the bridge of his nose. His too-blue eyes startle me. They are electric. His hair is dark blonde and so unlike Leonora's that for a second I doubt he could be her son. But there is something in the turn of his nose and the twist of his lips that reminds me strongly of her. And though their eyes are not the same color, there is no denying the twin intensity the eyes of mother and son both contain.

"I am surprised to find you here, Professor. I was under the impression that you taught at the university in Munich."

"Whatever would give you that notion?"

"A friend of mine," I say carefully, not sure how much to reveal yet, "provided me with the information."

"My dear lady, I have not set foot in the homeland of my father in over thirty years."

So Luc is a liar and possibly even a murderer. I cannot think of him harming Eric. "I've come on behalf of my husband, whom I do not know where to find."

"You've lost your husband..."

Is he mocking me? His tone of voice certainly suggests it. I must sound like a fool, but what else can I tell him?

The truth.

I cannot wait any longer. My desire to spare him pain has vanished. He does not seem to have any qualms about inflicting it on me. "If it weren't for your mother, we would have never come. I know of Constantinos, of Vladec Salei, of Leonora, your mother, who still lives."

He is off the desk and trembling with rage before me, his jaw taut as a bowstring, as soon as my words have been spoken. "You know *nothing* of Leonora," he says, his teeth clenched, his anger palpable. "I saw the life being sucked out of her. I saw her *die*."

"She lives, Zigmund. She has a son, another son."

"I was her only son!" he shrieks. His hands are balled into fists at his sides. For one dreadful instant, I fear he is going to strike me.

"Professor, is anything the matter?" Both of us turn our attention to the doorway. The gaunt man who I encountered in the hallway peeks through the door. He looks from me to Zigmund, then back to me, accusation in his eyes.

"Escort this woman from my office, Heinrich."

"There is no need, I assure you, Professor," I say, rising. "I'm quite capable of leaving on my own."

"I saw my mother die," he says again, as if I could forget the first time he told me. The wavering note in his voice gives me a moment's hope, but when I look into his eyes—eyes of flint—I know better than to count on his aid.

"I know, but sometimes what we think we see never happened."

"Get out of my office," he says, teeth gritted. "I don't know who sent you, but it was in extremely bad taste."

"Take this," I say, handing him the scrap of paper I have written my name and the address of the château upon. He grabs the note before it can flutter to the ground. "If you change your mind, that is where you can find me, though I hope it won't be too late."

I am halfway down the corridor when I hear footfalls behind me. "What is your game, Mrs. Bradburry?"

So he read the note.

"I'm not playing a game. I only want your help."

"I only help myself these days," he says, running his hand through his hair.

Tortured. I know that look. I saw it in my own eyes this morning. "I'm very sorry to hear that, and I'm sure your mother will be as well."

His eyes flash. The confusion of emotions I saw on his face a minute before is gone—gone so thoroughly I fear I must have deluded myself into believing I saw anything at all. "You read about these things, you study them practically all your life, but if you were to meet one in the flesh, you'd be so terrified you wouldn't be able to move. Don't tell me my business, Mrs. Bradburry."

"I *have* met one in the flesh, Professor. That's the problem." I turn and walk on, not waiting for him to answer nor expecting him to follow.

Snow blows against my face as I emerge from the University. The sun has already begun to set. Soon, darkness will envelop the streets of Prague.

A crowd has gathered in the square. Several little stands have been erected, all displaying wares for the Three Kings celebration. Epiphany is just days away. I wonder, as I hurry through the press of bodies, if I will be alive to celebrate it.

All around me, vendors hock their goods. The marionettes catch my eye. I am reminded of Steven and his request for one and consequently of my dearest friend, Molly, all those miles away. I miss her terribly and not just because I am homesick. If only she were here to help me decipher this puzzle; if only she were here to lend me even an ounce of her pluck.

I pass a man painting Hradcany Castle and then another carving a miniature St. Vitus from a block of wood. In the middle of the square, I see steam rising.

I remember the entry in Zigmund's book. One of the ways to dispatch a Vrykolakas is through burning.

I know I'll never be able to rest if I don't see it for myself, see the body turning to ash in the middle of the square.

Frantically, I push my way through the crowd, and feel like a fool when I discover the source of the steam. It is just a young man welding a sculpture into shape.

Hysterical, that's what I've become. I sigh and move on, gazing at the bustle of people milling through the stalls. All these people, these artisans and craftsmen, bakers and woodworkers, these *normal* people, are absorbed in their own little peaceful world, not knowing the horror that dwells just a few short miles beyond the safety of their town.

The thoughts threaten to overwhelm me. The panic in my chest is suffocating. I bite down hard on my tongue to keep from crying out. This has to end, but how? And who will put an end to it? *Me?* How can I when I feel so alone?

Yet I am not alone, not truly. I press my hands to my stomach. If not for Eric, then for the child—I must survive.

I walk on in a haze. The streets all start to look the same, as do the people. I do not know where my feet take me; all I know is that the day is waning, and I need comfort.

And then I see the church.

The square in front of the mustard-colored facade is deserted. Whatever crowds I witnessed have not invaded the almost tomb-like silence of this part of the city. I look up at the sun, already dangerously low in the sky. I should be getting back, but I cannot resist the pull of the church.

The air in here is close, cool, and I feel soothed as I walk down the narthex. The church is empty, save for a man near the altar. He eyes me with what I think is suspicion, but that can't possibly be what he feels. Curiosity maybe or perhaps I imagined the emotion. He is not looking at me at all anymore. I'm just being hysterical again.

I settle into a pew and draw my rosary out of my pocket. A shuddering breath escapes me as I stare at the beads pooled in my hands. I finger the beads, marveling once again at the rose pattern carved into each one. I remember Eric's face when he gave it to me—so full of love and hope for the future. The beads are beautiful—but gold. This is the one time I wish Eric had given me silver instead.

Near me, I hear a small sound, almost like a dove's coo. Startled, I look up and see a small, dark-haired head—a child's head. I do not know how I haven't seen him. Did he sneak in? Or was he here all along?

For a panic-stricken instant, I fear Stefan is here, too. The passage in Zigmund's book about holy objects not affecting him must not include setting foot in a church, but even *he* would not be bold enough to tread on hallowed ground.

I scan the church, but there is no one here except the child and the man dusting the statues around the altar. I know the child is a vampire, but still, he is only a child. How can he be turned loose into the city to fend for himself?

"Greydanus?" I whisper, coming to kneel at his side. His eyes are transfixed on the statue of the Infant of Prague. I do not think he has heard me. "Greydanus," I say again, and this time I touch his shoulder. I expect him to feel cold, as Eric has told me vampires are, as I know Stefan is, but he is warm—warm and soft and as full of life as any normal six-year-old child should be. He turns from his gazing, unclasping his hands, and looks up at me with eyes so full of sadness that my breath catches in my throat.

"Mrs. Bradburry?" he asks. He shakes his head slightly, his eyes squinted. He looks as though he does not recognize me or is astonished to find me here.

"Madelaine, call me Madelaine." He nods abstractedly, his Adam's apple bobbing as he swallows. "Why are you here?" I say after a moment, trying to reclaim his attention.

His eyes have been drawn once again to the statue of the Child Jesus.

"I had to get away. There is no peace in my father's house."

"But this is so far from home. How did you get all the way here on your own?"

"I did not come alone."

Terror claws my insides. "Your father?" I ask, barely above a whisper.

"No, me."

The voice jolts me as violently as an ice pick through the heart. I turn so suddenly that my shoulder smacks into the pew, the sound reverberating throughout the church, causing the attendant to look in our direction. I signal to him that everything is fine, but still he stares. How could he not? She is beautiful, after all, and looks unearthly in her coat of white fur.

"Leonora," I say, rubbing my shoulder as I rise to my feet. I have to crane my neck upward to see her. She towers over me, though I am by no means short. "Thank God you're here. Zigmund did not believe me and now he will not come and I only have so many days left to figure out how to end this before your husband ends *me*." My words tumble forth. I still cannot believe she is here in this church. A vampire has no soul. As I turn to look at Greydanus, I am beginning to doubt my own preconceptions. "We must go to him," I tell her, my eyes still focused on her son...*one* of her sons.

"I can't."

"What do you mean you *can't*? Leonora, we don't have the time..."

"I can't. He thinks I'm dead. I *should* be dead."

"But you're not." I step out of the pew, wanting to comfort her, to ease her fears. I can see she is on the verge of breaking.

"No, I can't...I...what am I doing here?!" It is as though she realizes for the first time that she is in the church. "I cannot be here." The hysteria in her voice is undeniable. I inch closer, holding out my hand, but she backs away. Her eyes dart about in horror as she recoils from the sight of all the holy objects that are anathema to her kind.

"But you are."

I look down to see Greydanus at my side. How did he get here when I was blocking the pew?

"Easy, Mother, there is no need to fear. There is peace here. Don't go back to Father's house." His pleading does no good. Leonora's eyes are savage, hunted, and something more.

"God preserve us…" The child sees it, too.

She is changing.

Once thought to denote a werewolf…

Oh, Zigmund, if only you had taken that analysis one step further, I think to myself. I latch onto her arm and lead her down the aisle, knowing that if I do not get her out of here soon, there is no telling what the people of this city will do to her once she has transformed.

"Greydanus, find us a conveyance. We must return to the château at once."

I rush her down the steps, her hand in mine. She is deathly cold, but her hand—God help me—her hand is no longer human. The rough pads of a wolf's paw scratch against my palm, the dagger-sharp claws digging into my flesh.

Her night-black, white-streaked hair streams out behind her. But that streak has turned to black. The rest of her hair is the color of snow as it retracts into her scalp, becoming fur. I wrench my hand out of her grasp and throw the hood over her head lest someone should see her and give us away.

I pace along the sidewalk, chafing my hands against the cold, my heart threatening to burst if Greydanus does not return soon with our means of escape.

I notice scratches on my hand and see the blood beginning to seep, but my attention is drawn to the sound of wheels clattering over the cobblestones. I look up to see the liveried footman sitting atop the box of the carriage I took to the city so many hours ago. The window on the side of the carriage is down, a small dark head leaning out of it.

"Open the door, now!" I command, hurling Leonora into the carriage.

Greydanus shifts to the far corner of the seat as we hurtle in, drawing up his knees and hugging them tightly. His eyes are filled with pure terror—fear of the creature his mother is becoming, though it cannot be the first time he has witnessed this transformation.

She is hunched over, clutching her stomach. Words in a language I cannot understand spill from her mouth. She looks at me. I can feel the heat of her gaze, feel it singeing my lungs. Her eyes are terrible to behold. I am transfixed to my seat, unable to move, unable to break the hold of those amber-white eyes, those two pools of hellfire.

"She's a hellhound."

"No, not my mother, you don't understand."

His hands claw at my arm, but I ignore him. I cannot look away from his mother, no matter how hard I wish it, and I wish it with all my might. The carriage rocks beneath us. I'm thrown back against Greydanus, shielding him. A wild shriek rattles the carriage, accompanied by the sickening sound of bones cracking through flesh. The carriage bucks again. Blinking, I force myself to look upon the chaos. I cannot believe what I am seeing. This cannot be real; this is a nightmare. Never, *never* in my life could I have expected to see a sight like this.

Leonora, her muscular, fur covered arms spanning the width of the cab, towers above us, her back pressed against the roof of the carriage. She has raised herself on her hind legs—hind legs, yes, for she has completely turned now into a gross distortion of a wolf, a wolf with a human, fur covered body. Spittle drips from her fangs onto the floor. Her eyes are still aflame, but I am no longer the object of her scrutiny. All her attention is focused on Greydanus, who has gone mute with terror. I feel him shivering behind me. I know that I must do something. The look in his mother's eyes fills me with dread.

She doesn't know us. She can no longer tell friend from enemy, not even her own son.

If I do not act, I fear she will tear him limb from limb, and me along with him, for I will not move. Inside of me, I feel a pressure welling. I cannot contain it anymore. I open my mouth and scream as though I have been damned to hell itself. Suddenly, my scream is joined by an earth-shaking howl. I clap my hands over my ears and Greydanus does as well. The sound is terrifying, but even more so because there still exists some shred of humanity within it.

My arms encircle Greydanus, my body creating a shield. Any minute now I will feel claws tearing into my back, but the attack never comes. The howl still rings within the carriage, but there is a new sound now—tearing canvas and the whistling of the wind. The carriage rocks and then subsides, steadying. I feel coolness against my face. I glance up. The wolf, Leonora, is gone, the only traces of her presence some stray tufts of fur that caught on the roof during her escape.

The entire top of the carriage is in tatters. I step onto the seat and raise myself up through the hole, searching the streets for some sign of her, but she is nowhere to be seen. The wind slapping against my face is so cold it feels like knives slashing my flesh. "Come," I shout down to Greydanus. "We must track her down before she gets beyond our reach."

As soon as I speak the words, I realize how absurd this sounds now, how absurd all of this is. I feel something inside me snap, and I crumple to the seat. This never made any sense, though I was trying to make it logical. How could I have thought I could solve this? This...what exactly *was* this? Hybrid vampires, werewolves who weren't... How could I have fooled myself into thinking I understood any of it?

Forgive me, Eric.

"Shall we be heading back to the château, Madam?"

"Where have you been?" I snap through my tears, shocked that the driver has reappeared and is so calm. "Where you deaf to all that?"

"All what, Madam?" he asks. His eyes sparkle unnaturally. I bite my tongue to keep from becoming hysterical. No wonder he didn't hear anything. He can't; he's one of them. His eyes are nearly as translucent as his master's.

"Oh, never mind. Drive on," I whisper, and slump back against the seat.

It is then that I notice Greydanus's tears. Fear shoots through me. I want to leap through the hole in the roof, yet something holds me back. Surely this child cannot be an abomination like his father?

Then why is he crying blood?

Tears stream down his face and splatter against his white shirt, the stains pooling together and making it look as though there is a mortal wound beneath the thin linen. No sobs shake his body; he is perfectly still. His head is turned toward the window. I would not be able to see the tears except that their color is so strikingly dark against his pale skin.

The tears are not thick and viscous like normal blood should be, but are watery, as though they are diluted.

A shadow crosses his face, obscuring my view. I look out the opposite window and see a line of trees—a familiar sight that makes me tremble.

We're almost home.

When I look back at Greydanus, it is all I can do not to scream. He has pulled a small vial from somewhere and is siphoning the tears into it. If he drinks the blood in my presence, I will lose whatever shred of reason I still possess.

"I'm sorry you had to witness this," he says quietly, not meeting my eyes. I am not sure if he is apologizing for his mother's transformation or the fact that he weeps blood. "It is the only nourishment I can take, but I will save it for later, when I am alone. I know you must think me a monster. I wish you didn't. I wish you could understand. This is how I survive," he says, slipping the stoppered vial into his vest pocket.

I may not understand everything, but I do understand one thing. The graveness of his features, the solemnity of his manner. If only I'd known before. How could a child be happy or vital when he is feeding off himself?

"I can only sustain myself," he continued, his voice scarcely louder than a whisper. "They do not understand this yet. I've no interest in feeding on others. Besides which, Grandfather says I am a complete waste in that department anyway."

I find it hard to swallow. I cannot decide if I am more unnerved by his matter-of-fact tone or by the mention of *Grandfather*. The painting in Zigmund's book flashes before my mind's eye.

Greydanus. He looks so fragile, so helpless. I want nothing more than to gather him into my arms and tell him everything will be all right, but that is nonsense. I am a fool to even think such thoughts. Then there is the other fact that I am conveniently forgetting: he is the child of vampires, a vampire himself, and if it were his will, he could snap me in two as easily as a twig.

He sighs and looks at his hands, which are shaking. This is all just a way of life for him and his kind, but you would have to be blind not to see that the strain on him is great—not only the obvious physical strain of bleeding himself dry, but the mental and emotional weight as well.

"Have you never tried..." I stumble, searching for the words, not knowing if what I want to say will sound as mad to him as it does to me, "...animals?"

"How could I? I'm half one myself."

A brownish-grey wolf gamboling at the edge of the forest. I'd known it was him.

"It would be cannibalistic. No, Father thinks it is a phase, but Mother knows it's permanent. She's the only one who's been there when I have to..."

"Bleed yourself?"

"*Yes*," he says on a sigh. He settles back into his seat, his breathing no longer labored. It is as though a great weight has been lifted from his heart. "I'm glad I've told you, Maddie."

I smile weakly, wishing I could return the sentiment. Yes, I am grateful he has confided in me, but glad? If it makes him happy to have shared his secret with someone mortal, then yes, I suppose I am glad for it...for him.

My hand strays to my stomach. It is an unconscious gesture that I have found myself doing since I discovered I was pregnant.

"I am happy for you."

"For what?" I ask, hiding my hand in the folds of my skirt, and not only because Greydanus's perception alarms me. The cuts from Leonora's claws are still bleeding.

"The baby. You will live, Madelaine. And that baby will never need to know that any of this has happened."

Is that a threat? I'm grasping at shadows. How could something so good, so pure, so childlike... But that's what he is—a child, albeit an undead one. The reality before me is hard to accept. I must stop thinking of him in human terms. A normal child of six would not have such a command of the language or the grace of manner he possesses.

"Yes, thank you," I say, putting my unwounded hand on my stomach. I feel more secure with it there, covering my child, protecting my child.

"How long has this been happening?"

"What?" He knows perfectly well what.

"With your mother, I mean..." I say awkwardly, trying to soften the blow.

"Oh, that, yes. As long as I can remember. Full sun, full moon, rage, fear, sorrow...it doesn't seem to matter what the trigger is. When the thought is there, transformation comes naturally."

"And for you as well?"

"I've learned to control it better, I suppose."

I find this strange, but then again, if two such strong creatures had created him, I suppose he could have a stronger will than his mother, though it seems unlikely.

We ride in silence, the tree branches beating a never-ending tattoo against the torn roof of the carriage as we roll through the forest. There is something that has been nagging at my heart throughout this entire ride. Who was that woman with Stefan this morning?

"Greydanus...I don't know how to say this..."

"It's about Zigmund, isn't it?"

Corcitura

I forget all about the woman in that instant. Greydanus sounds so hopeful, so full of curiosity, and his eyes are so bright, but not from hunger or any unnatural cravings.

"If you like…"

"Did you see him? Is he at all like me? What did he say?"

My heart aches for this child who isn't a child. Loneliness, abandonment, unworthiness—they've both suffered it in spades, the stoic professor and his undead child brother he has no idea exists. If only Zigmund had believed me.

"I noted a striking resemblance around the eyes," I say, which is not entirely a lie. There is intensity in his eyes as well as his little brother's—a quality they both inherited from their mother. Greydanus's face brightens even more at this news. "He is quite tall and carries himself well," I continue. What else can I say? That he didn't believe a word I said and was violently resentful when I brought up his mother? "I hope he will think better of what I had to say and come to our aid."

"I hope so, too. It is nice to know you are not alone in the world any longer."

"You have your mother…"

"Still…she cannot always protect me from them."

That small, impersonal word makes me sit up straighter in my seat. *Them.* There is so much meaning in that word.

"Who exactly is *them*…

"Father, Grandfather…"

"Yes, yes…" I say impatiently. He's told me of those two. I *know* of those two. But he has yet to tell me of the rest.

"My aunts."

So that woman is one of Stefan's sisters. It explains the resemblance.

"Wolfling, that's what they call me," he says bitterly.

They, I muse. "And how many of these aunts do you have?" I feel a beast questioning him so, but my survival—*our* survival—might hinge on this information.

"Four, well, four that live with us. Aunties Ruxandra, Magdalena, Dacia, and Irina. Auntie Ruxandra is the worst."

"R-really?" I can barely force the word out of my throat.

"She's always at Father's right hand. If they weren't related, I'd swear they were lovers."

It pains me to hear the child speak with such knowledge, yet based on what I saw of the pair at the edge of the forest this morning, it wouldn't take a stretch of the imagination to believe Greydanus's assessment.

"A short time after I was born, she went away for a good long while. Mother thought we'd finally got rid of her, but then she resurfaced more smug and vicious than ever."

"And the ones that don't live with you...what happened to them?"

"Auntie Nadia's gone missing. She doesn't associate with us, and we don't associate with her. I believe it has something to do with Grandfather."

"I can understand that."

"And then there is Auntie Olga, who was *ungrateful*."

"Ungrateful?"

"Auntie Ruxandra says Auntie Olga was a 'vapid, selfish creature who let the talk of priests and old women corrupt her mind against us,' and didn't understand the great gift Father wanted to give her. Apparently, Auntie Ruxandra was all for accepting this gift. I think that's the reason she went away, though I can't be sure. But Auntie Olga wouldn't agree. So she took her own life. Ungrateful, you see."

Good for her, I think, then am horrified that I've taken to approving of suicide. But when given the alternative, would I have chosen differently?

"We don't talk about her much, but I would have loved to have met her. Such courage. I wish I could have an ounce of that courage. Maybe Father would want me then."

"Don't ever say that!" I snap. "You don't owe him anything," I say in a quieter tone. "Certainly not love." Am I truly saying this? Am I counseling this child to hate his father? But given such a father...

Greydanus is silent, staring out the window. When he turns toward me, I want to crawl into a dark hole and never come out.

"I hate him, Madelaine. I hate him so much it terrifies me. And when I think of if I could kill him, I know the answer is yes. A thousand times yes. I'd do it without any remorse whatsoever because for the last six years, he's done worse to me."

Before I can answer, he pulls back his sleeve to reveal dozens of deep, crisscrossed scars snaking up his arm. I reach out to trace the furrows in his flesh, feeling nauseous as I see how deep they are. What must have been his pain when these lacerations were so viciously inflicted? There must have been gallons of blood. Did his father satiate himself with it afterward? What kind of monster would do such a thing to his own child?

"Grandfather comes every six weeks to check my progress. I told you I was a disappointment."

"These marks...your grandfather didn't inflict them, did he?"

He shakes his head and rolls down the sleeve.

No matter how hard he is struggling to keep his resolve, he is failing. I see his lip trembling, though he bites it to hide its quivering. He looks so childish and vulnerable that I forget all caution and take him into my arms. His tears come in torrents, the blood soaking into my sleeve. He cries with abandon, not caring that he is wasting his only source of nourishment. I feel the tears prick my own eyes. Although my tears aren't made of blood, they drain the energy from me. I do not know whether I am more terrified of the evidence of Stefan's savagery or the knowledge that *Grandfather* is a frequent visitor to the château.

I cry in silence, the tears falling atop Greydanus's head. As we turn a corner, panic engulfs me. I no longer hear the trees striking the carriage. We are in a clearing. All calm leaves me, and I cannot fight the sobs now racking my body. The promise of Zigmund's help was shattered hours ago, yet still I was holding on to hope.

I see now that was folly. There is no turning back. I cannot run anymore. I am alone, save for the unexpected ally I am cradling in my arms.

I have no choice but to fight. Once I step from this carriage, the countdown will begin. My murderer is waiting.

We have returned.

CB

I do not want to leave Greydanus unattended, but he insists he can look after himself. From the look in his eyes and the grim set of his mouth, I know better than to argue with him. I've seen his scars, I've witnessed the mental torture he suffers through daily, but that does not mean I have the authority to become a second mother, no matter how poorly the first is parenting him.

I have been alone, locked in my room for more than an hour, watching the hands of the clock tick by until my appointment with my jailer. A card has been left on my nightstand lest I forget that my presence is urgently desired. As if I could.

For the fiftieth time, I reread the blood red lettering.

I am expecting you at seven sharp in the dining hall. Bring your appetite. I have a surprise for you.

The visions I've conjured of what that surprise could be range from the ridiculous to the macabre to the downright grisly. Strangely, though, my heart stopped racing the minute I locked myself in this room. And when I went to the mirror a moment ago and lifted the back of my hair to pin it atop my head, I did not flinch when I saw several strands of dead looking white hair intermingled with the dark brown—white hair that hadn't been there this morning. There is no point in fretting over vanity now nor will there ever be again if I do not find a way to stop Stefan from killing me. Those white hairs are the least of my worries.

Which brings me to my next problem: should I even bother to bring a weapon with me to dinner? The only thing that I could consider a weapon is a letter opener I saw on the desk in the corner. Regardless of what I've read in Zigmund's book, I slip the letter opener into my pocket and keep my hand clutched around its hilt.

The hallway is lit by only a few candles. Slowly, feeling along the wall with one hand while keeping my grip on the letter opener with the other, I make my way toward the dining hall. Leonora is nowhere in sight. I haven't seen her since she abandoned us in front of the church in town. Nor is my husband to be found amid these corridors, but I was expecting this.

It is almost preternatural how quickly I reach my destination. I have not been here long enough to get a handle on this sprawling, labyrinthine manor, yet I arrive at the dining hall as though my path has been predestined since I set forth from my room.

I tighten my grip on the letter opener as I shoulder the door open.

"Ah! There she is. You're late."

I glance at the clock above the mantelpiece. It reads seven-oh-one. *Late indeed.*

"I've saved a seat for you at the head of the table."

Mutely, I follow his outstretched hand and sit at the opposite end of a table that seems much longer and older than the one I sat at last night. Eric had been with me then. God knows where he is now.

"Settle in, will you? I've arranged a splendid feast."

"And the surprise?" My voice is harsh, brittle, near to cracking.

"Patience. All will come in due course."

Just as he says this, two waiters bustle into the room, their arms loaded down with covered trays. Something about them makes me clutch the letter opener tighter. I do not know what it is, but they seem somehow wrong. Their skin is too ashen, their eyes too lifeless. When the waiter carrying my tray draws near, the stench of rotting meat fills my nostrils.

"Dinner, Madame," he rasps. I lean away, but I can still feel his foul breath against my face.

Whatever happens, I must not eat this food. I steel myself, expecting the worst, so when the corpse-like garcon uncovers the dish, I am relieved yet suspicious at the same time. I was expecting a feast from the charnel house, but all I see on the plate is a perfectly normal looking breast of chicken surrounded by some peas and potatoes.

I glance at my host. He has not uncovered his dish, but has signaled to the garcons to leave us. The room now seems dimmer from my vantage point. I realize with a sickening feeling in the pit of my stomach that Stefan has placed himself in the shadowed end on purpose.

"Have fun in town, did you?"

I wonder how much he knows and if it is worth the effort to dissemble. "Yes, actually. I met some friends."

"Oh?"

I cannot help smirking. Coy, that, but not coy enough for me to believe he is innocent. I remember Greydanus's scars and fight mightily to control my tongue.

"Yes." I am unwilling to say more lest he should chip away at my resolve or I should inadvertently divulge the incident with Leonora. I have a suspicion about her whereabouts. It is my final hope. If he were to discover what I suspect, I'd truly be lost.

"I don't suppose you met with Luc?"

I bite down on my tongue so hard I break the skin. Blood pools in my mouth. I quickly grab a crystal goblet and spit into it. I stare into the goblet, watching my blood mix with the hideous red liquid that already fills the glass. A sharp, coppery smell wafts up from the glass, but I know that smell is not from my blood alone. It is too pungent, too insistent. My hands begin to tremble. The crystal of the goblet feels suddenly very cold. Carefully, I set the goblet onto the table, thankful I didn't spill a drop. When I look up, I realize I might as well have waved a red flag in front of a bull for all my supposed caution.

A radical change has come over Stefan. His eyes are pulsating, radiating in the darkness. I can sense his hunger. His longing for my blood is almost a palpable force—a force so strong that I feel the weight of it pressing against my chest. I suck in a breath and lean back into the velvet of the seat, trying to calm my breathing and act as though nothing has changed between us.

"No, I haven't seen Luc since the night he brought us here," I lie with difficulty. My heart feels as though an iron band has been wrapped around it. I wheeze once again, trying to fill my lungs with air, but can only manage a shallow breath. "Should I have?"

"No, sadly, no," he says, waving his hand. A flash of red catches the candlelight at Stefan's end of the table. I lean forward in my chair, the pressure suddenly lifted from my heart. "Luc has left us. He did give me a marvelous gift before he went, though."

The candles flare up, fully illuminating the ring. I lean back in my chair and stifle a gasp.

The last time I saw that blood red ruby, it was on Luc's finger.

"Rather tasty, this," Stefan remarks, lifting a dark link of meat from his plate, which he has finally uncovered.

"What is that?" I feel as though I have eaten sand. I cannot swallow even if I try.

"Blood sausage," he says through a mouthful, the dark red sauce dripping down his chin. "Delicious."

My fork clatters against the plate, the sound echoing loudly through the empty, cavernous hall. I glance at my dish and am relieved to see that my food is still the same, sensible fare I looked at a minute ago. Still, I cannot help but wonder. Who is to say he does not have the power to conceal what the food truly is? I must be going mad to think such thoughts, but Stefan's relish has made up my mind for me: I will not eat this nor any other food prepared in this house. I've been subsisting on moldering bread for the last day and a half, and I intend to keep it that way. At least I can be sure that my own food was never human.

I've had quite enough of Stefan's company for one evening. I am about to rise, when he lifts his hand and motions for me to remain seated. "This is what happens to those who do not know their place," he says, savagely tearing off chunks from another sausage. I stare at him, watching the muscles in his mouth work the meat into oblivion, fascinated in spite of the gruesomeness of my suspicions.

"I am a patient and forgiving man, my dear Mrs. Bradburry, but *don't* push me too far."

I force myself to swallow. I will not be cowed. I push back my chair, but it collides with something solid. Before I can see what it is, I feel hands on my shoulders.

I'd know the touch of those hands anywhere.

"Madelaine..."

"*Eric!*"

He does not respond to my kisses nor is he moved by the tears streaming down my face. I stare into his eyes, willing him to show some sign of life, but he looks at me as though he does not recognize me.

"Eric..." I venture again, reaching out to embrace him. The moment my arms wrap around him, I feel all the hope go out of me. Whatever he has been through has made him thin and fragile, so frail that I can feel his bones. Memories flood my mind, and I resist the urge to cry out for all that I have lost. I feel as though I am holding a statue, not the man I've given my body and soul to, the man I love. I want him to return my warmth, to embrace me with the same feeling he once did, to kiss me and make love to me with the passion we shared before we got caught up in this madness, but he is limp in my arms. I have no choice but to shoulder his weight or he will collapse.

I want to rail against Stefan, beat him, stab him, *kill* him for what he's done to my husband. I feel the anger welling up in my throat, wanting to vent itself in screams of anguish, but suddenly peace washes over me, or if not peace, at least calmness and the will to get me through the next few moments.

"Ah, yes, my old friend. I'm glad you enjoyed your sojourn in the tower."

"If you will be so *kind*," I say, my teeth clenched, my face still bathed in tears, "I believe my husband has had enough excitement for one day."

"I know he has." The smile on Stefan's lips curdles my blood. I stare at him, and it is as if I am seeing him in his true form. The face that glares up at me in triumph is not the face of the man I have been sharing this unholy feast with. It is the face in the painting, no, the *faces* in the *paintings* in Zigmund's books.

Corcitura

"Now you know the truth, my dear. It remains to be seen what you will do with your newfound knowledge."

There is no need for me to speak. We understand each other perfectly. I close my mouth and guide Eric out of the room as quickly as I can.

Once we reach our room, I gently lay Eric down on the bed and turn my attention toward the door. I consider pushing one of the lowboys against it, but that will only waste time and energy. If Stefan wants in, nothing will stop him. I settle for bolting the door and pray that will be enough.

"Madelaine." Eric's voice is thin and reedy, barely above a whisper, so when I turn and see him thrashing about, blood seeping through his sleeve, his eyes rolled back into his head, I cannot reconcile the quietness of his voice with the violence of the fit he is having.

I scramble onto the bed and lay my hand against his forehead, wincing as the heat burns my skin.

"Eric, listen to me..."

"Non sum qualis eram," he mutters, his eyes boring into mine.

"Non sum qualis eram," I repeat. I know that phrase.

I am not what I once was.

"Eric, no," I say, slapping him on the cheek to get him to stop thrashing. "Listen to me, Eric, concentrate on me. Look at me!"

"I have to atone for my sins."

"What sins? What are you talking about? What has he filled your head with? Eric, look at me!" He thrashes insensibly. I look around for something to restrain him with, but then my attention is drawn to his arm. The blood has completely soaked through his sleeve. I rip back the cloth and look in horror on the ravaged flesh. My stomach churns as I remember the night on the boat when I pricked my finger after touching his skin.

This is what he was hiding.

With a shock, I realize the scars, or what soon will be scars, look exactly like the ones on Greydanus's arm.

"This is Stefan's work," I say, more to myself than Eric. I am trembling with fear, horror, rage. What more must I do to save my husband from that beast's influence? "What has he done to you, Eric? Eric, come back to me, I'm begging you."

I shake him by the shoulders. Suddenly, there is a dreadful change in him. I cry out as he grips my wrist and yanks me toward him so that our noses are almost touching. His eyes are so clear, so alien to the eyes I have known and loved. He searches my face, his mouth twisted into a sneer that terrifies me, for it is the mirror image of the smirk Stefan is always wearing. He turns his eyes toward his arm. I look from him to his arm then back to him. My stomach heaves as the truth blares in my mind.

Before he can lunge, I wrap my hand around his wrist, ignoring the blood washing over my fist. I turn my back on him to block his way. His teeth snap at the air above my shoulder, but I will not give in.

"You will not drink your own blood! So help me God, you *will* come back to me!"

I hazard a look over my shoulder and see his mouth twisting as he struggles to free himself from my grasp, but the exertion is too much for him. Exhausted, he slumps back against the pillows.

I release my grasp and wipe my hand against my skirt. We are both bloody messes, but thank God the madness has passed. When I lay my hand against his forehead again, I am relieved to feel coolness.

One outburst has passed, but when will the next occur? How long has this been going on? What did that monster do to my husband? He is not a vampire yet, thank God, but he is close to it, *very close.*

"Maddie..."

"Yes, Eric, I am here."

"Oh, Maddie, Maddie...what would you do for me?"

"I'd go to hell and back and cut off the devil's head myself for you, my own love," I say, tears choking me as I stroke his cheek.

"Yes," he says weakly, "I knew you would. You are my salvation."

Corcitura

The pain in my chest is unbearable. I cannot see him like this. Damned Stefan, his cursed wife, Greydanus...no, I cannot hate him. He is blameless.

"Maddie..." He is so weak, so deathly pale.

"Eric, *Eric*..." I say frantically. I lift his head to keep him from nodding off again. I cannot lose him. I *will not* lose him.

"Play me a nocturne. Soothe my soul."

I glance back at the door to make sure it is still bolted, then slide off the bed and settle in at the pianoforte. Not surprisingly, sheet music has been set out, a *Nocturne*, no less. I wonder, not for the first time, if all this is part of Stefan's plan. It has to be. It is too convenient.

This is how a marionette must feel—to have someone guiding your every step, pulling your strings, robbing you of your own free will.

My fingers brush against the cool ivory as I begin to play. The music is elegiac, something that would be better suited to a funeral Mass. But Eric has requested it. No matter how dirge-like it might sound, nor what it might presage, I will play it. I have come to believe that nothing that has been happening to us is an accident.

The tears are streaming freely down my face so that I can barely read the notes on the page any longer. As I reach the cadenza, I remember my violin. What a fool thought that was, to think music could be a balm in such a place as this.

A groan from the bed stays my hands. Eric tries to rise, but does not have the strength and falls back against the headboard.

"Sleep, rest, my love," I say, kissing his brow. He is cold, so cold.

"Don't leave me."

"Never."

"Forgive me?"

"There is nothing to forgive." I was furious with him once—furious that he'd lied to me, that he hadn't had the decency to tell me the truth—but that seems like a lifetime ago. I am here because of him, yet I would not want to be anywhere else in the world right now. He needs me, Greydanus needs me. I refuse to abandon them.

Eric smiles. For an instant I see a spark of his former self. "Shut your eyes," I say softly, stroking his forehead. "I'll keep watch." I may be powerless against Stefan in many regards, but I will not let him take Eric from me.

And so I keep watch and wait for I don't know what to happen. That something will happen, I am sure, but what it might be is as foreign to me as the language of this country I find myself a prisoner in. I focus on Eric, watching his chest rise and fall. Beneath his lids, his eyes dart back and forth rapidly. I wonder with alarm what or *who* is invading his dreams.

Weariness tugs at my eyes. I glance at the clock, blinking to make out the time. A quarter past one. I draw up my knees and rest my head against them, my eyelids closing. "Brace up, Maddie," I say aloud, trying to rouse myself. Just a few more hours and...what? I'll be dead? Or Eric? Sleep is not a luxury I can afford. I must plan. I must think of some way out of this.

I leave the bed and settle into the chair before the lowboy, willing myself to stay awake. My fingernails dig into the soft red velvet of the chair's arms. I must not drowse off. That's what he wants. I would be playing straight into his hands.

No, Stefan, I think as I jolt up in the chair. *Try me, torture me, break me. I will never let you win.*

ം

"Papa! Wait! Come back!"

I swing back and forth, looking down at my tiny legs kicking out in midair. The new dress from Paris is beautiful but restricting, and I long to change into my cotton shift.

"Papa, wait!" I shriek again as I catapult myself off the swing and race after my father. I hear his laughter as he dodges behind a hedge. He runs away from me as he always does when he wants me to follow. I know there is a new present waiting for me at the end of the race. Maybe a pony, or more likely, some new books, which is what Papa knows I truly want.

Corcitura

Breathless, my little legs pushing me onward, I race around the last hedge and stop short at the edge of the river.

"*Papa*?" I shout, turning in a circle. He couldn't have gone anywhere else. This is the last hedge before the river. He couldn't have...

"Papa!" I scream, racing frantically along the bank. I long to see his kind face, to feel the protection of his arms as he gathers me into his embrace. My vision blurs as tears flood my eyes. I spin around once more, searching under the hedges, and catch sight of something bobbing on the surface of the river.

Papa's derby.

But where is Papa?

I reach out carefully and pluck the hat from the river.

Then I see the blood.

My throat is raw by the time I stop screaming. I cradle father's derby in my hands, fingering the lining that is stained with his blood.

"How does one so young know such sorrow?"

The derby falls to the grass as I look up into a pair of glowing green eyes. I stare at the woman, wondering where she came from. Her blonde hair falls past her waist. At her throat is a necklace that makes me want to run back to the house and hide underneath my bed. The head of a golden wyvern, its eyes as green as the woman's, glares down at me from around her neck. I back away, but she extends one stark white hand and motions me to come nearer.

I hiccough as I swallow a mouthful of tears. "My father, he's..."

"Alive. Rest assured, small one. He's alive, but much more whole than he was before."

I know she means to comfort me, but her words make my stomach churn. I back further away, glancing over my shoulder to judge the distance from here to my home. I can make it if I sprint, provided she is not a good runner.

"I have a gift for you, *draguta*."

Warily, I take a step toward her, curious in spite of my fear. In her palm rests a gold bangle dotted with sparkling red stones.

"You like it, don't you?"

I nod, mesmerized, and reach out my hand, wanting nothing more than to claim that bangle for my own. I have never been greedy for jewelry before, but a fire has been lit in my blood. I cannot think of anything other than possessing that band of gold, though the shape of it terrifies me. As I draw closer, I see that the blood red stones are meant to be eyes. The bangle is crafted into the mirror image of the wyvern around the woman's neck, with one small difference: this wyvern is eating its tail.

I now know what it is—an ouroboros. Suddenly, I do not want that bracelet anymore. When I shrink back, arms encircle me. I try to break free, but the strength in those arms is crushing the breath from my lungs. The woman grabs my wrist. As I try to kick, bite, scratch, do anything to stop her, I hear a click. My arm falls heavily against my side.

My skin is pinched where the bracelet encircles my wrist. I feel it squeezing in tighter, feel its golden prongs digging into my flesh. I cry out, but the world suddenly goes dark. The grass is soft under me as I fall against it. My body is at peace, but my mind races feverishly. What has happened? Where did that woman go? I struggle vainly to keep my eyes open, but I cannot fight the impulse any longer. The back of my head throbs. I close my eyes to shut out the pain. The last vision I have is of those blood red stones glowing as bright as fire as the ouroboros cinches tighter and tighter around my flesh, devouring my wrist.

 co

A sea of masked faces surrounds me. For a second, I am too disoriented to know if I am at a gala or a danse macabre in hell.

The room looks familiar, but something is different, and it is not the massive chandelier hanging from the ceiling or the frescoed wall at the opposite end of the room. Those I remember. It is everything else that strikes me as odd, especially the people.

Corcitura

A memory tugs at the back of my mind, but it is only after a man brushes past me that I know where I am. Although he is masked, I would recognize him anywhere.

Eric.

I am at Riverhampton at the millionaires' ball the night Eric and I first met.

Twelve years have evaporated in an instant. I was a child a minute before, a child whose father was murdered by a woman with glowing green eyes. I am wondering how this could have happened, when I am swept up into Eric's arms. Through the slits in the Venetian devil's mask, I see his brown eyes dance. The breath escapes my lungs. His eyes are vibrant, smiling, unearthly. Something is not right, but the magnetic attraction that sparks through me every time our bodies touch is too strong to break away from. Or is it just that? For the first time, it feels like something more...something fiercer. My chest tightens in panic. I have to get away, but he twirls me through that mass of revelers, spinning me further and further away from them. I scan the crowd for a familiar face, but this is impossible to find, since the masks conceal everything. I am in the midst of animals, fools, devils. I cannot tell friend from foe.

Eric twirls me before a mirror, and I catch sight of myself for the first time. Can that really be me? I look like some dark pixie out of a madman's dream. My arms are bare and deathly pale beneath the glare of the chandelier. A black feathered swan mask covers my eyes. My hair, looking much darker than it should, is piled high atop my head. A black corset bodice imprisons me. I suck in a breath and wince as the whalebone stays dig into my stomach. My black tulle skirt mushrooms about me. I stare at myself, realizing for the first time that I have stopped spinning. Eric has finally released me.

When I turn back, Eric is gone. I see him receding through the crowd. I shout his name, but he does not turn round nor heed me when I call him more forcefully. Everyone seems to have surrounded me. The crowd blocks my path almost intentionally. I cannot reach my husband, no matter how hard I push or beg these people to let me through. They form a barricade. I look from one to the other, pleading with them to show me some shred of compassion, but they just cross their arms and remain as still as stone, their masks leering down on me with those same fixed, lifeless stares so natural to marionettes.

I stand on tiptoe to try and catch a last glimpse of my husband. He is standing half in shadow, half in light. I can just make out his face. I reach for him. He turns and puts his finger to his lips. I try to scream out but cannot. That one gesture has rendered me mute.

I turn back toward the room. Gone are all the guests. The floor is strewn with champagne flutes and remnants of confetti and crepe paper, all covered with a thick layer of dust, as though this room has been abandoned for years. The emptiness is oppressive, as is the cold. I hug my bare arms and chafe them, but it is no use. I am as cold as a corpse, save for the ouroboros bracelet, which burns when I touch it.

The air shimmers. I am once again transported somewhere both familiar and foreign. A copse of trees surrounds me. I hear the rattling of carriage wheels and walk toward the sound. As I exit the copse, my heart lightens. I have finally, *finally* seen two faces I recognize.

"Molly, *Molly*, thank God you're here!" I can speak again. I reach out my hands, but it is as though a wall separates us, an invisible wall. I can see but cannot touch her. Her eyes are downcast, her hand in Steven's. Twin sets of tears stain their faces. They pass me by without a sign of recognition. I am staring at them, aghast, when I hear a whinny and turn to see two black horses coming to a halt nearby. They rear up, the black plumes atop their heads flapping wildly. Something has frightened them. When I look behind them to see what they are pulling, I can understand why they are so skittish.

A hearse. I laugh morbidly, thinking this cannot get any worse. Through the windows of the hearse, I see a dark outline. As I draw nearer, the dark shape takes the form of an ebony coffin.

The thought that I am in that coffin flits across my mind. It would explain why Molly and Steven treated me as though I were invisible. But the pressure from the bracelet tells me I am still very much alive.

From behind the hearse, a party emerges. Aunt Robbie walks right by me without even a nod of recognition. And then comes my father, remarkably whole, not a spot of blood on his person. "Papa!" I call out, but he passes me by just as silently as all the rest.

I reach out for him, but my arm passes straight through him.

I *am* dead.

I race to the back of the hearse and fling open the doors, climbing up to reach the coffin. It shines brilliantly, its ebony wood so polished I can see my terrified face reflected in its surface. I run my hands over the wood, fumbling with the solid silver hasps, but they do not give beneath my fingers. After several minutes of trying to unlatch them, I give up, exhausted, my fingers bloodied. Whoever is inside this casket is sealed in forever.

I sit back on my heels and stare at the coffin, trying to think of a way to break those hasps. I must know who is inside, even if it means I will be confronted with my own cold, dead face.

My heart catapults into my throat as the hasps spring open and the lid of the casket snaps back.

I smell the blood before I even see it.

Cautiously, I lean over the side of the coffin. It is a blood*bath*, literally, and within the blood filled coffin rests the body of my husband.

I touch his forehead. His skin is like ice, the cold so fierce it burns my hand. I lay my fingers against his neck, feeling for a pulse, but I feel something else instead. I scream as his hand clamps around my wrist more tightly than the ouroboros bracelet.

"Non sum quails eram."

I shriek with all the power and all the anguish and all the fear I can. I tear at his grasp and pull so hard I hear my arm snap out of its socket. Fetid, hot breath lashes my face. I scream louder, but nothing can deter this monster that has already dragged me so low into the casket that the blood has stained my face.

His fangs brush against my neck. It is the last sensation I know.

◌ଓ

"NO!"

I am back in our room in our bed, Eric at my side. My hands fly to my neck, but there are no wounds. I breathe a sigh of relief and settle back against the pillows.

"Have a pleasant walk down memory lane, did you?"

The voice startles me. I glance toward the mirror above the lowboy.

Stefan is staring at me from within it. Cautiously, I make my way toward it and run my hands along the frame, searching for a clasp, a hidden catch, but there is nothing but his smirking face looking out at me from the glass.

"I assure you it is no trick. I never was one for legerdemain or sleight of hand. It all seemed so tawdry to me. So false."

"Of all the sadistic, wicked..."

"It takes very little work to be wicked," he says calmly. "You should try it some time."

"I think not."

"Yes, I know, that's the problem."

He is so maddeningly calm, almost jovial—as though he is already assured of his victory.

"How's that arm treating you, by the way?"

I ignore him and also the pain in my arm. It is a dull ache, but nothing as severe as I should be feeling after that sickening pop of bone coming out of socket. "Do you take issue with people thinking you're damned?" I venture. I have no idea where this conversation is taking me, but I feel emboldened. If he focuses on me, he is less likely to pay any attention to Eric lying prone and defenseless on the bed.

"Have there been whispers? Mob mentality, I take it, from the villages beyond the château's walls?"

"No, just a theory from a book I found at Charles University's library this afternoon."

That gets his attention. "A book?"

"Yes, it was enlightening," I say cryptically.

"I'm so glad for you."

I'll bet you are.

"I quite enjoy people thinking I'm damned. It's very liberating."

One death white hand caresses his chin. I cannot help staring. Deep, red scars crisscross the nearly translucent skin. How could I not have noticed those scars before?

"Curious, are you? My weaker nature had to be subdued. It tried to claw out for a time, to cut its way out of my own flesh. Oh, it was painful, *dreadfully* painful, but it was worth the sacrifice, I do assure you. In time, sense won out, and by then I had been overtaken...and here I am before you, my dear. Whole, unsullied, pure. The scars are but a reminder of my former, corporeal self."

"This can't be real. This is a dream." My voice is hollow, sepulchral, much like his eyes.

"That is debatable," he says, waving his scarred hands. "But I am, I do assure you, my dear Mrs. Bradburry, very, *very* real."

ᘓ

"Have you met your soul's demonic twin yet, my dear? None of us Belododias have. But that will change...*soon*."

I wake with a start, sweat coating my body. My back aches as I straighten up. I had fallen asleep sitting before the mirror. *Eric...*

He is still sleeping, thank God. I pull the covers back from his swathed head and find only a line of pillows arranged in a haphazard manner.

Eric is gone.

I scatter the pillows, stopping only as I notice something reflected in the mirror by the bedstead.

The bracelet Eric gave me. Thank God the other abomination was only a dream. I finger the clasp, but it is no longer there. I shake my wrist, hoping to hear the clinking of the heart charm against the circles of gold, but there is no sound.

Where the heart charm should be, the heart charm remains, only with this difference: the key is missing.

And the heart is bleeding and has sprouted eyes.

The ouroboros bracelet.

I stare dumbly at the circlet of gold that harpy gave to me in what I thought was a dream. The bangle is so tight, and my wrist so livid, that I *know* this supposedly inanimate piece of jewelry is somehow sucking the blood from my arm.

There is only one thought in my mind now. I look around for something to break the clasp.

Nothing on the desk, nothing on the lowboy.

And then I remember. I shove my hand into my pocket, thanking God when my fingers curl around the cool steel handle of the letter opener.

I slide the blade beneath the bracelet, but the ouroboros seems to have a life of its own.

"Get off me, you beast," I grunt through gritted teeth. I dig the letter opener in deeper, cutting myself in the process. Blood seeps from the wound, but I cannot stop now. I work the blade in further and hear a click. The bracelet snaps off and falls to the floor, somehow shattering into tiny fragments as it strikes the carpet. Blood oozes from the slash along my wrist. I put my wrist to my mouth, sucking on the wound, hoping to stop the bleeding,

It is then that I hear the laugh.

I have seen too much already. I am beyond fear now. Curiosity is too powerful an emotion for me to resist. I cross to the other side of the bed and stop astounded in front of the floor to ceiling mirror. My reflection is completely gone. Inside the mirror is a beautiful woman with long blonde curls and radiant green eyes.

Auntie Ruxandra is the worst.

The woman from my dream. The woman who corrupted the bracelet my husband gave me into a tool of vampiric destruction. A smile twists her lips, the cruelty in her knowing look shattering my confidence.

"Come closer, I won't hurt you, *draguta*." She speaks that word again, her voice so deadly persuasive—saying everything and nothing.

I step closer, unnerved yet fascinated. She is holding a chalice in her hands.

"Go on, drink. You know you want to."

"Where are you?" I demand. The voice that just spoke was not the woman's, but Stefan's.

"It's not important where I am. What's important is that you slake your thirst. I know you desire it. I have seen the way you look at blood."

I drop my hand to my side, rubbing away the traces of blood in the folds of my skirt. Blood still swirls in my mouth. Swallowing it seems like an abomination, but I refuse to spit it out and enflame their hunger.

I have no choice. I swallow.

"Your fortitude is amusing," he says, "but I have a feeling it will not last much longer."

As if to test my resolve, he holds the chalice closer so that I can see its contents. A thick, dark red wine fills the cup. Before I can look deeper, Stefan yanks the chalice back and puts it to his lips. I fight to control my nausea as he taps the bottom of the chalice to get the thick substance down his throat. My eyes are riveted to his neck, on his Adam's apple as it bobs up and down with each gulp. His skin is so pale and paper-thin that I almost believe I can see the blood coursing down his throat, reddening his veins. When he brings the glass away from his lips, I stare even harder, this time in horror. The liquid has left stains around his mouth—bloodstains.

I've read about this in books, imagined it in my mind countless times since I've been here, but to actually witness it is something entirely different. I thought I was prepared, but nothing—no amount of book learning or supposed life experience or bravado—can make you invulnerable to the sight of a vampire drinking blood.

"Your turn," he says when he is sated.

I swallow several times and lick my lips, unsuccessfully trying to rid my mouth of the sharp taste of my own blood.

The chalice is before me again, somehow refilled. All I have to do is reach through the mirror and take it of my own free will. I stare at the chalice, mesmerized. What harm would it do?

Just one little sip...

I reach for the chalice as if I have no will to resist, not even bothering to think of how I will pass my flesh and blood hand through the mirror. But then, I see that I do not have to worry over this. Ruxandra has erased all barriers.

How thoughtful of her.

The glass crackles as her hand passes through it. Shards of mirror rake across her flesh, drawing blood, which pools in her cuticles and drips into the chalice to mingle with whomever else's blood is contained within it. I stare at the red lines and bits of glass scarring her flesh, astounded that the mirror gave so easily without breaking into a million pieces.

"Anything is possible for one of us," she answers as if reading my thoughts. "All you have to do is drink."

"You've waited your whole life for this, Madelaine," Stefan coos from behind his sister. "The time to seize your destiny is now."

"Yes, yes, the time is now," she chants.

I take the chalice and cradle it in both my hands. I can feel the two of them gloating from inside the mirror. I can sense their exultation.

I hear his persuasive voice in my head, urging me to succumb. Now I know how Eric fell. With Stefan, the line between good and evil, right and wrong, becomes increasingly blurred.

I raise the chalice to my lips and let the coppery, pungent smell of the blood wash over me.

So this is how it is done...

Yes, I *am* finally ready to seize my destiny.

I lower the cup and stare into Stefan's glowing eyes. "I will not fall that easily."

His smile goes slack. His eyes, always so assured, look panicked. With a cry, I hurl the chalice at the mirror.

Corcitura

I drop to the floor and cover my head as glass splinters through the air. A cavernous roar shakes the ground beneath me, toppling me over onto a piece of mirror that slices into my arm. I stifle the urge to cry out as I carefully pull out the shard, thankful that the wound is not deep. Slowly, I rise to my feet and survey the damage. Blood is spattered across the coverlet, the lowboy, and nearly every surface around what once was the mirror, including me. I rip off a piece of my skirt and wipe the blood off my face before tying the fabric around my arm. I've had quite enough blood for one evening.

My breath catches in my throat, not so much because my tormentors are gone, but because of what the mirror left behind. The mirror was a door, a cover for the tunnel that snakes out into darkness before me. Wind so chill it sets my teeth chattering blows through the opening and stings my eyes. The blackness is so thick within that corridor, I have no idea how I shall see once I am in it, but I know I must follow this path. *If they've taken Eric this way...*

I step over the shards and into the corridor, feeling my way along the wall, my fingers dislodging lichen from the bricks. The smell is damp and earthy and ages old. I wonder, as I walk on through darkness that shows no signs of abating, how long it has been since any living soul traveled down this road—and whether what they found at the end of it was to their liking.

I am beginning to think this corridor has no end. As I trip around yet another corner, the corridor suddenly widens, and I find myself in a circular chamber. A torch gutters on the far wall. Beneath the flickering light, I see a pair of shackles affixed to the rock. Metal flakes off in my hands, leaving rust particles all over my fingers as I touch the manacles. Those obviously haven't been used in quite a while.

I heft the torch out of its holder and turn the light upon the room. "God help me!" I scream, stumbling back and dropping the torch.

My breath rattles in my chest. I fight to calm myself. I am not in danger, I now see, though I feel as if my heart might never beat normally again.

Melika Dannese Lux

The torch flickers on the ground, throwing an eerie light on the shape above the large cylindrical curio attached to the wall. A great beast with golden wings enfolds the top of the tubular encasement. I grab the torch and bring it near the glass. Within, the mirror image of the beast is carved atop an unsheathed staff that gleams in the torchlight. I finger the surface of the glass, wishing I could get my hands on that staff and arm myself for whatever I might encounter once I get out of this corridor, assuming I *ever* get out of this corridor. I move the torch higher and see the beast for what it is: a wyvern. Its eyes are emerald and menacing, its fangs bestial.

First the wyvern headed necklace, then the ouroboros bracelet. This had to be some sort of cult. What did the wyvern have to do with Stefan and his sisters and...me? There have been too many instances of that same symbol appearing to just be coincidental.

I lean in closer, raising the torch for a better look, and am punished for my curiosity. A gust of wind plunges me into darkness.

"Lovely," I say, disgusted. But then I think: that wind had to come from somewhere.

I peer ahead and see a white light shining farther down the corridor.

I follow the light, stumbling over the uneven stones in the path, until I feel the ground begin to slope up beneath me. The night air is crisp against my face as I step up into the grounds behind the château. A full moon hangs overhead, illuminating my former steps. When I look back, I see that the subterranean tunnel has led me to the back, ruined part of the grounds that I'd passed through the first night I came to the château. Before me stretches a circular plateau, in the midst of which is the ruin Eric and I passed that wretched night. Beyond that lies the graveyard, where my tombstone waits for me. I shudder and press on, making for the ruin.

The clouds are now paying court to the full moon, blocking its light so that I stumble and can barely see where I am walking. As I draw closer, a lone shaft of moonlight penetrates the gloom, and I see something lying on a catafalque in the center of the ruin.

By the time I step onto the crumbling stone floor, the moonlight has shifted, casting a pall over the corner where a white iron maiden rests, shining with ghostly radiance as though it possesses some life of its own.

In my haste to get away from the sphinxlike face carved into the iron maiden, I stumble backward and knock into the catafalque. A groan escapes whatever is lying atop it. I fall to my knees, leaning in close to the corpse that isn't a corpse at all. I know this face. It is the face of the man who betrayed us.

"Luc, wake up," I whisper. I try to raise him, but he is shackled to the catafalque. I look around for something to use as leverage to break him free, for I sense that I am running out of time. The hair on the back of my neck is prickling. I have the uncanny sensation I am being watched. Luc groans again and turns away from me.

That's when I see the bite marks on his neck.

And then I hear the sound of stone scraping against stone.

The iron maiden is opening.

I drop to the ground and scamper behind the catafalque. Cautiously, I peek over the edge. A pale hand is wedged beneath the lid of the iron maiden. The hand looks so frail, yet suddenly it grips the lid and forces it back, revealing something so mind-boggling I do not even believe I am seeing it.

A beautiful young girl is impaled on the spikes within—impaled, but somehow alive.

Her long brown hair hangs past her waist. Her eyes, when she opens them, are the same emerald green color as Ruxandra's. She has to be one of Stefan's sisters, one of the *Aunties* Greydanus spoke of.

There is no blood at all spewing out of her even though the spikes protrude through her skin. She is pierced through practically everywhere except her eyes and heart, which I suppose would kill her. I cannot tell if the spikes are silver, but logically, an *iron* maiden should have *iron* spikes. If they were silver, she would be dead. From what I see of them, they look old and coarse and rust-encrusted. Yes, definitely iron.

Still, why has she not lost blood? I lean back into the shadows as she steps out of the coffin, her thin, Grecian style dress catching on the spikes. She turns back, irritated, and yanks the dress off the spikes, then saunters out of the coffin and stretches, looking around with a self-satisfied air that makes me shrink further into the shadows. Her eyes are so cold and cruel.

As she turns toward me, I have to fight not to make any sound. A minute ago, her body was pierced with holes, but now they are corroding closed, the flesh returning to its milk-white sheen instead of the singed gray of a second before.

So those are the famed vampiric powers of regeneration and healing.

"Ah ha ha!" she laughs, prancing around like a nymph. "You still live?"

I fear she is talking to me, but then she leans down over the catafalque and I hear a sickening crunch. When she raises her head, the moonlight shines against her chin, revealing the blood spattered there.

"Only a few more days now, dearest. We will get our fill of sport out of you."

She leers at him devilishly, her blood-flecked fangs protruding over her plump lower lip. Suddenly, her body goes rigid. She cocks her head toward the hills behind us.

The graveyard. Through the mist shrouding the fen, I see two white-clad figures emerge. The leader is the woman I had seen with Stefan and in my dream and in the mirror. In her hand, she holds something small and furry and unmoving.

As she brushes past me, I have a better view of what that small furry shape is—a rabbit with its throat torn out. I can no longer contain the bile swirling in my mouth. I lean over as close to the ground as I can to spit out the vomit. When I glance up, the three of them have surrounded the catafalque and are staring down at Luc.

A thud sounds at my feet.

How many more horrors shall I be forced to witness this night?

The sucked dry body of a man not much younger than me lies inches away.

I bite my fist to keep from screaming.

The prancing one, the nymph, stands behind Luc's head, running her long-nailed fingers possessively through his hair.

"Good hunting, sisters?" she asks, her voice a sibilant hiss in the darkness.

"Not so much. Magdalena found *that*," the ringleader says disgustedly, pointing to the young man. I draw in my feet and flatten myself against the pillar. "Hardly an appetizer. But soon, we will have better fare, I guarantee."

They stare at each other, the raven-haired one that has yet to speak content to gnaw on the remains of the rabbit and nod her head in agreement. In my heart—my heart that is so cold I cannot believe it hasn't stopped beating—I know they are talking about me.

How I wish Leonora were with me now. I think back to her in her true form—how savage she looked, how brutal—and wish with even greater urgency that she were here to protect me.

"Where's the wolf?"

I gasp and immediately cover my mouth. Had she read my thoughts?

"Probably looking for the wolfling," the raven-haired one chortles between bites. A hideous, guttural sound escapes her throat as she bites down harder on the dead rabbit's flesh.

"Yes, but I doubt she'll find him. Or if he'll be able to get out. The little freak. He cannot possibly be immune to silver bars, even if he is a *Born Vampire*," she says, rolling her eyes.

My heart palpitates furiously. What have they done to Greydanus? And where is Leonora when we need her most?

Oh, Zigmund, why did you not believe me?

There is a disturbance near my feet. The youth, who I thought was dead, is stirring. I try to inch away from him, but it is no use. He has latched onto my foot and will not let go. His paper-like fingers rustle against the leather of my boots.

I nudge him with my foot, but he is holding on with inhuman force. I now understand where this surge of strength has come from. He's revivifying. His eyes light up.

He has taken his place in the ranks of the undead.

"What is that old saying, Ruxandra? Let sleeping dogs lie? It seems some of our group have not taken this to heart."

Before I can pull away, the raven-haired one swoops down on the youth and rips out his throat. The sight is too much for me. I cannot hold it in any longer. I scream.

"Useless," she says disgustedly, looking down at the thoroughly dead body of that poor young man.

But I cannot spare him a second thought. I've given myself away.

"What's this? A *spy*?"

"A very pretty spy, yes. Fresh, too." The escapee from the iron maiden clutches my neck so hard I can scarcely breathe. "With young blood pulsing through her veins." I flinch as she brings her mouth near my neck. Her breath is sickly sweet, like rotting flesh.

"Dacia! You do not take precedence here. Wait your turn. Go feast on the body you were enjoying before this little bit of flesh interrupted us," Ruxandra commands.

Her pout is grotesque because of her fangs. She shrugs and dances back to Luc's body.

The faces surrounding me are like a scene from hell. Their fangs protrude, saliva dripping off them and onto me. Their eyes flash—bright green and glistening black. In that instant, I see the outline of their skulls beneath their translucent skin.

"What's to be done with her," the raven-haired one says. I know very well what they want to do with me. I saw my fate etched into the granite of a tombstone the day before. I struggle against Ruxandra's hold, but she digs her nails into my scalp and twists my hair around her fist.

"Can we have some sport before the deed?" the raven-haired one asks excitedly. *Ghoul*, I think, and spit in her face.

She laughs at my defiance, but her sister is not amused and yanks so hard on my hair that some of it is ripped from my scalp.

"No," she says, hissing into my ear. "Not sport that will mar that perfect skin. But sport of a different kind. Yes, sport that would drive any sane person mad. And then...she will die."

"The master's new pet," Dacia sing-songs from the catafalque. "What a prize she is. Can we not, are you sure, Ruxandra?"

"Silence! I have orders, sister. You'd be wise to obey them, lest you end up like that," she says, nodding in the direction of the dead youth.

"Come, there's no time...*wretch*!"

I dig my fingernails into the soft flesh of her arm. She stumbles back and looks at the wound, mesmerized by the blood seeping from it.

This is my chance.

The air cleanses my skin of the touch of her dead fingers as I run through the night. The closest thing is the graveyard. Maybe I can lose them among the tombstones. I turn back to see if they are following and quicken my speed when I see how close they are. Winded, I crouch down behind a large obelisk, my breath coming in pants. Then it hits me.

There are supposed to be four sisters. Where is the other?

"Hello, darling."

I turn and come face-to-face with the missing Belododia. Her eyes are ruby red; blood is spattered across her chin. I scrabble for the obelisk, my fingernails breaking against the stone as I try to get a handhold on it. Blood streaks down my hands. I curse myself for being so hasty. Their bloodlust is like a sixth sense for them. They are upon me before I can move. The air is rent with shrieks. Their breath is hot against my neck. Ruxandra grabs me by the hair. I try to resist, but her grip is viselike. I claw at her hands as she brings my head down atop the tombstone. The pain is searing. The world goes dark before I can cry out to the night that I am being murdered.

※

The air is close and foul, stale. I cough, choking. There is no breeze in this room, no flow of air at all.

Something is terribly wrong. I try to remember what has happened. The sisters attacked me. I feel something wet against my neck. When I try to touch my fingers to it, I cannot. Something is tied around my finger. There is no light in here. I feel with the fingers of my left hand. A knot, a bit of string. Why would someone loop string around my finger?

My back is terribly cramped. I try to flex my toes, but my foot hits against something solid. I stretch my arms out, but my elbows cannot move farther than a hand span. It is as though I am trapped in a box. Suddenly, everything is blindingly clear. I know why I am so cramped, why I cannot move, why the air is so stale.

I am buried alive.

My throat constricts. I fight the urge to cry out. I must conserve my breath. I remember the string. There is a reason for it, there has to be. The wood of the coffin is becoming oppressive, and I cannot think clearly. In a rage, I claw at the ceiling, which is much closer than I expect. I tear and scratch until I break my skin. I have not even made a dent in the wood and have used up vital stores of air. Sweat covers every inch of my body. I can already feel the dead earth encrusted in my bones. My fingers are bloody and skewered with splinters. My lungs cannot take the lack of air.

The string on my finger feels like fire. I yank on it, but there is no sound. My mind races through memories of the morbid facts I've read about, the obscure, macabre history I used to think was interesting. There is something to this string. I think and think until my head feels as though it will explode and my eyes stream from the trapped heat of this suffocating box.

I close my eyes. And then I remember.

Thomas Bateson, inventor of The Bateson Belfry—used to help those mistakenly buried alive to alert people of their fate. When the person awakes and yanks on the string, a bell is supposed to sound, signaling that the body has been buried prematurely. So why does my bell not toll, now that I am yanking so violently on the string?

Something brushes against my leg. I bite my lips raw to keep from screaming. To be buried alive is one thing; to be interred with something that can eat you before you die is a fate I would not even wish on the sirens who put me in this coffin.

I try to shrink in on myself, but there is nowhere for me to hide.

Whatever it is slithers up my leg. I cannot keep my eyes shut to this horror any longer. I look down and see a snake, a little dragon, inching up my body. *Heaven help me...*

A wyvern.

It mirrors the head of the staff I have seen in the glass case in the cavern and around the she-devils' necks. But the difference is that this one is alive and watching me. There is something in its mouth, but all I care about are its eyes—hideous and green and staring into my own, mesmerizing me.

I blink to break the trance. The creature comes to a stop, glaring at me in what I can only think is delight. Something heavy drops onto my stomach. I reach for it blindly, my eyes still fixed on the shadow of the creature shambling off into the darkness. The beast should have collided with the end of the coffin. When I reach out with my foot, all I feel is the wall. The wyvern is gone.

I return my attention to the object. My fingers trace its shape—a pendulum, weighty as lead.

I shift it in my hand, trying to get a feel for its weight. I run my fingers over the shape again and drop the object as I realize what it is.

Stefan's maniacal laughter rips through the confines of my tomb.

"But Bateson's Belfry...the bell...how is this possible?" I manage to croak out.

"That's very simple, Madelaine. This is *not* Bateson's Belfry. It is mine. Belododia's Belfry."

I pick up the object that I know now is the clapper that should be inside the bell on the surface, the clapper without which the bell cannot toll.

A scream tears out of my lungs. I pound furiously on the lid of the coffin. The laughter fills my ears, my head, my heart, suffocating me faster than this airless tomb. I cannot die here. I *will not* die here, but what can I do to save myself? My vision is beginning to leave me. I can scarcely breathe.

All goes quiet. I hear no laughter. Am I already dead? Is this what it feels like to pass into the afterlife? I lie still, straining to hear.

And then, coming from very far away, I hear it.

A wolf's howl.

And after that, the most welcome sound in the universe.

A spade striking against the wood above my head.

Screams erupt all around me, but I do not care. Someone is digging me out, someone, *someone...*

Moonlight spills in through the hole above me. I feel myself being pulled up from the grave, dirt falling against my clothes.

The moonlight shines on a face I thought I'd never see again.

"Mrs. Bradburry," he says, his blue eyes grim. "I believe you now."

"Thank God for that."

Zigmund leans me against his shoulder and lifts me out of the hole. I glance around for Leonora. She must have been the one who brought him here, but I do not see her anywhere. As we walk away from the grave, I look back and catch sight of a black shape running away from the château. I have never seen that creature before. It cannot possibly be the author of my salvation...can it?

"How did you know?"

"I'll explain once you are safe in my home."

I suddenly pull up. Amid the screams and the commotion, I finally see the massive white wolf, but Leonora does not concern me now. She is keeping our enemies occupied, but not my mind.

"I cannot leave without my husband."

"I'm afraid you have no choice."

"Would you have left your mother behind?" I ask, not knowing what else to say.

"I didn't have to. She abandoned *me.*"

Corcitura

The wolf has rejoined us. Zigmund stares at it as though he doesn't realize it's his mother, but then her glowing eyes bore into him and he becomes grim once more. "Come, there is no time. If you want to save him, you will come with me. There is nothing you can do for him here."

"No!" I strain against his arms, crying until I am insensible, for I have seen a sight on the rampart where I stood this morning that makes my heart ache. Eric, standing on high, his arms outstretched, imploring me in a voice only I can here. "Can't you see him?! He is up on the turret! Look, *look*, why are you so blind?! My husband needs me!"

"That is not your husband."

His words silence me. "*Not* Eric?"

"I'm afraid not, Mrs. Bradburry. You do not know as much about our adversary as you think."

Our adversary. The words give me comfort. He is on my side. He will fight this evil with me.

I turn back one last time and see Stefan, his hand raised in a gesture of farewell. Though I am far away, I can see the dark stains around his mouth.

I let Zigmund lead me on. We follow the path Leonora is taking us down. I stare at her as she now holds the tiny brownish-grey wolf that is Greydanus in her mouth. The scene is surreal, yet I do not have the will to fight against the illogic of it any longer, and instead I focus my attention on the prints her gigantic paws leave in the snow. Greydanus glances at me once or twice, sorrow in his eyes. I cannot give him any reassurance that I have not lost my sanity. This is all too much.

I allow Zigmund to settle me into his carriage, Leonora and Greydanus, once more human, climbing in after me a moment later.

"It will be all right, Madelaine," Greydanus says, taking my hand. I cannot say anything in return. I've lost the will to respond, to put up the brave front.

"I'm sorry for that scene this afternoon," Leonora says. "I couldn't face the idea that my son was alive and thought me dead. But now that has been corrected."

"Has it?!" The forcefulness of my voice shocks me, but I cannot hold in my anger any longer. "Has it for you, for him, for me? For Eric?! Did you not see the way your son looked at you, Leonora? He probably thinks he's just as mad as I do. No, nothing has been remedied, nothing at all."

I cross my arms and shift to the farthest corner of the cab, not wanting to be near either of them. I can no longer offer Greydanus or his mother comfort. She is the cause of all of this. If it hadn't been for her accursed letter and my husband's foolhardy insistence on coming to her aid, I would be at home now, home and safe and loved by the man who has brought all this upon us.

"You'd never have been allowed to live a happy life. Not with this hanging over your head," she says, reading my thoughts. She reaches out her hand and takes mine. For once, I do not resist.

"Fix it," I murmur, suddenly feeling very old and very tired.

"I will. *We* will, now sleep."

I do as she commands, thankful that for the time being at least, this is no longer only *my* battle to fight.

ᑉ

"Thank you," I say, accepting the steaming mug of coffee from Zigmund's outstretched hand. I wrap the blanket about my shoulders and settle into the comfort of the armchair. We are in Zigmund's home in Mala Strana. Though I was nearly killed this night, I feel comforted by the warmth of this room. And even though I cannot quite call them friends, save maybe Greydanus, I feel safer being here with Leonora and Zigmund as well.

Leonora and Greydanus are curled up together on the sofa. Zigmund, as he settles down into his chair behind his desk, stares at them as though he still cannot believe they exist. I do not blame him. The next few hours will be crucial to all of us. I sense animosity in Zigmund and fear he will let this emotion consume him. I'm not certain he can set his ill-will aside.

He leans back in the chair, tents his fingers, and stares at his mother, who meets his eyes unflinchingly.

"You're supposed to be dead," he says finally, quietly, sounding like a little boy.

"As you can see, I'm not."

"You should be."

"Sometimes we see what we want to, Zigmund, not what really happened."

"What makes you think I wanted to believe you died?!" he shouts.

Leonora wraps her arms tighter around Greydanus and rests her chin atop his head. I look at Zigmund and wish I hadn't. The venom in the glance he turns on his brother makes the chillness between them seem insurmountable.

"Well, then, it seems I was mistaken. Leonora..."

"Mother."

"You lost the right to that name when you abandoned me thirty years ago."

"*Zigmund*," I cannot help chiding.

He turns on me a look of such hurt that I cannot help feeling sorry for him in spite of his harshness. What must his life have been like all these years?

He opens his mouth, turning his attention to his mother once again, when an unwelcome sound shatters the silence.

A knock at the door.

Stefan has found us, it has to be. Who else would call at this hour?

I look to Leonora, then Greydanus, whose eyes are shut, his whole body tensed as if waiting for the blow to fall.

The knock sounds again, more insistent this time.

Zigmund's eyes are trained on the door, his lips moving silently. He is half out of the chair when the door bursts inward.

I scamper higher on my chair, looking for something to fend off our attacker. I reach for the poker by the fire, bringing it up in front of me for protection. Leonora reels back, still clutching Greydanus, who is screaming something I cannot understand. The most horror-stricken of us all is

Zigmund, who keeps muttering, "It cannot be, it cannot be," as the creature moves into the room.

"After all these years, you've found me again," Zigmund says. "I'd know you anywhere, you devil. Show yourself!"

The figure steps unhurriedly into the room and throws back the black cowl of its cloak.

White-blonde hair trails down its back, a streak of black dividing the middle of its scalp. Its eyes are milky blue, save for the blacker than pitch pupils. Its face, though pale as death, is somehow beautiful.

"Not Constantinos?" Zigmund asks, looking at me in bewilderment.

"No," says the woman, fixing her eyes on him. "My name is Olga Belododia, and I have come to kill my brother."

Book the Third: The Narrative of Zigmund Fertig 1895: The Foundling

Specters of the Past

"*I* will not stand for this, Mattias Fertig! I forbid you to take my daughter and grandson to that godless bacchanal."

I tried to sneak away, but Father wouldn't let me. I should have known things would turn out badly this night and not only because I had seen an eclipse an hour ago. All of Greece was in convulsions over what it meant. But I was only seven years old and not yet superstitious. Grandfather, on the other hand, had never met a myth he didn't believe in wholeheartedly, which was why he was being so bull-headed now.

Father knew better than to argue with Grandfather when he was in one of his moods. Father should have given in by now. *I* would have given in by now.

"Father, it's only a festival," I whimpered. Things had gone downhill very quickly if I was the one who had to be the voice of reason.

Grandfather's nose looked even more aquiline and severe in the darkness of the hallway. His fine eyebrows were drawn together, making a dark line across his forehead. His dark hair looked even blacker in the gloom, especially since not a single strand of white ran through it, though Grandfather was nearly eighty.

"There, you see? Even the child sees sense. Listen to him, Dominic. It's only a festival."

"Only a festival?" Grandfather sputtered. "Can you not see how uneasy my daughter is?"

He waved his hands toward Mother, who stood in the doorway. I knew we'd get no help from her. She hated taking sides whenever anyone argued.

"Why are you consumed with such an unnatural desire to take part in this orgy, even at the expense of your wife and son's safety?"

"You of all people are the last to cast aspersions on my intentions. You've been to the festival every year."

"That doesn't mean I cannot see danger when it is right in front of me."

"As I said, it's only a festival. It's all in good fun."

"All in good fun?! *All in good fun?!* Basta, how dare you! Zigmund, come."

"Take your hands off my son, Dominic."

Grandfather's fingers tightened around my wrist. Father gripped my other arm and wouldn't let go. I looked up at them. Their faces looked as hard and cold as the statues of the Parthenon. I felt tightness in my chest as I wondered if they would rip me apart like the baby Solomon wanted to cut in half in the Bible. Neither of them wanted to give me up.

"Father, I'll stay," I mumbled.

"Silence, Zigmund," Father ordered. "I am the head of this family. I will decide who stays and who goes."

"Then you will also bear the consequences of your actions," Grandfather said.

"So be it."

Grandfather flung me away. "Take him and have done with the lot of you. I tried to warn you."

"Come along, Zigmund."

"Grandfather..." I whimpered, looking back at him. He'd turned his back on us. He stared down into the fire in the hearth, his hands gripping the mantle.

"Grandfather," I cried again. I suddenly felt very afraid. I called to him again, but he wouldn't answer me.

"Hurry, Zigmund, the hour grows late."

Father pushed me ahead of him. I looked back one last time, but he had already slammed the door. The three of us stood outside in the alley in the humid Grecian night.

"Pompous old wretch."

"Mattias!" Mother gasped. "You've never disagreed on anything before. You've always been so attuned. Maybe my father is right."

"Nonsense," he said, putting on his best devil-may-care smile and ruffling my hair. "Your father is clinging to old notions. This is not the middle ages, Nora. Why should we be afraid of having a little fun? That's exactly what we need after a hard day's digging, isn't that right, Zig?"

I nodded, not really knowing why I did so. I had wanted to go to the festival just as much as Father, but after the scene in Grandfather's house, I was beginning to feel sick.

I let them walk ahead, happy to fall behind and plod along at my own pace. Mother continued to nag him, but Father wouldn't budge. Once he set his mind on something, it was impossible to turn him off it.

I hated to hear them arguing. They hardly ever fought, but when they did, the rows were spectacular. Father blamed it on Mother's fiery Italian temper, and Mother said the fault lay with Father's stubborn Teutonic blood. Whatever the reason, I wished they would fight when I wasn't around. I wasn't used to seeing them at loggerheads. It was something foreign to me, just like the language of this country we had been spending so much time in lately.

Mother muttered something in Italian and left Father in her wake. Her long dark hair trailed out behind her like a black wave, contrasting sharply against her alabaster skin. She was like a statue brought to life, but she'd always been warm and attentive to me, though everyone's opinion was that she would have been just as happy with or without a son.

Father trailed after her, catching her hand, which she did not snatch away. Father was not nearly as striking as mother, but he was handsome in a bookish way. Sandy hair like mine crowned the trademark Fertig forehead—wider than most, but not too high, so therefore considered a good trait.

Corcitura

His eyes were large and blue like mine, too. Mother said I was the mirror image of Father. We'd make a striking pair once I grew into my face and took my place beside him at the university in Cologne. Our futures had already been planned out for us years in advance.

My mind wandered back to the festival. *Anthesteria*—the feast of wine and revelry and the dead. I rolled the strange name around on my tongue. The festival honored Dionysus, the Greek god of wine. It was said that everyone who took part outstripped the god in their ritual madness.

From what my parents had told me, Anthesteria was a time to expel ghosts and frolic with the dead, and though I did not know what this meant or what exactly I would have to do, I was fascinated.

And just *slightly* terrified.

"Zigmund, look! Rockets! Just like Carnival in Venice." I looked up to where my mother was pointing. Fireworks exploded into jewel-toned flames, brightening the starless sky. I smiled, forgetting my fear. Maybe Grandfather had been wrong to worry.

I linked hands with Mother and Father and wandered into the crowd.

I seemed to be the only child here. I really couldn't tell, though, since everyone was costumed in one way or another and *everyone* wore masks. There was a gaggle of shield bearing, helmet wearing, bristling plumed Hoplite soldiers in one corner. Across from them crouched a line of winged women who looked like harpies.

Something bumped into my back, knocking me from my parents' grasp. I was still on my knees when I felt bones encircling my neck.

I tried to scream, but the skeletal fingers closed around my throat, cutting off the sound.

"Come away with the daughters of Nyx, child," my kidnapper hissed into my ear. "Come away, come away. We will feast on your blood. We long to drink it. And we will, whether we ask your leave or not."

I reached up and ripped off one of her fingers. Her screams rattled through my body, but all I heard was the beating of my own heart as I stared down at the twitching bone in my hand.

I threw the finger on the ground and sprinted away, only to run straight into another black cloaked figure. I flailed in the folds of its robe, terrified that I'd feel bony hands strangling me any second.

Finally, I righted myself and looked up. The figure was not a woman. I wasn't sure if the figure was even human.

A death's head smiled down at me. All that was missing was a scythe.

"Back, Thanatos!"

Who had spoken? I looked behind me to see one of the Hoplites marching toward me. When I looked back, Thanatos, or whoever he was, was gone, but the other women were still there. One of them, not the one who had attacked me, glared at me over the rim of a chalice she held in her bony hands. Her brittle nails scraped across the glass, the sound setting my teeth on edge. She lurched toward me and the chalice overturned, spilling the liquid onto the ground. I edged away, narrowly missing getting sprayed with it. It was dark and red and smelled awful.

"Begone, Keres!" commanded the Hoplite, waving his sword. "Anthesteria is coming to an end!"

The Keres gnashed her teeth and reeled away, followed by her sisters. The death-masked Thanatos was nowhere in sight.

I screamed as something laid its hands on me.

"Father!" I shrieked, burying my face in his chest as he gathered me up.

"Having fun, little man?" he asked. Was he crazy? I'd come face-to-face with death and he found it funny?

I wriggled out of his arms and ran to Mother.

"Lost your way, my little love?" she asked as I slipped my hand into hers.

"I think the excitement's getting to him, Nora." This from Father, who was back at our side. I was so angry with him. I wished Thanatos and his sisters would come back and spirit him away.

"Maybe we should leave," Father said, noticing, probably for the first time, that I was less than thrilled to be surrounded by corpses on parade.

"So soon? The night is young yet and you have much, *so much*, to see."

The voice had come from a man who was gamboling in the middle of the circle of stalls. He whirled like a dervish, twirling streamers in the faces of the ladies who had gathered beside us. The man was handsome, darkly so, with the swarthy good looks of a gypsy. His accent was familiar to me. I'd heard men speak with that easiness of tone, but not in Greece. His speech was more Northern European, maybe French.

A large, gold ring pierced his earlobe. He wore a tall beaver skin hat that somehow managed not to fly off even though he was spinning like a top.

Sparks flew from his hands. I forgot Thanatos and the Keres sisters and was mesmerized by the magic this man had at his fingertips. His roquelaure looked like the wings of a giant bat as he spun closer and closer to us.

The roquelaure hit me in the face as the gypsy magician swiped me aside in his haste to reach Mother. Finally, he stopped his mad twirling.

I brushed the cloth away and looked up. The gypsy was staring at Mother in a way I didn't like. Father laughed, obviously thinking this was all a great jest. I was beginning to wonder if he'd visited the wine cellar before we left Grandfather's. He wasn't acting at all like himself.

"Bellissima," the gypsy said, his voice slithering around us. My skin prickled. Mother paled, which was a sight, since her skin was already marble-white.

From inside the folds of his cloak he drew out a mask.

"How did you know I was Italian?" she asked. She hadn't seen the mask yet, but I had. I couldn't take my eyes off it—the hellfire red of the leather; the sharp, long ears that looked more demonic than human; the long hooked nose.

Mother's hand hung in midair. The gypsy's mouth flicked up at the edges. He grabbed Mother's arm, shoving the mask into her palm.

"A face like yours could only have been born of the Eternal City. I hope you may keep that beauty—*eternally.*"

The mask shattered to the ground as Mother jerked her hand away. The gypsy laughed as though Mother's terror was a hysterical joke.

Suddenly, the gypsy's eyes were on me. I felt sweat beading the back of my neck. "It's nothing personal, mon ami," he said, patting me on the head. "I mean nothing by it. It's just good business."

I swiped at his hand, but he just shrugged and laughed and backed away.

"Nora, what is it?" Father wasn't amused anymore.

"I want to go, now. *Now,*" she repeated.

"All right, all right," he coaxed. Father was now as uneasy as I had been. The gypsy had unnerved us all, with his sparks and his magic and his second sight. He scared me, but I couldn't think about him now with Mother in such a state—a state he'd put her in.

I remembered the black robed figure. *Thanatos.* I tried to look for him in the crowd, but they were too tall for me to see anything and too tightly packed together for me to get a look through.

I'd be thinking about Thanatos for a long time, I knew, but the gypsy was different. I wanted to see him again, even if only for a second. I had to know that he was real. I had to know he wasn't another ghost of Anthesteria. And I had to know what he'd meant by saying he wished Mother would stay beautiful forever.

The crowd parted. I looked up into their masked faces, hoping for a sign, something to tell me that what I was seeing made sense.

All the booths had disappeared. Nothing remained—no sparks, no smoke, no sign of his wild face.

The gypsy was gone. It was as though he'd never existed.

"Come along, Zigmund, it's time to head home."

"But Father, Mother...the gypsy."

"What gypsy?" I glared up at my father. I knew he was lying for Mother's sake. But still, I feared maybe he wasn't.

Corcitura

That entire night, we'd frolicked with corpses and danced with ghouls. Now, as we walked down those wine-soaked streets, I felt like there were two ghouls walking beside me in the form of my parents.

I wished we were heading back to Grandfather's instead of to the rooms we'd rented in a local hotel Father was mad about staying in every time we came to Greece.

My skin prickled. I turned around, expecting to see that death-headed face, but there was nothing behind us except a large, mangy-looking black dog whose ribs I could see through its skin.

Father was oblivious to everything except Mother. This was how it had always been. Their world was the two of them. I was allowed a small place in it because I was their son. They loved me in their own flawed way, but I was never welcomed onto that other plane they shared. And I wasn't sure if I wanted to be, when it came down to it.

I wished he felt different tonight, especially after what happened to us at the festival. I could feel a tang in the air—something earthy and bitter and to be honest, evil.

Mother was on her guard. I think she was as attuned to me as she'd ever been. I'd caught her looking behind us at least five times already. She was nowhere near as oblivious as Father.

I reached up to take her hand and shivered when my fingers laced between hers. She was colder than a sheet of ice.

The alley behind our lodgings was deserted. Father fumbled with the key.

"Hurry, Mattias, *hurry.*"

"Easy, Nora. Just one more turn..." As calm and oblivious as ever. Finally, Father got the key to work and the door opened. Mother let go of my hand and darted inside. I stared at my palm. Blood rushed underneath my skin, returning it to its normal shade of pink. I flexed my fingers, hearing them crack as life was pushed back into them. Mother had nearly crushed me.

Father lit one of the lamps.

"Off to bed with you, little man," he said to me. My bed was a small lump on a straw pallet on the opposite side of the room. The gravel floor crunched under my feet as I walked to my cot. I was settled in under the thin sheet when Mother knelt at my side. The light from my lamp made her eyes glow like sulfur. I shrank into the pillow.

"Zigmund, you saw it too, didn't you?"

I nodded. I knew she was talking about the death-headed figure—Thanatos.

"I'm scared, Zigmund. Something is not right. Something evil is tracking us."

I nodded again. I'd felt the same.

"Whatever you do, do *not* open that door, no matter what."

I looked over at the door. It was bolted tightly. I did not have the strength to lift those bolts, and I didn't think Father would open the door to a stranger in the middle of the night. What was mother thinking?

"Do not answer it if it calls out."

"Answer...what?" My mouth had gone dry.

"The Vrykolakas."

It was not the first time I had heard that hideous word. Having a professor of archeology for a father, I'd learned all the superstitions of the places we visited from an early age. The Vrykolakas was neither a vampire nor a werewolf, but maybe a combination of both and deadlier than either.

I pulled the covers up to my chin and tried to look brave. Mother had always been given to superstition, but this was something different. There was real fear in her eyes. But the Vrykolakas was just a myth.

"Sleep now, my son."

I'd seen paintings of this creature in my father's books. It was plague-ravaged and had a barbed tongue with which it inflicted wounds its victims never healed from. How could I sleep when Mother and I both thought this creature was hunting us? When we both thought this creature was hiding behind the disguise of Thanatos?

Corcitura

"Good night, Mother," I said finally. She would have stayed there all night, looking like a ghost, if I had not spoken.

Her eyelids fluttered. She seemed to remember she was talking to me. It was almost as if she had been looking into the middle-distance at something she couldn't quite see. "Yes, good night, my angel." Her lips burned frigidly against my forehead. I swallowed hard. I did not want to let her walk the short distance to her side of the room. The space between her bed and mine seemed greater than a chasm. "Mother..."

"Sleep, little one, sleep," she soothed. I relaxed my grip on the covers and watched her fade into the shadows. Already I could hear my father's light snore. Nothing troubled him. He was a man of science. He did not waste thoughts on demons and ghouls.

I stared unblinking at the ceiling. I would not get to sleep tonight. My hands felt cold, so I shoved them beneath my pillow. I did not mean to cry out, but the straw that stuck beneath my fingernails seemed to hurt more than anything.

As the echo of my shriek died out, I heard the knock sounding against the door.

There was a rustling from the bed across the room as one of my parents rose. I would bet my life it was my mother.

I held my breath as we waited for something, anything, to happen. When it did, I wished I hadn't been so eager to hear more.

The door shook as something stabbed into it and was raked along the wood. I flinched and looked down at the floor, wondering how long it would take me to burrow into the gravel.

Father stirred. Mother whispered to him to keep silent, but she was too late.

"Who is it?" he called out, his voice ringing through the darkness.

The dagger-scraping ceased. In the long pause that followed, I got the feeling that whatever was on the other side of the door was leaning its ear against the wood, straining to hear.

"Mattiasssss Fertig."

I would not have answered that voice. It sounded like the hiss of a snake and was just as menacing. Gooseflesh broke out over my body. I could not move even if I had wanted to.

"Yes, what do you want at this hour?"

There was another pause. I had not swallowed since the scraping stopped.

"You have already given it to me."

The voice was not brash or triumphant. It was matter-of-fact. I think that was what terrified me the most.

The room suddenly flooded with light.

"Mattias, put out the light!" Mother whispered furiously.

"Some devil is playing us for fools, Nora, and I intend to see what this trick is about."

"Mattias, I'm begging you. A devil is right!"

Father's eyes searched Mother's face. I watched them without breathing, wondering in the back of my mind why there was silence outside. What had happened to that thing?

Father leaned down and caressed Mother's cheek. It was a tender gesture I had seen him do a thousand times.

"I must find out what that is," he said. His voice held the same note of purpose I'd heard every time he'd made up his mind to do something neither Mother or I could support him in.

What would he find when he opened that door?

As it happened, the choice was taken out of his hands.

He never made it across the room.

"Mattias!!!"

The last image I had of my father was of him sinking through the ground, his arms outstretched above him, clinging to my mother as she tried to pull him out of the grip of the thing that had burrowed up through the floor.

Long, dagger-like fingernails dug into my father's chest. A gurgling sound escaped his throat as he looked down and saw the blood spurting from his wounds.

I could not sit by and watch my father being murdered. I grabbed the closest thing I could find—a leather case he kept his maps in. It was tubular and so light it nearly flipped out of my hands as I lifted it off the floor. What damage could it do? Then I thought of the gravel. I poured out the contents of the case and dumped as many handfuls of gravel as I could into it. The result was not earth-shattering, but it would have to do.

The thing was halfway out of the hole by now. Father had stopped moving. His mouth was slack and his eyes were no longer blinking frantically. I still clung to my makeshift club, but I knew I couldn't help him.

Anguish bubbled up in my throat—anguish and rage, which grew even hotter when I looked upon the familiar death-headed creature that was crouching by my parents' bed.

Father had been a barrier to what it was really after. It was staring at Mother with unconcealed lust, its eyes roving over her half-clothed body. She could not move for terror, but I wasn't going to see another of my parents defiled and then murdered.

I hefted my club and brought it down against the beast's head.

That got its attention.

"Zigmund, no!"

I was too terrified to scream. The monster had thrown back the black cowl of its robe, leaving its bald head exposed. The beast's tongue whipped out and struck its face, the barbs wrapped around the tongue tearing off chunks of the creature's skin. I dropped the club and backed away, but there was nowhere to escape.

The long-nailed fingers closed around my throat, and I was hefted up to what seemed an outrageous height. My legs flailed in the air as I clawed at the dead-white hand.

"Little gnat, I will crusssh you," it hissed. Its grip closed tighter. I would have been suffocated if it had not been for Mother.

The beast flinched. I looked over its shoulder and saw Mother drop the club. Suddenly, it was as if the thought of crushing the life out of me no longer mattered to it. The creature flung me to the ground and crawled toward the bed.

Even with my infantile mind, I knew what it wanted. I knew what would happen. And I knew I had to stop it.

I leaped onto the beast's back and dug my nails into the dead flesh of its head. The creature spasmed and screamed and clawed at its back, trying to grab me. I evaded its searching hands, batting them away and digging my fingers into them when I could. But I did that one time too many and was finally caught.

My head was gripped in a vise. I was too shocked to understand that the beast was digging its nails into my face, but after a minute, the horror sunk in. I kicked and squirmed, but the creature held fast. I felt blood pouring out of me. The beast flexed its fingers and I whimpered in pain. A few inches higher and I'd have lost an eye. As it was, if I lived, I'd carry these scars with me forever.

"I alwaysss hated children. Even when I wasss one. Filthy little vermin that should be dessstroyed at the first chance."

The beast squeezed harder as it drew me toward its mouth. Its breath was disgustingly sweet, like garbage left out to bake in the sun. "Enjoy your sssstay in hell. I did while I wasss there."

I stretched out my fingers to claw at its eyes, but the monster flung me against the wall before I could do any damage. The stone bashed against my skull. Darkness hemmed me in, and I knew no more of my mother's shame.

***

My head throbbed as I woke. I felt like I had been put through a stone grinder. I could barely move. When I put my fingers to my face, my hand came away covered in blood.

I listened for any sound in the darkness, which was blacker than before. I wondered absently if I'd gone blind. Certainly having razor sharp nails stuck into your face inches from your eye could do that, but I was beginning to make out shapes in the gloom, so I knew I hadn't lost my sight...yet.

I felt around the gravel floor for something with which to see. All I could hear was a sucking sound, but I didn't know where it was coming from. I listened, though I was becoming more and more terrified by the noise. It sounded like an animal trying to suck the marrow out of the bones of its prey.

Finally, I felt something—broken glass from the lamp that father had dropped.

Father...

I pushed aside the shards and rifled through the gravel till my fingers closed around a match. I struck it, not even bothering to think of what I might see, or of if I'd like it.

I didn't.

The Vrykolakas—there could be no denying that's what the beast was—cradled Mother almost gently, as though she were an infant. Mother's arms hung lifelessly at her sides. I had to crane my head until I nearly toppled over to be able to look into her eyes. No living person's head should be skewed at such an angle.

My breath lodged in my throat. I'd seen that look before on Father's face.

Father's body was gone.

I didn't know whether to speak or slink off. But as it happened, I didn't have to decide. The Vrykolakas once again decided for a member of the Fertig family.

"Where do you think you are going?"

It dropped Mother to the ground. Her arm smacked against the floor, her wrist twitching reflexively. For a second, I wondered if she was really dead. Her dark eyes were glassy and unseeing. I could not deny the blood trickling from her mouth.

I shut my eyes and reopened them quickly, but the image was still there. I no longer saw my mother. All I saw were the gashes on her throat.

In the space of an hour, I'd become an orphan.

"I never leave anyone to tell the tale," the Vrykolakas said, crawling toward me.

Instinctively, I looked at Mother, but she couldn't help me. She'd never caress my head again, never tell me I was her bambino caro.

That was all the push I needed.

I fell to my knees.

"Sssmart of you to ssshow me honor."

Melika Dannese Lux

My hands closed around fistfuls of gravel. Slowly, I raised myself and glared up into the eyes of the monster who had murdered my parents.

Its lips split. The barbed tongue that had torn open my mother's throat peeked out through the cracked skin. I clenched my fists, knowing that if I didn't time this attack right, I'd feel the sting of that barb in my own neck.

Wait for it...wait for it...stop thinking of Mother's dead eyes watching you...

"I've never met with a more willing victim."

"And you never will again."

I hurled the gravel into its eyes. The walls shook from its shrieks, chunks of stone falling from the ceiling and smashing into my head as I raced past the monster and catapulted myself through the window above my pallet.

Once I hit the ground outside, I looked back to make sure the Vrykolakas wasn't following me. I could still hear its shrieks, but with that bloated stomach, the beast would never be able to squeeze itself through the tiny window I had barely gotten out of.

I needed to get to Grandfather. I ran off, knowing I was being hunted, knowing I was leading a rabid half-wolf, half-vampire to my grandfather's house. The beast had gotten a whiff of me and liked what it had smelled.

I knew I was exposing Grandfather, but I was a child who had just seen his parents eviscerated. If my mind wasn't very sound at the time, Grandfather would have to forgive me. He'd know what to do. He *always* knew what to do. He was the one who first told me about the creature that had killed my parents. He would know how to kill *it*.

The cobbled alley was deserted. Grandfather's varnished door shone red as blood in the moonlight. If Father hadn't been so stubborn, we could have stayed here. But no, we needed to stay in the city with the people—to live like locals. That was his logic.

And it had killed him.

"Grandfather, Grandfather!" I shouted, pounding on the door. Grandfather had exceptional hearing for a man his age, so why wasn't he answering?

Corcitura

I pounded again. The door didn't budge. All I had to show for my efforts were bruised hands. I stood back and looked over the door. Only then did I see that it was jammed.

This was going to take work. I barely had any strength left, but I had to try.

I leaned against the door, but I was too frail to make any headway. "Grandfather!" I yelled again. Still no answer. I slammed my shoulder into the wood again and again, ignoring the pain from my splitting skin, but the only thing I was destroying was myself.

My lungs felt raw. I could scarcely breathe, but finally, as my last bits of energy were giving out, the door cracked inward just enough for me to squeeze through. I ripped my pants in three places and caught my hair on a nail, but I managed to get in.

The minute my bare feet touched the floor on the other side of the threshold, I knew something was wrong. I smelled something harsh, burning.

I padded through the hall, making for Grandfather's study. As I rounded the corner, I saw a light underneath the door. A flickering light.

I reached for the door handle and howled as the brass burned my palm. That's what the smell had been—fire. But Grandfather was in there. Weak as I was, I had to get him out. I tore off whatever was left of my shirt, wrapped it around the handle, and pushed.

Grandfather was slumped over in his armchair in the only corner of the study not yet destroyed by flames. Papers curled and burned, wood crackled and turned to ash. No longer were the spines of his books green and brown and pebbled leather. Everything was red—violent, hungry, hellish red. His library was already half consumed by the fire his enemies must have set on purpose.

Grandfather had always been thin, but I still had trouble lifting him. I set him back against the cushions. His eyes were glassy, his jaw slack. There was a huge gash in his forehead. Blood trickled out of the corner of his mouth. If that were not enough evidence that he was dead, the knife sticking out of his chest pushed all doubt out of my mind.

Still, I felt for a pulse. I had to try. But there was no movement in the veins at his wrist. His hand was clenched around a piece of paper. I pried open his already stiff fingers and snatched the scrap, hoping for a clue. The writing was gibberish. Just more theories he'd been working out when someone had come into his house and murdered him.

I threw the paper on the fire.

There were no tears for Grandfather. Tears were a sign of weakness. And weakness got you killed.

A crash sounded in the hall. I knew it wasn't from burning timbers. The fire had not spread from this room.

My last recourse was dead. The creature had killed off my family, and now it had come for me. I could hear it scrabbling in the hallway. I should have fled by now, but I couldn't move.

Images stumbled over each other in my mind—the gravel spraying up around Father as he was sucked into the ground, the dead black eyes staring out at me from my mother's face, the rose blooming in Grandfather's chest.

And me, still bleeding from the face and leaving a trail of my blood for the Vrykolakas to follow.

I grabbed a towel from the wash basin in the corner and pressed it to my wounds. The sounds outside the room were drowned out by the roar of the fire. The Vrykolakas could have been standing behind me and I wouldn't have known.

Coughing and sputtering, blood mixing with my sweat and sticking to the skin around my eyes, I stumbled out into the alley on the other side of the house. I wiped away the muck and looked back. Grandfather's house was hardly recognizable. The roof had caved in over the study. My one hope was that the Vrykolakas was trapped inside, being burnt to cinders.

I didn't want to spend another minute in this country. I had no definite plans, but my mind kept pointing me in one direction—the harbor. I set off, hoping I'd be able to find my way aboard a ship.

That night, in a cupboard aboard the cutter I'd stowed away on, I lay awake and wondered.

Corcitura

I was miles away from that house of death. The Vrykolakas had followed me into the blaze, but I was the only one who had made it out. Why, then, could I hear its screams in my head?

***

That was thirty years ago. The memory was as fresh in my mind as if it had happened this morning. I had never been able to forget the screams. Torment, despair, rage, surprise—all these emotions threaded through that flesh-crawling howl.

I hadn't screamed since that night. When the wolf knocked down my door a few hours ago, it came as a shock that the sound coming from my own throat was a near replica of the shrieks of the animal that had murdered my parents.

I wasn't afraid for my life, but seeing a full grown, black streaked, snow white wolf in the middle of your study is enough to make even a grown man's courage falter.

I'd been on the verge of reaching for my revolver when the wolf looked into my eyes and addressed me by name. I thought I'd finally snapped. The years of strain, of struggle, of isolation had finally taken their toll.

Then the wolf began to transform. The fur retracted into its body. Long, silky black hair sprouted from its scalp and fell around its shoulders. The snout shrunk and reformed into a well-molded, patrician nose. Only the eyes remained unchanged—black and mysterious, like two pools of night. The woman drew herself upright and stared at me. Her glistening claws had turned into delicate fingernails. Warmth returned to my body as I stared at her graceful alabaster arms. I remembered the way they used to encircle me when I was a child.

How she had found me was a mystery. That she was even alive was impossible.

"Zigmund, do you not recognize me?"

The voice was the same. Lower pitched, sensuous—like liquid gold. But this was incredible. There was no explainable reason for the vision standing in my study, addressing me as if a chasm of thirty years did not separate us.

"Zigmund, please," she said, stepping toward me.

"Recognize you?" I finally answered, coming to my senses somewhat. I rose from my chair, but made no move to go to her, keeping the solidity of the desk between us. "How could I not? You haven't changed since the night I saw you die."

"Darling, please…"

"Don't touch me!"

I couldn't help my anger. Did she expect me to accept her resurrection in a minute's time? Why wasn't she as stunned to see me as I was to see her?

"Zigmund, you have to understand, I didn't know, I thought I'd killed you myself…"

I had found that hard to believe, but I let her talk. Apparently, she'd been "reborn" that night in Greece. The Vrykolakas's bite had already taken effect. Her throat had closed of its own accord, making her whole once more, but insatiable for blood. I did not want to dwell on the things she told me she did in those early days. She didn't blush, but I felt myself growing as red as a tomato.

I sat down heavily in my chair. My mother was alive, in her own way. What did this mean for me? What did she *think* it could mean—that I would rush into her arms and forgive her for abandoning me? For letting me fend for myself for so many years?

No. It was unforgivable, and I told her as much. Nor did I soften when she told me the reason she hadn't been able to find me was because I thought she was dead. I'd work out that logic when I had more time alone.

And then she told me she had a son—*another* son.

I think if I had had a knife, I would have killed her then. But she didn't give me much time to follow through on those thoughts. The name Madelaine Bradburry was flung at me before I could tell Leonora where I thought she deserved to be right now. I remembered the woman who had pleaded with me to help her, the woman who had told me my mother was alive. Maybe that's why I was more prepared for this apparition, if one can ever be prepared to meet a ghost.

Corcitura

I listened to the story, thankful that my mind could be focused on the details of my profession. Science had always been my sanctuary. I planned the course of action; I knew the weapons and tools I'd need to arm myself with for what was to come. Medals of St. Benedict, a shovel, my revolver with the silver coated bullets in case I met any undead—*other* undead—along the way.

And so I went with her and saved a woman from being buried alive.

How had my life come to this in the space of twenty-four hours? A day before, I'd been planning my next lecture. Since then, I'd been reunited with someone who should have been dead, discovered I had a vampiric half-brother, and been thrust into ridding the world of a pestilence that no one had ever even heard of besides the people in this room.

I glanced at Leonora, cradling the second son she had somehow birthed. The creature was pale yet well-favored in his way. He had the same large eyes as his mother, the same nose, hands, ears, hair. He looked more like her than I ever had. Something about him made me uncomfortable. I didn't like the way he looked at me, as though he knew exactly what I was thinking and didn't approve.

And then he had started to cry blood.

Not hysterically, but silently, unobtrusively, which was somehow worse than if he had had a tantrum. Twice I'd watched him surreptitiously lick the tears as they trickled down his face. Exsanguination. I'd never seen that in any creature before, but I was willing to bet my entire academic career on the fact that my half-brother kept himself alive by drinking his own blood.

If I thought any more about this, I'd go insane. I turned my attention to the other player in our morbid little quintet. She looked so much like the beast I'd been hunting my whole life. Chalk-white skin, her eyes nearly translucent but with slitted black pupils. Long white-blonde hair flowing well past her waist, with a striking black streak dividing the fair locks. She had his sense of style, too, although she had chosen to wear a black fur coat instead of the black shroud Constantinos preferred. As I noticed this fur, I wondered if she had inherited his penchant for transformation, as had Leonora. Her lips were full and ruddy. If I were pressed, I would admit that she was beautiful, in a dead bride sort of way.

Impossible that Constantinos had a daughter. Olga Belododia, that's what she'd called herself. She'd come to kill her brother, Stefan, the Corcitura, the one who was neither an Upyr nor a Vrykolakas, but the first of his kind. Had he done this to her? He must have. If she'd been turned by Constantinos, she would have retained her own appearance and not had such striking similarities to that monster. It must have been a consequence of being turned by the hybrid. *Family resemblance*, I thought.

During all this, the last member of our party had remained silent. I looked over at the dark-haired woman curled up in the chair by the fire. Her eyes were fixed on Olga, but Madelaine Bradburry was not seeing the woman before her. I'd seen her husband on the turret, or what Stefan Belododia wanted us all to believe was her husband. It would take Madelaine time to get over that sight.

I turned back to Olga. She reminded me so much of Constantinos. When she spoke, I'd noticed that she had been careful not to open her mouth too widely, which made me wonder if she had inherited that family trait as well—cursed with a tongue studded with barbs.

I cleared my throat. "What do you know of Constantinos?"

"Nothing, other than that he attacked my brother before Vladec Salei finished the job."

Her voice was husky but not unpleasant. There was something in her eyes that made me trust her. Maybe it was because they held the same cynicism, the same world-weariness I saw in my own every morning when I looked at myself in the mirror. "Vladec Salei, yes, the other party." I'd never even heard of Vladec Salei until Eric Bradburry put me on the scent. It was then that I began what would become my life's work, eventually discovering that Salei and Constantinos had joined forces to create a creature that could not be killed by any of the methods I'd used in the past. But never before had I even countenanced the thought that my mother was involved. How could I have been so stupid?

"Yes, Vladec Salei. The reason I look like *this*."

"What are you talking about?" She looked nothing like Vladec Salei.

"This. This! Are you blind?" I couldn't follow her logic. If anything, she looked like Constantinos wearing a wig.

"You're supposed to be dead, Olga." These were the first meaningful words Leonora had spoken since she'd dragged me off to the graveyard to unearth Madelaine Bradburry.

"Well, sorry to disappoint, Leonora, but as you can see, I'm not."

"Auntie Olga." The little creature sitting in Leonora's lap extricated himself from her stranglehold and walked to Olga's side, looking up at her with his blood-stained face.

"Who are you, child?" she asked, her voice trembling. In all my years of fieldwork, I'd never seen a vampire cry, not even when they begged me to spare them from the sun's rays. Olga was close to crying now as she bent down to eye-level with the elfish creature addressing her.

"I've wanted to meet you my whole life," he said in his small voice. "I'm glad you're here, no matter what you have to say. I love you. Know that."

She did not hold in the tears any longer. How could she? How could anyone in her position?

I guided her to my chair, which she collapsed into.

"Seven years I've lived with this curse," she said, her hands shaking as she brushed the tears from her cheeks. "Seven years. I was dead. I'd killed myself rather than be turned by my own brother, but I wasn't quick enough."

All of us leaned forward in our chairs, even Madelaine Bradburry, who seemed to have come out of her trance.

"Stefan turned me before I had the chance to die."

I couldn't help pitying her—to be so close to freedom and then have it ripped away to be turned into a monster.

"So what do you think, Professor?" Her lips twitched up in a bitter smile. "Do you like what you see? Because this is what you get when my brother feels the urge to play God."

I glanced at the company. Madelaine Bradburry's eyebrows were *V*-ed, my child brother's mouth was open in an expression of horror, and Leonora—I could not think of her in intimate terms—looked as though she was hearing nothing new.

"Why now? Why after all these years have you come to kill Stefan?" Leonora's eyes widened at her own words. Was she regretting her decision to ask for my help? Was she feeling kindly toward her *husband* now, the father of that freakish child once again curled on her lap?

"I've been trying ever since the day he did this to me. I have not stopped. He's been clever, oh, very clever indeed. He knows of me. He knows I've been after him. How could he not? I was his first turn. I finally picked up the trail in Romania after I'd had words with my sister."

"How many of there *are* you?" I couldn't help asking. The man seemed to be overrun with sisters.

"Four who have been turned by Vladec Salei, myself...and *Nadia*."

"And who is this Nadia?" The name intrigued me, as did the hatred with which Olga had spat it out.

"Nadia is the one who betrayed us all to Vladec Salei. The reason I look like *this*," she said again, pulling at her black robes.

"And where is Nadia?"

"In hell, for all I know or care."

"Yes, I'm sure," I said, trying to placate her, "but it would help if we knew where she was. Wait...she's not, um..."

"Diseased? Infected? Repulsive like me, you mean?"

"I was going to say a vampire."

Her eyes softened. She looked down at her hands. They were lovely hands, though the nails were overlong and yellowing. "No. She was canny enough to strike a deal with that devil Salei."

"...which is why she has remained untouched for all these years." Leonora rose and walked over to me. I made a pretense of looking for something on my desk so I would not have to be near her. She noticed, but did nothing to draw me back. She'd been dead to me for thirty years. Having her so close would take getting used to.

"Forever twenty-four, Zigmund?"

"How did you...?" I said sharply, aghast. "You can read my thoughts?"

"Now that you no longer think I am dead. Now that I am free of the guilt of being a murderer. But I didn't have to read your mind, my son. I can see it in your eyes."

I put on my glasses. Let her see through that.

She smiled sadly at me and fixed her eyes on the Corcitura's sister. "Olga. Nadia is in Romania, isn't she?"

Olga stared at Leonora suspiciously, then nodded.

"Where in Romania?"

"You should know. Weren't you Salei's mistress?"

"He never thought me worthy to share her exact whereabouts," she said. I noticed she hadn't answered the question. "Olga, please, is there any truth to the rumor of a weapon that can kill whatever it is Vladec and Constantinos have created?"

"You're talking about the cross?"

"The cross?" We all turned toward Madelaine, who had shot out of her chair at the mention of the cross. "My husband told me of a cross. There is a blood cabochon in it. It's supposed to contain the blood of Vladec and Constantinos and someone whose name I cannot remember."

"Florin Istratescu? You actually believe that lie?"

"Lie?!" This time *I* was the one to be incredulous.

"Of course a lie," Olga scoffed. "The cross is a myth. Something Vladec and my sister concocted to keep the superstitions of the people in check. You think if it existed, I wouldn't have found it and put it to good use by now?"

"No, that's impossible." The blood dagger concealed in the cross was what I'd based my entire theory on. It was the only way to kill the Corcitura. I'd dedicated the last seven years to this theory, traveling around the earth, picking up bits and pieces of legend and sifting through them to find the truth. I'd made countless trips to Romania looking for that artifact. I'd even learned the language to better endear myself to the people and to read the ancient texts. Yet I'd never heard of

Nadia Belododia, nor had I been able to locate that elusive cross. And now this wraith was sitting here telling me my work had been a waste?

"I've done the research, *Miss* Belododia," I sputtered. It seemed ridiculous to address her as such. She must have thought so, too. She smirked at me and laughed. "The cross has to exist. It *has* to. There is no other way of killing that beast."

"Yes, there is."

I scanned the faces of our group, then turned back to Olga. "Well?"

"Are you beginning to lose your memory, Professor? Did I not tell you when I came here that *I* was the way?"

"Don't be ridiculous. What could you possibly do?"

"I'm his creation. I can kill him. As far as we know, I'm the only turn."

"He has to eat. Who is to say he hasn't made any more like you?" This came from Madelaine Bradburry. I was grateful to her for that line of thought, though I didn't for an instant credit it.

"There is a difference between feasting and creating new life. I'm his sister. I was his first. And I intend to be his last."

"Then why are we all standing here wasting time?"

All of us, even Olga, stared at Madelaine.

"Let's go to Romania, or wherever your sister is, and find this cross."

"Why would we go to Romania when I'm *right here*?" Olga glared at Madelaine, who did not shrink back. I think she was past the point of being surprised or scared of anything supernatural.

"Because according to my husband and Professor Fertig, the cross exists. And I'd rather stake our lives on something we know can kill him, than on your own wild conjectures."

I suppose it was too much for a hybrid vampire to take. She hissed and she lunged and then my child brother brought her to her knees.

"Madelaine is right," he said, his tiny fingers latched around Olga's wrist, bending it backward. "If my brother has evidence and so does Eric, then I think we should listen to them."

"It is madness," said Olga weakly. Beads of sweat dotted her forehead as she tried to extricate herself from my brother's grasp. His cold eyes held hers in a stare neither of them seemed willing to break. Finally, he flicked his fingers. She fell back on her heels. Before she could cover her wrist with her robe, I caught sight of an ugly, purple bruise where my brother's fingers had been. What sort of strength did this child possess? He looked so frail and wan. And only a minute ago he'd told her he loved her. I guessed he'd only love her if she went along with his plans. If not...I only needed to look at that bruise to know what would happen if we crossed him.

"Right, let's go."

"No."

We all looked at Greydanus, who had somehow become our leader.

"No?" asked Madelaine, looking at the child in bewilderment

"No. I will stay here and protect you."

"Protect me?" The incredulity in Madelaine's voice couldn't be denied.

"Do you doubt I could?" he asked, nodding in Olga's direction.

The look Madelaine turned on Olga brought home to me exactly how she felt about the Corcitura's sister. If it came to it, Madelaine would take Greydanus's side. "No," Madelaine said quietly.

"Then it's settled."

"As your mother, I think I should have some say in this matter," Leonora said.

"That's rich."

The pained look she turned on me made me regret my words, but only momentarily. She would have to work much harder to get me to feel anything close to filial love for her any time soon.

"You know I can protect myself," Greydanus continued. "I've been doing it for years."

Had he been left to fend for himself as well?

"Yes, but I have always been there."

So much for my theory.

"I know, Mother, but now you have to stop putting me first and think of others. Of Madelaine and Eric and Olga and even my brother Zigmund...especially my brother Zigmund."

The child reached out and took my hand. I had to fight to keep from crumpling. His touch was not frigid, but that wasn't the reason I felt my knees go weak. The overwhelming power in those tiny fingers seared my limbs, making me feel sensations that I'd never felt before. It was ridiculous, but I felt like crying.

"The child is right," said Madelaine, looking from me to Greydanus.

She gave in so easily. I wondered if it was not mind-control he was working on her. Some form of mesmerism.

"I'm coming with you," Olga said gruffly, rising from the ground.

"Suddenly keen on the task, are you?" I asked.

"No, but you people do not look as though you can handle yourselves very well. I expect you will need a guide."

"I'm perfectly capable of tracking," said Leonora.

"So capable that you only found your son today after thirty years?"

The barb hit home. Leonora stayed silent.

"No, I must go, too," Olga said. There was not a shred of remorse in her voice, just of resignation. "She's my sister. It's my task, and if she cannot do it, which I know she *can't*, then it will fall to me. This entire trip is a waste of time, but I'll come. I'm not letting the pair of you out of my sight."

"When was the last time you saw your sister?" I asked her.

"Three weeks ago in Cluj. I nearly killed her."

"By accident?" Leonora asked.

Olga gave us a smile that was all the answer we needed. "After what happened, I doubt she's there still. If she's smart, and I know she is, she's moved on already."

"Do you have something of hers, something with her scent?" asked Leonora.

"Ah, a kindred, I see," Olga said knowingly. Something in her eyes told me she approved of Leonora's changeable status. It was something they could share. "Yes, as a matter of fact, I do."

She reached into the folds of her fur coat and pulled out a small wad of red fabric, which she unfurled to reveal a shawl. I thought something so personal would suffice, but the shawl was only concealing what the real objects were—two tiny, gold medallion earrings.

"I tore these off her ears in the struggle. Her blood is still caked on the wires."

I watched Leonora's face as she brought the earrings to her nose. Her neck stiffened and her eyes darkened till I could no longer distinguish iris from pupil. A small growl rumbled in her throat as her eyelids grew heavy and began to droop, like a drunk's after too much ale. *Bloodlust on full display*, I thought to myself. I wished I hadn't witnessed the hunger in Leonora's eyes when she finally reopened them.

"This is good," she said. "Deep. I'd recognize that scent anywhere. It was the same as Stefan's before he was turned. We must be quick. She'll have moved on from Cluj by now."

"Undoubtedly."

"So you're with us, then? No tricks?" I still was not sure of Olga.

"Just because I'm undead does not mean I have no heart, Zigmund. I'm with you to the end."

That was confirmation enough for me.

"Give me at least an hour to get things ready and to secure the house." I took Madelaine and Greydanus aside.

"She does not leave this house, and you do not let anyone enter." I was too well aware of what could happen if you answered an unexpected summons from outside. "Do you understand?"

"Yes, brother." He touched me again, and I felt different this time—no longer alone.

"And I shall stay by his side, you need not worry," said Madelaine, though I didn't believe her for one second. I'd seen the look in her eyes when she'd thought she saw her husband. I knew she would do anything, however reckless, if she thought she could break back into the château to save him. I worried for her, but it was her life in the end. I could not waste time over her any longer, not with our chances for locating Nadia growing slimmer by the minute.

"I don't believe you, you know," I whispered to Madelaine.

"Of course you don't, but you can't stop me." There it was again, the indomitable streak I'd noticed earlier.

"I know."

"Good. We understand one another, Professor. Now go before I will have no choice but to go back alone."

I squeezed her hand and went off to my room to gather a few possessions and books I'd need. Within half an hour, I had it all. My satchel was barely full, but in it was everything I wanted for this journey—maps, though I knew Romania intimately after all my trips there; books written by scholars who were not complete crackpots; my own book, though the contents were seared into my brain; and lastly, a *Mauser Zig-Zag* with a cache of silver coated bullets I had made. It never hurt to be too prepared.

When I crossed the threshold of the library, the first thing I saw was Leonora on eye-level with Greydanus.

"I've never left you before today, Grey. Be careful. No matter who tries to persuade you, do *not* open the door. I've seen what can happen when you open your lives to strangers. It is why I am this way."

"I know, Mother. I...love you."

"I love you more than I've ever loved anything in this world."

He reached out a finger and traced her tears. "No more tears, Mother. Soon it will be over...for all of us."

A shudder passed through her, a silent sob, as she pulled him to her chest. His little arms circled her neck, his hands balled into fists. I remembered that gesture. I'd done it so many times before she had died. Or hadn't. This was all too confusing to be real.

"Are we ready?" If my tone was gruff, it was meant to be. I could not stomach their good-byes. I pushed past Olga and was out the door before they could answer.

"Don't hate him because he has what you were robbed of, Zigmund."

Madelaine had followed me out of the library. I put down the satchel and fiddled with its straps, hoping she would take the hint.

She didn't.

"What are you talking about?" I asked disinterestedly.

"It's not her fault. He's all she has now. Don't begrudge her this happiness."

"It should have been mine."

"A lot of things should have been, Zigmund, but they aren't. Are you going to be miserable about the things you cannot change, or do something about the things you can?"

I knew the speech was more for her own benefit than mine. "What would you have done in her place?"

"I would have been terrified."

"But you would have fought to get away. You would have at least *tried* to find the ones you loved."

"Yes."

"Just like with Eric."

"Which is why we must hurry."

Leonora and Olga had joined us. This was the first time I noticed that Leonora's fur, when not affixed to her skin, became a floor length white fur coat. Olga wore an exact replica in black, but that was not what drew my attention to her. It was her eyes, slitted and predatory. I hoped she'd have the restraint to not kill her sister if we found her.

"Remember what I said," I told Madelaine. I pulled out the other revolver I had put into my waistband and handed it to her. "Use this only if necessary."

She turned the revolver over, studying it, her eyes hard. "I think I might need something a bit stronger," she said, attempting a smile.

"Use that only in an emergency and only on the sisters. If Stefan comes..."

"I'll be there to protect her, don't worry. Go."

I searched Greydanus's face for some trick. I'd studied him with almost clinical scrutiny in the short time I'd known he was my brother. His eyes held no deception. I knew I could trust him with my life.

Olga was already outside in the snow, her dark figure casting a long shadow on the ground. Leonora had left as soon as Greydanus appeared at my elbow. I didn't need to see her face to know the apprehension she felt at leaving her child behind, even though her child was probably stronger than all of us put together.

"Keep her safe."

I hoped, as I locked the door behind me, that those were not the last words I'd ever speak to Greydanus.

***

"If she is not in Sighisoara, shouldn't we be thinking of other options?" The small town in the region of Transylvania was the place we'd decided to search first. It was South of Cluj, and, I thought, the logical direction Nadia Belododia would be headed in.

"What of Brasov?" I asked as we passed through another tunnel and our cabin was plunged into darkness. Three days out and we'd just crossed the border into Romania. "You said Nadia was born in Brasov." I continued talking, though I could not see my companions in the gloom. "She's lived there her entire life. It is where she feels comfortable, her haven, her sanctuary. It makes sense to look there if our search of Sighisoara reveals nothing."

"Not Brasov," Olga said adamantly, her pupils reforming into slits as the darkness cleared. I'd never get used to that reptilian feature, nor the fact that her pupils changed every time light hit them directly. "She'd never return there, not after what happened."

"That's where Vladec found her seven years ago, when Eric and Stefan stumbled into their path," Leonora supplied.

"Believe me when I tell you, she wouldn't go back to Brasov." Olga looked from me to Leonora in consternation. "That's where Stefan killed our father."

I was silent and so was Leonora. I did not know what to say. Leonora pulled down the table from the wall and laid out one of my maps, smoothing out the creases.

"What do you need that for?" asked Olga. I suppose she was angry that we hadn't paid more attention to her revelation. At this point, knowing what we did, I don't think anything could have shocked us.

"I haven't been to Romania in a while," said Leonora.

"You don't need the stupid maps. I know my way around fine."

"Yes, but I don't, and I'm sorry, Olga, I just don't trust you."

"That's quite all right, the feeling is mutual. Besides, you should be more concerned with my sister. She's the one you cannot trust."

"You seem so sure of that, Miss Belododia," I said, again feeling like an idiot for addressing her in such normal, human terms. "But you have given us no reasons, concrete anyway, besides your obvious spite."

"Spite?"

"Jealousy, then."

"No, Zigmund, no. You don't understand. Everything in my life has been a lie since I died. Or since I was supposed to die. I had prepared my soul for God. I was so ready to die."

"I can imagine," I said uncomfortably. I had never wished for death before, but when I saw the sympathy on Leonora's face, it struck home painfully that this was a longing she must have known all too well.

"Nadia helped make me like this."

"She couldn't have been the one who attacked you?"

"No, but she stood by and did nothing. Madelaine Bradburry's husband was there, did you know that? My sister was the one who restrained him. I don't think he ever knew what happened to me. They were all standing around me. I can still see Salei's face lit up by the moonlight. Eric was too horrified to help me anyway. They would have killed him if he'd tried."

"I see," I said, though I didn't at all. "But about Nadia..."

"What about Nadia?" she said, standing abruptly and pacing to the window. "You are showing an unhealthy interest in my sister, do you know that, Professor?"

"My interest, I can assure you, Madam, is not unhealthy. It is merely that she could be our only hope."

"How many times do I have to explain..."

"You can explain as much as you want. Until I assess her character and motives for myself, I won't believe you."

"Fine," she said, turning her back on me.

"Fine," I responded, turning my back on *her*.

"Children."

"I beg your pardon?" I asked Leonora.

"You're both acting like two brats straight out of the nursery. If this is how it is going to be, I'd have better results going alone. I've picked up her scent."

"How? We haven't even gotten off the train yet." I stood and was nearly catapulted into Leonora's lap as the train screeched to a halt.

Leonora nodded toward the window, which Olga had opened.

"We must hurry. She's on the move."

By the time I'd gathered my effects, Leonora and Olga were gone. I stepped out into the corridor, pushing through the crowd, searching for my companions. I spotted them easily, Olga's fair head and Leonora's dark one towering over the hatted and shawled passengers exiting the train. That was another thing I'd just become aware of—how much taller they were than anyone around them.

I was pushed back in the shuffle so that when I finally reached the platform, I'd lost Leonora and Olga again. Only a few travelers remained, along with the porter. I looked back to make sure the train was even still there. I half expected it to have disappeared, too.

Then there was the fog—thick, dense, and blanketing everything. I'd forgotten the fog and how obscuring it could be. That was the thing about Romania. While I was away from it, it was mysterious and intriguing, a place I longed to return to. When I was actually in the country, I remembered all too well how much I hated that mystic evasiveness that had always hampered my searches here.

I swatted at the fog, but nothing broke that sheet of grey. There was nothing I could do but wait and hope they would find their way back to me soon. I set down my things and waited...*waited...*

"Planning to waste all your time standing about like a statue?"

I felt Leonora's hand on my arm. I could see nothing but her eyes, like two dark beacons glowing in the mist. The rest of her blended in too well.

"Where's Olga?"

"Right in front of you."

I wondered how I hadn't seen her before. She was outlined starkly, a black slash against the grey. With alarm, I saw that the fog was swirling away from her as though it was afraid to touch her.

"What do you expect will happen?" I asked as we set off.

"Actually, I have no idea what is going to happen. Isn't it liberating?"

I couldn't think of anything to say to that.

The spire of the citadel on the hill pierced the fog. I was so engrossed in being able to actually *see* something clearly in this town, that I didn't notice the angel until I walked straight into him.

"Are you all right, Professor?"

"Fine, although I think I've just been struck down by St. Michael."

The fog had cleared enough for me to see that the angel was no angel at all, but a man made of stone. In his hands, he held two swords—*real* swords, glistening with beads of moisture from the mist—both of which were striking the life out of the other statue on the dais.

I felt like I'd walked into one of my books. Though the other face was disfigured by rage and almost past being human, I knew who it was.

Vladec Salei.

But that was impossible. Vladec Salei, as far as we knew, was still alive.

The fog was encroaching again. I swatted at it, dispersing enough to cause a hole through which I could see the statue. Stone teeth curved down over the Upyr's lower lip, its forked tongue snaking out of its mouth. Ram's horns I'd never seen before in any representation of the creature sprouted from its skull and curled downward toward its neck. The eyes of the Upyr were the only things that were not made of stone. Red orbs with what looked like black ink swirling in the center—marbles, perhaps—had been set into the eye sockets. Huge, black stone wings fanned out behind the creature's back. Those wings frightened me even more than its gargoyle-like face. I'd only ever seen a wingspan like that on the back of a wyvern, and they did not exist outside of mythology books.

The Upyr was on its knees, its red-black eyes blazing up at the man who must have been Florin Istratescu. A glance at the carving at the base of the statue confirmed my suspicions.

Dispatching the Devil. That would have been a fitting title. Half the Upyr's head was cut off, with one blade slicing clean through its neck on the right side. The other blade pierced straight through the beast's heart and out its back. Its clawed hands were clasped futilely around this second blade.

Thorough, I thought. There was no way a vampire, not even one as strong and vicious as an Upyr, could come back from a dual attack like that.

"St. Florin Istratescu."

The fog dispersed completely as soon as I said his name. What power was here that I had not been able to discover? It was almost as if this hamlet, this treasure trove of lore, had been purposefully hidden from me during all my searches in this country. I should have found this place easily on all my trips, but I never had. What forces were at work here? I swallowed hard as I realized that I was in this much deeper than I knew.

"My ancestor." Olga's voice drew me out of my thoughts. "They're not squeamish about their history in these parts," she said as we pushed through the church's doors.

The pungent smell of melted candle wax and old books hit us as we stepped across the threshold. Dust motes danced in the light shining down through the stained glass windows. In the middle of the long, dark nave stood a baptismal font made of marble and covered over with gilded wood.

Something was weaving around next to the font—an indefinable figure that almost looked like a cloud of grey, as if the fog I thought we'd escaped from had somehow found its way into the church. Only as we drew closer did I discern that the nebulous mist was a man.

He was extraordinary looking, perhaps because he seemed alien to his surroundings, yet at the same time I could not imagine a better place for him to be. His close-cropped hair and pointed, clipped beard were completely white. His back was stooped and his cheeks slightly sunken. He was ageless and ancient all at once, but his eyes, his vibrant green eyes sparkled with vitality. Gaunt yet full of life; old yet preternaturally young, as though he'd been trapped in this place since time began.

As I watched him obliviously sweeping the floor, I was struck by how powerful his hands looked. They were large, bronzed, sinewy hands—hands that would be more comfortable grasped around the hilt of a sword than around that flimsy stick of wood.

Like everything about him besides his eyes, his clothes were colorless—nondescript grey garments that identified him as either a priest or friar. I hadn't been to church in years, so I wasn't sure which he was. He kept busily sweeping the ground around the font, so he did not notice us until we were upon him, or so I thought.

"You can tell your friend that the walls will not bleed if she enters the House of God."

"My friend?" I asked, confused, looking at Olga.

"The other one with the dark hair, who has yet to come into the sanctuary."

I looked behind me and saw Leonora still standing outside. I motioned to her, but she shook her head.

The priest righted himself and set the broom against the font. Once again, I was startled by the brilliance of his green eyes and the youthful spark that flickered in them. "I know what she is," he said, his voice grave.

My breath rattled in my throat. Were we that transparent? Did they honestly look so vampiric? Was I becoming immune to how otherworldly they actually *did* look? Or was this priest much more experienced with the undead than I had suspected?

I turned back to signal to Leonora, but there was no need. She was already standing at my side, looking at the priest intently.

"Do you?" she asked, her voice constricted.

"Yes. But I also know your heart. You are not responsible for what has happened. Forgive yourself and finally be at peace."

Her face crumpled as the tears leaked out of her eyes. She put her hand to her mouth and sobbed, but the priest, for all his words of comfort, showed no emotion whatsoever at her reaction. Instead, he turned his piercing eyes on me.

"You're here for the cross, then," he said, almost resignedly.

"The cross of Istratescu?" I asked, bewildered. Why was *I* the one to sound skeptical? Wasn't that what I was after?

"We saw the statue outside," said Leonora through her tears, her voice still unsteady. "Please tell us we haven't wasted our time coming here."

"Ah, the statue," said the priest, his grim line of a mouth ticking up slightly at the edges.

"It's quite impressive," I mumbled, feeling I had to contribute something to the conversation.

"I suppose it would be, to you. To me, it's just a painful reminder of the glory that has not yet been achieved, and possibly never will be, if the one appointed to the task should fail. St. Devil's Bane," he said, and spat out a laugh.

"What do you know of the Corcitura?"

The priest froze at the sound of Olga's voice. Slowly, he turned and fixed his narrowed eyes on her, and the transformation that came over his face was like a revelation.

"What do you know of such things?" he asked, his eyes burning with intensity as they roved over her face.

"He is my brother."

The priest let out a sigh. "Olga."

"Yes."

"I thought you were dead."

"I was, for half a minute."

"Then it is not too late. This changes things. Come, I will show you the book."

The book? I'd never heard of this book. I was as giddy as a child with a new toy as the priest led us behind the altar and down a flight of stairs to a chamber filled with books older than the four of us combined.

"Just a moment," he said, lighting a candle and setting it down on a marble topped pedestal that served as a makeshift altar. I would have thought he would have known exactly where a book of such importance was, but he didn't seem to have the slightest idea. He climbed up to the top of one bookcase first, muttered, "No, not there," then darted to a chest covered with crosses and other religious carvings in the corner. The book was apparently not in there either. I couldn't figure out what his game was or why he was doing this.

"Is it going to be much longer?" I asked, my tone gruff. His dithering was getting on my nerves.

"You've waited this long, you can afford to wait a few more seconds," he shot back over his shoulder. "Things are constantly shifting around here so that I never know where they'll show up in the morning."

And exactly who did the shifting, I wondered. He seemed to be the only one curating this place. I found the presence of others hard to fathom, and I was willing to bet that we, the priest, and the man who had written this mysterious book were the only ones to have ever seen it.

"And here we are at last," he said as he hefted a large, square object out of the chest. The object was covered with a nondescript brown cloth, which when pulled back revealed a book almost too beautiful and terrible to describe. Intertwined gold, red, and blue vines were tooled into the leather of the cover, in the middle of which was a brilliant, illuminated image of the man dispatching the Upyr with the twin silver swords, only this time, the man had been elevated. He now had angel's wings and looked more like St. Michael than ever.

"I'd forgotten how beautiful the cover was," the priest said wistfully as he ran his fingers over the leather. I watched his eyes lingering on the image until he finally must have felt my scrutiny and looked away. Clearing his throat, he seemed to come back to his senses, and said, "In this book are all of Florin's notes, case studies, and musings on how he dispatched every creature Vladec Salei ever created."

"May I?"

"Of course," he said, standing aside. I stood before the book, my hands trembling above the cover. Seven years of research, of mind-bending work, had led to this. I'd plumbed some very dark depths in Vladec Salei's past to find his connection to this man that some regarded as a mystic, others as a saint. Now, I was seconds away from knowing all the answers, from filling in all the holes I'd never been able to plug up.

Carefully, for the book was nearly five hundred years old, I leafed through the pages, my eyes roving over the lettering. Florin was a meticulous chronicler. Every single moment of every single day since that fateful morning in 1395 had been set down in the greatest detail, along with illuminated illustrations done in Florin's own hand.

I was nearing the end of the book when an entry caught my eye.

25th June 1474: Dispatched woman turned by Vladec Salei. Violent killing. She almost took me to the grave with her. Much blood was shed by both of us. Treated my wounds with poultice of blessed water, nettles, and mustard seed. This turn necessitated the use of both swords, as do all Vladec's turnings. Silver stakes through the heart afterward, just to be thorough. The turns are more vicious lately and more prone to attacking children, then finishing off the parents. I fear Vladec is tiring of just feeding. These creatures are undeniably vicious, but they do not satisfy Vladec's need to play God. I sensed this desire in him, even before he was transformed. Last confrontation, he confided that he grows sick of "the weak" and craves something stronger. What can he mean? I fear I may not be able to stop him much longer. My health is deteriorating. I am growing weak, old, brittle. There is no one to stop him once I die. And this is how it will remain forever. I have tried to keep him away from my family, but he marked us all for death that day he was attacked. Already I have used the swords against my mother and sisters.

I stopped reading and so did Olga, who had been peering over my shoulder. "So it goes back as far as that?"

I turned back to the book, leafing through to the end. The last entry was dated 13th January 1495.

Thirteenth January...

I grabbed Olga's hand and pointed to the date, though she'd already seen it. "Do you think this is what he is planning?"

"It's only a few days away. One hundred years after he was turned..."

"And five hundred years to the day since the Upyr made him what he is. It cannot be a coincidence, Olga. This is what he's been working toward."

We bent our heads and read on.

I killed his last creation, there is no more I can do. I am one hundred and eighteen years old today, and I am spent. That first Upyr's gift was meant for me—my birthday present. Vladec has never forgiven me for not getting away from it in time. He's never forgiven himself for not being strong enough to resist the call of the blood. How could an act of self-sacrifice lead to such hatred? I hear him at the door. I know this will be the end. There will be no turning for me. I am armed with the wyvern-headed staff as I write this. It is the only thing that can kill him, but I know my flesh will feel the bite of its silver blade on this day. God, I have tried to be a good and faithful servant, but I have failed. The plague will continue to walk the earth when I am gone. Forgive me...

Here the script trailed off, so that whatever else Florin had written was illegible.

I righted myself and breathed in deeply. What did all this mean? The twisted planning of Vladec Salei was coming full circle. Florin had known something wasn't right, but known it just barely, only having the smallest inkling. How could he have taken that next leap and pieced together Salei's plan, foreseeing the monster Salei would create some four hundred years later? And I had to wonder... If it had taken Salei so long to meet one he thought worthy enough to share in the creation of the Corcitura, what must he have created in the meantime?

"He was very near the edge when he wrote that," the priest said, barely above a whisper. "And then Salei drove him over it."

"How do you know?" I asked.

"Oral legends passed down through the generations," he said curtly, and from the look on his face, I knew that was all the elaboration I'd get from him.

I sat back on my heels and stared at the book. "May I keep this?" I said. For some odd reason, I felt the need to possess this treasure, no matter what.

"I'm afraid not," the priest said. "At least, not yet. This is really all that is left."

"That is not true, Father."

The priest looked at Olga, and in his eyes there was a knowing gleam. "I see. And does your sister feel the same way?"

"I do not need her."

"Be that as it may, she has a part to play before all this can be put to rest."

He sounded genuinely sorry. Once again I was intrigued by just why they feared Nadia so much.

I pulled my watch from my pocket. The hour was growing late. Though the book had been illuminating in more ways than I could have imagined—especially since I hadn't bargained on finding a book such as this at all—we still needed answers.

The priest had been eyeing me strangely since I had requested to keep the book. "I'm sorry about that, Father," I said as apologetically as I could. "The book is a treasure trove that I would love to call my own. I don't know what I was thinking."

"I do. The draw of the power is too great to resist. Imagine all that knowledge...it is like a shield. You would be more powerful than Vladec Salei, and you'd know all his secrets, which are legion. No, the book stays here. What you came for is the cross."

"And I'm guessing you'll let us take that away, since it is the only weapon that can kill Salei's creation."

"I'm afraid I can't."

"Why ever not?" The words, "Will no one rid me of this meddlesome priest?!" flashed through my mind. I imagined this was how Henry II must have felt. I was starting to lose patience with this riddling cleric. He was as nebulous as the fog I had originally taken him for.

"Because I don't have it."

Leonora uttered a curse, which I thought inappropriate in the presence of a priest, but he didn't seem to mind.

"I couldn't have put it better myself. The cross was stolen several years ago."

"Please tell me that the thief wasn't Vladec Salei," Olga said.

"Of course not," he said, sounding highly offended. "Do you think if he'd shown his face here, I'd have let him...well, never mind." A clap of thunder sounded overhead, shaking the church and upsetting our balance, but the priest stood deathly still. All his anger seemed to evaporate in a second. His hands did not shake; his eyes no longer shot green fire. He looked at Olga with infinite weariness as he passed his hand over his forehead. "No, no, it was your father, I'm afraid."

"My father?"

"Your father was in the pay of the one who made the hybrid. I'm sorry," he added, seeing Olga's reaction, "but your father stole the cross more than thirty years ago."

"Then all of this," she said, her voice shaking, "Nadia, Stefan..."

"It was all planned."

"What must I do?" I was startled by the quick change in Olga's voice. Just two seconds before, all her illusions, her world, had been shattered, and now she was ready to go on as if nothing had destroyed every notion she had clung to her entire life.

"The last known owner of the cross was your sister Nadia, but she hasn't been seen in these parts for years."

"Where can I find her?"

"Most probably Brasov."

"So she *did* return to Brasov. What blasted nerve, begging your pardon, Father."

The priest gave Olga a small half-smile, but remained silent.

"Then we must go," said Leonora, already halfway out of the cellar.

"Must we?"

"Olga, we've been through this already," I said as I followed Leonora and the priest up the stairs.

"Yes, I know, and you still don't believe me when I tell you we're walking into a trap. I can feel it Zigmund, why can't you?"

"Because I am not going to be cowed by *feelings* and superstition. She's in Brasov, then to Brasov we will go, even if I have to go alone." It was a threat I had been saving up for a moment such as this, though I wasn't sure I wanted to travel to the end of the nave without either of them to back me up. I could defend myself; I'd been on my own since I was seven, but having allies with their particular skills wouldn't hurt.

"Fine. Then I won't *feel* anything when she betrays you to Vladec Salei."

"*Olga*," I groaned, but she was already out of reach.

"Just one thing," said the priest. I glanced at him, annoyed with him just for being there. "Are you prepared to lose everything, even your life, to stop this plague from continuing? Is this a task worth fighting for?"

I hesitated. I'd been close to death many times before, none worse than when I had nearly been killed in Greece. Was I willing to give it all up for Olga, Eric...Leonora?

I searched my heart, my soul, and found the answer.

"Yes."

"And more importantly...are you willing to die without making peace with your mother?"

"My mother is dead," I said automatically.

"Oh, I do pity you for still believing that."

I stared at him, wondering why he'd asked about Leonora when he couldn't possibly have known she was my mother.

"The nose," he said, staring off into the distance. "And the inflection in your voices. Even some of your mannerisms—that way you have of tilting your head to the side when you are puzzling over something. I may be old, but I am not blind."

I followed his line of sight, but there was no longer any light streaming in through the windows set high in the upper reaches of the church. Still, I knew he was looking at her.

"They have much to atone for, those who did this to her and you. Do not let bitterness stop you from forgiving her before the end."

"Father, I..."

"Remember what I said. Now, go."

I stood there, uncertain of what to say, and not really sure if he wanted me to say anything at all.

"Thank you," I finally managed. It seemed the safest thing to say, and I *was* grateful for everything I had seen here.

"Don't thank me yet," he answered in his usual gruff manner as he walked me down the nave toward the doors. "This is far from over."

"Will we ever see you again?" I felt suddenly small, as though I were a child once again, alone in the world.

"You'll be hearing from me...if she succeeds."

"Nadia?" But as soon as I said the name, I knew Nadia was the farthest thing from his mind. He was staring straight at Olga with those penetrating green eyes that still guarded so many secrets.

"The first step has been taken. See that she follows through."

"I will," I responded, without really knowing what I was vowing to do.

"And Zigmund..."

"Yes, Father?"

"When you see Vladec Salei...tell him I'll be waiting for him on the other side. He owes me that wyvern-headed staff."

***

Florin Istratescu.

Florin Istratescu, who had been dead for nearly five hundred years.

I had spent an hour in the company of a ghost.

I had been dealing with dead men my whole life, but this was different. This was bigger, and it frustrated me that I couldn't figure out how I fit into it all.

My companions had noticed something was wrong with me as soon as we'd resumed our journey, but I was still too muddleheaded to tell them what had been revealed to me on the steps of that church. I needed time to think, but time was something that was slipping away from us.

"She's been here. I can smell the residue of her blood."

That statement was typical of Leonora. If I had been more innocent, I would have felt nauseous, but I'd become immune to statements like hers years ago.

Brasov was a dismal place, but at least we were spared the fog that had assailed us in Sighisoara. My feelings were in a horrendous jumble. On the one hand, I was excited to be finally closing in on Nadia. On the other hand, I was still walking in a fog, but a fog within my mind. How had I not known that the key to my past, Leonora's abandonment of me, the creature whose existence was based on conjecture, had been right underneath my fingertips? *So close...*

We walked through the town till we came to a row of houses surrounding the fountain in the center of the cobblestone square.

Leonora grew very still and held out her hand, signaling for us to wait. All was quiet around us. Olga and I waited to see what Leonora would do.

She raised her head and sniffed the air.

Just like a wolf.

"The scent is strong just here. I can smell her fear. She is close."

"No, she's not."

We both looked at Olga, startled to see she was no longer standing next to us. Her voice had sounded in my ear, yet she was halfway across the square, standing before the door of an unassuming stone house.

"I do not have the tracking powers you do, Leonora, but I can feel my sister's presence. She is not here. This was my sister's house."

"Was?" I asked, coming to a stop beside her. The roof was low, the lintel even lower. I would have to duck to not strike my head.

"Yes, *was*. I still cannot believe she came back here to live in this place that holds such evil for every member of our family. You can still see the farmer's house..."

She turned away and pushed against the door, which gave easily beneath her touch.

The house smelled warm and lived in, but the scene was anything but cozy. Overturned tables, torn curtains, chipped dishes, food thrown everywhere—the house was a shambles.

"All signs of a struggle," I mumbled as I walked further into the room. Olga searched beneath the uprooted furniture. Leonora tore coverings off every surface, while I searched for any clue Nadia might have left behind.

And then I saw it. In the corner lay a book. As I got closer, I saw that the book was a bible—old, torn, and coated in black leather with a single gold cross stamped onto the cover.

I leaned over and picked up the book, surprised at how light it was in my hands.

But it wasn't just light.

It was hollow.

I turned the book over. The pages had been carved out, forming the shape of...

"A cross."

"What?"

"Still think the cross is a myth, eh, Olga? Deny this to me now," I said, waving the desecrated bible in her face. "Deny the cross exists."

She remained silent. She was no longer staring at me or the book. Her eyes were riveted on the hearth.

What on earth could have caused her eyes to dilate in such fear? I almost didn't want to look. We must have been mistaken. The house was not empty, but occupied by someone I had no wish to see. Constantinos. Was he standing behind me? Leonora wouldn't have been so calm if that beast were in the same room.

"Olga..."

"Just look, Zigmund."

I did, and my stomach lurched when I saw the stain.

The stones were cold to my touch, but the liquid that made up the stain was warm. Too warm. God help us if we were too late.

"No wonder you smelled the scent so strongly," I said.

"She's being hunted," said Leonora.

"But not only by us."

"What do you mean?" asked Olga. I dried my hands on my pants and picked up the small sharp object I'd found within the pool of blood.

"Do either of you recognize this?" I said, holding out the object to them.

Leonora blanched and clutched the mantle. Olga remained expressionless, though her throat trembled as she tried to swallow.

"Constantinos."

"No, Leonora," Olga said, looking at her for affirmation. "It might belong to Stefan."

"Stefan's too busy with Madelaine's husband," I answered, rising and handing the barb to Olga.

"Don't say that," Leonora said weakly.

"You'd better hope he's still interested in that man. Once his game is over, he's coming after Madelaine...and your son." I shoved my hands in my pockets and stared down at the stain. "What does this mean? How do we even know she's still alive?"

"I can sense her," both Leonora and Olga said at the same time.

In all my years of study, after all that I had witnessed, I'd learned to be at home with the uncanny. But the way the two of them could almost read each other's thoughts and could *know* things intuitively made me feel out of my element and more terrified than a man of my age and experience had a right to be.

"We're going to Cluj." I'd made up my mind. This was turning into a wild-goose chase. I was getting tired of retracing my steps, but I had to pursue this lead—this one last lead. I wasn't willing to go back to Madelaine Bradburry empty-handed.

"How do you know she's not leading us on?"

"Don't tell me this was artifice. For whose benefit?"

"You don't know Nadia," Olga said, brushing past me.

I grabbed her fur-coated arm. "Trust me, Olga. We need her."

Olga made a sound that reminded me of the exasperated huff of a very large dog. She looked to Leonora, but it was clear Leonora was on my side.

"If they are hunting her, something must have gone wrong." Olga threw back her hood and absently ran her long-nailed fingers through her hair. "No, she's on the move. You're right. Cluj is closest to Prague, so if we need to leave in a hurry..."

She let the sentence hang in the air. We all knew what she meant.

"Just know that she could be taking us halfway across Europe for her own ends, Zigmund."

No one spoke. We'd all considered this at one point or another since we set out.

"And for all we know, that is exactly what they want her to do. I still think this is a trap. The blood, the barb, it could all be for our benefit."

"I don't think so."

"Neither do I."

I smiled gratefully at Leonora.

"Then we must hurry. The farther away she gets, the weaker the scent grows."

I did not argue, but followed behind Olga as Leonora led the way toward the train station. Back onto the train and off to Cluj. This was starting to get old.

They were always one step ahead of us. What if we made a mistake and went too far? What if they caught *our* scent?

Then who would be the hunted?

***

Cluj welcomed us with a dour face, which matched our mood perfectly. Rain pelted down as we stepped off the train. In a short time, this place would be blanketed by snow and the whole town would be paralyzed.

From the worry on Leonora's and Olga's faces, I knew the scent had gone dead. I was beginning to believe this was just another wasted venture—a diversion to keep us off track.

"Let's get something to eat and then see where that leaves us."

"Dead, that's where. I can't sense anything. I can't track the scent. It's a though she's disappeared."

"It's the same for me," said Olga.

I stared at the two women for a long while. Neither of them seemed happy about my suggestion—they had no appetite for the kind of food I ate—but the rain had already turned to snow, and I didn't think standing outside till I caught pneumonia would solve anything.

"Come," said Olga, putting up her hood and leading the way. "There's a place over here where you can get a good meal and some rest, not that we need any of those things," she said, glancing at Leonora with what I thought was the ghost of a smile. Leonora smirked back and walked on, leaving me alone.

Oh, mortality, how overrated you are.

I followed them into an ill-lit tavern, which was thankfully empty. We'd already met with our share of gawkers on this trip.

Corcitura

We chose the table in the farthest, darkest corner, and ordered bread and cheese and ale from the proprietor.

"This is getting us nowhere," I said, taking a sip of ale. I was desperate. We were running out of time. The thirteenth of January was only days away. "Something has to be done. If splitting up will help, I don't see how we can't."

"And how far do you think you'd get on your own?"

"Farther than I've gotten with you." Why did I feel the need to spar with Olga? She could be so prickly, so defensive. I wasn't helping any, especially when what I'd said wasn't true. I'd gotten farther with her in one week than I had in thirty years on my own.

"Listen to the pair of you." I shifted uncomfortably beneath Leonora's scornful gaze. "What can you do on your own, Zigmund, honestly?"

"I've managed this long without you."

"So, it is back to that again?"

"Of course it's back to that," I whispered, though there was no one around to overhear. "I thought you were dead. How can you expect me to forget what I saw so quickly? I saw you *die*."

"He turned me, Zigmund, I wasn't dead. Near to it, but once he left me, I came to and touched the blood at my throat. I touched the blood *in* my throat, Zigmund. I don't know how I didn't lose my mind then."

She paused, looked down at her hands. "I healed. And the first thing I wanted was blood. As soon as I awoke, I felt the urge. The thirst. But something else. I knew I wasn't only a vampire. I was more."

"A wolf, yes," said Olga quietly. "That's how I felt when I regained consciousness."

"An animal in all things. A monster. How had this happened? How had I survived? It was then that I knew what I'd become. I wasn't dead. I had to get out. I saw the blood spattered across the floor. You have to believe me when I say I thought you were dead. I thought I'd killed you, especially after Vladec appeared and convinced me that's what happened. My brain had been so starved of oxygen for those few minutes when I hovered between life and death, that I had no memory of what happened before my throat was ripped open. I couldn't deny what Vladec was accusing me of. I'd done terrible things, he said. And I believed him because he was offering me a second chance at life with him. And more importantly, he promised to give me what I needed to survive. I'm not proud of it, Zigmund, but I had no choice."

"Neither of us had," Olga said. Her ice blue eyes had grown darker with intensity. "Are those scars your fault?"

"Of course not!" I barked, more startled than offended. I'd thought about the scars off and on for years, but this was the first time the full horror of what my face must have looked like to someone else was brought home to me. Self-consciously, I put my hand to my face, trying to shield the marks that had marred my skin since I was a child. It had never even crossed my mind that she, of all people, would say anything about them. But now I felt vulnerable, ugly—an outcast.

"Then don't blame us for ours. Do you think we wanted this, Zigmund? I can assure you we did not. This was forced on us. We're the victims, so stop acting as though this is our fault. We didn't choose this."

"Zigmund, please, after so long, can you not find it in your heart to accept this?"

I looked from Olga to Leonora, riddled with guilt that I had never understood how they must have felt, how *all* vampires who hadn't chosen the path must have felt. *Olga, Olga, what have they done to you? Why?* I stared at her. She stared back at me until her eyes were too much to take, and I looked away.

*Leonora...*She hadn't asked for forgiveness because I knew she felt she had done nothing wrong. And wasn't she right? She had been blameless, a victim.

"What else can you tell us of your sister?" I asked Olga. I felt like a beast, but I wasn't ready to face the demons Leonora wanted me to exorcise. I couldn't meet her eyes, though I felt her staring at me. I knew I'd see disappointment in them, and that was something I couldn't handle right now. "How will I know her when I see her?"

"She's Stefan in a skirt. Not much else."

Corcitura

"Why do you hate her?" I asked. There was such venom in her voice every time she was forced to talk about her sister.

"Why do I hate her? You dare ask me that?"

"Yes, because you've told us next to nothing about her."

"I've told you enough. She's the reason I'm this way. She was the one who told them where to find me. I was happy, Zigmund. I was the only Belododia who had gotten away whole. She hated me for that. She hated me because I left her and Stefan to our father. Well, I had no choice. I could either leave or become my father's next plaything."

"What do you mean?"

"Figure it out, Professor. I will not defile the air by speaking the details."

"Tell me about your father."

"There's not much tell. He was a monster."

"*And...*"

"Why do you want to know all this?"

"Because I want to understand you. And, frankly, I need to know how to approach your sister."

"It's simple. Let *me* handle her."

"*No!*" Leonora and I said simultaneously. I thought back to the earrings and the dried blood on the hooks. I was not planning to let Olga anywhere near Nadia once we found her.

"Olga, please," I coaxed. "Tell us."

She picked at the splintered wood of the tabletop. "There never was any sense of normalcy in our lives," she went on, not looking at us. "Our parents were never married. No, don't interrupt, that is the truth. No matter what you've heard or been told to the contrary, Vladec never legitimized my parents' union. It was all a matter of convenience, but not for my mother. She never had a chance. So many times I begged her to leave, but she stayed. She was devoted to him, the fool. Even after what he did. Even after the beatings, the rapes. I remember her shrinking in the corner, blood streaming from her eyes, still professing love for the man who'd just split her lips and cracked open her skull. When she grew barren, after giving birth to seven children in as many years, she was no good to him any longer. That's when he started bringing in the harlots."

I sucked in a breath, not sure if I wanted to hear any more of this. But Olga pressed on. She was beyond stopping herself now. "Every night there was a different one, which she had to wait on hand and foot, as though they were the wife and she the harlot. And as if that were not humiliating enough, he'd tie her in the corner and make her witness his depravity. She had to watch them, Zigmund, and so did we."

I felt something pricking at my eyes and shook my head to clear my vision.

"And then one day," Olga said, her voice so soft I had to lean in to catch her words, "Father had enough. He was only dissolute up to a point. Even he had his limits. I tried to stop him and got thrashed for my trouble. The older girls were gone by then. Ruxandra, Dacia, Irina, Magdalena...it was just me, Stefan, and Nadia. They had each other. They'd always been fey like that, almost able to read each other's thoughts. It frightened me."

Here she paused and looked longingly at the glass of ale the proprietor had brought for her. *Fool*, I thought to myself, but he was not to know only one thing could quench her thirst.

"He eviscerated my mother before my eyes."

Even Leonora, who must have known this already, looked shocked. Maybe Salei had never told her this part of the story.

"I see you're surprised," Olga said to Leonora. "So Vladec kept his own counsel about that. Or maybe Stefan told you a different version? Yes, that would be like him. It was the way he coped, to lie about what really happened. Stefan always was a liar. And Nadia did nothing to beat the lie out of him, like I would have."

I stared into my glass, knowing that whatever words I was trying to string together would sound hollow to her.

"I hated their closeness," she continued, her voice fierce and hard. "They were one in their terror, twins in their sorrow. I was always on the outside looking in, and they never, *ever* let me in. I was caged behind iron bars. All my life, I was the one who had no one to pair up with, no partner for my adventures. My sisters had each other, and they all left together. Nadia had Stefan. I had *no one*, so it made sense that I was the one my father singled out for his vengeance."

"Go on."

"For pity's sake, Zigmund, haven't you heard enough?"

"I'll know when it's enough," I said to Leonora.

"No, it's all right." Olga pushed the glass of ale away. The longing must have been too great. "When the other girls left, I was the whipping boy, you might say. My father made me what I am today. Not this, obviously, but inside. I always knew how he valued me. With one look, he told me every time I came into his presence. With one look, I knew just how worthless I was."

She was close to tears, but pressed on.

"Yet even after all these years, even after Stefan killed him, I still love my father in some way. Some sick, twisted way, isn't that pathetic?" she said, her hands shaking as she wiped at her eyes. I feared for her. Her voice had been much too light, too high—hysterical. "Don't misunderstand me, I'd have probably killed him if Stefan hadn't, but you never do stop loving your parents, no matter how weak or despicable they are."

Now it was my turn to stare uncomfortably at my glass of ale.

"And there's something else. I haven't been entirely truthful with you, Zigmund."

"What are you talking about?" How many more revelations could she make? I was still reeling from what I'd heard already.

"Stefan isn't the only reason I'm this way. He didn't get to me first. For that, I have my sister Magdalena to thank."

I glanced at Leonora. This was obviously news to her, too.

"It happened once the orgy in the courtyard of Castle Bran had subsided. I heard them leaving as I lay there between consciousness and death. I could feel my soul leaving my body. And then I felt something else—a pain so searing it was as though two needles had been stabbed into my neck. I remember spasming so badly I thought my ribs would pop out through my chest. I felt blood swilling down my neck and I heard something...eating. Lapping up my blood like a dog. Suddenly, I was whole again—whole and bitterly thirsty. And I wasn't alone. Magdalena was near me, feeding on me. I attacked her. I was crazed. All I could think of was blood and how badly I needed it. And my revenge. I wanted to destroy her for bringing me back. I should have just let her have her way, because all that commotion brought Stefan back. That's when he finished the job she'd started. If he hadn't shown up, I would have killed her. I would have had my vengeance and finished her off right there. I've waited for another chance these seven years. My revenge will not be put off, Zigmund. Her time has come. When we find them, she's *mine*."

I leaned back in my chair, winded. I had lived her turning with her. It was almost as if she'd taken me there to witness everything. With a jolt I had come out of her trance, broken the pull of those two arctic eyes, and returned to the relative calm and safety of this tavern.

Something else had happened to me in those few moments. I didn't know what, but Olga had done something to me, thrown back the cover on something I'd kept hidden inside of me for thirty years. And I was infuriated that I didn't understand what I was feeling.

I felt Leonora's eyes on me. But her scrutiny was not what was making the hair on the back of my hands rise. Something in the atmosphere had changed. It was colder in here and more oppressive, as though a foreign presence had been introduced and weighed us down.

That's when I heard the voices. One was familiar, the other vaguely so, as if heard in a dream and immediately forgotten.

"All thisss, coming back to thisss sssstupid country, for thisss sssstupid girl who meansss nothing to usss. All for your twisted delusssionsss of grandeur and vainglory. Folly, it'sss folly, and ssstupidity. You tricked me. It was ssssupposed to be *that boy* I was attacking, not Ssstefan."

"Stop blathering. You served your purpose. We had an agreement. It's not my fault you're blind as a bat in the dark."

"Bloody fool agreement."

"Oh, shut up and drink your blood. Have you any idea what I had to go through just to get you that pint? That poor girl was blameless. Now, I'll have to make a fine present to her father to compensate for her loss...or I could just kill him."

"She'ss the wrong type."

"Don't be petulant. You've always been petulant. I don't know why I even decided to go into business with you in the first place. "

"Connveeeeniencsssse."

"Desperation is what it was. After nearly five hundred years of searching, you think I could have found someone more, I don't know...grateful? You're nothing but a nag. And stop looking at me with that ugly face of yours. Thank the devil Stefan only inherited the barbed tongue."

"Sssss..."

"Oh, get that lisp fixed. I'm sick of you sounding like a leaky pipe all the time."

"Would the two of you just stop?!"

"Give up the act, my dear. You know you love it when we argue."

I reached into my satchel, my fingers closing around the handle of the *Mauser*. As I pulled it out, a snarl rattled the table, knocking the wood into my arm and nearly jolting the revolver out of my hand.

Leonora had knocked over her goblet. Ale washed over her white-knuckled hands. Her fingernails, looking more like claws now, were embedded into the table. Her dark eyes were horrifying because they did not look like her eyes at all. Rage, terror, anger—one or all of those emotions had made them turn a hellish shade of amber.

But the snarl had not come from her.

It had come from Olga. The creature sitting across from me bore almost no resemblance to the woman who had shared her dark past with me a minute ago. She still looked human, but a human with fangs extending over bloodless lips. Her eye blazed, literally, as though fire burned in them. Her back was arched, the fur of her coat receding and covering her like a second skin.

She was transforming and all because of something that was behind us. Something I was too cowardly to turn around and face.

"Ah, yes, I thought I smelled wet dog in here."

The voice was smooth, like liquid silver, but harsh and cruel as iron. Olga flinched as though she had been struck. She knew the voice, too, it was obvious. Instead of becoming even more enraged, she seemed to shrink in on herself. Was that fear in her eyes? Fear of which of them?

I couldn't take it anymore.

I turned around.

There were three figures sitting at a table across from ours, but I only had eyes for one. The suffocating darkness of that hole in Greece came back to me, pressing against my chest, weighing me down. I heard my father's screams, I saw the blood spilling out of his chest.

I remembered the figure of a woman, my mother, lying limp in its arms.

It hadn't changed. The eyes were still red-rimmed, the hooded cloak was black as a reaper's, the creature's stomach bulging beneath the garment's folds. Lolling out of its mouth was that tongue, *that cursed barbed tongue* that had torn into my mother's throat.

Constantinos.

I fired before I realized I'd pulled the trigger. The beast rocketed back, but only a silver bullet to the heart or a swift blade through the neck would kill it. I knew the creature better than it knew itself, and yet I'd missed. Missed at point-blank range.

"You ssstill fear me, Zigmund," it hissed, looking down in fascination at the blood that was pouring from the wound in its arm.

I could not stop shaking. I raised the revolver higher this time, level with the beast's heart. The hold it had had on me, on my family, was about to end. I would not miss this time.

"No!"

The gun flew out of my hand and landed on the opposite side of the room. I had no idea who had shouted *no*, but it had been a female voice that did not belong to either of the women with me.

I glanced back at Leonora and Olga, then looked up at the tall, dignified man and the monster who had ruined my life. Olga, Leonora, and the Vrykolakas glowered at each other across a divide, fangs bared, claws scraping against the floor like bulls before a charge, each of them looking more animal than human.

Time was at a standstill. I saw no end to this stalemate, other than one or all of us getting ripped to pieces. But then the girl came into the middle, and I forgot about everything else.

Stefan in a skirt. That's how Olga said I would know her. I had only seen Stefan a few times, but Olga was right. Her hair wasn't as red as his, but the eyes were the same, though not translucent like her brother's. She was staring at me, pleading with me with those emerald green eyes now. I shrugged and shook my head, not knowing what to do or say, or why she should be appealing to me. And then I understood.

She was their prisoner.

That's when Nadia started to scream.

"Smart girl," the dignified man who I knew was Vladec Salei said, smirking, his eyes on me. "So we finally meet, my son. You could have been my son. You *should* have been my son, in another time and place. But I thought it best your mother forgot you ever existed. Worked out wonderfully, don't you agree?"

Out of the corner of my eye, I saw Olga, or what used to be Olga. The sight of her in wolf form gave me courage. I lunged at Constantinos.

"Get her away!" I yelled to Olga and Leonora. "She's your sister. Save her!"

"Sssscars," Constantinos hissed in my ear. I had to fight to keep from retching, his breath was so foul. "I ssstill see them. Sssshall we make them deeper, do you think?" His nails fitted perfectly into the grooves in my face, just as though I were still that terrified seven-year-old boy. I felt the blood trickling out of the reopened wounds, but then something happened. The Vrykolakas released me from its iron grasp. A spasm passed through Constantinos's body and his arm suddenly jerked back, freeing me. A howl the likes of which I hadn't heard in thirty years tore through my ears. I wondered absently if I'd ever be able to hear right again.

I stumbled to my feet and stared down at my attacker. He was clutching his other arm, from which blood was gushing freely.

"Thank me when we get out of this," the wolf that was Olga growled. I was dazed, but lucid enough to see the blood and gore on her muzzle.

Red in tooth and claw.

She was the one who had set me free. The wounds on Constantinos's arm were deep, and his flesh hung down around them in ragged strips. I smirked when I saw the look on his face—he was terrified. I'd never seen him so vulnerable before.

I wanted to enjoy this, to gloat, to tear into him with words as savagely as he'd torn into me with his claws. I had rehearsed this moment over and over in my mind, but I was robbed of my triumph. Arms, legs—fur coated and strong—wrapped around me and dragged me toward the tavern's door.

I could scarcely hear, not to mention breathe. Through the all-encompassing fur, I dimly heard Nadia Belododia screaming. I hoped she was screaming at her captors, not screaming because her sister was tearing her to ribbons. Salei uttered an oath and scratched my arm as I was yanked out of his reach. Everything went black.

When I opened my eyes, I was out in the streets not far from the tavern. The air was too cold, too shocking after the suffocation of the fur.

"I don't know why we are even running. We're just delaying the inevitable," Olga said. She'd returned to her human form, but was panting like the wolf she'd been just a minute ago. "They will track us back to the château. They know it is where we are headed."

"Then let them come." Leonora stared balefully at the battered remains of the tavern.

"What on earth have you done?!" I screamed. The building was a fire-ravaged shell. Smoke rose from the blackened hulk of broken wood and masonry.

"It had to be done. Don't worry, I shunted the proprietor out the back before I set fire to the place."

"Olga..."

"It has to come to that, after all, though, doesn't it? He's already on his way back there for his triumph. Well, I'll tell you something, Vladec Salei, you are in for a surprise." Leonora had apparently not heard a word of our exchange. She was still staring at the remains of the tavern. I didn't like the way her eyes were shining nor the way she was muttering to herself. After all these years, had this finally pushed her over the edge? Had seeing Salei and Constantinos together finally driven her mad?

"There goes Nadia."

"What?" I looked up to see Nadia Belododia sprinting toward the church on the other side of the square.

A roar from the ashes sent us all running after her.

"Nadia, stop!" Olga shouted, her voice ringing off the rafters of the church.

"Get away from me!" Nadia screamed, backing toward the altar. "You cannot harm me here!"

"Who do you think you are, some blasted medieval queen? This church will not give you any sanctuary from me and certainly not from them. Unless you want them to find you, Nadia? Do you? DO YOU?!"

"Stop it, the pair of you." The command was so fierce that it silenced the sisters at once. "Have you forgotten the others?" Leonora continued, her voice shrinking to a whisper. "They are out there. It will do no good for our cause if you keep shrieking like a couple of harridans."

Nadia had fallen to her knees behind the altar and was sobbing pitifully. She looked so childish and alone.

"Get that look out of your eyes, Zigmund, she is not what she seems," Olga ordered.

"You are a damned soul, and I will have nothing to do with you! You took the coward's way out! You left Stefan and me for dead to save yourself!"

"I left because I didn't want to be raped by my own father!"

"But that was fine for me?"

"It wouldn't have happened to you. You had Stefan, you *always* had Stefan. Stefan killed for you. He never would have done it for me."

"Yes, you're right. You weren't worthy."

I grabbed Olga before she could gouge her sister's eyes out.

"Thank God for Stefan," Nadia continued, driving home the knife.

"You see, Zigmund?" Olga said, looking up at me, her eyes desperate. "What makes you think this creature, who just betrayed her loyalties, will kill our brother? Leave it to me. This trip was a waste of time. You have your proof about the cross, yet where is it?"

"Is this what you're looking for?"

All three of us stared at the silver cross Nadia pulled from the pocket of her overcoat.

"After all these years..." I said, reaching out my hands. The cross was larger than I had been led to believe, larger and more intricate. The blood cabochon was nearly black in the gloom of the church. Only one thing more and my research would be confirmed. I felt for the clasp that would release the blood dagger. It was there. This was the cross I had staked my academic career, and more, on finding. It was finally mine.

"Let me do this," she whispered. "I am not tainted like my sister. I am the only one who can kill him. I must, to set him free."

I ran my fingers over the cross. It was cold to the touch, biting into my flesh like ice.

"I am the last of the untainted Istratescu-Belododia line."

"That line was tainted from the beginning, thanks to your friend," snapped Olga.

"*What?*" This sudden lack of self-possession that had taken hold of Nadia was surprising.

"Need I mention Vladec Salei? And you were perfectly content with him and that beast in the tavern until we came along, or was that just a trick of the mind? Salei is so good at those."

Nadia looked from me to Olga. I willed Nadia to say the words that would disprove her sister's accusations, but she seemed unsure of how to answer.

"You see?" Olga said. "There is no need for me to say anything else. You and Salei are intimately acquainted and have been for years."

"I do not love him."

"Who mentioned anything about love?" I shot in. I didn't like the way her eyes narrowed when Olga mentioned Vladec Salei.

"She cannot help herself, Zigmund."

"I'd never betray my family to that...that..."

"Spare us the histrionics, Nadia. You betrayed us all to save your own skin years ago. Who do you think that farmer was who Father was going to sell you to? Vladec Salei. He almost got Stefan then. Eventually he did, thanks to you. Remember the night in Castle Bran? Oh, yes, you told him where to find me, too. And you held back Eric Bradburry so he couldn't come to my aid, you little *witch*. I have you to thank for this," she said, opening her mouth to reveal the barbs encircling her tongue. "God only knows how you've debased yourself with that monster to preserve your worthless life."

"I've never..." she wavered.

"Be silent! You sicken me. I can see your soul, Nadia. Thank God you can't or you'd go mad."

"Wretch!" Nadia flung herself at her sister, her nails drawn. A snarl rent the church as Leonora intervened with wolf-like quickness, laying Nadia on the floor in less time than it took me to blink.

"*What are you?*"

Leonora glared down on the fallen girl. "I don't like this, Zigmund," she said, still staring at Nadia. "I don't trust her."

"Take me with you, I'm begging you," Nadia said desperately. "I am the only one who can kill Stefan. I am not proud of what I did to preserve myself, but I never once intended for it to go this far."

"So you admit it?" Olga pressed.

"Yes, of course I do. What would you have done in my situation?"

"Do you not remember? I killed myself. Magdalena and our brother didn't think it was enough."

"God forgive me, Olga, I *am* sorry. I know nothing I say will convince you. So let it be something I do."

Olga flinched as Nadia rose and put her hands on Olga's shoulders. "All the proof I can give you is to do the deed. I want you to be there, standing behind me, as I plunge the cross into his heart. My brother is dead to me. It's time we make him dead to the world."

They stood there in silence, these two sisters who were so different, yet so alike in their determination to rid the world of the creature who had once been their brother.

"Leonora," said Olga. I wasn't surprised to hear the lack of feeling in her voice. She and I were quite similar—both unwilling to forgive, both too stubborn to accept the chances we were given to start over. "Make sure the way to the train station is clear. We're going back. We're going home."

***

The train ride back to Prague was hardly convivial. Nadia barely looked at me, let alone spoke two words the whole trip. It was as if she had focused all her hatred on me, and I couldn't figure out why. I was the one who'd wanted to find her to begin with. I had next to no experience with the opposite sex, so for all I knew, this could have been her way of showing her thanks.

I doubted it.

Corcitura

Leonora and Olga were in constant conversation—planning, conjecturing, sharing life histories. They had more in common than I'd ever know. Sometimes, they seemed to be talking wordlessly, with only the slightest movements of their lips. It was a language I hoped I never had the opportunity to learn.

The hotel on the border was isolated—perfect for our purposes. Thankfully, we had not met up with Vladec Salei or Constantinos, nor had there been any signs of them following us. Their destination was the same as ours. We'd meet up soon enough.

Leonora and Olga were worried about Nadia bolting in the middle of the night, but it was ridiculous to keep fearing she'd escape. She was settled now; there was no fight left in her. She knew the alternatives. I saw the weariness in her eyes every time I looked at her. If anything, what she wanted most was to get the deed over with so she could go back to whatever she had been doing before our paths crossed.

I was on guard duty that night in Nadia's room, mostly because Leonora didn't want to have anything to do with her, and also because I didn't trust Olga not to kill her sister in the middle of the night.

I settled a chair by the half open door and watched Nadia as she slept. Or tried to sleep. She was so restless, so careworn. I couldn't help feeling sorry for her.

"Why are you staring at me, Professor?"

"I didn't realize I was." I shifted my chair closer to the door; she had risen in the bed. Though she was swaddled in a robe, I felt uncomfortable that she was conversing with me in such a state of undress.

"You do believe me, don't you? Please tell me you do."

"Of course." I wasn't so sure of this, but what other choice did we have? Olga could have turned out to be just as much of a fraud as she claimed her sister was.

Really, Zigmund, how likely is that?

"I've done terrible things, Zigmund," she said, looking down at the floor. "Things even my father would have been ashamed of. This is my chance to make it right. Olga will never forgive me..."

"You don't know that."

"You don't know my sister. She inherited all the stubbornness of both our parents. Maybe in time, after what is going to happen, she will come to understand why I did what I did. It is my one hope."

Her green eyes glowed in the darkness. I studied her as she looked at me with that smile that I wasn't sure how to interpret.

Suddenly, I felt the urge to get away. Something about her eyes was drawing me to her. If I stayed, I suspected my resolve would disintegrate under the power of those twin emerald orbs. "Sleep well, Nadia," I said, rising and stepping halfway out the door. "We have a long journey ahead of us."

She smiled at me again, as if she knew what I'd been thinking, almost as if she knew she was rattling me by her presence. "Good night, Professor. Sweet dreams."

I turned back and looked at her nestled under the covers, covers that clung tightly to her, outlining her slender body.

What's wrong with you, Zigmund? This was nonsense, but there was something about her that fascinated me, intrigued me, made me feel excited and terrified all at once—and I didn't know why.

I secured the door behind me and lingered in the hallway. I didn't feel like going back to my room, nor did I think Leonora and Olga would want me to leave my post.

Leonora at least wouldn't want me to. But I could not stay in that suffocating room with Nadia all night, for various reasons, most of which I didn't want to think about.

Moonlight shone through a bay window at the end of the hall. A threadbare window seat took up the space beneath the glass. It would have to do for the night. I settled onto the seat and leaned my head against the cool panes.

"What are you thinking, Professor?

I bolted upright, startled. I looked around, but all was in darkness beyond the shaft of light. The swish of a long coat sounded against the floorboards as Olga emerged from the shadows and sat down next to me.

"We're so close, Olga, so close," I said, rubbing my eyes, "and yet I feel as though we are just beginning."

"I feel the same."

Her profile looked stark and ghostly, silhouetted against the darkness. Her skin shone eerily in the light of the moon. She was so pale, her skin looking as fragile as porcelain.

"I can't help feeling that something is still not right. We're missing a connection somehow."

It was now or never. She'd given me an opening to voice my own fears, to tell her the truth about the specter we both thought was dead.

I cleared my throat. "Olga," I ventured. "I should have told you this sooner, but...that man we talked with was no ordinary priest."

Seeing no reaction from her, I pressed on. "He was Florin Istratescu. Somehow, someway, he came back to warn us...to help us, though I'm not really sure how."

"A ghost," she whispered, thunderstruck. "But that's impossible."

"Is any of this possible?" I asked, waving my hands to encompass everything and nothing. "Are *you* possible? Is Leonora? No, Olga, however improbable all this is, it is hideously real."

"Then why was it kept hidden?"

"I have no idea. And I doubt if we'll ever really know."

"I can't accept that," she said, breaking eye contact with me to stare out the window. "There *has* to be a reason. There has to be some logic behind this, otherwise it is...it's just too hopeless. It means we all really *were* doomed from the start."

"Not you." Florin's words flashed through my mind. She had a part to play in this...and so did Nadia.

Olga turned her eyes on me, and just as quickly looked away. "What's killing me," I said, disturbed by the brief intensity of her searching eyes, "is why, after all this time, I still can't figure it out. What does it all mean?"

"I don't know, Zigmund. I wish with everything that I did. But I'm just as confused as you are. I wonder if it would have been better if we'd never come at all."

"Don't say that," I said, reaching out and taking her hand in mine. Her hand wasn't cold, but it wasn't warm either.

It was brought home to me then that this was how it felt to be caught between life and death, with no possibility of ever reconciling the two states. Flesh that is neither cold nor warm just...*there*, hovering uncertainly, somewhere in the middle.

She looked down at our joined hands, but made no move to pull away. "Nadia's here," I said with more assurance than I felt. "She'll have to see it through."

The moment was lost. Olga slid her hand out of mine.

"And what of you, Professor? What are you gaining in all this?"

"Stefan's death."

"And Constantinos's? And Vladec Salei's? You forget they have to die, too."

"Of course," I said. It was the first time I'd actually thought of them as things that once were alive. I didn't know why that should have struck me as significant after so many years of hunting them, but the situation now seemed much graver than simply doing my duty.

"Then we're really no better than they are, are we? Murderers. That's what we've become. That's what *I've* become, been forced to do, every time I feel the hunger...which is frequent."

"You must have found a way to subsist on...other means of food?"

Florin was forgotten as I watched her sink deeper into the folds of her coat, pulling up the collar to almost shield her face. "I am what I am, Zigmund. What use is there in denying it? I can only hope that those I've *selected* led dishonorable lives. It makes the pain easier to bear."

"Not for them." My tone was sharper than I'd meant it to be. God knew I'd killed my fair share of vampires, but I'd convinced myself that most of them had been monsters before they had decided to live forever.

"I suppose if I ever do die, God will not look kindly on what I've done. It's funny, though, because in life, my sisters used to mock me for being too pious. Nadia, especially. Haughty, that's what they used to say. Well, pride comes before the fall, and I've fallen lower than any of them. I'm not proud of it, but I'm not going to apologize or feel guilty forever because of what they did to me."

She was so near, yet so remote. Porcelain, yes, as cold as a statue. But I refused to believe she was heartless.

"Olga." My fingers brushed against hers and she pulled back, edging into the corner of the seat. I could tell my touch pained her, but why should it have? Did she crave my blood? Was the hunger too much of a strain to fight? Or did I truly repulse her? In some sick way, I hoped it was only bloodlust that kept her from yielding to my touch.

Only bloodlust.

What's happening to you, Zigmund? I thought. *What's happening to you?* You've dedicated your life to hunting creatures like her, and now...what? You're falling in love with a woman who's been dead for nearly seven years. Absurd...morbid...insane.

"It's late," she said in the low, husky voice I had grown used to hearing. What would I do when I couldn't hear that voice every day once this was over? "Go get some rest," she continued. "I'll keep watch."

"No!"

"Ah," she said, smiling and ducking her head, but it was too late. I'd already seen the barbs and the gleam of teeth sharper than a serrated knife. "You're getting to know me too well, Professor."

"Zigmund."

"Zigmund," she repeated. When she looked at me, her smile faded. "The moonlight does strange things."

For the first time since I'd known her—all of a week—color rushed into her cheeks. She looked beautiful flushed. *Even more beautiful than...*

A moment like this would not happen again. I knew I was going to lose her, be it to Stefan, Constantinos, Vladec Salei, or whatever dark fate Florin had hinted at. Or even to herself. I was on the verge of succumbing to an emotion I'd never felt before. How could I be so fickle? Ten minutes ago, I'd been lusting after her sister. Now I wanted nothing more than to take Olga into my arms.

"Olga..."

Her eyes were fearful, uncertain, as she lifted them to my face, but I did not care. This was our moment, our time, our last time.

I kissed her.

Her lips felt like silk, brushing against my own. I drew her to me. She laced her arms around my neck, only hesitating a moment before kissing me back, first gently, then so passionately I felt the breath strangling in my throat. My blood quickened. I knew I should stop. If I could feel my own blood racing, so could she. I wasn't sure if she could control her urge to feed.

Before I could push her away, she stiffened. I opened my eyes. Something was wrong. She was too quiet. Too horror struck. I pulled away.

"What is it?

"This is wrong."

"How could this be wrong," I breathed into her hair, pulling her toward me again. I knew I was being suicidal. I knew she could tear into my jugular if I brought her any closer, but I couldn't stop thinking about how tantalizing the feeling of her lips on mine had been.

"I was on the edge of death, Zigmund."

"So was I. Are you going to let death be a barrier between us forever? Or are we finally going to put an end to the cycle of destruction?"

"How?"

Now was the moment. I knew what it was she had stirred in me. And I finally knew how to put those feelings into words.

"I do believe I love you, Olga."

"Folly," she scoffed.

"Is it?"

"Of course it is. How could you expect me to go along with such nonsense?" she asked without an ounce of conviction. "Life, for us at least, is not that simple."

"Normally, I would agree, but not now."

I tried to kiss her, but she turned away.

"I'm as good as dead, Zigmund," she said flatly. She was like a statue in my grasp, her arms like two lead weights at her sides. "I will never have real, human life in me again. I won't damn you to the same fate."

"I'm not asking you to turn me into a vampire," I said, my lips brushing against her cheek.

"But that's what I'd end up doing."

My sharp exhale ruffled her hair. I released her, holding her at arm's length and staring into her eyes—those twin crystals that were so uncannily translucent, save for the vertical black slits dividing them. She did not blink; she did not look away.

And I knew she was right.

"You'd be much better off with Nadia." It must have destroyed her to say that, to give voice to a lie neither of us believed. "If circumstances were different. If I could be trusted not to rip open your throat..."

She turned from me and laughed sadly, hopelessly. "Barbed tongues are remarkably good at that."

The image of another woman flashed before me. Her throat had once been as swan-like as Olga's, but in the vision, it was mutilated, savaged—ripped open by a tongue made of Devil's Rope.

"Zigmund, I didn't mean, I didn't think..."

"No," I said, but she was absolutely right. She was a vampire, a wolf, a thing of nightmare, no matter how beautiful her face might be, how hurt she had been, how much I longed to kiss her again right now.

"Saying it just wouldn't work between us seems trite, doesn't it?"

"Yes," I breathed.

"But it's the truth." Her reserve had returned. She lowered her eyes and took a step back—cutting herself off from me again. She'd withdrawn, as I'd done so many times over the years. No, we weren't as different as she thought.

And we would never be together.

She laid her hand against my cheek, tracing the indentations Constantinos's nails had made. I closed my eyes, turning my face into her palm, but that must have been too much for her to take. She shoved her hands into her pockets and walked off into the darkness. "Why, Stefan...why?" I heard her whisper.

Twice, I'd been robbed of the women I loved. Twice, those barbs had torn apart my life. After all these years, I still wasn't sure of myself, of my theories, of my ability to kill Stefan Belododia. But I was sure of one thing.

By the time I got through with him, Stefan Belododia would be *begging* for death.

***

I turned the key in the lock of my front door on the night of January twelfth. We'd made it home, and I hadn't said a word to either Olga or Nadia since that night at the hotel. Olga seemed content to ignore what had passed between us. And Nadia, well, I couldn't speak for her. Her eyes had followed me everywhere I went during the remainder of our journey. Apparently, I was hiding my longing for her behind a mask of indifference.

As I stepped into my darkened study, I could tell something was wrong. The sound of labored breathing came to me from across the room. Cautiously, I stepped over the threshold and nearly skidded across the floor.

"Stay back," I said, holding my arm out to bar Olga's way. There was nothing in that room that could have harmed her nor any sight that would have shocked her. But I could not be depended on to think rationally when it came to her safety.

I reached into my pocket and pulled out a box of matches. The light the match threw across the room was dim, but bright enough for me to see the blood trailing away toward the darkest part of the study where my armchair was.

"Who's there?"

"They've taken Greydanus."

"Madelaine?" I asked, uncertain. Our enemies had many tactics, disguising their voices being one of them. Leonora bounded into the room as soon as she heard her child's name. I trailed in her wake, almost afraid of what I would see. Madelaine's voice had been so weak. When I finally came upon her, I understood why.

She was almost unrecognizable. Across her knees rested a wyvern-headed staff. It was the mirror image of the one we'd seen in Florin's last illuminated illustration, the one he wanted back when Vladec Salei was dead. Blood trailed down the front of Madelaine's dress, but the blood that worried me the most was dribbling out of her mouth. She looked near death.

"I killed the leader. I killed Ruxandra."

"Are you injured?" I asked, dropping to my knees in front of her. Gently, I pressed against her stomach. She winced and bit her lip, but I had not felt anything broken. I could not account for where the blood was coming from.

"Not externally," she said, trying to rise and falling back, exhausted.

"Look at all the blood." I turned to see Olga behind me, her eyes glazed over. Nadia was standing cautiously by the door, but Olga...

"Get out of the room *now*, for all our sakes. You're not yourself."

"I am myself, Zigmund, that's the problem," she said, mesmerized by the blood pooled around Madelaine's feet.

Around her feet...staining the front of her dress, the hem.

Suddenly, I knew. Madelaine had never had the chance to confide in me, but from the amount of blood and the placement of the stain... "Madelaine, please tell me it isn't true."

"Your theories better be right, Professor. I better not have lost my baby for nothing."

Full Circle

"My son. What have they done with him?" asked Leonora.

"She's just lost her child. You can sympathize, I'm sure, having now lost more than one." I said that last part under my breath. I tried to lay my hand against Madelaine's forehead, but she pushed me away and grabbed the armrests of the chair, raising herself slightly. "He's been taken captive."

"Tell me what happened," I coaxed.

Her glassy eyes stared past me and focused on a spot above my head. She clenched her teeth as she struggled to somehow master herself. "Your brother," she said with effort, "took it into his head that he could kill his aunts on his own. I knew it was foolishness. I tried to convince him not to go, but he wouldn't take no for an answer. I told him of the passageway I'd gone through the night you found me," she said, grimacing.

"Steady, Maddie," I said, slipping a pillow behind her back.

"*Please*, Zigmund, don't call me that, I beg you." She bit her lip to hold in her tears. She'd been so strong up until I'd stupidly forgotten myself. I took her hand, and she seemed to rally.

"I wasn't going on without a weapon. I took the revolver you gave me, Zigmund, but Greydanus thought we should have a weapon that had some history behind it. I shattered the glass and took this," she said, nodding at the staff. "The report of the revolver was not that loud. We were underground. The walls are thick down there, and the passage out of the tunnel was some distance away. I thought we were secure. I thought we'd be safe. I was so wrong."

She swallowed with difficulty, her eyes narrowing at the memories she was having trouble putting into words.

"I had my back turned. I was taking the staff off the hook when they found us."

Leonora dropped to her knees beside me. Unshed tears coated her eyes. I took her hand in mine and joined ours with Madelaine's, which seemed to give both of them courage.

"The revolver lay among the shattered glass. By the time I got to it, Ruxandra had already wrenched the muzzle off. She was coming for me, Zigmund. Thank God I had the staff. I was able to kill Ruxandra, which probably saved my life. I think they were afraid of what I'd do to them, since I'd sliced off their leader's head. But they took Grey. I'm sorry, Zigmund, but I knew if I went after them, they wouldn't think twice about finishing me off. I'd...I'd..."

"It's all right," I said. She was being so strong. I'd have lost my sanity by now.

"I'd lost my baby by then. I just couldn't make myself lose anything more. Forgive me."

"There is nothing to forgive," said Leonora. Madelaine looked at her suspiciously at first, then her brow relaxed as she realized Leonora was sincere.

I squeezed Madelaine's hand. The poor girl had come close to annihilation more than once already. How could she even think for one second we'd hold what had happened against her?

"The key to finding him," she continued, "lies with the sisters."

Olga had ventured into the center of the room. The sheen of bloodlust had faded from her eyes. "To get to Greydanus," she said, "we need to break their hold, their power. First, we need to get rid of *my* sisters, though I do not know how I can call them that any longer."

"I'm sure they feel the same way about you."

I turned back to Madelaine, who was the only one of our group to have witnessed the sisters at close range.

"What can you tell me about these...girls?"

"*Girls?*" scoffed Olga.

"Well, harpies, if you prefer."

"Dacia likes to sleep in an iron maiden," Madelaine muttered.

"Perfect, I met one of those before."

"Which you killed?"

"Please, Nadia, now is not the time for false piety."

I shot Olga a grateful look. Nadia was one to talk, given her little speech to me about how killing her brother was the only option—an option that I was pushing her toward, I reminded myself, but still. Her life until this point hadn't exactly been spotless.

I turned back to Madelaine. She'd gone shockingly pale. "Get me some brandy," I said to Leonora. I gave the glass to Madelaine, who drank it down in one draught. I was relieved to see some pink coming back into her cheeks.

"There's no need to go into any gory details," I said. We'd have gory details aplenty to deal with soon enough.

"There are only two left after her," Madelaine said. Her voice was growing stronger. "Magdalena and Irina, I believe. She's the one who set them onto me in the graveyard."

Olga nodded, her eyes hard. I could tell she was making special plans for the sister who had dragged her from heaven to hell.

"Magdalena doesn't seem to be that difficult. She was crunching on a squirrel or a rabbit or something and hardly seemed interested in what was going on. From what I remember of that night they first...attacked me, there was a body on the catafalque, so if you could find some way to...I can't believe I'm saying this. What's happening to me, Zigmund? How can I talk about killing so easily?"

"Don't think about it, Madelaine. Don't even try to understand it. They're too far gone for you to waste any pity on."

She swallowed hard. The way she looked at me made me feel hollow, as though I was no better than the soulless creatures we were talking about destroying. But to give them human qualities, to think of them as anything other than evil, would have given them power over us. At the first sign of weakness, they'd make their play. By the time we realized where our pity had gotten us, they'd have their fangs buried in our necks.

"Very well...if you could somehow poison it? They seem to like feasting on it whenever they get the chance." Her mouth puckered in disgust.

"Yes," I said, hitting upon a method I'd used before in Bavaria, thankful to be dealing with facts. I'd always been better at facts than emotions. "I have a way for that, too. Come, the night is waning. We haven't much time, since they are most likely night feeders. Can you walk?"

"I once told Eric I would go to hell and back for him, and I meant it." She declined my hand and rose on her own. The blood was now dried on her dress, and the stain not as large as I had once thought. Still, to be walking about so soon after losing a child.

"Madelaine, you've been through too much, I'm not sure..."

"*I* am sure, Zigmund." She gripped the staff so hard her knuckles turned chalk-white. "Doing nothing to avenge my husband, our child, to stop these monsters from doing this to any other living creatures, would be an even greater tragedy."

She stumbled past me toward the door.

"Not that way," I said, catching up to her and guiding her toward the door near the back of the room. I felt her stiffen in my arms, but she finally relented and let me support her.

"Follow me," I said to the others. I led them up to the attic then down the stairs behind the house, which led out onto a sheltered patch of grass not visible from the other houses surrounding my own. "Douse the light," I said, handing Olga the candle I'd been using to illuminate our path.

"But the darkness?" protested Nadia.

"I have no problem with it, do you, Leonora?" asked Olga, mockingly.

"None whatsoever."

They were enjoying ganging up on the living members of our party, though Madelaine did not seem to flinch at the idea of going on in the dark.

"It will only be a few steps before we reach a light source," I explained. "Then we shall be able to see fine, Nadia, do not worry."

I looked up at the moon and sighed. "Do it," I said. Olga snuffed out the light.

I kicked off the false patch of grass covering the hatch and lifted the lock.

"What in the world…"

"Just follow me," I said, guiding Nadia down the stairs. I was always shocked by how cool the air was underground. Nadia slipped her hand into mine and I shivered, but not because of the cold. Her changes in mood were grating. One minute, she was pursuing me with what I could only guess was romantic interest; the next, she treated me like some plague-ridden corpse to be avoided at all costs.

"Just a few more paces and we'll be there," I mumbled. She tightened her grip on my arm, making me wince. Who knew such delicate fingers had so much strength in them. "And here we are." I could have gathered everything we needed in the dark if I had to. I knew this place blind. It had been my sanctuary, my laboratory, my safe haven for so many years, but now that feeling of security had been destroyed.

I pried Nadia's fingers from my arm and stood in the dark in silence. How could I have known, day by day when I came down here to work, that the creature I'd hunted for so long was only a few miles north of this very place?

I pulled down the lever, and the room buzzed into light.

"What's that?" Nadia asked, pointing to a jar on one of the shelves lining the brick walls.

"Blessed salt. One of my first discoveries and one of my most potent weapons. Extremely fast acting and deadly. That's the first thing we'll need. It'll teach them not to toy with their food," I said, unable to keep from smiling. Nadia looked horrified. I pushed on. "Then the silver coated spikes."

"Resourceful," said Madelaine, coming to my side and fingering the spikes I'd just removed from the glass case in which I kept them. I'd fashioned them in such a way that they fit over whatever spike I encountered and were held there by mere suction. They were cone shaped and completely made of silver. Most of the time, they'd worked, being of a standard size. The trick was to make sure they stayed fastened long enough to do the job.

"I did some...fieldwork, you could say, in Bavaria several years ago. A pretty nasty specimen, the creature was. Had been terrorizing the wardens of a local castle for years. He was very fond of sleeping in an iron maiden. When I learned that, well, these were the implements of his destruction." I carefully slid each spike over the other and shoved them into a satchel I had taken off a hook in the wall.

"And you mean to use these for the same purpose? Will it work?"

"Hopefully. Some vampires are obsessed with danger, almost to the point of it becoming a fetish to them. She probably doesn't mind the spikes piercing the rest of her body."

"Sick, unnatural creature," muttered Olga.

"But not the heart, am I correct?" I asked Madelaine. This point was crucial.

"Yes, there were no spikes near her heart, nor her eyes. And the spikes were made of iron, not silver."

"Just as I thought. She's a temptress, always trying to put one over on death."

"She was no different in life," Olga said bitterly, looking at Nadia.

"For once we are in agreement, Sister."

"Then let's be off," I said, arming myself with my equipment. I tried to focus on the outcome, the results of ridding the world of these pestilent creatures. It was the only thing that kept me from feeling like a murderer.

"Just one moment, Zigmund." We all turned to look at Olga, who had put up her hood, cloaking her face in shadow. She walked over to Madelaine and held out her hand, which was encased in a black leather glove. "I'll be needing this, Mrs. Bradburry."

Madelaine glanced at me, then returned her gaze to Olga. "I'll want it back cleaned when you are finished. I'm not done with that staff yet."

"You have my word."

Madelaine placed the silver staff in Olga's hand. A slight shudder racked Olga's body as silver touched leather, but she quickly mastered herself.

"Let's move out," I said, cutting the electricity.

Darkness enveloped us again, and for the first time in years, I welcomed it.

***

The body on the catafalque was not dead, but that wasn't the reason I hesitated. I knew this man, even though he should have died years ago, or if not died, then at least aged.

He didn't look a day older than when I'd last seen him, on the night my parents were murdered.

I looked down into the face of the gypsy who had given my mother the Venetian devil's mask thirty years ago. He'd led the Vrykolakas to us. He was the messenger, the scout who had marked my mother for death.

"Zigmund, what is it? *Zigmund*," Madelaine said, shaking my arm. I could not look away. The syringe was freezing against my skin. I held it aloft, poised, but I could not make myself inject him with the mixture of blessed salt and water. That would have been merciful; mercy was something he'd not shown us.

Dead leaves whispered around our feet on the areas of ground that were not blanketed in snow. The man's face was ashen, nearly drained of blood, but his eyes still had that fiery, maniacal spark I remembered too well.

"Inject the salt into Luc's wounds and be done with it."

Luc. So that was his name. I'd been right to think he was French.

This was my moment to gloat, to literally rub salt into the wounds of the man I'd hated for so long. Now, standing here, holding the power of life and death between my fingers, I had no taste for revenge. It wasn't personal, and it certainly wasn't good business to me, as it had been to him.

"Zigmund, you must hurry."

I flicked the syringe and put the needle to his neck.

"When will it take effect?" Madelaine asked.

"Any moment now," I said. Just as I had spoken the words, a tremor shook the body. Luc's eyes skewered me. I dropped the syringe. He'd recognized me. He knew I was the boy he'd patted on the head and called *mon ami.*

"Fer-Fer," he stuttered.

"Yes," I answered. "Fertig."

His eyes flashed with alarm, then realization, and finally with something that I took for gratitude. Before he took his last breath, his mouth formed two words. "Forgive me."

I felt my throat constrict. How could I answer him? I hadn't even decided if I would forgive Leonora, and now he was asking me to absolve him from destroying my entire family?

"Zigmund, he's gone."

"What?"

"You don't have to say anything. You don't have to explain. You've done your part to exorcise his demons. We have other matters to attend to now."

I glanced at Madelaine, then looked back at the body. His eyes stared straight up at the decayed, spider-webbed molding on the ceiling. Twice he'd flickered in and out of my life, like a crazed, elusive flame. I'd hated him on sight then, but I didn't hate him now. He lay there as still as a rock. The man who had sacrificed us to Thanatos was dead.

And I found I didn't even care.

"Give me the spikes," I said to Madelaine. She disappeared behind one of the crumbling pillars and reemerged with the satchel. Madelaine had been a brick since I'd met her. In some ways, I trusted her more than Olga, trusted her strength, her reasoning, even though she was more involved than any of us and had much more to lose.

I glanced at her as I set the satchel down next to the dead man's body. The blood was still caked on her face and dress. She'd lost a child, was very likely going to lose a husband, and yet here she was, her mouth set in a hard line, ready to do whatever it took to strike these creatures from the face of the earth—even, I was starting to believe, if it meant giving her life.

I removed the conical silver stakes and slipped them over the spikes in the iron maiden. The only spikes that truly needed covering were the ones that would pierce Dacia just above and below her heart. They'd form a cage around that organ, pinioning it. The effect would be nearly instantaneous. Dacia would only just have a second or two to realize what had happened before she died.

"Zigmund, Madelaine, *hurry.*" I couldn't spare a moment to tell Olga we were moving as fast as we could. The smell in the air had changed. The scent was different, more spiced, more pungent.

I knew that smell.

Blood.

I slipped on the last of the cones. There were too many spikes left, but I'd run out of my silver coated coverings. And I'd run out of time.

I grabbed Madelaine and rushed her to the safety of the shadows. Leonora was at our side, a streak of white against the blackness. Olga completely blended in with the night.

The wind had died, magnifying every other sound. But that was the trouble. There were no other sounds. Not a breath, for none of us were breathing; not a rustle, for the ground beneath our feet was covered with snow.

Laughter sliced through the night—laughter that raised bumps on my flesh and snaked its way into my mind, making me think wretched, suicidal things. My eyes flitted toward the iron maiden. *Those silver stakes, so sparkling in the moonlight, so inviting...*

I gasped as Olga put her hands over my ears, not because her hands were cold, but because I felt as though her touch had released me from the stranglehold of a nameless beast. "I'll not have them playing at being sirens with *your* mind, Zigmund," Olga whispered. She said it to me, but her eyes were riveted to a space above my head.

I looked up and over the barrier that separated us from the vampiresses' midnight playground.

The sisters had returned.

From the looks of them, one would have never known that their eldest sister had just been killed. They laughed and shoved each other, their eyes glittering unnaturally. The three of them seemed to be reveling in their new freedom. I shouldn't have been surprised, having witnessed this kind of internecine jockeying for power before. Ruxandra's death meant that there was one less Belododia sister to hunt for and take orders from.

The sisters had brought with them a fresh sampling of delicacies—conies, stripped bare and sucked dry; dead rats that the sisters twirled by the tails and struck each other with playfully; and something wrapped in a bloodied sheet that I think must have once been a small boy.

A large, heavy object clanked over the broken stones, the snow crunching through its wheels. Moonlight pierced through the clouds and illuminated what it was—a large cage, the sort of cage one would use to hold a circus animal. It was being pulled by the smallest and youngest looking of the sisters—the redheaded Irina.

In that cage, his small, blood-spattered hands clinging limply to the bars, was my brother.

"Greydanus!" Leonora gasped. I tried to hold her back, but wasn't quick enough. Thankfully, Olga got to her before Leonora could give us away.

"Not until the time is right," she warned.

Leonora's eyes had already taken on the angry yellow sheen that was preparatory to her transformation into a wolf. I watched in amazement as her nails, which had already lengthened to claws, retracted into her flesh as her mania subsided. She panted through Olga's fingers and glared at the woman who had stopped her from rescuing her son. I didn't want to think what would have happened if Olga hadn't been so quick, or strong. This mission called for secrecy. Better for Stefan to think that Madelaine and I had found this spot through sheer cunning than that his wife and sister were helping us kill Vladec Salei's turns.

"Come, wolfling, it will not be so bad. You need to learn how to hunt like a proper vampire."

"Yes," the red-headed minx hissed, abandoning the cage and prancing over to Luc's dead body.

Oh, my dearest Irina, you are in for a surprise.

"Enough vacillating," she said, brushing the hair back from the man's neck and caressing his flesh. "You don't want to go the way of your mother, do you, little Grey? Where is she, I wonder?"

"Bother her," said the one with night black hair, the one who must have taken over leadership from Ruxandra. This was Magdalena—she was next in line—and Olga had marked her for death. My eyes flickered to Olga, who tightened her grip on the staff.

"She is so tiresome. 'Am I a vampire, am I a wolf, am I a vampire, am I a wolf, I cannot decide, so I'll be both!'"

A low growl rumbled in Leonora's throat, but the sisters' cackling clanged off the stonework, ricocheting through the ruin, making it impossible for them to hear us.

"I will not have my nephew, Stefan's heir, in such a situation," Magdalena continued, all trace of laughter now gone. Her eyes were cold and dark and dead—like a shark's. "He must decide what he wants to be, before Stefan and Vladec and that plague return. And tonight he will. Irina!"

The redhead pulled back guiltily, her fangs drawn. "Stay away from him," Magdalena warned, "he is for Greydanus. It will be his first turn."

"No!"

"Are we to be witnesses to this sparring match?" asked Madelaine.

"No, because if Irina does not take a bite of that dead traitor soon, *I* will not wait any longer."

"You will wait until I tell you to," I said, alarmed by Olga's fierceness. "You will destroy everything if you act before we have planned. You will get your revenge, just wait for it."

I turned my attention to Greydanus, trying to catch his eye. I knew he could see in the darkness; I knew he could sense we were near. What had he been put through since I last saw him? What had they done? He'd been beaten, that much I could see. Welts and open, bloody wounds covered his arms. His hands were completely covered in scratches, so much so that it looked as though he had been attacked by a cat.

How I wanted to kill those harpies then. Greydanus was a child, but to them, nothing more than an annoyance, a burden that had to be taught what was right and proper for one of his kind to do. But that was the problem: there'd never been one like him before. They could rip him and tear him and beat him till he bled, but that blood would just find its way back into his body for nourishment, continuing the vicious cycle that forced him to suffer in order to replenish his strength. It made no sense, but one thing did to me now. I cared for that solemn little creature. Despite the reality that I would most probably never forgive Leonora, I was growing to love my brother so much that I was willing to sacrifice myself to set him free.

"He is your brother. Of course you would love him. I knew it would come in time."

I shied away from Leonora, still unnerved by her ability to read my thoughts so well.

When I looked back at the cage, Greydanus was staring straight at me. I nodded and so did he, which was our undoing.

"What are you looking at?" Magdalena shrieked. I felt the life drain from my limbs as she turned her dark eyes on me, but her hold didn't last.

From inside the iron maiden, Dacia was screaming.

Three things seemed to happen at once. Magdalena stood frozen in horror, unsure of where to look. Dacia writhed in agony, trying to tear herself free of the spikes. And Irina hung back, her eyes shifting from one stricken sister to the other. Of all of them, Irina disturbed me the most; she made no move to come to her sisters' aid. I shouldn't have been surprised, though. There was no honor amongst thieves, so why should vampiresses be any different? Each in her own way was entirely without compassion for the other.

Irina acted first, taking the opportunity to sink her teeth into Luc's dead body, ripping off a chunk of his flesh. In all my years of dealing with their kind, I had never seen one so overcome by bloodlust. She was trembling as she rose from the side of the catafalque. Her hands shook so violently that she was forced to reach out and steady herself. Blood poured down her chin, splashing onto the wyvern pendant at her throat.

And then the moment I'd been waiting for finally happened.

"Irina?! Your throat! What's happening to you?! Dacia, no, *no!*"

Magdalena could not decide where to look. A more inexperienced man would have pitied her, but I couldn't, not after what I knew she'd done. The silver spikes pierced every inch of Dacia's body. The two that I had thought most important, the two that would form a cage around her heart, were having a devastating effect. Madelaine gasped and turned away. Even she, who had killed for the first time not so long ago, couldn't stand the sight.

Blood soaked the ground beneath Dacia's feet—every last drop of blood that had drained from her body. The girl who just a minute earlier had had hair like silk was reduced to a husk of ashen flesh. Grey, wispy hair hung around her drooping head, her body dangling limply on the spikes. She no longer twitched; she no longer moved. The creature that had been Dacia Belododia was dead.

Magdalena stretched her hands toward the iron maiden, but the mere brush of Magdalena's fingers caused Dacia to crumble to dust.

Magdalena whimpered pitifully, sounding like an animal caught in a trap. She didn't know where to turn. Destruction surrounded her, hemming her in. She scampered backward, trying to escape from one corpse, only to be faced with another the minute she turned around. Her black eyes shone with fear, terror, the realization that she wasn't getting out of this the usual way—by killing off her prey. *She* was the prey now. I'd seen that look so many times before, and I knew that once they gave in to the fear they were as good as dead, no matter their strength.

Magdalena crab-walked backward, colliding with Irina, which was Irina's undoing. Up until that point, Irina had been concentrating all her power on trying to keep her throat from ripping open. The collision with Magdalena sent Irina sprawling.

Irina was lost. I *did* pity Magdalena then. If she still had a conscience, the last few moments of her life would be torture. She would have to suffer the guilt of knowing she'd hastened her sister's death.

Irina clawed at her throat. The blessed salt was burning through her skin, burning the evil out of her too quickly for her or her sister to do anything to stop it. Her bones were showing through her corroded skin by the time I decided I'd finally seen enough.

I'd wasted too much time watching them die. My focus shifted to Greydanus, who stared in mute horror as his aunt literally came apart at the seams.

"Don't look, Greydanus," I said, trying to find a way into the cage, which was completely made of silver. "I thought silver didn't have any effect on him," I said to Leonora. Grey's face was bloodless; he was paler than usual. He did not look as though he would last much longer in this prison.

"A little silver will not harm him, but this much could be fatal if he's been exposed to it for too long," she answered. "He'll die of poisoning or suffocation if we don't get him out of there soon. I cannot touch the bars, Zigmund," she continued desperately. "You will have to do it."

"*Me*, how?!"

"Trust me."

Leonora stood behind me. I didn't know what she was doing, until she reached out her arms and covered my hands with hers. Power surged through my muscles at her touch. I had to stop myself from thinking that this was the first embrace she'd given me since I was a child.

Concentrate, Zigmund, I ordered myself as I wrapped my hands around the bars of Greydanus's cage.

This needed to be quick. I couldn't risk Leonora's skin coming into contact with the silver. I shut my eyes and focused my mind on breaking the bars. Leonora would take care of the rest.

The silver between my fingers grew hot and caved in on itself. It felt like I was no longer gripping solid bars, but tin that was somehow crumpling at the touch of my hands. Leonora released me after a moment. When I opened my eyes, I saw a gaping hole where the bars had been a second before. On the floor surrounding the cage was a mound of crushed silver.

I looked down at my hands. I was whole and so was Leonora, thank God.

I reached inside and took Greydanus's hand. The strength of his grip heartened me, as did the color that rushed back into his face when I pulled him from the cage.

"Thank you, brother," he said as I laid him in Leonora's arms.

I nodded and ruffled his hair, then stopped myself when I realized what I was doing. He was a child, he was my brother, but he was still a vampire more powerful than the one who had just crushed the bars of his prison.

"You!"

I dodged to the left, shoving Leonora and Greydanus out of the reach of Magdalena's bloodstained nails. The breath was knocked from my lungs as she rammed into my back. When I turned and faced her, I knew something was wrong. She stood motionless, a peculiar look twisting her face—a look of shock, surprise, disbelief.

Slowly, she looked down and saw the blade sticking through her heart.

"Rest in peace, *sister*," Olga said, twisting the sword out of Magdalena's back. I scrambled out of the way as Magdalena thudded to the ground. Already she was beginning to shrivel, but there was more that needed to be done. Olga had not yet cleaned off the blade nor returned it to Madelaine. I turned away, wincing as I heard the slice of the blade against Magdalena's neck. That was a sound I could never get used to.

So it was done. Dacia was dust and Irina would soon be so herself. I tapped her body with the toe of my boot. She was lifeless, the wound on her throat ghastly and impossible to recover from. I leaned down, intending to close her eyelids, when Olga intercepted and bent over the body. Once more I heard the blade cutting through vertebrae.

"There's no harm in being thorough," she said, rising and cleaning the sword on her cloak.

Madelaine was by us in a trice, holding out her hand for the sword.

"Cleaned and ready to use again if the occasion arises," said Olga, handing the sword back to its new owner.

"I know it will," Madelaine said grimly.

"The news will be out soon enough," I said to them. "We must hurry. We don't want them descending on us now when we are vulnerable to attack. Vladec Salei won't be pleased that his seraglio has been disbanded."

"How can you be so callous?" Nadia asked. She had hidden in the shadows through the entire ordeal and was now holding herself apart from us as though we all had some contagious disease.

"In my line of work, there is no time to dwell on human traits, Nadia," I said, regretting that I sounded so cold. "Your sisters ceased to be human years ago."

"One could argue they never were," said Olga, her eyes boring into her sister's so that for a second I doubted the sincerity of Nadia's tears.

"Don't lecture me on humanity. You never had any toward me."

To my surprise, Olga restrained herself. Maybe the killings *had* taken their toll, or maybe she was storing up her rage for another time.

I led them back toward the road and the cab that would take us home.

"When you've seen the things I have over the years, Nadia...."

"I have."

"No, my dear," I answered, "you haven't. You've barely scratched the surface."

I tried to take her arm, but she pulled out of my reach, preferring to walk beside Greydanus, who I remembered was seeing her for the first time. He didn't look pleased that she had chosen to walk beside him. He tried to keep Madelaine—whose hand he had grabbed at the first chance—between him and his newfound aunt.

The cab, when we reached it, had thankfully not yet been found or destroyed in an all-out vampiric rage. I had already put Leonora and Madelaine into the cab and was in the process of bundling Greydanus in after them, when Nadia dropped to one knee, grabbed Greydanus by the hand, and turned him to face her.

"This child," she said, curling a lock of hair behind his ear. Greydanus flinched. I didn't blame him. She was staring at him so intently, so possessively, so...*hungrily*. "This child, this beautiful child of dead parents is my nephew? Come here, angel..."

It wasn't a request. It was a command. Greydanus let himself be pulled to her chest. He was predisposed to be frail. After his ordeal, he was even weaker, so it wasn't helpful that Nadia was hugging him as though she wanted to snuff out whatever life he had left.

And yet...and yet he did nothing to break free from her iron embrace. His body was stiff in her arms. His eyes flitted from mine to Olga's and settled there. I looked between them. The expression in their eyes was the same. I knew them to be linked by a stronger bond than simply a family bloodline. Their experiences were similar, though they could never be identical. I still did not know what exactly Greydanus truly was. Yet they understood each other in that single glance—and in that single glance they conveyed a sentiment toward their sister and aunt that made me despair of ever winning them to my side.

They would never see Nadia as our salvation.

"There, Pet, I think you and I understand each other." Greydanus looked shaken and even paler than before. "Shall we be off?" Nadia said brightly. Her quick change of mood startled me. Maybe seeing the child had put things into perspective for her. I certainly hoped so. One less liability on this fool's errand would be a blessing I wouldn't begrudge.

I jumped up onto the box and took the reins. I'd made the journey up top alone going out, but I was not to be alone on the way back.

"For your own protection," said Olga as she settled in beside me.

"Not just drawn to my magnetic personality?"

She smiled at me briefly, then settled back, withdrawing into herself once more.

So much for levity. Nothing but Stefan's death could bring peace to any of us now.

***

I wanted nothing more than to be alone that night. I needed time to figure things out, time to plan. Tomorrow was the day we were staking all our hopes on: 13th January 1895, the five hundredth anniversary of Vladec Salei's initiation into the ranks of the damned. Leonora and Olga felt him drawing close. And they felt Stefan even more powerfully now that his *fathers* would soon join him.

Madelaine was the one I had worried about the most, but she seemed to be holding up well, especially since Greydanus had become her unofficial protector. He was in awe that she had had the courage and the skill to bring down Ruxandra without getting killed herself. He hadn't left her side since we returned. It was touching to see this child so solicitous of a woman he barely knew. But the way she responded to his concern was anything but a cause for celebration. I could tell she had attached herself to him more fiercely than she should have. If there was something left to worry about in regards to Madelaine Bradburry, it was how she would cope when the time came for Greydanus to be taken from her.

My mind shifted back to Olga. Olga, whose very presence disturbed and excited me. She was a catalyst. I hadn't had time to think over it before, but now, in the solitude of my bedroom, I saw in my mind's eye the vision of her in Romania with that fog swirling away from her body. I wondered if she'd discovered her seeming power over it. And I wondered if that power was something I'd needed all these years—all these years I'd spent trying to unravel this complex tapestry of myth and legend.

Nadia, the missing link, the linchpin of my entire dispatching theory, had been so close this whole time. How had I never found her? How had I been kept in the dark about her existence? She was the living embodiment of the last blood relative I had so strongly believed could kill the creature. Something had put that in my mind and something had kept me from discovering the means of carrying out my theory. I wasn't a superstitious man, but this smacked strangely of intervention, and not the divine kind, either.

Then there was Vladec Salei. I hadn't even known Vladec Salei existed until Eric Bradburry told me so. I'd been tailing Stefan and Eric as they passed through Greece, but only because I was tracking Constantinos. I followed them because of *him*. Everything I'd done in life after that night thirty years ago, I'd done because of *him*. And I'd never known that because of *him*, my mother was still alive.

Leonora was dead to me, dead and gone, the victim of a Vrykolakas attack. Having seen her as I did that night, who in their right mind would have suspected her of being alive and well and the mistress of the Upyr who was turning out to be the puppet master of us all? Never had I even dared to consider the possibility that Leonora was involved with Salei, too. I'd simply thought of him as a megalomaniac who randomly selected Constantinos from a pool of unsuitable and unstable vampires. It was all a question of luck, a question of chance. Only now was I beginning to understand just how predetermined all of Salei's moves had been.

Maybe I'd been too obsessed with Constantinos to the exclusion of everything else. I didn't know. All I knew was that the last seven years had been a waste. How could I have not seen?

A glass of Helles and a smoke were all that could comfort me now. I'd noticed, lately, that my memory had been failing me in certain areas. Perhaps it was the influence of that pernicious fog I'd come up against, but more probably it was due to over-memorization of bits of information and overexposure to creatures that by all rights shouldn't even exist. The strain of countless years of killing, of dealing with unspeakable things, seemed to be piling up one by one this night, and I felt suddenly very, *very* old.

Before I did anything else, I would recheck some facts in my lexicon and then make everything ready for tomorrow. And then, if I was lucky, I would sleep, but I didn't hold out much hope for that.

I unlocked my study door and hesitated on the threshold. A strange scent hung in the air, something alien and unidentifiable. Cautiously, I stepped into the room.

A fire raged in the hearth. A plate of smoking, basil scented chicken had been laid out on the table by the fire. One glass of my best cognac had been poured, yet I could see a faint circle of moisture on the table, indicating that someone had poured themselves another glass and let it sit there long enough for it to leave a mark.

"Dinner and a chat by the fire."

I grabbed the poker and braced myself for an attack, but my fears were groundless. The voice did not belong to Vladec Salei nor to that hissing beast nor Stefan. "I thought you had retired," I said, stoking the fire. The flames blazed up, illuminating Nadia's eyes, which were greener than ever—green and seductive and as inviting as a soft patch of grass.

Zigmund, stop thinking this way.

Nadia settled down on the rug before the fire and twirled the stem of the other glass of cognac between her fingers. I noticed that the glass was already half drained. I wondered how many drinks she'd had before I got here.

"Couldn't sleep. I thought you could use some *nourishment.*"

The way she purred that last word, I wasn't sure what kind of nourishment she had in mind. I broke off a piece of the chicken and handed it to her, but she declined it.

I settled down opposite her, placing the plate of chicken and the bottle of cognac as a barrier between us. There were questions I wanted to ask her, but I wasn't sure I'd like the answers. She was still an enigma to me. I thought back to everything Olga had said, and also what Florin had mentioned. We couldn't trust Nadia, but she was our only hope. I couldn't very well make small talk at such a time as this, but I was not the first who spoke.

"How much do you know of Vladec Salei?"

"I beg your pardon?"

"You studied him, you knew of him, yet for all those years, he kept your mother hidden, right...beneath...*this*," she said, leaning over to tweak my nose.

Had I somehow given her the impression that she and I were on a familiar enough footing to allow such liberties as this?

"Don't you find that odd, Zigmund? Don't you find that the least bit *fascinating*?"

"What's your game? Where are you going with this?"

"I just want you to know what you're up against, that's all, Professor." She leaned back and stretched luxuriously, exposing more of her throat than was seemly. I suddenly noticed how flimsy the blouse she was wearing was. I turned my eyes away and focused on the fire.

"I *can* say..." I mumbled, "that yes, he is gifted, and *yes*, he is an expert at his particular brand of evil."

"You have no idea how good," she said, her lids drooping a fraction of an inch.

"And I assume you do?"

"No, alas, no, but I can imagine, from what I've been told."

She wrapped her fingers around the neck of the bottle and poured herself another drink. I tried not to look at her, preferring to stare at the fire instead. It was the safest thing to do with her so tantalizingly close.

"You look parched, Professor. Drink," she said, shoving the bottle into my lap. She pushed the plate out of the way and sidled up beside me, dangerously near. I did as I was told, finding that I had no will or desire to resist her. Something in her eyes made me believe she wasn't finished with me for the night.

She leaned back on her palms and half-closed her eyes. "I'm sure you know his history."

It wasn't a question, and I didn't take it as such. "Turned in Russia during a holiday to the Black Sea," I rattled off mechanically, reciting facts I'd dredged up through my research, which I had to admit was practically all secondhand. "Went berserk and killed his father. Vampire creator unknown," I said, cutting off my words with a swig of the cognac, which I immediately wished I hadn't tasted. My mind clouded, my eyes grew blurry. The last thing I needed was to feel uninhibited.

"Wrong on most accounts," she said with a laugh. I darted my head around to see her drinking the cognac down in a single gulp. "These histories were all gathered by non-witnesses."

I laughed at this, but she continued undaunted. What was she but a non-witness, preparing to blow all my research out of the water with more secondhand stories?

"Yes, Vladec Salei killed Constantin Belododia. But not *our* Vladec Salei."

I nearly choked on my cognac. "*What?*"

"See, Professor? I *can* catch you off guard." She poured herself another drink and sat there staring into the liquid gold in her goblet until I thought I'd die from the tension of waiting to hear what she was keeping to herself.

"Vladec Salei was the name of the Upyr. Vladec Salei no longer exists. After he killed his creator, Constantin Belododia took on the creature's name and all the vengeance that went with it."

"But why would he do such a thing?"

"Because he wanted to strike out all traces of his weaker self. And what better way to do that than to take on the identity of his attacker, the one he claimed had made him whole?"

"Bloody, self-loathing Romanian. It's impossible. It can't be true. I would have known."

"Like you knew about him and your mother? Would you have really known, Professor? Secondhand research," she said, tapping my chest to emphasize each word. "Vladec killed the Upyr with his bare hands only moments after he'd been turned. The transformation hadn't even taken hold yet and he was able to do that. That murderous rage passed down through generations. Whatever they told you, it was wrong. Vladec wasn't only an Istratescu on his mother's side."

"No," I said, not believing that this much interbreeding and calculation could happen in one family.

"The name does not lie, Zigmund. He was a Belododia on his father's side. So you see," she said, refilling her glass and mine, though mine was in no need of replenishment, "all of us, Stefan included, were doomed from the beginning."

I set down the glass and put my head in my hands. All my research and I had never discovered this link—this binding, indestructible link that soldered this cursed line more strongly than I had ever guessed. "So what is he to you, then, a great grandfather seven times removed?"

"Something like that."

"But if he was turned, why aren't you all vampires? Why are you even *here*? Logically, with a vampire ancestor, some trace of the curse would have passed to each child."

"Ah, and I have you at my mercy yet again," she said, her eyes sparkling, with drink or desire, I wasn't sure. "We Belododias and Istratescus never bother with formalities. Vladec had already gotten Flavia Istratescu pregnant before the Upyr did its work. No matter that they weren't married and Flavia was only fifteen and a cousin of his. They took care of these things young back then."

I leaned away from her, sickened, but not by the sour smell of the drink on her breath.

"I just want you to be prepared, Zigmund," she said, laying her hand on my arm with a tenderness I had done nothing to encourage.

"Thank you. Thank you for scaring the life out of me and destroying everything that I have believed to be the truth," I said, pulling away from her.

"What does it matter when he's as good as dead?"

"He's not dead *yet*," I reminded her, shying away; she was leaning in closer than she should have been. "And from what you've just told me, Vladec, or whatever his name really is, was able to kill a raging vampire with his bare hands before the transformation had taken root. Not to mention that you've poked holes in all my theories in a matter of minutes. Oh, yes, Nadia, your supposed capabilities fill me with *so* much confidence."

"You don't believe what Olga said about me, do you?" she asked, looking up at me through her lashes.

"Of course not."

"Good. Don't let her convince you that I'm not good for you, or vice versa."

"I had no intention of doing that," I said. Had I given her the impression I was interested in her that way? I went over my conduct of the past days and found that I had been blameless.

"I've never been in love before, Professor," she said, sliding her hand into mine.

"*Love*?!" I choked.

Nadia's blouse had slipped over her shoulders— deliberately, I believed. The gypsy-like garment was much lower-cut than the one she had worn yesterday and exposed more of her flesh than was appropriate. Her head was tilted to the left, which made her corkscrew curls fall all on that side and allowed her milk-white neck to remain bare. I got the unmistakable feeling she was trying to entice me to kiss her exposed throat. I looked away and thought of Olga, which instantly brought me back to my senses.

And while I was thinking about her, something I had overlooked in the heated seconds came back to me like a punch in the stomach.

Constantin. Constantin*os*.

"They have the same name."

"Who?"

I hadn't realized I'd spoken aloud. I raced behind my desk and rifled through my satchel, emerging a few moments later with the lexicon in my hands.

"Page 475. There's a lovely illustration there," I said, tossing the book into Nadia's lap.

That got her to forgo her cognac orgy. Slowly, she leafed through the pages and gasped when she reached the one I had mentioned.

"Constantinos in all his glory. You've met him before. There's no need to feign shock."

"I've never...I've just never seen him so...so..."

"Clearly? Exposed? So true to what he really is? Well, my dear, I find that hard to believe. Now tell me why your damned ancestor and that beast have the same name."

She ran her fingers over the page as if to absorb the reality her eyes could not see. "Similarity, symbiosis."

"What are you jabbering about?"

"I can't explain it. Vladec, *Constantin*, wanted it in everything he did, even in the choosing of the one who would help him create the Corcitura. I'm sure that if he'd found another vampire named Constantin first, he would have never sought out a Vrykolakas. It is our bad fortune that he became partners with probably the most vicious vampire of its kind. So much for luck."

"How do you know all this?"

"It is my family history. I was the only one brave enough to dig deeper. I was the only one savvy enough to survive to tell you now."

"No, no, you couldn't possibly have learned all this on your own." *I* hadn't, how could she?

"I did."

"Nadia, don't lie to me!"

"I'm not lying!"

"You're holding something back. For once in your life, speak the truth!"

She looked down at her long, pale fingers. My words had stung her. Was that guilt in her eyes when she turned them on me? Or was it weariness? For a second I truly believed I saw Nadia's soul...and there was no fight left in it.

"He told me," she said quietly, "this last time."

"This last time? And how often has he taken you captive?"

"At least three," she said, wiping her nose with the back of her hand. The action was so childish that I softened toward her. I truly did not know what she had gone through. Who was I to judge?

"The time before was nearly seven years ago," she continued, "when Stefan found me again. It's why I did what I did, why I led them all to Castle Bran. I had to, Zigmund, don't you see? I would have been just like Olga if I hadn't. Stefan was already well on his way to becoming the Corcitura. There was nothing I could have done."

"There is always something you can do if you are willing to try hard enough."

Self-preservation. That's what this was all about. What would I have done in her place? It could have been argued that I abandoned Leonora to Constantinos, but I was seven years old and believed both my parents to be beyond any help I could give them. Nadia had known exactly what she was doing. So why did I feel that I was somehow guiltier than her?

We sat in front of the fireplace in silence. The situation was awkward to begin with. I'd stayed longer than I should have and was going to suggest we each retire for the night, when I felt Nadia draw closer. Her fingers entwined with mine. Her skin was warm and alive...so different from Olga's. My heart began to pound. I sensed what she wanted from me. And I knew if I gave in, I wouldn't be able to stop myself.

I turned away, but she pulled me back and suddenly her lips were on mine—crushingly, devouringly. Fire flooded my entire body. I couldn't resist. I had no will for it. I returned her kiss, clutching her to my chest, my fingers ravaging her hair. For one, agonizing second, I gave in to her, but then a savage pain ripped through my head as the truth was brought home.

What the devil was I doing? And the devil it was, because I felt like I had no control over my impulses, my actions, my desire. I had to stop. I tried to push her away, but her will was stronger than mine, as was her grip. She coiled her arms around me, locking me in a hold I could not break. Her hands trailed up my back, latching around my throat so tightly and in such a way that if she had wanted to, she could have snapped my neck.

"Na..." I tried to cry out, but she pushed me on my back and crushed the breath out of me. She was far more experienced than I was. Had Vladec Salei taught her? The thought disgusted me. To think that this mouth that was latched onto my own had kissed dead flesh and enjoyed it. From somewhere far away, I heard laughter, and the face affixed to mine no longer looked like Nadia's. It no longer even looked human.

And then I knew what her aim was. If I didn't find a way to rip this leech off, she'd suffocate me.

I sensed the presence in the room before I even heard her speak.

"Zigmund, I..."

Nadia's hold relaxed. I drank in the air as she raised her head to look at the woman who had intruded upon us. I pushed Nadia off me and glanced down, horrified to see my shirt ripped open. How could I deny that this was not what it looked like? No one would have believed me, least of all *her*.

Shock was etched in the small lines around her eyes, small lines that had not been there the first day we met. And now she saw me like this. I couldn't have wounded her deeper had I stabbed her through the heart.

I looked down at Nadia's face and saw there no look of shame. She had not even made a move to straighten her clothes.

Nadia's eyebrows were arched challengingly. As my eyes roved over her disheveled body, I felt suddenly obscene. An overwhelming sense of shame took hold of me.

Corcitura

I moved toward Madelaine, but she shook her head and recoiled from me.

"Madelaine, I can explain."

Her eyes were glossy with tears, but she bit her lip to keep them from spilling out.

"Maddie, please!"

"Don't call me that!" she shrieked, swatting my hand away. "Only one man has the right to call me that. And he's probably dead by now, not that you care. All you care about is dallying with that...that...*thing*."

I grabbed her arm and held it so that she couldn't run away. She fought me for a moment, then seemed to lose all her will to resist. Her shoulders sagged and she looked at me with such sorrow that I felt as though my own heart would break.

"Zigmund, how could you?"

"This is not what you think."

"You monster, how could you? I leave you alone for not even three quarters of an hour and you're...you're...Zigmund, *why?*"

"You don't understand, Madelaine."

"Don't I? You came in here to prepare for tomorrow, which is quite an important day to all of us, in case you had forgotten. Do you not have anything better to do than to *conjoin* yourself with the woman who is supposedly here to save us all?"

"And what if he wants to? That is his choice. We all relieve our stresses in different ways."

I turned shocked eyes on Nadia. "What are you implying? You have the gall to accuse me of going into this willingly?"

"Let her see us, Zigmund, for all I care. If we choose to come together, it is none of her business."

Madelaine's mouth formed an *o* of shock. "So it's true, then?"

"Of course it's not true!" I said, buttoning my shirt. "What do you take me for, Madelaine?"

"Frankly, Zigmund, I have not known you long enough to form a judgment of your character."

"Don't be pedantic. You trusted me with saving your husband's life."

"I see now that I was mistaken."

"Don't say that," I pleaded. Her eyes wavered between me and the minx sprawled out on the hearthrug. Madelaine was uncertain, which was a point in my favor. A few more minutes and I would have won Madelaine to my side, but then Leonora and Greydanus and Olga burst in and chaos erupted.

"What's this?"

"Nothing," I said, avoiding Leonora's eyes. I hadn't thought of her as my mother in years, so why did I feel like a child caught stealing now?

"I was overwrought and Zigmund was comforting me."

"I was doing nothing of the kind!"

"Oh, no, I think it is much more than just comforting." Olga's scorn was understandable, but no less painful than I had imagined. What must she think of me? Especially after we had nearly declared ourselves to each other less than three days ago. In her eyes, I must have been a cad, a monster, or worse.

Yet of all of them, the one who was hardest to face was Greydanus. His face looked pained. Was he so hurt because he did not understand what had almost just happened between Nadia and me, or was it something else that disturbed him?

He shook his head and turned away, and I knew the look for what it was.

Disappointment.

"All right, all of you, out! Now!" I ordered, herding them toward the door. I would brook no dissent, especially not from Nadia, who acted as though she were exempt from my command. "Up with you too, witch," I said, grabbing her arm and practically lifting her off the floor.

"Leonora," I said, taking her aside, "watch that one all night. I do not trust her, but she is our one hope, much as I regret it. See that she stays protected."

"From you?"

"Mother, please think better of me than that."

I froze. How had that word slipped out? I'd never meant to say that word again.

"Things change, Zigmund. *People* change. I knew one day it would happen for you. I knew one day you'd forgive me." She didn't cry, she didn't smile, but something about her seemed to finally be at rest, at peace. "I'll watch her."

I closed my eyes as she laid her hand against my cheek. When I opened them, she was gone.

And I was alone once more.

***

Dawn would break in less than two hours.

Dawn of the day that would bring everything full circle.

I preferred darkness at this hour, though darkness hid many things. The thought of sunlight pouring through the now-shaded windows made me sink deeper into the comforting embrace of my chair.

I lit my pipe and leaned back, propping my feet on the desk and giving myself up to questions I had no answers to.

What had Nadia tried to do to me? Did I have that much draw for women that she could not resist me? It was highly unlikely. That couldn't be it. There was something deeper there, something I did not want to think about, something that puzzled me as much as Olga's seeming power to dispel the fog around me as well as in my mind. I couldn't call Nadia into question now. She could have been a reprobate for all I cared. Hers was the only blood left in that accursed family that was not tainted. She had to stay.

What of Olga, then? Olga, who was more of a mystery to me than ever. It was her eyes that I had shied away from, her searching eyes that looked upon me with scorn. Could she not see that *she* had been the one to awaken my dormant feelings? Did she not know that her sister repulsed me? Just because I had been hollow inside for so many years didn't mean someone couldn't come along one day and spark something I thought I'd never feel—and that person had *not* been the one who tried to suffocate me upon my hearthrug.

How would I ever be able to convince Olga I hadn't betrayed her?

And then there was Leonora. Beautiful, remote, half-wolf Leonora.

My mother.

"Why are you so afraid to call her that aloud, Zigmund?"

I nearly tipped over the chair as I bolted up from it. I was blinder than a bat without my glasses, and the darkness I had prized so much a minute ago made it nearly impossible for me to see a thing in the gloom now. I reached for my spectacles and turned up the lamp on my desk.

In the corner by the fireplace, I saw a small figure sitting in the armchair. The child's feet stuck out over the lip of the chair. I thought, somewhat abstractedly, that those little feet would not get anywhere near to touching the floor for at least another two years. I was thankful I couldn't see his eyes. I feared they would hold the same reproach our mother's had.

"What are you doing here, Greydanus? You should be in bed." It was an idiotic thing to say to a vampire.

"Sleep is not something I require," he said stiffly. He was so formal, so much older than his years. It was like talking to Methuselah in the form of a child. "Why did you do it, Zigmund? Why did you betray Mother?"

"I didn't betray anyone," I said, knocking the ashes out of my pipe. What could he know of betrayal? Leonora had coddled him and loved him since birth. She was willing to kill for him. Greydanus knew nothing of what she had done in her past, what she had done to me. "My feelings are my feelings, I cannot help what I feel," I babbled, losing patience with his placid face. Why wasn't he showing any emotion?! "My life is my own. I'm not going to be lectured by a six-year-old."

"I am your brother."

"Regardless."

"Your actions are not conducted in a vacuum, Zigmund. They have effects. Don't be selfish."

"Selfish?" I asked, stepping out from behind the desk to do I didn't know what. Even if I'd wanted to, I couldn't bring myself to harm him, not that my flimsy attempts would have done any good. He was beyond my power to kill, more so even than his father. Greydanus was an unknown. This fact frustrated me most of all. "You want to know what's selfish? Your mot..." I couldn't even say it. "Leonora abandoning a son she already had to become a vampire's mistress. Then, as if that weren't transgression enough, becoming the wife of said vampire's son and creating a little monster of their own. Tell me that's not selfish. How much more human wreckage can that woman leave in her wake?"

"Why do you hate her so?" he asked, wide-eyed.

"You wouldn't understand. You're too young to hate."

"Try me."

I stopped pacing and stared at him, unsure if he was telling the truth. He was so guileless, he had to be sincere.

"I don't want to end up like you, brother," he said, his eyes locked onto mine. "So full of hatred, so racked with guilt and regret. I've been to those depths and they are blacker than night, blacker than the most evil soul, which I have had the occasion to meet, to *know* intimately. Do not make the mistake of believing you are the only one to ever suffer at the hands of your family. The difference is I was persecuted on purpose. You were much more fortunate."

"Fortunate? You call being abandoned fortunate?"

"If you had been my father's son, you would have wished every waking second of your life that there had been some mistake. Do not be so quick to discount your past. Everything happens for a reason."

I sank into my seat. Why was he telling me all this? What was it to him if I forgave her or not, or if I lived or died?

"So, I was abandoned for a reason?"

"Yes. If she had found you after the transformation, she would have killed you. In some ways, it was a blessing that Grandfather convinced her she had murdered you."

"A blessing, don't be ridiculous."

"You do not know what happens to those who wake from eternal sleep only to find that they have been cursed with eternal life. I have been forced to witness it more times than any of our kind should. You, with all your training, all your knowledge, all your courage, would not be able to stand the sight of so much blood, nor the screaming, the tearing, the rupturing of flesh, the shattering of bone. You'd shoot yourself sooner than see more. Human beings were not meant to witness the rebirth of those who should remain dead."

I felt a lump harden in my throat. In all my years, I'd always taken life—*their* lives. This child had witnessed the creation of it—creation in its most perverse form. I had always thought myself a man who was afraid of practically nothing, but when faced with a scene such as he described, I had my first prickings of doubt. Everything I had ever done in my life had counted for nothing in the world Greydanus lived in.

One thing had bothered me ever since I discovered I had a vampire for a brother. It was impossible, to my scientific mind, to understand how this had happened. "How are you here, Greydanus? How were you even born?"

"What artifact are you obsessed with, Zigmund?" he asked. I felt like our roles had reversed. Now I was the knowledge-seeking student and he the learned professor.

"The Cross of Istratescu, you know that," I said uncomfortably.

"Now think of the dagger concealed within it," he said, tenting his fingers to complete the illusion. All that was missing was a pair of glasses pushed down to the end of his nose. "When the hinge is depressed, the dagger springs out, but not before the blood in the cabochon coats the dagger with its protection. That is exactly what the blood of a vampire does to the organs of those it attacks. If they are unfortunate enough to survive, the blood serves as a protector, coating their insides, preserving the function of their organs, but making them supercharged, if you will. Think of the power of a locomotive and you will get a sense of just how strong and nearly invincible the inner workings of the vampiric reproductive system are. Why do you think it's so hard to kill us? And why do you think they always drive a stake through our hearts? If our hearts were not so powerful, no one would bother with them. They'd just cut off our heads and be done with it. Or throw us into furnaces, which is a death none of us can ever come back from."

I stared at him, feeling as though I'd been attending a lecture in the operating theater. He was so formal, so scientific, so un-childlike, that it was a minute before I could make myself believe I'd really been talking to Greydanus and not a doctor seventy years his senior. Of course he would know all this. I shouldn't have been surprised. He'd been born of this system, however unnatural it was. It still seemed too fantastic to be real.

"I assure you it's not."

"How did you know what I was thinking?"

"You spoke aloud. I do not read minds like Mother. I'm afraid I didn't inherit that, though there are worse things I did. Like eternal youth."

"Is that such a bad thing?"

"Maybe not to some, but to me it is. It's all a lie, Zigmund. I will grow until I reach the age at which my father was turned. And then I will stop and forever be nineteen. No one wants to outlive one's friends...or one's family."

I understood his meaning instantly. Madelaine, myself...we'd all die one day, but he would linger on. Age upon age would pass. He'd make new friends, maybe even have new loves. Then they would die and he'd have to start anew, investing his emotions, his immortal heart, over and over and over again.

"Don't listen to the ramblings of fools," he said, smiling grimly. "When it comes down to it, if they knew the truth, no one would want to live on this earth forever."

I had wondered why his brow was always troubled, his eyebrows perpetually v-eed, other worlds swirling in the two black pits set into his face. After sharing his secret knowledge with me, he looked even graver. And I finally understood why.

"Zigmund, I beg you to listen to me. I will not see you become a slave to your resentment over something Mother did years ago. Something you should have forgiven her for. You will never know what it is like to be one of us. You will never know how lucky you are to be human. You take for granted the great gift you have been given, that one day you will be able to see the face of the One who created you. I have seen my creator's face. I no longer have any illusions."

"Lucky?" I laughed, completely disregarding his confession. It was too alien for me to understand. I, who had not bothered about such things in years. "Sometimes I wish I were as stony as you and she," I said, my tone unnecessarily fierce. "As unfeeling as an immortal. Sometimes, anything would be better than to *feel*, Greydanus. Tell me you can understand this, because from what I've seen, I don't believe your kind can feel anything."

"We can, even more acutely than you, because we envy you. Your foibles, your fears, your needs. It sounds ridiculous to you, I know, but once you lose the ability to experience the normal, everyday things of life, you crave them more fiercely than anything else...even blood. Do you know what it is to feel like a block of marble? To feel dead inside? That's how Mother feels. That's how she's felt since the day she was condemned—the day you thought she died."

"She's told you all this?"

"I didn't need for her to confide in me. You can feel the longing in her every movement, her every look. But she confided in me regardless of this. For as long as I can remember, which was shortly after I was born, I've known of you. I've dreamed of you. I've wondered why she let herself believe she murdered you. I've wondered everything. But you see, you're wrong, Zigmund. She never stopped loving you, she never forgot you. She never abandoned you."

"But she can read minds, Greydanus!" I said, falling to my knees before this child who was wiser than me in ways I couldn't even understand. "She must have known I was alive. She could have found me, if only to show me she hadn't died. That would have been enough."

"In all the years, she never knew. She thought you were dead. But even if she had discovered that Grandfather was lying to her, it would not have done any good. You shut her out. Her power is only as strong as you make her. You thought she was dead from the outset. And in that you killed her. She wouldn't have been able to find you because you'd already buried her in your mind, in your heart. To you she was dead, and that's how it remained."

I settled back on my heels, thunderstruck. All those years I had pursued Constantinos, and then Vladec Salei, she was always there, just beyond my reach. If only I'd believed. Yet how could I? I'd seen her throat torn open. What idiot would have believed someone could live through that? Was it really as simple as closing my mind to her influence? Or was this child lying to save her?

"I don't believe you."

"I really don't care if you do or not," he said, rising. I stared at him in wonder.

"You don't mean that."

He turned his eyes on me. I shrank back. Oh, but he did mean it—he meant every word he had said, and it shook me to my core.

"Condemn yourself to living in the dark for however long life remains in you. I have done what I can. I've tried, Zigmund. I've offered you the answers you have been searching for. It is up to you to accept them or not. I pray you will for your sake, as well as ours."

My hand closed around air as I reached out to stop him. He had vanished—vanished so quickly, I was left wondering if the entire interview had been a fabrication of my overheated imagination.

The words of a child had shattered all my carefully constructed notions. I remained on my knees, unable to find the will to move.

A vampire would pray for me. I hadn't prayed since my parents died. Nor had I cried. I'd promised, on that night in Greece, that I would never do either again.

Tonight, I was breaking all my vows.

***

There was no moon that night. *Pity*, I thought. The light that would have reflected off the snow piled on the ground would have illuminated our way.

Darkness was to be our companion for the evening. In a way, we were fortunate. Our enemies could sense us. I was pretty sure they could see in the darkness, too. Whatever cover we had now, for however short a time, would be a blessing. Stealth, silence, subtlety—we'd need all three of these in abundance if we had any hope of surviving the night.

"The ruin. It's where my sisters were killed. It's where all the destruction has taken place in this accursed hole. It is there that we will find them."

"No, not there," said Leonora as she walked between Olga and me through the graveyard behind Château Belododia.

"Then where should we head?" asked Nadia in an exasperated tone. I looked at her quickly, reassured when I saw Olga standing behind her, blocking her path. Whatever madness had possessed Nadia the night before had apparently been a onetime occurrence. Since then, she'd treated me like an evil to be tolerated until her part in our play was done. I had caught her several times—mainly whenever Olga was near—staring at me in a way that made me uncomfortable, but I suspected she was just trying to make her sister jealous. I prayed Olga still felt even *that* emotion where I was concerned and counted it a mercy that she was even being sociable to me after that scene in my study.

"The crypt atop the hill," Leonora said. "It's the highest peak in this district and the most suited to what we all think they are planning for Eric."

A sharp intake of breath to my right reminded me of Madelaine's presence. She had refused to give up the staff, and I had stopped trying to coax it from her. I was armed with my own silver staff, not nearly as old or fierce as Florin's wyvern-headed sword, but it had served me well in the past.

"No one is to separate at any time," I said to our group. We'd pulled up at the base of the hill. Faintly, the low murmur of voices floated down from above. Someone was already up there—intoning, chanting—preparing for the ritual that would turn Eric into a replica of Stefan Belododia.

"If things go poorly," I said to Olga, "I want you to get Madelaine out of here."

"I'm not leaving without Eric," Madelaine said, her grip on the staff tightening, her eyes trained on the hill above us. I nodded at Olga, who inclined her head in return. She knew what to do. No matter how strongly Madelaine might try to resist, I would not have her blood on my hands. I'd enough blood on them already.

"Then may God help us. Let us be off."

"There isss no hurry."

The dual snarls that ripped from Leonora's and Olga's throats were somehow less terrifying than the hiss of that quiet voice. Had it really only been a few days since I last heard it? After not hearing it for so long, that voice still had the power to make me feel like my heart would turn to ash if its owner got too close.

I could feel its breath from where I stood. I could smell that stench of decay.

Two red eyes stared out at me from the darkness to my left less than three feet away. Something lumbered out of the shadows. I instinctively brought my staff higher, ready to strike.

Nothing could have prepared me for the sight of the creature in its other form—a wolf as black as pitch and as large as a bear, its fur bristling from the growl that rumbled through its whole body.

Death stalked toward us on padded feet.

And it was not alone.

"Fancy meeting all of you here," said the man who had gone by an assumed name for five hundred years. "A family reunion of the most bizarre variety. Then again, I was never one for conventionality."

"Retrieve Greydanus and get Madelaine out of here," Leonora said to Olga. She was crouched down on all fours, the fur already half retracted into her flesh, coating her limbs and soldering to her body like armor. In the time it took me to blink, she had retaken the form I had come to believe she was most comfortable in, that of an enormous white wolf. Constantinos's eyes narrowed, crinkling at the edges. I got the feeling he was pleased by her transformation.

Melika Dannese Lux

"Greydanus is quite safe, trust me. And there is no reason to spirit Madelaine away," Vladec Salei said, studying his nails. "She's already gone."

I looked behind me. Nadia was the only one of us still there, holding the Cross of Istratescu. I shoved my hands in my pockets. I had never given the cross back to her, so how in the world had she taken it off me without my feeling anything?

"You wouldn't give it back to me, so I took it," she said, her eyes downcast.

"Resourceful girl," murmured Vladec Salei.

"You stay out of this!"

"Ssshe-wolf, you have returned to me." The wolf's voice silenced everyone. My hands dropped to my sides. Everything inside me felt limp and lifeless. The creature's voice was still sibilant, still a hiss, yet if it were possible for a hiss to grow cavernous, this one had.

Leonora circled closer, her eyes riveted on her maker.

"How touching," Salei continued, angling himself toward the hill. He was going to make a run for it. I clutched my staff, and he laughed. "That cannot kill me, boy, and you know it."

"Don't call me boy, I'm not a child."

"I've known you since you *were* a child, *boy*. Have you forgotten?"

He stared at me as if he expected me to enlighten him with something I had no memory of. What was he getting at? I never knew him when I was a child.

"If I'd known you, don't you think I would have done something about it? Constantinos is the one I've been hunting all these years. Not you."

"You honestly never knew? Leonora, I'm surprised at you. But then again, I never did tell you, so I cannot cast blame at your feet, er, paws. But Zigmund, honestly. Such a man of science! Such an historian of all things esoteric. How did you never make the connection? How could you possibly be so ignorant of your history?"

I looked to Leonora, who seemed just as bewildered as I was.

"You disappoint me yet again, Zigmund. I should think that in all the years that have passed, you would have figured out what really happened to your grandfather."

I clutched the staff and backed away from him. My mind ricocheted back to the blazing, ransacked study. There was my grandfather's body, slumped back in his armchair, the great gash in his head, the blood dripping from the side of his mouth, the knife stuck into his chest up to the hilt. I had always known there was something wrong with that knife. It was too showy, too amateurish, added as an afterthought.

"Ah, so you *do* remember. That's good. I thought you might, given some time for reflection."

I remembered Grandfather's books and papers smoldering in the blaze his killer had set. There was one paper especially that stood out in my memory—the scrap clutched in his hand that I had torn out and forgotten until now. I'd looked at it fleetingly, searching for a clue, then thrown it on the flames that were devouring half the study. What did that piece of paper matter to me then—then when I was desperate to see if my grandfather still had life left in him, then when I was frantically trying to save the last member of my family?

The script wavered in my mind's eye, the script in my grandfather's strong hand.

Black Sea, Vrykolakas, Constantin...

Constantin. It hadn't been about Constantinos as I had thought, as I'd once believed when it suited my vendetta against the beast who had murdered my parents. Nadia's revelation had soldered the pieces together. I knew why my grandfather had been killed. He'd been on the scent, the *true* scent, long before I even had an inkling of just how intricate Salei's web of deceit really was.

"*You,* Constantin Belododia. *You* murdered my grandfather."

"It took you long enough to figure it out."

Grandfather had known. And he'd been killed for it. My world shifted off its axis as the truth came home.

"He knew too much, he was getting dangerously close to discovering my secrets—my plans for Constantinos and my creation. Your grandfather knew *exactly* why I had chosen a Vrykolakas as my associate. If I committed any crimes, I'd give my real name, *his* name, Constantin...*os*. No one would suspect. But your grandfather, he was smarter than any of you and infinitely more dangerous. He knew of Florin's manuscript, he knew of *me*, he'd discovered what really happened along the Black Sea. So he had to be taken care of. I am sorry."

"Liar."

"You do know me too well, my dear," he said to Leonora.

"My father was dying," she continued. "No one knew it but me. He didn't want to tell you, Zigmund. You were his favorite; he loved you best of us all. He did not have long to live. By the time I found out he'd died, a month had gone past."

"Yes, well, you were otherwise engaged during that month, if you recall."

The wolf that was Leonora looked down at the snow-covered ground. I sensed that she was ashamed of something, but I was not going to learn any more secrets from her now.

"I suppose I owe Con an apology, too, but then again, maybe not. You liked notoriety in those days, old devil. You still do, I think. The crime of Dominic Bianchetti's death in that great conflagration, like all other unexplainable crimes, was blamed on Constantinos. It suited both our purposes. Of course, while Constantinos was busy terrorizing the authorities, I took care of your mother, Zigmund. I'd seen her with that fop of a husband, and I wanted her. I would have done the turning much more delicately than Constantinos, of course, but one must make allowances when one's plans go awry. Still, she owes me a great deal, I assure you..."

"What do you mean?" He was so confident, so cocky.

"*I* was there to save your mother from herself. *I* was the one who saved half of Greece from her destruction. She couldn't control herself in the early days. I taught her how to be...human. I taught her how to feed, to survive, to combat her thirst until the opportune moment arose. So you see, she owes me everything. I think you'd do well to show a little more gratitude."

All of us, even Constantinos, looked bewildered by this statement.

"Especially since your mother gave me Stefan and brought us all back here—completing the circle, you might say."

"What is he talking about?" I demanded of the white wolf beside me.

"I *should* have been a Vrykolakas," Salei rattled on, "but no, the Upyr had to find me first, and I had to make do with the hand I was dealt. We had some good times, old friend, until Leonora came between us. What a plague you were, Con. The Plague of Athens. All those years, whenever a disease hit or a crime went unsolved, they thought it was because of the plague, or the curse of the Night Feeder, but it was you. So smart, taking advantage of superstition like that."

If it were possible for a wolf to preen, Constantinos did so at that moment.

"But in most ways, you were always an animal. He had no refinement," Salei said, speaking to me as though Constantinos was not there. "His methods were effective, undeniably effective, but so, *so* messy. Most of the time, the victims never recovered. Because, you see, Constantinos had no desire to create life."

"He is what he is. He's always been a monster," I said. I ignored the growl that shook the ground as powerfully as a minor earthquake. For the first time in years, I wasn't afraid of the chimera that had haunted my nightmares for so long.

"Quite. I kept my plans apart from Leonora to an extent. She knew I wanted to create a new species, my Corcitura, my hybrid, mongrel vampire nothing could destroy."

"You forget the cross."

"Well, *almost* nothing. It is never good to be *too* immortal, is it? Achilles would have something to say to this."

"Just how old *are* you?" Nadia said. Her eyes were open so wide, I was surprised her eyeballs hadn't fallen out of their sockets.

"High marks for theatricality, dearest. I should think you'd know exactly how old I am, especially since we've had such a lengthy association. I *am* old, but not ancient. Besides which, I was speaking associatively. But back to my point. Mongrel here was fairly easy to persuade. You remember that rash of murders a few years back? No, of course you wouldn't, you were on the run then and quite young."

I took a step toward him. This monologue was beginning to try my patience.

"How many times do I have to tell you that flimsy piece of metal will do you no good?" he asked, tenting his fingers and walking past me, circling me. "They were all women who were murdered. Constantinos never did get over your mother."

"You monster," I snarled.

"Ah, ta-ta, *temper*, Zigmund," he said, placing one long-nailed finger beneath my chin and completely immobilizing me. "Have respect for your elders. Savage beast, Constantinos was, but then I gave him purpose. I cut him a deal, as it were. He would help me create my species in exchange for...visiting rights, you might say. But then things went wrong in a hurry. They always do, don't they? I didn't count on Eric Bradburry. But it all worked out right in the end, after a little detour, which I had too much fun planning, if you must know the truth. I love making people think they are losing their minds. When you've lived for over half a millennium, amusements of a new variety are few and far between. Not that I don't enjoy the perks of my existence. I love blood, I really do, I need it to survive, but it can only sate me so much."

Despite his control over me, I managed to tighten the grip on the staff, which drew his attention.

"You really are a thick-headed imbecile," he said, and this time there was nothing patronizing in his tone.

"Maybe this blade cannot kill you, but there is something that can," I said through gritted teeth. "And, by the way...Florin sends his love."

"*Florin?*" He'd spat out the name so violently that I shook from the force of his voice.

I kept silent, watching his face, glorying in the anger I saw there. But it wasn't just anger. Fear, if only for a second, wavered in those cool, steel eyes.

"How quaint," he said, his voice like acid.

"Yes...and as for what can kill you...Florin wants it back."

"Oh, *does* he?"

"And soon..."

"Then I'm so sorry to disappoint him." For all of a minute, he had been unnerved, vulnerable, exposed, but now he was master of himself again. "It really doesn't matter one way or the other..."

"Why do you keep babbling on like this?" I snapped, cutting him off.

"I should think it is obvious, Zigmund. I'm stalling so that my son can finish the preparations. One more blood sacrifice and my triumph will be secured. And then I'm going to kill you, like I should have done the minute I found out who you were."

"I lost my son once, you're not going to take him from me again."

"Sons, sons, all this talk about *sons!*" he said on a laugh, turning to Leonora and releasing me from his control. "It makes me so grateful to have such a large family. I'm afraid you've all stumbled upon my secrets too late. Even if I die, Stefan is my legacy. He will carry on in my stead."

"I wouldn't count on it..."

"Tut-tut, Zigmund, so *unwise.*"

The staff fell from my hands. The pressure of his eyes as he turned them on me was so fierce that I stumbled where I stood. I struggled to regain my wits, but that feeling of being bashed around the head by a heavy wind remained.

"Well, Constantinos," Salei continued, ignoring me as I finally willed myself to pick up the staff, "I would be lying if I said it has been a pleasure. You provided a service and for that I thank you," he said, bowing.

The wolf's eyes widened in surprise. "We had an arrangement," he growled, advancing on Salei. Why was Leonora still between them? She was shielding Salei. *She was betraying me again.* I saw her eyes focused on

Constantinos. No, she wasn't protecting Salei. She wanted her revenge.

And in her single-mindedness, she would doom us all.

"Mother!"

Saying the word she longed to hear had done nothing to break her concentration. "Silence, Zigmund! You do not understand what I must do!"

"Of course he doesn't," Salei cooed. He was enjoying this more than he had a right to.

"We had an agreement!" the wolf growled again, and suddenly he was standing upright, changed back into the plague-ridden living corpse I knew so well.

"Taking this a bit personally, aren't you, Con?"

"You wouldn't have your creation without me! He'sss half mine. It isss only right that I get to be there for hisss firssst turn."

"Are you blind? Did you not see that lovely, pale creature, the living image of yourself, minus the boils and sores? *That*, my dear fellow, was Stefan's first turn. It's not my fault you missed it."

The beast hissed. Something strange was happening to him. His head began to shake as though he had been stricken with palsy. "He isss half mine," he insisted, stepping closer.

"No, that is where you are wrong. You didn't finish your job. You never do or this little whelp would not be here today," he said, indicating me. "Stefan is more than half mine...he's *all* mine...especially since you'll not be a problem for much longer."

Constantinos's jaw dropped open, looking practically unhinged. "*What?*" he choked, his eyes darting between Salei and Leonora, who had retaken human form. I looked at her, but either she didn't notice me or chose to ignore my alarm.

"It's time we parted ways, old friend. It's time I settled a score."

"That score is not yours to settle, Salei. It is mine."

Salei looked at her almost lovingly. She stood apart from us all, in more ways than one—cloaked in white, her white-streaked black hair streaming out behind her, her skin as pale as moonlight.

"You have finally come into your own," he said wistfully. "Deal with him as you see fit, my love."

Disgust rippled across Leonora's face. She fell to the ground so that I thought Salei's words had struck her dead. By the time I turned to face him, he was gone.

My hands dropped to my sides, the staff striking against my leg.

"Zigmund..."

I looked behind me. Leonora was leaning over the prone body of Constantinos. There had been no scream, there had been no fight.

I knelt beside her, trying to search her eyes, but I could barely see them through the strands of the long dark hair that had fallen over her cheek, shading her face. Her skin was livid, her chest heaving.

I reached for her hand.

Absently, as though I was staring through someone else's eyes, I saw another hand clamped over ours—a hand that looked shockingly like a wolf's foreleg.

That's funny, I don't remember Mother ever turning into a black wolf.

"You cannot kill me. You're not sssstrong enough."

Constantinos's claws wrapped around our wrists, soldering our hands together. I didn't try to struggle free. I held back and not because of the look of sheer triumph on that death's head gloating up at us.

I stared at Mother and she at me. In that look, I knew what she meant for us to do.

"No, Constantinos, you're right. I'm not strong enough."

"But *we* are."

I reached into my pocket with my left hand and drew out the small, silver whistle I'd grabbed before we left my house.

"A whissstle?" he cackled. "What are you going to do, trill me to death? Play until my eardrumssss bursssst?" He tucked his chin and shook with laughter.

"You've always been so sensitive to small sounds. I can't imagine why," I said.

"What do you mean?!" His death's head stilled, his body grew taught. He was all attention now.

"You love being a wolf. I can tell. It is your greatest pride," I taunted. His grip lessened. I felt blood rushing back into my arm. "But there are downsides to being essentially..."

"No, I beg you, *no*!!!!"

"Just an oversized dog."

I pressed my lips to the whistle and blew.

His hand, the only part of him that had transformed, slipped off ours. I kept the whistle between my teeth, blowing for all I was worth. I could hear no sound, but I knew it was working.

Constantinos writhed in the snow, his hands clapped over his ears, his tongue lolling out.

I shifted the staff to my other hand and nodded to Leonora.

Constantinos's screams died in his throat as Mother lunged down on his neck. His bloodshot eyes bulged as I drove the sword into his heart. There would be no regeneration for him this time.

Fur retracted into his arm, turning it pale and scarred again.

I reached out to Leonora, and she slid her palm into mine. Our hands remained joined over the dead body of the murderer of my father, the killer of my mother's mortal life.

We looked down at him in silence. A memory from that dark night came back to me—a memory of how my mother looked when I thought she was dead. Mangled flesh, blood pooling from the wound, near decapitation.

There was nothing near about the Vrykolakas's decapitation. Leonora was much more thorough than Constantinos had been.

I helped her to her feet. "It is over for us, Zigmund," she whispered, slipping into my arms. Her flesh was cold even through the fabric of my shirt. "But it is not over for our friends. Madelaine, Olga, Eric..."

"*Nadia.*"

"Go, Zigmund, I'll follow."

I scrambled up the hill, thinking back to Mother's words—and the words of Vladec Salei, or Constantin Belododia, as I now knew him.

I'd instinctively added Nadia to the list of our friends, but I wasn't sure if she deserved the distinction. *A lengthy association.*

I stumbled, lost my foothold, and regained it all in the time it took me to realize that I had no idea what any of Salei's confession had meant. In a way, I was glad I couldn't waste precious time pondering the imponderable anymore. I had reached my destination.

As soon as I crested the rim of the hill, I wished I could send someone else to take my place.

Eric—it had to be him—lay on a catafalque in the middle of what must have at one time been a stone gazebo. I had talked with this boy once, nearly seven years ago, but the pale consumptive on the stone slab bore little to no resemblance to that young man.

The two figures on either side of the catafalque were mirror images of each another, Salei on the left, his protégé on the right. Stefan Belododia had looked nothing like this when I had seen him break out of a police wagon in London. He had been pale and scrawny and nowhere near as self-confident as he was now. The smirk on his face was a new addition as well, one that I hated immediately. It was the same smile contorting the lips of his mentor.

A bright light shot out from underneath the catafalque. I stumbled back, dazed. The light was as bright as fire, but there could be nothing underneath the stone slab. The hill was solid.

I was wrong. There was just enough space between the catafalque and the light to allow something to emerge.

Fingers stripped of flesh snaked between the crevices. Moans, thousands of moans, filled the air. Soulless, glaring, malevolent eyes stared out at me from that slit in the earth.

I knew what they were planning to do. I knew what that pit contained.

A pit full of Salei's turns. A pit full of vampires.

All anxious to welcome Eric with open arms.

I looked for Nadia, but she wasn't here. I hadn't seen Madelaine until this moment. She stood with her back to one of the pillars, gripping it as though she was afraid to let go. She had a full view of what they were about to do to her husband. Her eyes were feverishly drawn to his body. I feared she had snapped. Any other woman would have turned away by this point. The look in her eyes was too hopeful, too blind to what was about to happen.

Stefan looked down at Eric, stroking the hair back from his forehead as if Eric were a child. "Soon, Brother, very soon. You do not know the great gift you have been chosen for. My first true turn outside my own bloodline. I would not want it to be anyone but you."

"Are you sure about this, my son?"

Vladec Salei, uneasy? This gave me hope, even as my mind reeled at the sight of such an ostensibly young looking man calling Stefan his son. I still did not understand the bond between them, nor did I want to.

"Yes, Father. I've never been surer about anything. Eric will fall to my will. He was always solicitous of me, always willing to recede into the background and let me take the forefront. He will be amenable, Father. It is why he was chosen. He is the last blood sacrifice that you need for your transformation to be complete. He will be our minion, our scavenger, our slave."

"Then we should not wait any longer. It is time, no matter what Florin threatens," Salei spat, his eyes flickering toward me as he reached out and untied the black scarf that had been encircling Eric's neck.

"God, no, please," both Madeleine and I said in unison. There were two small puncture wounds on Eric's neck. I hoped against reason that those were only exploratory bites. He could not be infected, not after all we'd gone through to save him.

"Five hundred years ago, I was saved," Salei said, looking down on Eric's still form. "Now, my son will bestow this gift on you. You have been chosen, Eric, be grateful. You will be part of a race that cannot be destroyed. You will help me to become that which I have dreamed of for half a millennium. We do not need to fear the one who can kill us."

Nadia, where are you?

"The time is now. Embrace your destiny. And help me step into mine."

Like a coward, I wished Madelaine would do something so I did not have to intervene, but how much more could I ask her to give? She had already sacrificed her unborn child.

I stepped forward, drawing Salei's attention again. His eyes bored into me, but he did not lunge. He did not even move. He looked serene, terrible, triumphant.

My stomach heaved at that look. I knew I had failed.

"It is too late. It has already begun. *He* cannot stop us now."

"You will be the strongest of my creations, Eric," Stefan said, completely oblivious to my presence. "Where Olga and Greydanus have failed me, you will succeed."

"Think again, *brother*."

Eric Bradburry's voice sliced through the night, as did the blade of the staff he had been holding beneath him all this time.

The wyvern-headed staff Madelaine had used to kill Ruxandra.

The wyvern-headed staff a ghost was waiting to reclaim.

The silver blade arced through the air and plunged into Stefan's heart. The Corcitura slumped forward, clutching the catafalque.

High marks for theatricality, I thought, hearkening back to his *father's* words. No mere silver sword could kill Stefan Belododia.

"Eric, Eric, defiant to the end. Have we not done all this before?"

There was no fear in Eric's eyes, no regret, only a look that I imagined Berserker warriors must have worn into battle. His mouth was set in a hard, grim line.

"You know you cannot kill me so easily," Stefan said.

"You may be indestructible, but not all vampires are."

"What? *No!!*"

In one fluid motion, Eric ripped the staff from Stefan's chest and swung it against the neck of Vladec Salei.

The blade embedded in the pale flesh, blood suppurating as steel severed artery. Shock twisted those aristocratic features that had bedeviled countless queens, courtiers, and commoners for five hundred years.

Eric, pale and exhausted, tried to rip the blade through Salei's neck, but the blade wouldn't give. It was lodged.

And Vladec Salei was changing.

Horns broke through his scalp and curled down toward his neck. Ashen, pebbled skin stretched across his fingers, wrapping around them and coating his arms. Teeth that had been suavely menacing now grew savage, vicious in their length, protruding over cracked lips. But his eyes were worst of all. Large, red, slit, reptilian. Eyes of a snake, a beast, a monster.

A wyvern that in some grotesque way still had the features of a man.

And as I witnessed this transformation, it was as though the puzzle pieces in my mind finally locked into place. The constant presence of that dragon-headed symbol, the infestation of wyverns around this place, Eric's resistance, Stefan's subjugation, his total disregard for everything he had once held dear, the fiat he had pledged to Salei on his knees.

The last blood sacrifice.

Salei needed all these things to fully come into his own.

Now, eye-to-eye with this spawn of hell, I finally knew what Vladec Salei was.

The living personification of the dragon that lies in wait to devour us all.

And I, for one, was tired of him having so much power.

"I can't do this alone," I heard Eric mutter, his eyes darting about, looking for help.

"Fight it, Father!" Stefan shrieked. "Come into your own!" I felt Stefan's tension. I had to act. I had to help Eric kill this demon that had corrupted so many souls.

I hefted up my staff. *Aim for the heart, drive the blade home.*

"Maddie! I can't do this alone!"

Corcitura

A flurry of black stayed my hand. Shoulder to shoulder with her husband, Madelaine Bradburry wrapped her hands over his and forced the blade clean through Vladec Salei's neck.

The half-man, half-wyvern screeched, reaching up its talons, but there was nothing it could do to stop the sweep of the blade.

I could not turn away. And I did not want to. I watched as the beast shrunk in on itself, retaking the form of Salei. His proud head tumbled to the ground. His body twitched as his hands reached up of their own accord to feel the mangled flesh around the stump of his neck. Nothing could bring him back now.

Nothing was as final as decapitation.

The earth beneath our feet began to shake as the moans of the damned turned to shrieks. "Madelaine, Eric, hold on!" I yelled. I threw my arms around them both, shielding them as light shot up out of the pit and encircled us. Sand whipped against my face, sharp sand that pierced the skin around my eyes.

"Zigmund, shut your eyes!" Madelaine screamed into my chest. "It's not sand, it's glass!"

I pushed their heads down. The whirlwind of fire that surrounded us was so hot, the sand and dirt and pieces of gravel beneath the catafalque had turned to glass. Shards clashed against each other, clinking through the maelstrom of fire. I winced as bits of glass broke from the inferno and hurtled against us, slashing through our clothes. I bent my head and hugged Madelaine and Eric closer, pressing them against me.

I forced my eyes up, peering through the chaos. The roof of the ruin had been blown off. We were in the eye of a giant whirlwind of flames, and that was probably the only reason we were still alive. Nothing could touch us here but the stray bits of glass that had already scarred our hands. Our clothes were unsigned and our skin unburned.

I looked behind me and saw Stefan Belododia in the wall of fire. He was whole, unhurt, staring straight at me. Despite the heat, gooseflesh broke out over my body. He was waiting, glaring. If the fire didn't finish me, he would.

A blinding light as bright as a sunburst streaked through the whirlwind. For one, terrifying second, all I could see was that shocking white light. And then I felt myself being lifted off the ground by a howling, savage wind, fierce as a sirocco. Madelaine and Eric clamped their hands onto my shoulders as I braced myself against the catafalque. The wind ripped my shirt clean off my back.

The vortex shifted. I felt myself being returned to earth. The whirlwind funneled down wildly, rapidly, straight into the earth, sucked back into the pit beneath our feet.

I lifted my head. Bits of glass that had once been sand still hung suspended in the air, then fell to the ground, shattering against the stone floor.

And then everything was silent.

Madelaine raised her head, her eyes searching her husband's face. She pried his fingers from around the staff and threw it to the ground.

"Madelaine?" he asked, as though he couldn't believe she was there.

"I'm here, Eric," she said through her tears. She took his hand and kissed it.

"My saving grace..."

"Your saving grace," she said, catching him as he slumped forward into her arms.

"You came through. I knew you would," he said weakly.

"I promised you, Eric. I promised you," she repeated, kissing his eyes, his forehead, everything.

"You went into hell itself."

"And cut off the devil's head to save you."

"Can you manage?" I asked her.

"This is one burden I am thankful for."

"And it will be the last you ever bear on this earth."

"*Zigmund!*"

I threw my body between Madelaine and the Corcitura as he lunged for her throat. The edge of the stone slammed into my side as Stefan crashed into my back. His fangs snapped at my neck, but I used my body as a shield. I *would not* let him get near Madelaine. I *would not* let him take anything more from her.

Leonora might have been too weak to help me, but there was still another—one I would trust with my life.

"Olga! *Olga!* Get them away!" From the corner of my eye, I saw a figure with black streaked, white-blonde hair canter up the hillside behind me. I ignored the fear in Madelaine's eyes as Olga wrapped her cloak around her and Eric and hustled them away.

I jabbed Stefan in the ribs. He was so enraged with grief, anger, and every other dark emotion that nothing could weaken him.

"You and your theories and your blasted interference!" he shrieked in my ear. I shied away from him, his spittle lashing my face.

"So now you're going to turn *me* into a monster, eh?" I said through my teeth, sucking vainly for air as he pummeled me in the kidneys. Already I felt the blood seeping from my nose and lip where he had raked his nails.

"I have no intention of prolonging your life," he hissed. "I am no longer interested in wasting my gifts. *No*, no more Corcitura will there be on this earth. It is time I became the vampire I was born to be. Father's dream died with him. Now, it is *my* time."

I felt his fangs against my jugular, but the pressure immediately relaxed. Against all logic, I was free.

I fell to the ground, slicing my hands on the bits of glass that were scattered there. I ignored the pain, grateful to still be alive. My vision was still blurred, but my mind was whip-sharp. I remembered that before I'd nearly lost consciousness, I had heard a shriek.

A female shriek. In fact, I heard it still.

Nadia.

I crawled to the ridge and leaned out over the lip of the hill, my fingers brushing against Nadia's. Her nails scrabbled against my hand as she tried to pull herself up and out of Stefan's grasp.

"Nadia, *reach!*" I commanded, stretching, trying to grab her hand. It was no good.

Nadia, cross in hand, tumbled over the edge with Stefan. "Zigmund."

Leonora and Greydanus emerged from the gloom behind me. A light encircled Greydanus's head so that I believed I really had died and he had come to take me into the afterlife. As he got closer, I saw that the glow was being thrown by a lantern he carried in his left hand. If I survived this night, I would have to get my head checked.

"She will not be able to hold him by herself," said Leonora. Thank God she had recovered enough to help me now. "Hurry."

We were halfway down the hill when we heard an inhuman scream. The earth rumbled beneath us, making us slip the rest of the way down. A low moan that sounded more animal than human rose from the tomb-pocked ground.

Leonora grabbed my arm, halting me. "It is finished," she said. Her eyes dared me to tell her it was true. I shook my head, unsure. "He is dead?"

I took the lantern from Greydanus and set off for the graveyard.

She's dead, I thought when I finally reached the spot where Stefan and Nadia lay. Her body was sprawled on the ground, blood staining her face and blouse.

"Nadia," I said. She was not breathing. I put my lips to hers and blew air into her lungs, pushing on her chest, until finally she gasped and threw her arms around me.

"Zigmund," she choked, fingering my arms as though she could not believe I was actually there.

"Concentrate on me," I ordered her, but her eyes traveled to the thing rotting beside her.

The skeleton next to Nadia was blackened and charred. The extreme decomposition must have been an effect of the blood in the cabochon of Florin's cross. But the transformation had happened so quickly. Skin, vital fluids, organs—everything had disintegrated in a matter of minutes.

I lifted the skeleton's arm, studying its bone structure. I had to admit that the frame was much slimmer and smaller in stature than I would have suspected one of Stefan's strength to be. Maybe when the curse was lifted, he reverted to his slight human form. That must have been it.

That *had* to have been it.

"It's over, Zigmund, it's over," Nadia said, nestling herself against my arm.

"You've done it," I said, more shocked than admiring. I still felt uneasy in her presence, and the thought that I had to find some way of providing for her welfare, if only for a short while, did not do anything to make me like her better. I shifted my weight and moved away, trying not to smirk when she stumbled without me to support her.

"Are you proud of me, Zigmund?" she asked sharply. I did not look at her. I was too busy studying the skeleton's bones.

"You've saved us all," I said uneasily.

"Then I am glad."

"So, you have your prize after all?" Startled, I pivoted on my heels to see Olga standing behind me.

I hadn't realized Nadia had sidled up against me. "Not now, Olga, please," she whispered, turning her head into my arm. "Can you not let me be happy for once?"

"Of course, as long as you're not happy with *him*."

"That suits me fine," I said, rising, once more causing Nadia to stumble.

"Olga, we need to talk."

She waved me away and bent to look at the skeleton.

I sighed as I wandered away from the body. I needed to think. All my life had seemed to be leading up to this moment. Now that it was over, I felt somehow less alive— hollowed out, like an empty shell. And what had we to show for our efforts? I'd nearly been savaged by a vampire; Madelaine had lost a baby, but had regained her husband. And Leonora had finally tasted vengeance...and so had I.

And now I had Olga, or hoped I would soon enough. She was living on a border between life and death, something I had been doing these past thirty years. Her nature would have seemed an insurmountable barrier to me a week ago, but not after what we'd been through since then. She'd need to be convinced I was no longer troubled by her threading the needle with the otherworld, and I would have to convince *her* not to be scrupulous on my behalf. This was my choice. I was finally mature enough to make it.

And then there was the matter of Nadia and what she had tried to do to me. Olga might not believe me now, but I would do everything I could to make her see that I was blameless. I was not going to let that minx come between me and the only woman I knew I could ever love.

"Zigmund, this is not right."

Olga's voice seemed to come to me from across a divide.

"What?" I asked, looking back blearily.

"This skeleton. It can't be my brother's."

"Of course it is," Nadia said. "Are you calling me a liar? After what I've done, you have the nerve to suggest I didn't kill him? He nearly killed *me*! You're more damned than I thought."

A snarl tore from Olga's throat, but I was between her and her sister in an instant. I leaned down to examine the bones again, but something caught my eye and drew my attention away from the body.

I hadn't seen the cross lying in the dirt bedside the skull. The blood cabochon was smashed and the ironwork had been charred up to where the glass used to be, as though it had been melted by fire. The metal would not have been so altered if the cross hadn't been plunged into the Corcitura's flesh.

"This skeleton is Stefan's, without a doubt," I said, willing myself to believe my own words. Certainly it was. It *had* to be. Everyone else was dead, and Stefan was nowhere to be found.

"Exactly as I said," Nadia persisted. She pushed past me and headed off in the direction of the château.

"Follow her," I said to Leonora. She linked hands with Greydanus and the two of them trailed along in Nadia's wake. I watched their receding forms, feeling satisfied when Nadia turned around and give a little gasp as she saw that my mother and brother were no longer human. *Thank God for wolves*, I thought grimly.

I gathered the cross into my hands, studying its charred and broken edges, trying to make sense of everything and failing miserably. How could I be sure I hadn't been mistaken? Was Nadia the right one? Of course she was. She was the only untainted member of that family left.

"Zigmund..."

The warning note in Olga's voice made my stomach lurch. I knelt beside her, leaning over to study the golden charm she cradled in her hands.

"Why would this skeleton be wearing a wyvern-headed necklace?"

I had no answer to her question. Somewhere, deep within me, I had the feeling that Nadia had betrayed us all.

Epilogue

Cologne, Germany: 13 February 1895

"*A* package has come for you, Zigmund. And some letters, too."

I looked up from the files strewn across my desk to see Nadia carrying the parcel and two envelopes toward me. A month had passed—a month of uncertainty, of being stuck in limbo—and *still* she was here. And I couldn't for the life of me see a way out.

"Who are they from, Nadia?"

She ran her fingers along the desk's edge. "Obviously someone whom you gave this address to, dear. And there are only a few souls who know we have settled in Cologne."

We, there it was again. That word that had no basis in reality, at least not where I was concerned. *We* had come back to Cologne; *we* had settled in the house directly across from the one I'd been born in; *we* were making a life together. According to Nadia, *we* were to be married the second I realized I loved her.

The truth of the matter was that I hadn't been able to think of a way of getting rid of her. Admittedly, Nadia was better company to me than no one, as horrible as that logic sounded to me now. She would have to fill the void Olga left. But not in that way, *never* in that way.

Until I decided what to do, I let Nadia keep her wild notions, while I continued with my work and counted the few blessings that were still left to me. First among these was that none of my parents' friends were alive to question Young Fertig's strange appearance and cohabitation with a woman being passed off as my distant cousin. Never mind that she looked nothing like me, clung to me in a most un-cousinly way whenever she forced me to take her out of the house (which only happened on Market Day, thank God), and did not speak a lick of German, nor Italian, which would have come in handy. Then at least I could have laid a claim to my mother's side of the family.

The times—probably at least fifty a day—when I'd broached the subject of Nadia returning home, I'd gotten three differing reactions, depending on whatever mood my houseguest was in. The chief argument was that she claimed to love me and wished to marry me when I came around to the idea. Therefore, it made no sense for her to take herself off, especially, she hinted darkly, since her virtue was already tarnished beyond repair in the eyes of the townsfolk.

Secondly, how could I even think of throwing a defenseless girl out into the world to fend for herself? I must be a beast more heinous than the creatures I'd dedicated my life to hunting down. There had been much haranguing, hysterics, childlike tantrums, and threats to do herself harm in conjunction with argument number two. I'd found her in my study three days later with my stolen razor pressed against her wrist. Thank God the walls of this house were thick enough to hold in the abuse she hurled at me when I took the razor away. And thank God, too, that I had absolutely no servants to spread tales through the city. A nonexistent retinue was a safe retinue, at least until I could figure out what to do with the pariah who styled herself the chatelaine of my home.

Nadia's moods were as varied as the seasons. When she was feeling pious, I'd be reminded that it was my fault she was even here in the first place, since I was the one who had kidnapped her from her homeland. But in the same breath she would forswear any desire to return to the "wild and savage land" of her birth. Romania held too many horrible memories for her. I was also conveniently forgetting that the tavern I'd found her in had burned to the ground, a calamity she would no doubt be blamed for, since she was seen (by whom, she never said) fleeing the scene. If she hadn't been ostracized from society before, she would most certainly be now.

For all her arguments, all her histrionics and pledges of love, what had stayed my hand in the end was the unnatural fierceness and animosity with which I'd caught her staring at me so many times. Nadia was secretive to begin with, but ever since she'd come here, our roles had reversed. She was supposedly my "guest," yet I'd never felt like anything but a prisoner in my own home. And though I did not want to believe it, I wasn't sure I'd seen the last of her brother. I'd brought the bones back to Germany with me. They were in a strongbox I'd hidden underneath my bed. Until I could decide for certain that those bones were his, and that Nadia wasn't hatching some diabolical plan to bring her brother back from the dead, she would stay put and like it.

"Certainly there must be some markings on them?" I prodded, turning my thoughts back to the present.

"There is no address on any of them." The statement was said in a murmur, yet there was an edge to her voice that put me on guard.

"Who sent the letter you have not relinquished, my *dear*?" I fought to keep my voice level, but failed. My eyes were riveted on the note she had nearly crushed between her fingers.

Say it, Nadia, say it. I'd waited for this moment since that night. She'd promised to write. I'd been expecting it. Why, then, did I fear to read her words?

"Madelaine Bradburry."

The name shattered the air between us as thoroughly as if it had been a suit of armor crashing against the floor. I reached out my hand and snatched the letter from Nadia before she could do any further damage to it.

"I've set some tea out on a table by the fire. I think you should drink it *now*."

A hint of defiance lifted her eyebrows. The letter felt like a burning coal in my hands, but I would not open it with her watching me with those cat eyes I had once thought were beautiful.

"As you wish," she said, and shuffled over to the wing chair near the hearth. Trust was another thing that had not blossomed between us this past month. The night her brother died had seemed too well-constructed, too easy. I believed Nadia knew more than she'd concealed beneath that mask of innocence.

I turned my attention to Madelaine's letter, placing the other one on top of the book-shaped package. Madelaine came first. I owed her precedence after what she had given up for all of us.

My Dear Friend,

By the time you receive this, Eric and I will already be settled into our new home. Where exactly that is, it is not in me to reveal, hence the absence of an address on this letter. Just know that we are safe and happy, for the time being. I find it difficult to entirely dispel the feeling that all has been for naught, but when I look at Eric and see how he has improved, I take heart that our efforts were not in vain.

My one consolation is that we escaped before Stefan had the chance to exert his influence any further. Had we been under that pernicious influence even one hour more, Eric would now be dead or worse. Thank God you were right. Those marks were only test bites. Only. I cannot help but laugh at that, at what I have been reduced to—counting as a blessing that a monster only attacked my husband a little.

Though the five of us did so much, united as we were in our mutual cause, none of it would have been possible without Nadia. We owe our lives to her. I don't pretend to doubt her courage, and yet I wonder...could any of us have proved equal to the task of killing the one we loved most in the world as easily as she? Olga told me that they always seemed somehow fey, somehow more than just brother and sister. Maybe she was right.

Corcitura

I pray you will not let her become familiar with the contents of this letter. In fact, I pray you have found a way to rid yourself of her in the most delicate manner, giving no harm to either of you. But I fear that if you let her see what I have written here, the thoughts I am speculating on, you would be putting yourself in danger. I write these words only for your eyes. Take them as a warning. Be watchful.

Enough of Nadia. The time will come for you to decide what to do on that front, if you haven't decided already. I hope for your sake and Olga's that you have.

And now I must thank you, Zigmund, for believing me before the end. Thank you for saving my life. Have you saved yours? I pray you'll see in time what is confronting you. I pray you'll act before you find yourself in a situation you have no hope of extricating yourself from.

My thoughts overtake me. I apologize. I cannot seem to focus on what I am truly writing to tell you. I must get back to my world, Zigmund, but it is hard, so hard, for both of us.

Eric thanks you. He has not forgotten you, though his memory of that night is sketchy at best, but he does remember that we killed that creature. That makes two he and I have killed, Zigmund. But Eric found the half-dead body of a third. I fear for his mind if he continues to dwell on those thoughts, yet how can he ever rid himself of them? They are seared into his mind. And my mind as well. I told him everything, as he told me. For most of what he went through, I was not there, but hearing it was just as bad. I cannot forget now.

And I've gone off again. Forgive me. The doctors say Eric is recovering beautifully, though their diagnosis is only based on physicality. I don't think he will ever be the same Eric Bradburry on the inside. I am thankful that we are safe for the time being, and Eric is happy in our new home—and I am happy to have my beloved returned to me. Perhaps in time we will be able to see you. I know we would both dearly love to see you again, absent the strain of the days we spent together...

I wish I had more time, Zigmund, or perhaps more courage to tell you what I fear outright, instead of couching my suspicions in shadow and secrecy. But the hour grows late, and Eric needs me. And I suspect that if you have not already become aware of everything I myself have come to know as the truth, Olga and your mother and brother will help you see it in time...and that time will be soon in coming. For how can it not be when you have been with her every waking hour of the day? She is bound to be unguarded at one moment or another. Then you will have the entire story, the whole affair laid bare before your unbelieving eyes. But I have said too much already.

I will write again, I promise, as soon as our lives start to regain a semblance of normalcy. I have great hopes that our futures will be free of any more tragedy than we have already experienced. But somehow, I don't think this is possible, either for you or me.

Hopefully, I am wrong, but I have seen too much of the darker side of human nature to make me believe otherwise.

I am and always will remain,
    Your faithful friend,
      Madelaine Bradburry

I stared at the letter for several minutes. There was no denying Madelaine's implications, especially since they dovetailed into my own, the suspicions I'd thought of over and over during the last thirty days. What was she trying to tell me? Nothing that I hadn't already thought of myself.

I glanced toward Nadia. Firelight danced across her profile, making her features seem sharper than they normally were, more hawk-like.

Her eyes had closed. Sleep had finally overtaken her, or had it? Dark suspicions clouded my mind. She'd been far too adamant that she couldn't leave me, far too willing to put everything else on hold to make sure I was "settled," as she said. I suspected she was trying to whittle down my resolve, maybe hoping that I would warm to her given her constant presence. If I'd learned anything within this month, it was that I had been a fool to ever trust her in the first place.

I reached for the next letter. This one had no name. I was beginning to wonder, as I drew the leaves from the envelope, at the state of the German postal service, but then I saw the salutation and could not blame the mail carriers at all. There was subterfuge of a vampiric nature at work here.

My darling son,

For thirty days I have lived by the hands of the clock. For thirty days I have been missing you. We have been missing you. Your brother was more affected by that night than I thought he would be, but not for the reasons you would expect. Not because his father and grandfather were killed.

I have begun to understand things about Greydanus that were hidden from me until now. I have begun to hope that he can be the one to put an end to this.

Do not doubt what you have just read, Zigmund. I have not taken leave of my senses. I meant to write that. This is not over.

I have my reasons for not writing my feelings down, Nadia's presence being first amongst them. I hope she has not poisoned your mind during this month. I hope she has not turned you against Olga. She went away for you, for us, because she, too, knew the night of 13th January did not mark the end. I hope she has discovered what she was seeking, for all our sakes.

Think back to that night, Zigmund. It is not a very difficult task. I have not been able to strike the memories of that night from my mind, and I believe I never will. But think now. Remember the scream. There was something inhuman about it. And by inhuman I do not mean vampiric. I know what my kind sound like when they are in agony, and that scream did not come from a vampire.

There is a farm on the outskirts of the château, down the hill. I've been back there since then, to look at the place I was incarcerated in, the place where your brother was born. The house is the same, though emptier. All those souls set free. And the farm... I spoke with the man down there. He seemed less inclined to fear me than he did a month ago. Zigmund, one of the farmer's prize bulls was killed that night and not because the farmer desired meat for supper. I do not need to write any further. I believe you can infer what that means.

Nadia cannot speak Italian, of this I am thankful. I hope you remember the little I taught you before we were parted. Know this:
  Guardare per la mia venuta. La vedrò di nuovo...presto.
    ~Your Mother

My hand shook as I set the letter down. Of course I remembered Italian. The language was a part of me, as I was a part of her and always would be.

Watch for my coming. I will see you again...soon.

Sooner than soon from the tone of that letter. She was here, I could feel her.

Her fears had been my own. That hellish night rushed back to me. The charred iron of the cross, the smashed blood cabochon. Voices raised in anguish, an animal scream...

An animal scream.

The words beat against my skull. I'd always known there had been something wrong with that scream. I'd gone against years of fieldwork, years of knowing those creatures for what they were, all because I'd been too stubborn to face the possibility that Stefan had somehow survived.

The structure of that skeleton and that wyvern-headed necklace were more pieces of the puzzle that I could not explain, though I had tried like a madman to discount them.

I glanced over at Nadia again and saw that she was looking at me through half-closed lids, smiling. Was that smile a grin of triumph or of simple contentment that I hadn't thrown her out on her rear yet? I had kept Nadia at hand because I didn't trust her. But there was more to it than that. Somewhere in the back of my thoughts, I'd known that if I'd gotten rid of her, *he* would have come, though I'd almost deluded myself into thinking the cross had obliterated him from this earth. And she, cunning viper that she was, must have clung to my side because she knew her brother was not through with any of us.

So, had the cross been a lie? Maybe its vaunted powers were nothing more than a fabrication. I thought back to Florin and that manuscript. Was it all an elaborate hoax? Of course not. I had spoken to the author himself. There was something deeper at work here. Either the cross was a sham, or Nadia had deliberately destroyed it.

I reached for the package. The brown paper wrapping came off easily in my hands, given that someone had gotten to it first. My eyes flicked toward Nadia again, but she'd turned her attention to the fire.

Which was just as well. If she didn't already know the contents of the package, my face would have given the game away once I discovered what the wrapping concealed.

Florin's manuscript.

How was this possible? He had been adamant about the book not leaving the confines of the church. To think I was holding in my hands the book that had been hidden from me, the tome I had only been allowed to hold for a few precious minutes...

In my fever of excitement, I'd let my fancies run rampant. This was not Florin's manuscript. This book was much less thick than the one I'd held in Sighisoara and nowhere near as finely tooled.

I ran my fingers over the scratched brown leather of the cover, feeling particles coming off on my hand. Carefully, I tilted the book up, keeping my eyes on Nadia for any sudden movements, any sign that she was aware of what I was doing.

Something fell against my leg. When I looked down, I saw a small, yellowed envelope resting on my knee. I set the book down and picked up the envelope, examining it. There was nothing on it but a name.

My name.

I broke the seal and slid the pages from the envelope. The handwriting was not familiar, but I knew it was from her. She was the only one left of the triumvirate of women I'd come to trust.

I wasn't expecting any modifiers of endearment. That was not my Olga's way. The one word scratched onto the top of the sheet meant more to me than any sentimental appellation.

Zigmund,

And how have you been this past month? I trust well, if my sister has not put an end to your life yet. I know we didn't part on the best of terms, but I've had much time to think since I saw you last. I have forgiven you, Zigmund, because I know you could not be as treacherous as Nadia would have me believe. I see now that I was mistaken. It was wrong of me to misjudge you so harshly. Will you now forgive me? I was blinded by other emotions the day you asked me to marry you.

I set the letter down, feeling acute pain in my chest as I recalled the memory. Olga, remote and cloaked in black as usual, holding herself away from me. Cold, distant, undead. I couldn't accept it, and I told her so, but she would not be dissuaded. I'd compared her to marble once and statue-like was how she'd remained. Deaf to my pleas, my tears, my declarations of love. Nothing I'd said had changed her mind.

But now I had reason to hope. She'd forgiven me and asked for my forgiveness in return. What did that mean? Was this merely a letter acknowledging the fact? To let me know there was no longer any ill-will between us? Was that the extent of it? Was that all I'd ever be entitled to? That seemed a cold response, even from her. I sensed the meaning behind her words, however unemotional she tried to make them. My heart raced as I read on.

I should tell you that I've seen your mother and my nephew many times since the night of 13th January. They've been my eyes and ears in Prague and Romania. Leonora would never tell you for modesty's sake what her help to me has meant. And still she cannot believe you are alive, even after seeing you in the flesh, holding you, caressing your face like I once did. She does not like to talk about her intelligence, Zigmund, or her strength, but she has both brains and courage in spades. I'd have been lost without her and Greydanus and so would you. I hope you realize this now.

You once asked me if I would let "death" be a barrier between us forever. I can say, now that I am far away, now that I do not have you near to persuade me...I can say with conviction that no, I will not. I <u>cannot</u>. Not after what I've seen cold dispassion do to so many lives, not after I've spent countless hours wondering what I am missing being parted from you. I refuse to be a shade. I refuse to be a memory to you, Zigmund. I'm tired of living in darkness. I'm through with denying what I am. For as long as mortal life allows us, I will bind myself to you. You accepted me unconditionally that night. It's time I return the favor.

Which is why I've stayed away. A hundred times I've made up my mind to return to you, and a hundred times I've talked myself out of this plan, but I cannot wander in the dark anymore. This month has been a month of searching, both within and outside of myself. I knew there were things Nadia had hidden from us, possibly things she didn't even understand herself. Nadia is a fanatic, Zigmund. She sold her family, she sold us, all of us—my damned vampiric sisters, me, our brother—to save herself. She sold her soul to save her body. God have mercy on her.

I have threaded the void between the living and the dead yet again, Zigmund. The book that is now in your possession came from a vault even deeper than the one we were shown. Florin held nothing back this time, especially when he saw that it was I who had returned to discover the true means of lifting this curse that had been laid on our family for five hundred years. Now it must all make sense to you—the hiddenness of the place, the fog swirling away from me as if it were afraid...the secrecy. That small patch of land was stuck in the shadow world for half a millennium until one of this cursed family went against the call of the blood and proved their worth. I learned much during my time with him, Zigmund, the most important thing being that Vladec Salei's precious plans were not foolproof.

In the journal are all the details, all Florin's research into the history of his battle against not Vladec's creations, but Vladec Salei himself, or Constantin Belododia, as I now know him to be named. I thought I was so knowledgeable about my history, but it turns out I was mistaken about that, among other things. My ancestor was named after his birthplace, his true birthplace, not where the vampire turned him when he was nineteen. It turns out he was from the Black Sea, but not the Russian side like he wanted us to believe all this time. He was born on the Romanian side, in Constanta. No matter how hard he tried, he could not deny the blood, our blood, the blood of the Romany people. Sooner or later, we would have figured it out. I hope he knows I found out his secret. I hope that knowledge tortures him even more than the flames of hell.

Forgive me for that. I got sidetracked with my thoughts of revenge. You've seen what that can do to me. You know firsthand how obsessed with vengeance I can be. But back to the book. Though slim, it contains not only the truth about Salei's history, but also all Florin's suppositions on the nature of the Corcitura, the beast we now know Salei had longed to create since almost immediately after his turning. Maybe it was the Upyr's desire, or maybe it was all my ancestor's idea, I don't know. Florin is quiet on that point. But on the nature of the cross, the true nature, the one that he didn't share with anyone, the one that would have pieced all your theories together—he keeps nothing hidden.

I learned things about Nadia, too, because of what I read of the cross. Why do you think she was so terrified to let it out of her possession? Once Salei was dead, she would have no reason to fear. She became brazen, defiant. I have a feeling she only consented to do whatever she did for him to trap him in the end. I highly doubt she would have killed him herself. Cross or no cross, she was not suicidal. Nadia always did love to delegate. She must have known that Salei's days were numbered, especially after Eric came into the picture. When she saw Madelaine and Eric cut off Salei's head, she destroyed the cross, the only thing that had been protecting her from him until then.

Why do you suppose she was the only one of us who was never turned? Because she had the cross's protection. The cross was charmed in that way. The combined blood of Salei, Constantinos, and Florin most of all, served as a shield against Salei's power. He could not touch her as long as she was the cross's keeper.

Yet something puzzled me, as I know it did you, for you never were able to figure out the science behind that blood cabochon. Where did Constantinos fit in all of this? And how could the cross kill the Corcitura if the cabochon only contained the blood of St. Devil's Bane and Vladec Salei? That mixture would not kill it, since there was still one party's blood missing. Without the Vrykolakas, there wouldn't be a Corcitura. So how did Nadia get Constantinos's blood?

I've been somewhat of a world traveler in the last month, Zigmund. And I have Eric Bradburry to thank for putting me onto this line of thought. He—though weak and not himself at all—Madelaine, Leonora, Greydanus, and I visited Greece and did some not so savory investigative work, the details of which I will spare you. Suffice it to say that even though the cross was first stolen by our father, Nadia re-stole it before his death when she learned that Vladec Salei was the one she was about to be sold to. Lucky fool that she was, she stumbled across Constantinos when he and Salei were passing through Brasov, and it was there that she collected his blood. I do not want to think what she had to give up to get it, but she is cunning. She's preserved herself well. But there are other ways of satisfying a Vrykolakas. She must have made a trade. I'm almost certain she gave Constantinos a bit of her blood in exchange for his.

Armed with this weapon, and as the last surviving untainted member of our family, she thought, as did almost everyone, that she was the only one who could kill our brother. But she couldn't have killed him, though she possessed what everyone thought of as the only thing that could kill the Corcitura. She never had any intention of killing the only person she loved, in her own fanatical way. She sacrificed him to Salei, yet she loves Stefan more than she loves herself. It was madness to think she'd ever be amenable to our wishes. But for all her precaution, for all her cleverness, Nadia was wrong. The cross cannot kill our brother.

I imagine your brow furrowing, your eyes narrowing then opening in astonishment as you take in what I've just said. I long to be near you now, to see that look on your face in person; it is one of my favorite remembrances of you. I want to be by your side to fight this, Zigmund, to take your hand in mine and not care what the world says about us loving each *other. But I must wait. There is more you must know, more we both must do before that dream can become a reality.*

Think back to that fog as I tell you this. It seems my dear ancestor's ploy had a chink in its armor. A divine chink. Florin told me it was part of the agreement. When he killed himself, Florin incurred the wrath of God, so God let that devil Salei (I cannot stomach using my family's name to refer to that demon) have free reign over that place of secrecy for five hundred years. If the creature's descendants were to choose to fight against the thirst that consumes all vampires and find this place before the five hundred years were up, then the curse would be lifted, the fog would disperse, and knowledge would dawn.

I pity Nadia for her ignorance, for her misguided loyalty, for her fatalistic devotion to the boy who killed for her. She really had no chance. I know you would say, as you've said before, that we all have a chance. I believe you are right. We all have a chance at redemption. We all have the freedom to choose to put an end to the destruction of our fathers, if only we have the courage to do it.

If she had known the truth, maybe things would have been different for her. Maybe she would have joined us, believed us, believed me. She was against me from the start. I wonder if it was because she knew the real reason or if it was just her natural animosity for me coming to the fore. I still can't imagine she knew that you <u>cannot</u> be untainted to kill the beast. Her purity of blood was her entire argument. She couldn't have known the truth. The greatest desire of the Corcitura is to create life, or as near to life as you can call what we are. Its desire to play God is boundless. It needs to create replicas of itself, clones, to feel whole, however abominable and unnatural its progeny might turn out to be.

Although I broke the curse on that fog-shrouded patch of Sighisoara, I was mistaken, too, Zigmund. I cannot kill him either, though I was so sure of my power. I was too blind to understand that it is not enough to just be tainted. You must be of the blood, of his blood. The creature's greatest desire is its downfall, because you see, Zigmund, the only thing that can kill the Corcitura...

"Is its child."

"You have finally fitted all the pieces of the puzzle together, Zigmund. I congratulate you."

The touch of cold flesh seeped through the fabric of my shirt. I groaned as the hand squeezed my shoulder, my entire arm going numb. When I tried to flex my fingers, I gritted my teeth in pain; it felt like there were chips of ice in my joints.

What had he done to me?

I slid lower in my chair as his hand clamped down tighter and tighter, knife-sharp nails digging into my skin. Absently, I thought that if I lived through this encounter, I'd have scars to match the marks on my face that this creature's Grecian father had gifted to me.

"You must have known I would return for you in my own time. I was a wreck after that night. I needed time to think things over, to reassess my strategy. I'd been betrayed, Zigmund, did you know that? Had your little brain figured that out yet? It turns out my father didn't trust me as much as I thought. I've had extraordinarily bad luck with fathers, haven't I? Constantinos wasn't there long enough to finish what he started, so I cannot turn into a wolf at will, though I do have this lovely reminder of my Greek papa," he said.

I felt the prick of his barbed tongue against my skull.

"Ironic, isn't it? In all other ways, I am exactly like Vladec Salei. I didn't think the monster's death would affect me so. I didn't think I'd be so *weak*. I thought all those disgusting traces of humanity had been sucked out of me. And although I never cared about Constantinos and would have ripped his head off myself if given the chance, still, one must account for the loss of *both* of one's fathers in a single night. *Thank you for that.*"

I tried to jerk away as he stabbed his nails deeper into my skin. Frantically, I looked toward Nadia, my eyes pleading with her, begging her to help me. I'd lost the power to speak. All I could manage was a pitiful whimper, which did not move that hardhearted witch at all.

"Oh, Zigmund, you look so pathetic," she said, laughing like a maniac. I'd been a fool, an absolute imbecile to take pity on her. Was it her fine eyes that had bewitched me? No; I knew I did not love her, nor ever had. She might not have been a vampire, but she was somehow more damned to me now than the monster that was trying to purge me of my blood.

"Nadia's always been my right hand. She got me into this, and she got me out. She deserves a reward for what she's done, and I intend to give it to her, as soon as I'm through with *you*."

"What are you laughing about?" Nadia demanded. I might not have been able to speak, but the weak, choking sound coming from my throat was indeed a laugh, which shocked me. There'd been something horror-stricken in Nadia's face when Stefan had spoken of his gift that had made me giddy, and I couldn't say why.

"Pay no attention to him, sister. This is the reaction some of his kind have before the end, when they know they do not have much time left. You truly are an idiot where women are concerned," he said, his breath coming quick and fast, his words shooting into my ear. I'd lost all will to fight. I didn't even care that I was being taunted. All I wanted was for it to be over and done with. "Did you think she loved you, Zigmund? Did you really believe she stayed with you all this time because she couldn't take care of herself? What a gallant fool you are!"

He allowed himself a laugh. I found that I could move a fraction of an inch, so I turned my head and faced him. I wanted the hatred in my eyes to be the last thing he saw before he killed me.

"Oh, don't look at me so wrathfully, old son. I'm only speaking the truth. It's no secret. How could anyone ever possibly love *you*? How could you even *think* Olga would give you a second thought? Pathetic weakling. No one is coming for you now. You're still just a child, all alone, defenseless. This is what should have happened to you all those years ago. Your mother has abandoned you again, Zigmund, and now Olga has, too."

"Never presume to speak for me, *brother*."

The words did not register, but Nadia's shriek did.

"Surprised to see me again, Nadia?"

Her milk-white hand lay atop my other shoulder. Instantly, I felt Stefan's hold weaken. Blood flowed through my paralyzed limbs. I could move again. I tried to rise to my feet, but did not yet have the strength.

"Stay, Zigmund." Her voice warmed my blood. Every second that passed made me stronger. Seeing her after I'd been so certain I'd never set eyes on her again was more bracing than a shot of brandy.

"That's right," Stefan said, backing away from us, edging closer to Nadia. "Protect *him*. You cannot kill both of us, Olga. One of us will get to him, and you will have failed. And how do you expect to kill me? There is only one of you, however powerful you might fancy yourself. Nadia or I will finish him off. Make your choice, Olga. You cannot have it both ways. One of us is going to die. You don't have the power to stop us."

"But I do."

The sound of that voice destroyed whatever lethargy remained in my bones. Feeling came back into my jaw. I could talk.

"Greydanus, help me to rise." I leaned down and took my brother's tiny hand in mine. His grasp was firm, strong, unafraid.

"A family reunion. How charming. Nadia, sister dear, you remember my *wife*? And my little son, how dreadful it is to see you again."

Leonora stood behind me, supporting me. "It seems the tables have turned, Stefan," I said with effort. My jaw muscles were still not working properly. I feared my threat sounded hollow; he did not seem at all intimidated. I must have looked a sight, ripped and bloodied and unable to speak a sentence without halting every few syllables to make my meaning clear. He was so unmoved by the presence of Leonora, Olga, and Greydanus. I couldn't understand why, until he grabbed Nadia, and I knew all too well what he planned to do.

"Stefan, what are you doing?" she said frantically, trying to pull out of his hands, which were clamped over her arms, pinning them behind her. "Let me go. Brother, *please*, what are you doing?!"

"I can't let you go, Nadia," he said, his voice deathly calm. "I can't let you go on in this state."

"What s-state? Why c-can't you?" Her voice had been brittle, choked with phlegm, hitched on that *c*. Her eyes roved over his face, searching it for a warmth, a kindness he hadn't possessed in years. Olga might have argued her brother had never possessed it at all.

"Aren't you grateful to me?" Nadia asked. Her eyelids fluttered furiously as tears streamed down her face. Her throat spasmed convulsively as she tried and failed to swallow. I could sense her terror almost as strongly as I felt Stefan's hatred for her.

"Oh, yes, I'm grateful for your love, but not your interference. You never wanted the gift. You sacrificed so much to safeguard your mortality."

"Please, Stefan, no, no," she whimpered, pleading with him, her chest heaving as she fought to keep from screaming.

I couldn't bear it. Not even Nadia, who had betrayed us and exposed us to her brother's rage, deserved to die like this.

"Stay back, Zigmund, unless you want to die, too." Olga slid her hand in mine, pulling me back with a mere tug.

"Olga, she's your sister."

"It's too late. It's already begun. The best we can do now for Nadia is to free her from what Stefan is about to turn her into."

"I'm afraid all your efforts, all your self-preservation, have been in vain."

"Stefan, remember what we meant to each other, please, Stefan, *please*!"

He held her in his iron grip, immune to her cries, her tears, her pleas for mercy. "Never make deals with the devil, dearest. He always comes to collect in the end."

"*Stefan, no! No!!!*"

I looked away. I'd no desire to witness the horror of the scene and add it to the spate of gruesome memories already burned into my brain. The sound of his teeth ripping into the soft flesh of her neck was enough evidence of the savagery occurring less than ten feet away from me. A strangled gasp escaped Nadia. I forced myself to turn in her direction. I thought she was dead. She'd gone ashen, lying limp in Stefan's arms. His mouth was still affixed to her neck, his fangs completely embedded in her veins, his tongue gouging deeper and deeper, enlarging the wound. The blood loss was immense. I'd never seen a creature as obsessed with blood as this one. Even for a vampire, he was taking an inordinate amount of pleasure in feeding off his sister. Her eyes stared vacantly at the ceiling as her body lurched with each successive bite.

How much blood did he need? He must have sucked all the life out of her by now. Her cheeks had shrunken in a matter of seconds. The skin underneath her eyes had wrinkled and hollowed. She looked like a corpse.

A growl signaled the end of the orgy as Stefan pulled his head back, his barbed tongue licking the remnants of viscera from his chin. He'd gripped her bare forearms so tightly that her flesh had turned blue from the pressure of his fingers.

She had to be dead. He'd loosed his fury on her. He'd overdone it. She had been too weak.

He tilted her forward, her auburn hair shielding her face. She lurched, but he held her firm, as though he were not yet done with her. I winced at the sight. The only thing that was supporting her was the man standing behind her—the brother who had just murdered her.

"You killed her," I said. *What a profound observation, Zigmund*, I thought to myself.

Stefan glared at me, his lips twisted into a terrifying smile. "Patience."

The fingers on Nadia's hands began to twitch. Slowly, haltingly, like an automaton that has not been oiled in a generation, she straightened her back. A second before, her head had almost been wrenched around. Now, bones creaked and settled as she fitted her skull back into place. Her hair slid back, parting, revealing a face that was chalk white and slack jawed. She looked more like a revenant than any vampire I'd ever come up against.

Her lids fluttered. Lashes rose, unveiling eyes that glowed greener than they had been in life.

"I give you my latest creation," Stefan said, stepping aside. "Go forward, my lovely. Make me proud. You deal with her, and I'll deal with *him*."

"As you wish."

The thing that had been Nadia smiled at her brother, smiled with a mouthful of fangs so jumbled it was a miracle she could even talk. Twisted teeth snaked out from between lips that were parched and cracked. She looked more animal than human, as though some madman had decided to cross a woman with an angler fish.

Olga backed up a step, since it was toward Olga that the creature was shambling.

"Jealous, sister?" the revenant taunted. I could no longer think of her as Nadia. She'd changed too thoroughly to be called by such a human name.

"Of a succubus? I think not," Olga said, leading Nadia out into the open, farther from Stefan, whose eyes were focused on Greydanus.

"Father's little contingency plan," Stefan said sourly.

"Leave my son alone."

"Which one? Certainly not Zigmund? What do I care for Zigmund? He can wait his turn. I was looking at that sallow, stunted corpse in front of you," he said, pointing to Greydanus, "the one my father insisted had to be born to keep me in line."

"Zigmund, what's happening to her?"

Greydanus was forgotten as all of us, even Stefan, looked at the creature. She'd stalled in the middle of the room, her legs seemingly rooted to the ground. The look of bewilderment on her face was simultaneously terrifying and pathetic.

She held out an arm to steady herself. She seemed in danger of toppling over, as though she were weakening. I darted a look at Stefan, who stood mute with horror or surprise, I could not tell.

She leaned down and lifted the hem of her skirt, shrieking when she saw what had happened to her legs.

Small cuts crisscrossing her pale flesh had begun to ooze. But that wasn't why she was panicking. The blood that was seeping from her wounds was white...and it was burning through her skin.

"She's not strong enough to withstand the transformation. The changed blood is burning through her. Olga, think of Magdalena," I said, suddenly understanding why this was really happening to Nadia.

Olga turned to me, her eyes widening.

"Follow it through," I urged her.

"Magdalena saved me," Olga said slowly. "She might not have known it, but she did."

"You would have been a straight turn," I said, my mind furiously working it out, "if she had not bitten you first."

"Magdalena was an Upyr, yes."

"She was the counterbalance to the acidity, the poison of the Corcitura's bite. If she hadn't gotten to you first..."

"I'd have ended up like this. Oh, Zigmund, no."

"Make it quick, Olga. And as painless as you can. I believe she's suffered enough."

The creature's eyes went wide as another globule of the white blood erupted from her wounds, singeing her flesh. But her panic was forgotten as Olga drew closer. The creature that had been Nadia was consumed with one desire. I could sense the bloodlust oozing from her as tangibly as the sticky white blood that was now draining from her neck.

For the first time, I saw compassion in Olga's eyes. She'd talked about revenge, she'd taken it swiftly when she'd killed Magdalena, but now that she knew the truth, vengeance was no longer as sweet. As she advanced on her sister, there was nothing menacing about her. Even as she crouched down on all fours and began her transformation into the white-streaked black wolf, I knew she didn't have the stomach for what she was about to do.

"God have mercy on you for what you've done, Nadia. And may He forgive me for what I'm about to do."

Bone cracked against bone, fur met flesh, and with one final, blood-chilling screech, Nadia Belododia passed into oblivion.

Olga, her body lengthening out, her claws tapering into delicate fingers, crouched over her sister's corpse. Gradually, the signs of destruction vanished from Nadia's ravaged body. Her teeth retracted, once more becoming human, but her eyes, those striking eyes, lost their violent green sheen and became nondescript—sightless, milky white...dead.

"It was a mistake to come back here, Stefan."

"Don't lecture me, my darling wife. I think you should be more worried about your son." Stefan raced past me, covering the distance in less time than it took me to swallow. He glowered triumphantly at me from where he'd stood a second before. This time, he was not alone.

"Stefan, no, have mercy! Please!"

Stefan held Greydanus to his chest, his hands clamped around the child's neck, the barbed tongue poised inches from my brother's throat.

"You thought you killed one son. Why shouldn't I kill the other? Especially one as dangerous as this. One who was born to make sure I stayed subservient to Vladec Salei forever. Well, Vladec's dead now. It's time I did things my way."

"What's this? What unholy mischief is this?!"

Olga stumbled back from her sister's body, holding in her hands something that looked like a pocket watch.

"Yet another secret my devoted sister took to her grave. You could call it *my* contingency plan. Father wasn't the only one who thought ahead."

I grabbed the watch from Olga's hands. As it clicked open, I saw that it was a locket with two pictures set into the corroded gold holders. In one picture were a gorgeous woman and a child that I thought was Greydanus. In the second picture, the child stood in front of Stefan, who was flanked on either side by a beaming Vladec Salei and a dour-as-usual Constantinos. I turned the locket to the light. The child was small with fair hair and large eyes that I would have bet my life were green.

"A Corcitura's child."

"How could you, Stefan? How could you do something so abominable?"

"I'd no choice but to be unfaithful, Leonora," he said, raking a finger across Grey's chin, drawing blood. My brother twisted and squirmed like a wolf in a trap, but Stefan hung on. "I knew Greydanus would fail me. I knew it from the moment he was born. I couldn't take that chance. He's a failure to me now. Look at him," he said, holding Grey out by the neck. The child was turning blue, the life being crushed out of him by his own father.

Any mother would have fought like a tigress to save her child from such a beast. In this instance, the child had the good fortune to have a mother who was also a wolf. Leonora crouched to the ground. The floorboards trembled as a growl thundered through the room. Her long, black hair receded into her scalp, painting a huge dark swath against the white fur of her back. I'd seen her transform before, but never with such ferocity, with such deadly intent.

Stefan's eyes were fixed on her. Her canines were bared, spittle trailing down them, the low, menacing snarl rumbling in her throat. Foam flecked the edges of her mouth.

Rabid dog.

"Mother wolf come to save her cub," Stefan taunted. He pulled Greydanus to his chest. I could not move, and Olga seemed to be frozen over the body of her sister. She'd reclaimed the locket and cradled it in her hand. "Impossible, impossible," she muttered over and over. "Ruxandra...how could you?"

"I'm afraid you are too late. Only one of my sons is loyal to me. The other is a liability I have no intention of living with."

"Then I think it's time for you to die, Father."

The hand now clamped around Stefan's forearm no longer bore any resemblance to the childish one I had held ten minutes ago. This hand was covered in fur, brownish-grey fur, its gleaming claws extending and sinking into the flesh of its victim.

I stood in an agony of indecision. Olga was too distracted by the discovery of more family atrocities. She didn't need my help, at least physically, but Greydanus did. Our mother was in full-fledged wolf mode, but she was hesitating. I could feel her fear, her indecision, as she gauged how to attack her husband without crushing her son.

The task had fallen to me. I needed to be the one to right the wrongs.

"*You?*" Stefan scoffed, squeezing his son's neck tighter. "What the devil can *you* do? I'm stronger than you, stronger than your half-wolf, half-vampire mother. You've lost, Greydanus. *Greydanus*, what a ridiculous name that is. If I'd had my way, I'd have named you Dragos after my father, after a murderer. I have him to thank for so much. Maybe the name would have toughened you up, made you more like me."

That seemed to rally Greydanus. I saw his canines extending. Already, fur coated most of his body. With a savage swipe, he raked his claw against his father's arm, slashing through the flesh.

Stefan looked down at his wounds in disbelief. "*You little ingrate.* You think I'd let you kill me? When it came to whose brains you inherited, I believe you got your mother's. Just...like...your...brother."

I couldn't take it any longer. Leonora was paralyzed by fear that Stefan would snuff Grey out with one more squeeze if she pounced. I had to drive her into action. He'd insulted me enough. He'd tried to kill us all. He'd ruined so many lives. He had to die. *Again.*

I lowered my shoulder and screamed like a maniac, hoping to draw his attention. His legs, his knees, if I could ram them, maybe I'd throw him off balance. Maybe he'd be so shocked he would release Greydanus. Then my brother could finish him off.

When I slammed into Stefan, I felt like a thousand pound weight had crashed against my back. Greydanus yelped as he fell from his father's grasp, fully transforming into a small grey wolf before his paws touched the ground.

Whatever was behind me was incredibly strong and breathing incredibly heavily. The breath was hot and gamey—the breath of a large dog.

I turned my head to look straight into the glowing yellow eyes of my mother. Behind her, the clear blue, nearly transparent eyes of Olga stared into my own.

A family attack, that's what it had been, and Greydanus had indeed finished it.

I pushed myself off the ground and peered over Greydanus at the broken, bloodied corpse of Stefan Belododia. The flesh of his neck was ragged. Grey stared solemnly at the carnage he'd inflicted. Blood mingled with the grey fur of his muzzle; blood dulled the shine of his silver claws.

I reached out and ruffled his head, forgetting for a second that he was not some stray harmless pup. He came out of his trance at my touch and turned his small, fuzzy head around, looking at me with eyes sad yet flinty, which reminded me immediately that he was much more than a wolf and much more than a vampire.

A Corcitura's child. What a burden that must have been for him to bear on his own.

Not on his own any longer.

I watched in silence as he lowered his head and transformed into the grave, quiet child I had come to love. I looked to Leonora and Olga, who had already returned to their "human" forms. Leonora knelt behind me, wrapping her arm around my shoulders. Greydanus shuffled over, crouching before me and nestling back into my arms. And Olga, *my* Olga, had forgotten the locket and her sister and was at my side, her hand in mine. My family was whole again.

"You stupid fool."

I rocked back on my heels, stunned that he was speaking. *How* was he speaking?

"It is not over."

"What do you mean it's not over? You're dead."

"You're wrong. *Dead* wrong, my distinguished professor."

I collared him. He choked on the blood that was bubbling in his lungs, but somehow continued laughing, reveling in tormenting us to the last.

"Tell me. Be honest for once before you die."

"I am being honest. I haven't hidden anything. By now, he's in safe hands. Everything is working as I planned. I have left a legacy. Now you must find him. He will come for you. All of you. Rejoice in that knowledge and die."

"Who? Belododia, tell me!"

"I will live again through him...Greydanus's demonic twin."

"Speak! *Tell me!*"

"My son...Ducaine."

I released his collar, letting him drop from my hands. His head smacked against the wood floor, but still he continued to laugh. Greydanus crawled to his side and pressed his hands against his father's wound. The air escaped Stefan's lungs in a last, startled gasp. His limbs stiffened. His eyes rolled back into his head. His mouth dropped open, forever frozen in a silent scream.

"If he is speaking the truth..." I said, knowing it was foolish to still deny it. I'd seen the pictures in the locket. I'd noted the likeness.

"I know he is," Olga said. "He was my brother. I can still tell when he is lying. He wasn't just now."

"How will we find him? Where should we even start to look?"

"I don't know, Zigmund. I don't know."

I held out my hand for her. She sidled over and nestled into my arms. I held her close, comforted by her presence. I'd gained everything that had been taken from me and more. I no longer felt alone and forsaken. I was not the lost boy who'd been forced to flee from monsters. *I* would seek out the monsters this time; *I* would hunt down this new threat. I was no longer the child who had searched in vain for something he would never find.

"I will not give up looking." Leonora held out her hand. I took it in mine.

"Nor will I," I answered.

"Nor I," said Olga."

"I'm with you, Zigmund. We'll find him...my other brother."

Corcitura

We would always be a family of five. Greydanus would never stop searching. He was not content to give up yet another brother so easily, nor was I.

It was not only our lives that depended on the outcome of our mission. Madelaine, Eric, every single person we came into contact with over the years—all of us would be in danger if we gave up now, and that was a risk I was unwilling to take.

I stroked Greydanus's head. We would fight this. It seemed it was our destiny to always be on the run, always searching. My family was with me now, our immediate ghosts laid to rest. That in and of itself gave me comfort and strength.

"We'll find him, Grey. We have to."

I glanced at my mother and Olga, who both looked quite wolfish. A secret smile passed between them. I felt the corners of my own lips lifting in grim solidarity. So this was what we'd been called on to do. This was the task that had been set before us. We had been chosen to carry on Florin's legacy.

"Let the hunt begin."

Postscript

Legacy

"This way, if you please, Mr. and Mrs. Rathbourne. There are just a few more papers we must go over before the adoption is finalized."

"I must say, Mr. Filipov, we were thrilled to bits when we received your letter. *Thrilled to bits*, weren't we, Charles?"

"Jubilant."

"Now, Charles, don't be sarcastic. It doesn't suit you. Honestly, I despair of you sometimes."

"It's just that we have three grown children. What do we want with a waif from Romania?"

"I'm surprised at you, dearest. David and Marishka were forever trying to convince us to adopt. And now that they are gone, God rest their souls, I should think you'd understand that there is no better way to honor their memory than to welcome one of those poor little scamps into our home."

"I should think a donation would suffice to honor their memory."

"If you would like to contribute that, too, Sir..."

"No, Mr. Filipov, I'm afraid not, as much as you would appreciate it."

"We at the Ratliff Home for the Dispossessed are concerned about the children firstly, I do assure you, Mr. Rathbourne, but every little bit helps. Now, if you will come into my study."

"Can you believe this, Charles? The boy is almost ours! How exciting!"

"That's hardly the word I would use."

"You are determined to be petulant about this, aren't you?"

"If you want to know the truth, yes. There is something about him I do not like. Something about the eyes. They're too unnaturally bright."

"How can you tell that from a black and white photograph?"

"I can, never mind how."

"I hope you are not letting the child's ancestry put you off, Mr. Rathbourne?"

"I don't know very much *about* his ancestry, Mr. Filipov, other than the scant information you've relayed to us."

"If you wouldn't mind, Mr. Filipov..."

"Certainly not, Mrs. Rathbourne. He's been with us a little over a month. Poor thing was as thin as a rail when he got here. If you'd seen him then, his little legs like two sticks, you would not have put up any barriers to his adoption, I do assure you, Mr. Rathbourne."

"Yes, yes, of course, go on."

"He is quite precocious for a six-year-old. Head and tails above everyone else here. I can vouch for his scholarship. High marks on all his exams. He's quite proficient in everything we teach here as well. A remarkable child. He has the intelligence and command of the language of a child of at least fourteen."

"Oh, Charles! A genius! How wonderful for us. Imagine what the Duncans will say. Lilia will be seething with envy."

"Quite. But what of his parents? Was there much known of them, that is, before they passed on?"

"The father is a mystery. We haven't been able to get much information out of the child on that front. He seems unduly reticent about it. He doesn't even know his surname, poor dear."

"That seems strange."

"Yes, well...um..."

"You hesitate, Mr. Filipov! Could it be because you are hiding something you wish us not to know? Is he the son of Leather Apron? John Pizer's child, eh?"

"Oh, really, Charles, scandalmongering will get you nowhere. And to bring that poor man into it. Was it not enough he was suspected of being Jack the Ripper?"

"I'm inclined to agree with you, Mrs. Rathbourne. Ridiculous accusations, Sir, I do assure you. As I was saying, his mother is another story entirely. He remembers her first name."

"How fortuitous."

"Yes. Ruxandra, I believe. Yes, Ruxandra it was. Apparently, she was a beauty, but died of some rare blood disease."

"How tragic."

"Charles! Stop being so unfeeling!"

"I must agree with your wife yet again, Sir. You are being most difficult about the matter. I cannot think what has put you in such a state."

"Oh, but I think you can."

"What are you implying?"

"Really, you two, all we want is the boy. Charles, *please.*"

"And I am more than happy to give him to you."

"Relieved, no doubt."

"Charles! There, Mr. Filipov, that's the last of it. Now, can we see him?"

"Of course, he should just be coming down for lunch. Won't he be surprised!"

"Oh, I am about to burst!"

"If you feel so inclined, dearest, I do wish you would explode in here. The cab is hired, after all."

"Oh, Charles, really."

"Right this way. Ah, there he is."

"Oh, what a perfect angel! Look at all that lustrous blonde hair. And his eyes aren't the least bit abnormal, Charles. Look how green they are. So shining and bright, like emeralds! How enchanting!"

"Unnatural. I say, Mr. Filipov, there is no way we could get out of this now, is there?"

"Why ever would you want to?"

"I do not like the look of the boy. There's something secretive in his face that strikes me as...

"Yes..."

"Charles, look how affectionate he is! Easy, love, not so tight around the neck. Mummy cannot breathe. Oh, he's so ardent!"

"How wonderful for you, Isadora. Mr. Filipov..."

"You still haven't told me what it is you don't like about the boy, Sir."

"Well..."

"Yes..."

"Well, I just have a feeling, and I'd like to know if there is any way we can break the agreement."

"You mean return the boy if he doesn't prove satisfactory?"

"Must you put it like that?"

"That is how I see it."

"I thought you would."

"I am afraid that, no, there is no way of returning your product should it not meet your expectations. There is just no way."

"There is always a way, as far as I and my solicitor are concerned."

"Is that a threat, Mr. Rathbourne?"

"More like a warning, Mr. Filipov."

"What are you two men squabbling about? Dearest, look. How do you like your new son? Say hello to your new papa, darling."

"He's not my papa."

"Of course he is, dearest. His name is Charles, just like yours."

"My name is not Charles. And he is *not* my papa. My papa is dead."

"You must forget all about that now, Charlie. You have a new life."

"And you will not talk of your other parents again, do you hear, my boy?"

"Tell him, Charles. Mildly and firmly, follow your family's motto."

"Isadora...I don't think you should let him cling to you so."

"Pay no attention to your papa. Charles, look what you've done. My poor little man is put out. That's right, cling to Mama as much as you want, and do not cry, my love. It'll be all right in time. Oh, what a sweet boy! Did you see that, Charles? He's mellowing. He gave me a peck on the neck. Oh, dear, but I do think we will have to have those teeth filed, Charlie, dearest. They are a tad sharp. Thank you again, Mr. Filipov. We'll let you know of his progress. I'm sure he will be right as rain in a few days, once he is settled."

"I am sure you are right, Mrs. Rathbourne. I wish you all the best of luck."

"Come, Charles, let us take Charlie to the park. He is so pale. He could use the fresh air."

"I do not think the air will make a difference."

"Good-bye, Mr. Filipov, and thank you!"

The door closed behind the happy family. Mr. Filipov leaned against the wood and exhaled, feeling as though the weight of the world had been lifted off his shoulders. It had been a month of confusion, a month of disasters. Now his world could return to the ordered routine he so loved, at least for the next twenty-four hours. No more wild outbursts, no more broken furniture, no more uncanny wanderings in the night. The child had been placed in a happy home. How long it would remain happy, Mr. Filipov could not say. That was Mr. and Mrs. Charles Rathbourne's problem now.

"Sasha, is he gone? Has that devil child finally been placed?"

"Yes, Liddie, thank God."

The harried little housekeeper ran to the head of the Ratliff Home for the Dispossessed and threw her arms around his neck. "Oh, Sasha, Sasha, we're saved! All my prayers have been answered. I do pity those people. God have mercy on them."

"I pray He will, too, Liddie, darling. But I've seen that boy for what he is. I'm afraid there's not much hope. I think it's time we put our plans into action. My replacement will be here in three days. Will you be ready by then, my love?"

"Yes, darling. I can be ready tonight if you need it to be so."

"All the better. Mr. Adamson is willing to step into the breach until Mr. Moncrieff arrives. The sooner we leave this place, the better. You will love Novgorod. It is much colder than you are used to, but it is safe...and far away from here."

"Do you think it will go poorly, then?"

"Undoubtedly. I saw something in that child's eyes the moment he arrived on our doorstep. Something..."

"Evil."

"Yes. I do not envy his new parents. The child is obstinate. The woman is so blinded by the idea of him being *her* child that she hardly noticed the look in his eyes when she told him he had a new name and a new father. I think her husband suspects, though he can have *no* idea of what is coming."

"There is nothing we can do. The other children were in danger. *We* were in danger. It is a terrible thing, deception, but better them than us. And I'm not sorry for feeling that way."

"No, my love, nor am I, as callous as that sounds. There is nothing I wouldn't have done to rid myself of that child. Charles Rathbourne the Third. That's what they're calling him."

"That will never last. The child won't stand for it."

"I know. He's got the mind of a man of fifty and the heart of a sinner. Mrs. Rathbourne was taken in heart and soul by that face."

"Oh, Sasha, Sasha, why did this have to happen?"

"I don't know, Liddie. But I do know this. No matter if we go to Novgorod or the deepest wilds of Siberia, I fear we have not seen the last of Ducaine Belododia."

ABOUT THE AUTHOR

Melika is also the author of the historical novel *City of Lights: The Trials and Triumphs of Ilyse Charpentier*, which takes place amid the glamour of fin de siècle 19th century Paris. She is currently working on the sequel to *Corcitura*, a collection of comedy/horror/fantasy stories set in Eastern Europe in the 1800s, and the first book of a planned fantasy duology. To learn more, please visit www.booksinmybelfry.com

www.ingramcontent.com/pod-product-compliance
Lightning Source LLC
Chambersburg PA
CBHW030858050726
47500CB00008B/3